"**R**azor-sharp horrors . . . You'll be turning pages almost as fast as you can breathe. In Coyne, Hill has created a vivid protagonist. . . . And as villains go, Craddock is a whopper: a cruel, manipulative apparition who shadows his victims everywhere, climbs into their brains, and drives them to madness. . . . Horror fans, and anyone who likes a fast-paced read, will probably enjoy this inventive thriller."

Salt Lake Tribune

"[Hill] adds so many twists that readers will be white-knuckling their armchairs by story's end. . . . The book moves from eerie haunting to suspense-filled thriller. . . . *Heart-Shaped Box* is a fine mix of psychological terror and gruesome horror. . . . Hill's voice rings out loud and clear in this remarkable, moving, and well-crafted first novel."

Denver Post

"[*Heart-Shaped Box*] rocks. It's a flat-out, white-line, turbo-charged, relentless, bleakly humorous, and, above all, honest story. . . . Hill's fealty to the autumnal suspirations of the darkest sorts of dread is instantly apparent. And this, as they say, is just the beginning."

Austin Chronicle (Texas)

"**J**oe Hill has written a vivid, convincing tale that puts the tropes of old-fashioned ghost stories to work in the world of an almost-washed-up rock star. . . . This is a fast-paced journey on wheels borrowed from Hell's used-car lot, and there aren't a lot of comfort breaks."

Plain Dealer (Cleveland)

"**S**eriously freaky . . . Is the book any good? It is, actually, and enormously fun to read. . . . A plot that unfolds at a gripping, runaway pace. Judas and his girlfriend, Georgia, are strong, well-defined characters who remain immensely likable despite their mistakes and imperfections. . . . Genuinely scary . . . Tightly paced . . . It's an auspicious debut from a writer in the very early stages of establishing his career. . . . Expect more scares from him."

Lexington Herald Leader

"**A**n entertaining and . . . frightening read . . . All hell breaks loose . . . The urgency of the story and the pace at which Hill tells it are turbocharged to the point where readers will likely be racing through the pages to see what happens next. . . . *Heart-Shaped Box* is a worthy novel."

Chicago Sun-Times

"**T**he story moves with an exhilarating urgency. . . . Hill's prose is lean and precise, and he renders Jude's world with impressive confidence. It feels solid, every detail both correct and fresh. . . . Hill has a flawless sense of pacing. His narrative never flags. . . . And one can sense his literary ambition pushing at the margins of the genre. . . . Delightfully gory . . . Not only well-written and terrifying, but also—as it draws to its close—surprisingly moving. So go ahead, take a chance, and open his *Heart-Shaped Box*. I think you'll be happy you did."

Scott Smith,
New York Times bestselling author of *The Ruins*

© Shane Leonard

About the Author

A two-time Bram Stoker Award-winner and a recipient of the World Fantasy Award, Joe Hill is the author of the critically acclaimed *New York Times* bestseller *Heart-Shaped Box* and the critically acclaimed story collection *20th Century Ghosts*. His stories have appeared in numerous journals and Year's Best collections. He calls New England home.

Find out more at *www.joehillfiction.com*

BOOKS BY JOE HILL

20th Century Ghosts (stories)
Heart-Shapted Box

And coming soon in hardcover:
Horns

HEART-SHAPED BOX

♥

JOE HILL

WM

WILLIAM MORROW
An Imprint of HarperCollins*Publishers*

wm

WILLIAM MORROW
An Imprint of HarperCollins*Publishers*

The excerpt from *Voice of the Fire*, copyright © by Alan Moore, is used by permission of Top Shelf Productions.

A hardcover edition of this book was published in 2007 by William Morrow, an imprint of HarperCollins Publishers. A rack-size edition of this book was published in 2008 by Harper paperbacks.

FIRST HARPER PAPERBACK PUBLISHED 2010.

Designed by Susan Yang

The Library of Congress has catalogued the hardcover edition as follows:

Hill, Joe.
  Heart-shaped box / Joe Hill. — 1st ed.
    p.   cm.
  ISBN 978-0-06-114793-7
  I. Title.

  PS3608.I4342H43 2007
  813'.6—dc22   2006046548

ISBN 978-0-06-194489-5 (pbk.)

  20   WBC/LSC   30 29 28 27 26 25 24 23

For my dad, one of the good ones

HOW MAY THE DEAD HAVE DESTINATIONS?

—Alan Moore, *Voice of the Fire*

BLACK DOG

1

Jude had a private collection.

He had framed sketches of the Seven Dwarfs on the wall of his studio, in between his platinum records. John Wayne Gacy had drawn them while he was in jail and sent them to him. Gacy liked golden-age Disney almost as much as he liked molesting little kids; almost as much as he liked Jude's albums.

Jude had the skull of a peasant who had been trepanned in the sixteenth century, to let the demons out. He kept a collection of pens jammed into the hole in the center of the cranium.

He had a three-hundred-year-old confession, signed by a witch. "I did spake with a black dogge who sayd hee wouldst poison cows, drive horses mad and sicken children for me if I wouldst let him have my soule, and I sayd aye, and after did give him sucke at my breast." She was burned to death.

He had a stiff and worn noose that had been used to hang a man in England at the turn of the nineteenth century, Aleister Crowley's childhood chessboard, and a snuff film. Of all the items in Jude's collection, this last was the thing he felt most uncomfortable about possessing. It had come to him by way of a police officer, a man who had worked security at some shows in L.A. The cop had said the video was diseased. He said it with some enthusiasm. Jude had watched it and felt that he was right. It was diseased. It had also, in an indirect way, helped hasten the end of Jude's marriage. Still he held on to it.

Many of the objects in his private collection of the grotesque and the bizarre were gifts sent to him by his fans. It was rare for him to actually buy something for the collection himself. But when Danny Wooten, his personal assistant, told him there was a ghost for sale on the Internet and asked did he want to buy it, Jude didn't even need to think. It was like going out to eat, hearing the special, and deciding you wanted it without even looking at the menu. Some impulses required no consideration.

Danny's office occupied a relatively new addition, extending from the northeastern end of Jude's rambling, 110-year-old farmhouse. With its climate control, OfficeMax furniture, and coffee-and-cream industrial carpet, the office was coolly impersonal, nothing at all like the rest of the house. It might have been a dentist's waiting room, if not for the concert posters in stainless-steel frames. One of them showed a jar crammed with staring eyeballs, bloody knots of nerves dangling from the backs of them. That was for the All Eyes On You tour.

No sooner had the addition been built than Jude had come to regret it. He had not wanted to drive forty minutes from Piecliff to a rented office in Poughkeepsie to see to his business, but that would've probably been preferable to having Danny Wooten right here at the house. Here Danny and Danny's work were too close. When Jude was in the kitchen, he could hear the phones ringing in there, both of the office lines going off at once sometimes, and the sound was maddening to him. He had not recorded an album in years, had hardly worked since Jerome and Dizzy had died (and the band with them), but still the phones rang and rang. He felt crowded by the steady parade of petitioners for his time, and by the never-ending accumulation of legal and professional demands, agreements and contracts, promotions and appearances, the work of Judas Coyne Incorporated, which was never done, always ongoing. When he was home, he wanted to be himself, not a trademark.

For the most part, Danny stayed out of the rest of the house. Whatever his flaws, he was protective of Jude's private space. But Danny considered him fair game if Jude strayed into the office—something Jude did, without much pleasure, four or five times a day. Passing through the office was the fastest way to the barn and the dogs. He could've avoided Danny by going out through the front door and walking all the way around the house, but he refused to sneak around his own home just to avoid Danny Wooten.

Besides, it didn't seem possible Danny could always have something to bother him with. But he always did. And if he didn't have anything that demanded immediate attention, he wanted to talk. Danny was from Southern California originally, and there was no end to his talk. He would boast to total strangers about the benefits of wheatgrass, which included making your bowel movements as fragrant as a freshly mowed lawn. He was thirty years old but could talk skateboarding and PlayStation with the pizza-delivery kid like he was fourteen. Danny would get confessional with air-conditioner repairmen, tell them how his sister had OD'd on heroin in her teens and how as a young man he had been the one to find his mother's body after she killed herself. He was impossible to embarrass. He didn't know the meaning of shy.

Jude was coming back inside from feeding Angus and Bon and was halfway across Danny's field of fire—just beginning to think he might make it through the office unscathed—when Danny said, "Hey, Chief, check this out." Danny opened almost every demand for attention with just this line, a statement Jude had learned to dread and resent, a prelude to half an hour of wasted time, forms to fill out, faxes to look at. Then Danny told him someone was selling a ghost, and Jude forgot all about begrudging him. He walked around the desk so he could look over Danny's shoulder at his computer screen.

Danny had discovered the ghost at an online auction site, not eBay but one of the wannabes. Jude moved his gaze over the item description while Danny read aloud. Danny would've cut his food for him if Jude gave him the chance. He had a streak of subservience that Jude found, frankly, revolting in a man.

"'Buy my stepfather's ghost,'" Danny read. "'Six weeks ago my elderly stepfather died, very suddenly. He was staying with us at the time. He had no home of his own and traveled from relative to relative, visiting for a month or two before moving on. Everyone was shocked by his passing, especially my daughter, who was very close to him. No one would've thought. He was active to the end of his life. Never sat in front of the TV. Drank a glass of orange juice every day. Had all his own teeth.'"

"This is a fuckin' joke," Jude said.

"I don't think so," Danny said. He went on, "'Two days after his funeral, my little girl saw him sitting in the guest room, which is directly across from her own bedroom. After she saw him, my girl didn't like to be alone in her room anymore, or even to go upstairs. I told her that her grandfather wouldn't ever hurt her, but she said she was scared of his eyes. She said they were all black scribbles and they weren't for seeing anymore. So she has been sleeping with me ever since.

"'At first I thought it was just a scary story she was telling herself, but there is more to it than that. The guest room is cold all the time. I poked around in there and noticed it was worst in the closet, where his Sunday suit was hung up. He wanted to be buried in that suit, but when we tried it on him at the funeral home, it didn't look right. People shrink up a little after they die. The water in them dries up. His best suit was too big for him, so we let the funeral home talk us into buying one of theirs. I don't know why I listened.

"'The other night I woke up and heard my stepfather walking around overhead. The bed in his room won't stay made, and the door opens and slams shut at all hours. The cat won't go upstairs either, and sometimes she sits at the bottom of the steps looking at things I can't see. She stares awhile, then gives a yowl like her tail got stepped on and runs away.

"'My stepfather was a lifelong spiritualist, and I believe he is only here to teach my daughter that death is not the end. But she is eleven and needs a normal life and to sleep in her own room, not in mine. The only thing I can think is to try and find Pop another home, and the world is full of people who want to believe in the afterlife. Well, I have your proof right here.

"'I will "sell" my stepfather's ghost to the highest bidder. Of course a soul cannot really be sold, but I believe he will come to your home and abide with you if you put out the welcome mat. As I said, when he died, he was with us temporarily and had no place to call his own, so I am sure he would go to where he was wanted. Do not think this is a stunt or a practical joke and that I will take your money and send you nothing. The winning bidder will have something solid to show for their investment. I will send you his Sunday suit. I believe if his spirit is attached to anything, it has to be that.

"'It is a very nice old-fashioned suit made by Great Western Tailoring. It has a fine silver pinstripe,' blah-blah, 'satin lining,' blah-blah. . . ." Danny stopped reading and pointed at the screen. "Check out the measurements, Chief. It's just your size. High bid is eighty bucks. If you want to own a ghost, looks like he could be yours for a hundred."

"Let's buy it," Jude said.

"Seriously? Put in a bid for a hundred dollars?"

Jude narrowed his eyes, peering at something on the screen, just below the item description, a button that said YOURS NOW: $1,000. And beneath that: *Click to Buy and End Auction Immediately!* He put his finger on it, tapping the glass.

"Let's just make it a grand and seal the deal," he said.

Danny rotated in his chair. He grinned and raised his eyebrows. Danny had high, arched, Jack Nicholson eyebrows, which he used to great effect. Maybe he expected an explanation, but Jude wasn't sure he could've explained, even to himself, why it seemed reasonable to pay a thousand dollars for an old suit that probably wasn't worth a fifth of that.

Later he thought it might be good publicity: *Judas Coyne buys a poltergeist*. The fans ate up stories like that. But that was later. Right then, in the moment, he just knew he wanted to be the one who bought the ghost.

Jude started on, thinking he would head upstairs to see if Georgia was dressed yet. He had told her to put on her clothes half an hour ago but expected to find her still in bed. He had the sense she planned to stay there until she got the fight she was looking for. She'd be sitting in her underwear, carefully painting her toenails black. Or she'd have her laptop open, surfing Goth accessories, looking for the perfect stud to poke through her tongue, like she needed any more goddam . . . And then the thought of surfing the Web caused Jude to hold up, wondering something. He glanced back at Danny.

"How'd you come across that anyway?" he asked, nodding at the computer.

"We got an e-mail about it."

"From who?"

"From the auction site. They sent us an e-mail that said 'We notice you've bought items like this before and thought you'd be interested.'"

"We've bought items like this before?"

"Occult items, I assume."

"I've never bought anything off that site."

"Maybe you did and just don't remember. Maybe I bought something for you."

Jude said, "Fuckin' acid. I had a good memory once. I was in the chess club in junior high."

"You were? That's a hell of a thought."

"What? The idea that I was in the chess club?"

"I guess. It seems so . . . geeky."

"Yeah. But I used severed fingers for pieces."

Danny laughed—a little too hard, convulsing himself and wiping imaginary tears from the corners of his eyes. The sycophantic little suck-ass.

2

The suit came early Saturday morning. Jude was up and outside with the dogs.

Angus lunged as soon as the UPS truck ground to a halt, and the leash was yanked out of Jude's hand. Angus leaped against the side of the parked truck, spit flying, paws scuffling furiously against the driver's-side door. The driver remained behind the wheel, peering down at him with the calm but intent expression of a doctor considering a new strain of Ebola through a microscope. Jude caught the leash and pulled on it, harder than he meant to. Angus sprawled on his side in the dirt, then twisted and sprang back up, snarling. By now Bon was in on the act, straining at the end of her leash, which Jude held in his other hand, and yapping with a shrillness that hurt his head.

Because it was too far to haul them all the way back to the barn and their pen, Jude dragged them across the yard and up to the front porch, both of them fighting him the whole time. He shoveled them in through the front door and slammed it behind them. Immediately they set to flinging themselves against it, barking hysterically. The door shuddered as they slammed into it. Fucking dogs.

Jude shuffled back down into the driveway, and reached the UPS truck just as the rear door slid open with a steely clatter. The deliveryman stood inside. He hopped down, holding a long, flat box under his arm.

"Ozzy Osbourne has Pomeranians," the UPS guy said. "I saw them on TV. Cute little dogs like house cats. You ever think about getting a couple cute little dogs like that?"

Jude took the box without a word and went inside.

He brought the box through the house and into the kitchen. He put it on the counter and poured coffee. Jude was an early riser by instinct and conditioning. When he was on the road, or recording, he had become accustomed to rolling into bed at five in the morning and sleeping through most of the daylight hours, but staying up all night had never come naturally. On the road he would wake at four in the afternoon, bad-tempered and headachy, confused about where the time had gone. Everyone he knew would seem to him clever impostors, unfeeling aliens wearing rubber skin and the faces of friends. It took a liberal quantity of alcohol to make them seem like themselves again.

Only it had been three years since he'd last gone on tour. He didn't have much interest in drinking when he was home, and was ready for bed most nights by nine. At the age of fifty-four, he had settled back into the rhythms that had guided him since his name was Justin Cowzynski and he was a boy on his father's hog farm. The illiterate son of a bitch would have dragged him out of bed by the hair if he'd found him in it when the sun came up. It was a childhood of mud, barking dogs, barbed wire, dilapidated farm buildings, squealing pigs with their flaking skin and squashed-in faces, and little human contact, beyond a mother who sat most of the day at the kitchen table wearing the slack, staring aspect of someone who had been lobotomized, and his father, who ruled their acres of pig shit and ruin with his angry laughter and his fists.

So Jude had been up for several hours already but had not eaten breakfast yet, and he was frying bacon when Georgia wandered into the kitchen. She was dressed only in a pair of black panties, her arms folded across her small, white, pierced breasts, her black hair floating around her head in a soft, tangly nest. Her name wasn't really Georgia. It wasn't Morphine either, although she had stripped under that name for two years. Her name was Marybeth Kimball, a handle so simple, so plain, she'd laughed when she first told him, as if it embarrassed her.

Jude had worked his way through a collection of Goth girlfriends who stripped, or told fortunes, or stripped *and* told fortunes, pretty girls who wore ankhs and black fingernail polish, and whom he always called by their state of origin, a habit few of them cared for, because they didn't like to be reminded of the person they were trying to erase with all their living-dead makeup. She was twenty-three.

"Goddam stupid dogs," she said, shoving one of them out of her way with her heel. They were whisking around Jude's legs, excited by the perfume of the bacon. "Woke me the fuck up."

"Maybe it was time to get the fuck up. Ever think?" She never rose before ten if she could help it.

She bent into the fridge for the orange juice. He enjoyed the view, the way the straps of her underwear cut into the almost-too-white cheeks of her ass, but he looked away while she drank from the carton. She left it on the counter, too. It would spoil there if he didn't put it away for her.

He was glad for the adoration of the Goths. He appreciated the sex even more, their limber, athletic, tattooed bodies and eagerness for kink. But he had been married once, to a woman who used a glass and put things away when she was done, who read the paper in the morning, and he missed their talk. It was grown-up talk. She hadn't been a stripper. She didn't believe in fortune-telling. It was grown-up companionship.

Georgia used a steak knife to slice open the UPS box, then left the knife on the counter, with tape stuck to it.

"What's this?" she asked.

A second box was contained within the first. It was a tight fit, and Georgia had to tug for a while to slide the inner box out onto the counter. It was large, and shiny, and black, and it was shaped like a heart. Candies sometimes came in boxes like that, although this was much too big for candies, and candy boxes were pink or sometimes yellow. A lingerie box, then—except he hadn't ordered anything of the kind for her. He frowned. He didn't have any idea what might be in it and at the same time felt somehow he *should* know, that the heart-shaped box contained something he'd been expecting.

"Is this for me?" she asked.

She pried the lid loose and took out what was inside, lifting it for him to see. A suit. Someone had sent him a suit. It was black and old-fashioned, the details blurred by the plastic dry-cleaning bag pulled over it. Georgia held it up by the shoulders, in front of her body, almost as if it were a dress she was thinking of trying on but she wanted his opinion of it first. Her gaze was questioning, a pretty furrow between her eyebrows. For a moment he didn't remember, didn't know why it had come.

He opened his mouth to tell her he had no clue, but then instead heard himself say, "The dead man's suit."

"What?"

"The ghost," he said, remembering as he spoke. "I bought a ghost. Some woman was convinced her stepfather was haunting her. So she put his restless spirit up for sale on the Internet, and I bought it for a grand. That's his suit. She thinks it might be the source of the haunting."

"Oh, cool," Georgia said. "So are you going to wear it?"

His own reaction surprised him. His skin crawled, went rough and strange with gooseflesh. For one unconsidered moment, the idea struck him as obscene.

"No," he said, and she flicked a surprised glance at him, hearing something cold and flat in his voice. Her smirk deepened a little, and he realized he had sounded . . . well, not frightened but momentarily weak. He added, "It wouldn't fit." Although, in truth, it looked as if the poltergeist had been about his height and weight in life.

Georgia said, "Maybe I'll wear it. I'm a bit of a restless spirit myself. And I look hot in men's clothing."

Again: a sensation of revulsion, a crawling of the skin. She shouldn't put it on. It unsettled him that she would even joke about it, although he couldn't have said why. He wasn't going to let her put it on. In that one instant, he could not imagine anything more repellent.

And that was saying something. There wasn't much that Jude found too distasteful to contemplate. He was unused to feeling disgust. The profane didn't trouble him; it had made him a good living for thirty years.

"I'll stick it upstairs until I figure out what to do with it," he said, trying for a dismissive tone—and not quite making it.

She stared at him, interested at this wavering of his usual self-possession, and then she pulled off the plastic dry-cleaning bag. The coat's silver buttons flashed in the light. The suit was somber, as dark as crow feathers, but those buttons, the size of quarters, gave it something of a rustic character. Add a string tie and it was the sort of thing Johnny Cash might've worn onstage.

Angus began to bark, high, shrill, panicked barking. He shoved himself back on his haunches, tail lowered, rearing away from the suit. Georgia laughed.

"It *is* haunted," she said.

She held the suit in front of her and waved it back and forth, walking it through the air toward Angus, flapping it at him, a bullfighter with cape. She moaned as she closed in on him, the throaty, drawn-out cry of a wandering haunt, while her eyes gleamed with pleasure.

Angus scrambled back, hit a stool at the kitchen counter, and knocked it over with a ringing crash. Bon stared out from beneath the old, blood-stained chopping block, ears flattened against her skull. Georgia laughed again.

"Cut it the fuck out," Jude said.

She shot him a snotty, perversely happy look—the look of a child burning ants with a magnifying glass—and then she made a face of pain and shouted. Swore and grabbed her right hand. She flung the suit aside onto the counter.

A bright drop of blood fattened at the tip of her thumb and fell, *plink*, onto the tiled floor.

"Shit," she said. "Fucking pin."

"You see what you get."

She glared, flipped him the bird, and stalked out. When she was gone, he got up and put the juice back into the fridge. Jude dropped the knife in the sink, got a hand towel to wipe the blood off the floor—and then his gaze caught on the suit, and he forgot whatever it was he'd been about to do.

He smoothed it out, folded the arms over the chest, felt carefully around. Jude couldn't find any pins, couldn't figure out what she'd stuck herself on. He laid it gently back into its box.

An acrid odor caught his attention. He glanced into the pan and cursed. The bacon was burnt.

He put the box on the shelf in the back of his closet and decided to stop thinking about it.

4

He was passing back through the kitchen, a little before six, to get sausages for the grill, when he heard someone whispering in Danny's office.

The sound jumped him and halted him in his tracks. Danny had gone home more than an hour ago, and the office was locked, should've been empty. Jude tilted his head to listen, concentrating intently on the low, sibilant voice . . . and in another moment he identified what he was hearing, and his pulse began to slow.

There was no one in there. It was only someone talking on the radio. Jude could tell. The low tones weren't low enough, the voice itself subtly flattened out. Sounds could suggest shapes, painted a picture of the pocket of air in which they'd been given form. A voice in a well had a deep, round echo, while a voice in a closet sounded condensed, all the fullness squeezed out of it. Music was also geometry. What Jude was hearing now was a voice clapped into a box. Danny had forgotten to turn off the radio.

He opened the door to the office, poked his head in. The lights were off, and with the sun on the other side of the building, the room drowned in blue shadow. The office stereo was the third-worst in the house, which was still better than most home stereos, a stack of Onkyo components in a glass cabinet by the water cooler. The readouts were lit a vivid, unnatural green, the color of objects viewed through a night-vision scope, except for a single, glowing, vertical slash of red, a ruby mark showing the frequency to which the radio was tuned. The mark was a narrow slit, the shape of a cat's pupil, and seemed to stare into the office with an unblinking, alien fascination.

". . . How cold is it going to get tonight?" said the man on the radio in a husky, almost abrasive tone. A fat man, judging by the wheeze when he exhaled. "Do we have to worry about finding bums frozen to the ground?"

"Your concern for the welfare of the homeless is touching," said a second man, this one with a voice that was a little thin, reedy.

It was WFUM, where most of the bands were named after fatal diseases (Anthrax), or conditions of decay (Rancid), and where the DJs tended to be preoccupied with crotch lice, strippers, and the amusing humiliations that attended the poor, the crippled, and the elderly. They were known to play Jude's music, more or less constantly, which was why Danny kept the stereo tuned to them, as an act of both loyalty and flattery. In truth, Jude suspected that Danny had no particular musical preferences, no strong likes or dislikes, and that the radio was just background sound, the auditory equivalent of wallpaper. If he had worked for Enya, Danny would've happily hummed along to Celtic chanting while answering her e-mails and sending faxes.

Jude started across the room to turn off the stereo but had not gone far before his step hitched, a memory snagging at his thoughts. An hour ago he'd been outside with the dogs. He had stood at the end of the dirt turnaround, enjoying the sharpness of the air, the sting on his cheeks. Someone down the road was burning a waste pile of deadfall and autumn leaves, and the faint odor of the spiced smoke had pleased him as well.

Danny had come out of the office, shrugging on his jacket, headed home. They stood talking for a moment—or, to be more accurate, Danny stood jawing at him while Jude watched the dogs and tried to tune him out. You could always count on Danny Wooten to spoil a perfectly good silence.

Silence. The office behind Danny had been silent. Jude could remember the crows going *crawk-crawk* and Danny's steady stream of exuberant chatter, but not the sound of the radio coming from the office behind him. If it had been on, Jude thought he would've heard. His ears were still as sensitive as they'd ever been. They had, against long odds, survived all that he'd inflicted upon them over the last thirty years. By comparison, Jude's drummer, Kenny Morlix, the only other surviving member of his original band, had severe tinnitus, couldn't even hear his wife when she was yelling right in his face.

Jude started forward once more, but he was ill at ease again. It wasn't any one thing. It was all of it. It was the dimness of the office and the glaring red eye staring out from the face of the receiver. It was the idea that the radio hadn't been on an hour ago, when Danny had stood in the open office door zipping his jacket. It was the thought that someone had recently passed through the office and might still be close by, maybe watching from the darkness of the bathroom, where the door was open a crack—a paranoid thing to think and unlike him, but in his head all the same. He reached for the power button on the stereo, not really listening anymore, his gaze on that door. He wondered what he would do if it started to open.

The weatherman said, ". . . cold and dry as the front pushes the warm air south. The dead pull the living down. Down into the cold. Down into the hole. You will di—"

Jude's thumb hit the power button, switching off the stereo, just as he registered what was being said. He twitched, startled, and stabbed the power button again, to get the voice back, figure out what the hell the weatherman had just been going on about.

Except the weatherman was done talking, and it was the DJ instead: ". . . going to freeze our asses off, but Kurt Cobain is warm in hell. Dig it."

A guitar whined, a shrill, wavering sound that went on and on without any discernible melody or purpose except perhaps to drive the listener to madness. The opening of Nirvana's "I Hate Myself and I Want to Die." Was that what the weatherman had been talking about? He'd said something about dying. Jude clicked the power button once more, returning the room to stillness.

It didn't last. The phone went off, right behind him, a startling burst of sound that gave Jude's pulse another unhappy jump. He shot a look at Danny's desk, wondering who would be calling on the office line at this hour. He shifted around behind the desk for a glance at caller ID. It was a 985 number, which he identified immediately as a prefix for eastern Louisiana. The name that came up was COWZYNSKI, M.

Only Jude knew, even without picking up the phone, that it wasn't really Cowzynski, M., on the other end. Not unless a medical miracle had transpired. He almost didn't pick up at all, but then the thought came that maybe Arlene Wade was calling to tell him Martin was dead, in which case he would have to talk to her sooner or later, whether he wanted to or not.

"Hello," he said.

"Hello, Justin," said Arlene. She was an aunt by marriage, his mother's sister-in-law, and a licensed physician's assistant, although for the last thirteen months her only patient had been Jude's father. She was sixty-nine, and her voice was all twang and warble. To her he would always be Justin Cowzynski.

"How are you, Arlene?"

"I'm the same as ever. You know. Me and the dog are gettin' along. Although he can't get up so much now because he's so fat and his knees pain him. But I'm not callin' to tell you about myself or the dog. I'm callin' about your father."

As if there could be anything else she might call about. The line hissed with white noise. Jude had been interviewed over the phone by a radio personality in Beijing and taken calls from Brian Johnson in Australia, and the connections had been as crisp and clear as if they were phoning him from down the street. But for some reason calls from Moore's Corner, Louisiana, came in scratchy and faint, like an AM radio station that's just a little too far away to be received perfectly. Voices from other phone calls would bleed in and out, faintly audible for a few moments and then gone. They might have high-speed Internet connections in Baton Rouge, but in the little towns in the swamps north of Lake Pontchartrain, if you wanted a high-speed connection with the rest of the world, you souped up a car and got the fuck out.

"Last few months I been spoonin' him food. Soft stuff he don't have to chew. He was likin' them little stars. Pastina. And vanilla custard. I never met a dyin' person yet didn't want some custard on their way out the door."

"I'm surprised. He never used to have a sweet tooth. Are you sure?"

"Who's takin' care of him?"

"You are."

"Well, I guess I'm sure, then."

"All right."

"This is the reason I'm callin'. He won't eat custard or little stars or anything else. He just chokes on whatever I put in his mouth. He can't swallow. Dr. Newland was in to see him yesterday. He thinks your dad had another infarction."

"A stroke." It was not quite a question.

"Not a fall-down-and-kill-you kind of stroke. If he had another one of those, there wouldn't be any question of it. He'd be dead. This was one of the little blow-outs. You don't always know when he's had one of the little ones. Especially when he gets like he is now, just starin' at things. He hasn't said a word to anyone in two months. He isn't ever going to say a word to anyone again."

"Is he at the hospital?"

"No. We can care for him just as well or better here. Me livin' with him and Dr. Newland in every day. But we can send him to the hospital. It would be cheaper there, if that matters to you."

"It doesn't. Let 'em save the beds at the hospital for people who might actually get better in them."

"I won't argue you on that one. Too many people die in hospitals, and if you can't be helped, you have to wonder why."

"So what are you going to do about him not eating? What happens now?"

This was met by a moment of silence. He had an idea that the question had taken her by surprise. Her tone, when she spoke again, was both gently reasonable and apologetic, the tone of a woman explaining a harsh truth to a child.

"Well. That's up to you, not me, Justin. Doc Newland can poke a feedin' tube in him and he'll go on a while longer, that's what you want. Till he has another little blowout and he forgets how to breathe. Or we can just let him be. He isn't ever goin' to recover, not at eighty-five years old. It's not like he's bein' robbed of his youth. He's ready to let go. Are you?"

Jude thought, but did not say, that he'd been ready for more than forty years. He had occasionally imagined this moment—maybe it was fair to say he'd even daydreamed of it—but now it had come, and he was surprised to find that his stomach hurt.

When he replied, though, his voice was steady and his own. "Okay, Arlene. No tube. If you say it's time, that's good enough for me. Keep me updated, all right?"

But she wasn't done with him yet. She made an impatient sound, a kind of stiff exhalation of breath, and said, "Are you comin' down?"

He stood at Danny's desk, frowning, confused. The conversation had taken a leap from one thing to another, without warning, like a needle skipping across a record from one track to the next. "Why would I do that?"

"Do you want to see him before he's gone?"

No. He had not seen his father, stood in the same room with him, in three decades. Jude did not want to see the old man before he was gone, and he did not want to look at him after. He had no plans to so much as attend the funeral, although he would be the one to pay for it. Jude was afraid of what he might feel—or what he wouldn't. He would pay whatever he had to pay not to have to share his father's company again. It was the best thing the money could buy: distance.

But he could no more say this to Arlene Wade than he could tell her he'd been waiting on the old man to die since he was fourteen. Instead he replied, "Would he even know if I was there?"

"It's hard to say what he knows and what he doesn't. He's aware of people in the room with him. He turns his eyes to watch folks come and watch folks go. He's been less responsive lately, though. People get that way, once enough lights have burned out."

"I can't make it down. This week isn't good," Jude said, reaching for the easiest lie. He thought maybe the conversation was over, and was prepared to say good-bye. Then he surprised himself by asking a question, one he hadn't known was even on his mind until he heard himself speaking it aloud. "Will it be hard?"

"For him to die? Naw. When an old fella gets to this stage, they waste away pretty quick without bein' hooked to the feed bag. They don't suffer none."

"You sure on that?"

"Why?" she asked. "Disappointed?"

5

Forty minutes later Jude drifted into the bathroom to soak his feet—size 14, flat arches, and a constant source of pain to him—and found Georgia leaning over the sink sucking her thumb. She had on a T-shirt and pajama bottoms with a cute pattern of tiny red figures that might've been hearts printed on them. It was only when you got close that you could see that all those tiny red figures were actually images of shriveled dead rats.

He leaned into her and pulled her hand out of her mouth to inspect her thumb. The tip was swollen and had a white, soft-looking sore on it. He let go of her hand and turned away, disinterested, pulling a towel off the heated rack and throwing it over his shoulder.

"Ought to put something on that," he said. "Before it festers and rots. There's less work for pole dancers with visible disfigurements."

"You're a sympathetic son of a bitch, you know that?"

"You want sympathy, go fuck James Taylor."

He glanced over his shoulder at her as she stalked out. As soon as he said it, a part of him wished he could take it back. But he didn't take it back. In their metal-studded bracelets and glossy black, dead-girl lipstick, they wanted harshness, the girls like Georgia. They wanted to prove something to themselves about how much they could take, to prove they were hard. That was why they came to him, not in spite of the things he said to them or the way he treated them but because of those things. He didn't want anyone to go away disappointed. And it was just understood that sooner or later they *would* go away.

Or at least *he* understood it, and if they didn't at first, then they always figured it out eventually.

One of the dogs was in the house.

Jude woke just after three in the morning at the sound of it, pacing in the hallway, a rustle and a light swish of restless movement, a soft bump against the wall.

He had put them in their pens just before dark, remembered doing this very clearly, but didn't worry about that fact in the first few moments after coming awake. One of them had got into the house somehow, that was all.

Jude sat for a moment, still drunk and stuporous from sleep. A blue splash of moonlight fell across Georgia, sleeping on her belly to his left. Dreaming, her face relaxed and scrubbed of all its makeup, she looked almost girlish, and he felt a sudden tenderness for her—that, and also an odd embarrassment to find himself in bed with her.

"Angus?" he murmured. "Bon?"

Georgia didn't stir. Now he heard nothing in the hallway. He slid out of bed. The damp and the cold took him by surprise. The day had been the coolest in months, the first real day of fall, and now there was a raw, clinging chill in the air, which meant it had to be even colder outside. Maybe that was why the dogs were in the house. Maybe they had burrowed under the wall of the pen and somehow forced their way in, desperate to be warm. But that didn't make sense. They had an indoor-outdoor pen, could go into the heated barn if they were cold. He started toward the door, to peek into the hall, then hesitated at the window and twitched aside the curtain to look outside.

The dogs were in the outdoor half of the pen, both of them, up against the wall of the barn. Angus roamed back and forth over the straw, his body long and sleek, his sliding, sideways movements agitated. Bon sat primly in one corner. Her head was raised, and her gaze was fixed on Jude's window—on him. Her eyes flashed a bright, unnatural green in the darkness. She was too still, too unblinking, like a statue of a dog instead of the real thing.

It was a shock to look out the window and see her staring directly back at him, as if she'd been watching the glass for who knew how long, waiting for him to appear. But that was not as bad as knowing that something else was in the house, moving around, bumping into things in the hallway.

Jude glanced at the security panel next to the bedroom door. The house was monitored, inside and out, by a collection of motion detectors. The dogs weren't big enough to set them off, but a grown man would trip them, and the panel would note movement in one part of the house or another.

The readout, however, showed a steady green light and read only SYSTEM READY. Jude wondered if the chip was smart enough to tell the difference between a dog and a naked psychotic scrambling around on all fours with a knife in his teeth.

Jude had a gun, but it was in his private recording studio, in the safe. He reached for the Dobro guitar leaning against the wall. Jude had never been one to smash a guitar for effect. His father had smashed his very first guitar for him, in an early attempt to rid Jude of his musical ambitions. Jude hadn't been able to repeat the act himself, not even onstage, for show, when he could afford all the guitars he wanted. He was, however, perfectly willing to use one as a weapon to defend himself. In a sense he supposed he had always used them as weapons.

He heard one floorboard creak in the hall, then another, then a sigh, as of someone settling. His blood quickened. He opened the door.

But the hallway was empty. Jude plashed through long rectangles of icy light, cast by the skylights. He stopped at each closed door, listened, then glanced within. A blanket tossed across a chair looked, for a moment, like a deformed dwarf glaring at him. In another room he found a tall, gaunt figure standing behind the door, and his heart reared in his chest, and he almost swung the guitar, then realized it was a coatrack, and all the breath came rushing unsteadily out of him.

In his studio, at the end of the hall, he considered collecting the gun, then didn't. He didn't want it on him—not because he was afraid to use it but because he wasn't afraid enough. He was so keyed up he might react to a sudden movement in the dark by pulling the trigger and wind up blowing a hole in Danny Wooten or the housekeeper, although why they would be creeping about the house at this hour he couldn't imagine. He returned to the corridor and went downstairs.

He searched the ground floor and found only shadow and stillness, which should've reassured him but didn't. It was the wrong kind of stillness, the shocked stillness that follows the bang of a cherry bomb. His eardrums throbbed from the pressure of all that quiet, a dreadful silence.

He couldn't relax, but at the bottom of the stairs he pretended to, a charade he carried on for himself alone. He leaned the guitar against the wall and exhaled noisily.

"What the fuck are you doing?" he said. By then he was so ill at ease the sound of his own voice unnerved him, sent a cool, prickling rush up his forearms. He had never been one to talk to himself.

He climbed the stairs and started back down the hall to the bedroom. His gaze drifted to an old man, sitting in an antique Shaker chair against the wall. As soon as Jude saw him, his pulse lunged in alarm, and he looked away, fixed his gaze on his bedroom door, so he could only see the old man from the edge of his vision. In the moments that followed, Jude felt it was a matter of life and death not to make eye contact with the old man, to give no sign that he saw him. He did not see him, Jude told himself. There was no one there.

The old man's head was bowed. His hat was off, resting on his knee. His hair was a close bristle, with the brilliance of new frost. The buttons down the front of his coat flashed in the gloom, chromed by moonlight. Jude recognized the suit in a glance. He had last seen it folded in the black, heart-shaped box that had gone into the rear of his closet. The old man's eyes were closed.

Jude's heart pounded, and it was a struggle to breathe, and he continued on toward the bedroom door, which was at the very end of the hallway. As he went past the Shaker chair, against the wall to his left, his leg brushed the old man's knee, and the ghost lifted his head. But by then Jude was beyond him, almost to the door. He was careful not to run. It didn't matter to him if the old man stared at his back, as long as they didn't make eye contact with each other, and besides, there was no old man.

He let himself into the bedroom and clicked the door shut behind him. He went straight to his bed and got into it and immediately began to shake. A part of him wanted to roll against Georgia and cling to her, let her body warm him and drive away the chills, but he stayed on his side of the bed so as not to wake her. He stared at the ceiling.

Georgia was restless and moaned unhappily in her sleep.

7

He didn't expect to sleep but dozed off at first light and then woke uncharacteristically late, after nine. Georgia was on her side, her small hand resting lightly on his chest and her breath soft on his shoulder. He slipped out of bed and away from her, let himself into the hall and walked downstairs.

The Dobro leaned against the wall where he had left it. The sight of it gave his heart a bad turn. He'd been trying to pretend he had not seen what he'd seen in the night. He had set himself a goal of not thinking about it. But there was the Dobro.

When Jude looked out the window, he spotted Danny's car parked by the barn. He had nothing to say to Danny and no reason to bother him, but in another moment he was at the door of the office. He couldn't help himself. The compulsion to be in the company of another human, someone awake and sensible and with a head full of everyday nonsense, was irresistible.

Danny was on the phone, craned back in his office chair, laughing about something. He was still in his suede jacket. Jude didn't need to ask why. He himself had a robe over his shoulders and was hugging himself under it. The office was filled with a damp cold.

Danny saw Jude looking around the door and winked at him, another favorite ass-kissing Hollywood habit of his, although on this particular morning Jude didn't mind it. Then Danny saw something on Jude's face and frowned. He mouthed the words *You okay?* Jude didn't answer. Jude didn't know.

Danny got rid of whoever he was talking to, then rotated in his chair to turn a solicitous look upon him. "What's going on, Chief? You look like fucking hell."

Jude said, "The ghost came."

"Oh, did it?" Danny asked, brightening. Then he hugged himself, mock-shivered. Tipped his head toward the phone. "That was the heating people. This place is a fucking tomb. They'll have a guy out here to check on the boiler in a little while."

"I want to call her."

"Who?"

"The woman who sold us the ghost."

Danny lowered one of his eyebrows and raised the other, making a face that said he had lost Jude somewhere. "What do you mean, the ghost came?"

"What we ordered. It came. I want to call her. I want to find some things out."

Danny seemed to need a moment to process this. He swiveled partway back to his computer and got the phone, but his gaze remained fixed on Jude. He said, "You sure you're all right?"

"No," he said. "I'm going to see to the dogs. Find her number, will you?"

He went outside in his bathrobe and his underwear, to set Bon and Angus loose from their pens. The temperature was in the low fifties, and the air was white with a fine-grained mist. Still, it was more comfortable than the damp, clinging cold of the house. Angus licked at his hand, his tongue rough and hot and so real that for a moment Jude felt an almost painful throb of gratitude. He was glad to be among the dogs, with their stink of wet fur and their eagerness for play. They ran past him, chasing each other, then ran back, Angus snapping at Bon's tail.

His own father had treated the family dogs better than he ever treated Jude, or Jude's mother. In time it had rubbed off on Jude, and he'd learned to treat dogs better than himself as well. He had spent most of his childhood sharing his bed with dogs, sleeping with one on either side of him and sometimes a third at his feet, had been inseparable from his father's unwashed, primitive, tick-infested pack. Nothing reminded him of who he was, and where he had come from, faster than the rank smell of dog, and by the time he reentered the house, he felt steadier, more himself.

As he stepped through the office door, Danny was saying into the phone, "Thanks so much. Can you hold a moment for Mr. Coyne?" He pressed a button, held out the receiver. "Name's Jessica Price. Down in Florida."

As Jude took the receiver, he realized that this was the first time he'd ever heard the woman's full name. When he had put down his money on the ghost, he'd simply not been curious, although it seemed to him now that it was the kind of thing he should've made a point to know.

He frowned. She had a perfectly ordinary sort of name, but for some reason it caught his attention. He didn't think he had ever heard it before, but it was so inherently forgettable it was hard to be sure.

Jude put the receiver to his ear and nodded. Danny pressed the button again to take it off hold.

"Jessica. Hello. Judas Coyne."

"How'd you like your suit, Mr. Coyne?" she asked. Her voice carried a delicate southern lilt, and her tone was easy and pleasant . . . and something else. There was a hint in it, a sweet, teasing hint of something like mockery.

"What did he look like?" Judas asked. He had never been one to take his time getting to the point. "Your stepfather."

"Reese, honey," the woman said, talking to someone else, not Jude. "Reese, will you turn off that TV and go outside?" A girl, away in the background, registered a sullen complaint. "Because I'm on the phone." The girl said something else. "Because it's private. Go on, now. Go on." A screen door slapped shut. The woman sighed, a bemused, "you know kids" sound, and then said to Jude, "Did you see him? Why don't you tell me what *you* think he looks like, and I'll say if you're right."

She was fucking with him. *Fucking* with him.

"I'm sending it back," Jude told her.

"The suit? Go ahead. You can send the suit back to me. That doesn't mean he'll come with it. No refunds, Mr. Coyne. No exchanges."

Danny stared at Jude, smiling a puzzled smile, his brow furrowed in thought. Jude noticed then the sound of his own breath, harsh and deep. He struggled for words, to know what to say.

She spoke first. "Is it cold there? I bet it's cold. It's going to get a lot colder before he's through."

"What are you out for? More money? You won't get it."

"She came back home to kill herself, you asshole," she said, Jessica Price of Florida, whose name was unfamiliar to him, but maybe not quite as unfamiliar as he would've liked. Her voice had suddenly, without warning, lost the veneer of easy humor. "After you were done with her, she slashed her wrists in the bathtub. Our stepdaddy is the one who found her. She would've done anything for you, and you threw her away like she was garbage."

Florida.

Florida. He felt a sudden ache in the pit of his stomach, a sensation of cold, sick weight. In the same moment, his head seemed to come clear, to shake off the cobwebs of exhaustion and superstitious fear. She had always been Florida to him, but her name was really Anna May McDermott. She told fortunes, knew tarot and palmistry. She and her older sister both had learned how from their stepfather. He was a hypnotist by trade, the last resort of smokers and self-loathing fat ladies who wanted to be done with their cigarettes and their Twinkies. But on the weekends Anna's stepfather hired himself out as a dowser and used his hypnotist's pendulum, a silver razor on a gold chain, to find lost objects and to tell people where to drill their wells. He hung it over the bodies of the ill to heal their auras and slow their hungry cancers, spoke to the dead with it by dangling it over a Ouija board. But hypnotism was the meal ticket: *You can relax now. You can close your eyes. Just listen to my voice.*

Jessica Price was talking again. "Before my stepfather died, he told me what to do, how I should get in touch with you and how to send you his suit and what would happen after. He said he'd see to you, you ugly, no-talent motherfucker."

She was Jessica Price, not McDermott, because she had married and was a widow now. Jude had the impression her husband had been a reservist who bought it in Tikrit, thought he recalled Anna telling him that. He wasn't sure Anna had ever mentioned her older sister's married name, although she'd told him once that Jessica had followed their stepfather into the hypnotism trade. Anna had said her sister made almost seventy thousand dollars a year at it.

Jude said, "Why did I have to buy the suit? Why didn't you just send it to me?" The calm of his own voice was a source of satisfaction to him. He sounded calmer than she did.

"If you didn't pay, the ghost wouldn't really belong to you. You had to pay. And, boy, are you goin' to."

"How'd you know I'd buy it?"

"I sent you an e-mail, didn't I? Anna told me all about your sick little collection . . . your dirty little oh-cult pervert shit. I figured you couldn't help yourself."

"Someone else could've bought it. The other bids—"

"There weren't any other bids. Just you. I put all those other bids up there, and the biddin' wasn't goin' to be done until you made an offer. How do you like your purchase? Is it what you were hopin' for? Oh, you have got some fun ahead of you. I'm goin' to spend that thousand dollars you paid me for my stepdad's ghost on a bouquet for your funeral. Goin' to be one hell of a nice spread."

You can just get out, Jude thought. *Just get out of the house. Leave the dead man's suit and the dead man behind. Take Georgia for a trip to L.A. Pack a couple suitcases, be on a flight in three hours. Danny can set it up, Danny can . . .*

As if he had said it aloud, Jessica Price said, "Go ahead and check into a hotel. See what happens. Wherever you go, he'll be right there. When you wake up, he'll be settin' at the foot of your bed." She was starting to laugh. "You're goin' to die, and it's goin' to be his cold hand over your mouth."

"So Anna was living with you when she killed herself?" he said. Still in possession of himself. Still perfectly calm.

A pause. The angry sister was out of breath, needed a moment before she could reply. Jude could hear a sprinkler running in the background, children shouting in the street.

Jessica said, "It was the only place she had. She was depressed. She'd always been bad depressed, but you made it worse. She was too miserable to go out, get help, see anyone. You made her hate herself. You made it so she wanted to die."

"What makes you think she killed herself because of me? You ever think it was the pleasure of your company drove her over the edge? If I had to listen to you all day, I'd probably want to slash my wrists, too."

"You're going to die—" she spat.

He cut her off. "Think up a new line. And while you're working on that, here's something else to think about: I know a few angry souls myself. They drive Harleys, live in trailers, cook crystal meth, abuse their children, and shoot their wives. You call 'em scumbags. I call 'em fans. Want to see if I can find a few who live in your area to drop in and say hello?"

"No one will help you," she said, voice strangled and trembling with fury. "The black mark on you will infect anyone who joins your cause. You will not live, and no one who gives you aid or comfort will live."

Reciting it through her anger, as if it were a speech she had rehearsed, which perhaps she had. "Everyone will flee from you or be undone like you will be undone. You're goin' to die alone, you hear me? *Alone*."

"Don't be so sure. If I'm going down, I might like some company," he said. "And if I can't get help, maybe I'll come see you myself." And banged the phone down.

8

Jude glared at the black phone, still gripped in his white-knuckled hand, and listened to the slow, martial drumbeat of his heart.

"Boss," Danny breathed. "Ho. Lee. Shit. *Boss.*" He laughed: thin, wheezing, humorless laughter. "What the hell was all that?"

Jude mentally commanded his hand to open, to let go of the phone. It didn't want to. He knew that Danny had asked a question, but it was like a voice overheard through a closed door, part of a conversation taking place in another room, nothing to do with him.

It was beginning to settle in that Florida was dead. When he had first heard she'd killed herself—when Jessica Price threw it in his face—it had not meant anything, because he couldn't let it mean anything. Now, though, there was no running from it. He felt the knowledge of her death in his blood, which went heavy and thick and strange on him.

It did not seem possible to Jude she could be gone, that someone with whom he'd shared his bed could be in a bed of dirt now. She was twenty-six—no, twenty-seven; she'd been twenty-six when she left. When he sent her away. She'd been twenty-six, but she asked questions like a four-year-old. *You go fishin' much on Lake Pontchartrain? What's the best*

dog you ever owned? What do you think happens to us when we die?
Enough questions to drive a man mad.

She'd been afraid she was going mad. She was depressed. Not fash-
ionably depressed, in the way of some Goth chicks, but clinically. She
had been overcome with it in their last couple of months together, didn't
sleep, wept for no reason, forgot to put on her clothes, stared at the TV
for hours without bothering to turn it on, answered the phone when it
rang but then wouldn't say anything, just stood there holding it, as if
she'd been switched off.

But before that there'd been summer days in the barn while he rebuilt the Mustang. There'd been John Prine on the radio, the sweet
smell of hay baking in the heat, and afternoons filled with her lazy, pointless questions—a never-ending interrogation that was, at turns, tiresome,
amusing, and erotic. There'd been her body, tattooed and icy white, with
the bony knees and skinny thighs of a long-distance runner. There'd been
her breath on his neck.

"Hey," Danny said. He reached out, and his fingers grazed Jude's
wrist. At his touch, Jude's hand sprang open, releasing the phone. "Are
you going to be all right?"

"I don't know."

"Want to tell me what's going on?"

Slowly Jude lifted his gaze. Danny half stood behind his desk. He
had lost some of his color, his ginger freckles standing out in high relief
against the white of his cheeks.

Danny had been her friend, in the unthreatening, easygoing, slightly
impersonal way he made himself a friend to all of Jude's girls. He played
the role of the urbane, understanding gay pal, someone they could trust
to keep their secrets, someone they could vent to and gossip with, someone who provided intimacy without involvement. Someone who would
tell them things about Jude that Jude wouldn't tell them himself.

Danny's sister had OD'd on heroin when Danny was just a freshman
in college. His mother hanged herself six months later, and Danny had

been the one who discovered her. Her body dangled from the single rafter in the pantry, her toes pointed downward, turning in small circles above a kicked-over footstool. You didn't need to be a psychologist to see that the double-barreled blast of the sister and the mother, dying at almost the same time, had wiped out some part of Danny as well, had frozen him at nineteen. Although he didn't wear black fingernail polish or rings in his lips, in a way Danny's attraction to Jude wasn't so different from Georgia's, or Florida's, or any of the other girls'. Jude collected them in almost exactly the same way the Pied Piper had collected rats, and children. He made melodies out of hate and perversion and pain, and they came to him, skipping to the music, hoping he would let them sing along.

Jude didn't want to tell Danny about what Florida had done to herself, wanted to spare him. It would be better not to tell him. He wasn't sure how Danny would take it.

He told him anyway. "Anna. Anna McDermott. She cut her wrists. The woman I was just talking to is her sister."

"Florida?" Danny said. He settled back into his chair. It creaked beneath him. He looked winded. He pressed his hands to his abdomen, then leaned forward slightly, as if his stomach were cramping up. "Oh, shit. Oh, fucking shit," Danny said sweetly. No words had ever sounded less obscene.

A silence followed. Jude noticed, for the first time, that the radio was on, murmuring softly. Trent Reznor sang that he was ready to give up his empire of dirt. It was funny hearing Nine Inch Nails on the radio just then. Jude had met Florida at a Trent Reznor show, backstage. The fact of her death hit him fresh, all over again, as if he were just realizing it for the first time. *You go fishin' much on Lake Pontchartrain?* And then the shock began to coalesce into a sickened resentment. It was so pointless and stupid and self-involved that it was impossible not to hate her a little, not to want to get her on the phone and curse her out, except he couldn't get her on the phone, because she was dead.

"Did she leave a note?" Danny asked.

"I don't know. I didn't get much information from her sister. It wasn't the world's most helpful phone call. Maybe you noticed."

But Danny wasn't listening. He said, "We used to go out for margaritas sometimes. She was one hell of a sweet kid. Her and her questions. She asked me once if I had a favorite place to watch the rain when I was a kid. What the hell kind of question is that? She made me shut my eyes and describe what it looked like outside my bedroom window when it was raining. For ten minutes. You never knew what she was going to ask next. We were big-time compadres. I don't understand this. I mean, I know she was depressed. She told me about it. But she really didn't want to be. Wouldn't she have called one of us if she was going to do something like . . . ? Wouldn't she have given one of us a chance to talk her out of it?"

"I guess not."

Danny had dwindled somehow in the last few minutes, shrunk into himself. He said, "And her sister . . . her sister thinks it's your fault? Well, that's . . . that's just crazy." But his voice was weak, and Jude thought he didn't sound entirely sure of himself.

"I guess."

"She had emotional problems going back before she met you," Danny said, with a little more confidence.

"I think it runs in her family," Jude said.

Danny leaned forward again. "Yeah. *Yeah*. I mean—what the Christ? Anna's sister is the person who sold you the ghost? The dead man's suit? What the fuck is going on here? What happened that made you want to call her in the first place?"

Jude didn't want to tell Danny about what he'd seen last night. In that moment—pushed up against the stony truth of Florida's death—he wasn't entirely sure *what* he'd seen last night anymore. The old man sitting in the hallway, outside his bedroom door at 3:00 A.M., just didn't seem as real now.

"The suit she sent me is a kind of symbolic death threat. She tricked us into buying it. For some reason she couldn't just send it to me, I had to pay for it first. I guess you could say sanity isn't her strong suit. Anyway, I could tell there was something wrong about it as soon as it came. It was in this fucked-up black heart-shaped box and—this will maybe sound a little paranoid—but it had a pin hidden inside to stick someone."

"There was a needle hidden in it? Did it stick you?"

"No. It poked Georgia good, though."

"Is she all right? Do you think there was something on it?"

"You mean like arsenic? No. I don't get the sense Jessica Price of Psychoville, Florida, is actually that stupid. Deeply and intensely crazy, but not stupid. She wants to scare me, not go to jail. She told me her stepdaddy's ghost came with the suit and he's going to get me for what I did to Anna. The pin was probably, I don't know, part of the voodoo. I grew up not far from the Panhandle. Place is crawling with toothless, possum-eating trailer trash full of weird ideas. You can wear a crown of thorns to your job at the Krispy Kreme and no one will bat an eye."

"Do you want me to call the police?" Danny asked. He was finding his footing now. His voice wasn't so winded, had regained some of its self-assurance.

"No."

"She's making threats on your life."

"Who says?"

"You do. Me, too. I sat right here and heard the whole thing."

"What did you hear?"

Danny stared for a moment, then lowered his eyelids and smiled in a drowsy kind of way. "Whatever you say I heard."

Jude grinned back, in spite of himself. Danny was shameless. Jude could not, at the moment, recall why it was he sometimes didn't like him.

"Naw," Jude said. "That's not how I'm going to deal with this. But you can do one thing for me. Anna sent a couple letters after she went home. I don't know what I did with them. You want to poke around?"

"Sure, I'll see if I can lay a hand on them." Danny was eyeing him uneasily again, and even if he had recovered his humor, he had not got back his color. "Jude . . . when you say that's not how you're going to deal with this . . . what's *that* mean?" He pinched his lower lip, brow screwed up in thought again. "That stuff you said when you hung up. Talking about sending people after her. Going down there yourself. You were pretty pissed. Like I've never heard you. Do I need to be worried?"

"You? No," Jude said. "Her? Maybe."

9

His mind leaped from one bad thing to another, Anna nude and hollow-eyed and floating dead in scarlet bathwater, Jessica Price on the phone—*You're goin' to die, and it's goin' to be his cold hand over your mouth*—the old man sitting in the hall in his black Johnny Cash suit, slowly lifting his head to look at Jude as Jude walked by.

He needed to quiet the noise in his head, a thing usually best accomplished by making some noise with his hands. He carried the Dobro to his studio, strummed at it experimentally, and didn't like the tuning. Jude went into the closet to look for a capo to choke the strings and found a box of bullets instead.

They were in a heart-shaped box—one of the yellow heart-shaped boxes his father used to give to his mother, every Valentine's Day and every Mother's Day, on Christmas and on her birthday. Martin never gave her anything else—no roses or rings or bottles of champagne—but always the same big box of chocolates from the same department store.

Her reaction was as unvarying as his gift. Always, she smiled, a thin, uncomfortable smile, keeping her lips together. She was shy about her teeth. The uppers were false. The real ones had been punched in. Always, she offered the box first to her husband, who, smiling proudly, as if

his gift were a diamond necklace and not a three-dollar box of chocolates, would shake his head. Then she presented them to Jude.

And always Jude picked the same one, the one in the center, a
chocolate-covered cherry. He liked the *gloosh* of it when he bit into it,
the faintly corrupt, sticky-sweet sap, the rotten-soft texture of the cherry
itself. He imagined he was helping himself to a chocolate-covered eyeball.
Even in those days, Jude took pleasure in dreaming up the worst, reveled
in gruesome possibilities.

Jude found the box nestled in a rat's nest of cables and pedals and
adapters, under a guitar case leaned against the back of his studio closet.
It wasn't just any guitar case, but the one he'd left Louisiana with thirty
years before, although the used, forty-dollar Yamaha that had once occupied it was long gone. The Yamaha he had left behind, onstage in San
Francisco, where he'd opened for Zeppelin one night in 1975. He'd been
leaving a lot of things behind in those days: his family, Louisiana, swine,
poverty, the name he'd been born with. He did not waste a lot of time looking back.

He picked the candy box up, then dropped it just as quickly, his
hands going nerveless on him. Jude knew what was in it without even
opening it, knew at first sight. If there was any doubt at all, though, it
fled when the box hit the ground and he heard the brass shells jingle-
jangle inside. The sight of it caused him to recoil in an almost atavistic
terror, as if he'd gone digging through the cables and a fat, furry-legged
spider had crawled out across the back of his hand. He had not seen the
box of ammo in more than three decades and knew he'd left it stuck between the mattress and the box spring of his childhood bed, back in
Moore's Corner. It had not left Louisiana with him, and there was no
way it could be lying there behind his old guitar case, only it was.

He stared at the yellow heart-shaped box for a moment, then forced
himself to pick it up. He pulled off the lid and tipped the box over. Bullets spilled onto the floor.

He had collected them himself, as avid for them as some children were for baseball cards: his first collection. It had started when he was eight, when he was still Justin Cowzynski, years and years before he'd ever imagined that someday he would be someone else. One day he was tramping across the east field and heard something snap underfoot. He bent to see what he'd stepped on and picked an empty shotgun shell out of the mud. One of his father's, probably. It was fall, when the old man shot at turkeys. Justin sniffed the splintered, flattened case. The whiff of gunpowder itched his nostrils—a sensation that should've been unpleasant but which was strangely fascinating. It came home with him in his dungaree pocket and went into one of his mother's empty candy boxes.

It was soon joined by two live shells for a .38, swiped from the garage of a friend, some curious silver empties he had discovered at the rifle range, and a bullet from a British assault rifle, as long as his middle finger. He had traded for this last, and it had cost him dear—an issue of *Creepy* with a Frazetta cover—but he felt he had got value for value. He would lie in bed at night looking his bullets over, studying the way the starlight shone on the polished casings, smelling the lead, the way a man might sniff at a ribbon scented with a lover's perfume; thoughtfully, with a head full of sweet fantasy.

In high school he strung the British bullet on a leather thong and wore it around his throat until the principal confiscated it. Jude wondered that he had not found a way to kill someone in those days. He'd possessed all the key elements of a school shooter: hormones, misery, ammunition. People wondered how something like Columbine could happen. Jude wondered why it didn't happen more often.

They were all there—the crushed shotgun shell, the silver empties, the two-inch bullet from the AR-15, which couldn't be there, because the principal had never given it back. It was a warning. Jude had seen a dead man in the night, Anna's stepfather, and this was his way of telling Jude that their business was not done.

It was a crazy thing to think. There had to be a dozen more reasonable explanations for the box, for the bullets. But Jude didn't care what was reasonable. He wasn't a reasonable man. He only cared what was true. He had seen a dead man in the night. Maybe, for a few minutes, in Danny's sun-splashed office, he'd been able to block it out, pretend it hadn't happened, but it had.

He was steadier now, found himself considering the bullets coolly. It came to him that maybe it was more than a warning. Perhaps it was also a message. The dead man, the ghost, was telling him to arm himself.

Jude considered the .44, his Super Blackhawk, in the safe, under his desk. But what would he shoot at? He understood that the ghost existed first and foremost within his own head. That maybe ghosts always haunted minds, not places. If he wanted to take a shot at it, he'd have to turn the barrel against his own temple.

He brushed the bullets back into his mother's candy box, pushed the lid back on. Bullets wouldn't do him any good. But there were other kinds of ammunition.

He had a collection of books on the shelf at one end of the studio, books about the occult and the supernatural. Around the time Jude was just beginning his recording career, Black Sabbath came out big, and Jude's manager advised him that it couldn't hurt to at least imply that he and Lucifer were on a first-name basis with each other. Jude had already taken up the study of group psychology and mass hypnosis, on the theory that if fans were good, cultists were even better. He added volumes by Aleister Crowley and Charles Dexter Ward to the reading list, and he worked his way through them with a careful, joyless concentration, underlining concepts and key facts.

Later, after he was a celebrity, Satanists and Wiccans and spiritualists, who from listening to his music mistakenly thought he shared their enthusiasms—he really didn't give a fuck; it was like wearing leather pants, just part of the costume—sent him even more (admittedly fascinating) reading: an obscure manual, printed by the Catholic Church in the thirties, for performing exorcisms; a translation of a five-hundred-year-old book of perverted, unholy psalms written by a mad Templar; a cookbook for cannibals.

Jude placed the box of bullets up on the shelf among his books, all thoughts of finding a capo and playing some Skynyrd gone. He ran his thumbnail along the spines of the hardcovers. It was cold enough in his studio to make his fingers stiff and clumsy, and it was hard to turn pages, and he didn't know what he was looking for.

For a while he struggled to make his way through a strangled discourse on animal familiars, creatures of intense feeling who were bound by love and blood to their masters, and who could deal with the dead directly. But it was written in dense eighteenth-century English, without any punctuation. Jude would labor over a single paragraph for ten minutes, then wouldn't know what he'd read. He set it aside.

In another book he lingered on a chapter about possession, by way of demon or hateful spirit. One grotesque illustration showed an old man sprawled on his bed, among tangled sheets, his eyes bulging in horror and his mouth gaping open, while a leering, naked homunculus climbed out from between his lips. Or, a worse thought: Maybe the thing was climbing in.

Jude read that anyone who held open the golden door of mortality, for a peek at the other side, risked letting something through, and that the ill, the old, and those who loved death were especially in danger. The tone was assertive and knowledgeable, and Jude was encouraged until he read that the best method of protection was to wash yourself in urine. Jude had an open mind when it came to depravity, but he drew the line at water sports, and when the book slipped from his cold hands, he didn't bother to pick it up. Instead he kicked it away.

He read about the Borley rectory, about contacting spirit companions by way of the Ouija board, and about the alchemical uses of menstrual blood, his eyes going in and out of focus, and then he was flinging books, lashing them about the studio. Every word was crap. Demons and familiars and enchanted circles and the magical benefits of piss. One volume swept a lamp off his desk with a crash. Another hit a framed platinum record. A spiderweb of gleaming shatter lines leaped through the glass over the silver disk. The frame dropped from the wall, hit the floor, tilted onto its face with a crunch. Jude's hand found the candy box full of bullets. It struck the wall, and ammo sprayed across the floor in a ringing clatter.

He grabbed another book, breathing hard, his blood up, just looking to do some damage now and never mind to what, then caught himself, because the feel of the thing in his hand was all wrong. He looked and saw a black, unlabeled videotape instead. He didn't know right away what it was, had to think awhile before it came to him. It was his snuff film. It had been sitting on the shelf with the books, apart from the other videos for . . . what? Four years? It had been there so long he'd stopped seeing it among the hardcovers. It had become just a part of the general clutter on the shelves.

Jude had walked into the studio one morning and found his wife, Shannon, watching it. He was packing for a trip to New York and had come looking for a guitar to take with him. He stopped in the doorway at the sight of her. Shannon stood in front of the television, watching a man suffocate a naked teenage girl with a clear plastic bag, while other men watched.

Shannon frowned, her brow wrinkled in concentration, watching the girl in the movie die. He didn't worry about her temper—anger didn't impress him—but he'd learned to be wary of her when she was like this, calm and silent and drawn into herself.

At last she said, "Is this real?"

"Yes."

"She's really dying?"

He looked at the TV. The naked girl had gone slack and boneless on the floor. "She's really dead. They killed her boyfriend, too, didn't they?"

"He begged."

"A cop gave it to me. He told me the two kids were Texas junkies who shot up a liquor store and killed someone, then ran for Tijuana to hide out. Cops keep some sick shit lying around."

"He begged for her."

Jude said, "It's gruesome. I don't know why I still have it."

"I don't either," she said. She rose and ejected the movie, then stood looking at it, as if she had never seen a videotape before and was trying to imagine what purpose one might serve.

"Are you all right?" Jude asked.

"I don't know," she said. She turned the glassy, confused look upon him. "Are you?"

When he didn't reply, she crossed the room and slipped past him. At the door Shannon caught herself and realized she was still holding the tape. She set it gently on the shelf before she walked out. Later the housekeeper shoved the video in with the books. It was a mistake Jude never bothered to correct, and soon enough he forgot it was even there.

He had other things to think about. After he returned from New York, he found the house empty, Shannon's side of the closet cleaned out. She didn't bother with a note, no Dear John saying their love had been a mistake or that she'd loved some version of him that didn't really exist, that they'd been growing apart. She was forty-six and had been married and divorced once before. She didn't do junior-high theatrics. When she had something to say to him, she called. When she needed something from him, her lawyer called.

Looking at the tape now, he really didn't know why he had held on to it—or why it had held on to him. It seemed to him he should've sought it out and got rid of it when he came home and found her gone. He was not even sure why he had accepted it in the first place, when the tape had been offered to him. Jude teetered then on the edge of an uncomfortable thought, that he had, over time, become a little too willing to take what he was offered, without wondering at the possible consequences. And look at the trouble it had led to. Anna had offered herself to him, and he had taken, and now she was dead. Jessica McDermott Price had offered him the dead man's suit, and now it was his. Now it was his.

He had not gone out of his way to own a dead man's suit, or a videotape of Mexican death-porn, or any of the rest of it. It seemed to him instead that all these things had been drawn to him like iron filings to a magnet, and he could no more help drawing them and holding on to them than a magnet could. But this suggested helplessness, and he had never been helpless. If he was going to throw something into the wall, it ought to be this tape.

But he'd stood too long thinking. The cold in the studio sapped him, so that he felt tired, felt his age. He was surprised he couldn't see his own breath; that was how cold it felt. He couldn't imagine anything more foolish—or weak—than a fifty-four-year-old man pitching his books in a fit of rage, and if there was one thing he despised, it was weakness. He wanted to drop the tape and crunch it underfoot, but instead he turned to put it back on the shelf, feeling that it was more important to recover his composure, to act, at least for a moment, like an adult.

"Get rid of it," Georgia said from the door.

His shoulders twitched in reflexive surprise. He turned and looked. She was naturally pale to begin with, but now her face was bloodless, like polished bone, so she resembled a vampire even more than usual. He wondered if it was a trick of makeup before he saw that her cheeks were damp, the fine black hairs at her temples pasted down with sweat. She stood in pajamas, clutching herself and shivering in the cold.

"You sick?" he asked.

"I'm fine," she said. "Picture of health. Get rid of it."

He gently set the snuff film back on the shelf. "Get rid of what?"

"The dead man's suit. It smells bad. Didn't you notice the way it smelled when you took it out of the closet?"

"It isn't in the closet?"

"No, it isn't in the closet. It was lying on the bed when I woke up. It was spread out right next to me. Did you forget to put it back? Or forget you took it out in the first place? I swear to God, it's a surprise sometimes you remember to put your dick back in your pants after you take a piss. I hope all the pot you smoked in the seventies was worth it. What the hell were you doing with it anyway?"

If the suit was out of the closet, then it had walked out on its own.

There was no percentage in telling Georgia that, though, so he said nothing, pretended an interest in cleaning up.

Jude went around the desk, bent, and turned over the framed record that had dropped to the floor. The record itself was as busted as the plate of glass on top of it. He popped the frame apart and tipped it on its side. Broken glass slid with a musical clash into the wastebasket by his desk. He plucked out the pieces of his smashed platinum album—*Happy Little Lynch Mob*—and stuck them in the trash, six gleaming scimitar blades of grooved steel. What to do now? He supposed a thinking man would go and have another look at the suit. He rose and turned to her.

"Come on. You should lie down. You look like hell. I'll put the suit away, and then I'll tuck you in."

He put his hand on her upper arm, but she pulled free. "No. The bed smells like it, too. It's all over the sheets."

"So we'll get new sheets," he said, taking her arm again.

Jude turned her and guided her into the hallway. The dead man was sitting two-thirds of the way down the corridor, in the Shaker chair on the left, his head lowered in thought. A drape of morning sunshine fell across where his legs should have been. They disappeared where they passed into the light. It gave him the look of a war veteran, his trousers ending in stumps, midway down his thighs. Below this splash of sunshine were his polished black loafers, with his black-stockinged feet stuck in them. Between his thighs and his shoes, the only legs that were visible were the legs of the chair, the wood a lustrous blond in the light.

No sooner had Jude noticed him than he looked away, did not want to see him, did not want to think about him being there. He glanced at Georgia, to see if she had spotted the ghost. She was staring at her feet as she shuffled along with Jude's hand on her arm, her bangs in her eyes. He wanted to tell her to look, wanted to know if she could see him as well, but he was too in dread of the dead man to speak, afraid the ghost would hear him and glance up.

It was crazy to think somehow the dead man wasn't going to notice them walking past, but for no reason he could explain, Jude felt that if they were both very quiet, they could slip by unseen. The dead man's eyes were closed, his chin almost touching his chest, an old man who had nodded off in the late-morning sun. More than anything Jude wanted him to stay just as he was. Not to stir. Not to wake. Not to open his eyes; please, not to open his eyes.

They drew closer, but still Georgia didn't glance his way. Instead she laid a sleepy head on Jude's shoulder and closed her eyes. "So you want to tell me why you had to trash the studio? And were you shouting in there? I thought I heard you shouting, too."

He didn't want to look again but couldn't help himself. The ghost remained as he was, head tipped to the side, smiling just slightly, as if musing on a pleasant thought or a dream. The dead man didn't seem to hear her. Jude had an idea then, unformed, difficult to articulate. With his closed eyes and his head tilted just so, the ghost seemed not so much to be asleep as to be *listening* for something. Listening for *him*, Jude thought. Waiting, perhaps, to be acknowledged, before he would (or could) acknowledge Jude in return. They were almost on top of him now, about to walk past him, and Jude shrank against Georgia to avoid touching him.

"That's what woke me up, the noise, and then the smell—" She made a soft coughing sound and lifted her head to squint blearily at the bedroom door. She still didn't notice the ghost, although they were crossing directly in front of him now. She came up short, stopped moving. "I'm not going in there until you do something about that suit."

He slipped his hand down her arm to her wrist and squeezed it, shoving her forward. She made a thin sound of pain and protest and tried to pull away from him. "What the fuck?"

"Keep walking," he said, and then realized a moment later, with a pitiful throb in the chest, that he had spoken.

He glanced down at the ghost, and at the same time the dead man lifted his head and his eyes rolled open. But where his eyes belonged was only a black scribble. It was as if a child had taken a Magic Marker—a truly magic marker, one that could draw right on the air—and had desperately tried to ink over them. The black lines squirmed and tangled among one another, worms tied into a knot.

Then Jude was past him, shoving Georgia down the hallway while she struggled and whined. When he was at the door to the bedroom, he looked back.

The ghost came to his feet, and as he rose, his legs moved out of the sunlight and painted themselves back into being, the long black trouser legs, the sharp crease in his pants. The dead man held his right arm out to the side, the palm turned toward the floor, and something fell from the hand, a flat silver pendant, polished to a mirror brightness, attached to a foot of delicate gold chain. No, not a pendant but a curved blade of some kind. It was like a dollhouse version of the pendulum in that story by Edgar Allan Poe. The gold chain was connected to a ring around one of his fingers, a wedding ring, and the razor was what he had married. He allowed Jude to look at it for a moment and then twitched his wrist, a child doing a trick with a yo-yo, and the little curved razor leaped into his hand.

Jude felt a moan struggling to force its way up from his chest. He shoved Georgia through the door, into the bedroom, and slammed it.

"What are you doing, Jude?" she cried, pulling free at last, stumbling away from him.

"Shut up."

She hit him in the shoulder with her left hand, then slugged him in the back with her right, the hand with the infected thumb. This hurt her more than it hurt him. She made a sick gasping sound and let him be.

He still held the doorknob. He listened to the corridor. It was quiet.

Jude eased the door back and looked through a three-inch opening, ready to slam it again, expecting the dead man to be there with his razor on a chain.

No one was in the hallway.

He shut his eyes. He shut the door. He put his forehead against it, pulled a deep breath down into his lungs and held it, let it go slowly. His face was clammy with sweat, and he lifted a hand to wipe it away. Something icy and sharp and hard lightly grazed his cheek, and he opened his eyes and saw the dead man's curved razor in his hand, the blue-steel blade reflecting an image of his own wide, staring eyeball.

Jude shouted and flung it down, then looked at the floor, but already it wasn't there.

11

He backed away from the door. The room was filled with the sound of strained breathing, his own and Marybeth's. In that moment she was Marybeth. He couldn't recall what it was he usually called her.

"What kind of shit are you on?" she asked, in a voice that hinted at a hillbilly drawl, faint but distinctly southern.

"Georgia," he said, remembering then. "Nothing. I couldn't be more sober."

"Oh, the hell. What are you taking?" And that subtle, barely-there drawl was gone, receding as quickly as it had come. Georgia had lived a couple years in New York City, where she'd made a studied effort to lose her accent, didn't like being taken for a cornpone hick.

"I got off all my shit years ago. I told you."

"What was that in the hall? You saw something. What'd you see?"

He glared a warning at her, which she ignored. She stood huddled before him in her pajamas, her arms crossed under her breasts, hands tucked out of sight against her sides. Her feet were spread slightly apart, as if, should he try to move past her into the rest of the bedroom, she would block his way—an absurd prospect for a girl a hundred pounds lighter than he was.

"There was an old man sitting out in the hall. In the chair," he said at last. He had to tell her something and didn't see any reason to lie. Her opinion of his sanity didn't trouble him. "We walked right by him, but you didn't see him. I don't know if you *can* see him."

"That's lunatic bullshit." She said it with no special conviction.

He started toward the bed, and she got out of his way, pressed herself to the wall.

The dead man's suit was spread neatly across his side of the mattress. The deep, heart-shaped box lay on the floor, the black lid resting next to it, white tissue paper hanging out. He caught a whiff of the suit when he was still four paces away from it and flinched. It hadn't smelled that way when it first came out of the box, he would've noticed. Now it was impossible not to notice it. It had the ripe odor of corruption, something dead and spoiling.

"Christ," Jude said.

Georgia stood at a distance, a hand cupped over her mouth and nose. "I know. I was wondering if there was something in one of the pockets. Something going bad. Old food."

Breathing through his mouth, Jude patted down the jacket. He thought it very likely he was about to discover something in an advanced state of decomposition. It would not have surprised him to find that Jessica McDermott Price had stuffed a dead rat into the suit, a little something extra to go with his purchase, at no additional charge. Instead, though, he felt only a stiff square of what was maybe plastic in one pocket. He slipped it out for a look.

It was a photograph, one he knew well, Anna's favorite picture of them. She had taken it with her when she left. Danny snapped it one afternoon in late August, the sunlight reddish and warm on the front porch, the day swarming with dragonflies and glittering motes of dust. Jude perched on the steps in a worn denim jacket, his Dobro over one knee. Anna sat beside him, watching him play, her hands squeezed between her thighs. The dogs were sprawled in the dirt at their feet, staring quizzically up at the camera.

It had been a good afternoon, maybe one of the last good afternoons before things started to go bad, but looking at the photograph now brought him no pleasure. Someone had taken a Sharpie to it. Jude's eyes had been marked out in black ink, covered over by a furious hand.

Georgia was saying something from where she stood a few feet away, her voice shy, uncertain. "What did he look like? The ghost in the hall?"

Jude's body was turned so she couldn't see the photograph, a lucky thing. He didn't want her to see it.

He struggled to find his voice. It was hard to get past the unhappy shock of those black scribbles blotting out his eyes in the picture. "An old man," he managed at last. "He was wearing this suit."

And there were these awful fucking black scribbles floating in front of his eyes and they looked just like this, Jude imagined telling her, turning to show her the snapshot at the same time. He didn't do it, though.

"He just sat there?" Georgia asked. "Nothing else happened?"

"He stood up and showed me a razor on a chain. A funny little razor."

On the day Danny took the picture, Anna was still herself, and Jude thought she'd been happy. Jude had spent most of that late-summer afternoon beneath the Mustang, and Anna had stayed close by, crawling under herself to pass him tools and necessary parts. In the photo there was a smear of motor oil on her chin, dirt on her hands and knees—an appealing, well-earned grime, the kind of filth you could take pride in. Her eyebrows were bunched up, a pretty dimple between them, and her mouth was open, as if she were laughing—or, more likely, about to ask him a question. *You go fishin' much on Lake Pontchartrain? What's the best dog you ever owned?* Her with her questions.

Anna had not asked him why he was sending her away, however, when it was over. Not after the night he found her wandering the side of the highway in a T-shirt and nothing else, people honking at her as they went past. He hauled her into the car and pulled back his fist to hit her, then slugged the steering wheel instead, punching it until his knuckles bled. He said enough was enough, that he was going to pack her shit for her, send her on her way. Anna said she'd die without him. He said he'd send flowers to the funeral.

So: She at least had kept her word. It was too late to keep his.

"Are you messing with me, Jude?" Georgia asked. Her voice was close. She was creeping toward him, in spite of her aversion to the smell. He slid the picture back into the pocket of the dead man's suit before she could see. "Because if this is a joke, it sucks."

"It isn't a joke. I guess it's possible I'm losing my mind, but I don't think that's it either. The person who sold me the . . . suit . . . knew what she was doing. Her little sister was a fan who committed suicide. This woman blames me for her death. I talked to her on the phone just an hour ago, and she told me so herself. That's one part of this thing I'm sure I didn't imagine. Danny was there. He heard me talking to her. She wants to get even with me. So she sent me a ghost. I saw him just now in the hall. And I saw him last night, too."

He began to fold the suit, intending to return it to its box.

"Burn it," Georgia said, with a sudden vehemence that surprised him. "Take the fucking suit and burn it."

Jude felt, for an instant, an almost overpowering impulse to do just that, find some lighter fluid, douse it, cook it in the driveway. It was an impulse he immediately mistrusted. He was wary of any irrevocable action. Who knew what bridges might be burned along with it? He felt the slightest flicker of an idea, something about the awful-smelling suit and how it might be of use, but the thought drifted away before he could fix on it. He was tired. It was hard to pin a solid thought in place.

His reasons for wanting to hold on to the suit were illogical, superstitious, unclear even to himself, but when he spoke, he had a perfectly reasonable explanation for keeping it. "We can't burn it. It's evidence. My lawyer is going to want it later, if we decide to build a case against her."

Georgia laughed, weakly, unhappily. "What? Assault with a deadly spirit?"

"No. Harassment, maybe. Stalking. It's a death threat anyway, even if it's a crazy one. There's laws on that."

He finished folding the suit and set it back in its nest of tissue paper, inside the box. He breathed through his mouth as he did it, head turned from the stink.

"The whole room smells. I know this is pussy, but I feel like I might yak," she said.

He slipped a sideways look at her. She was absentmindedly clutching her right hand to her chest, staring blankly at the glossy black heart-shaped box. She had, until just a few moments before, been hiding the hand against her side. The thumb was swollen, and the place where the pin had gone in was now a white sore, the size of a pencil eraser, glistening with pus. She saw him looking at it, glanced down at herself, then up again, smiling miserably.

"You got a hell of an infection there."

"I know. I been putting Bactine on it."

"Maybe you ought to see someone about it. If it's tetanus, Bactine won't take care of it."

She closed her fingers around the injured thumb, squeezed it gently. "I pricked it on that pin hidden in the suit. What if it was poisoned?"

"I guess if it had cyanide on it, we'd know by now."

"Anthrax."

"I spoke to the woman. She's country-fried stupid, not to mention in need of some superior fucking psychiatric drugs, but I don't think she would've sent me anything with poison on it. She knows she'd go to jail for that." He touched Georgia's wrist, pulled her hand toward him, and studied the thumb. The skin around the area of infection was soft and rotten and pruned up, as if it had been soaking in water for a long time. "Why don't you go and set in front of the TV. I'll have Danny book an appointment with the doctor."

He let go of her wrist and nodded toward the door, but she didn't move.

"Will you look and see if he's in the hall?" she asked.

He stared for a moment, then nodded and went to the door. He opened it half a foot and peeked out. The sun had shifted or moved behind a cloud, and the hallway was in cool shadow. No one sat in the Shaker chair against the wall. No one stood in the corner with a razor on a chain.

"All clear."

She touched his shoulder with her good hand. "I saw a ghost once. When I was a kid."

He wasn't surprised. He hadn't met a Goth girl yet who hadn't had some kind of brush with the supernatural, who didn't believe, with utter, embarrassing sincerity, in astral forms or angels or Wiccan spellcraft.

"I was living with Bammy. My grandmother. This was just after the first time my daddy threw me out. One afternoon I went in the kitchen to pour myself a glass of her lemonade—she makes real nice lemonade— and I looked out the back window, and there was this girl in the yard. She was picking dandelions and blowing on them to make them fly apart, you know, like kids do, and she was singing to herself while she was doing it. This girl a few years younger than myself, in a real cheap dress. I pushed up the window to yell out to her, find out what she was doing in our yard. When she heard the window squeak, she looked up at me, and that's when I knew she was dead. She had these messed-up eyes."

"How do you mean messed-up?" Jude asked. The skin on his fore- arms prickled and tightened, going rough with gooseflesh.

"They were black eyes. No, they weren't even like eyes at all. It was more like . . . like they were covered over."

"Covered over," Jude repeated.

"Yes. Marked out. Black. Then she turned her head and seemed to look over at the fence. In another moment she hopped up and walked across the yard. She was moving her mouth, like she was talking to someone, only no one was there, and I couldn't hear any words coming out of her. I could hear her when she was picking dandelions and singing to herself, but not when she got up and seemed to be talking to someone. I always thought that was a strange thing—how I could only hear her when she sang. And then she reached up, like there was an invisible person standing in front of her, just on the other side of Bammy's fence, and she was taking his hand.

"And I got scared all of a sudden, like got chills, because I felt something bad was going to happen to her. I wanted to tell her to let go of his hand. Whoever was taking her hand, I wanted her to get away from him. Only I was too scared. I couldn't get my breath. And the little girl looked back at me one more time, kind of sad, with her marked-over eyes, and then she came up off the ground—I swear to God—and floated over the fence. Not like she was flying. Like she was being picked up by invisible hands. The way her feet dangled in the air. They bumped into the pickets. She went over, and then she was gone. I got the flop sweats and had to sit down on the kitchen floor."

Georgia darted a look at Jude's face, maybe to see if he thought she was being foolish. But he only nodded that she should go on.

"Bammy came in and cried out and said, 'Girl, what's the matter?' But when I told her what I saw, that was when she got really upset and started crying. She sat down on the floor with me and said she believed me. She said I had seen her twin sister, Ruth.

"I knew about Ruth, who died when Bammy was little, but it wasn't until then that Bammy told me what really happened to her. I always thought she got run over by a car or something, but it wasn't like that. One day, when they were both about seven or eight—this was 1950-something—their mother called them in for lunch. Bammy went, but Ruthie stayed out, because she didn't feel like eating and because she was just naturally disobedient. While Bammy and her folks were inside, someone snatched her out of the backyard. She wasn't ever seen again. Except now and then, people at Bammy's house spot her blowing on dandelions and singing to herself, and then someone who isn't there takes her away. My mother saw Ruth's ghost, and Bammy's husband seen her once, and some of Bammy's friends, and Bammy, too.

"Everyone who saw Ruth was just like me. They wanted to tell her not to go, to stay away from whoever was on the other side of the fence. But everyone who sees her is too scared by the sight of her to speak. And Bammy said she thought it wouldn't ever be over until someone found their voice and spoke up. That it was like Ruth's ghost was in a kind of dream, stuck repeating her last minutes, and she'll be that way until someone calls out to her and wakes her up."

Georgia swallowed, fell silent. She bowed her head, so her dark hair hid her eyes.

"I can't believe the dead want to hurt us," she said finally. "Don't they need our help? Don't they always need our help? If you see him again, you should try to talk to him. You should find out what he wants."

Jude didn't believe that it was a matter of if, only when. And he already knew what the dead man wanted.

"He didn't come for talk," Jude said.

12

Jude wasn't sure what to do next, so he made tea. The simple, automatic gestures of filling the kettle, spooning loose tea into the strainer, and finding a mug had a way of clearing his head and slowing time, opening a useful silence. He stood at the range listening to the kettle tick.

He did not feel panicked, a realization that brought him some satisfaction. He was not ready to run, had doubts there was anything to gain from running anyway. Where could he go that would be better than here? Jessica Price had said the dead man belonged to him now and would follow him wherever he went. Jude flashed to an image of himself sliding into a first-class seat on a flight to California, then turning his head to see the dead man sitting next to him, with those black scribbles floating in front of his eyes. He shuddered, shook off the thought. The house was as good a place as any to make a stand—at least until he figured out some spot that made more sense. Besides, he hated to board the dogs. In the old days, when he went on tour, they always came on the bus with him.

And no matter what he'd said to Georgia, he had even less interest in calling the police or his lawyer. He had an idea that dragging the law into it might be the worst thing he could do. They could bring a case against

Jessica McDermott Price, and there just might be some pleasure in that, but getting even with her wouldn't make the dead man go away. He knew that. He'd seen lots of horror movies.

Besides, calling in the police to rescue him rubbed against his natural grain, no small matter. His own identity was his first and single most forceful creation, the machine that had manufactured all his other successes, which had produced everything in his life that was worth having and that he cared about. He would protect that to the end.

Jude could believe in a ghost but not a boogeyman, a pure incarnation of evil. There had to be more to the dead man than black marks over his eyes and a curved razor on a golden chain. He wondered, abruptly, what Anna had cut her wrists with, became conscious all over again of how cold it was in the kitchen, that he was leaning toward the kettle to absorb some of its ambient heat. Jude was suddenly certain she had slashed her wrists with the razor on the end of her father's pendulum, the one he'd used to mesmerize desperate suckers and to search for well water. He wondered what else there was to know about how Anna had died and about the man who'd been a father to her and who had discovered her body in a cold bath, the water darkened with her blood.

Maybe Danny had turned up Anna's letters. Jude dreaded reading them again and at the same time knew that he had to. He remembered them well enough to know now that she'd been trying to tell him what she was going to do to herself and he'd missed it. No—it was more terrible than that. He had not wanted to see, had willfully ignored what was right in front of him.

Her first letters from home had conveyed a breezy optimism, and their subtext was that she was getting her life together, making sound, grown-up decisions about her future. They arrived on rich white card stock and were composed in delicate cursive. As with her conversation, these letters were filled with questions, although, in her correspondence at least, she didn't seem to expect any answers. She would write that she had spent the month sending out job applications, then rhetorically ask if it was a mistake to wear black lipstick and motorcycle boots to an interview at a day-care center. She would describe two colleges and wonder at length about which would be better for her. But it was all a con, and Jude knew it. She never got the job at the day care, never mentioned it again after that one letter. And when the spring semester rolled around, she had moved on to applying for a spot at a beauticians' academy, college forgotten.

Her last few letters were a truer picture of the place she'd been in mentally. They came on plain, ruled paper, torn out of a notebook, and her cursive was cramped, hard to read. Anna wrote that she couldn't get any rest. Her sister lived in a new development, and there was a house going up right next door. She wrote she heard them hammering nails all day long and that it was like living next to a coffin maker after a plague. When she tried to sleep at night, the hammers would start up again, just as she was drifting off, and never mind that there was no one over there. She was desperate to sleep. Her sister was trying to get her on a treatment plan for her insomnia. There were things Anna wanted to talk about, but she didn't have anyone to talk to, and she was tired of talking to herself. She wrote that she couldn't stand to be so tired all the time.

Anna had begged him to call, but he had not called. Her unhappiness wore on him. It was too much work to help her through her depressions. He'd tried, when they were together, and his best hadn't been good enough. He'd given it his best, it hadn't panned out, and still she wouldn't leave him alone. He didn't know why he even read her letters, let alone sometimes responded to them. He'd wished they would just stop coming. Finally they had.

Danny could dig them out and then make a doctor's appointment for Georgia. As plans went, it wasn't much, but it was better than what he had ten minutes before, which was nothing. Jude poured the tea, and time started up again.

He drifted with his mug into the office. Danny wasn't at his desk. Jude stood in the doorway, staring at the empty room, listening intently to the stillness for some sign of him. Nothing. He was in the bathroom, maybe—but no. The door was slightly ajar, as it had been the day before, and the crack revealed only darkness. Maybe he had taken off for lunch.

Jude started over toward the window, to see if Danny's car was in the driveway, then held up before he got there, took a detour to Danny's desk. He flipped through some stacks of paper, looking for Anna's letters. If Danny had found them, however, he'd tucked them somewhere out of sight. When Jude didn't turn them up, he settled into Danny's chair and launched the Web browser on his computer, intending to do a search on Anna's stepdaddy. It seemed like there was something about everyone online. Maybe the dead man had his own MySpace account. Jude laughed—choked, ugly laughter—down in his throat.

He couldn't remember the dead man's first name, so he ran a search for "McDermott hypnosis dead." At the top of Jude's search results was a link to an obituary, which had appeared in last summer's *Pensacola News Journal,* for a Craddock James McDermott. That was it: Craddock.

Jude clicked on it—and there he was.

The man in the black-and-white photograph was a younger version of the man Jude had seen twice now in the upstairs hallway. In the picture he looked a vigorous sixty, his hair cut in that same close-to-the-scalp military bristle. With his long, almost horsey face, and wide thin lips, he bore more than a passing resemblance to Charlton Heston. The most startling thing about the photograph was discovering that Craddock, in life, had eyes like any man's eyes. They were clear and direct and stared into Forever with the challenging self-assurance of motivational speakers and evangelical preachers everywhere.

Jude read. It said that a life of learning and teaching, exploring and adventuring, had ended when Craddock James McDermott had died of a cerebral embolism at his stepdaughter's home in Testament, Florida, on Tuesday, August 10. A true son of the South, he had grown up the only child of a Pentecostal minister and had lived in Savannah and Atlanta, Georgia, and later Galveston, Texas.

He was a wide receiver for the Longhorns in 1965 and enlisted in the service upon graduation, where he served as a member of the army's psychological operations division. It was there that he discovered his calling, when he was introduced to the essentials of hypnosis. In Vietnam he earned a Purple Heart and a Bronze Star. He was discharged with honors and settled in Florida. In 1980 he was wed to Paula Joy Williams, a librarian, and became stepfather to her two children, Jessica and Anna, whom he later adopted. Paula and Craddock shared a love built upon quiet faith, deep trust, and a mutual fascination with the unexplored possibilities of the human spirit.

At this, Jude frowned. It was a curious sentence—"a mutual fascination with the unexplored possibilities of the human spirit." He didn't even know what it meant.

Their relationship endured until Paula passed away in 1986. In his life Craddock had attended to almost ten thousand "patients"—Jude snorted at the word—using deep hypnotic technique to alleviate the suffering of the ill and to help those in need to overcome their weaknesses, work that his oldest stepdaughter, Jessica McDermott Price, carried on still, as a private consultant. Jude snorted again. She had probably written the obituary herself. He was surprised she hadn't included the phone number for her service. *Mention that you heard about us in my stepfather's obit and receive 10 percent off your first session!!!*

Craddock's interest in spiritualism and the untapped potential of the mind led him to experiment with "dowsing," the old country technique of discovering underground water sources with the use of a rod or pendulum. But it was the way in which he led so many of his fellow life travelers to discover their own hidden reservoirs of strength and self-worth for which he will be best remembered by his surviving adopted daughter and his loved ones. "His voice may have fallen silent, but it will never be forgotten."

Nothing about Anna's suicide.

Jude passed his gaze over the obit again, pausing on certain combinations of words that he didn't much care for: "psychological operations," "unexplored possibilities," "the untapped potential of the mind." He looked again at Craddock's face, taking in the chilly confidence of his pale black-and-white eyes and the almost angry smile set on his thin, colorless lips. He was a cruel-looking son of a bitch.

Danny's computer pinged to let Jude know that an e-mail had come through. Where the hell was Danny anyway? Jude glanced at the computer's clock, saw he'd been sitting there for twenty minutes already. He clicked over to Danny's e-mail program, which picked up messages for both of them. The new e-mail was addressed to Jude.

He flicked a glance at the address of the sender, then shifted in the chair, sitting up straight, muscles tightening across his chest and abdomen, as if he were readying himself for a blow. In a way he was. The e-mail was from craddockm@box.closet.net.

Jude opened the e-mail and began to read.

dear jude

we will ride at nightfall we will ride to the hole i am dead you will die anyone who gets too close will be infected with the death on you us we are infected together we will be in the death hole together and the grave dirt will fall in on top of us lalala the dead pull the living down if anyone tries to help you i us we will pull them down and step on them and no one climbs out because the hole is too deep and the dirt falls too fast and everyone who hears your voice will know it is true jude is dead and i am dead and you will die you will hear my our voice and we will ride together on the night road to the place the final place where the wind cries for you for us we will walk to the edge of the hole we will fall in holding each other we will fall sing for us sing at our at your grave sing lalala

Jude's chest was an airless place, stuck full of icy-hot pins and needles. *Psychological operations,* he thought almost randomly, and then he was angry, the worst kind of angry, the kind that had to stay bottled up, because there was no one around to curse at, and he wouldn't allow himself to break anything. He had already spent a chunk of the morning throwing books, and it hadn't made him feel better. Now, though, he meant to keep himself under control.

He clicked back to the browser, thinking he might have another glance at his search results, see what else he could learn. He looked blankly at the *Pensacola News* obituary one more time, and then his gaze fixed on the photograph. It was a different picture now, and in it Craddock was grinning and old, face lined and gaunt, almost starved, and his eyes were scribbled over with furious black marks. The first lines of the obituary said that a life of learning and teaching, exploring and adventuring, had ended when Craddock James McDermott died of a cerebral embolism at his stepdaughter's home and now he was coming lalala and it was cold he was cold Jude would be cold too when he cut himself he was going to cut himself and cut the girl and they would be in the deathhole and Jude could sing for them, sing for all of them—

Jude stood up so quickly, and with such sudden force, that Danny's chair was flung back and toppled over. Then his hands were on the computer, under the monitor, and he lifted, heaving it off the desk and onto the floor. It hit with a short, high-pitched chirp and a crunch of breaking glass, followed by a sudden pop of surging electricity. Then quiet. The fan that cooled the motherboard hushed slowly to a stop. He had hurled it instinctively, moving too quickly to think. Fuck it. Self-control was overrated.

His pulse was jacked. He felt shaky and weak in the legs. Where the fuck was Danny? He looked at the wall clock, saw it was almost two, too late in the day for lunch. Maybe he'd gone out on an errand. Usually, though, he paged Jude on the intercom to let him know he was headed out.

Jude came around the desk and finally made it to the window with the view of the drive. Danny's little green Honda hybrid was parked in the dirt turnaround, and Danny was in it. Danny sat perfectly still in the driver's seat, one hand on the steering wheel, his face ashy, rigid, blank.

The sight of him, just sitting there, going nowhere, looking at nothing, had the effect of cooling Jude off. He watched Danny through the window, but Danny didn't do anything. Never put the car in drive to leave. Never so much as glanced around. Danny looked—Jude felt an uneasy throb in his joints at the thought—like a man in a trance. A full minute passed, and then another, and the longer he watched, the more ill at ease Jude felt, the more sick in his bones. Then his hand was on the door and he was letting himself out, to find out what was wrong with Danny.

13

The air was a cold shock that made his eyes water. By the time he got to the side of the car, Jude's cheeks were burning, and the tip of his nose was numb. Although it was going on early afternoon, Jude was still in his worn robe, a muscle shirt, and striped boxers. When the breeze rose, the freezing air burned his bare skin, raw and lacerating.

Danny didn't turn to look at him but went on peering blankly through the windshield. He looked even worse close up. He was shivering, lightly and steadily. A drop of sweat trickled across his cheekbone.

Jude rapped his knuckles on the window. Danny started, as if springing awake from a light doze, blinked rapidly, fumbled for the button to roll down the glass. He still didn't look directly up at Jude.

"What are you doing in your car, Danny?" Jude asked.

"I think I should go home."

"Did you see him?"

Danny said, "I think I should go home now."

"Did you see the dead man? What did he do?" Jude was patient. When he had to be, Jude could be the most patient man on earth.

"I think I have a stomach flu. That's all."

Danny lifted his right hand from his lap to wipe his face, and Jude saw it was clutching a letter opener.

"Don't you lie, Danny," Jude said. "I just want to know what you saw."

"His eyes were black marks. He looked right at me. I wish he didn't look right at me."

"He can't hurt you, Danny."

"You don't know that. You don't know."

Jude reached through the open window to squeeze his shoulder. Danny shrank from his touch. At the same time, he made a whisking gesture at Jude with the letter opener. It didn't come anywhere close to cutting him, but Jude withdrew his hand anyway.

"Danny?"

"Your eyes are just like his," Danny said, and clunked the car into reverse.

Jude jumped back from the car before Danny could back out over his foot. But Danny hesitated, his own foot on the brake.

"I'm not coming back," he said to the steering wheel.

"Okay."

"I'd help you if I could, but I can't. I just can't."

"I understand."

Danny eased the car back down the driveway, tires grinding on the gravel, then turned it ninety degrees and rolled down the hill, toward the road. He watched until Danny passed through the gates, turned left, and disappeared from sight. Jude never saw him again.

14

He set out for the barn and the dogs.

Jude was grateful for the sting of the air on his face and the way each inhalation sent a stunned tingle through his lungs. It was real. Ever since he had seen the dead man that morning, he felt increasingly crowded by unnatural, bad-dream ideas leaking into everyday life where they didn't belong. He needed a few hard actualities to hold on to, clamps to stop the bleeding.

The dogs watched him mournfully as he undid the latch to their pen. He slipped in before they could clamber out past him, and hunkered down, let them climb on him, smell his face. The dogs: They were real, too. He stared back at them, into their chocolate eyes and long, worried faces.

"If there was something wrong with me, you'd see it, wouldn't you?" he asked them. "If there were black marks over my eyes?"

Angus lapped his face, once, twice, and Jude kissed his wet nose. He stroked Bon's back, while she sniffed anxiously at his crotch.

He let himself out. He wasn't ready to go back inside and found his way into the barn instead. He wandered over to the car and had a look at himself in the mirror on the driver's-side door. No black marks. His eyes were the same as always: pale gray under bushy black brows and intense, like he meant murder.

Jude had bought the car in sorry shape from a roadie, a '65 Mustang, the GT fastback. He'd been on tour, almost without rest, for ten months, had gone out on the road almost as soon as his wife left him, and when he came back, he found himself with an empty house and nothing to do. He spent all of July and most of August in the barn, gutting the Mustang, pulling out parts that were rusted, burnt out, shot, dented, corroded, caked in oils and acids, and replacing them: HiPo block, authentic cranks and heads, transmission, clutch, springs, white pony seats—everything original except for the speakers and the stereo. He installed a bazooka bass in the trunk, affixed an XM radio antenna to the roof, and laid in a state-of-the-art digital sound system. He drenched himself in oil, banged knuckles, and bled into the transmission. It was a rough kind of courtship, and it suited him well.

Around that time Anna had come to live with him. Not that he ever called her by that name. She was Florida then, although somehow, since he'd learned of her suicide, he'd come to think of her as Anna again.

She sat in the backseat with the dogs while he worked, her boots sticking out a missing window. She sang along with the songs she knew and talked baby talk to Bon and kept at Jude with her questions. She asked him if he was ever going to go bald ("I don't know"), because she'd leave him if he did ("Can't blame you"), and if he'd still think she was sexy if she shaved off all her hair ("No"), and if he'd let her drive the Mustang when it was done ("Yes"), and if he'd ever been in a fistfight ("Try to avoid them—hard to play guitar with a broken hand"), and why he never talked about his parents (to which he said nothing), and if he believed in fate ("No," he said, but he was lying).

Before Anna and the Mustang, he had recorded a new CD, a solo disc, and had traveled to some twenty-four nations, played more than a hundred shows. But working on the car was the first time since Shannon had left him that he felt gainfully employed, doing work that mattered, in the truest sense—although why rebuilding a car should feel like honest work instead of a rich man's hobby, while recording albums and playing arenas had come to seem like a rich man's hobby instead of a job, he couldn't have said.

The idea crossed his mind once more that he ought to go. Put the farm in the rearview mirror and take off, it didn't matter for where.

The thought was so urgent, so demanding—*get in the car and get out of here*—that it set his teeth on edge. He resented being made to run. Throwing himself into the car and taking off wasn't a choice, it was panic. This was followed by another thought, disconcerting and unfounded, yet curiously convincing: the thought that he was being herded, that the dead man *wanted* him to run. That the dead man was trying to force him away from . . . from what? Jude couldn't imagine. Outside, the dogs barked in concert at a passing semi.

Anyway, he wasn't going anywhere without talking to Georgia about it. And if he did eventually decide to light out, he would probably want to get dressed beforehand. Yet in another moment he found himself inside the Mustang, behind the wheel. It was a place to think. He'd always done some of his best thinking in the car, with the radio on.

He sat with the window halfway down, in the dark, earth-floored garage, and it seemed to him if there was a ghost nearby, it was Anna, not the angry spirit of her stepfather. She was as close as the backseat. They had made love there, of course. He had gone into the house to get beer and had come back, and she was waiting in the rear of the Mustang in her boots and no more. He dropped the open beers and left them foaming in the dirt. In that moment nothing in the world seemed more important than her firm, twenty-six-year-old flesh, and her twenty-six-year-old sweat, and her laughter, and her teeth on his neck.

He leaned back against the white leather, feeling his exhaustion for the first time all day. His arms were heavy, and his bare feet were half numb from the cold. At one time or another, he had left his black leather duster in the backseat. He reached for it and spread it over his legs. The keys were in the ignition, so he clicked the engine over to the battery to run the radio.

Jude was no longer sure why he had climbed into the car, but now that he was sitting, it was hard to imagine moving. From what seemed a long way off, he could hear the dogs barking again, their voices strident and alarmed. He turned up the volume to drown them out.

John Lennon sang "I Am the Walrus." Jude let his head rest on the back of the seat, relaxing into the pocket of warmth under his jacket. Paul McCartney's slinky bass kept drifting away, getting lost under the low mutter of the Mustang's engine, which was funny, since Jude hadn't turned the engine on, only the battery. The Beatles were followed by a parade of commercials. Lew at Imperial Autos said, "You won't find offers like ours anywhere in the tristate area. We're pulling deals our competition can't come close to matching. The dead pull the living down. Come on in and get behind the wheel of your next ride and take it for a spin on the nightroad. We'll go together. We'll sing together. You won't ever want the trip to end. It won't."

Ads bored Jude, and he found the strength to flip to another station. On FUM they were playing one of his songs, his very first single, a thunderous AC/DC ripoff titled "Souls for Sale." In the gloom it seemed as if ghostly shapes, unformed wisps of menacing fog, had begun to swirl around the car. He shut his eyes and listened to the faraway sound of his own voice.

> *More than silver and more than gold,*
> *You say my soul is worth,*
> *Well, I'd like to make it right with God,*
> *But I need beer money first.*

He snorted softly to himself. It wasn't selling souls that got you into trouble, it was buying them. Next time he would have to make sure there was a return policy. He laughed, opened his eyes a little. The dead man, Craddock, sat in the passenger seat next to him. He smiled at Jude, to show stained teeth and a black tongue. He smelled of death, also of car exhaust. His eyes were hidden behind those odd, continuously moving black brushstrokes.

"No returns, no exchanges," Jude said to him. The dead man nodded sympathetically, and Jude shut his eyes again. Somewhere, miles away, he could hear someone shouting his name.

". . . ude! Jude! Answer me Ju . . ."

He didn't want to be bothered, though, was dozy, wanted to be left alone. He cranked the seat back. He folded his hands across his stomach. He breathed deeply.

He had just nodded off when Georgia got him by the arm and hauled him out of the car, dumped him in the dirt. Her voice came in pulses, drifting in and out of audibility.

". . . get out of there Jude get the fuck . . .

. . . on't be dead don't be . . .

. . . leeeeeese, please . . .

. . . eyes open your fucking . . ."

He opened his eyes and sat up in one sudden movement, hacking furiously. The barn door was rolled back, and the sunshine poured through it in brilliant, crystalline beams, solid-looking and sharp-edged. The light stabbed at his eyes, and he flinched from it. He inhaled a deep, cold breath, opened his mouth to say something, to let her know he was all right, and his throat filled with bile. He rolled onto all fours and retched in the dirt. Georgia had him by the arm and bent over him while he horked up.

Jude was dizzy. The ground tilted underneath him. When he tried to look outside, the world spun, as if it were a picture painted on the side of a vase, turning on a lathe. The house, the yard, the drive, the sky, streamed by him, and a withering sensation of motion sickness rolled through him, and he upchucked again.

He clutched the ground and waited for the world to stop moving. Not that it ever would. That was one thing you found out when you were stoned, or wasted, or feverish: that the world was always turning and that only a healthy mind could block out the sickening whirl of it. He spat, wiped at his mouth. His stomach muscles were sore and cramped, as if he'd just done a few dozen abdominal crunches, which was, when you thought about it, very close to the truth. He sat up, turned himself to look at the Mustang. It was still running. No one was in it.

The dogs danced around him. Angus leaped into his lap and thrust his cold, damp nose into his face, lapped at Jude's sour mouth. Jude was too weak to push him away. Bon, always the shy one, gave Jude a worried, sidelong look, then lowered her head to the thin gruel of his vomit and covertly began to gobble it up.

He tried to stand, grabbing Georgia's wrist, but didn't have the strength in his legs and instead pulled her down with him, onto her knees. He had a dizzying thought—*the dead pull the living down*—that spun in his head for a moment and was gone. Georgia trembled. Her face was wet against his neck.

"Jude," she said. "Jude, I don't know what's happening to you."

He couldn't find his voice for a minute, didn't have the air yet. He stared at the black Mustang, shuddering on its suspension, the restrained idling force of the engine shaking the entire chassis.

Georgia continued, "I thought you were dead. When I grabbed your arm, I thought you were dead. Why are you out here with the car running and the barn door shut?"

"No reason."

"Did I do something? Did I fuck it up?"

"What are you talking about?"

"I don't know," she said, beginning to cry. "There must be some reason you're out here to kill yourself."

He turned on his knees. He found he was still holding one of her thin wrists, and now he took the other. Her nest of black hair floated around her head, bangs in her eyes.

"Something's wrong, but I wasn't out here trying to kill myself. I sat in the car to listen to some music and think for a minute, but I didn't turn the engine on. It turned itself on."

She wrenched her wrist away. "Stop it."

"It was the dead man."

"Stop it. Stop it."

"The ghost from the hall. I saw him again. He was in the car with me. Either he started the Mustang or I started it without knowing what I was doing, because he wanted me to."

"Do you know how crazy that sounds? How crazy all of this sounds?"

"If I'm crazy, then Danny is, too. Danny saw him. That's why he's gone. Danny couldn't hack it. He had to go."

Georgia stared at him, her eyes lucid and bright and fearful behind the soft curl of her bangs. She shook her head in an automatic gesture of denial.

"Let's get out of here," he said. "Help me stand."

She hooked an arm under his armpits and pushed off the floor. His knees were weak springs, all loose bounce and no support. No sooner had he come to his heels than he started to roll forward. He put his hands out to stop his fall and caught himself on the warming hood of the car.

He said, "Shut it off. Get the keys."

Georgia picked his duster off the ground—it had spilled out of the Mustang with him—and threw it back in the driver's seat. She coughed, waving her hands at the fog of exhaust, climbed into the car, and shut it off. The silence was sudden and alarming.

Bon pressed herself against Jude's leg, looking for reassurance. His knees threatened to fold. He drove her aside with his knee, then put his heel to her ass. She yelped and leaped away.

"Fuck off me," he said.

"Whyn't you leave her be?" Georgia asked. "The both of them saved your life."

"How do you figure?"

"Didn't you hear them? I was coming out to shut them up. They were hysterical."

He regretted kicking Bon then and looked around to see if she was close enough to put a hand on. She had retreated into the barn, though, and was pacing in the dark, watching him with morose and accusing eyes. He wondered about Angus and glanced around for him. Angus stood in the barn door, his back to them, his tail raised. He was staring steadily down the driveway.

"What does he see?" Georgia asked, an absurd thing to ask. Jude had no idea. He stood bracing himself against the car, too far from the sliding barn door to see out into the yard.

Georgia pushed the keys into the pocket of her black jeans. She had dressed somewhere along the line and wrapped her right thumb in bandages. She slipped past Jude and went to stand next to Angus. She ran her hand over the dog's spine, glanced down the drive, then back at Jude.

"What is it?" Jude asked.

"Nothing," she said. She held the right hand against her breastbone and grimaced a little, as if it were paining her. "Do you need help?"

"I'm managing," he said, and shoved off the Mustang. He was conscious of a building black pressure behind his eyeballs, a deep, slow, booming pain that threatened to become one of the all-time great headaches.

At the big sliding barn doors, he paused, with Angus between himself and Georgia. He peered down the drive of frozen mud, to the open gates of his farm. The skies were clearing. The thick, curdled gray cloud cover was coming apart, and the sun blinked irregularly through the rents.

The dead man, in his black fedora, stared back at him from the side of the state highway. He was there for a moment, when the sun was behind a cloud, so that the road was in shadow. As sunshine fluttered around the edges of a cloud, Craddock flickered away. His head and hands disappeared first, so that only a hollow black suit remained, standing empty. Then the suit disappeared, too. He stammered back into being a moment later, when the sun retreated under cover once more.

He lifted his hat to Jude and bowed, a mocking, oddly southern gesture. The sun came and went and came again, and the dead man flashed like Morse code.

"Jude?" Georgia asked. He realized he and Angus were standing there staring down the drive in just the same way. "There isn't anything there, is there, Jude?" She didn't see Craddock.

"No," he said. "Nothing there."

The dead man faded back into existence long enough to wink. Then the breeze rose in a soft rush and, high above, the sun broke through for good, at a place where the clouds had been pulled into strings of dirty wool. The light shone strongly on the road, and the dead man was gone.

15

Georgia led him into the music library on the first floor. He did not notice her arm around his waist, supporting and guiding him, until she let go. He sank onto the moss-colored couch, asleep almost as soon as he was off his feet.

He dozed, then woke, briefly, his vision swimmy and unclear, when she bent to lay a throw blanket across him. Her face was a pale circle, featureless, except for the dark line of her mouth and the dark holes where her eyes belonged.

His eyelids sank shut. He could not remember the last time he'd been so tired. Sleep had him, was pulling him steadily under, drowning reason, drowning sense, but as he went down again, that image of Georgia's face swam before him, and he had an alarming thought, that her eyes had been missing, hidden behind black scribbles. She was dead, and she was with the ghosts.

He struggled back toward wakefulness and for a few moments almost made it. He opened his eyes fractionally. Georgia stood in the door to the library, watching him, her little white hands balled into little white fists, and her eyes were her own. He felt a moment of sweet relief at the sight of her.

Then he saw the dead man in the hallway behind her. His skin was pulled tight across the knobs of his cheekbones, and he was grinning to show his nicotine-stained teeth.

Craddock McDermott moved in stop motion, a series of life-size still photographs. In one moment his arms were at his sides. In the next, one of his gaunt hands was on Georgia's shoulder. His fingernails were yellowed and long and curled at the end. The black marks jumped and quivered in front of his eyes.

Time leaped forward again. Abruptly Craddock's right hand was in the air, held high above Georgia's head. The gold chain dropped from it. The pendulum at the end of it, a curved three-inch blade, a slash of silvery brightness, fell before Georgia's eyes. The blade swung in slight arcs before her, and she stared straight at it with eyes that were suddenly wide and fascinated.

Another stop-motion twitch ahead in time and Craddock was bent forward in a frozen pose, his lips at her ear. His mouth wasn't moving, but Jude could just hear the sound of him whispering, a noise like someone sharpening the blade of a knife on a leather strop.

Jude wanted to call to her. He wanted to tell her to watch out, the dead man was right next to her, and she needed to run, to get away, not to listen to him. But his mouth felt wired shut, and he couldn't produce any sound except for a fitful moan. The effort it took even to keep his eyelids open was more than he could sustain, and they rolled shut. He flailed against sleep, but he was weak—an unfamiliar sensation. He went down once more, and this time he stayed down.

Craddock was waiting for him with his razor, even in sleep. The blade dangled at the end of its gold chain before the broad face of a Vietnamese man, who was naked save for a white rag belted around his waist, and seated in a stiff-backed chair in a dank concrete room. The Vietnamese's head had been shaved, and there were shiny pink circles on his scalp, where he'd been burnt by electrodes.

A window looked out on Jude's rainy front yard. The dogs were right up against the glass, close enough so their breath stained it white with condensation. They were yapping furiously, but they were like dogs on TV, with the volume turned all the way down; Jude heard no sound of them at all.

Jude stood quietly in the corner, hoping he would not be seen. The razor moved back and forth in front of the Vietnamese's amazed, sweat-beaded face.

"The soup was poisoned," Craddock said. He was speaking in Vietnamese, but in the way of dreams, Jude understood just what he was saying. "This is the antidote." Gesturing with his free hand at a massive syringe resting inside a black heart-shaped box. In the box with it was a wide-bladed bowie knife with a Teflon handle. "Save yourself."

The VC took the syringe and stuck it, without hesitation, into his own neck. The needle was perhaps five inches long. Jude flinched, looked away.

His gaze leaped naturally to the window. The dogs remained just on the other side of the glass, jumping against it, no sound coming from them. Beyond them Georgia sat on one end of a seesaw. A little tow-headed girl in bare feet and a pretty flowered dress sat on the other end. Georgia and the girl wore blindfolds, diaphanous black scarves made of some sort of crepelike material. The girl's pale yellow hair was tied into a loose ponytail. Her expression was an unreadable blank. Although she looked vaguely familiar to Jude, it was still a long-drawn-out moment before it came to him, with a jolt of recognition, that he was looking at Anna, as she had been at nine or ten. Anna and Georgia went up and down.

"I'm going to try to help you," Craddock was saying, speaking to the prisoner in English now. "You're in trouble, you hear? But I can help you, and all you need to do is listen close. Don't think. Just listen to the sound of my voice. It's almost nightfall. It's almost time. Nightfall is when we turn on the radio and listen to the radio voice. We do what the radio man says to do. Your head is a radio, and my voice is the only broadcast."

Jude looked back, and Craddock wasn't there anymore. In his place, where he had sat, was an old-fashioned radio, the face lit up all in green, and his voice came out of it. "Your only chance to live is to do just as I say. My voice is the only voice you hear."

Jude felt a chill in his chest, didn't like where this was going. He came unstuck and in three steps was at the side of the table. He wanted to rid them of Craddock's voice. Jude grabbed the radio's power cord, where it was plugged into the wall, and yanked. There was a pop of blue electricity, which stung his hand. He recoiled, throwing the line to the floor. And still the radio chattered on, just as before.

"It's nightfall. It's nightfall at last. Now is the time. Do you see the knife in the box? You can pick it up. It's yours. Take it. Happy birthday to you."

The VC looked with some curiosity into the heart-shaped box and picked out the bowie knife. He turned it this way and that, so the blade flashed in the light.

Jude moved to look down at the face of the radio. His right hand still throbbed from the jolt it had taken, was clumsy, hard to manipulate. He didn't see a power button, so he spun the dial, trying to get away from Craddock's voice. There was a sound Jude at first took for a burst of static, but which in another moment resolved into the steady, atonal hum of a large crowd, a thousand voices chattering all together.

A man with the knowing, streetwise tone of a fifties radio personality said, "Stottlemyre is hypnotizing them today with that twelve-to-six curve-ball of his, and down goes Tony Conigliaro. You've probably heard that you can't make people do things they don't want to do when they've been hypnotized. But you can see here it just isn't true, because you can tell that Tony C. sure didn't want to swing at that last pitch. You can make anyone do any awful thing. You just have to soften them up right. Let me demonstrate what I mean with Johnny Yellowman here. Johnny, the fingers of your right hand are poisonous snakes. Don't let them bite you!"

The VC slammed himself back into his chair, recoiling in shock.

His nostrils flared, and his eyes narrowed, with a sudden look of fierce determination. Jude turned, heel squeaking on the floor, to cry out, to tell him to stop, but before he could speak the Vietnamese prisoner whacked the knife down.

His fingers fell from his hand, only they were the heads of snakes, black, glistening. The VC did not scream. His damp, almond-brown face was lit with something like triumph. He lifted the right hand to show the stumps of his fingers, almost proudly, the blood bubbling out of them, down the inside of his arm.

"This grotesque act of self-mutilation has been brought to you courtesy of orange Moxie. If you haven't tried a Moxie, it's time to step up to the plate and find out why Mickey Mantle says it's the bee's knees. Side retired in order. . . ."

Jude turned, reeled toward the door, tasting vomit in the back of his throat, smelling vomit when he exhaled. At the very periphery of his vision, he could see the window, and the seesaw. It was still going up and down. No one was on it. The dogs lay on their sides, asleep in the grass.

He shoved through the door and banged down two warped steps and into the dusty dooryard behind his father's farm. His father sat with his back to him, on a rock, sharpening his straight razor with a black strop. The sound of it was like the dead man's voice, or maybe it was the other way around, Jude no longer knew for sure. A steel tub of water sat in the grass next to Martin Cowzynski, and a black fedora floated in it. That hat in the water was awful. Jude wanted to scream at the sight of it.

The sunshine was intense and direct on his face, a steady glare. He staggered in the heat, swayed back on his heels, and brought a hand up to shield his eyes from the light. Martin drew the blade across the strop, and blood fell from the black leather in fat drops. When Martin scraped the blade forward, the strop whispered "death." When he jerked the razor back, it made a choked sound like the word "love." Jude did not slow to speak with his father but kept going on around the back of the house.

"Justin," Martin called to him, and Jude flicked a sidelong look at him, couldn't help himself. His father wore a pair of blind man's sunglasses, round black lenses with silver frames. They gleamed when they caught the sunlight. "You need to get back in bed, boy. You're burnin' up. Where do you think you're goin' all dressed up like that?"

Jude glanced down and saw he was wearing the dead man's suit. Without breaking stride he began to pull at the buttons of the coat, undoing them as he reeled forward. But his right hand was numb and clumsy—it felt as if he were the one who had just chopped off his fingers—and the buttons wouldn't come free. In a few more steps, he gave up. He felt sick, cooking in the Louisiana sun, boiling in his black suit.

"You look like you're headed to someone's funeral," his father said. "You want to watch out. Could be your'n."

A crow was in the tub of water where the hat had been, and it took off, fanning its wings furiously, throwing spray, as Jude went past it in his stumbling, drunkard's gait. In another step he was at the side of the Mustang. He fell into it, slammed the door behind him.

Through the windshield the hardpack wavered like an image reflected in water, shimmering through the heat. He was sodden with sweat and gasping for breath in the dead man's suit, which was too hot, and too black, and too restricting. Something stank, faintly, of char. The heat was worst of all in his right hand. The feeling in the hand couldn't be described as pain, not anymore. It was, instead, a poisonous weight, swollen not with blood but liquefied ore.

His digital XM radio was gone. In its place was the Mustang's original, factory-installed AM. When he thumbed it on, his right hand was so hot it melted a blurred thumbprint in the dial.

"If there is one word that can change your life, my friends," came the voice on the radio, urgent, melodious, unmistakably southern. "If there is just one word, let me tell you, that word is 'holyeverlastinJesus'!"

Jude rested his hand on the steering wheel. The black plastic immediately began to soften, melting to conform to the shape of his fingers. He watched, dazed, curious. The wheel began to deform, sinking in on itself.

"Yes, if you keep that word in your heart, hold that word to your heart, clasp it to you like you clasp your children, it can save your life, it really can. I believe that. Will you listen to my voice, now? Will you listen only to my voice? Here's another word that can turn your world upside down and open your eyes to the endless possibilities of the living soul. That word is 'nightfall.' Let me say it again. Nightfall. Nightfall at last. The dead pull the living down. We'll ride the glory road together, hallelujah."

Jude took his hand off the wheel and put it on the seat next to him, which began to smoke. He picked the hand up and shook it, but now the smoke was coming out of his sleeve, from the inside of the dead man's jacket. The car was on the road, a long, straight stretch of blacktop, punching through southern jungle, trees strangled in creepers, brush choking the spaces in between. The asphalt was warped and distorted in the distance, through the shimmering, climbing waves of heat.

The reception on the radio fizzed in and out, and sometimes he could hear a snatch of something else, music overlapping the radio preacher, who wasn't really a preacher at all but Craddock using someone else's voice. The song sounded plaintive and archaic, like something off a Folkways record, mournful and sweet at the same time, a single ringing guitar played in a minor key. Jude thought, without sense, *He can talk, but he can't sing.*

The smell in the car was worse now, the smell of wool beginning to sizzle and burn. Jude was beginning to burn. The smoke was coming out both his sleeves now and from under his collar. He clenched his teeth and began to scream. He had always known he would go out this way: on fire. He had always known that rage was flammable, dangerous to store under pressure, where he had kept it his whole life. The Mustang rushed along the unending back roads, black smoke boiling from under the hood, out the windows, so he could hardly see through the fog of it. His eyes stung, blurred, ran with tears. It didn't matter. He didn't need to see where he was going. He put the pedal down.

Jude lurched awake, a feeling of unwholesome warmth in his face. He was turned on his side, lying on his right arm, and when he sat up, he couldn't feel the hand. Even awake he could still smell the reek of something burning, an odor like singed hair. He looked down, half expecting to find himself dressed in the dead man's suit, as in his dream. But no; he was still in his tatty old bathrobe.

The suit. The key was the suit. All he had to do was sell it again, the suit and the ghost both. It was so obvious he didn't know why it had taken so long for the idea to occur to him. Someone would want it; maybe lots of people would want it. He'd seen fans kick, spit, bite, and claw over drumsticks that had been thrown into the crowd. He thought they would want a ghost, straight from the home of Judas Coyne, even more. Some hapless asshole would take it off his hands, and the ghost would have to leave. What happened to the buyer after that didn't much trouble Jude's conscience. His own survival, and Georgia's, was a matter that concerned him above all others.

He stood, swaying, flexed his right hand. The circulation was coming back into it, accompanied by a sensation of icy prickling. It was going to hurt like a bitch.

The light was different, had shifted to the other side of the room, pale and weak as it came through the lace curtains. It was hard to say how long he'd been asleep.

The smell, that stink of something burning, lured him down the darkened front hall, through the kitchen, and into the pantry. The door to the backyard patio was open. Georgia was out there, looking miserably cold, in a black denim jacket and a Ramones T-shirt that left the smooth, white curve of her midriff exposed. She had a pair of tongs in her left hand. Her breath steamed in the cold air.

"Whatever you're cooking, you're fuckin' it up," he said, waving his hand at all the smoke.

"No I'm not," she said, and flashed him a proud and challenging smile. She was, in that instant, so beautiful it was a little heartbreaking—the white of her throat, the hollow in it, the delicate line of her just-visible collarbones. "I figured out what to do. I figured out how to make the ghost go away."

"How's that?" Jude asked.

She picked at something with the tongs and then held it up. It was a burning flap of black fabric.

"The suit," she said. "I burned it."

16

An hour later it was dusk. Jude sat in the study to watch the last of the light drain out of the sky. He had a guitar in his lap. He needed to think. The two things went together.

He was in a chair, turned to face a window that looked over the barn, the dog pen, and the trees beyond. Jude had it open a crack. The air that came in had a crisp bite to it. He didn't mind. It wasn't much warmer in the house, and he needed the fresh air, was grateful for the mid-October perfume of rotten apples and fallen leaves. It was a relief from the reek of exhaust. Even after a shower and a change of clothes, he could still smell it on him.

Jude had his back to the door, and when Georgia came into the room, he saw her in reflection. She had a glass of red wine in each hand. The swaddling of bandages around her thumb forced her to grip one of the glasses awkwardly, and she spilled a little on herself when she sank to her knees beside his chair. She kissed the wine off her skin, then set a glass in front of him, on the amp near his feet.

"He isn't coming back," she said. "The dead man. I bet you. Burning the suit got rid of him. Stroke of genius. Besides, that fucking thing had to go. *Whoo-ee*. I wrapped it in two garbage bags before I brought it downstairs, and I still thought I was going to gag from the stink."

It was in his mind to say, *He wanted you to do it,* but he didn't. It wouldn't do her any good to hear it, and it was over and done with now.

Georgia narrowed her eyes at him, studying his expression. His doubts must've been there in his face, because she said, "You think he'll be back?" When Jude didn't reply, she leaned toward him and spoke again, her voice low, urgent. "Then why don't we go? Get a room in the city and get the hell out of here?"

He considered this, forming his reply slowly, and only with effort. At last he said, "I don't think it would do any good, just to up and run. He isn't haunting the house. He's haunting me."

That was part of it—but only part. The rest was too hard to put into words. The idea persisted that everything to happen so far had happened for reasons—the dead man's reasons. That phrase, "psychological operations," rose to Jude's mind with a feeling of chill. He wondered again if the ghost wasn't trying to make him run, and why that would be. Maybe the house, or something in the house, offered Jude an advantage, although, try as he might, he couldn't figure what.

"You ever think *you* ought to take off?" Jude asked her.

"You almost died today," Georgia said. "I don't know what's happening to you, but I'm not going anywhere. I don't think I'm going to let you out of my sight ever again. Besides, your ghost hasn't done anything to me. I bet he can't touch me."

But Jude had watched Craddock whispering in her ear. He had seen the stricken look on Georgia's face as the dead man held his razor on a chain before her eyes. And he had not forgotten Jessica Price's voice on the telephone, her lazy, poisonous, redneck drawl: *You will not live, and no one who gives you aid or comfort will live.*

Craddock could get to Georgia. She needed to go. Jude saw this clearly now—and yet the thought of sending her away, of waking alone in the night and finding the dead man there, standing over him in the dark, made him weak with dread. If she left him, Jude felt she might take what re-mained of his nerve with her. He did not know if he could bear the night and the quiet without her close—an admission of need that was so stark and unexpected it gave him a brief, bad moment of vertigo. He was a man afraid of heights, watching the ground lunge away beneath him, while the Ferris wheel yanked him helplessly into the sky.

"What about Danny?" Jude said. He thought his own voice sounded strained and unlike him, and he cleared his throat. "Danny thought he was dangerous."

"What did this ghost do to Danny? Danny saw something, got scared, and ran for his life. Wasn't like anything got done to him."

"Just because the ghost *didn't* do anything doesn't mean he *can't*. Look at what happened to me this afternoon."

Georgia nodded at this. She drank the rest of her wine in one swal-low, then met his gaze, her eyes bright and searching. "And you swear you didn't go into that barn to kill yourself? You swear, Jude? Don't be mad at me for asking. I need to know."

"Think I'm the type?" he asked.

"Everyone's the type."

"Not me."

"Everyone. I tried to do it. Pills. Bammy found me passed out on the bathroom floor. My lips were blue. I was hardly breathing. Three days after my last day of high school. Afterward my mother and father came to the hospital, and my father said, 'You couldn't even do that right.'"

"Cocksucker."

"Yup. Pretty much."

"Why'd you want to kill yourself? I hope you had a good reason."

"Because I'd been having sex with my daddy's best friend. Since I was thirteen. This forty-year-old guy with a daughter of his own. People found out. His daughter found out. She was my friend. She said I ruined her life. She said I was a whore." Georgia rolled her glass this way and that in her left hand, watching the glimmer of light move around and around the rim. "Pretty hard to argue with her. He'd give me things, and I'd always take them. Like, he gave me a brand-new sweater once with fifty dollars in the pocket. He said the money was so I could buy shoes to go with it. I let him fuck me for shoe money."

"Hell. That wasn't any good reason to kill yourself," Jude told her. "It was a good reason to kill him."

She laughed.

"What was his name?"

"George Ruger. He's a used-car salesman now, in my old hometown. Head of the county Republican steering committee."

"Next time I get down Georgia way, I'll stop in and kill the son of a bitch."

She laughed again.

"Or at least thoroughly stomp his ass into the Georgia clay," Jude said, and played the opening bars of "Dirty Deeds."

She lifted his glass of wine off the amp, raised it in a toast to him, and had a sip.

"Do you know what the best thing about you is?" she asked.

"No idea."

"Nothing grosses you out. I mean, I just told you all that, and you don't think I'm . . . I don't know. Ruined. Hopelessly fucked up."

"Maybe I do and I just don't care."

"You care," she said. She put a hand on his ankle. "And nothing shocks you."

He let that pass, did not say he could've guessed the suicide attempt, the emotionally cold father, the family friend who molested her, almost from the first moment Jude saw her, wearing a dog collar, her hair hacked into uneven spikes and her mouth painted in white lipstick.

She said, "So what happened to you? Your turn."

He twitched his ankle out of her grasp.

"I'm not into feel-bad competitions."

He glanced at the window. Nothing remained of the light except for a faint, reddish bronze flush behind the leafless trees. Jude considered his own semitransparent reflection in the glass, his face long, seamed, gaunt, with a flowing black beard that came almost to his chest. A haggard, grim-visaged ghost.

Georgia said, "Tell me about this woman who sent you the ghost."

"Jessica Price. She didn't just send him to me either. Remember, she tricked me into paying for him."

"Right. On eBay or something?"

"No. A different site, a third-rate clone. And it only looked like a regular Internet auction. She was orchestrating things from behind the scenes to make sure I'd win." Jude saw the question forming in Georgia's eyes and answered it before she could speak. "Why she went to all that trouble I can't tell you. I get the feeling, though, that she couldn't just mail him to me. I had to agree to take possession of him. I'm sure there's some profound moral message in that."

"Yeah," Georgia said. "Stick with eBay. Accept no substitutes." She tasted some wine, licked her lips, then went on. "And this is all because her sister killed herself? Why does she think that's your fault? Is it because of something you wrote in one of your songs? Is this like when that kid killed himself after listening to Ozzy Osbourne? Have you written anything that says suicide is okay or something?"

"No. Neither did Ozzy."

"Then I don't see why she's so pissed off at you. Did you know each other in some way? Did you know the girl who killed herself? Did she write you crazy fan letters or something?"

He said, "She lived with me for a while. Like you."

"Like me? Oh."

"Got news for you, Georgia. I wasn't a virgin when I met you." His voice sounded wooden and strange to him.

"How long did she live here?"

"I don't know. Eight, nine months. Long enough to overstay her welcome."

She thought about that. "I've been living with you for about nine months."

"So?"

"So have I overstayed mine? Is nine months the limit? Then it's time for some fresh pussy? What, was she a natural blonde, and you decided it was time for a brunette?"

He took his hands off his guitar. "She was a natural psycho, so I threw her ass out. I guess she didn't take it well."

"What do you mean, she was a psycho?"

"I mean manic-depressive. When she was manic, she was a hell of a lay. When she was depressive, it was a little too much work."

"She had mental problems, and you just chucked her out?"

"I didn't sign on to hold her hand the rest of her life. I didn't sign on to hold yours either. I'll tell you something else, Georgia. If you think our story ends 'and they lived happily ever after,' then you've got the wrong fuckin' fairy tale." As he spoke, he became aware that he'd found his chance to hurt her and get rid of her. He had, he understood now, been steering the conversation toward this very moment. The idea recurred that if he could sting her badly enough to make her leave—even if it was just for a while, a night, a few hours—it might be the last good thing he ever did for her.

"What was her name? The girl who killed herself?"

He started to say "Anna," then said "Florida" instead.

Georgia stood quickly, so quickly she tottered, looked as if she might fall over. He could've reached out to steady her but didn't. Better to let her hurt. Her face whitened, and she took an unsteady half step back. She stared at him, bewildered and wounded—and then her eyes sharpened, as if she were suddenly bringing his face into focus.

"No," she breathed softly. "You're not going to drive me away like that. You say any shitty thing you want. I'm sticking, Jude."

She carefully set the glass she was holding on the edge of his desk.

She started away from him, then paused at the door. She turned her head but didn't quite seem able to look into his face.

"I'm going to get some sleep. You come on to bed, too." Telling him, not asking.

Jude opened his mouth to reply and found he had nothing to say. When she left the room, he gently leaned his guitar against the wall and stood up. His pulse was jacked, and his legs were unsteady, the physical manifestations of an emotion it took him some time to place—he was that unused to the sensation of relief.

17

Georgia was gone. That was the first thing he knew. She was gone, and it was still night. He exhaled, and his breath made a cloud of white smoke in the room. He shoved off the one thin sheet and got out of bed, then hugged himself through a brief shivering fit.

The idea that she was up and wandering the house alarmed him. His head was still muddy with sleep, and it had to be close to freezing in the room. It would've been reasonable to think Georgia had gone to figure out what was wrong with the heat, but Jude knew that wasn't it. She'd been sleeping badly as well, tossing and muttering. She might have come awake and gone to watch TV—but he didn't believe that either.

He almost shouted her name, then thought better of it. He quailed at the idea that she might not reply, that his voice might be met with a ringing silence. No. No yelling. No rushing around. He felt if he went slamming out of the bedroom and rushing through the unlit house, calling for her, it would tip him irrevocably toward panic. Also, the darkness and quiet of the bedroom appalled him, and he understood that he was afraid to go looking for her, afraid of what might be waiting beyond the door.

As he stood there, he became aware of a guttural rumble, the sound of an idling engine. He rolled his eyes back, looked at the ceiling. It was

lit an icy white, someone's headlights, pointing in from the driveway below. He could hear the dogs barking.

Jude crossed to the window and shifted aside the curtain.

The pickup parked out front had been blue once, but it was at least
twenty years old and had not seen another coat in all that time, had
faded to the color of smoke. It was a Chevy, a working truck. Jude had
whiled away two years of his life twisting a wrench in an auto garage for
$1.75 an hour, and he knew from the deep, ferocious mutter of the idling
engine that it had a big block under the hood. The front end was all ag-
gression and menace, with a wide silver bumper like a boxer's mouth-
piece and an iron brush guard bolted over the grill. What he had taken at
first for headlights were a pair of floods attached to the brush guard, two
round spots pouring their glare into the night. The pickup sat almost a
full foot off the ground on four 35s, a truck built for running on washed-
out swamp roads, banging through the ruts and choking brush of the
Deep South, the bottoms. The engine was running. No one was in it.

The dogs flung themselves against the chain-link wall of the pen, a
steady crash and clang, yapping at the empty pickup. Jude peered down
the driveway, in the direction of the road. The gates were closed. You had
to know a six-digit security code to get them open.

It was the dead man's truck. Jude knew the moment he saw it,
knew with a calm, utter certainty. His next thought was, *Where we going, old man?*

The phone by the bed chirped, and Jude half jumped in surprise, letting go of the curtain. He turned and stared. The clock beside the phone
read 3:12. The phone rang again.

Jude moved toward it, tiptoeing quickly across cold floorboards.
Stared down at it. It rang a third time. He didn't want to answer. He had
an idea it would be the dead man, and Jude didn't want to talk to him.
Jude didn't want to hear Craddock's voice.

"Fuck it," he said, and he answered. "Who is it?"

"Hey, Chief. It's Dan."

"Danny? It's three in the morning."

"Oh. I didn't know it was so late. Were you asleep?"

"No." Jude fell silent, waited.

"I'm sorry I left like I did."

"Are you drunk?" Jude asked. He looked at the window again, the blue-tinted glare of the floodlights shining around the edges of the curtains. "Are you calling drunk because you want your job back? Because if you are, this is the wrong fuckin' time—"

"No. I can't . . . I can't come back, Jude. I was just calling to say I'm sorry about everything. I'm sorry I said anything about the ghost for sale. I should've kept my mouth shut."

"Go to bed."

"I can't."

"What the fuck is wrong with you?"

"I'm out walking in the dark. I don't even know where I am."

Jude felt the back of his arms prickling with goose bumps. The thought of Danny out on the streets somewhere, shuffling around in the dark, disturbed him more than it should've, more than made sense.

"How'd you get there?"

"I just went walking. I don't even know why."

"Jesus, you're drunk. Take a look around for a street sign and call a fuckin' cab," Jude said, and hung up.

He was glad to let go of the phone. He hadn't liked Danny's tone of spaced-out, unhappy confusion.

It wasn't that Danny had said anything so incredible or unlikely. It was just that they'd never had a conversation like it before. Danny had never called in the night, and he'd never called drunk. It was difficult to imagine him going for a walk at 3:00 A.M., or walking so far from his home as to get lost. And whatever his other flaws, Danny was a problem solver. That was why Jude had kept him on the payroll for eight years. Even shitfaced, Danny probably wouldn't call Jude first if he didn't know where he was. He'd walk to a 7-Eleven and get directions. He'd flag down a cop car.

No. It was all wrong. The phone call and the dead man's truck in the driveway were two parts of the same thing. Jude knew. His nerves told him so. The empty bed told him so.

He glanced again at the curtain, lit from behind by those floods. The dogs were going crazy out there.

Georgia. What mattered now was finding Georgia. Then they could figure out about that truck. Together they could get a handle on the situation.

Jude looked at the door to the hallway. He flexed his fingers, his hands numb from the cold. He didn't want to go out there, didn't want to open the door and see Craddock sitting in that chair with his hat on his knee and that razor on a chain dangling from one hand.

But the thought of seeing the dead man again—of facing whatever was next—held him for only a moment more. Then he came unstuck, went to the door, and opened it.

"Let's do it," he said to the hallway before he had even seen if anyone was there.

No one was.

Jude paused, listening past his own just slightly haggard breathing to the quiet of the house. The long hall was draped in shadows, the Shaker chair against the wall empty. No. Not empty. A black fedora rested in the seat.

Noises—muffled and distant—caught his attention: the murmur of voices on a television, the distant crash of surf. He pulled his gaze away from the fedora and looked to the end of the hallway. Blue light flickered and raced at the edges of the door to the studio. Georgia was in there, then, watching TV after all.

Jude hesitated at the door, listening. He heard a voice shouting in Spanish, a TV voice. The sound of surf was louder. Jude meant to call her name then, Marybeth—not Georgia, Marybeth—but something bad happened when he tried: His breath gave out on him. He was able to produce only a wheeze in the faint sound of her name.

He opened the door.

Georgia was across the room in the recliner, in front of his flat-screen TV. From where he stood, he couldn't see anything of her but the back of her head, the fluffy swirl of her black hair surrounded by a nimbus of unnatural blue light. Her head also largely blocked the view of whatever was on the TV, although he could see palm trees and tropical blue sky. It was dark, the lights in the room switched off.

She didn't respond when he said, "Georgia," and his next thought was that she was dead. When he got to her, her eyes would be rolled up in their sockets.

He started toward her, but had only gone a couple of steps when the phone rang on the desk.

Jude could view enough of the TV now to see a chubby Mex in sunglasses and a beige jogging suit, standing at the side of a dirt track in jungly hill country somewhere. Jude knew what she was watching then, although he hadn't looked at it in several years. It was the snuff film.

At the sound of the phone, Georgia's head seemed to move just slightly, and he thought he heard her exhale, a strained, effortful breath. Not dead, then. But she didn't otherwise react, didn't look around, didn't get up to answer.

He took a step to the desk, caught the phone on the second ring.

"That you, Danny? Are you still lost?" Jude asked.

"Yeah," Danny said with a weak laugh. "Still lost. I'm on this pay phone in the middle of nowhere. It's funny, you almost never see pay phones anymore."

Georgia did not glance around at the sound of Jude's voice, did not shift her gaze from the TV.

"I hope you aren't calling because you want me to come looking for you," Jude said. "I've got my hands full at the moment. If I have to come looking for you, you better hope you stay lost."

"I figured it out, Chief. How I got here. Out on this road in the dark."

"How's that?"

"I killed myself. I hung myself a few hours ago. This road in the dark . . . this is dead."

Jude's scalp crawled, a trickling, icy sensation, almost painful.

Danny said, "My mother hung herself just the same way. She did a better job, though. She broke her neck. Died instantly. I lost my nerve at the last second. I didn't fall hard enough. I strangled to death."

From the television across the room came gagging sounds, as if someone were strangling to death.

"It took a long time, Jude," Danny went on. "I remember swinging for a long time. Looking at my feet. I'm remembering lots of things now."

"Why'd you do it?"

"He made me. The dead man. He came to see me. I was going to come back to the office and find those letters for you. I was thinking I could at least do that much. I was thinking I shouldn't have bailed out on you like I did. But when I went in my bedroom to get my coat, he was waiting there. I didn't even know how to knot a noose until he showed me," Danny said. "That's how he's going to get you. He's going to make you kill yourself."

"No he's not."

"It's hard not to listen to his voice. I couldn't fight it. He knew too much. He knew I gave my sister the heroin she OD'd on. He said that was why my mother killed herself, because she couldn't live knowing what I had done. He said I should've been the one to hang, not my mom. He said if I had any decency, I would've killed myself a long time ago. He was right."

"No, Danny," Jude said. "No. He wasn't right. You shouldn't—"

Danny sounded short of breath. "I did. I *had* to. There was no arguing with him. You can't argue with a voice like that."

"We'll see," Jude said.

Danny had no reply for that. In the snuff film, two men were bickering in Spanish. The choking sounds went on and on. Georgia still did not look away. She was moving just slightly, shoulders hitching now and then in a series of random, almost spastic shrugs.

"I have to go, Danny." Still Danny said nothing. Jude listened to the faint crackle on the line for a moment, sensing that Danny was waiting for something, some final word, and at last he added, "You keep walking, boy. That road must go somewhere."

Danny laughed. "You aren't as bad as you think, Jude. You know that?"

"Yeah. Don't tell."

"Your secret is safe," Danny said. "Good-bye."

"Good-bye, Danny."

Jude leaned forward, gently set the phone back in its cradle. As he was bent across the desk, he glanced down and behind it and saw that the floor safe was open. His initial thought was the ghost had opened it, an idea he discarded almost immediately. Georgia, more likely. She knew the combination.

He pivoted, looked at the back of her head, at the halo of flickering blue light, at the television beyond.

"Georgia? What are you doin', darlin'?"

She didn't reply.

He came forward, moving silently across the thick carpet. The picture on the flat-screen came into view first. The killers were finishing off the skinny white kid. Later they would get his girlfriend in a cinder-block hut close to a beach. Now, though, they were on an overgrown track somewhere in the bush, in the hills above the Gulf of California. The kid was on his stomach, his wrists bound together by a pair of white plastic flexi-cuffs. His skin was fish-belly pale in the tropical sunlight. A diminutive, walleyed Anglo, with a clownish Afro of crinkly red hair, stood with one cowboy boot on the kid's neck. Parked down the road was a black van, the back doors thrown open. Next to the rear fender was the chubby Mex in the warm-up suit, an affronted expression hung on his face.

"Nos estamos yendo," said the man in the sunglasses. "Ahora."

The walleyed redhead made a face and shook his head, as if in dis-agreement, but then pointed the little revolver at the skinny kid's head and pulled the trigger. The muzzle flashed. The kid's head snapped forward, hit the ground, bounced back. The air around his head was suddenly clouded with a fine spray of blood.

The Anglo took his boot off the boy's neck and stepped daintily away, careful to get no blood on his cowboy boots.

Georgia's face was a pale, rigid blank, her eyes wide and unblinking, gaze fixed on the television. She wore the Ramones T-shirt she'd had on earlier, but no underwear, and her legs were open. In one hand—the bad hand—she had clumsy hold of Jude's pistol, and the barrel was pushed deep into her mouth. Her other hand was between her legs, thumb moving up and down.

"Georgia," he said, and for an instant she shot a sidelong glance at him—a helpless, pleading glance—then immediately looked back to the TV. Her bad hand rotated the gun, turning it upside down, to point the barrel against the roof of her mouth. She made a weak choking sound on it.

The remote control was on the armrest. Jude hit the power button. The television blinked off. Her shoulders leaped, a nervous, reflexive shrug. The left hand kept working between her legs. She shivered, made a strained, unhappy sound in her throat.

"Stop it," Jude said.

She pulled the hammer back with her thumb. It made a loud snap in the silence of the studio.

Jude reached past her and gently pried the gun out of her grip. Her whole body went abruptly, perfectly still. Her breath whistled, short and fast. Her mouth was wet, glistening faintly, and it came to him then that he was semihard. His cock had begun to stiffen at the smell of her in the air and the sight of her fingers teasing her clit, and she was at just the right height. If he moved in front of the chair, she could suck his dick while he held the gun to her head, he could stick the barrel in her ear while he shoved his cock—

He saw a flicker of motion, reflected in the partly open window beyond his desk, and his gaze jumped to the image in the glass. He could see himself there and the dead man standing beside him, hunched and whispering in his ear. In the reflection Jude could see that his own arm had come up, and he was holding the pistol to Georgia's head.

His heart lurched, all the blood rushing to it in a sudden, adrenalized burst. He looked down, saw it was true, he was holding the gun to her head, saw his finger squeezing the trigger. He tried to stop himself, but it was already too late—he pulled it, waited in horror for the hammer to fall.

It didn't fall. The trigger wouldn't depress the last quarter inch. The safety was on.

"Fuck," Jude hissed, and lowered the gun, trembling furiously now. He used his thumb to ease the hammer back down. When he had settled it into place, he flung the pistol away from himself.

It banged heavily against the desk, and Georgia flinched at the sound. Her stare, however, remained fixed on some abstract point off in the darkness before her.

Jude turned, looking for Craddock's ghost. No one stood beside him. The room was empty, except for himself and Georgia. He turned back to her and tugged on her slender white wrist.

"Get up," he said. "Come on. We're going. Right now. I don't know where we're going, but we're getting out of here. We're going someplace where there are lots of people and bright lights, and we're going to try to figure this out. You hear me?" He could no longer recall his logic for staying. Logic was out the window.

"He isn't done with us," she said, her voice a shuddering whisper.

He pulled, but she didn't rise, her body rigid in the chair, uncooperative. She still wouldn't look at him, wouldn't look anywhere except straight ahead.

"Come on," he said. "While there's time."

"There is no more time," she said.

The television blinked on again.

18

It was the evening news. Bill Beutel, who had started his journalism career when the assassination of Archduke Ferdinand was the breaking story of the day, sat stiffly behind the news desk. His face was a network of spiderweb wrinkles, radiating out from around his eyes and the corners of his mouth. His features were set in their grief expression, the look that said there was more bad news in the Middle East or that a school bus had gone off the interstate and rolled, killing all passengers, or a tornado in the South had inhaled a trailer park and coughed out a mess of ironing boards, splintered shutters, and human bodies.

". . . there will be no survivors. We'll bring you more as the situation continues to unfold," Beutel said. He turned his head slightly, and the reflected blue screen of the teleprompter floated in the lenses of his bifocals for a moment. "Late this afternoon the Dutchess County sheriff's department confirmed that Judas Coyne, the popular lead singer of Jude's Hammer, apparently shot and killed his girlfriend, Marybeth Stacy Kimball, before turning the weapon on himself to take his own life."

The program cut to video of Jude's farmhouse, framed against a sky of dingy, featureless white. Police cruisers had parked haphazardly in the turnaround, and an ambulance stood backed up almost to the door of Danny's office.

Beutel continued to speak in voice-over: "Police are only beginning to piece together the picture of Coyne's last days. But statements from those who knew him suggest he had been distraught and was worried about his own mental health."

The footage jumped to a shot of the dogs in their pen. They were on their sides in the short, stubbly grass, neither of them moving, legs stretched stiffly away from their bodies. They were dead. Jude tightened up at the sight of them. It was a bad thing to see. He wanted to look away but couldn't seem to pry his gaze free.

"Detectives also believe that Coyne played a role in the death of his personal assistant, Daniel Wooten, thirty, who was found in his Woodstock home earlier this morning, also an apparent suicide."

Cut to two paramedics, one at either end of a sagging blue plastic body bag. Georgia made a soft, unhappy sound in her throat, watching one of the paramedics climb backward into the ambulance, hefting his end.

Beutel began to talk about Jude's career, and they cut away to file footage of Jude onstage in Houston, a clip six years old. Jude was in black jeans and black steel-toed boots, but bare-chested, his torso glowing with sweat, the bearish fur on it plastered to his breast, stomach heaving. A sea of a hundred thousand half-naked people surged below him, a rioting flood of raised fists, crowd surfers tumbling this way and that along the flow of humanity beneath.

Dizzy was already dying by then, although at the time almost no one except Jude knew. Dizzy with his heroin addiction and his AIDS. They played back-to-back, Dizzy's mane of blond hair in his face, the wind blowing it across his mouth. It was the last year the band had been together. Dizzy died, and Jerome, and then it was over.

In the file footage, they were playing the title song off their final album as a group, "Put You in Yer Place"; their last hit, the last really good song Jude had written, and at the sound of those drums—a furious cannonade—he was jolted free from whatever hold the television seemed to have over him. That had been real. Houston had happened, that day had happened. The engulfing, mad rush of the crowd below and the engulfing, mad rush of the music around him. It was real, it had happened, and all the rest was—

"Bullshit," Jude said, and his thumb hit the power button. The television popped off.

"It isn't true," Georgia said, her voice hardly more than a whisper. "It isn't true, is it? Are we . . . are you . . . Is that going to happen to us?"

"No," Jude said.

And the television popped back on. Bill Beutel sat behind the news desk again, a sheaf of papers clasped in his hands, his shoulders squared to the camera.

"Yes," Bill said. "You will both be dead. The dead pull the living down. You will get the gun, and she will try to get away, but you will catch her, and you will—"

Jude hit the power button again, then threw the remote control at the screen of the television. He went after it, put his foot on the screen and then straightened his leg, shoved the television straight through the open back of the cabinet. It hit the wall, and something flared, a white light going off like a flashbulb. The flat-screen dropped out of sight into the space between cabinet and wall, hit with a crunch of plastic and a short, electrical, fizzing sound that lasted for only a moment before ending. Another day of this and there would be nothing left to the house.

He turned, and the dead man stood behind Georgia's chair. Craddock's ghost reached around the back to cup her head between his hands. Black lines danced and shimmered before the old man's eye sockets.

Georgia did not try to move or look around, was as still as a person faced with a poisonous snake, afraid to do anything—even to breathe—for fear of being struck.

"You didn't come for her," Jude said. As he spoke, he was stepping to the left, circling along one side of the room and toward the doorway to the hall. "You don't want her."

In one instant Craddock's hands were gently cradling Georgia's head. In the next his right arm had come up to point out and away from his body: *Sieg heil.* Around the dead man, time had a way of skipping, a scratched DVD, the picture stuttering erratically from moment to moment, without any transitions in between. The golden chain fell from his raised right hand. The razor, shaped like a crescent moon, gleamed brilliantly at the end. The edge of the blade was faintly iridescent, the way a rainbow slick of oil is on water.

Time to ride, Jude.

"Go away," Jude said.

If you want me to go, you just have to listen to my voice. You have to listen hard. You have to be like a radio, and my voice is the broadcast. After nightfall it's nice to have some radio. If you want this to end, you have to listen hard as you can. You have to want it to end with all your heart. Don't you want it to end?

Jude tightened his jaw, clamped his teeth together. He wasn't going to answer, sensed somehow it would be a mistake to give any reply, then was startled to find himself nodding slowly.

Don't you want to listen hard? I know you do. I know. Listen. You can tune out the whole world and hear nothing but my voice. Because you are listening so hard.

And Jude went on nodding, bobbing his head slowly up and down, while around him all the other sounds of the room fell away. Jude had not even been aware of these other noises until they were gone: the low rumble of the truck idling outside, the thin whine of Georgia's breath in her throat, matched by Jude's own harsh gasping. His ears rang at the sudden utter absence of sound, as if his eardrums had been numbed by a shattering explosion.

The naked razor swayed in little arcs, back and forth, back and forth. Jude dreaded the sight of it, forced himself to look away.

You don't need to look at it, Craddock told him. *I'm dead. I don't need a pendulum to get inside your mind. I'm there already.*

And Jude found his gaze sliding back to it anyway, couldn't help himself.

"Georgia," Jude said, or tried to say. He felt the word on his lips, in his mouth, in the shape of his breath, but did not hear his own voice, did not hear anything in that awful, enveloping silence. He had never heard any noise as loud as that particular silence.

I am not going to kill her. No, sir, said the dead man. His voice never varied in tone, was patient, understanding, a low, resonant hum that brought to mind the sound of bees in the hive. *You are. You will. You want to.*

Jude opened his mouth to tell him how wrong he was, said, "Yes," instead. Or assumed he said it. It was more like a loud thought.

Craddock said, *Good boy.*

Georgia was beginning to cry, although she was making a visible effort to hold herself still, not to tremble. Jude couldn't hear her. Craddock's blade slashed back and forth, whisking through the air.

I don't want to hurt her, don't make me hurt her, Jude thought.

It ain't going to be the way you want it. Get the gun, you hear? Do it now.

Jude began to move. He felt subtly disconnected from his body, a witness, not a participant in the scene playing itself out. He was too empty-headed to dread what he was about to do. He knew only that he had to do it if he wanted to wake up.

But before he reached the gun, Georgia was out of the chair and bolting for the door. He didn't have any idea she could move, thought that Craddock had been holding her there somehow, but it had just been fear holding her, and she was already almost by him.

Stop her, said the only voice left in the world, and as she lunged past him, Jude saw himself catch her hair in one fist and snap her head back. She was wrenched off her feet. Jude pivoted and threw her down. The furniture jumped when she hit the floor. A stack of CDs on an end table slid off and crashed to the floor without a sound. Jude's foot found her stomach, a good hard kick, and she jerked herself into a fetal position. The moment after he'd done it, he didn't know why he'd done it.

There you go, said the dead man.

It disoriented Jude, the way the dead man's voice came at him out of the silence, words that had an almost physical presence, bees whirring and chasing one another around the inside of his head. His head was the hive that they flew into and out of, and without them there was a waxy, honeycombed emptiness. His head was too light and too hollow, and he would go mad if he didn't get his own thoughts back, his own voice. The dead man was saying now, *You need to show that cunt. If you don't mind me sayin' so. Now get the gun. Hurry.*

Jude turned to get the gun, moving quickly now. Across the floor, to the desk, the gun at his feet, down on one knee to pick it up.

Jude did not hear the dogs until he was reaching for the revolver. One high-strung yap, then another. His attention snagged on that sound like a loose sleeve catching on a protruding nail. It shocked him, to hear anything else in that bottomless silence besides Craddock's voice. The window behind the desk was still parted slightly, as he had left it. Another bark, shrill, furious, and another. Angus. Then Bon.

Come on now, boy. Come on and do it.

Jude's gaze flitted to the little wastebasket next to the desk and to the pieces of the platinum record shoved into it. A nest of chrome knife blades sticking straight up into the air. The dogs were both barking in unison now, a tear in the fabric of the quiet, and the sound of them called to mind, unbidden, their smell, the stink of damp dog fur, the hot animal reek of their breath. Jude could see his face reflected in one of those silver record shards, and it jolted him: his own rigid, staring look of desperation, of horror. And in the next moment, mingled with the relentless yawping of the dogs, he had a thought that was his own, in his own voice. *The only power he has, over either one of you, is the power you give him.*

In the next instant, Jude reached past the gun and put his hand over the wastebasket. He set the ball of his left palm on the sharpest, longest-looking spear of silver and lunged, driving all his weight down onto it. The blade sank into meat, and he felt a tearing pain lance through his hand and into the wrist. Jude cried out, and his eyes blurred, stung with tears. He instantly yanked his palm free from the blade, then clapped his right hand and the left together. Blood spurted between them.

What the fuck are you doin' to yourself, boy? Craddock's ghost asked him, but Jude wasn't listening anymore. Couldn't pay attention through the feeling in his hand, a sensation of having been deeply pierced, almost to the bone.

I'm not through with you, Craddock said, but he was, he just didn't know it. Jude's mind reached for the sound of the barking dogs like a drowning man grasping at a life preserver, found it and clasped it to him. He was on his feet, and he began to move.

Get to the dogs. His life—and Georgia's—depended on it. It was an idea that made no rational sense, but Jude did not care what was rational. Only what was true.

The pain was a red ribbon he held between his hands, following it away from the dead man's voice and back to his own thoughts. He had a great tolerance for pain, always had, and at other times in his life had even willfully sought it out. There was an ache way down in his wrist, in the joint, a sign of how deep his wound was, and some part of him appreciated that ache, wondered at it. He caught sight of his reflection in the window as he rose. He was grinning in the straggles of his beard, a vision even worse than the expression of terror he'd glimpsed in his own face a moment before.

Get back here, said Craddock, and Jude slowed for an instant, then found his step and kept on.

He shot a look at Georgia on his way by—couldn't risk a glance back to see what Craddock was doing—and she was still curled on the floor, her arms around her stomach and her hair in her face. She glanced back at him from under her bangs. Her cheeks were damp with sweat. Her eyelids fluttered. The eyes beneath pleaded, questioned, fogged over with pain.

He wished there were time to say he hadn't meant to hurt her. He wanted to tell her that he wasn't running, wasn't leaving her, that he was leading the dead man away, but the pain in his hand was too intense. He couldn't think past it to line words up into clear sentences. And besides, he didn't know how long he'd be able to think for himself, before Craddock would get ahold of him again. He had to control the pace of what happened next, and it had to happen fast. That was fine. It was better that way. He had always been at his best operating in 5/4 time.

He heaved himself down the hall, made the stairs and took them fast, too fast almost, four at a time, so it was like falling. He crashed down the last few steps to the red clay tiles of the kitchen. One ankle turned under him. He stumbled into the chopping block, with its slender legs and scarred surface stained with old blood. A cleaver was buried in the soft wood at one edge, and the wide, flat blade glinted like liquid mercury in the dark. He saw the stairs behind him reflected in it and Craddock standing on them, his features blurred, his hands raised over his head, palms out, a tent-revival preacher testifying to the flock.

Stay, Craddock said. *Get the knife.* But Jude concentrated on the throbbing in the palm of his hand. It was the deep hurt of pierced muscle and had the effect of clearing his head and centering him. The dead man couldn't make Jude do what he wanted if Jude was in too much pain to hear him. He shoved himself back from the chopping block, and his momentum carried him away from it and down the length of the kitchen.

He hit the door into Danny's office, pushed through it, and rushed on into darkness.

19

Three steps through the door, he pulled up, hesitated for a moment to get his bearings. The shades were drawn. There was no light anywhere. He could not see his way in all that darkness and had to move forward more slowly, shuffling his feet, hands stretched before him, feeling for objects that might be in his path. The door wasn't far, and then he would be outside.

As he went forward, though, he felt an anxious constriction in his chest. It was a little more work to breathe than he liked. He felt at any moment his hands would settle on Craddock's cold, dead face in the dark. At the thought he found himself fighting not to panic. His elbow struck a standing lamp, and it crashed over. His heart throbbed. He kept moving his feet forward in halting baby steps, but he had no sense of getting any closer to where he was going.

A red eye, the eye of a cat, opened slowly in the darkness. The speakers that flanked the stereo cabinet came on with a thump of bass and a low, empty hum. The constriction was around Jude's heart, a sickening tightness. *Keep breathing,* he told himself. *Keep moving. He's going to try to stop you from getting outside.* The dogs barked and barked, voices rough, strained, not far away now.

The stereo was on, and there should've been radio, but there was no radio. There was no sound at all. Jude's fingers brushed the wall, the doorframe, and then he grasped the doorknob with his punctured left hand. An imaginary sewing needle turned slowly in the wound, producing a cold flare of pain.

Jude twisted the doorknob, pulled the door back. A slash opened in the darkness, looking out into the glare of the floodlights on the front of the dead man's truck.

"You think you're something special because you learnt how to play a fuckin' guitar?" said Jude's father from the far end of the office. He was on the stereo, his voice loud and hollow.

In the next moment, Jude became aware of other sounds coming from the speakers—heavy breathing, scuffling shoes, the thud of someone bumping a table—noises that suggested a quiet, desperate wrestling match, two men struggling with each other. There was a little radio play going. It was a play Jude knew well. He had been one of the actors in the original.

Jude stopped with the door half open, unable to plunge out into the night, pinned in place by the sounds coming from the office stereo.

"You think knowin' how to do that makes you better than me?" Martin Cowzynski, his tone amused and hating all at the same time. "Get over here."

Then came Jude's own voice. No, not Jude's voice—he hadn't been Jude then. It was Justin's, a voice in a slightly higher octave, one that cracked sometimes and lacked the resonance that had come with the development of his adult pipes. "Momma! Momma, help!"

Momma did not say anything, did not make a sound, but Jude remembered what she'd done. She had stood up from the kitchen table and walked to the room where she did her sewing and gently closed the door behind her, without daring to look at either of them. Jude and his mother had never helped each other. When they needed it most, they had never dared.

"I said get the fuck over here," Martin told him.

The sound of someone knocking into a chair. The sound of the chair banging against the floor. When Justin cried out again, his voice wavered with alarm.

"Not my hand! No, Dad, not my hand!"

"Show you," his father said.

And there came a great booming sound, like a door slamming, and Justin-the-boy-on-the-radio screamed and screamed again, and at the sound of it Jude pitched himself out into the night air.

He missed a step, stumbled, dropped to his knees in the frozen mud of the driveway. Picked himself up, took two running steps, and stumbled again. Jude fell onto all fours in front of the dead man's pickup. He stared over the front fender at the brutal framework of the brush guard and the floodlights attached to it.

The front of a house or a car or a truck could sometimes look like a face, and so it was with Craddock's Chevy. The floodlights were the bright, blind, staring eyes of the deranged. The chrome bar of the fender was a leering silver mouth. Jude expected it to lunge at him, tires spinning on the gravel, but it didn't.

Bon and Angus leaped against the chain-link walls of their pen, barking relentlessly—deep, throaty roars of terror and rage, the eternal, primitive language of dogs: *See my teeth, stay back or you will feel them, stay back, I am worse than you.* He thought for an instant they were barking at the truck, but Angus was looking past him. Jude glanced back to see at what. The dead man stood in the door to Danny's office. Craddock's ghost lifted his black fedora, set it carefully on his head.

Son. You come on back here, son, the dead man said, but Jude was trying not to listen to him, was concentrating intently on the sound of the dogs. Since their barking had first disrupted the spell he'd been under, up in the studio, it had seemed like the most important thing in the world to get to them, although he could not have explained to anyone, including himself, why it mattered so. Only that when he heard their voices, he remembered his own.

Jude hauled himself up off the gravel, ran, fell, got up, ran again, tripped at the edge of the driveway, came crashing down on his knees once more. He crawled through the grass, didn't have the strength in his legs to launch himself onto his feet again. The cold air stung in the pit of his wounded hand.

He glanced back. Craddock was coming. The golden chain dropped from his right hand. The blade at the end of it began to swing, a silver slash, a streak of brilliance tearing at the night. The gleam and flash fascinated Jude. He felt his gaze sticking to it, felt the thought draining out of him—and in the next instant he crawled straight into the chain-link fence with a crash and dropped to his side. Rolled onto his back.

He was up against the swinging door that held the pen shut. Angus banged into the other side, eyes turned up in his head. Bon stood rigidly behind him, barking with a steady, shrill insistency. The dead man walked toward them.

Let's ride, Jude, said the ghost. *Let's go for a ride on the nightroad.*

Jude felt himself going empty, felt himself surrendering to that voice again, to the sight of that silver blade cutting back and forth through the dark.

Angus hit the chain-link fence so hard he bounced off it and fell on his side. The impact brought Jude out of his trance again.

Angus.

Angus wanted out. He was already back on his feet, barking at the dead man, scrabbling his paws against the chain link.

And Jude had a thought then, wild, half formed, remembered something he had read yesterday morning, in one of his books of occultism. Something about animal familiars. Something about how they could deal with the dead directly.

The dead man stood at Jude's feet. Craddock's gaunt, white face was rigid, fixed in an expression of contempt. The black marks shivered before his eyes.

You listen, now. You listen to the sound of my voice.

"I've heard enough," Jude said.

He reached up and behind him found the latch to the pen, released it.

Angus hit the gate an instant later. It crashed open, and Angus leaped at the dead man, making a sound Jude had never heard from his dog before, a choked and gravelly snarl that came from the deep barrel of his chest. Bon shot past a moment later, her black lips drawn back to show her teeth and her tongue lolling.

The dead man took a reeling step backward, his face confused. In the seconds that followed, Jude found it difficult to make sense of what he was actually seeing. Angus leaped at the old man—only it seemed in that instant that Angus was not one dog but two. The first was the lean, powerfully built German shepherd he'd always been. But attached to this shepherd was an inky darkness in the shape of a dog, flat and featureless but somehow solid, a living shadow.

Angus's material body overlapped this shadow form, but not perfectly. The shadow dog showed around the edges, especially in the area of Angus's snout—and gaping mouth. This second, shadowy Angus struck the dead man a fraction of an instant ahead of the real Angus, coming at him from his left-hand side, away from the hand with the gold chain and the swinging silver blade. The dead man cried out—a choked, furious cry—and was *spun,* staggered backward. He shoved Angus off him, clipped him across the snout with an elbow. Only no; it wasn't Angus he was shoving, it was that other, black dog that dipped and leaned like a shadow thrown by candle flame.

Bon launched herself at Craddock's other side. Bon was two dogs as well, had a wavering shadow twin of her own. As she leaped, the old man snapped the gold chain at her, and the crescent-shaped silver blade whined in the air. It passed through Bon's front right leg, up around the shoulder, without leaving a mark. But then it sank into the black dog attached to her, snagged its leg. The shadow Bon was caught and, for one moment, pulled a little out of shape, deformed into something not quite dog, not quite . . . anything. The blade came loose, snapped back to the dead man's hand. Bon yelped, a horrid, piercing shout of pain. Jude did not know which version of Bon did the yelping, the shepherd or the shadow.

Angus threw himself at the dead man once more, jaws agape, reaching for his throat, his face. Craddock couldn't spin fast enough to get him with his swinging knife. The shadow Angus put his front paws on his chest and heaved, and the dead man stumbled down into the driveway. When the black dog lunged, it could stretch itself almost a full yard away from the German shepherd it was attached to, lengthening and going slim like a shadow at the end of day. Its black fangs snapped shut a few inches from the dead man's face. Craddock's hat flew. Angus—both the German shepherd and the midnight-colored dog attached to him—scrambled on top of him, gouging at him with his claws.

Time skipped.

The dead man was on his feet again, backed against the truck. Angus had skipped through time with him, was ducking and tearing. Dark teeth ripped through the dead man's pant leg. Liquid shadow drizzled from scratches in the dead man's face. When the drops hit the ground, they hissed and smoked, like fat falling in a hot frying pan. Craddock kicked, connected, and Angus rolled, came up on his feet.

Angus crouched, that deep snarl boiling up from inside him, his gaze fixed on Craddock and Craddock's swinging gold chain with its crescent-shaped blade on the end of it. Looking for an opening. The muscles in the big dog's back bunched under the glossy short fur, coiled for the spring. The black dog attached to Angus leaped first, by just a fraction of an instant, mouth yawning open, teeth snapping at the dead man's crotch, going for his balls. Craddock shrieked.

Skip.

The air reverberated with the sound of a slamming door. The old man was inside his Chevy. His hat was in the road, mashed in on itself.

Angus hit the side of the truck, and it rocked on its springs. Then Bon hit the other side, paws scrabbling frantically on steel. Her breath steamed the window, her slobber smeared the glass, just as if it were a real truck. Jude didn't know how she had got all the way over there. A moment ago she'd been cowering next to him.

Bon slipped, turned in a circle, threw herself at the pickup truck once more. On the other side of the truck, Angus jumped at the same time. In the next instant, though, the Chevy was gone, and the two dogs bounded into each other. Their heads audibly knocked, and they crashed down onto the frozen mud where the truck had been only an instant before.

Except it wasn't gone. Not entirely. The floodlights remained, two circles of light floating in midair. The dogs sprang back up, wheeled toward the lights, then began barking furiously at them. Bon's spine was humped up, her fur bristling, and she backed away from the floating, disembodied lights as she yapped. Angus had no throat left for barking, each roaring yawp hoarser than the one before. Jude noted that their shadow twins had vanished, fled with the truck, or had gone back inside their corporeal bodies, where they'd always been hiding, perhaps. Jude supposed—the thought seemed quite reasonable—that those black dogs attached to Bon and Angus had been their souls.

The round circles of the floodlights began to fade, going cool and blue, shrinking in on themselves. Then they winked out, leaving nothing behind except faint afterimages printed on the backs of Jude's retinas, wan, moon-colored disks that floated in front of him for a few moments before fading away.

20

J ude wasn't ready until the sky in the east was beginning to lighten
with the first show of false dawn. Then he left Bon in the car and brought
Angus inside with him. He trotted up the stairs and into the studio. Georgia was where he'd left her, asleep on the couch, under a white cotton
sheet he'd pulled off the bed in the guest room.

"Wake up, darlin'," he said, putting a hand on her shoulder.

Georgia rolled toward him at his touch. A long strand of black hair
was pasted to her sweaty cheek, and her color was bad—cheeks flushed
an almost ugly red, while the rest of her skin was bone white. He put the
back of his hand against her forehead. Her brow was feverish and damp.

She licked her lips. "Whafuck time is it?"

"Five."

She glanced around, sat up on her elbows. "What am I doing here?"

"Don't you know?"

She looked up at him from the bottoms of her eyes. Her chin began
to tremble, and then she had to look away. She covered her eyes with
one hand.

"Oh, God," she said.

Angus leaned past Jude and stuck his snout against her throat, under her jaw, nudging at it, as if telling her to keep her chin up. His great staring eyes were moist with concern.

She jumped when his wet nose kissed her skin, sat the rest of the way up. She gave Angus a startled, disoriented look and laid a hand on his head, between his ears.

"What's he doing inside?" She glanced at Jude, saw he was dressed, black Doc Martens, ankle-length duster. At almost the same time, she seemed to register the throaty rumble of the Mustang idling in the driveway. It was already packed. "Where are you going?"

"Us," he said. "South."

RIDE ON

21

The daylight began to fail when they were just north of Fredericksburg, and that was when Jude saw the dead man's pickup behind them, following at a distance of perhaps a quarter mile.

Craddock McDermott was at the wheel, although it was hard to make him out clearly in the weak light, beneath the yellow shine of the sky, where the clouds glowed like banked embers. Jude could see he was wearing his fedora again, though, and drove hunched over the wheel, shoulders raised to the level of his ears. He had also put on a pair of round spectacles. The lenses flashed with a weird orange light, beneath the sodium-vapor lamps over I-95, circles of gleaming flame—a visual match for the floods on the brush guard.

Jude got off at the next exit. Georgia asked him why, and he said he was tired. She hadn't seen the ghost.

"I could drive," she said.

She had slept most of the afternoon and now sat in the passenger seat with her feet hitched under her and her head resting on her shoulder.

When he didn't reply, she took an appraising look at his face and said, "Is everything all right?"

"I just want to get off the road before dark."

Bon stuck her head into the space between the front seats to listen to them talk. She liked to be included in their conversations. Georgia stroked her head, while Bon stared up at Jude with a look of nervous misgiving visible in her chocolate eyes.

They found a Days Inn less than half a mile from the turnpike. Jude sent Georgia to get the room, while he sat in the Mustang with the dogs. He didn't want to take a chance on being recognized, wasn't in the mood. He hadn't been in the mood for about fifteen years.

As soon as Georgia was out of the car, Bon scrambled into her empty seat, curled up in the warm ass print Georgia had left in the leather. As Bon settled her chin on her front paws, she gave Jude a guilty look, waiting for him to yell, to tell her to get in the back with Angus. He didn't yell. The dogs could do what they wanted.

Not long after they first got on the road, Jude had told Georgia about how the dogs had gone after Craddock. "I'm not sure even the dead man knew that Angus and Bonnie could go at him like that. But I do think Craddock sensed they were some kind of threat, and I think he would've been glad to scare us out of the house and away from them, before we figured out how to use the dogs against him."

At this, Georgia had twisted around in her seat, to reach into the back and dig behind Angus's ears, leaning far enough into the rear to rub her nose against Bon's snout. "Who are my little hero dogs? Who is it? Yeah, you are, that's right," and so forth, until Jude had started to feel half mad with hearing it.

Georgia came out of the office, a key hooked over one finger, which she wiggled at him before turning and walking around the corner of the building. He followed in the car and parked at an empty spot, in front of a beige door among other beige doors, at the rear of the motel.

She went inside with Angus while Jude walked with Bon along a tangle of scrub woods at the edge of the parking lot. Then he came back and left Bon with Georgia and took Angus for the walk. It was important for neither of them to stray far from the dogs.

These woods, behind the Days Inn, were different from the forest around his farmhouse in Piecliff, New York. They were unmistakably southern woods, smelled of sweet rot and wet moss and red clay, of sulfur and sewage, orchids and motor oil. The atmosphere itself was different, the air denser, warmer, sticky with dampness. Like an armpit. Like Moore's Corner, where Jude had grown up. Angus snapped at the fireflies, blowing here and there in the ferns, beads of ethereal green light.

Jude returned to the room. In the ten minutes it took to pass through Delaware, he had stopped at a Sunoco for gas and thought to buy a half dozen cans of Alpo in the convenience store. It had not occurred to him, however, to buy paper plates. While Georgia used the bathroom, Jude pulled one of the drawers out of the dresser, opened two cans, and slopped them in. He set the drawer on the floor for the dogs. They fell upon it, and the sound of wet slobbering and swallowing, harsh grunts and gasps for air, filled the room.

Georgia came out of the bathroom, stood in the door in faded white panties and a strappy halter that left her midriff bare, all evidence of her Goth self scrubbed away, except for her shiny, black-lacquered toenails. Her right hand was wrapped in a fresh knot of bandage. She looked at the dogs, nose wrinkled in an expression of amused disgust.

"Boy, are we livin' foul. If housekeepin' finds out we been feedin' our dogs from the dresser drawers, we will *not* be invited back to the Fredericksburg Days Inn." She spoke in cornpone, putting on for his bemusement. She had been dropping *g*'s and drawing out her vowels off and on throughout the afternoon—doing it sometimes for laughs and sometimes, Jude believed, without knowing she was doing it. As if in leaving New York she was also traveling away from the person she'd been there, unconsciously slipping back into the voice and attitudes of who she'd been before: a scrawny Georgia kid who thought it was a laugh to go skinny-dipping with the boys.

"I seen people treat a hotel room worst," he said. "Worst" instead of "worse." His own accent, which had become very slight over the years, was thickening up as well. If he wasn't careful, he would be talking like an extra from *Hee Haw* by the time they got to South Carolina. It was hard to venture back near the place you'd been bred without settling into the characteristics of the person you'd been there. "My bassist, Dizzy, took a shit in a dresser drawer once, when I wouldn't get out of the bathroom fast enough."

Georgia laughed, although he saw her watching him with something close to concern—wondering, maybe, what he was thinking. Dizzy was dead. AIDS. Jerome, who'd played rhythm guitar and keyboards and pretty much everything else, was dead, too, had run his car off the road, 140 miles an hour, hit a tree, and crushed his Porsche like a beer can. Only a handful of people knew that it wasn't a drunk-driving accident, but that he had done it cold sober, on purpose.

Not long after Jerome cashed out, Kenny said it was time to call it a day, that he wanted to spend some time with his kids. Kenny was tired of nipple rings and black leather pants and pyrotechnics and hotel rooms, had been faking it for a while anyway. That was it for the band. Jude had been a solo act ever since.

Maybe he wasn't even that anymore. There was his box of demos in the studio at home, almost thirty new songs. But it was a private collection. He had not bothered to play them for anyone. It was just more of the same. What had Kurt Cobain said? Verse chorus verse. Over and over. Jude didn't care anymore. AIDS got Dizzy, the road got Jerome. Jude didn't care if there was any more music.

It didn't make sense to him, the way things had worked out. He had always been the star. The band had been called Jude's Hammer. He was the one who was supposed to die tragically young. Jerome and Dizzy were meant to live on, so they could tell PG-13 stories about him years later, on a VH1 retrospective—the both of them balding, fat, manicured, at peace with their wealth and their rude, noisy pasts. But then Jude had never been good at sticking to the script.

Jude and Georgia ate sandwiches they'd picked up in the same Delaware gas station where Jude had bought the Alpo. They tasted like the Saran Wrap they'd come wrapped in.

My Chemical Romance was on Conan. They had rings in their lips and eyebrows, their hair done up in spikes, but beneath the white pancake makeup and black lipstick they looked like a collection of chubby kids who had probably been in their high-school marching band a few years earlier. They leaped around, falling into each other, as if the stage beneath them were an electrified plate. They played frantically, pissing themselves with fear. Jude liked them. He wondered which of them would die first.

After, Georgia switched off the lamp by the bed and they lay together in the dark, the dogs curled up on the floor.

"I guess it didn't get rid of him," she said. "Burning his suit." No Daisy Duke accent now.

"It was a good idea, though."

"No it wasn't." Then: "He made me do it, didn't he?"

Jude didn't reply.

"What if we can't figure out how to make him go away?" she asked.

"Get used to smellin' dog food."

She laughed, her breath tickling his throat.

She said, "What are we going to do when we get where we're going?"

"We're going to talk to the woman who sent me the suit. We're going to find out if she knows how to get rid of him."

Cars droned on I-95. Crickets thrummed.

"Are you going to hurt her?"

"I don't know. I might. How's your hand?"

"Better," she said. "How's yours?"

"Better," he said.

He was lying, and he was pretty sure she was, too. She had gone into the bathroom to re-dress the hand when they first got into the room. He had gone in after, to re-dress his, and found her old wraps in the trash. He pulled the loops of gauze out of the wastebasket to inspect them. They stank of infection and antiseptic cream, and they were stained with dried blood and something else, a yellow crust that had to be pus.

As for his own hand, the gouge he'd put in it probably needed stitches. Before leaving the house that morning, he had tugged a first-aid kit out of an upper cabinet in the kitchen and used some Steri-Strips to pull the gash closed, then wound it in white bandages. But the gouge continued to seep, and by the time he took the wraps off, blood was beginning to soak through them. The hole in his left hand bulged open between the Steri-Strips, a red, liquid eye.

"The girl who killed herself," Georgia began. "The girl this is all about . . ."

"Anna McDermott." Her real name now.

"Anna," Georgia repeated. "Do you know why she killed herself? Was it because you told her to scram?"

"Her sister obviously thinks so. Her stepdaddy, too, I guess, since he's haunting us."

"The ghost . . . can make people do things. Like getting me to burn the suit. Like making Danny hang himself."

He'd told her about Danny in the car. Georgia had turned her face to the window, and he'd heard her crying softly for a while, making little damp, choked sounds, which evened out after a time into the slow, regular inhalations of sleep. This was the first either of them had mentioned Danny since.

Jude continued, "The dead man, Anna's stepdaddy, learned hypnotism torturing Charlie in the army and stayed with it after he got out. Liked to call himself a mentalist. In his life he used that chain of his, with the silver razor on the end of it, to put people into trances, but now he's dead, he don't need it anymore. Something about when he says things, you just have to do it. All of a sudden, you're just sitting back, watching him run you here and there. You don't even feel anything. Your body is a suit of clothes, and he's the one wearing it, not you." *A dead man's suit,* Jude thought, with a shuddery feeling of revulsion. Then he said, "I don't know much about him. Anna didn't like to talk on him. But I know she worked for a while as a palm reader, and she said her stepdaddy was the one who taught her how. He had an interest in the less-understood aspects of the human mind. Like, for example, on the weekends he'd hire himself out as a dowser."

"Those are people who find water by waving sticks in the air? My grandma hired an old hillbilly with a mouthful of gold teeth to find her a fresh spring after her well went dry. He had a hickory stick."

"Anna's stepdaddy, Craddock, didn't bother with a stick. He just used that pretty razor on a chain he's got. Pendulums work about as well, I guess. Anyway, the psycho bitch who sent me the suit, Jessica McDermott Price, wanted me to know that her pop had said he'd get even with me after he was dead. So I think the old man had some ideas about how to come back. In other words, he's not an accidental ghost, if that makes sense. He got the way he is now on purpose."

A dog yapped somewhere in the distance. Bon lifted her head, gazed thoughtfully in the direction of the door, then lowered her chin back to her forepaws.

"Was she pretty?" Georgia asked.

"Anna? Yeah. Sure. You want to know if she was good in the sack?"

"I'm just asking. You don't got to be a son of a bitch about it."

"Well, then. Don't ask questions you don't really want to know the answers to. Notice I never inquire about your past lays."

"Past lays. Goddammit. Is that the way you think of me? The present lay, soon to be the past lay?"

"Christ. Here we go."

"And I'm not being a snoop. I'm trying to figure this out."

"How is knowing whether she was pretty going to help you figure anything out about our ghost problem?"

She held the sheet to her chin and stared at him in the dark.

"So she was Florida and I'm Georgia. How many other states has your dick visited?"

"I couldn't tell you. I don't have a map somewhere with pins in it. You really want me to make an estimate? While we're on the subject, why stop with states? I've had thirteen world tours, and I always took my cock along with me."

"You fuckin' asshole."

He grinned in his beard. "I know that's probably shocking, to a virgin such as yourself. Here's some news for you: I got a past. Fifty-four years of it."

"Did you love her?"

"You can't leave it alone, can you?"

"This is important, goddammit."

"How's it important?"

She wouldn't say.

He sat up against the headboard. "For about three weeks."

"Did she love you?"

He nodded.

"She wrote you letters? After you sent her home?"

"Yeah."

"Angry letters?"

He didn't reply at first, considering the question.

"Did you even fuckin' read 'em, you insensitive shitbird?" There it was again, an unmistakably rural and southern cadence in her voice. Her temper was up, and she'd forgotten herself for a moment. Or maybe it was not a case of forgetting herself, Jude thought, so much as the opposite.

"Yeah, I read 'em," he said. "I was hunting around for them when the shit blew up in our faces back in New York."

He was sorry Danny had not found them. He had loved Anna and lived with her and talked with her every day they were together but now understood he had not learned nearly enough about her. He knew so little of the life she'd lived before him—and after.

"You deserve whatever happens to you," she said. Georgia rolled away from him. "We both deserve it."

He said, "They weren't angry. Sometimes they were emotional. And sometimes they were scary, because there was so little emotion in them. In the last one, I remember she said something about how she had things she wanted to talk about, things she was tired of keeping secret. She said she couldn't stand to be so tired all the time. Which should've been a warning sign to me right there. Except she said stuff like that other times, and she never . . . anyway. I been trying to tell you she wasn't right. She wasn't happy."

"But do you think she still loved you? Even after you put your boot in her ass?"

"I didn't—" he started, then let out a thin, seething breath. Wouldn't let himself be baited. "I suppose probably she did."

Georgia didn't speak for a long time, her back to him. He studied the curve of her shoulder. At last she said, "I feel bad for her. It's not a lot of fun, you know."

"What?"

"Being in love with you. I've been with a lot of bad guys who made me feel lousy about myself, Jude, but you're something special. Because I knew none of them really cared about me, but you do, and you make me feel like your shitty hooker anyway." She spoke plainly, calmly, without looking at him.

It made him catch his breath a little, what she said, and for an instant he wanted to tell her he was sorry, but he shied from the word. He was out of practice at apologies and loathed explanations. She waited for him to reply, and when he didn't, she pulled the blanket up to cover her shoulder.

He slid down against the pillow, put his hands behind his head.

"We'll be passing through Georgia tomorrow," she said, still not turning toward him. "I want to stop and see my grandma."

"Your grandma," Jude repeated, as if he weren't sure he'd heard her right.

"Bammy is my favorite person in the world. She bowled a perfect three hundred once." Georgia said it as if the two things followed each other naturally. Maybe they did.

"You know the trouble we're in?"

"Yeah. I was vaguely aware."

"Do you think it's a good idea to start making detours?"

"I want to see her."

"How about we stop in on our way back? You two can catch up on old times then. Hell, maybe the two of you could go bowl a couple strings."

Georgia was a little while in answering. At last she said, "I was feelin' like I ought to see her now. It's been on my mind. I don't think it's any sure thing we'll be makin' the trip back. Do you?"

He pulled his beard, staring at the shape of her under the sheet. He didn't like the idea of slowing for any reason but felt the need to offer her something, some concession, to make her loathe him a little less. Also, if Georgia had things she wanted to say to someone who loved her, he supposed it made sense not to wait around. Putting off anything that mattered no longer seemed like sensible planning.

"She keep lemonade in the fridge?"

"Fresh made."

"Okay," Jude said. "We'll stop. Not too long, though, okay? We can be in Florida this time tomorrow if we don't mess around."

One of the dogs sighed. Georgia had opened a window to air out the odor of Alpo, the window that looked into the courtyard at the center of the motel. Jude could smell the rust of the chain-link fence and a dash of chlorine, although there was no water in the pool.

Georgia said, "Also, I used to have a Ouija board, once upon a time. When we get to my grandma's, I want to poke around for it."

"I already told you. I don't need to talk to Craddock. I already know what he wants."

"No," Georgia said, her voice short with impatience. "I don't mean so we can talk to *him*."

"Then what do you mean?"

"We need it if we're going to talk to Anna," Georgia said. "You said she loved you. Maybe she can tell us how to get out of this mess. Maybe she can call him off."

22

Lake Pontchartrain, huh? I didn't grow up too far from there. My parents took us campin' there once. My stepdaddy fished. I can't remember how he did. You go fishin' much on Lake Pontchartrain?"

She was always after him with her questions. He could never decide if she listened to the answers or just used the time when he was talking to think of something else to pester him about.

"Do you like to fish? Do you like raw fish? Sushi? I think sushi is disgusting, except when I'm drinkin', and then I'm in the mood. Repulsion masks attraction. How many times have you been to Tokyo? I hear the food is really nasty—raw squid, raw jellyfish. Everything is raw there. Did they not invent fire in Japan? Have you ever had bad food poisonin'? Sure you have. On tour all the time.

"What's the hardest you ever puked? You ever puked through your nostrils? You have? That's the worst.

"But did you fish Lake Pontchartrain much? Did your daddy take you? Isn't that the prettiest name? Lake Pontchartrain, Lake Pontchartrain, I want to see the rain on Lake Pontchartrain. You know what the most romantic sound in the world is? Rain on a quiet lake. A nice spring rain. When I was a kid, I could put myself into a trance just sittin' at my window watchin' the rain. My stepdad used to say he never met anyone as easy to put into a trance as me. What were you like growin' up? When'd you decide to change your name?

"Do you think I should change my name? You should pick out a new name for me. I want you to call me whatever you want to call me."

"I already do," *he said.*

"That's right. You do. From now on, my name is Florida. Anna Mc-Dermott is dead to me. She's a dead girl. All gone. I never liked her anyway. I'd rather be Florida. Do you miss Louisiana? Isn't it funny we only lived four hours apart from each other? We coulda crossed paths. Do you think you and I were ever in the same room, at the same time, and didn't know it? Probably not, though, right? Because you blew out of Louisiana before I was even born."

It was either her most endearing habit or her most infuriating. Jude was never sure. Maybe it was both at the same time.

"You ever shut up with the questions?" *he asked her the first night they slept together. It was two in the morning, and she'd been interrogating him for an hour.* "Were you one of those kids who would drive their momma crazy going, 'Why is the sky blue? Why doesn't the earth fall into the sun? What happens to us when we die?'"

"What do you think happens to us when we die?" *Anna asked.* "You ever seen a ghost? My stepdaddy has. My stepdaddy's talked to them. He was in Vietnam. He says the whole country is haunted."

By then he already knew that her stepfather was a dowser as well as a mesmerist, and in business with her older sister, also a hypnotist by trade, the both of them back in Testament, Florida. That was almost the full extent of what he knew about her family. Jude didn't push for more—not then, not later—was content to know about her what she wanted him to know.

He had met Anna three days before, in New York City. He'd come down to do a guest vocal with Trent Reznor for a movie sound track—easy money—then stuck around to see a show Trent was doing at Roseland. Anna was backstage, a petite girl, violet lipstick, leather pants that creaked when she walked, the rare Goth blonde. *She asked if he wanted an egg roll and got it for him and then said,* "Is it hard to eat with a beard like that? Do you get food in it?" *At him with the questions almost from hello.* "Why do you think so many guys, bikers and stuff, grow beards to look threatening? Don't you think they'd actually work against you in a fight?"

"How would a beard work against you in a fight?" *he asked.*

She grabbed his beard in one fist and yanked at it. He bent forward, felt a tearing pain in the lower half of his face, ground his teeth, choked on an angry cry. She let go, continued, "Like if I was ever in a fight with a bearded man, that's the first thing I'd do. ZZ Top would be pushovers. I could take all three of them myself, little itty-bitty me. Course, those guys are stuck, they *can't* shave. If they ever shaved, no one would know who they were. I kind of guess you're in the same boat, now I think about it. It's who you are. That beard gave me bad dreams as a little girl, when I used to watch you in videos. Hey! You know, you could be completely anonymous without your beard. You ever think of that? Instant vacation from the pressures of celebrity. Plus, it's a liability in combat. Reasons to shave."

"My face was a liability to getting laid," *he said.* "If my beard gave you bad dreams, you should see me without it. You'd probably never sleep again."

"So it's a disguise. An act of concealment. Like your name."

"What about my name?"

"That isn't your real name. Judas Coyne. It's a pun." *She leaned toward him.* "Name like that, are you from a nutty Christian family? I bet. My stepdaddy says the Bible is all bunk. He was raised Pentecostal, but he wound up a spiritualist, which is how he raised us. He's got a pendulum— he can hang it over you and ask you questions and tell if you're lying by the way it swings back and forth. He can read your aura with it, too. My aura is black as sin. How about yours? Want me to read your palm? Palm reading is nothing. Easiest trick in the book."

She told his fortune three times. The first time she was kneeling naked in bed beside him, a gleaming line of sweat showing in the crease between her breasts. She was flushed, still breathing hard from their exertions. She took his palm, moved her fingertips across it, inspecting it closely.

"Look at this lifeline," *Anna said.* "This thing goes on for miles. I guess you live forever. I wouldn't want to live forever myself. How old is too old? Maybe it's metaphorical. Like your music is forever, some malarkey along those lines. Palm reading ain't no exact science."

And then once, not long after he finished rebuilding the Mustang, they had gone for a drive into the hills overlooking the Hudson. They wound up parked at a boat ramp, staring out at the river, the water flecked with diamond scales beneath a high, faded-blue sky. Fluffy white clouds, thousands of feet high, crowded the horizon. Jude had meant to drive Anna to an appointment with a psychiatrist—Danny had set it up—but she'd dissuaded him, said it was too nice a day to spend it in a doctor's office.

They sat there, windows down, music low, and she picked up his hand, lying on the seat between them. She was having one of her good days. They'd been coming less and less often.

"You love again after me," *she said.* "You get another chance to be happy. I don't know if you'll let yourself take it. I kind of think not. Why don't you want to be happy?"

"What do you mean, after you?" *he asked. Then he said,* "I'm happy now."

"No you aren't. You're still angry."

"With who?"

"Yourself," *she said, as if it were the most obvious thing.* "Like it's your fault Jerome and Dizzy died. Like anyone could've saved them from themselves. You're still real pissed with your daddy, too. For what he did to your mother. For what he did to your hand."

This last statement stole his breath. "What are you talking about? How do you know about what he did to my hand?"

She flicked her gaze toward him: an amused, cunning look. "I'm starin' at it right now, aren't I?" *She turned his hand over, moved her thumb across his scarred knuckles.* "You don't have to be psychic or anything. You just have to have sensitive fingers. I can feel where the bones healed. What'd he hit this hand with to smash it? A sledgehammer? They healed real bad."

"The basement door. I took off one weekend to play a show in New Orleans. A battle-of-the-bands thing. I was fifteen. Helped myself to a hundred bucks' bus fare out of the family cash box. I figured it wouldn't be like stealing, 'cause we'd win the contest. Five-hundred-dollar cash prize. Pay it all back with interest."

"How'd you do?"

"Took third. We all got T-shirts," *Jude said.* "When I came back, he dragged me over to the basement door and smashed my left hand in it. My chord-making hand."

She paused, frowning, then glanced at him in confusion. "I thought you made chords with the other hand."

"I do now."

She stared.

"I kinda taught myself how to make them with my right hand while my left was healing, and I just never went back."

"Was that hard?"

"Well. I wasn't sure my left would ever be good for making chords again, so it was either that or stop playing. And it would've been a lot harder to stop."

"Where was your mom when this happened?"

"Can't remember." *A lie. The truth was, he couldn't forget. His mother had been at the table when his father started to pull him across the kitchen, toward the basement door, and he had screamed for her to help, but she only got up and put her hands over her ears and left for the sewing room. He could not, in truth, blame her for refusing to intervene. Supposed he had it coming, and not for taking a hundred dollars out of the cash box ei-ther.* "S'okay. I wound up playing better guitar after I had to switch hands anyway. It just took about a month of making the most horrible fuckin' noises you ever heard. Eventually someone explained I had to restring my guitar backwards if I was going to play with my hands reversed. After that I picked it up pretty easy."

"Plus, you showed your daddy, didn't you?"

He didn't answer. She examined his palm once more, and rolled her thumb across his wrist. "He isn't through with you yet. Your daddy. You'll see him again."

"No I won't. I haven't looked at him for thirty years. He doesn't figure in my life anymore."

"Sure he does. He figures into it every single day."

"Funny, I thought we decided to skip visiting the psychiatrist this afternoon."

She said, "You have five luck lines. You're luckier than a cat, Jude Coyne. The world must still be payin' you back for all your daddy did to you. Five luck lines. The world is never going to be done payin' you back." *She laid his hand aside.* "Your beard and your big leather jacket and your big black car and your big black boots. No one puts on all that armor unless they been hurt by someone who didn't have no right to hurt them."

"Look who's talking," *he said.* "Is there any part of you, you won't stick a pin in?" *She had them in her ears, her tongue, one nipple, her labia.* "Who are you trying to scare away?"

Anna gave him his final palm reading just a few weeks before Jude packed her stuff. He looked out the kitchen window early one evening and saw her trudging through a cold October rain to the barn, wearing only a black halter and black panties, her naked flesh shocking in its paleness.

By the time he caught up to her, she had crawled into the dog pen, the part of it that was inside the barn, where Angus and Bon went to get out of the rain. She sat in the dirt, mud smeared on the backs of her thighs. The dogs whisked here and there, shooting worried looks her way and giving her space.

Jude climbed into the pen on all fours, angry with her, sick to death of the way it had been the last two months. He was sick of talking to her and getting dull, three-word answers, sick of laughter and tears for no reason. They didn't make love anymore. The thought repelled him. She didn't wash, didn't dress, didn't brush her teeth. Her honey-yellow hair was a rat's nest. The last few times they had attempted to have sex, she'd turned him off with the things she wanted, had embarrassed and sickened him. He didn't mind a certain amount of kink, would tie her up if she wanted, pinch her nipples, roll her over and put it in her ass. But she wasn't happy with that. She wanted him to hold a plastic bag over her head. To cut her.

She was hunched forward, with a needle in one hand. She pushed it into the thumb of the other, working intently and deliberately—pricking herself once, then again, producing fat, gem-bright drops of blood.

"The hell you doing?" he asked her, struggling to keep the anger out of his voice and failing. He took her by the wrist, to stop her sticking herself.

She let the needle drop into the mud, then reversed his grip, squeezed his hand in hers and stared down at it. Her eyes glowed with fever in their dark, bruised-looking hollows. She was down to sleeping three hours a night at best.

"You're running out of time almost as fast as I am. I'll be more useful when I'm gone. I'm gone. We have no future. Someone is going to try and hurt you. Someone who wants to take everything away from you." *She rolled her eyes up to look into his face.* "Someone you can't fight. You'll fight anyway, but you can't win. You won't win. All the good things in your life will soon be gone."

Angus whined anxiously and slipped in between them, burrowing his snout in her crotch. She smiled—first smile he'd seen in a month—and dug behind his ears.

"Well," *she said.* "You'll always have the dogs."

He twisted free of her grip, took her by the arms, lifted her to her feet. "I don't listen to nothing you say. You've told my fortune three times at least, and it comes out a different way every time."

"I know," *she said.* "But they're all true anyway."

"Why were you sticking yourself with a needle? Why you want to do that?"

"I done it since I was a girl. Sometimes if I stick myself a couple times, I can make the bad thoughts go away. It's a trick I taught myself to clear my head. Like pinchin' yourself in a dream. You know. Pain has a way of wakin' you up. Of remindin' you who you are."

Jude knew.

Almost as an afterthought, she added, "I guess it isn't workin' too good anymore." *He led her out of the pen and back across the barn. She spoke again, said,* "I don't know what I'm out here for. In my underwear."

"I don't either."

"You ever dated anyone as crazy as me, Jude? Do you hate me? You've had a lot of girls. Tell me honest, am I the worst? Who was your worst?"

"Why do you got to ask so many damn questions?" *he wanted to know.*

As they went back out into the rain, he opened his black duster and closed it over her thin, shivering body, clasped her against him.

"I'd rather ask questions," *she said,* "than answer them."

23

He woke a little after nine with a melody in his head, something with the feel of an Appalachian hymn. He nudged Bon off the bed—she had climbed up with them in the night—and pushed aside the covers. Jude sat on the edge of the mattress, mentally running over the melody again, trying to identify it, to remember the lyrics. Only it couldn't be identified, and the lyrics couldn't be recalled, because it hadn't existed until he thought it up. It wouldn't have a name until he gave it one.

Jude rose, slipped across the room and outside, onto the concrete breezeway, still in his boxers. He unlocked the trunk of the Mustang and pulled out a battered guitar case with a '68 Les Paul in it. He carried it back into the room.

Georgia hadn't moved. She lay with her face in the pillow, one bone-white arm above the sheets and curled tight against her body. It had been years since he dated anyone with a tan. When you were a Goth, it was important to at least imply the possibility you might burst into flames in direct sunlight.

He let himself into the john. By now Angus and Bon were both trailing him, and he whispered at them to stay. They sank to their bellies outside the door, staring forlornly in at him, accusing him with their eyes of failing to love them enough.

He wasn't sure how well he could play with the puncture wound in his left hand. The left did the picking and the right found the chords. He lifted the Les Paul from its case and began to fiddle, bringing it into tune. When he strummed a pick across the strings, it set off a low flare of pain—not bad, almost just an uncomfortable warmth—in the center of his palm. It felt as if a steel wire were sunk deep into the flesh and beginning to heat up. He could play through that, he thought.

When the guitar was in tune, he searched for the proper chords and began to play, reproducing the tune that had been in his head when he woke. Without the amp the guitar was all flat, soft twang, and each chord made a raspy, chiming sound. The song itself might have been a traditional hill-country melody, sounded like something that belonged on a Folkways record or a Library of Congress retrospective of traditional music. Something with a name like "Fixin' to Dig My Grave." "Jesus Brung His Chariot." "Drink to the Devil."

"'Drink to the Dead,'" he said.

He put the guitar down and went back into the bedroom. There was a small notepad on the night table, and a ballpoint pen. He brought them into the bathroom and wrote down "Drink to the Dead." Now it had a title. He picked up the guitar and played it again.

The sound of it—the sound of the Ozarks, of gospel—gave him a little prickle of pleasure, which he felt along his forearms and across the back of his neck. A lot of his songs, when they started out, sounded like old music. They arrived on his doorstep, wandering orphans, the lost children of large and venerable musical families. They came to him in the form of Tin Pan Alley sing-alongs, honky-tonk blues, Dust Bowl plaints, lost Chuck Berry riffs. Jude dressed them in black and taught them to scream.

He wished he had his DAT recorder, wanted to get what he had down on tape. Instead he put the guitar aside once more, and scribbled the chords on the notepad, beneath his title. Then he took up the Les Paul and played the lick again, and again, curious to see where it would take him. Twenty minutes later there were spots of blood showing through the bandage around his left hand, and he had worked out the chorus, which built naturally from the initial hook, a steady, rising, thunderous chorus, a whisper to a shout: an act of violence against the beauty and sweetness of the melody that had come before.

"Who's that by?" Georgia asked, leaning in through the bathroom door, knuckling the sleep out of her eyes.

"Me."

"I like that one."

"It's okay. Sound even better if this thing was plugged in."

Her soft black hair floated around her head, had a swirled, airy look to it, and the shadows under her eyes drew his attention to how large they were. She smiled drowsily down at him. He smiled back.

"Jude," she said, in a tone of almost unbearable, erotic tenderness.

"Yeah?"

"You think you could get your ass out of the bathroom, so I could pee?"

When she shut the door, he dropped his guitar case on the bed and stood in the dimness of the room, listening to the muffled sound of the world beyond the drawn shades: the drone of traffic on the highway, a car door slamming, a vacuum cleaner humming in the room directly above. It came to him then that the ghost was gone.

Ever since the suit had arrived at his house in its black heart-shaped box, he had sensed the dead man lingering close to him. Even when Jude couldn't see him, he was conscious of his presence, felt it almost as a barometric weight, a kind of pressure and electricity in the air, such as precedes a thunderstorm. He had existed in that atmosphere of dreadful waiting for days, a continuous crackle of tension that made it difficult to taste his food or find his way into sleep. Now, though, it had lifted. He had somehow forgotten the ghost while he'd been writing the new song—and the ghost had somehow forgotten him, or at least not been able to intrude into Jude's thoughts, into Jude's surroundings.

He walked Angus, took his time. Jude was in short sleeves and jeans, and the sun felt good on the back of his neck. The smell of the morning—the pall of exhaust over I-95, the swamp lilies in the brush, the hot tarmac—got his blood going, made him want to be on the road, to be driving somewhere, anywhere. He felt good: an unfamiliar sensation. Maybe he was randy, thought about the pleasant tousle of Georgia's hair and her sleep-puffy eyes and lithe white legs. He was hungry, wanted eggs, a chicken-fried steak. Angus chased a groundhog into waist-high grass, then stood at the edge of the trees, yapping happily at it. Jude went back to give Bon a turn to stretch her legs and heard the shower.

He let himself in the bathroom. The room was steamy, the air hot and close. He undressed, slipped in around the curtain, and climbed into the tub.

Georgia jumped when his knuckles brushed her back, twisted her head to look at him over her shoulder. She had a black butterfly tattooed on her left shoulder and a black heart on her hip. She turned toward him, and he put his hand over the heart.

She pressed her damp, springy body against his, and they kissed. He leaned into her, over her, and to balance herself, Georgia put her right hand against the wall—then inhaled, a sharp, thin sound of pain, and pulled the hand back as if she had burned it.

Georgia tried to lower her hand to her side, but he caught her wrist and lifted it. The thumb was inflamed and red, and when he touched it lightly, he could feel the sick heat trapped inside it. The palm, around the ball of the thumb, was also reddened and swollen. On the inside of the thumb was the white sore, glittering with fresh pus.

"What are we going to do about this thing?" he asked.

"It's fine. I'm putting antiseptic cream on it."

"This isn't fine. We ought to run you to the emergency room."

"I'm not going to sit in some emergency room for three hours to have someone look at the place I poked myself with a pin."

"You don't know what stuck you. Don't forget what you were handling when this happened to you."

"I haven't forgotten. I just don't believe that any doctor is going to make it better. Not really."

"You think it's going to get better on its own?"

"I think it'll be all right—if we make the dead man go away. If we get him off our backs, I think we'll *both* be all right," she said. "Whatever's wrong with my hand, it's part of this whole thing. But you know that, don't you?"

He didn't know anything, but he had notions, and he was not happy to hear they matched her own. He bowed his head, considering, wiped at the spray on his face. At last he said, "When Anna was at her worst, she'd poke herself in the thumb with a needle. To clear her head, she told me. I don't know. Maybe it's nothing. It just makes me uneasy, you getting stuck like she used to stick herself."

"Well. It doesn't worry me. Actually, that almost makes me feel better about it." Her good hand moved across his chest as she spoke, her fingers exploring a landscape of muscle beginning to lose definition and skin going slack with age, and all of it overgrown with a mat of curling silver hairs.

"It does?"

"Sure. It's something else her and I got in common. Besides you. I never met her, and I don't hardly know anything about her, but I feel connected to her somehow. I'm not afraid of that, you know."

"I'm glad it's not bothering you. I wish I could say the same. Speaking for myself, I don't much like thinking about it."

"So don't," she said, leaning into him and pushing her tongue into his mouth to shut him up.

24

Jude took Bon for her overdue walk while Georgia busied herself in
the bathroom, dressing and rebandaging her hand and putting in her
studs. He knew she might be occupied for twenty minutes, so he stopped
by the car and pulled her laptop out of the trunk. Georgia didn't even
know they had it with them. He'd packed it automatically, without thinking, because Georgia took it with her wherever she went and used it to
stay in touch with a gaggle of geographically far-flung friends by way of
e-mail and instant message. And she dribbled away countless hours
browsing message boards, blogs, concert info, and vampire porn (which
would've been hilarious if it weren't so depressing). But once they were
on the road, Jude had forgotten they had the laptop with them, and
Georgia had never asked about it, so it had spent the night in the trunk.

Jude didn't bring his own computer—he didn't have one. Danny had
handled his e-mail and all the rest of his online obligations. Jude was
aware that he belonged to an increasingly small segment of the society,
those who could not quite fathom the allure of the digital age. Jude did
not want to be wired. He had spent four years wired on coke, a period of
time in which everything seemed hyperaccelerated, as in one of those
time-lapse movies, where a whole day and night pass in just a few

seconds, traffic reduced to lurid streaks of light, people transformed into blurred mannequins rushing jerkily here and there. Those four years now felt more like four bad, crazy, sleepless days to him—days that had begun with a New Year's Eve hangover and ended at crowded, smoky Christmas parties where he found himself surrounded by strangers trying to touch him and shrieking with inhuman laughter. He did not ever want to be wired again.

He had tried to explain the way he felt to Danny once, about compulsive behavior and time rushing too fast and the Internet and drugs. Danny had only lifted one of his slender, mobile eyebrows and stared at him in smirking confusion. Danny did not think coke and computers were anything alike. But Jude had seen the way people hunched over their screens, clicking the refresh button again and again, waiting for some crucial if meaningless hit of information, and he thought it was almost exactly the same.

Now, though, he was in the mood to score. He lugged her laptop back to the room, plugged in, and went online. He didn't make any attempt to access his e-mail account. In truth, he wasn't sure *how* to access his e-mail. Danny had a program all set up to reel in Jude's messages from the Net, but Jude couldn't have said how to get at that information from someone else's computer. He knew how to Google a name, however, and he Googled Anna's.

Her obituary was short, half the length her father's had been. Jude was able to read it in a glance, which was all it merited. It was her photograph that caught his attention and gave him a brief hollow sensation in the pit of his stomach. He guessed it had been taken close to the end of her life. She was glancing blankly into the camera, some strands of pale hair blown across a face that was gaunt, her cheeks sunken hollows beneath her cheekbones.

When he had known her, she'd sported rings in her eyebrows and four apiece in each of her ears, but in the photo they were gone, which made her too-pale face that much more vulnerable. When he looked closely, he could see the marks left by her piercings. She'd given them up, the silver hoops and crosses and ankhs and glittering gems, the studs and fishhooks and rings she had stuck into her skin to make herself look dirty and tough and dangerous and crazy and beautiful. Some of it was true, too. She really had been crazy and beautiful; dangerous, too. Dangerous to herself.

The obituary said nothing about a suicide note. It said nothing about suicide. She had died not three months before her stepfather.

He ran another search. He tapped in "Craddock McDermott, dowsing," and half a dozen links popped up. He clicked on the topmost result, which brought him to a nine-year-old article in the *Tampa Tribune*, from their living/arts section. Jude looked at the pictures first—there were two—and stiffened in his chair. It was a while before he could unlock his gaze from those photographs and shift his attention to the text beside them.

The story was titled "Dowsing for the Dead." The slug line read: *20 years after Vietnam, Capt. Craddock McDermott is ready to lay some ghosts to rest . . . and raise some others.*

The article opened with the story of Roy Hayes, a retired biology professor, who at the age of sixty-nine had learned to fly light planes and who had, one fall morning in 1991, taken an ultralight up over the Everglades to count egrets for an environmental group. At 7:13 A.M. a private strip south of Naples had received a transmission from him.

> "I think I'm having a stroke," Hayes said. "I'm dizzy. I can't tell how low I am. I need help."

That was the last anyone had heard from him. A search party, involving more than thirty boats and a hundred men, had not been able to find a trace of either Hayes or his plane. Now, three years after his disappearance and presumed death, his family had taken the extraordinary step of hiring Craddock McDermott, Captain U.S. Army (ret.), to lead a new search for his remains.

> "He didn't go down in the 'Glades," McDermott states with a confident grin. "The search parties were always looking in the wrong place. The winds that morning carried his plane farther north, over Big Cypress. I put his position less than a mile south of I-75."
>
> McDermott believes he can pinpoint the site of the crash to an area the size of a square half mile. But he didn't work out his estimate by consulting meteorological data from the morning of the disappearance, or by examining Dr. Hayes's final radio transmissions, or by reading eyewitness reports. Instead he dangled a silver pendulum above an outsize map of the region. When the pendulum began to swing rapidly back and forth, over a spot in south Big Cypress, McDermott announced he had found the impact zone.
>
> And when he takes a private search team into the Big Cypress swamp later this week, to look for the downed ultralight, he will not be bringing with him sonar, metal detectors, or hound dogs. His plan for locating the vanished professor is much more simple—and unnerving. He means to appeal to Roy Hayes directly—to call upon the deceased doctor himself to lead the party to his final resting place.

The article shifted to backstory, exploring Craddock's earliest encounters with the occult. A few lines were spent detailing the more gothic details of his early family life. It touched briefly on his father, the Pentecostal minister with a penchant for snake handling, who had disappeared when Craddock was just a boy. It lingered for a paragraph on his mother, who had twice moved them across the country, after seeing a phantom she called "the walking-backwards man," a vision that foretold of ill luck. After one such visit from the walking-backwards man, little Craddock and his mother departed an Atlanta apartment complex, not three weeks before the building burned to the ground in an electrical fire.

Then it was 1967, and McDermott was an officer stationed in Vietnam, where he was placed in charge of interrogating the captured elite of the People's Liberation Army. He found himself assigned to the case of one Nguyen Trung, a chiromancer, who had reportedly learned his fortune-telling arts from Ho Chi Minh's own brother and who had offered his services to a variety of higher-ups among the Vietcong. To put his prisoner at ease, McDermott asked Trung to help him understand his spiritual beliefs. What followed was a series of extraordinary conversations on the subjects of prophecy, the human soul, and the dead, discussions McDermott said had opened his eyes to the supernatural all around him.

> "In Vietnam the ghosts are busy," McDermott avers. "Nguyen Trung taught me to see them. Once you know how to look for them, you can spot them on every street corner, their eyes marked out and their feet not touching the ground. The living are often known to employ the dead over there. A spirit that believes it has work to do won't leave our world. It'll stay until the job is done.
>
> "That was when I first began to believe we were going to lose the war. I saw it happen on the battlefield. When our boys died, their souls would come out of their mouths, like steam from a teakettle, and run for the sky. When the Vietcong died, their spirits remained. Their dead went right on fighting."

After their sessions had concluded, McDermott lost track of Trung, who disappeared around the time of Tet. As for Professor Hayes, McDermott believed that his final fate would be known soon enough.

> "We'll find him," McDermott said. "His spirit is unemployed at the moment, but I'll give him some work. We're going to ride together— Hayes and I. He's going to lead me right to his body."

At this last—*We're going to ride together*—Jude felt a chill crawling on the flesh of his arms. But that was not as bad as the peculiar feeling of dread that came over him when he looked at the photographs.

The first was a picture of Craddock leaning against the grill of his smoke-blue pickup. His barefoot stepdaughters—Anna was maybe twelve, Jessica about fifteen—sat on the hood, one to either side of him. It was the first time Jude had ever seen Anna's older sister, but not the first time he'd ever looked upon Anna as a child—she was just the same as she'd been in his dream, only without the scarf over her eyes.

In the photograph Jessica had her arms around the neck of her smiling, angular stepfather. She was almost as rangy as he was, tall and fit, her skin honey-colored and healthy with tan. But there was something off about her grin—toothy and wide, maybe too wide, too enthusiastic, the *sell-sell-sell* grin of a frantic real estate salesperson. And there was something off about her eyes, too, which were as bright and black as wet ink, and disconcertingly avid.

Anna sat a little apart from the other two. She was bony, all elbows and knees, and her hair came almost to her waist—a long, golden spill of light. She was also the only one not putting on a smile for the camera. She wasn't putting on any kind of expression at all. Her face was dazed and expressionless, her eyes unfocused, the eyes of a sleepwalker. Jude recognized it as the expression she wore when she was off in the monochromatic, upside-down world of her depression. He was struck with the troubling idea that she had wandered that world for most of her childhood.

Worst of all, though, was a second, smaller photograph, this one of Captain Craddock McDermott, in fatigues and a sweat-stained fishing hat, M16 slung over one shoulder. He posed with other GIs on hardpacked yellow mud. At his back were palms and standing water; it might've been a snapshot of the Everglades, if not for all the soldiers, and their Vietnamese prisoner.

The prisoner stood a little behind Craddock, a solidly built man in a black tunic, with shaved head, broad, handsome features, and the calm eyes of a monk. Jude knew him at first glance as the Vietnamese prisoner he had encountered in his dream. The fingers missing from Trung's right hand were a dead giveaway. In the grainy, poorly colored photo, the stumps of those fingers had been freshly stitched with black thread.

The same caption that identified this man as Nguyen Trung described the setting as a field hospital in Dong Tam, where Trung had received care for combat-related injuries. That was almost right. Trung had lopped off his own fingers only because he thought they were about to attack—so it had been combat of a sort. As for what had happened to him, Jude thought he knew. Jude thought it was likely that after Trung had no more to tell Craddock McDermott—about ghosts and the work ghosts did—he'd gone for a ride on the nightroad.

The article did not say if McDermott had ever found Roy Hayes, retired professor and ultralight pilot, but Jude believed he had, although there was no rational reason to think such a thing. To satisfy himself he did another search. Roy Hayes's remains had been laid to rest five weeks later, and in fact Craddock had not found him—not personally. The water was too deep. A state police scuba team had gone in and pulled him out, in the place where Craddock told them to dive.

Georgia threw open the bathroom door, and Jude quit her browser.

"Whatchu doin'?" she asked.

"Trying to figure out how to check my mail," he lied. "You want a turn?"

She looked at her computer for a moment, then shook her head and wrinkled her nose. "No. I don't have the least interest in going online. Isn't that funny? Usually you can't peel me off."

"Well, see? Running for your life ain't all bad. Just look at how it's building character."

He pulled out the dresser drawer again and slopped another can of Alpo into it.

"Last night the smell of that shit was making me want to gag," Georgia said. "Strangely, this morning it's getting me hungry."

"Come on. There's a Denny's up the street. Let's go for a walk."

He opened the door, then held out his hand to her. She was sitting on the edge of the bed, in her stone-washed black jeans, heavy black boots, and sleeveless black shirt, which hung loose on her slight frame. In the golden beam of sunlight that fell through the door, her skin was so pale and fine it was almost translucent, looked as if it would bruise at the slightest touch.

Jude saw her glance at the dogs. Angus and Bon bent over the drawer, heads together as they went snorkeling in their food. He saw Georgia frown, and he knew what she was thinking, that they'd been safe as long as they kept the dogs close. But then she squinted back at Jude, standing in the light, took his hand, and let him pull her to her feet. The day was bright. Beyond the door the morning waited for them.

He was, for himself, not scared. He still felt under the protection of the new song, felt that in writing it he had drawn a magic circle around the both of them that the dead man could not penetrate. He had driven the ghost away—for a time anyhow.

But as they crossed the parking lot—thoughtlessly holding hands, a thing they never did—he happened to glance back at their hotel room. Angus and Bon stared out through the picture window at them, standing side by side on their hind legs, with their front paws on the glass and their faces wearing identical looks of apprehension.

25

The Denny's was loud and overcrowded, thick with the smell of bacon fat and burnt coffee and cigarette smoke. The bar, just to the right of the doors, was a designated smoking area. That meant that after five minutes of waiting up front to be seated, you could plan on smelling like an ashtray by the time you were led to your table.

Jude didn't smoke himself and never had. It was the one self-destructive habit he'd managed to avoid. His father smoked. On errands into town, Jude had always willingly bought him the cheap, long boxes of generics, had done it even without being asked, and they both knew why. Jude would glare at Martin across the kitchen table, while his father lit a cigarette and took his first drag, the tip flaring orange.

"If looks could kill, I'd have cancer already," Martin said to him one night, without any preamble. He waved a hand, drew a circle in the air with the cigarette, squinting at Jude through the smoke. "I got a tough constitution. You want to kill me off with these, you're gonna have to wait a while. You really want me dead, there's easier ways to do it."

Jude's mother said nothing, concentrated on shelling peas, face screwed up in an expression of intent study. She might have been a deaf-mute.

Jude—Justin then—did not speak either, simply went on glaring at him. He was not too angry to speak but too shocked, because it was as if his father had read his mind. He'd been staring at the loose, chicken-flesh folds of Martin Cowzynski's neck with a kind of fury, wanting to will a cancer into it, a lump of black-blossoming cells that would devour his father's voice, choke his father's breath. Wanting that with all his heart: a cancer that would make the doctors scoop out his throat, shut him up forever.

The man at the next table had had his throat scooped out and used an electrolarynx to talk, a loud, crackling joy buzzer that he held under his chin to tell the waitress (and everyone else in the room): "YOU GOT AIR-CONDITIONIN'? WELL, TURN IT ON. YOU DON'T BOTHER TO COOK THE FOOD, WHY YOU WANNA FRAH YOUR PAYIN' CUSTOMERS? JE-SUS CHRIST. I'M EIGHTY-SEVEN." This was a fact he felt to be of such overwhelming importance that he said it again after the waitress walked away, repeating himself to his wife, a fantastically obese woman who didn't look up from her newspaper as he spoke. "I'M EIGHTY-SEVEN YEARS OLD. CHRIST. FRAH US LIKE AIGS." He looked like the old man from that painting, *American Gothic,* down to the gray strands of hair combed over his balding dome.

"Wonder what sort of old couple we'd make," Georgia said.

"Well. I'd still be hairy. It would just be white hair. And it would probably be growing in tufts out of all the wrong places. My ears. My nose. Big, crazy hairs sticking out of my eyebrows. Basically like Santa, gone horribly fuckin' wrong."

She scooped a hand under her breasts. "The fat in these is going to drain steadily into my ass. I got a sweet tooth, so probably my teeth will fall out on me. On the bright side, I'll be able to pop out my dentures for toothless, old-lady blow jobs."

He touched her chin, lifted her face toward his. He studied her high cheekbones and the eyes in deep, bruised hollows, eyes that watched with a wry amusement that did not quite mask her desire to meet with his approval.

"You got a good face," he said. "You got good eyes. You'll be all right. With old ladies it's all about the eyes. You want to be an old lady with lively eyes, so it looks like you're always thinking of something funny. Like you're looking for trouble."

He drew his hand away. She peered down into her coffee, smiling, flattered into an uncharacteristic shyness.

"Sounds like you're talking about my grandma Bammy," she said. "You'll love her. We could be there by lunch."

"Sure."

"My grandma looks like the friendliest, most harmless old thing. Oh, but she likes tormenting people. I was living with her by the time I was in the eighth grade. I'd have my boyfriend Jimmy Elliott over—to play Yahtzee, I said, but really we were sneaking wine. Bammy would leave a half-full bottle of red in her fridge most days, leftover from dinner the night before. And she knew what we were doing, and one day she switched purple ink for the booze and left it for us. Jimmy let me take the first slug. I got a mouthful and went and coughed it all down myself. When she came home, I still had a big purple ring on my mouth, purple stains all down my jaw, purple tongue. It didn't come out for a week either. I expected Bammy to paddle me good, but she just thought it was funny."

The waitress came for their order. When she was gone, Georgia said, "What was it like being married, Jude?"

"Peaceful."

"Why did you divorce her?"

"I didn't. She divorced me."

"She catch you in bed with the state of Alaska or something?"

"No. I didn't cheat—well, not too often. And she didn't take it personal."

"She didn't? Are you for real? If we were married and you helped yourself to a piece, I'd throw the first thing came to hand at you. And the second. I wouldn't drive you to the hospital either. Let you bleed." She paused, bent over her mug, then said, "So what did it?"

"It would be hard to explain."

"Because I'm too stupid?"

"No," he said. "More like I'm not smart enough to explain it to myself, let alone anyone else. For a long time, I wanted to work at being a husband. Then I didn't. And when I didn't anymore—she just knew it. Maybe I made sure she knew it." And as he said it, Jude was thinking how he'd started staying up late, waiting for her to get tired and go to bed without him. He'd slip in later, after she was asleep, so there was no chance of making love. Or how he would sometimes start playing guitar, picking at a tune, in the middle of her telling him something—playing right over her talk. Remembering how he'd held on to the snuff movie instead of throwing it away. How he'd left it out where she could find it—where he supposed he knew she *would* find it.

"That doesn't make sense. Just all of a sudden, you didn't feel like making the effort? That doesn't seem like you. You aren't the type to give up on things for no reason."

It wasn't for no reason, but what reason there was defied articulation, could not be put into words in a way that made sense. He had bought his wife the farmhouse, bought it for both of them. He bought Shannon one Mercedes, then another, a big sedan and a convertible. They took weekends, sometimes, in Cannes, and flew there on a private jet where they were served jumbo shrimp and lobster tail on ice. And then Dizzy died—died as badly and painfully as a person could die—and Jerome killed himself, and still Shannon would come into Jude's studio and say, "I'm worried about you. Let's go to Hawaii" or "I bought you a leather jacket—try it on," and he would begin to strum at his guitar, hating the chirp of her voice and playing over it, hating the thought of spending more money, of owning another jacket, of going on another trip. But mostly just hating the contented, milk-fed look of her face, her fat fingers with all their rings, the cool look of concern in her eyes.

At the very end, when Dizzy was blind and raging with fever and soiling himself almost hourly, he got the idea in his head that Jude was his father. Dizzy wept and said he didn't want to be gay. He said, "Don't hate me anymore, Dad, don't hate me." And Jude said, "I don't. I never." And then Dizzy was gone, and Shannon went right on ordering Jude clothes and thinking about where they should eat lunch.

"Why didn't you have children with her?" Georgia asked.

"I was worried I'd have too much of my father in me."

"I doubt you're anything like him," she said.

He considered this over a forkful of food. "No. He and I have pretty much exactly the same disposition."

"What scares me is the idea of having kids and then them finding out the truth about me. Kids always find out. I found out about my folks."

"What would your kids find out about you?"

"That I dropped out of high school. That when I was thirteen I let a guy turn me into a prostitute. The only job I was ever good at involved taking my clothes off to Mötley Crüe for a roomful of drunks. I tried to kill myself. I been arrested three times. I stole money from my grandma and made her cry. I didn't brush my teeth for about two years. Am I missing anything?"

"So this is what your kid would find out: No matter what bad thing happens to me, I can talk to my mother, because she's been through it all. No matter what shitty thing happens to me, I can survive it, because my mom was through worse, and she made it."

Georgia lifted her head, smiling again, her eyes glittering bright with pleasure and mischief—the kind of eyes Jude had been talking about only a few minutes before.

"You know, Jude," she said, reaching for her coffee with the fingers of her bandaged hand. The waitress was behind her, leaning forward with the coffeepot to refill Georgia's mug and not looking at what she was doing, staring instead down at her check pad. Jude saw what was going to happen but couldn't force the warning out of his throat in time. Georgia went on talking, "Sometimes you're such a decent guy, I can almost forget what an assh—"

The waitress poured just as Georgia moved her cup and dumped coffee over the bandaged hand. Georgia wailed and yanked the hand back, drawing it tight against her chest, her face twisting in a hurt, sickened grimace. For a moment there was glassy shock in her eyes, a flat and empty shine that made Jude think she might be about to pass out.

Then she was up, clutching the bad hand in her good one. "Want to watch where the fuck you're pourin' that, you dumb bitch?" she shouted at the waitress, that accent coming over her again, her voice going country on her.

"Georgia," Jude said, starting to rise.

She made a face and waved him back to his chair. She thudded the waitress with her shoulder, on her way by her, stalking toward the hall to the bathrooms.

Jude nudged his plate aside. "Guess I'll take the check when you get a chance."

"I am so sorry," the waitress said.

"Accidents happen."

"I am so sorry," the waitress repeated. "But that is no reason for her to talk to me that way."

"She got burnt. I'm surprised you didn't hear worse."

The waitress said, "The two of you. I knew what I was serving the moment I laid eyes on you. And I served you just as nice as I'd serve anyone."

"Oh? You knew what you were serving? What was that?"

"Pair of lowlifes. You look like a drug peddler."

He laughed.

"And you only got to take one glance at her to know what she is. You payin' her by the hour?"

He stopped laughing.

"Get me the check," he said. "And get your fat ass out of my sight."

She stared at him a moment longer, her mouth screwed up as if she were getting ready to spit, then hurried away without another word.

The people at the tables immediately around him had stopped their conversations to gawk and listen. Jude swept his gaze here and there, staring back at anyone who dared stare at him, and one by one they returned to their food. He was fearless when it came to making eye contact, had looked into too many crowds for too many years to lose a staring contest now.

Finally the only people left watching him were the old man out of *American Gothic* and his wife, who might've been a circus fat lady on her day off. She at least made an effort to be discreet, peeping at Jude from the corners of her eyes while pretending to be interested in the paper spread before her. But the old man just stared, his tea-colored eyes judging and also somehow amused. In one hand he held the electrolarynx to his throat—it hummed faintly—as if he were about to comment. Yet he said nothing.

"Got something on your mind?" Jude asked, when staring right into the old man's eyes didn't embarrass him into minding his own business.

The old man raised his eyebrows, then wagged his head back and forth: *No, nothing to say.* He lowered his gaze back to his plate with a comic little sniff. He set the electrolarynx down beside the salt and pepper.

Jude was about to look away, when the electrolarynx came to life, vibrating on the table. A loud, toneless, electric voice buzzed forth: "YOU WILL DIE."

The old man stiffened, sat back in his wheelchair. He stared down at his electrolarynx, bewildered, maybe not really sure it had said anything. The fat lady curled her paper and peered over the top of it at the device, a wondering frown set on a face as smooth and round as the Pillsbury Doughboy's.

"I AM DEAD," the electrolarynx buzzed, chattering across the surface of the table like a cheap windup toy. The old man plucked it up between his fingers. It made joy-buzzer sounds from between them. "YOU WILL DIE. WE WILL BE IN THE DEATH HOLE TOGETHER."

"What's it doin'?" said the fat woman. "Is it pickin' up a radio station again?"

The old man shook his head: *Don't know*. His gaze rose from the electrolarynx, which now rested in the cup of his palm, to Jude. He peered at Jude through glasses that magnified his astonished eyes. The old man held his hand out, as if offering the device to Jude. It hummed and jittered about.

"YOU WILL KILL HER KILL YOURSELF KILL THE DOGS THE DOGS WON'T SAVE YOU WE'LL RIDE TOGETHER LISTEN NOW LISTEN TO MY VOICE WE WILL RIDE AT NIGHTFALL. YOU DON'T OWN ME. I OWN YOU. I OWN YOU NOW."

"Peter," the fat woman said. She was trying to whisper, but her voice choked, and when she forced her next breath up, it came out shrill and wavering. "Make it stop, Peter."

Peter just sat there holding it out to Jude, as if it were a phone and the call was for him.

Everyone was looking, the room filled with crosscurrents of worried murmuring. Some of the other customers had come up out of their chairs to watch, didn't want to miss what might happen next.

Jude was up, too, thinking, *Georgia*. As he rose and started to turn toward the hallway to the restrooms, his gaze swept the picture windows that looked out front. He stopped in midmovement, his gaze catching and holding on what he saw in the parking lot. The dead man's pickup idled there, waiting close to the front doors, the floodlights on, globes of cold white light. No one sitting in it.

A few of the onlookers were standing around, at tables just behind his, and he had to shove through them to reach the corridor to the bathrooms. Jude found a door that said WOMEN, slammed it in.

Georgia stood at one of the two sinks. She didn't glance up at the sound of the door banging against the wall. She stared at herself in the mirror, but her eyes were unfocused, not really fixed on anything, and her face wore the wistful, grave expression of a child almost asleep in front of the television.

She cocked her bandaged fist back and drove it into the mirror, hard as she could, no holding back. She pulverized the glass in a fist-size circle, with shatter lines jagging out away from the hole in all directions. An instant later silver spears of mirror fell with a ringing crash, broke musically against the sinks.

A slender, yellow-haired woman with a newborn in her arms stood a yard away, beside a changing table that folded out from the wall. She grabbed the baby to her chest and began to scream, "Oh, my God! Oh, my *God!*"

Georgia grabbed an eight-inch scythe blade of silver, a gleaming crescent moon, raised it to her throat, and tipped her chin back to gouge into the flesh beneath. Jude broke out of the shock that had held him in the doorway and caught her wrist, twisted it down to her side, then bent it back, until she made a pitiful cry and let go. The mirrored scythe fell to the white tiles and shattered with a pretty clashing sound.

Jude spun her, twisting her arm again, hurting her. She gasped and shut her eyes against tears but let him force her forward, march her to the door. He wasn't sure why he hurt her, if it was panic or on purpose, because he was angry at her for going off or angry at himself for letting her.

The dead man was in the hall outside the bathroom. Jude didn't register him until he'd already walked past him, and then a shudder rolled through him, left him on legs that wouldn't stop trembling. Craddock had tipped his black hat at them on their way by.

Georgia could barely hold herself up. Jude shifted his grip to her upper arm, supporting her, as he rammed her across the dining room. The fat lady and the old man had their heads together.

". . . WASN'T NO RADIO STATION . . ."

"Weirdos. Weirdos playing a prank."

"SHADDAP, HERE THEY COME."

Others stared, jumped to get out of the way. The waitress who only a minute before had accused Jude of being a drug peddler and Georgia of being his whore stood by the front counter talking to the manager, a little man with pens in his shirt pocket and the sad eyes of a basset hound. She pointed at them as they crossed the room.

Jude slowed at his table long enough to throw down a pair of twenties. As they went by the manager, the little man lifted his head to regard them with his tragic gaze but did not say anything. The waitress went on sputtering in his ear.

"Jude," Georgia said when they went through the first set of doors. "You're hurting me."

He relaxed his grip on her upper arm, saw that his fingers had left waxy white marks in her already pale flesh. They thumped through the second set of doors and were outside.

"Are we safe?" she asked.

"No," he said. "But we will be soon. The ghost has a healthy fear of them dogs."

They walked quickly past Craddock's empty and idling pickup truck. The passenger-side window was rolled down about a third of the way. The radio was on inside. One of the AM right-wingers was talking, in a smooth, confident, almost arrogant voice.

". . . it feels good to embrace those core American values, and it feels good to see the right people win an election, even if the other side is going to say it wasn't fair, and it feels good to see more and more people returning to the politics of common Christian good sense," said the deep, dulcet voice. "But you know what would feel even better? To choke that bitch standing next to you, choke that bitch, then step into the road in front of a semi, lay down for it, lay down and . . ."

Then they were past, the voice out of earshot.

"We're going to lose this thing," Georgia said.

"No we aren't. Come on. It isn't a hundred yards back to the hotel."

"If he doesn't get us now, he's going to get us later. He told me. He said I might as well kill myself and get it over, and I was going to. I couldn't help myself."

"I know. That's what he does."

They started along the highway, right at the edge of the gravel breakdown lane, with the long stalks of sawgrass whipping at Jude's jeans.

Georgia said, "My hand feels sick."

He stopped, lifted it for a look. It wasn't bleeding, either from punching the mirror or from lifting up the curved blade of glass. The thick, muffling pads of the bandage had protected her skin. Still, even through the wraps he could feel an unwholesome heat pouring off it, and he wondered if she had broken a bone.

"I bet. You hit the mirror pretty hard. You're lucky you aren't all hacked up." Nudging her forward, getting them moving again.

"It's beating like a heart. Going *whump-whump-whump.*" She spat, spat again.

Between them and the motel was an overpass, a stone train trestle, the tunnel beneath narrow and dark. There was no sidewalk, no room even for the breakdown lane at the sides of the road. Water dripped from the stone ceiling.

"Come on," he said.

The overpass was a black frame, boxed around a picture of the Days Inn. Jude's eyes were fixed on the motel. He could see the Mustang. He could see their room.

They did not slow as they passed into the tunnel, which stank of stagnant water, weeds, urine.

"Wait," Georgia said.

She turned, doubled over, and gagged, bringing up her eggs, lumps of half-digested toast, and orange juice.

He held her left arm with one hand, pulled her hair back from her face with the other. It made him edgy, standing there in the bad-smelling dark, waiting for her to finish.

"Jude," she said.

"Come on," he said, tugging at her arm.

"Wait—"

"Come on."

She wiped her mouth, with the bottom of her shirt. She remained bent over. "I think—"

He heard the truck before he saw it, heard the engine revving behind him, a furious growl of sound, rising to a roar. Headlights dashed up the wall of rough stone blocks. Jude had time to glance back and saw the dead man's pickup rushing at them, Craddock grinning behind the wheel and the floodlights two circles of blinding light, holes burned right into the world. Smoke boiled off the tires.

Jude got an arm under Georgia and pitched himself forward, carrying her with him and out the far end of the tunnel.

The smoke-blue Chevy slammed into the wall behind him with a shattering crash of steel smashing against stone. It was a great clap of noise that stunned Jude's eardrums, set them ringing. He and Georgia fell onto wet gravel, clear of the tunnel now. They rolled away from the side of the road, tumbled down the brush, and landed in dew-damp ferns. Georgia cried out, clipped him in the left eye with a bony elbow. He put a hand down into something squishy, the cool unpleasantness of swamp muck.

He lifted himself up, breathing raggedly. Jude looked back. It wasn't the dead man's old Chevy that had hit the wall but an olive Jeep, the kind that was open to the sky, with a roll bar in the back. A black man with close-cropped, steel-wool hair sat behind the steering wheel, holding his forehead. The windshield was fractured in a network of connected rings where his skull had hit it. The whole front driver's side of the Jeep had been gouged down to the frame, steel twisted up and back in smoking, torn pieces.

"What happened?" Georgia asked, her voice faint and tinny, hard to make out over the droning in his ears.

"The ghost. He missed."

"Are you sure?"

"That it was the ghost?"

"That he missed."

He came to his feet, his legs unsteady, knees threatening to give. He took her wrist, helped her up. The whining in his eardrums was already beginning to clear. From a long way off, he could hear his dogs, barking hysterically, barking mad.

26

Heaping their bags into the back of the Mustang, Jude became aware of a slow, deep throb in his left hand, different from the dull ache that had persisted since he stabbed himself there yesterday. When he looked down, he saw that his bandage was coming unraveled and was soaked through with fresh blood.

Georgia drove while he sat in the passenger seat, with the first-aid kit that had accompanied them from New York open in his lap. He undid the wet, tacky dressings and dropped them on the floor at his feet. The Steri-Strips he'd applied to the wound the day before had peeled away, and the puncture gaped again, glistening, obscene. He had torn it open getting out of the way of Craddock's truck.

"What are you going to do about that hand?" Georgia asked, shooting him an anxious look before turning her gaze back to the road.

"Same thing you're doing about yours," he said. "Nothing."

He began to clumsily apply fresh Steri-Strips to the wound. It felt as if he were putting a cigarette out on his palm. When he'd closed the tear as best he could, he wrapped the hand with clean gauze.

"You're bleeding from the head, too," she said. "Did you know that?"

"Little scrape. Don't worry about it."

"What happens next time? Next time we wind up somewhere without the dogs to look out for us?"

"I don't know."

"It was a public place. We should've been safe in a public place. People all around, and it was bright daylight, and he went and come at us anyway. How are we supposed to fight somethin' like him?"

He said, "I don't know. If I knew what to do, I'd be doing it already, Florida. You and your questions. Lay off a minute, why don't you?"

They drove on. It was only when he heard the choked sound of her weeping—she was struggling to do it in silence—that he realized he'd called her Florida, when he had meant to say Georgia. It was her questions that had done it, one after another, that and her accent, those Daughter of the Confederacy inflections that had steadily been creeping into her voice the last couple days.

The sound of Georgia trying not to cry was somehow worse than if she wept openly. If she would just go ahead and cry, he could say something to her, but as it was, he felt it necessary to let her be miserable in private and pretend he hadn't noticed. Jude sank low in the passenger seat and turned his face toward the window.

The sun was a steady glare through the windshield, and a little south of Richmond he fell into a disgusted, heat-stunned trance. He tried to think what he knew about the dead man who pursued them, what Anna had told him about her stepfather when they were together. But it was hard to think, too much effort—he was sore, and there was all that sun in his face and Georgia making quiet, wretched noises behind the steering wheel—and anyway he was sure Anna hadn't said much.

"I'd rather ask questions," *she told him,* "than answer them."

She had kept him at bay with those foolish, pointless questions for almost half a year: *Were you ever in the Boy Scouts? Do you shampoo your beard? What do you like better, my ass or my tits?*

What little he knew should have invited curiosity: the family business in hypnotism, the dowser father who taught his girls to read palms and

talk to spirits, a childhood shadowed by the hallucinations of preadoles-
cent schizophrenia. But Anna—Florida—didn't want to talk about who
she'd been before meeting him, and for himself, he was happy to let her
past be past.

Whatever she wasn't telling him, he knew it was bad, a certain kind
of bad. The specifics didn't matter—that's what he believed then. He
had thought, at the time, that this was one of his strengths, his willingness to accept her as she was, without questions, without judgments.
She was safe with him, safe from whatever ghosts were chasing her.

Except he hadn't kept her safe, he knew that now. The ghosts always
caught up eventually, and there was no way to lock the door on them.
They would walk right through. What he'd thought of as a personal
strength—he was happy to know about her only what she wanted him to
know—was something more like selfishness. A childish willingness to
remain in the dark, to avoid distressing conversations, upsetting truths.
He had feared her secrets—or, more specifically, the emotional entan-
glements that might come with knowing them.

Just once had she risked something like confession, something close
to self-revelation. It was at the end, shortly before he sent her home.

She'd been depressed for months. First the sex went bad, and then
there was no sex at all. He'd find her in the bath, soaking in ice water,
shivering helplessly, too confused and unhappy to get out. Thinking on it
now, it was as if she were rehearsing for her first day as a corpse, for the
evening she would spend cooling and wrinkling in a tub full of cold water and blood. She prattled to herself in a little girl's crooning voice but
went mute if he tried to talk to her, stared at him in bewilderment and
shock, as if she'd just heard the furniture speak.

*Then one night he went out. He no longer remembered for what. To
rent a movie maybe, or get a burger. It was just after dark as he drove home.
Half a mile from the house, he heard people honking their horns, the oncoming cars blinking their headlights.*

Then he passed her. Anna was on the other side of the road, running in the breakdown lane, wearing nothing but one of his oversize T-shirts. Her yellow hair was windblown and tangled. She saw him as he passed, going the other way, and lunged into the road after him, waving her hand frantically and stepping into the path of an oncoming eighteen-wheeler.

The truck's tires locked and shrieked. The trailer's rear end fishtailed to the left while the cab swung right. It banged to a stop, two feet from rolling over her. She didn't appear to notice. Jude had stopped himself by then, and she flung open the driver's-side door, fell against him.

"Where did you go?" *she screamed.* "I looked for you everywhere. I ran, I ran, and I thought you were gone, so I ran, I ran lookin'."

The driver of the semi had his door open, one foot out on the step-down. "What the fuck is up with that bitch?"

"I got it," *Jude said to him.*

The trucker opened his mouth to speak again, then fell silent as Jude hauled Anna in across his legs, an act that hiked up her shirt and raised her bare bottom to the air.

Jude threw her into the passenger seat, and immediately she was up again, falling into him, shoving her hot, wet face against his chest.

"I was scared I was so scared and I ran—"

He shoved her off him with his elbow, hard enough to slam her into the passenger-side door. She fell into a shocked silence.

"Enough. You're a mess. I've had it. You hear? You aren't the only one who can tell fortunes. You want me to tell you about your future? I see you holding your fuckin' bags, waitin' for a bus," *he said.*

His chest was tight, tight enough to remind him he wasn't thirty-three but fifty-three, almost thirty years older than she. Anna stared. Her eyes round and wide and uncomprehending.

He put the car into drive and began to roll for home. As he turned in to the driveway, she bent over and tried to unzip his pants, to give him a blow job, but the thought turned his stomach, was an unimaginable act, a thing he could not let her do, so he hit her with the elbow again, driving her back once more.

He avoided her most of the next day, but the following night, when he came in from walking the dogs, she called from the top of the back stairs. She asked if he would make her some soup, just a can of something. He said all right.

When he brought it to her, a bowl of chicken noodle on a small tray, he could see she was herself again. Washed out and exhausted, but clear in her head. She tried to smile for him, something he didn't want to see. What he had to do was going to be hard enough.

She sat up, took the tray across her knees. He sat on the side of the bed and watched her take little swallows. She didn't really want it. It had only been an excuse to get him up to the bedroom. He could tell from the way her jaw tightened before each tiny, fretful sip. She had lost twelve pounds in the last three months.

She set it aside after finishing less than a quarter of the broth, then smiled, in the way of a child who has been promised ice cream if she'll choke down her asparagus. She said thank you, it was nice. She said she felt better.

"I have to go to New York next Monday. I'm doing *Howard Stern,*" Jude said.

An anxious light flickered in her pale eyes. "I . . . I don't think I ought to go."

"I wouldn't ask you to. The city would be the worst thing for you."

She looked at him so gratefully he had to glance away.

"I can't leave you here either," *he said.* "Not by yourself. I was thinking maybe you ought to stay with family for a while. Down in Florida." *When she didn't reply, he went on,* "Is there someone in your family I can call?"

She slid down into her pillows. She drew the sheet up to her chin. He was worried she would start crying, but when he looked, she was staring calmly at the ceiling, her hands folded one atop the other on her breastbone.

"Sure," *she said finally.* "You were good to put up with me for as long as you did."

"What I said the other night . . ."

"I don't remember."

"That's good. What I said is better forgotten. I didn't mean any of it anyhow." *Although in fact what he'd said was exactly what he meant, had only been the harshest possible version of what he was telling her now.*

The silence drew out between them until it was uncomfortable, and he felt he should prod her again, but as he was opening his mouth, she spoke first.

"You can call my daddy," *she said.* "My stepdaddy, I mean. You can't call my real daddy. He's dead, of course. You want to talk to my stepdaddy, he'll drive all the way up here to pick me up in person if you want. Just give him the word. My stepdaddy likes to say I'm his little onion. I bring tears to his eyes. Isn't that a cute thing to say?"

"I wouldn't make him come get you. I'll fly you private."

"No plane. Planes are too fast. You can't go south on a plane. You need to drive. Or take a train. You need to watch the dirt turn to clay. You need to look at all the junkyards full of rustin' cars. You need to go over a few bridges. They say that evil spirits can't follow you over running water, but that's just humbug. You ever notice rivers in the North aren't like rivers in the South? Rivers in the South are the color of chocolate, and they smell like marsh and moss. Up here they're black, and they smell sweet, like pines. Like Christmas."

"I could take you to Penn Station and put you on the Amtrak. Would that take you south slow enough?"

"Sure."

"So I'll call your da— your stepfather?"

"Maybe I better call him," *she said. It crossed his mind then how rarely she spoke to anyone in her family. They'd been together more than a year. Had she ever called her stepfather, to wish him happy birthday, to tell him how she was doing? Once or twice Jude had come into his record library and found Anna on the phone with her sister, frowning with concentration, her voice low and terse. She seemed unlike herself then, someone engaged in a disagreeable sport, a game she had no taste for but felt obliged to play out anyway.* "You don't have to talk to him."

"Why don't you want me to talk to him? 'Fraid we won't get along?"

"It's not that I'm worried he'll be rude to you or nothin'. He isn't like that. My daddy is easy to talk to. Everybody's friend."

"Well then, what?"

"I never talked to him about it yet, but I just know what he thinks about us taking up with each other. He won't like it. You the age you are and the kind of music you play. He hates that kind of music."

"There's more people don't like it than do. That's the whole point."

"He doesn't think much of musicians at all. You never met a man with less music in him. When we were little, he'd take us on these long drives, to someplace where he'd been hired to dowse for a well, and he'd make us listen to talk radio the whole way. It didn't matter what to him. He'd make us listen to a continuous weather broadcast for four hours." *She pulled two fingers slowly through her hair, lifting a long, golden strand away from her head, then letting it slip through her fingers and fall. She went on,* "He had this one creepy trick he could do. He'd find someone talkin', like one of those Holy Rollers that are always kickin' it up for Jesus on the AM. And we'd listen and listen, until Jessie and me were beggin' him for anything else. And he wouldn't say anything, and he wouldn't say anything, and then, just when we couldn't stand it anymore, he'd start to talk to himself. And he'd be sayin' exactly what the preacher on the radio was sayin', at exactly the same time, only in his own voice. Recitin' it. Deadpan, like. 'Christ the Redeemer bled and died for you. What will you do for Him? He carried His own cross while they spat on Him. What burden will you carry?' Like he was readin' from the same script. And he'd keep going until my momma told him to quit. That she didn't like it. And he'd laugh and turn the radio off. But he'd keep talkin' to himself. Kind of mutterin'. Sayin' all the preacher's lines, even with the radio off. Like he was hearin' it in his head, gettin' the broadcast on his fillings. He could scare me so bad doing that."

Jude didn't reply, didn't think a reply was called for, and anyway was not sure whether the story was true or the latest in a succession of self-delusions that had haunted her.

She sighed, let another strand of her hair flop. "I was sayin', though, that he wouldn't like you, and he has ways of gettin' rid of my friends when he doesn't like them. A lot of daddies are overprotective of their little girls, and if someone comes around they don't care for, they might try and scare 'em off. Lean on 'em a little. Course that never works, because the girl always takes the boy's side, and the boy keeps after her, either because he can't be scared or doesn't want her to *think* he can be scared. My stepdaddy's smarter than that. He's as friendly as can be, even with people he'd like to see burnt alive. If he ever wants to get rid of someone he doesn't want around me, he drives them off by tellin' 'em the truth. The truth is usually enough.

"Give you an example. When I was sixteen, I started running around with this boy I just knew my old man wouldn't like, on account of this kid was Jewish, and also we'd listen to rap together. Pop hates rap worst of all. So one day my stepdaddy told me it was going to stop, and I said I could see who I wanted, and he said sure, but that didn't mean the kid would keep wantin' to see me. I didn't like the sound of that, but he didn't explain himself.

"Well, you've seen how I get low sometimes and start thinkin' crazy things. That all started when I was twelve, maybe, same time as puberty. I didn't see a doctor or anything. My stepdaddy treated me himself, with hypnotherapy. He could hold things in check pretty good, too, as long as we sat down once or twice a week. I wouldn't get up to any of my crazy business. I wouldn't think there was a dark truck circling the house. I wouldn't see little girls with coals for eyes watchin' me from under the trees at night.

"But he had to go away. He had to go to Austin for some conference on hypnogogic drugs. Usually he took me along when he went on one of his trips, but this time he left me at home with Jessie. My mom was dead by then, and Jessie was nineteen and in charge. And while he was gone I started havin' trouble sleepin'. That's always the first sign I'm gettin' low, when I start havin' insomnia.

"After a couple nights, I started seein' the girls with the burning eyes. I couldn't go to school on Monday, because they were waitin' outside under the oak tree. I was too scared to go out. I told Jessie. I said she had to make Pop come home, that I was gettin' bad ideas again. She told me she was tired of my crazy shit and that he was busy and I would be all right till he got back. She tried to make me go to school, but I wouldn't. I stayed in my room and watched television. But pretty soon they started talkin' to me through the TV. The dead girls. Tellin' me I was dead like they was. That I belonged in the dirt with them.

"Usually Jessie got back from school at two or three. But she didn't come home that afternoon. It got later and later, and every time I looked out the window, I saw the girls starin' back at me. My stepdad called, and I told him I was in trouble and please come home, and he said he'd come quick as he could, but he wouldn't be back until late. He said he was worried I might hurt myself and he'd call someone to come be with me. After he hung up, he phoned Philip's parents, who lived up the street from us."

"Philip? Was this your boyfriend? The Jewish kid?"

"Uh-huh. Phil came right over. I didn't know him. I hid under the bed from him, and I screamed when he tried to touch me. I asked him if he was with the dead girls. I told him all about them. Jessie showed up pretty soon afterward, and Philip ran off quick as he could. After that he was so freaked out he didn't want to have anything to do with me. And my stepdaddy just said what a shame. He thought Philip was my friend. He thought Philip, more than anyone else, could be trusted to look out for me when I was havin' a rough time."

"So is that what's worrying you? Your old man is going to let me know you're a lunatic and I'll be so shocked I won't ever want to see you again? 'Cause I got to tell you, Florida, hearing you get kind of crazy now and then wouldn't exactly be a newsflash."

She snorted, soft breathy laughter. Then she said, "He wouldn't say that. I don't know what he'd say. He'd just find somethin' to make you like me a little less. If you *can* like me any less."

"Let's not start with that."

"No. No, on second thought maybe you best call my sister instead. She's an unkind bitch—we don't get along a lick. She never forgave me for being cuter than her and gettin' better Christmas presents. After Momma died, she had to be Susie Homemaker, but I still got to be a kid. Jessie was doin' our laundry and cookin' our meals by the time she was fourteen, and no one has ever been able to appreciate how hard she had to work or how little fun she got to have. But she'll arrange to get me home without any nonsense. She'll like havin' me back, so she can boss me around and make rules for me."

But when Jude called her sister's house, he got the old man anyway, who answered on the third ring.

"What'n I do for you? Go ahead and talk. I'll help you if I can."

Jude introduced himself. He said Anna wanted to come home for a while, making it out to be more her idea than his. Jude wrestled mentally with how to describe her condition, but Craddock came to his rescue.

"How's she sleepin'?" *Craddock asked.*

"Not too well," *Jude said, relieved, understanding somehow that this said it all.*

Jude offered to have a chauffeur drive Anna from the train station in Jacksonville to Jessica's house in Testament, but Craddock said no, he would meet her at the Amtrak himself.

"A drive to Jacksonville will suit me fine. Any excuse to get out in my truck for a few hours. Put the windows down. Make faces at the cows."

"I hear that," *Jude said, forgetting himself and warming to the old man.*

"I appreciate you takin' care of my little girl like you done. You know, when she was just a pup, she had posters of you all over her walls. She always did want to meet you. You and that fella from . . . what was their name? That Mötley Crüe? Now, she *really* loved them. She followed them for half a year. She was at all their shows. She got to know some of them, too. Not the band, I guess, but their road team. Them were her wild years. Not that she's real settled now, is she? Yeah, she loved all your albums. She loved all kinds of that heavy metal music. I always knew she'd find herself a rock star."

Jude felt a dry, ticklish sensation of cold spreading behind his chest. He knew what Craddock was telling him—that she had fucked roadies to hang with Mötley Crüe, that star fucking was a thing with her, and if she wasn't sleeping with him, she'd be in the sack with Vince Neil or Slash—and he also knew why Craddock was telling him. For the same reason he had let Anna's Jewish friend see her when she was out of her head, to put a wedge between them.

What Jude had not foreseen was that he could know what Craddock was doing and it could work anyway. No sooner had Craddock said it than Jude started thinking where he and Anna had met, backstage at a Trent Reznor show. How had she got there? Who did she know, and what did she have to do for a backstage pass? If Trent had walked into the room right then, would she have sat at his feet instead and asked the same sweet, pointless questions?

"I'll take care of her, Mr. Coyne. You just send her back to me. I'll be waitin'," *Craddock told him.*

Jude took her to Penn Station himself. She'd been at her best all morning—was trying very hard, he knew, to be the person he'd met, not the unhappy person she really was—but whenever he looked at her, he felt that dry sensation of chill in his chest again. Her elfish grins, the way she tucked her hair behind her ears to show her studded little pink earlobes, her latest round of goofy questions, seemed like cold-blooded manipulations and only made him want to get away from her even more.

If she sensed, however, that he was holding her at a distance, she gave no sign, and at Penn Station she stood on tiptoe and put her arms around his neck in a fierce hug—an embrace without any sexual connotations at all.

"We had us some fun, didn't we?" *she asked. Always with her questions.*

"Sure," *he said. He could've said more—that he'd call her soon, that he wanted her to take better care of herself—but he didn't have it in him, couldn't wish her well. When the urge came over him, to be tender, to be compassionate, he heard her stepdaddy's voice in his head, warm, friendly, persuasive:* "I always knew she'd find herself a rock star."

Anna grinned, as if he had replied with something quite clever, and squeezed his hand. He stayed long enough to watch her board but didn't remain to see the train depart. It was crowded and loud on the platform, noisy with echoing voices. He felt harried and jostled, and the stink of the place—a smell of hot iron, stale piss, and warm, sweating bodies—oppressed him.

But it wasn't any better outside, in the rainy fall cool of Manhattan. The sense of being jostled, hemmed in from all sides, remained with him all the way back to the Pierre Hotel, all the way back even to the quiet and emptiness of his suite. He was belligerent, needed to do something with himself, needed to make some ugly noises of his own.

Four hours later he was in just the right place, in Howard Stern's broadcasting studio, where he insulted and hectored, humiliated Stern's entourage of slow-witted ass kissers when they were foolish enough to interrupt him, and delivered his fire sermon of perversion and hate, chaos and ridicule. Stern loved him. His people wanted to know when Jude could come back.

He was still in New York City that weekend, and in the same mood, when he agreed to meet some of the guys from Stern's crew at a Broadway strip club. They were all the same people he had mocked in front of an audience of millions earlier in the week. They didn't take it personally. Being mocked was their job. They were crazy for him. They thought he had killed.

He ordered a beer he didn't drink and sat at the end of a runway that appeared to be one long, frosted pane of glass, lit from beneath with soft blue gels. The faces gathered in the shadows around the runway all looked wrong to him, unnatural, unwholesome: the faces of the drowned. His head hurt. When he shut his eyes, he saw the lurid, flashing fireworks show that was prelude to a migraine.

When he opened his eyes, a girl with a knife in one hand sank to her knees in front of him. Her eyes were closed. She folded slowly backward, so the back of her head touched the glass floor, her soft, feathery black hair spread across the runway. She was still on her knees.

She moved the knife down her body, a big-bladed hunting bowie with a wide, serrated edge. She wore a dog collar with silver rings on it, a teddy with laces across the bosom that squeezed her breasts together, black stockings.

When the handle of the knife was between her legs, blade pointing at the ceiling—parody of a penis—she flung it into the air, and her eyes sprang open, and she caught it when it came down and arched her back at the same time, raising her chest to the ceiling like an offering, and sliced the knife downward.

She hacked the black lace down the middle, opening a dark red slash, as if slitting herself from throat to crotch. She rolled and threw off the costume, and beneath she was naked except for the silver rings through her nipples, which swung from her breasts, and a G-string pulled up past her hard hip bones. Her supple, sealskin-smooth torso was crimson with body paint.

AC/DC was playing "If You Want Blood You Got It," and what turned him on wasn't her young, athletic body or the way her breasts swung with the hoops of silver through them or how, when she looked right at him, her stare was direct and unafraid.

It was that her lips were moving, just barely. He doubted if anyone else in the whole room besides him even noticed. She was singing to herself, singing along to AC/DC. She knew all the words. It was the sexiest thing he'd seen in months.

He raised his beer to her, only to find that it was empty. He had no *memory of drinking it. The waitress brought him another a few minutes later. From her he learned that the dancer with the knife was named Morphine and was one of their most popular girls. It cost him a hundred to get her phone number and to find out she'd been dancing for around two years, almost to the day she stepped off the bus from Georgia. It cost him another hundred to get that when she wasn't stripping, she answered to Marybeth.*

27

Jude took the wheel just before they crossed into Georgia. His head hurt, an uncomfortable feeling of pressure on his eyeballs more than anything else. The sensation was aggravated by the southern sunshine glinting off just about everything—fenders, windshields, road signs. If not for his aching head, the sky would've been a pleasure, a deep, dark, cloudless blue.

As the Florida state line approached, he was conscious of a mounting anticipation, a nervous tickle in the stomach. Testament was by then perhaps only four hours away. He would be at her house tonight, Jessie Price, née McDermott, sister to Anna, elder stepdaughter to Craddock, and he did not know what he might do when he reached the place.

It had crossed his mind that when he found her, it might end in death for someone. He had thought already that he could kill her for what she'd done, that she was *asking* for it, but for the first time, now that he was close to facing her, the idea became more than angry speculation.

He'd killed pigs as a boy, had picked up the fall-behinds by the legs and smashed their brains out on the concrete floor of his father's cutting room. You swung them into the air and then hit the floor with them, silencing them in midsqueal with a sickening and somehow hollow splitting sound, the same noise a watermelon would make if dropped from a great height. He'd shot other hogs with the bolt gun and imagined he was killing his father as he did it.

Jude had made up his mind to do whatever he had to. He just didn't know what that was yet. And when he thought about it closely, he dreaded learning, was almost as afraid of his own possibilities as he was of the thing coming after him, the thing that had once been Craddock McDermott.

He thought Georgia was dozing, did not know she was awake until she spoke.

"It's the next exit," she said in a sand-grain voice.

Her grandmother. Jude had forgotten about her, had forgotten he'd promised to stop.

He followed her instructions, hung a left at the bottom of the off-ramp and took a two-lane state highway through the shabby outskirts of Crickets, Georgia. They rolled by used-car lots, with their thousands of red, white, and blue plastic pennants flapping in the wind, let the flow of traffic carry them into the town itself. They cruised along one edge of the grassy town square, past the courthouse, the town hall, and the eroded brick edifice of the Eagle Theater.

The route to Bammy's house led them through the green grounds of a small Baptist college. Young men, with ties tucked into their V-neck sweaters, walked beside girls in pleated skirts, with combed, shining hairdos straight out of the old Breck shampoo commercials. Some of the students stared at Jude and Georgia, in the Mustang, the shepherds standing up in the backseat, Bon and Angus breathing steam on the rear windows. A girl, walking beside a taller boy who sported a yellow bow tie, shrank back against her companion as they went past. Bow Tie put a comforting arm around her shoulders. Jude did not flip them off and then drove for a few blocks feeling good about himself, proud of his restraint. His self-control, it was like iron.

Beyond the college they found themselves on a street lined with well-kept Victorians and Colonials, shingles out front advertising the practices of lawyers and dentists. Farther down the avenue, the houses were smaller, and people lived in them. At a lemon Cape with yellow roses growing on a flower trellis to one side, Georgia said, "Turn in."

The woman who answered the door was not fat but stocky, built like a defensive tackle, with a broad, dark face, a silky mustache and clever, girlish eyes, a brown shot through with jade. Her flip-flops smacked against the floor. She stared at Jude and Georgia for a beat, while Georgia grinned a shy, awkward grin. Then something in her grandmother's eyes (Grandmother? How old was she? Sixty? Fifty-five? The disorienting thought crossed Jude's mind that she might even be younger than himself) sharpened, as if a lens had been brought into focus, and she screamed and threw open her arms. Georgia fell into them.

"M.B.!" Bammy cried. Then she leaned away from her, and, still holding her by the hips, stared into her face. "What is wrong with you?"

She put a palm to Georgia's forehead. Georgia twisted from her touch. Bammy saw her bandaged hand next, caught her by the wrist, gave it a speculative look. Then she let go of the hand—almost flung it away.

"You strung out? Christ. You smell like a dog."

"No, Bammy. I swear to God, I am not on no drugs right now. I smell like a dog because I've had dogs climbin' all over me for most of two days. Why do you always got to think the worst damn thing?" The process that had begun almost a thousand miles before, when they started traveling south, seemed to have completed itself, so that everything Georgia said sounded country now.

Only had her accent really started reasserting itself once they were on the road? Or had she started slipping into it even earlier? Jude thought maybe he'd been hearing the redneck in her voice going all the way back to the day she stuck herself with the nonexistent pin in the dead man's suit. Her verbal transformation disconcerted and unsettled him. When she talked that way—*Why do you always got to think the worst damn thing?*—she sounded like Anna.

Bon squeezed into the gap between Jude and Georgia and looked hopefully up at Bammy. The long pink ribbon of Bon's tongue hung out, spit plopping from it. In the green rectangle of the yard, Angus tracked this way and that, whuffing his nose at the flowers growing around the picket fence.

Bammy looked first at Jude's Doc Martens, then up to his scraggly black beard, taking in scrapes, the dirt, the bandage wrapped around his left hand.

"You the rock star?"

"Yes, ma'am."

"You both look like you been in a fight. Was it with each other?"

"No, Bammy," Georgia said.

"That's cute, with the matchin' bandages on your hands. Is that some kind of romantic thing? Did you two brand each other as a sign of your affection? In my day we used to trade class rings."

"No, Bammy. We're fine. We were drivin' through on our way to Florida, and I said we should stop. I wanted you to meet Jude."

"You should've called. I would've started dinner."

"We can't stay. We got to get to Florida tonight."

"You don't got to get anywhere except bed. Or maybe the hospital."

"I'm fine."

"The hell. You're the furthest thing from fine I've ever laid eyes on." She plucked at a strand of black hair stuck to Georgia's damp cheek. "You're covered in sweat. I know sick when I see it."

"I'm just boiled, is all. I spent the last eight hours trapped inside that car with those ugly dogs and bad air-conditionin'. Are you going to move your wide ass out of the way, or are you going to make me climb back into that car and drive some more?"

"I haven't decided yet."

"What's the holdup?"

"I'm tryin' to figure what the chances are you two are here to slaughter me for the money in my purse and take it to buy OxyContin. Everyone is on it these days. There's kids in junior high prostitutin' themselves for it. I learned about it on the news this morning."

"Lucky for you we aren't in junior high."

Bammy seemed about to reply, but then her gaze flicked past Jude's elbow, fixed on something in the yard.

He glanced back to see what. Angus was in a squat, body contracted as if his torso contained an accordion, the shiny black fur of his back humped up into folds, and he was dropping shit after shit into the grass.

"I'll clean up. Sorry about that," Jude said.

"I'm not," Georgia said. "You take a good look, Bammy. If I don't see a toilet in the next minute or two, that's gonna be me."

Bammy lowered her heavily mascaraed eyelids and stepped out of the way. "Come on in, then. I don't want the neighbors seein' you standin' around out here anyway. They'll think I'm startin' my own chapter of the Hells Angels."

28

When they had been introduced, formally, Jude found out her name was Mrs. Fordham, which is what he called her from then on. He could not call her Bammy; paradoxically, he could not really think of her as Mrs. Fordham. Bammy she was, whatever he called her.

Bammy said, "Let's put the dogs out back where they can run."

Georgia and Jude traded a look. They were all of them in the kitchen then. Bon was under the kitchen table. Angus had lifted his head to sniff at the counter, where there were brownies on a plate under green Saran Wrap.

The space was too small to contain the dogs. The front hallway had been too small for them, too. When Angus and Bon came running down it, they had struck a side table, rattling the china on top of it, and reeled into walls, thudding them hard enough to knock pictures askew.

When Jude looked at Bammy again, she was frowning. She'd seen the glance that had passed between Jude and Georgia and knew it meant something, but not what.

Georgia spoke first. "Aw, Bammy, we can't put them out in a strange place. They'll get into your garden."

Bon clouted aside a few chairs to squirm out from under the table.

One fell over with a sharp bang. Georgia leaped toward her, caught her by the collar.

"I'll take her," Georgia said. "Is it all right if I run through the shower? I need to wash and maybe lie down. She can stay with me, where she won't get into trouble."

Angus put his paws up on the counter to get his snout closer to the brownies.

"Angus," Jude said. "Get your ass over here."

Bammy had cold chicken and slaw in the fridge. Also homemade lemonade, as promised, in a sweating glass pitcher. When Georgia went up the back stairs, Bammy fixed Jude a plate. He sat with it. Angus flopped at his feet.

From his place at the kitchen table, Jude had a view of the backyard. A mossy rope hung from the branch of a tall old oak. The tire that had been attached to it once was long gone. Beyond the back fence was an alley, unevenly floored in old bricks.

Bammy poured herself a lemonade and leaned with her bottom against the kitchen counter. The windowsill behind her was crowded with bowling trophies. Her sleeves were rolled up to show forearms as hairy as his.

"I never heard the romantic story of how you two met."

"We were both in Central Park," he said. "Picking daisies. We got to talking and decided to have a picnic together."

"It was either that or you met in some perverted fetish club."

"Come to think of it, it might've been a perverted fetish club."

"You're eating like you never seen food before."

"We overlooked lunch."

"What's your hurry? What's happenin' in Florida you're in such a rush to get to? Some friends of yours havin' an orgy you don't want to miss?"

"You make this slaw yourself?"

"You bet."

"It's good."

"You want the recipe?"

The kitchen was quiet except for the scrape of his fork on the plate and the thud of the dog's tail on the floor. Bammy stared at him.

At last, to fill in the silence, Jude said, "Marybeth calls you Bammy. Why's that?"

"Short for my first name," Bammy said. "Alabama. M.B.'s called me that since she was wetting her didies."

A dry mouthful of cold chicken lodged partway down Jude's windpipe. He coughed and thumped his chest and blinked at watering eyes. His ears burned.

"Really," he said, when his throat was clear. "This may be out of left field, but you ever go to one of my shows? Like, did you maybe see me on a twin bill with AC/DC in 1979?"

"Not likely. I didn't care for that kind of music even when I was young. Buncha gorillas stompin' around the stage, shoutin' swearwords and screamin' their throats out. I might've caught you if you were openin' for the Bay City Rollers. Why?"

Jude wiped at the fresh sweat on his forehead, his insides all queer with relief. "I knew an Alabama once. Don't worry about it."

"How'd the two of you both get so beat up? You got scrapes on your scrapes."

"We were in Virginia, and we walked to Denny's from our motel. On the way back, we were nearly run down."

"You sure about the 'nearly' part?"

"Going under a train trestle. Fella ran his Jeep right into the stone wall. Bashed his face a good one on his windshield, too."

"How'd he make out?"

"All right, I guess."

"Was he drunk?"

"I don't know. I don't think so."

"What happened when the cops got there?"

"We didn't stay to talk to them."

"You didn't stay—" she started, then stopped and threw the rest of her lemonade into the sink, wiped her mouth with the back of her forearm. Her lips were puckered, as if her last swallow of lemonade had been more sour than she liked.

"You are in some hurry," she said.

"A mite."

"Son," she said, "just how much trouble are the two of you in?"

Georgia called to him from the top of the stairs.

Come lie down, Jude. Come upstairs. We'll lie down in my room. You wake us up, Bammy, in an hour? We still got some drivin' to do."

"You don't need to go tonight. You know you can stay over."

"Better not," Jude said.

"I don't see the sense. It's almost five already. Wherever you're going, you won't get there till late."

"It's all right. We're night people." He put his plate in the sink.

Bammy studied him. "You won't leave without dinner?"

"No, ma'am. Wouldn't think of it. Thank you, ma'am."

She nodded. "I'll fix it while you nap. What part of the South are you from, anyway?"

"Louisiana. Place called Moore's Corner. You wouldn't have heard of it. There's nothing there."

"I know it. My sister married a man who took her to Slidell. Moore's Corner is right next to it. There's good people around there."

"Not my people," Jude said, and he went upstairs, Angus bounding up the steps after him.

Georgia was waiting at the top, in the cool darkness of the upstairs hallway. Her hair was wrapped in a towel, and she had on a faded Duke University T-shirt and a pair of loose blue shorts. Her arms were crossed under her breasts, and in her left hand was a flat white box, split at the corners and repaired with peeling brown tape.

Her eyes were the brightest thing in the shadows of the hall, greenish sparks of unnatural light, and in her wan, depleted face was a kind of eagerness.

"What's that?" he asked, and she turned it so he could read what was written on the side.

OUIJA ⟶ PARKER BROS. ⟶ TALKING BOARD

29

She led him into her bedroom, where she removed the towel from her head and slung it over a chair.

It was a small room, under the eaves, with hardly enough space in it for them and the dogs. Bon was already curled up on the twin bed tucked against one wall. Georgia made a clicking sound with her tongue and patted the pillow, and Angus leaped up beside his sister. He settled.

Jude stood just inside the closed door—he had the Ouija board now—and turned in a slow circle, looking over the place where Georgia had spent most of her childhood. He had not been prepared for anything quite so wholesome as what he found. The bedspread was a hand-stitched quilt, patterned after an American flag. A herd of dusty-looking stuffed unicorns, in various sherbet colors, were corralled in a wicker basket in one corner.

She had an antique walnut dresser, with a mirror attached to it, one that could be tilted back and forth. Photos had been stuck into the mirror frame. They were sun-faded and curled with age and showed a toothy, black-haired girl in her teens, with a skinny, boyish build. In this picture she wore a Little League uniform a size too big for her, her ears jutting out under the cap. In that picture she stood between girlfriends, all of them sunburned, flat-chested, and self-conscious in their bikini tops, on a beach somewhere, a pier in the background.

The only hint of the person she was to become was in a final still, a graduation picture, Georgia in the mortarboard and black gown. In the photo she stood with her parents: a shriveled woman in a flower-print dress, straight off the rack in Wal-Mart, a potato-shaped man with a bad comb-over and a cheap checked sport coat. Georgia posed between them, smiling, but her eyes sullen and sly and resentful. And while she held her graduation certificate in one hand, the other was raised in the death-metal salute, pinkie and index finger sticking up in devil horns, her fingernails painted black. So it went.

Georgia found what she was looking for in the desk, a box of kitchen matches. She leaned over the windowsill to light some dark candles. Printed on the rear of her shorts was the word VARSITY. The backs of her thighs were taut and strong from three years of dancing.

"Varsity what?" Jude asked.

She glanced back at him, brow furrowed, then saw where he was looking, took a peek at her own backside, and grinned.

"Gymnastics. Hence most of my act."

"Is that where you learned to chuck a knife?"

It had been a stage knife when she performed, but she could handle a real one, too. Showing off for him once, she'd thrown a Bowie into a log from a distance of twenty feet, and it had hit with a solid thunk, followed by a metallic, wobbling sound, the low, musical harmonic of trembling steel.

"Naw. Bammy taught me that. Bammy has some kind of throwing arm. Bowling balls. Softballs. She has a mean curve. She was pitching for her softball team when she was fifty. Couldn't no one hit her. Her daddy taught her how to chuck a knife, and she taught me."

After she lit the candles, she opened both windows a few inches, without raising the plain white shades. When the breeze blew, the shades moved and pale sunshine surged into the room, then abated, soothing waves of subdued brightness. The candles didn't add much light, but the smell of them was pleasant, mixed with the cool, fresh, grassy scent of the outdoors.

Georgia turned and crossed her legs and sat on the floor. Jude lowered himself to his knees across from her. Joints popped.

He set the box between them, opened it, and took out the gameboard—was a Ouija board a game board, exactly? Across the sepia-colored board were all the letters of the alphabet, the words **YES** and **NO**, a sun with a maniacally grinning face, and a glowering moon. Jude set upon the board a black plastic pointer shaped like a spade in a deck of cards.

Georgia said, "I wasn't sure I could turn it up. I haven't looked at the damn thing in probably eight years. You remember that story I told you, 'bout how once I saw a ghost in Bammy's backyard?"

"Her twin."

"It scared hell out of me, but it made me curious, too. It's funny how people are. Because when I saw the little girl in the backyard, the ghost, I just wanted her to go away. But when she vanished, pretty soon I got to wishin' I'd see her again. I started wantin' to have another experience like it sometime, to come across another ghost."

"And here you are now with one hot on your tail. Who says dreams don't come true?"

She laughed. "Anyway. A while after I saw Bammy's sister in the backyard, I picked this up at the five-and-dime. Me and one of my girlfriends used to play around with it. We'd quiz the spirits about boys at school. And a lot of times I'd be movin' the pointer in secret, makin' it say things. My girlfriend, Sheryll Jane, she knew I was makin' it say things, but she'd always pretend like she really believed we were talkin' to a ghost, and her eyes would get all big and round and stick out of her head. I'd slide the pointer around, and the Ouija board would tell her some boy at school had a pair of her underwear in his locker, and she'd let out a screech and say, 'I always knew he was weird about me!' She

was sweet to hang around with me and be so silly and play my games."
Georgia rubbed the back of her neck. Almost as an afterthought, she
added, "One time, though, we were playin' Ouija and it started workin'
for real. I wasn't movin' the pointer or anything."

"Maybe Sheryll Jane was moving it."

"No. It was movin' on its own, and we both knew it. I could tell it was
movin' on its own because Sheryll wasn't puttin' on her act with them big
eyes of hers. Sheryll wanted it to stop. When the ghost told us who it
was, she said I wasn't being funny. And I said I wasn't doin' nothin', and
she said stop it. But she didn't take her hand off the pointer."

"Who was the ghost?"

"Her cousin Freddy. He had hung himself in the summer. He was fifteen. They were real close . . . Freddy and Sheryll."

"What'd he want?"

"He said there was pictures in his family's barn of guys in their underwear. He told us right where to find them, hidden under a floorboard.
He said he didn't want his parents to know he was gay and be any more
upset than they were. He said that's why he killed himself, because he
didn't want to be gay anymore. Then he said souls aren't boys and aren't
girls. They're only souls. He said there is no gay, and he'd made his
momma sorrowful for nothin'. I remember that exactly. That he used the
word 'sorrowful.'"

"Did you go look for the pictures?"

"We snuck into the barn, next afternoon, and we found the loose
floorboard, but there was nothin' hidden under it. Then Freddy's father
came up behind us and gave us a good shoutin' at. He said we had no
business snoopin' around his place and sent us runnin'. Sheryll said not
finding any pictures proved it was all a lie and that I had faked the whole
thing. You wouldn't believe how mad she was. But I think Freddy's father
came across the pictures before us and got rid of them, so no one would
know his kid was a fairy. The way he shouted at us was like he was

scared about what we might know. About what we might be lookin' for."
She paused, then added, "Me and Sheryll never really made it up. We
pretended like we put it behind us, but after that we didn't spend as
much time together. Which suited me fine. By then I was sleepin' with
my daddy's pal George Ruger, and I didn't want a whole bunch of friends
hangin' around askin' me questions about how come I had so much
money in my pockets all of a sudden."

The shades lifted and fell. The room brightened and dimmed. Angus
yawned.

"So what do we do?" Jude said.

"Haven't you ever played with one of these?"

Jude shook his head.

"Well, we each put a hand on the pointer," she said, and started to
reach forward with her right hand, then changed her mind and tried to
draw it back.

It was too late. He reached out and caught her wrist. She winced—as
if even the wrist were tender.

She had removed her bandages before showering and not yet put on
fresh. The sight of her naked hand drove the air out of him. It looked as
if it had been soaking in bathwater for hours, the skin wrinkly, white,
and soft. The thumb was worse. For an instant, in the gloom, it looked
almost skinless. The flesh was inflamed a startling crimson, and where
the thumbprint belonged was a wide circle of infection, a sunken disk,
yellow with pus, darkening to black at the center.

"Christ," Jude said.

Georgia's too-pale, too-thin face was surprisingly calm, staring back
at him through the wavering shadows. She pulled her hand away.

"You want to lose that hand?" Jude asked. "You want to see if you can
die from blood poisoning?"

"I am not as scared to die as I was a couple days ago. Isn't that funny?"

Jude opened his mouth for a reply and found he had none to make.

His insides were knotted up. What was wrong with her hand would kill her if nothing was done, and they both knew it, and she wasn't afraid.

Georgia said, "Death isn't the end. I know that now. We both do."

"That isn't any reason to just *decide* to die. To not take care of yourself."

"I haven't just decided to die. I've decided there isn't goin' to be any hospital. We've already talked that idea in circles. You know we can't bring the dogs into no emergency room with us."

"I'm rich. I can make a doctor come to us."

"I told you already, I don't believe that what's wrong with me can be helped by any doctor." She leaned forward, rapped the knuckles of her left hand on the Ouija board. "This is more important than the hospital. Sooner or later Craddock is going to get by the dogs. I think sooner. He'll find a way. They can't protect us forever. We are livin' minute to minute, and you know it. I don't mind dyin' as long as he isn't waitin' for me on the other side."

"You're sick. That's the fever thinking. You don't need this voodoo. You need antibiotics."

"I need you," she said, her bright, vivid eyes steady on his face, "to shut the fuck up and put your hand on the pointer."

Georgia said she would do the talking, and she put the fingers of
her left hand next to his on the pointer—it was called the planchette,
Jude remembered now. He looked up when he heard her draw a steadying breath. She shut her eyes, not as if she were about to go into a mys-
tic trance but more as if she were about to leap from a high diving board
and was trying to get over the churning in her stomach.

"Okay," she said. "My name is Marybeth Stacy Kimball. I called myself Morphine for a few bad years, and the guy I love calls me Georgia,
even though it drives me nuts, but Marybeth is who I am, my true
name." She opened her eyes to a squint, peeped at Jude from between
her eyelashes. "Introduce yourself."

He was about to speak when she held up a hand to stop him.

"Your real name, now. The name that belongs to your true self. True
names are very important. The right words have a charge in them.
Enough charge to bring the dead back to the living."

He felt stupid—felt that what they were doing couldn't work, was a
waste of time, and they were acting like children. His career had afforded
him a variety of occasions to make a fool out of himself, however. Once,
for a music video, he and his band—Dizzy, Jerome, and Kenny—had run

in mock horror through a field of clover, chased by a dwarf dressed in a dirty leprechaun suit and carrying a chain saw. In time Jude had developed something like an immunity to the condition of feeling stupid. So when he paused, it wasn't out of a reluctance to speak but because he honestly didn't know what to say.

Finally, looking at Georgia, he said, "My name is . . . Justin. Justin Cowzynski. I guess. Although I haven't answered to that since I was nineteen."

Georgia closed her eyes, withdrawing into herself. A dimple appeared between her slender eyebrows, a little thought line. Slowly, softly, she spoke. "Well. There you go. That's us. We want to talk to Anna McDermott. Justin and Marybeth need your help. Is Anna there? Anna, will you speak to us today?"

They waited. The shade moved. Children shouted in the street.

"Is there anyone who would like to speak to Justin and Marybeth? Will Anna McDermott say somethin' to us? Please. We're in trouble, Anna. Please hear us. Please help us." Then, in a voice that approached a whisper, she said, "Come on. Do somethin'." Speaking to the planchette.

Bon farted in her sleep, a squeaking sound, like a foot skidding across wet rubber.

"She didn't know me," Georgia said. "You ask for her."

"Anna McDermott? Is there an Anna McDermott in the house? Could you please report to the Ouija information center?" he asked, in a big, hollow, public announcer's voice.

Georgia smiled, a wide, humorless grin. "Ah, yes. I knew it was only a matter of time before the fuckin'-around would commence."

"Sorry."

"Ask for her. Ask for real."

"It's not workin'."

"You haven't tried."

"Yes I have."

"No you haven't."

"Well, it just isn't workin'."

He expected hostility or impatience. Instead her smile broadened even more, and she regarded him with a quiet sweetness that he instantly mistrusted. "She was waitin' for you to call, right up to the day she died. Like there was any chance of that. What, did you wait a whole week, before moving on in your state-by-state tour of America's easiest snatch?"

He flushed. Not even a week. "You might not want to get too hot under the collar," he said, "considering you're the easy snatch in question."

"I know, and it disgusts me. Put! Your! Hand! Back on the motherfuckin' pointer. We are *not* done here."

Jude had been withdrawing his hand from the planchette, but at Georgia's outburst he set his fingers back upon it.

"I'm disgusted with the both of us. You for bein' who you are and me for lettin' you stay that way. Now, you call for her. She won't come for me, but she might for you. She was waitin' for you to call right to the end, and if you ever had, she would've come running. Maybe she still will."

Jude glared down at the board, the old-timey alphabet letters, the sun, the moon.

"Anna, you around? Will Anna McDermott come on and talk to us?" Jude said.

The planchette was dead, unmoving plastic. He had not felt so grounded in the world of the real and the ordinary in days. It wasn't going to work. It wasn't right. It was hard to keep his hand on the pointer. He was impatient to get up, to be done.

"Jude," Georgia said, then corrected herself. "Justin. Don't quit on this. Try again."

Jude. Justin.

He stared at his fingers on the planchette, the board beneath, and tried to think what wasn't right, and in another moment it came to him. Georgia had said that true names had a charge in them, that the right words had the power to return the dead to the living. And he thought then that Justin wasn't his true name, that he had left Justin Cowzynski in Louisiana when he was nineteen, and the man who got off the bus in New York City forty hours later was someone different entirely, capable of doing and saying things that had been beyond Justin Cowzynski. And what they were doing wrong now was calling for Anna McDermott. He had never called her that. She had not been Anna McDermott when they were together.

"Florida," Jude said, almost sighed. When he spoke again, his voice was surprising to him, calm and self-assured. "Come on and talk to me, Florida. It's Jude, darlin'. I'm sorry I didn't call you. I'm calling now. Are you there? Are you listening? Are you still waiting for me? I'm here now. I'm right here."

The planchette jumped under their fingers, as if the board had been struck from beneath. Georgia jumped with it and cried out weakly. Her bad hand fluttered to her throat. The breeze shifted direction and sucked at the shades, snapping them against the windows and darkening the room. Angus lifted his head, eyes flashing a bright, unnatural green in the weak light from the candles.

Georgia's good hand had remained on the pointer, and no sooner had it rattled back to rest on the board than it began to move. The sensation was unnatural and made Jude's heart race. It felt as if there were another pair of fingers on the planchette, a third hand, reaching into the space between his hand and Georgia's and sliding the pointer around, turning it without warning. It slipped across the board, touched a letter, stayed there for a moment, then *spun* under their fingers, forcing Jude to twist his wrist to keep his hand on it.

"W," Georgia said. She was audibly short of breath. "H. A. T."

"What," Jude said. The pointer went on finding letters, and Georgia continued calling them out: a **K**, an **E**. Jude listened, concentrating on what was being spelled.

Jude: "Kept. You."

The planchette made a half turn—and stopped, its little casters squeaking faintly.

"What kept you," Jude repeated.

"What if it isn't her? What if it's him? How do we know who we're talking to?"

The planchette surged, before Georgia had even finished speaking. It was like having a finger on a record that has suddenly begun to turn.

Georgia: "W. H. Y. I. . . ."

Jude: "Why. Is. The. Sky. Blue." The pointer went still. "It's her. She always said she'd rather ask questions than answer them. Got to be kind of a joke between us."

It was her. Pictures skipped in his head, a series of vivid stills. She was in the backseat of the Mustang, naked on the white leather except for her cowboy boots and a feathered ten-gallon hat, peeking out at him from under the brim, eyes bright with mischief. She was yanking his beard backstage at the Trent Reznor show, and he was biting the inside of his cheek to keep from shouting. She was dead in the bathtub, a thing he hadn't ever seen except in his mind, and the water was ink, and her stepfather, in his black undertaker's suit, was on his knees beside the tub, as if to pray.

"Go on, Jude," Georgia said. "Talk to her."

Her voice was strained, pitched to just above a whisper. When Jude glanced up at Georgia, she was shivering, although her face was aglow with sweat. Her eyes glittered from deep in their dark and bony hollows . . . fever eyes.

"Are you all right?"

Georgia shook her head—*Leave me alone*—and shuddered furiously. Her left hand remained on the pointer. "Talk to her."

He looked back at the board. The black moon stamped on one corner was laughing. Hadn't it been glowering a moment before? A black dog at the bottom of the board was howling up at it. He didn't think it had been there when they first opened the board.

He said, "I didn't know how to help you. I'm sorry, kiddo. I wish you fell in love with anyone but me. I wish you fell in love with one of the good guys. Someone who wouldn't have just sent you away when things got hard."

"A. R. E. Y. O. . . ." Georgia read, in that same effortful, short-of-breath voice. He could hear, in that voice, the work it took to suppress her shivering.

"Are. You. Angry."

The pointer went still.

Jude felt a boil of emotions, so many things, all at once, he wasn't sure he could put them into words. But he could, and it turned out to be easy.

"Yes," he said.

The pointer flew to the word **NO**.

"You shouldn't have done that to yourself."

"D. O. N. . . ."

"Done. What." Jude read. "Done what? You know what. Killed your—"

The pointer skidded back to the word **NO**.

"What do you mean, no?"

Georgia spoke the letters aloud, a **W**, an **H**, an **A**.

"What. If. I. Can't. Answer." The pointer came to rest again. Jude stared for a moment, then understood. "She can't answer questions. She can only ask them."

But Georgia was already spelling again. "I. S. H. E. A. . . ."

A great fit of shivering overcame her, so her teeth clattered, and when Jude glanced at her, he saw the breath steam from her lips, as if she were standing in a cold-storage vault. Only the room didn't feel any warmer or colder to Jude.

The next thing he noticed was that Georgia wasn't looking at her hand on the pointer, or at him, or at anything. Her eyes had gone unfocused, fixed on the middle distance. Georgia went on reciting the letters aloud, as the planchette touched them, but she wasn't looking at the board anymore, couldn't see what it was doing.

"Is." Jude read as Georgia spelled the words in a strained monotone. "He. After. You."

Georgia quit calling the letters, and he realized a question had been asked.

"Yes. Yeah. He thinks it's my fault you killed yourself, and now he's playing get-even."

NO. The planchette pointed at it for a long, emphatic moment before beginning to scurry about again.

"W. H. Y. R. U. . . ." Georgia muttered thickly.

"Why. Are. You. So. Dumb." Jude fell silent, staring.

One of the dogs on the bed whined.

Then Jude understood. He felt overcome for a moment by a sensation of light-headedness and profound disorientation. It was like the head rush that comes from standing up too quickly. It was also a little like feeling rotten ice give way underfoot, the first terrible moment of plunge. It staggered him, that it had taken him so long to understand.

"Fucker," Jude said. "That fucker."

He noticed that Bon was awake, staring apprehensively at the Ouija board. Angus was watching, too, his tail thumping against the mattress.

"What can we do?" Jude said. "He's coming after us, and we don't know how to get rid of him. Can you help us?"

The pointer swung toward the word **YES**.

"The golden door," Georgia whispered.

Jude looked at her—and recoiled. Her eyes had rolled up in her head, to show only the whites, and her whole body was steadily, furiously trembling. Her face, which had already been so pale it was like wax, had lost even more color, taking on an unpleasant translucence. Her breath steamed. He heard the planchette beginning to scrape and slide wildly across the board, looked back down. Georgia wasn't spelling for him anymore, wasn't speaking. He strung together the words himself.

"Who. Will. Be. The. Door. Who will be the door?"

"I will be the door," Georgia said.

"Georgia?" Jude said. "What are you talking about?"

The pointer began to move again. Jude didn't speak now, just watched it finding letters, hesitating on each for only an instant before whirring on.

Will. U. Bring. Me. Thru.

"Yes," Georgia said. "If I can. I'll make the door, and I'll bring you through, and then you'll stop him."

Do. You. Swear.

"I swear," she said. Her voice was thin and compressed and strained with her fear. "I swear I swear oh God I swear. Whatever I have to do, I just don't know what to do. I'm ready to do whatever I have to do, just tell me what it is."

Do. You. Have. A. Mirror. Marybeth.

"Why?" Georgia said, blinking, her eyes rolling back down to look blearily about. She turned her head toward her dresser. "There's one—"

She screamed. Her fingers sprang up off the pointer, and she pressed her hands to her mouth to stifle the cry. In the same instant, Angus came to his feet and began to bark from where he stood on the bed. He was staring at what she was staring at. By then Jude was twisting to see for himself, his own fingers leaving the planchette—which began to spin around and around on its own, a kid doing doughnuts on his dirt bike.

The mirror on the dresser was tilted forward to show Georgia, sitting across from Jude, with the Ouija board between them. Only in the mirror her eyes were covered by a blindfold of black gauze and her throat was slashed. A red mouth gaped obscenely across it, and her shirt was soaked in blood.

Angus and Bon bounded from the bed in the same moment. Bon hit the floor and launched herself at the planchette, snarling. She closed her jaws on the pointer, the way she might have attacked a mouse scampering for its hole, and it burst into pieces in her teeth.

Angus hurled himself against the dresser and put his front paws on the top of it, barking furiously at the face in the mirror. The force of his weight rocked the dresser onto its rear legs. The mirror could be rotated forward and back, and now it swung back, tilting to show its face to the ceiling. Angus dropped to all fours, and an instant later the dresser did the same, coming down onto its wooden legs with a ringing crash. The mirror swung forward, pivoting to show Georgia her own reflection once more. It was only her reflection. The blood—and the black blindfold—were gone.

31

In the late-afternoon cool of the room, Jude and Georgia stretched out together on the twin bed. It was too small for the both of them, and Georgia had to turn on her side and throw a leg over him to fit beside him. Her face nestled into his neck, the tip of her nose cold against his skin.

He was numb. Jude knew he needed to think about what had just happened to them, but he could not seem to turn his thoughts back to what he'd seen in the mirror, back to what Anna had been trying to tell them. His mind wouldn't go there. His mind wanted away from death for a few moments. He felt crowded by death, felt the promise of death all around, felt death on his chest, each death a stone heaped on top of him, driving the air out of him: Anna's death, Danny's, Dizzy's, Jerome's, the possibility of his own death and Georgia's waiting just down the road from them. He could not move for the weight of all those deaths pressing down on him.

Jude had an idea that as long as he was very still and said nothing, he and Georgia could stay in this quiet moment together indefinitely, with the shades flapping and the dim light wavering around them. Whatever bad thing that was waiting for them next would never arrive. As long as he remained in the little bed, with Georgia's cool thigh over him and her body clasped to his side, the unimaginable future wouldn't come for them.

It came anyway. Bammy thumped softly on the door, and when she spoke, her voice was hushed and uncertain.

"You all right in there?"

Georgia pushed herself up on one elbow. She swiped the back of a hand across her eyes. Jude had not known until now that she'd been crying. She blinked and smiled crookedly, and it was *real,* not a smile for show, although for the life of him he couldn't imagine what she had to smile about.

Her face had been scrubbed clean by her tears, and that smile was heartbreaking in its easy, girlish sincerity. It seemed to say, *Oh, well. Sometimes you get a bad deal.* He understood then that she believed what they'd both seen in the mirror was a kind of vision, something that was going to happen, that maybe they could not avert. Jude quailed at the idea. No. No, better Craddock should get him and be done with it than Georgia should die gasping in her own blood, and why would Anna show them that, what could she want?

"Honey?" Bammy asked.

"We're fine," Georgia called back.

Silence.

Then: "You aren't fightin' in there, are you? I heard bangin' around."

"*No,*" Georgia said, sounding affronted by the very suggestion. "Swear to God, Bammy. Sorry about the racket."

"Well," Bammy said. "Do you need anything?"

"Fresh sheets," Georgia said.

Another silence. Jude felt Georgia trembling against his chest, a sweet shivering. She bit down on her lower lip to keep from laughing. Then he was fighting it, too, was overcome with a sudden, convulsive hilarity. He jammed a hand into his mouth, while his insides hitched with trapped, strangled laughter.

"Jesus," said Bammy, who sounded like she wanted to spit. "Jesus Christ." Her tread moving away from the door as she said it.

Georgia fell against Jude, her cool, damp face pressed hard to his neck. He put his arms around her, and they clutched each other while they gasped with laughter.

32

After dinner Jude said he had some phone calls to make and left Georgia and Bammy in Bammy's living room. He didn't really have any-one to call but knew that Georgia wanted some time with her grand-mother and that they would be more themselves without him there.

But once he was in the kitchen, a fresh glass of lemonade before him and nothing to occupy himself with, he found the phone in his hand any-way. He dialed the office line to pick up his messages. It felt queer, to be busy with something so entirely grounded in the ordinary after all that had happened in the day, from their run-in with Craddock at Denny's to the encounter with Anna in Georgia's bedroom. Jude felt disconnected from who he'd been before he first saw the dead man. His career, his liv-ing, both the business and the art that had preoccupied him for more than thirty years, seemed matters of no particular importance. He dialed the phone, watching his hand as if it belonged to someone else, feeling he was a passive spectator to the actions of a man in a play, an actor per-forming the part of himself.

He had five messages waiting for him. The first was from Herb Gross, his accountant and business manager. Herb's voice, which was usually oily and self-satisfied, was, in the recording, grainy with emotion.

"I just heard from Nan Shreve that Danny Wooten was found dead in his apartment this morning. Apparently he hanged himself. We're all dismayed here, as I'm sure you can imagine. Will you call me when you get this message? I don't know where you are. No one does. Thank you."

There was a message from an Officer Beam, who said that the Piecliff police were trying to reach Jude about an important matter, and would he call back. There was a message from Nan Shreve, his lawyer, who said she was handling everything, that the police wanted to collect a statement from him about Danny, and he should call as soon as he could.

The next message was from Jerome Presley, who had died four years ago, after he drove his Porsche into a weeping willow at just under 140 miles an hour. "Hey, Jude, I guess we're getting the band back together soon, huh? John Bonham on drums. Joey Ramone on backup vocals." He laughed, then went on in his familiar, weary drawl. Jerome's croak of a voice had always reminded Jude of the comic Steven Wright. "I hear you're driving a souped-up Mustang now. That's one thing we always had, Jude—we could talk cars. Suspensions, engines, spoilers, sound systems, Mustangs, Thunderbirds, Chargers, Porsches. You know what I was thinking about, night I drove my Porsche off the road? I was thinking about all the shit I *never* said to you. All the shit we didn't talk about. Like how you got me hooked on your coke, and then you went and got straight and had the balls to tell me if I didn't do the same, you'd throw me out of the band. Like how you gave Christine money to set herself up with her own place after she left me, when she ran off with the kids without a word. How you gave her money for a lawyer. There's loyalty for you. Or how you wouldn't make a simple fucking loan when I was losing everything—the house, the cars. And here I let you sleep on the bed in my basement when you were fresh off the bus from Louisiana and you didn't have thirty dollars in your pocket." Jerome laughed again—his harsh, corrosive, smoker's laugh. "Well, we'll get a chance to finally talk about all that stuff soon. I guess I'll be seeing you any day. I hear you're on the nightroad now. I know where that road goes. Straight into a fucking tree. They picked me out of the branches, you know. Except for the parts I left on the windshield. I miss you, Jude. I'm looking forward to putting my arms around you. We're going to sing just like the old days. Everyone sings here. After a while it kind of sounds like screaming. Just listen. Listen and you can hear them screaming."

There was a clattering sound as Jerome took the phone from his ear and held it out so Jude could hear. What came through the line was a noise like no other Jude had ever heard before, alien and dreadful, a noise like the hum of flies, amplified a hundred times, and the punch and squeal of machinery, a steam press that banged and seethed. When listened to carefully, it was possible to hear words in all that fly hum, inhuman voices calling for Mother, calling for it to stop.

Jude was primed to delete the next message, expecting another dead person, but instead it was a call from his father's housekeeper, Arlene Wade. She was so far from his thoughts that it was several moments before he was able to identify her old, warbly, curiously toneless voice, and by then her brief message was almost done.

"Hello, Justin, it's me. I wanted to update you on your father. Hasn't been conscious in thirty-six hours. Heartbeat is all fits and starts. Thought you'd want to know. He isn't in pain. Call if you like."

After Jude hung up, he leaned over the kitchen counter, looking out into the night. He had his sleeves rolled to his elbows, and the window was open, and the breeze that drifted in was cool on his skin and perfumed with the smell of the flower garden. Insects hummed.

Jude could see his father in his head: the old man stretched out on his narrow cot, gaunt, wasted, his chin covered in a mangy white bristle, his temples sunken and gray. Jude even half believed he could smell him, the rank bad sweat, the stink of the house, an odor that included but was not limited to chicken shit, pig, and the ashtray smell of nicotine absorbed into everything—curtains, blankets, wallpaper. When Jude had finally lit out of Louisiana, he'd been fleeing that smell as much as escaping his father.

He had run and run and run, made music, made millions, spent a lifetime trying to put as much distance between himself and the old man as he could. Now, with a little luck, he and his father might die on the same day. They could walk the nightroad together. Or maybe they would ride, share the passenger seat of Craddock McDermott's smoke-colored pickup. The two of them sitting so close to each other that Martin Cowzynski could rest one of his gaunt claws on the back of Jude's neck. The smell of him filling the car. The smell of home.

Hell would smell like that, and they would drive there together, father and son, accompanied by their hideous chauffeur, with his silver crew cut and Johnny Cash suit and the radio turned to Rush Limbaugh. If hell was anything, it was talk radio—and family.

In the living room, Bammy said something in a low, gossipy murmur. Georgia laughed. Jude tilted his head at the sound and a moment later was surprised to find himself smiling in automatic response. How it was she could be in stitches again, with everything that was up against them and everything they'd seen, he couldn't imagine.

Her laughter was a quality he prized in her above all others—the deep, chaotic music of it and the way she gave herself over to it completely. It stirred him, drew him out of himself. It was just after seven by the clock on the microwave. He would step back into the living room and join the two of them for a few minutes of easy, pointless talk, and then he would get Georgia's attention and shoot a meaningful look at the door. The road was waiting.

He had made up his mind and was turning from the kitchen counter when a sound caught his attention, a lilting, off-key voice, singing: *bye-bye, bay-bee*. He turned on his heel, glanced back into the yard behind the house.

The rear corner of the yard was lit by a street lamp in the alley. It cast a bluish light across the picket fence and the big leafy oak with the rope hanging from one branch. A little girl crouched in the grass beneath the tree, a child of perhaps six or seven, in a simple red-and-white-checkered dress and with her dark hair tied in a ponytail. She sang to herself, that old one by Dean Martin about how it was time to hit the road to dreamland, digya in the land of nod. She picked a dandelion, caught her breath, and blew. The seed parachutes came apart, a hundred drifting white umbrellas that soared out into the gloom. It should've been impossible to see them, except that they were faintly luminescent, drifting about like improbable white sparks. Her head was raised, so she seemed almost to be staring directly at Jude through the window. It was hard to be sure, though. Her eyes were obscured by the black marks that jittered before them.

It was Ruth. Her name was Ruth. She was Bammy's twin sister, the one who had disappeared in the 1950s. Their parents had called them in for lunch. Bammy had come running, but Ruth lingered behind, and that was the last anyone ever saw of her . . . alive.

Jude opened his mouth—to say what, he didn't know—but found himself unable to speak. The breath caught in his chest and stayed there.

Ruth stopped singing, and the night went still, no sound even of insects now. The little girl turned her head, to glance into the alley behind the house. She smiled, and a hand flapped up in a small wave, as if she'd just noticed someone standing there, someone she knew, a friendly neighborhood acquaintance. Only there wasn't anyone in the alley. There were old pages from a newspaper stuck to the ground, some broken glass, weeds growing between the bricks. Ruth rose from her crouch and walked slowly to the fence, her lips moving—talking soundlessly to a person who wasn't there. When had Jude become unable to hear her voice? When she gave up singing.

As Ruth approached the fence, Jude felt a rising alarm, as if he were watching a child about to stray onto a busy highway. He wanted to call to her but could not, couldn't even inhale.

He remembered then what Georgia had told him about her. That people who saw little Ruth always wanted to call to her, to warn her that she was in danger, to tell her to run, but that no one could manage it. They were too stricken by the sight of her to speak. A thought formed, the sudden, nonsensical thought that this was every girl Jude had ever known who he hadn't been able to help; it was Anna and Georgia both. If he could just speak her name, get her attention, signal to her that she was in trouble, anything was possible. He and Georgia might beat the dead man yet, survive the impossible fix they had got themselves in.

And still Jude could not find his voice. It was maddening to stand there and watch and not be able to speak. He slammed his bandaged, injured hand against the counter, felt a shock of pain travel through the wound in his palm—and still could not force any sound up through the tight passage of his throat.

Angus was at his side, and he jumped when Jude pounded the counter. He lifted his head and lapped nervously at Jude's wrist. The rough, hot stroke of Angus's tongue on his bare skin startled him. It was immediate and real and it yanked him out of his paralysis as swiftly and abruptly as Georgia's laughter had pulled him out of his feeling of despair only a few moments before. His lungs grabbed some air, and he called through the window.

"Ruth!" he shouted—and she turned her head. She heard him. She *heard* him. "Get away, Ruth! Run for the house! Right now!"

Ruth glanced again at the darkened, empty alley, and then she took an off-balance, lunging step back toward the house. Before she could go any farther, her slender white arm came up, as if there were an invisible line around her left wrist and someone was pulling on it.

Only it wasn't an invisible line. It was an invisible hand. And in the next instant, she came right off the ground, hauled into the air by someone who wasn't there. Her long, skinny legs kicked helplessly, and one of her sandals flew off and disappeared into the dark. She wrestled and fought, suspended two feet in the air, and was pulled steadily backward. Her face turned toward Jude's, helpless and beseeching, the marks over her eyes blotting out her desperate stare, as she was carried by unseen forces over the picket fence.

"Ruth!" he called again, his voice as commanding as it had ever been onstage, when he was shouting to his legions.

She began to fade away as she was hauled off down the alley. Now her dress was gray-and-white checks. Now her hair was the color of moonsilver. The other sandal fell off, splashed in a puddle, and disappeared, although ripples continued to move across the shallow muddy water—as if it had fallen, impossibly, right out of the past and into the present. Ruth's mouth was open, but she couldn't scream, and Jude didn't know why. Maybe the unseen thing that was tugging her away had a hand over her mouth. She passed under the bright blue glare of the street lamp and was gone. The breeze caught a newspaper, and it flapped down the empty alley with a dry, rattling sound.

Angus whined again and gave him another lick. Jude stared. A bad taste in his mouth. A feeling of pressure in his eardrums.

"Jude," Georgia whispered from behind him.

He looked at her reflection in the window over the sink. Black squiggles danced in front of her eyes. They were over his eyes, too. They were both dead. They just hadn't stopped moving yet.

"What happened, Jude?"

"I couldn't save her," he said. "The girl. Ruth. I saw her taken away." He could not tell Georgia that somehow his hope that they could save themselves had been taken with her. "I called her name. I called her name, but I couldn't change what happened."

"Course you couldn't, dear," said Bammy.

33

Jude pivoted toward Georgia and Bammy. Georgia stood across the kitchen from him, in the doorway. Her eyes were just her eyes, no death marks over them. Bammy touched her granddaughter on the hip to nudge her aside, then eased into the kitchen around her and approached Jude.

"You know Ruth's story? Did M.B. tell you?"

"She told me your sister got taken when you were little. She said sometimes people see her out in the yard, getting grabbed all over again. It isn't the same as seeing it yourself. I heard her sing. I saw her taken away."

Bammy put her hand on his wrist. "Do you want to set?"

He shook his head.

"You know why she keeps coming back? Why people see her? The worst moments of Ruth's life happened out in that yard, while we all sat in here eating our lunch. She was alone and scared, and no one saw when she was taken away. No one heard when she stopped singing. It must've been the most awful thing. I've always thought that when something really bad happens to a person, other people just have to know about it. You can't be a tree falling in the woods with no one to hear you crash. Can I at least get you something else to drink?"

He nodded. She got the pitcher of lemonade, almost drained now, and sloshed the last of it into his glass.

While she poured, Bammy said, "I always thought if someone could speak to her, it might take a weight off her. I always thought if someone could make her feel not so alone in those last minutes, it might set her free." Bammy tipped her head to the side—a curious, interrogatory gesture Jude had seen Georgia perform a million times. "You might've done her some good and not even know it. Just by saying her name."

"What did I do? She still got taken." Downing the glass in a swallow and then setting it in the sink.

"I never thought for a moment anyone could change what happened to her. That's done. The past is gone. Stay the night, Jude."

Her last statement was so completely unrelated to the one that had preceded it, Jude needed a moment to understand she had just made a request of him.

"Can't," Jude said.

"Why?"

Because anyone who offered them aid would be infected with the death on them, and who knew how much they had risked Bammy's life just by stopping a few hours? Because he and Georgia were dead already, and the dead drag the living down. "Because it isn't safe," he said at last. That was honest, at least.

Bammy's brow knotted, screwing up in thought. He saw her struggling for the right words to crack him open, to force him to talk about the situation they were in.

While she was still thinking, Georgia crept into the room, almost tiptoeing, as if afraid to make any sound. Bon was at her heels, gazing up with a look of idiot anxiety.

Georgia said, "Not every ghost is like your sister, Bammy. There's some that are real bad. We're having all kinds of trouble with dead people. Don't ask either one of us to explain. It would just sound crazy."

"Try me anyway. Let me help."

"Mrs. Fordham," Jude said, "you were good to have us. Thank you for dinner."

Georgia reached Bammy's side and tugged on her shirtsleeve, and when her grandmother turned toward her, Georgia put her pale and skinny arms around her and clasped her tight. "You are a good woman, and I love you."

Bammy still had her head turned to look at Jude. "If I can do something . . ."

"But you can't," Jude said. "It's like with your sister there in the backyard. You can shout all you want, but it won't change how things play out."

"I don't believe that. My sister is dead. No one paid any attention when she quit singing, and someone took her away and killed her. But you are not dead. You and my granddaughter are alive and here with me in my house. Don't give up on yourself. The dead win when you quit singing and let them take you on down the road with them."

Something about this last gave Jude a nervous jolt, as if he'd touched metal and caught a sudden stinging zap of static electricity. Something about giving up on yourself. Something about singing. There was an idea there, but not one he could make sense of yet. The knowledge that he and Georgia had about played out their string—the feeling that they were both as dead as the girl he'd just seen in the backyard—was an obstacle no other thought could get around.

Georgia kissed Bammy's face, once, and again: kissing tears. And at last Bammy turned to look at her. She put her hands on her granddaughter's cheeks.

"Stay," Bammy said. "Make him stay. And if he won't, then let him go on without you."

"I can't do that," Georgia said. "And he's right. We can't bring you into this any more than we already have. One man who was a friend to us is dead because he didn't get clear of us fast enough."

Bammy pressed her forehead to Georgia's breast. Her breath hitched and caught. Her hands rose and went into Georgia's hair, and for a moment both women swayed together, as if they were dancing very slowly.

When her composure returned—it wasn't long—Bammy looked up into Georgia's face again. Bammy was red and damp-cheeked, and her chin was trembling, but she seemed to be done with her crying.

"I will pray, Marybeth. I will pray for you."

"Thank you," Georgia said.

"I am countin' on you coming back. I am countin' on seeing you again, when you've figured out how to make things right. And I know you will. Because you're clever and you're good and you're my girl." Bammy inhaled sharply, gave Jude a watery, sidelong look. "I hope he's worth it."

Georgia laughed, a soft, convulsive sound almost like a sob, and squeezed Bammy once more.

"Go, then," Bammy said. "Go if you got to."

"We're already gone," Georgia said.

34

He drove. His palms were hot and slick on the wheel, his stomach churning. He wanted to slam his fist into something. He wanted to drive too fast, and he did, shooting yellow lights just as they turned red. And when he didn't make a light in time and had to sit in traffic, he pumped the pedal, revving the engine impatiently. What he had felt in the house, watching the little dead girl get dragged away, that sensation of helplessness, had thickened and curdled into rage and a sour-milk taste in his mouth.

Georgia watched him for a few miles, then put a hand on his forearm. He twitched, startled by the clammy, chilled feel of her skin on his. He wanted to take a deep breath and recover his composure, not so much for himself as for her. If one of them was going to be this way, it seemed to him it ought to be Georgia, that she had more right to rage than he did, after what Anna had shown her in the mirror. After she had seen herself dead. He did not understand her quiet, her steadiness, her concern for him, and he could not find it in him to take deep breaths. When a truck in front of him was slow to get moving after the light turned green, he laid on the horn.

"Head out of your ass!" Jude yelled through the open window as he tore by, crossing the double yellow line to go past.

Georgia removed her hand from his arm, set it in her lap. She turned her head to stare out the passenger-side window. They drove a block, stopped at another intersection.

When she spoke again, it was in a low, amused mumble. She didn't mean for him to hear, was talking to herself, and maybe not even completely aware she'd spoken aloud.

"Oh, look. My least favorite used-car lot in the whole wide world. Where's a hand grenade when you need one?"

"What?" he asked, but as he said it, he already knew and was yanking at the steering wheel, pulling the car to the curb, and jamming on the brake.

To the right of the Mustang was the vast sprawl of a car lot, brightly illuminated by sodium-vapor lights on thirty-foot-tall steel posts. They towered over the asphalt, like ranks of alien tripods, a silent invading army from another world. Lines had been strung between them, and a thousand blue and red pennants snapped in the wind, adding a carnival touch to the place. It was after 8 P.M., but they were still doing business. Couples moved among the cars, leaning toward windows to peer at price stickers pasted against the glass.

Georgia's brow furrowed, and her mouth opened in a way that suggested she was about to ask him what in the hell he thought he was doing.

"Is this his place?" Jude asked.

"What place?"

"Don't act stupid. The guy who molested you and treated you like a hooker."

"He didn't . . . It wasn't . . . I wouldn't exactly say he—"

"I would. Is this it?"

She looked at his hands clenched on the wheel, his white knuckles.

"He's probably not even here," she said.

Jude flung open the car door and heaved himself out. Cars blasted past, and the hot, exhaust-smelling slipstream snatched at his clothes. Georgia scrambled out on the other side and stared across the hood of the Mustang at him.

"Where are you goin'?"

"To look for the guy. What's his name again?"

"Get in the car."

"Who am I looking for? Don't make me go around slugging used-car salesmen at random."

"You're not goin' in there alone to beat the shit out of some guy you don't even know."

"No. I wouldn't go alone. I'd take Angus." He glanced into the Mustang. Angus's head was already sticking into the gap between the two front seats, and he was staring out at Jude expectantly. "C'mon, Angus."

The giant black dog leaped onto the driver's seat and then into the road. Jude slammed the door, started around the front of the car, the dense, sleek weight of Angus's torso pressed against his side.

"I'm not gonna tell you who," she said.

"All right. I'll ask around."

She grabbed his arm. "What do you mean, you'll ask around? What are you going to do? Start askin' salesmen if they used to fuck thirteen-year-olds?"

Then it came back to him, popped into his head without any fore-warning. He was thinking he'd like to stick a gun in the son of a bitch's face, and he remembered. "Ruger. His name was Ruger. Like the gun."

"You're going to get arrested. You're not goin' in there."

"This is why guys like him get away with it. Because people like you go on protecting them, even when they ought to know better."

"I'm not protectin' *him,* you asshole. I'm protectin' *you.*"

He yanked his arm out of her grip and started to turn back, ready to give up and already seething about it—and that was when he noticed Angus was gone.

He cast a swift look around and spotted him an instant later, deep in the used-car lot, trotting between a row of pickups and then turning and disappearing behind one of them.

"Angus!" he shouted, but an eighteen-wheeler boomed past, and Jude's voice was lost in the diesel roar.

Jude went after him. He glanced back and saw Georgia right behind him, her own face white, eyes wide with alarm. They were on a major highway, in a busy lot, and it would be a bad place to lose one of the dogs.

He reached the row of pickups where he'd last seen Angus and turned, and there he was—ten feet away, sitting on his haunches, allowing a skinny, bald man in a blue blazer to scratch him behind the ears. The bald man was one of the dealers. The tag on his breast pocket said RUGER. Ruger stood with a rotund family in promotional T-shirts, their ample bellies doing double duty as billboards. The father's gut was selling Coors Silver Bullet; the mother's breast made an unpersuasive pitch for Curves fitness; the son, about ten, had on a Hooters shirt, and probably could've fit into a C cup himself. Standing next to them, Ruger seemed almost elflike, an impression enhanced by his delicate, arched eyebrows and pointy ears with their fuzzy earlobes. His loafers had tassels on them. Jude despised loafers with tassels.

"There's a good boy," Ruger said. "Look at this good boy."

Jude slowed, allowing Georgia to catch up. She was about to go past Jude but then saw Ruger and shrank back.

Ruger looked up, beaming politely. "Your dog, ma'am?" His eyes narrowed. Then a puzzled recognition passed across his face. "It's little Marybeth Kimball, all grown up. Look at you! Are you down visiting? I heard you were in New York City these days."

Georgia didn't speak. She glanced sidelong at Jude, her eyes bright and stricken. Angus had led them right to him, as if he'd known just who they were looking for. Maybe Angus *did* know somehow. Maybe the dog of black smoke who lived inside Angus had known. Georgia began shaking her head at Jude—*No, don't*—but he paid her no mind, stepped around her, closing in on Angus and Ruger.

Ruger shifted his gaze to Jude. His face came alive with amazement and pleasure. "Oh, my God! You're Judas Coyne, the famous rock-and-roll fellow. My teenage son has every single one of your albums. I can't say I quite care for the volume he plays them at"—digging a pinkie in one ear, as if his eardrums were still ringing from just such a recent encounter with Jude's music—"but I'll tell you what, you've made quite a mark on him."

"I'm about to make quite a mark on you, asshole," Jude said, and drove his right fist into Ruger's face, heard his nose snap.

Ruger staggered, half doubled over, one hand cupping his nose. The roly-poly couple behind him parted to let him stumble past. Their son grinned and stood on his toes to watch the fight from around his father's shoulder.

Jude sank a left into Ruger's breadbasket, ignoring the burst of pain that shot through the gouge in his palm. He grabbed the car dealer as he started to drop to his knees, and threw him onto the hood of a Pontiac with a sign stuck inside the windshield: **IT'S YOURS IF YOU WANT IT!!! CHEAP!!!**

Ruger tried to sit up, and Jude grabbed him by the crotch, found his scrotum, and squeezed, felt the stiff jelly of Ruger's balls crunch in his fist. Ruger sat bolt upright and shrieked, dark arterial blood gouting from his nostrils. His trousers were hiked up, and Angus jumped, snarling, and clamped his jaws on Ruger's foot, then yanked, tearing off one of his loafers.

The fat woman covered her eyes but kept two fingers apart to peek between them.

Jude only had time to get a couple more licks in before Georgia had him by the elbow and was hauling him off. Halfway to the car she began to laugh, and as soon as they were packed back into the Mustang, she was all over him, chewing his earlobe, kissing him above his beard, shivering against his side.

Angus still had Ruger's loafer, and once they were on the interstate, Georgia traded him a Slim Jim for it, then tied it from the rearview mirror by the tassels.

"Like it?" she asked.

"Better than fuzzy dice," Jude said.

HURT

35

Jessica McDermott Price's house was in a new development, an assortment of handsome Colonials and Capes with vinyl siding in various ice-cream-shop colors—vanilla, pistachio—laid out along streets that twisted and looped in the way of intestines. They drove by it twice before Georgia spotted the number on the mailbox. Home was a Day-Glo yellow, like mango sherbet, like the caution light, and it wasn't in any particular architectural style, unless big, bland, American suburban was a style. Jude glided past it and continued down the block about a hundred yards. He turned into an unpaved driveway and rolled across dried red mud to an unfinished house.

The garage had only just been framed, beams of new pine sticking up from the cement foundation and more beams crisscrossing overhead, the roof covered in plastic sheeting. The house attached to it was only a little further along, plywood panels nailed up between the beams, with gaping rectangles to show where windows and doors belonged.

Jude turned the Mustang so the front end was facing the street and backed into the empty, doorless bay of the garage. From where they parked, they had a good view of the Price house. He switched off the engine. They sat for a while, listening to the engine tick as it cooled.

They had made good time coming south from Bammy's. It was just going on one in the morning.

"Do we have a plan?" Georgia asked.

Jude pointed across the street, at a couple large trash cans on the curb. Then he gestured down the road, toward more green plastic barrels.

"Looks like tomorrow is garbage day," Jude said. He nodded toward Jessica Price's house. "She hasn't brought her cans out yet."

Georgia stared at him. A streetlight down the road cast a wan beam of light across her eyes, which glittered, like water at the bottom of a well. She didn't say anything.

"We'll wait until she carries out the trash, and then we'll make her get in the car with us."

"Make her."

"We'll drive around awhile. We'll talk some—the three of us."

"What if her husband brings out the trash?"

"He isn't going to. He was in the reserves, and he got wiped out in Iraq. It's one of the few things Anna told me about her sister."

"Maybe she has a boyfriend now."

"If she's got a boyfriend, and he's a lot bigger than me, we wait and look for another shot. But Anna never said anything about a boyfriend. The way I heard it, Jessica was just living here with their stepdad, Craddock, and her daughter."

"Daughter?"

Jude looked meaningfully at a pink two-wheeler leaned against Price's garage. Georgia followed his gaze.

Jude said, "That's why we're not going in tonight. But tomorrow is a school day. Sooner or later Jessica is going to be alone."

"And then?"

"Then we can do what we need to do, and we don't have to worry about her kid seeing."

For a while they were both quiet. Insect song rose from the palms

and the brush behind the unfinished house, a rhythmic, inhuman pulsing. Otherwise the street was quiet.

Georgia said, "What are we gonna do to her?"

"Whatever we have to."

Georgia lowered the seat all the way back and stared into the dark at
the ceiling. Bon leaned into the front and whined urgently in her ear.
Georgia rubbed her head.

"These dogs are hungry, Jude."

"They'll have to wait," he said, staring at Jessica Price's house.

He was headachy and his knuckles were sore. He was overtired, too,
and his exhaustion made it difficult to follow any one line of reasoning
for long. His thoughts, instead, were black dogs that chased their own
tails, going around and around in maddening circles without ever getting
anywhere.

He had done some bad things in his life—putting Anna on that train,
for starters, sending her back to her kin to die—but nothing like what he
thought might be ahead of him. He wasn't sure what he would have to
do, if it would end in killing—it might end in killing—and he had Johnny
Cash in his head singing "Folsom Prison Blues," Momma told me be a
good boy, don't play with guns. He considered the gun he had left at
home, his big John Wayne .44. It would be easier to get answers out of
Jessica Price if he had the gun with him. Only, if he had the gun with
him, Craddock would've persuaded him to shoot Georgia and himself by
now, and the dogs, too, and Jude thought about guns he'd owned, and
dogs he'd owned, and running barefoot with the dogs in the hillocky
acres behind his father's farm, the thrill of running with the dogs in the
dawn light, and the clap of his father's shotgun as he fired at ducks, and
how his mother and Jude had run away from him together when Jude
was nine, only at the Greyhound his mother lost her nerve and called her
parents, and wept to them, and they told her to take the boy back to his
father and try to make peace, make peace with her husband and with
God, and his father was waiting with the shotgun on the porch when

they returned, and he smashed her in the face with the gun stock and then put the barrel on her left breast and said he'd kill her if she ever tried to run away again, and so she never ran away again. When Jude—only he was Justin then—tried to walk inside the house, his father said, "I'm not mad at you, boy, this ain't your fault," and caught him in one arm and hugged him to his leg. He bent for a kiss and said he loved him, and Justin automatically said he loved him back, a memory he still flinched from, a morally repugnant act, an act so shameful he could not bear to be the person who had done it, so he had eventually needed to become someone else. Was that the worst thing he'd ever done, planted that Judas kiss on his father's cheek while his mother bled, taken the worthless coin of his father's affection? No worse than sending Anna away, and now he was back where he'd started, wondering about tomorrow morning, wondering if he could, when he had to, force Anna's sister into the back of his car and take her away from her home and then do what needed to be done to make her talk.

Although it was not hot in the Mustang, he wiped at the sweat on his brow with the back of one arm, before it could drip into his eyes. He watched the house and the road. A police car went by once, but the Mustang was tucked well out of sight, in the shadows of the half-built garage, and the cruiser didn't slow.

Georgia dozed beside him, her face turned away. A little after two in the morning, she began fighting something in her sleep. Her right hand came up, as if she were raising it to get the attention of a teacher. She had not rebandaged it, and it was white and wrinkled, as if it had been soaking in water for hours. White and wrinkled and terrible. She began to lash at the air, and she moaned, a cringing sound of terror. She tossed her head.

He leaned over her, saying her name, and firmly but gently took one shoulder to jostle her awake. She slapped at him with her bad hand. Then her eyes sprang open, and she stared at him without recognition, gazed up with complete, blind horror, and he knew in those first few moments she was seeing not his face but the dead man's.

"Marybeth," he said again. "It's a dream. *Shh*. You're all right. You're all right now."

The fog cleared from her eyes. Her body, which was clenched up and rigid, sagged, the tension going out of it. She gasped. He brushed back some hair that was stuck to the sweat on her cheek and was appalled at the heat coming off her.

"Thirsty," she said.

He reached into the back, dug through a plastic bag of groceries they'd picked up at a gas station, found her a bottled water. Georgia unscrewed the top and drank a third of it in four big swallows.

"What if Anna's sister can't help us?" Georgia asked. "What if she can't make him go away? Are we gonna kill her if she can't make Craddock go away?"

"Why don't you just rest? We're going to be waiting awhile."

"I don't want to kill anyone, Jude. I don't want to use my last hours on earth to murder anyone."

"These aren't your last hours on earth," he said. He was careful not to include himself in that statement.

"I don't want you to kill anyone either. I don't want you to be that person. Besides, if we kill her, then we'll have two ghosts hauntin' us. I don't think I can take any more ghosts after me."

"You want some radio?"

"Promise me you won't kill her, Jude. No matter what."

He turned on the radio. Low on the FM dial, he found the Foo Fighters. David Grohl sang that he was hanging on, just hanging on. Jude turned the volume low, to the faintest of murmurs.

"Marybeth," he began.

She shivered.

"You okay?"

"I like when you call me by my real name. Don't call me Georgia anymore, okay?"

"Okay."

"I wish you didn't first see me takin' my clothes off for drunks. I wish we didn't meet in a strip club. I wish you could've known me before I started with that kind of thing. Before I got like I am. Before I did all the things I wish I could take back."

"You know how people pay more money to buy furniture that's been roughed up a little? What do they call it? Things that have been distressed? That's because something that's seen a little wear is just more interesting than something brand-new that hasn't ever had a scuff on it."

"That's me," she said. "Attractively distressed." She was shivering again, steadily now.

"How you holding up?"

"Okay," she said, voice trembling along with the rest of her.

They listened to the radio through the faint hiss of static. Jude felt himself settling, his head clearing, felt muscles he hadn't known were knotted up beginning to loosen and relax. For the moment it didn't matter what was ahead of them or what they would have to do come morning. It didn't matter what was behind them either—the days of driving, the ghost of Craddock McDermott with his old truck and his scribbled-over eyes. Jude was somewhere in the South, in the Mustang, with the seat cranked back and Aerosmith on the radio.

Then Marybeth had to ruin it.

"If I die, Jude, and you're still alive," she said, "I'm gonna try to stop him. From the other side."

"What are you talking about? You aren't going to die."

"I know. I'm just sayin'. If things don't break our way, I'll find Anna, and us girls will try and make him stop."

"You aren't going to die. I don't care what the Ouija board said or what Anna showed you in the mirror either." He had decided this very thing a few hours back down the road.

Marybeth frowned thoughtfully. "Once she started talking to us, it got cold in my room. I couldn't stop shakin'. I couldn't even feel my hand on the pointer. And then you'd ask Anna somethin', and I'd just know how she was gonna answer. What she was tryin' to say. I wasn't hearin' voices or anything. I just knew. It all made sense then, but it doesn't now. I can't remember what she wanted me to do or what she meant by bein' a door. Except . . . I think she was saying that if Craddock can come back, so can she. With a little help. And somehow I can help. It's just—and I got this loud and clear—I might have to die to do it."

"You aren't going to die. Not if I have any say in it."

She smiled. It was a tired smile. "You don't have any say in it."

He didn't know how to reply, not at first. It had crossed his mind already that there was *one* way he could assure her safety, but he wasn't about to put it into words. It had occurred to him that if *he* died, Craddock would go away and Marybeth would live. That Craddock only wanted him, maybe only had a claim on this world as long as Jude was alive. After all, Jude had bought him, paid to own him and his dead man's suit. Craddock had spent most of a week now trying to make Jude kill himself. Jude had been so busy resisting he hadn't stopped to wonder if the price of surviving would be worse than giving the dead man what he wanted. That he was sure to lose, and that the longer he held out, the more likely he would drag Marybeth with him. Because the dead pull the living down.

Marybeth stared at him, her eyes a wet, lovely ink in the dark. He stroked the hair away from her forehead. She was very young and very beautiful, her brow damp with her fever sweat. The idea that her death should precede his was worse than intolerable, it was obscene.

He slid toward her, reached and took her hands in his. If her forehead was damp and too warm, her hands were damp and too cold. He turned them over in the gloom. What he saw was a nasty sort of shock. Both of her hands were pruned up, white and shriveled, not just the right one—although the right was more terrible, the entire pad of her thumb a glistening, rotted sore and the thumbnail itself gone, dropped off. On the surface of both palms, red lines of infection followed the delicate branches of her veins, down into her forearms, where they spread out, to etch diseased-looking crimson slashes across her wrists.

"What's happening to you?" he asked, as if he didn't already know. It was the story of Anna's death, written on Marybeth's skin.

"She's a part of me somehow: Anna. I'm carryin' her around inside me. I have been for a while, I think." A statement that should've surprised but didn't. He had sensed it, on some level, that Marybeth and Anna were coming together, merging somehow. He'd heard it in the way Marybeth's accent had resurfaced, becoming so like Anna's laconic, country-girl drawl. He had seen it in the way Marybeth played with her hair now, like Anna used to. Marybeth went on, "She wants me to help her back into our world, so she can stop him. I am the doorway—she told me that."

"Marybeth," he began, then couldn't find anything else to say.

She closed her eyes and smiled. "That's my name. Don't wear it out. Actually. On second thought. Go ahead and wear it out. I like when you say it. The way you say all of it. Not just the Mary part."

"Marybeth," he said, and let go of her hands and kissed her just above the left eyebrow. "Marybeth." He kissed her left cheekbone. She shivered—pleasantly this time. "Marybeth." He kissed her mouth.

"That's me. That's who I am. That's who I want to be. Mary. Beth. Like you're gettin' two girls for the price of one. Hey—maybe you really are gettin' two girls now. If Anna's inside of me." She opened her eyes and found his gaze. "When you're lovin' me, maybe you're lovin' her, too. Isn't that a good deal, Jude? Aren't I one hell of a bargain? How can you resist?"

"Best deal I've ever had," he said.

"Don't you forget it," she said, kissing him back.

He opened the door and told the dogs to get, and for a while Jude and Marybeth were alone in the Mustang, while the shepherds lay about on the cement floor of the garage.

36

He started awake, heart beating too fast, to the sound of the dogs barking, and his first thought was, *It's the ghost. The ghost is coming.*

The dogs were back in the car, had slept in the rear. Angus and Bon stood on the backseat together, the both of them peering out the windows at an ugly yellow Labrador. The Lab stood with her back rigid and her tail up, yapping repetitively at the Mustang. Angus and Bon watched her with avid, anticipatory expressions and barked occasionally themselves, booming, harsh woofs that hurt Jude's ears in the close confines of the Mustang. Marybeth twisted in the passenger seat, grimacing, not asleep anymore, but wishing she were.

Jude told them all to shut the fuck up. They didn't listen.

He looked out the windshield and straight into the sun, a copper hole punched through the sky, a bright and merciless spotlight pointed into his face. He made a complaining sound at the glare, but before he could lift a hand to shade his eyes, a man stepped in front of the car, and his head blocked the sun.

Jude squinted at a young man wearing a leather tool belt. He was a literal redneck, skin cooked to a fine, deep shade of carmine. He frowned at

Jude. Jude waved and nodded to him and started the Mustang. When the clock on the radio face lit up, he saw it was seven in the morning.

The carpenter stepped aside, and Jude rolled out of the garage and around the carpenter's parked pickup. The yellow Lab chased them down the driveway, still yapping, then stopped at the edge of the yard. Bon woofed back at her one last time as they pulled away. Jude eased past the Price house. No one had put the garbage out yet.

He decided there was still time and drove out of Jessica Price's little corner of suburbia. He walked first Angus, then Bon, in the town square, and got tea and doughnuts at a Honey Dew Drive-Thru. Marybeth rebandaged her right hand with some gauze from the dwindling supplies in the first-aid kit. She left her other hand, which at least had no visible sores, as it was. He gassed up the car at a Mobil, and then they parked at one edge of the concrete apron and snacked. He tossed plain crullers to the dogs.

Jude steered them back to Jessica Price's. He parked on the corner, half a block from her house, on the opposite side of the street and a long walk down the road from the construction site. He didn't want to take a chance on being seen by the laborer who'd been hovering over the car when they woke up.

It was after seven-thirty, and he hoped Jessica would bring the garbage out soon. The longer they sat, the more likely they were to draw attention, the two of them in their black Mustang, dressed in their black leather and black jeans, with their visible wounds and their tattoos. They looked like what they were: two dangerous lowlifes staking out a place where they planned to commit a crime. A NEIGHBORHOOD WATCH sign on a nearby lamppost stared them in the face.

By then his blood was flowing and his head was clear. He was ready, but there was nothing to do except wait. He wondered if the carpenter had recognized him, what he would say to the other men when they arrived on-site. *I still can't believe it. This guy who looks just like Judas Coyne, sleepin' it off in the garage. Him and some amazingly hot chick. He looked so much like the real guy, I almost asked him if he was takin' requests.*

And then Jude thought that the carpenter was also one more person who could positively identify them, after they were done doing whatever it was they were about to do. It was hard to live the outlaw life when you were famous.

He wondered idly who among rock stars had spent the most time in jail. Rick James, maybe. He did—what?—three years? Two? Ike Turner had done a couple years at least. Leadbelly had been in for murder, broke rocks for ten years, then was pardoned after putting on a good show for the governor and his family. Well. Jude thought if he played his cards right, he could do more time than all three of them put together.

Prison didn't frighten him especially. He had a lot of fans in there.

The garage door at the end of Jessica McDermott Price's concrete driveway rumbled open. A weedy girl, about eleven or twelve years old, her golden hair clipped into a short, flouncy bob, hauled a garbage can down to the side of the road. The sight of her gave him a tingle of surprise, the resemblance to Anna was so close. With her strong, pointy chin, towhead, and wide-spaced blue eyes, it was as if Anna had stepped out of her childhood in the eighties and straight into the bright, full morning of today.

She left the trash can, crossed the yard to the front door, and let herself in. Her mother met her just inside. The girl left the door open, allowing Jude and Marybeth to watch mother and daughter together.

Jessica McDermott Price was taller than Anna had been, her hair a shade darker, and her mouth bracketed by frown lines. She wore a peasant blouse, with loose, frilly cuffs, and a crinkly flower-print skirt, an outfit that Jude surmised was meant to make her look like a free spirit, an earthy and empathic Gypsy. But her face had been too carefully and professionally made up, and what he could see of the house was all dark, oiled, expensive-looking furniture and seasoned wood paneling. It was the home and the face of an investment banker, not a seer.

Jessica handed her little girl a backpack—a shiny purple-and-pink thing that matched her windbreaker and sneakers as well as the bike outdoors—and air-kissed her daughter's forehead. The girl tripped out, slammed the door, and hurried over the yard, pulling the pack onto her shoulders. She was across the street from Jude and Marybeth, and on her way by she shot them a look, measuring them up. She wrinkled her nose, as if they were some litter she'd spotted in someone's yard, and then she was around the corner and gone.

The moment she was out of sight, Jude's sides began to prickle, under his arms, and he became aware of the tacky sweat gluing his shirt to his back.

"Here we go," he said.

He knew it would be dangerous to hesitate, to give himself time to think. He climbed out of the car. Angus bounded after him. Marybeth got out on the other side.

"Wait here," Jude said.

"Hell, no."

Jude walked around to the trunk.

"How we goin' in?" Marybeth asked. "Were we just gonna knock on the front door? Hi, we've come to kill you?"

He opened the trunk and pulled out the tire iron. He pointed it at the garage, which had been left open. Then he slammed the trunk and started across the street. Angus dashed ahead, came back, raced ahead again, lifted a leg, and pissed on someone's mailbox.

It was still early, the sun hot on the back of Jude's neck. He held one end of the tire iron in his fist, the socket-wrench end, and clasped the rest of it against the inner part of his forearm, trying to hide it alongside his body. Behind him a car door slammed. Bon lunged past him. Then Marybeth was at his side, short of breath and trotting to keep up.

"Jude. Jude. What if we just . . . just try and talk to her? Maybe we can . . . persuade her to help us willingly. Tell her you never . . . never wanted to hurt Anna. Never wanted her to kill herself."

"Anna didn't kill herself, and her sister knows it. That's not what this is about. Never has been." Jude glanced at Marybeth and saw she had fallen a few steps behind him, was regarding him with a look of unhappy shock. "There's always been more to this than we figured at first. I'm not so sure we're the bad guys in this story."

He walked up the driveway, the dogs loping along, one on either side of him, like an honor guard. He took a passing glance at the front of the house, at windows with white lace curtains in them and shadows behind. If she was watching them, he couldn't tell. Then they were in the gloom of the garage, where a cherry two-door convertible with a vanity plate that read HYPNOIT was parked on the clean-swept concrete floor.

He found the inside door, put his hand on the knob, tilted his head toward the house, and listened. The radio was on. The most boring voice in the world said blue chips were down, tech stocks were down, futures all across the spectrum were looking down. Then he heard heels clicking across tile, just on the other side of the door, and he instinctively leaped back, but it was too late, the door was opening and Jessica McDermott Price was coming through.

She almost walked right into him. She wasn't looking. She had her car keys in one hand and a garishly colored purse of some kind in the other. As she glanced up, Jude grabbed the front of her blouse, gathering a bunch of silky fabric in his fist, and shoved her back through the door.

Jessica reeled backward, tottering in her heels, then twisted an ankle, her foot coming out of one shoe. She let go of her small, unlikely purse. It fell at their feet, and Jude kicked it aside, kept going.

He drove her across the mudroom and into a sun-splashed kitchen in the rear of the house, and that was when her legs gave out. The blouse tore as she went down, buttons popping off and ricocheting around the room. One of them nailed Jude in the left eye—a black spoke of pain. The eye watered over, and he blinked furiously to clear it.

She slammed hard against the island in the center of the kitchen and grabbed the edge to stop her fall. Plates rattled. The counter was at her back—she was still turned to face Jude—and she reached behind her without looking and grabbed one of the plates and broke it over Jude's head as he came at her.

He didn't feel it. It was a dirty plate, and toast crusts and curds of scrambled egg went flying. Jude shot out his right arm, let the tire iron slip down, grabbed the upper end, and, holding it like a club, swatted her across her left kneecap, just below the hem of her skirt.

She dropped, as if both legs had been jerked out from under her. Started to shove herself up, and then Angus flattened her again, climbed on top of her, paws scrabbling against her chest.

"Get off her," Marybeth said, and grabbed Angus by the collar, wrenched him back so hard he flipped over, rolling in one of those faintly ridiculous doggy somersaults, his legs kicking in the air for an instant before getting up on his paws again.

Angus heaved himself at Jessica once more, but Marybeth held him back. Bon ambled into the room, shot a guilty-nervous look at Jessica Price, then stepped over pieces of shattered plate and began snarfing up a toast crust.

The droning voice on the radio, a small pink boom box on the counter, said, "Book clubs for kids are a hit with parents, who look to the written word as a place to shelter their children from the gratuitous sexual content and explicit violence that saturate video games, television programs, and movies."

Jessica's blouse was torn open to the waist. She wore a lacy peach-colored bra that left the tops of her breasts exposed, and they shuddered and fell with her breath. She bared her teeth—was she grinning?—and they were stained with blood.

She said, "If you came to kill me, you ought to know I'm not afraid of dying. My stepfather will be on the other side to receive me with open arms."

"I bet you're looking forward to that," Jude said. "I get the picture you and him were pretty close. Least until Anna was old enough and he started fucking her instead of you."

37

One of Jessica McDermott Price's eyelids twitched irregularly, a drop of sweat in her lashes, ready to fall. Her lips, which were painted the deep, almost black red of bing cherries, were still stretched wide to show her teeth, but it wasn't a grin anymore. It was a grimace of rage and confusion.

"You aren't fit to speak of him. He scraped uglier messes than you off the heel of his boot."

"You got that about half right," Jude said. He was also breathing fast, but a little surprised by the evenness of his own voice. "You both stepped in a pile when you screwed with me. Tell me something, did you help him kill her, to keep her from talking about what he did? Did you watch while your own sister bled to death?"

"The girl who came back to this house wasn't my sister. She wasn't anything like her. My sister was already dead by the time you got through with her. You ruined her. The girl who came back to us was poison inside. The things she said. The threats she made. Send our stepdaddy to prison. Send me to prison. And Craddock didn't harm a hair on her goddam disloyal head. Craddock loved her. He was the best, the best man."

"Your stepdaddy liked to fuck little girls. First you, then Anna. It was right in front of me the whole time."

He was bending over her now. He felt a little dizzy. Sunlight slashed through the windows above the sink, and the air was warm and close, smelled overpoweringly of her perfume, a jasmine-flavored scent. Just beyond the kitchen, a sliding glass door was partly open and looking out onto an enclosed back porch, floored in seasoned redwood and dominated by a table covered in a lace cloth. A gray longhaired cat was out there, watching fearfully from up on the table, fur bristling. The radio voice was droning now about downloadable content. It was like bees humming in a hive. A voice like that could hum you right to sleep.

Jude looked around at the radio, wanting to give it a whack with the tire iron, shut it off. Then he saw the photograph next to it and forgot about taking out the radio. It was an eight-by-ten picture in a silver frame, and Craddock grinned out from it. He wore his black suit, the silver-dollar-size buttons gleaming down the front, and one hand was on his fedora, as if he were about to lift it in greeting. His other hand was on the shoulder of the little girl, Jessica's daughter, who so resembled Anna, with her broad forehead and wide-set blue eyes. Her sunburned face, in the picture, was an unsmiling, unreadable blank, the face of someone waiting to get off a slow elevator, a look that was entirely empty of feeling. That expression caused the girl to resemble Anna more than anything, Anna at the height of one of her depressions. Jude found the similarity disturbing.

Jessica was squirming back over the floor, using his distraction to try to get some distance between them. He grabbed her blouse again as she pulled away, and another button flew. Her shirt was hanging off her shoulders now, open to the waist. With the back of one arm, Jude wiped at the sweat on his forehead. He wasn't done talking yet.

"Anna never came right out and said she'd been molested as a kid, but she worked so hard to avoid being asked it was kind of obvious. Then, in her last letter to me, she wrote that she was tired of keeping secrets, couldn't stand it anymore. On the face of it, sounds like a suicidal statement. It took me a while to figure out what she really meant by it, that she wanted to get the truth off her chest. About how her stepfather used to put her into trances so he could do what he liked with her. He was good—he could make her forget for a while, but he couldn't completely wipe out the memories of what he'd done. It kept resurfacing, whenever she'd have one of her emotional crack-ups. Eventually, in her teens, I guess, she tipped to it, understood what he'd been up to. Anna spent a lot of years running from it. Running from him. Only I put her on a train and sent her back, and she wound up facing him again. And saw how old he was and how close to dying. And maybe decided she didn't need to run from anything anymore.

"So she threatened to tell what Craddock did to her. Is that right? She said she'd tell everyone, get the law after him. That's why he killed her. He put her in one more trance and cut her wrists in the bath. He fucked with her head and put her in the bath and slashed her open and watched her bleed out, sat there and watched—"

"You shut up about him," Jessica said, her voice spiking, high-pitched and harsh. "That last night was awful. The things she said and did to him were awful. She spat on him. She tried to kill him, tried to shove him down the stairs, a weak old man. She threatened us, all of us. She said she was going to take Reese away from us. She said she'd use you and your money and your lawyers and send him to jail."

"He was only doing what he had to, huh?" Jude said. "It was practically self-defense."

An expression flickered across Jessica's features, there and gone so quickly Jude half thought he'd imagined it. But for an instant the corners of her mouth seemed to twitch, in a dirty, knowing, appalling sort of smile. She sat up a little straighter. When she spoke again, her tone both lectured and crooned. "My sister was sick. She was confused. She'd been suicidal for a long time. Anna cut her wrists in the bath like everyone always knew she was going to, and there isn't anyone who can say different."

"Anna says different," Jude said, and when he saw the confusion on Jessica's face, he added, "I been hearing from all kinds of dead folks lately. You know, it never did make sense. If you wanted to send a ghost to haunt me, why not her? If her death was my fault, why send Craddock? But your stepfather isn't after me because of what *I* did. It's because of what *he* did."

"Who do you think you are, anyway, calling *him* a child molester? How many years you got on that whore behind you? Thirty? Forty?"

"Take care," Jude said, hand tightening on the tire iron.

"My stepfather deserved anything he asked of us," Jessica went on, couldn't shut up now. "I always understood that. My daughter understood it, too. But Anna made everything dirty and horrible and treated him like a rapist, when he didn't do anything to Reese she didn't like. She would've spoiled Craddock's last days on this earth, just to win favor with you, to make you care about her again. And now you see where it gets you, turning people against their families. Sticking your nose in."

"Oh, my God," Marybeth said. "If she's sayin' what I think she's sayin', this is about the most wrong fuckin' conversation I ever heard."

Jude put his knee between Jessica's legs and forced her back against the floor with his bad left hand. "That's enough. I hear any more about what your stepdaddy deserved and how much he loved all of you, I'm going to puke. How do I get rid of him? Tell me how to make him go away, and we'll walk out of here, and that'll be the end of it." Saying it without knowing if it was really true.

"What happened to the suit?" Jessica asked.

"What the fuck does it matter?"

"It's gone, isn't it? You bought the dead man's suit, and now it's gone, and there's no getting rid of him. All sales are final. No returns, especially not after the merchandise has been damaged. It's over. You're dead. You and that whore with you. He won't stop until you're both in the ground."

Jude leaned forward, set the tire iron across her neck, and applied some weight. She began to choke. Jude said, "No. I do not accept that. There better be another fucking way, or— Get the fuck off me." Her hands were tugging at his belt buckle. He recoiled from her touch, drawing the tire iron off her throat, and she began to laugh.

"Come on. You already got my shirt pulled off. Haven't you ever wanted to say you fucked sisters?" she asked. "I bet your girlfriend would like to watch."

"Don't touch me."

"Listen to you. Big tough man. Big rock star. You're afraid of me, you're afraid of my father, you're afraid of yourself. Good. You ought to be. You're going to die. By your own hand. I can see the death marks on your eyes." She flicked her glance at Marybeth. "They're on you, too, honey. Your boyfriend is going to kill you before he kills himself, you know. I wish I could be there to see it happen. I'd like to see how he does it. I hope he cuts you, I hope he cuts your little hooker face—"

Then the tire iron was back across Jessica's throat and he was squeezing as hard as he could. Jessica's eyes popped open wide, and her tongue poked out of her mouth. She tried to sit up on her elbows. He slammed her back down, banging her skull on the floor.

"Jude," Marybeth said. "Don't, Jude."

He relaxed the pressure on the tire iron, allowed her to take a breath—and Jessica screamed. It was the first time she'd screamed. He pushed down again, cutting off the sound.

"The garage," Jude said.

"Jude."

"Close the door to the garage. The whole fucking street is going to hear."

Jessica raked at his face. His reach was longer than hers, and he leaned back from her hands, which were bent into claws. He rapped her skull against the floor a second time.

"You scream again, I'll beat you to death right here. I'm going to ease this thing off your throat, and you better start talking, and you better be telling me how to make him go away. What about if you communicate with him directly? With a Ouija board or something? Can you call him off yourself?"

He relaxed the pressure again, and she screamed a second time—a long, piercing note, that dissolved into a cackle of laughter. He drove a fist into her solar plexus and knocked the air out of her, shut her up.

"Jude," Marybeth said again, from behind him. She had gone to shut the garage door but was back now.

"Later."

"Jude."

"What?" he said, twisting at the waist to glare at her.

In one hand Marybeth held Jessica Price's shiny, squarish, brightly colored purse, holding it up for him to look at. Only it wasn't a purse at all. It was a lunch box, with a glossy photo of Hilary Duff on the side.

He was still staring at Marybeth and the lunch box in confusion— didn't understand why she wanted him to see it, why it mattered—when Bon began to bark, a full, booming bark that came from the deepest part of her chest. As Jude turned his head to see what she was barking at, he heard another noise, a sharp, steely click, the unmistakable sound of someone snapping back the hammer of a pistol.

The girl, Jessica Price's daughter, had entered through the sliding glass door of the porch. Where the revolver had come from, Jude didn't know. It was an enormous Colt .45, with ivory inlays and a long barrel, so heavy she could barely hold it up. She peered intently out from beneath her bangs. A dew of sweat brightened her upper lip. When she spoke, it was in Anna's voice, although the really shocking thing was how calm she sounded.

"Get away from my mother," she said.

38

The man on the radio said, "What's Florida's number one export? You might say oranges—but if you did, you'd be mistaken."

For a moment his was the only voice in the room. Marybeth had Angus by the collar again and was holding him back, no easy task. He strained forward with all his considerable will and muscle, and Marybeth had to keep both heels planted to prevent him going anywhere. Angus began to growl, a low, choked rumble, a wordless yet perfectly articulate message of threat. The sound of him got Bon barking again, one explosive yawp after another.

Marybeth was the first to speak. "You don't need to use that. We'll go. Come on, Jude. Let's get out of here. Let's get the dogs and go."

"Watch 'em, Reese!" Jessica cried. "They came here to kill us!"

Jude met Marybeth's gaze, tossed his head in the direction of the garage door. "Get out of here." He rose, one knee popping—old joints—put a hand on the counter to steady himself. Then he looked at the girl, making good eye contact, staring right over the .45 pointed into his face.

"I just want to get my dog," he said. "And we won't trouble you anymore. Bon, come here."

Bon barked, on and on, in the space between Jude and Reese. Jude took a step toward her to grab for Bon's collar.

"Don't let him get too close to you!" Jessica screamed. "He'll try and take the gun!"

"Stay back," the little girl said.

"Reese," he said, using her name to soothe and to create trust. Jude was a man who knew a thing or two about psychological persuasion himself. "I'm putting this down." He held up the tire iron so she could see it, then set it on the counter. "There. Now you have a gun and I'm unarmed. I just want my dog."

"Let's go, Jude," Marybeth said. "Bonnie will follow us. Let's just get out of here."

Marybeth was in the garage now, staring back through the doorway. Angus barked for the first time. The sound of it rang off the concrete floor and high ceiling.

"Come to me, Bon," Jude said, but Bon ignored him, actually made a nervous half jump at Reese instead.

Reese's shoulders twitched in a startled shrug. She swung the gun toward the dog for a moment, then back to Jude.

Jude took another shuffling step toward Bon, was almost close enough to reach her collar.

"Get away from her!" Jessica screamed, and Jude saw a flash of movement at the edge of his vision.

Jessica was crawling across the floor, and when Jude turned, she shoved herself to her feet and fell upon him. He saw a gleam of something smooth and white in one hand, didn't know what it was until it was in his face—a dagger of china, a wide shard of broken plate. She drove it at his eye, but he turned his head and she stabbed it into his cheek instead.

He brought his left arm up and clipped her across the jaw with one elbow. He pulled the spike of broken plate out of his face and threw it away. His other hand found the tire iron on the counter, and he swung it into the side of Jessica's neck, felt it connect with a solid, meaty thud, saw her eyes straining from their sockets.

"No, Jude, no!" Marybeth screamed.

He pivoted and ducked as she shouted. He had a glimpse of the girl, her face startled and her eyes wide and stricken, and then the cannon in her hands went off. The sound of it was deafening. A vase, filled with white pebbles and with a few waxy fake orchids sticking out of it, exploded on the kitchen counter. Splinters of glass and pieces of rock flailed through the air around him.

The little girl stumbled backward. Her heel caught on the edge of a carpet, and she almost fell. Bon jumped at her, but Reese righted herself, and as the dog hit her—crashing into her hard enough to sweep her off her feet—the gun went off again.

The bullet struck Bon low, in the abdomen, and flipped her rear end into the air, so she did a twisting, head-over-heels somersault. She slammed into the cabinet doors beneath the sink. Her eyes were turned up to show the whites, and her mouth lolled open, and then the black dog of smoke that was inside her leaped out from between her jaws, like a genie spilling from the spout of an Arabian lamp, and rushed across the room, past the little girl, out onto the porch.

The cat that was crouched on the table saw it coming and screeched, her gray hair spiking up along her spine. She dived to the right as the dog of black smoke bounded lightly onto the table. The shadow Bon took a playful snap at the cat's tail, then leaped after her. As Bon's spirit dropped toward the floor, she passed through a beam of intense, early-morning sunshine and winked out of being.

Jude stared at the place where the impossible dog of black shadow had vanished, too stunned for a moment to act, to do anything but feel. And what he felt was a thrill of wonder, so intense it was a kind of galvanic shock. He felt he had been honored with a glimpse of something beautiful and eternal.

And then he looked over at Bon's dead, empty body. The wound in her stomach was a horror show, a bloody maw, a blue knot of intestines spilling out of it. The long pink strip of her tongue hung obscenely from her mouth. It didn't seem possible that she could be blown so completely open, so it seemed she had not been shot but eviscerated. The blood was everywhere, on the walls, the cabinets, on him, spreading out across the floor in a dark pool. Bon had been dead when she hit the ground. The sight of her was another kind of galvanic shock, a jolt to his nerve endings.

Jude returned his disbelieving gaze to the little girl. He wondered if she had seen the dog of black smoke when it ran past her. He almost wanted to ask but couldn't speak, was momentarily at a loss for words. Reese sat up on her elbows, pointing the Colt .45 at him with one hand.

No one spoke or moved, and into the stillness came the droning voice on the radio: "Wild stallions in Yosemite Park are starving after months of drought, and experts fear many will die if there isn't swift action. Your mother will die if you don't shoot him. You will die."

Reese gave no sign that she heard what the man on the radio was saying. Maybe she didn't, not consciously. Jude glanced toward the radio. In the photograph next to the boom box, Craddock still stood with his hand on Reese's shoulder, but now his eyes had been blotched out with death marks.

"Don't let him get any closer. He's here to kill you both," said the radio voice. "Shoot him, Reese. Shoot him."

He needed to silence the radio, should've followed his impulse to smash it earlier. He turned toward the counter, moving a little too quickly, and his heel shot out from under him, slipping in the blood underfoot with a high-pitched squeak. He tottered and took a lunging, off-balance step back in Reese's direction. Her eyes widened in alarm as he lurched toward her. He raised his right hand, in a gesture he meant to calm, to reassure, then realized at the last instant that he was holding the tire iron and that it would look to her as if he were lifting it to swing.

She pulled the trigger, and the bullet struck the tire iron with a ringing *bong,* corkscrewed up, and took off his index finger. A hot spray of blood hit him in the face. He turned his head and gaped at his own hand, as stunned by the wonder of his vanishing finger as he'd been by the miracle of the vanishing black dog. The hand that made the chords. Almost the whole finger was gone. He was still gripping the tire iron with his remaining fingers. He let it go. It clanged to the floor.

Marybeth screamed his name, but her voice was so far away she might've been out on the street. He could barely hear it through the whine in his ears. He felt dangerously light in the head, needed to sit down. He did not sit down. He put his left hand on the kitchen counter and began backpedaling, retreating slowly in the direction of Marybeth and the garage.

The kitchen stank of burnt cordite, hot metal. He held his right hand up, pointing at the ceiling. The stump of his index finger wasn't bleeding too badly. Blood wetted his palm, dribbled down the inside of his arm, but it was a slow dribble, and that surprised him. Nor was the pain so bad. What he felt was more an uncomfortable sensation of weight, of pressure concentrated in the stump. He could not feel his slashed face at all. He glanced at the floor and saw he was leaving a trail of fat drops of blood and red boot prints.

His vision seemed both magnified and distorted, as if he wore a fishbowl on his head. Jessica Price was on her knees, clutching her throat. Her face was crimson and swollen, as if she were suffering a severe allergic reaction. He almost laughed. Who wasn't allergic to a pipe across the neck? Then he thought he'd managed to mutilate both hands in the space of barely three days and fought an almost convulsive need to giggle. He'd have to learn to play guitar with his feet.

Reese stared at him through the pall of filthy gunsmoke, her eyes wide and shocked—and somehow apologetic—the revolver on the floor next to her. He flapped his bandaged left hand at her, although what this gesture meant, even he wasn't sure. He had an idea he was trying to reassure her he was okay. He was worried about how pale she looked.

The kid was never going to be right after this, and none of it was her fault.

Then Marybeth had him by the arm. They were in the garage. No, they were out of the garage and into the white blaze of the sun. Angus put his front paws on his chest, and Jude was almost knocked flat.

"Get off him!" Marybeth screamed, but she still sounded a long distance away.

Jude really did want to sit down—right here in the driveway, where he could have the sun on his face.

"Don't," Marybeth said as he began to sink to the concrete. "No. The car. Come on." She hauled on his arm with both hands to keep him on his heels.

He swayed forward, staggered into her, got an arm over her shoulder, and the two of them reeled down the incline of the driveway, a pair of stoned teenagers at the prom, trying to dance to "Stairway." He did laugh this time. Marybeth looked at him with fright.

"Jude. You have to help. I can't carry you. We won't make it if you fall."

The need in her voice concerned him, made him want to do better. He drew a deep, steadying breath and stared at his Doc Martens. He concentrated on shuffling them forward. The blacktop underfoot was tricky stuff. He felt a little as if he were trying to walk across a trampoline while drunk. The ground seemed to flex and wobble beneath him, and the sky tilted dangerously.

"Hospital," she said.

"No. You know why."

"Got to—"

"Don't have to. I'll stop the bleeding." Who was replying to her? It sounded like his own, surprisingly reasonable voice.

He looked up, saw the Mustang. The world wheeled around him, a kaleidoscope of too-bright green yards, flower gardens, Marybeth's chalky, horrified face. She was so close that his nose was practically stuck into the dark, floating swirl of her hair. He inhaled deeply, to breathe in her sweet, reassuring scent, then flinched at the stink of cordite and dead dog.

They went around the car, and she dumped him in on the passenger side. Then she hurried around the front of the Mustang, caught Angus by the collar, and began to haul him toward the driver's-side door.

She was fumbling it open when Craddock's pickup screamed out of the garage, tires spinning on concrete, greasy smoke roiling, and Craddock behind the wheel. The truck jumped the side of the driveway and thudded across the lawn. It hit the picket fence with a crack, swatted it flat, slammed over sidewalk, banged into the road.

Marybeth let go of Angus and threw herself across the hood of the car, sliding on her belly, just before Craddock's truck nailed the side of the Mustang. The force of the impact threw Jude into the passenger-side door. The collision spun the Mustang, so the rear end swung into the road and the front was shoved up over the curb, with such suddenness that Marybeth was catapulted off the hood and thrown to earth. The pickup struck their car with a strangely plastic crunch, mixed with a piercing yelp.

Broken glass fell tinkling into the road. Jude looked and saw Jessica McDermott Price's cherry convertible in the street next to the Mustang. The truck was gone. It had never been there in the first place. The white egg of the airbag had exploded from the steering wheel, and Jessica sat holding her head in both hands.

Jude knew he should be feeling something—some urgency, some alarm—but was instead dreamy and dull-witted. His ears were plugged up, and he swallowed a few times to clear them, make them pop.

He peeled himself off the passenger-side door, looked to see what had happened to Marybeth. She was sitting up on the sidewalk. There was no reason to worry. She was all right. She looked as dazed as Jude felt, blinking in the sunlight, a wide scrape on the point of her chin and her hair in her eyes. He glanced back at the convertible. The driver's-side window was down—or had fallen into the road—and Jessica's hand hung limply out of it. The rest of her had slumped down out of sight.

Somewhere, someone began to scream. It sounded like a little girl. She was screaming for her mother.

Sweat, or maybe blood, dripped into Jude's right eye and stung. He lifted his right hand, without thinking, to wipe at it and brushed the stump of his index finger across his brow. It felt as if he had stuck his hand against a hot grill. The pain shot all the way up his arm and into his chest, where it bloomed into something else, a shortness of breath and an icy tingling behind his breastbone—a sensation both dreadful and somehow fascinating.

Marybeth walked unsteadily around the front of the Mustang and pulled the driver's-side door open with a screech of bent metal. She stood with what looked like a giant black duffel bag in her arms. The bag was dripping. No—not a duffel bag. Angus. She pulled the driver's seat forward and slung him into the back before getting in.

Jude turned as she started the car, both needing and desperately not wanting to look back at his dog. Angus lifted his head to stare at him with wet, glazed, bloodshot eyes. He whined softly. His rear legs were smashed. A red bone stuck through the fur of one of them, just above the joint.

Judas looked from Angus to Marybeth, her scraped jaw set, her lips a thin, grim line. The wraps around her dreadful, shriveled right hand were soaked through. Them and their hands. They'd be hugging each other with hooks before this was over.

"Look at the three of us," Jude said. "Aren't we a picture?" He coughed. The pins-and-needles feeling in his chest was subsiding . . . but only slowly.

"I'll find a hospital."

"No hospital. Get on the highway."

"You could die without a hospital."

"If we go to a hospital, I'm going to die for sure, and you, too.

Craddock will finish us off easy. As long as Angus is alive, we got a chance."

"What's Angus going to—"

"Craddock's not scared of the dog. He's scared of the dog *inside* the dog."

"What are you talking about, Jude? I don't understand."

"Get going. I can stop my finger bleeding. It's only one finger. Just get on the highway. Go west." He held his right hand up in the air, by the side of his head, to slow the bleeding. He was beginning to think now. Not that he needed to think to know where they were going. The only place they could go.

"What the fuck is west?" Marybeth asked.

"Louisiana," he said. "Home."

39

The first-aid kit that had accompanied them from New York was on the floor of the backseat. There was one small roll of gauze left, and pins, and Motrin in shiny, difficult-to-open pouches. He took the Motrin first, tearing the packets open with his teeth and dry-swallowing them, six in all, 1,200 milligrams. It wasn't enough. His hand still felt as if it were a lump of hot iron resting on an anvil, where it was slowly but methodically being pounded flat.

At the same time, the pain kept the mental cloudiness at bay, was an anchor for his consciousness, a tether holding him to the world of the real: the highway, the green mile-marker signs zipping past, the rattling air conditioner.

Jude wasn't sure how long he would remain clear in the head, and he wanted to use whatever time he had to explain things. He spoke haltingly, through clenched teeth, as he rolled the bandage around and around the ruined hand.

"My father's farm is just across the Louisiana line, in Moore's Corner. We can be there in less than three hours. I'm not going to bleed out in three hours. He's sick, rarely conscious. There's an old woman there, an aunt by marriage, a registered nurse. She looks after him. She's on the payroll. There's morphine. For his pain. And he'll have dogs. I think he's got— Oh, motherfucker. Oh, Mother. Fucker. Two dogs. Shepherds, like mine. Savage fuckin' animals."

When the gauze was gone, he pinned it tight with alligator clips. He used his toes to force off his boots. He pulled a sock over his right hand. He wound the other sock around his wrist and knotted it tight enough to slow, but not cut off, the circulation. He stared at the sock puppet of his hand and tried to think if he could learn to make chords without the index finger. He could always play slide. Or he could switch back to his left hand, like he'd done when he was a kid. At the thought he began to laugh again.

"Quit that," Marybeth said.

He clenched his back teeth together, forced himself to stop, had to admit he sounded hysterical, even to himself.

"You don't think she'll call the cops on us? This old auntie of yours? You don't think she'd want to get a doctor for you?"

"She's not going to do that."

"Why not?"

"We aren't going to let her."

Marybeth didn't say anything for a while after that. She drove smoothly, automatically, slipping by people in the passing lane, then sliding back into the cruising lane, keeping at a steady seventy. She held the steering wheel gingerly with her white, wrinkled, sick left hand, and she didn't touch it with the infected right hand at all.

At last she said, "How do you see all this endin'?"

Jude didn't have an answer for that. Angus replied instead—a soft, miserable whine.

40

He tried to keep an eye on the road behind them, watching for police, or the dead man's truck, but in the early afternoon Jude laid his head against the side window and closed his eyes for a moment. The tires made a hypnotic sound on the road, a monotonous *thum-thum-thum*. The air conditioner, which had never rattled before, rattled in sudden bursts. That had something of a hypnotic effect as well, the cyclical way the fans vibrated furiously and fell silent, vibrated and fell silent.

He had spent months rebuilding the Mustang, and Jessica McDermott Price had made it junk again in a single instant. She'd done things to him he thought only happened to characters in country-western songs, laying waste to his car, his dogs, driving him from his home, and making an outlaw of him. It was almost funny. And who knew that getting a finger blown off and losing half a pint of blood could be so good for your sense of humor?

No. It wasn't funny. It was important not to laugh again. He didn't want to frighten Marybeth, didn't want her thinking he was drifting out of his head.

"You're out of your head," Jessica Price said. "You aren't going anywhere. You need to calm down. Let me get something to relax you, and we'll talk."

At the sound of her voice, Jude opened his eyes.

He sat in a wicker chair, against the wall, in the dim upstairs hallway of Jessica Price's house. He'd never seen the upstairs, had not got that far into her home, but knew immediately where he was all the same. He could tell from the photographs, the large framed portraits that hung from the walls of dark-paneled hardwood. One was a soft-focus school picture of Reese, about age eight, posing in front of a blue curtain and grinning to show braces. Her ears stuck out: goofy-cute.

The other portrait was older, the colors slightly faded. It showed a ramrod-straight, square-shouldered captain who, with his long, narrow face, cerulean eyes, and wide, thin-lipped mouth, bore more than a passing resemblance to Charlton Heston. Craddock's stare in this picture was faraway and arrogant at the same time. Drop and give me twenty.

Down the corridor to Jude's left was the wide central staircase, leading up from the foyer. Anna was halfway up the steps, with Jessica close behind her. Anna was flushed, too thin, the knobs of her wrists and elbows protruding under her skin and her clothes hanging loose on her. She wasn't a Goth anymore. No makeup, no black fingernail polish, no earrings or nose rings. She wore a white tunic, faded pink gym shorts, and untied tennis sneakers. It was possible her hair hadn't been brushed or combed in weeks. She should've looked terrible, bedraggled and starved, but she wasn't. She was as beautiful now as she ever had been the summer they spent out in the barn working on the Mustang with the dogs underfoot.

At the sight of her, Jude felt an almost overwhelming throb of emotion: shock and loss and adoration all together. He could hardly bear to feel so much at once. Maybe it was more feeling than the reality around him could bear as well—the world bent at the edges of his vision, became blurred and distorted. The hall turned into a corridor out of *Alice in Wonderland*, too small at one end, with little doors only a house cat could fit through, and too big at the other, the portrait of Craddock stretching until he was life-size. The voices of the women on the stairs deepened and dragged to the point of incoherence. It was like listening to a record slow down after the record player has been abruptly unplugged.

Jude had been about to cry out to Anna, wanted more than anything to go to her—but when the world warped all out of shape, he pressed himself back into the chair, his heartbeat racing. In another moment his vision cleared, the hallway straightened out, and he could hear Anna and Jessica clearly again. He grasped, then, that the vision surrounding him was fragile and that he could not put much strain on it. It was important to be still, to take no rash action. To do and feel as little as possible; to simply watch.

Anna's hands were closed into small, bony fists, and she went up the steps in an aggressive rush, so her sister stumbled trying to keep up, catching the banister to avoid a pratfall down the staircase.

"Wait—Anna—*stop!*" Jessica said, steadying herself, then lunging up the stairs to catch at her sister's shirtsleeve. "You're hysterical—"

"No I'm not don't touch me," Anna said, all one sentence, no punctuation. She yanked her arm away.

Anna reached the landing and turned toward her older sister, who stood rigid two steps below her, in a pale silk skirt and a silk blouse the color of black coffee. Jessica's calves were bunched up, and the tendons showed in her neck. She was grimacing, and in that moment she looked old—not a woman of about thirty but one approaching fifty—and afraid. Her pallor, especially at her temples, was gray, and the corners of her mouth were pinched, webbed with crow's-feet.

"You *are.* You're imagining things, having one of your terrible fantasies. You don't know what's real and what isn't. You can't go anywhere like you are."

Anna said, "Are these imaginary?" Holding up the envelope in her hand. "These pictures?" Taking out Polaroids, fanning them in one hand to show Jessica, then throwing them at her. "Jesus! It's your daughter. She's eleven."

Jessica Price flinched from the flying snapshots. They fell on the steps, around her feet. Jude noticed that Anna still held one of them, which she shoved back into the envelope.

"I know what's real," Anna said. "First time ever, maybe."

"Craddock," Jessica said, her voice weak, small.

Anna went on, "I'm going. Next time you see me, I'll be back with his lawyers. To get Reese."

"You think *he'll* help you?" Jessica said, her voice a tremulous whisper. *He? His?* It took Jude a moment to process that they were talking about him. His right hand was beginning to itch. It felt puffy and hot and insect-bitten.

"Sure he will."

"Craddock," Jessica said again, her voice louder now, wavering.

A door popped open, down the dark hallway to Jude's right. He glanced toward it, expecting to see Craddock, but it was Reese instead. She peeked around the edge of the doorframe, a kid with Anna's pale golden hair, a long strand of it hanging across one of her eyes. Jude was sorry to see her, felt a twinge of pain at the sight of her large, stricken eyes. The things some children had to see. Still—it was not as bad as some of what had been done to her, he supposed.

"It's going to come out, Jessie. All of it," Anna said. "I'm glad. I want to talk about it. I hope he goes to jail."

"Craddock!" Jessica screamed.

And then the door directly across from Reese's room opened, and a tall, gaunt, angular figure stepped into the hallway. Craddock was a black cutout in the shadows, featureless except for his horn-rimmed spectacles, the ones he seemed to put on only every now and then. The lenses of his glasses caught and focused the available light, so they glowed, a faint, livid rose in the gloom. Behind him, back in his room, an air conditioner was rattling, a steady, cyclical buzzing sound, curiously familiar.

"What's the racket?" Craddock asked, his voice a honeyed rasp.

Jessica said, "Anna's leaving. She says she's going back to New York, back to Judas Coyne, and she's going to get his lawyers—"

Anna looked down the hall, toward her stepfather. She didn't see Jude. Of course she didn't. Her cheeks were a dark, angry red, with two spots of no color at all showing high on her cheekbones. She was shaking.

"—get lawyers, and police, and tell everyone that you and Reese—"

"Reese is right here, Jessie," Craddock said. "Calm yourself. Calm down."

"—and she . . . she found some pictures," Jessica finished lamely, glancing at her daughter for the first time.

"Did she?" Craddock said, sounding perfectly at ease. "Anna, baby. I'm sorry you're worked up. But this is no time of day to run off upset like you are. It's late, girl. It's almost nightfall. Why don't you sit down with me, and we'll talk about what's bothering you. I'd like to see if I can't put your mind at ease. You give me half a chance, I bet I can."

Anna seemed to be having trouble finding her voice all of a sudden. Her eyes were flat and bright and frightened. She looked from Craddock to Reese and finally back to her sister.

"Keep him away from me," Anna said. "Or so help me I'll kill him."

"She can't go," Jessica said to Craddock. "Not yet."

Not yet? Jude wondered what that could mean. Did Jessica think there was more to talk about? It looked to him as if the conversation was already over.

Craddock glanced sidelong at Reese.

"Go to your room, Reese." He reached out toward her as he spoke, to put a reassuring hand on her small head.

"Don't touch her!" Anna screamed.

Craddock's hand stopped moving, hung in the air, just above Reese's head—then fell back to his side.

Something changed then. In the dark of the hall, Jude could not see Craddock's features well, but he thought he detected some subtle shift in body language, in the set of his shoulders or the tilt of his head or the way his feet were planted. Jude thought of a man readying himself to grab a snake out of the weeds.

At last Craddock spoke to Reese again, without turning his gaze away from Anna. "Go on, sweetheart. You let the grown-ups talk now. It's nightfall, and it's time for the grown-ups to talk without little girls underfoot."

Reese glanced down the hall at Anna and her mother. Anna met her gaze, moved her head in the slightest of nods.

"Go ahead, Reese," Anna said. "Just grown-ups talkin'."

The little girl ducked her head back into her room and pulled her door shut. A moment later the sound of her music came in a muffled blast through the door, a barrage of drums and a screech of train-coming-off-the-tracks guitar, followed by children jubilantly shrieking in rough harmony. It was the Kidz Bop version of Jude's last Top 40 hit, "Put You in Yer Place."

Craddock jerked at the sound of it, and his hands closed into fists.

"That man," he whispered.

As he came toward Anna and Jessica, a curious thing happened. The landing at the top of the staircase was illuminated by the failing sunshine that shone through the big bay window at the front of the house, so that as Craddock approached his stepdaughters, the light rose into his face, etching fine details, the tilt of cheekbone, the deep-set brackets around his mouth. But the lenses of his spectacles darkened, hiding his eyes behind circles of blackness.

The old man said, "You haven't been the same since you came home to us from living with that man. I can't tell what's got into you, Anna darling. You've had some bad times—no one knows that better than me— but it's like that Coyne fella took your unhappiness and cranked up the volume on it. Cranked it up so loud you can't hear my voice anymore when I try and talk to you. I hate to see you so miserable and mixed up."

"I ain't mixed up, and I ain't your darlin'. And I am tellin' you, if you come within four feet of me, you'll be sorry."

"Ten minutes," Jessica said.

Craddock whisked his fingers at her, an impatient, silencing gesture.

Anna darted a look at her sister, then back to Craddock. "You are both wrong if you think you can keep me here by force."

"No one is going to make you do anything you don't want," Craddock said, stepping past Jude.

His face was seamed and his color bad, his freckles standing out on his waxy-white flesh. He didn't walk so much as shuffle, bent over with what Jude guessed was some permanent curvature of the spine. He looked better dead.

"You think Coyne is going to do you any favors?" Craddock went on. "I seem to recall he threw your ass out. I don't think he even answers your letters anymore. He didn't help you before—I don't see why he will now."

"He didn't know how. I didn't know myself. I do now. I'm gonna tell him what you did. I'm gonna tell him you belong in jail. And you know what? He'll line up the lawyers to put you there." She flicked a look at Jessica. "Her, too—if they don't put her in the nut farm. Doesn't make a difference to me, as long as they stick her a long way off from Reese."

"Daddy!" Jessica cried, but Craddock gave his head a quick shake: *Shut up*.

"You think he'll even see you? Open the door when you come knocking? I imagine he's shacked up with someone else by now. There's all sorts of pretty girls happy to lift their skirts for a rock star. It's not like you have anything to offer him he can't get elsewhere, minus the emotional headaches."

At this a look of pain flickered across Anna's features, and she sagged a little: A runner winded and sore from the race.

"It doesn't matter whether he's with someone else. He's my friend," she said in a small voice.

"He won't believe you. No one will believe you, because it just isn't true, dear. Not a word of it," Craddock said, taking a step toward her. "You're getting confused again, Anna."

"That's right," Jessica said fervently.

"Even the pictures aren't what you think. I can clear this up for you if you'll let me. I can help you if—"

But he had gone too close. Anna leaped toward him. She put one hand on his face, snatching off his round, horn-rimmed spectacles and crushing them. She placed the other hand, which still clutched the envelope, in the center of his chest and shoved. He tottered, cried out. His left ankle folded, and he went down. He fell away from the steps, not toward them—Anna had come nowhere near throwing him down the staircase, no matter what Jessica had said about it.

Craddock landed on his scrawny rear with a thud that shook the whole corridor and jarred the portrait of him on the wall out of true. He started to sit up, and Anna put her heel on his shoulder and shoved, driving him down onto his back. She was shaking furiously.

Jessica squealed and dashed up the last few steps, swerving around Anna and dropping to one knee, to be by her stepfather's side.

Jude found himself climbing to his feet. He couldn't sit still any longer. He expected the world to get bent again, and it did, distending absurdly, like an image reflected in the side of an expanding soap bubble. His head felt a long way off from his feet—miles. And as he took his first step forward, he felt curiously buoyant, almost weightless, a scuba diver crossing the floor of the ocean. As he made his way down the hall, though, he *willed* the space around him to recover its proper shape and dimensions, and it did. His will meant something, then. It was possible to move through the soap-bubble world around him without popping it, if he took care.

His hands hurt, both of them, not only the right. It felt as if they were swollen to the size of boxing gloves. The pain came in steady, rhythmic waves, beating in time with his pulse, *thum-thum-thum,* like tires on blacktop. It mingled with the rattle and buzz of the air conditioner in Craddock's room, to create an oddly soothing chorus of background nonsense sound.

He wanted desperately to tell Anna to get out, to get downstairs and out of the house. He had a strong sense, though, that he could not shove himself into the scene before him without tearing through the soft tissue of the dream. And anyway, past was past. He couldn't change what was going to happen now any more than he'd been able to save Bammy's sister, Ruth, by calling her name. You couldn't change, but you could bear witness.

Jude wondered why Anna had even come upstairs, then thought that probably she wanted to throw some clothes in a bag before she left. She wasn't afraid of her father and Jessica, didn't think they had any power over her anymore—a beautiful, heartbreaking, fatal confidence in herself.

"I told you to stay away," Anna said.

"You doin' this for him?" Craddock asked. Until this moment, he had spoken with courtly southern inflections. There was nothing courtly about his voice now, though, his accent all harsh twang, a good ol' boy with nothing good about him. "This all part of some crazy idea you have to win him back? You think you're going to get his sympathy, you go crawlin' off to him, with your sob story about how your pop made you do terrible things and it ruined you for life? I bet you can't wait to boast to him 'bout how you told me off and shoved me down, an old man who cared for you in times of sickness and protected you from yourself when you were out of your mind. You think he'd be proud of you if he was standin' here right now and saw you attack me?"

"No," Anna said. "I think he'd be proud of me if he saw this." She stepped forward and spat into his face.

Craddock flinched, then let out a strangled bellow, as if he'd caught an eyeful of some corrosive agent. Jessica started to haul herself to her feet, fingers hooked into claws, but Anna caught her by the shoulder and shoved her back down next to their stepfather.

Anna stood over them, trembling, but not as furiously as she had been a moment before. Jude reached tentatively for her shoulder, put his bandaged left hand on it, and squeezed lightly. Daring finally to touch her. Anna didn't seem to notice. Reality warped itself out of shape for an instant when his hand settled upon her, but he thought everything back to normality by focusing on the background sounds, the music of the moment: *thum-thum-thum*, rattle and hum.

"Good for you, Florida," he said. It was out before he could catch himself. The world didn't end.

Anna wagged her head back and forth, a dismissive little shake. When she spoke, her tone was weary. "And I was scared of you."

She turned, slipping out of Jude's grasp, and went down the hall, to a room at the end. She closed the door behind her.

Jude heard something go *plink,* looked down. His right hand was in the sock, soaked through with blood and dripping on the floor. The silver buttons on the front of his Johnny Cash coat flashed in the very last of the salmon-colored light of day. He hadn't noticed he was wearing the dead man's suit until just now. It really was a hell of a good fit. Jude had not wondered for one second how it was possible he could be seeing the scene before him, but now an answer to that unasked question occurred. He had bought the dead man's suit and the dead man, too— owned the ghost and the ghost's past. These moments belonged to him, too, now.

Jessica crouched beside her stepfather, the both of them panting harshly, staring at the closed door to Anna's room. Jude heard drawers opening and closing in there, a closet door thudding.

"Nightfall," Jessica whispered. "Nightfall at last."

Craddock nodded. He had a scratch on his face, directly below his left eye, where Anna had caught him with a fingernail as she tore off his glasses. A teardrop of blood trickled along his nose. He swiped at it with the back of his hand and made a red smear along his cheek.

Jude glanced toward the great bay window into the foyer. The sky was a deep, still blue, darkening toward night. Along the horizon, beyond the trees and rooftops on the other side of the street, was a line of deepest red, where the sun had only just disappeared.

"What'd you do?" Craddock asked. He spoke quietly, voice pitched just above a whisper, still tremulous with rage.

"She let me hypnotize her a couple times," Jessica told him, speaking in the same hush. "To help her sleep at night. I made a suggestion."

In Anna's room there was a brief silence. Then Jude distinctly heard a glassy *tink,* a bottle tapping against glass, followed by a soft gurgling.

"What suggestion?" Craddock asked.

"I told her nightfall is a nice time for a drink. I said it's her reward for getting through the day. She keeps a bottle in the top drawer."

In Anna's bedroom a lingering, dreadful quiet.

"What's that going to do?"

"There's phenobarbital in her gin," Jessica said. "I got her sleeping like a champ these days."

Something made a clunking sound on the hardwood floor in Anna's room. A tumbler falling.

"Good girl," Craddock breathed. "I knew you had something."

Jessica said, "You need to make her forget—the photos, what she found, *everything.* Everything that just happened. You have to make it all go away."

"I can't do that," Craddock said. "I haven't been able to do that in a long while. When she was younger . . . when she trusted me more. Maybe you . . ."

Jessica was shaking her head. "I can't take her deep like that. She won't let me—I've tried. The last time I hypnotized her, to help with her insomnia, I tried to ask her questions about Judas Coyne, what she wrote in her letters to him, and if she ever said anything to him about . . . about you. But whenever I got too personal, whenever I'd ask her something she didn't want to tell me, she'd start singing one of his songs. Holdin' me back, like. I never seen anything like it."

"Coyne did this," Craddock said again, his upper lip curling. "He ruined her. *Ruined her.* Turned her against us. He used her for what he wanted, wrecked her whole world, and then sent her back to us to wreck ours. He might as well have sent us a bomb in the mail."

"What are we going to do? There's got to be a way to stop her. She can't leave this house like she is. You heard her. She'll take Reese away from me. She'll take you, too. They'll arrest you, and me, and we'll never see each other again, except in courtrooms."

Craddock was breathing slowly now, and all the feeling had drained from his face, leaving behind only a look of dull, saturnine hostility. "You're right on one thing, girl. She can't leave this house."

It was a moment before this statement seemed to register with Jessica. She turned a startled, confused glance upon her stepfather.

"Everyone knows about Anna," he went on. "How unhappy she's always been. Everyone's always known how she was going to wind up. That she was going to slit her wrists one of these days in the bath."

Jessica began to shake her head. She made to rise to her feet, but Craddock caught her wrists, pulled her back to her knees.

"The gin and the drugs make sense. Lots of 'em knock back a couple drinks and some pills before they do it. Before they kill themselves. It's how they quiet their fears and deaden the pain," he said.

Jessica was still shaking her head, a little frantically, her eyes bright and terrified and blind, not seeing her stepfather anymore. Her breath came in short bursts—she was close to hyperventilating.

When Craddock spoke again, his voice was steady, calm. "You stop it, now. You want Anna to take Reese away? You want to spend ten years in a county home?" He tightened his hold on her wrists and drew her closer, so he was speaking directly into her face. And at last her eyes refocused on his and her head stopped wagging back and forth. Craddock said, "This isn't our fault. It's Coyne's. He's the one backed us into this corner, you hear? He's the one sent us this stranger who wants to tear us down. I don't know what happened to our Anna. I haven't seen the real Anna since I can't remember when. The Anna you grew up with is dead. Coyne saw to that. Far as I'm concerned, he finished her off. He might as well have cut her wrists himself. And he's going to answer for it. Believe it. I'll teach him to meddle with a man's family. Shh, now. Catch your breath. Listen to my voice. We'll get through this. I'm going to get you through this, same as I've got you through every other bad thing in your life. You trust in me now. Take one deep breath. Now take another. Better?"

Her blue-gray eyes were wide and avid: entranced. Her breath whistled, one long, slow exhalation, then another.

"You can do this," Craddock said. "I know you can. For Reese, you can do whatever has to be done."

Jessica said, "I'll try. But you have to tell me. You have to say what to do. I can't think."

"That's all right. I'll think for both of us," Craddock said. "And you don't need to do anything except pick yourself up and go draw a warm bath."

"Yes. Okay."

Jessica started to rise again, but Craddock tugged at her wrists, held her beside him a moment longer.

"And when you're done," Craddock said, "run downstairs and get my old pendulum. I'll need something for Anna's wrists."

At that he let her go. Jessica rose to her feet so quickly she stumbled and put a hand against the wall to steady herself. She stared at him for a moment, then turned in a kind of trance and opened a door just to her left, let herself into a white-tiled bathroom.

Craddock remained on the floor until there came the sound of water rushing into the tub. Then he helped himself to his feet and stood shoulder to shoulder with Jude.

"You old cocksucker," Jude said. The soap-bubble world flexed and wobbled. Jude clenched his teeth together, pulled it back into shape.

Craddock's lips were thin and pale, stretched back across his teeth in a bitter, ugly grimace. The old flesh on the backs of his arms wobbled. He made his slow way down to Anna's room, reeling a little—getting shoved down had taken something out of him. He pushed the door in. Jude followed at his heels.

There were two windows in Anna's room, but they both faced the back of the house, away from where the sun had gone down. It was already night in there, the room sunk into blue shadows. Anna sat at the very end of the bed, an empty tumbler on the floor between her sneakers. Her duffel bag was on the mattress behind her, some laundry hastily thrown into it, the sleeve of a red sweater hanging out. Anna's face was a pleasant blank, her forearms resting on her knees, her eyes glassy and fixed on a point in the impossible distance. The cream-colored envelope with the Polaroid of Reese in it—her evidence—was in one hand, forgotten. The sight of her that way made Jude ill.

Judas sank onto the bed beside her. The mattress creaked beneath him, but no one—not Anna, not Craddock—seemed to notice. He put his left hand over Anna's right. His left hand was bleeding again from the puncture wound, the bandages stained and loose. When had that started? He couldn't even lift the right hand, which was too heavy now and too painful. The thought of moving it made him dizzy.

Craddock paused before his stepdaughter, bent to peer speculatively into her face.

"Anna? Can you hear me? Can you hear my voice?"

She went on smiling, did not reply at first. Then she blinked and said, "What? Did you say something, Craddock? I was listening to Jude. On the radio. This is my favorite song."

His lips tightened until there was no color in them. "That man," he said again, almost spitting it. He took one corner of the envelope and jerked it out of her hands.

Craddock straightened up, turned toward one of the windows to pull down the shade.

"I love you, Florida," Jude said. The bedroom around him bulged when he spoke, the soap bubble swelling so that it threatened to explode, then shrank again.

"Love you, Jude," Anna said softly.

At this, Craddock's shoulders jumped in a startled shrug. He looked back, wondering. Then the old man said, "You and him are going to be back together soon. That's what you wanted, and that's what you'll get. I'm going to see to it. I'm going to put you two together just as soon as I can."

"Goddam you," Jude said, and this time when the room bloated and stretched itself out of shape, he couldn't, no matter how hard he concentrated on *thum-thum-thum,* make it go back the way it was supposed to be. The walls swelled and then sank inward, like bed linens hanging on a line and moving in a breeze.

The air in the room was warm and close and smelled of exhaust and dog. Jude heard a soft whining sound behind him and looked back at Angus, who lay on the bed where Anna's duffel bag had been only a moment before. His breathing was labored, and his eyes were gummy and yellow. A sharp-tipped red bone stuck through one bent leg.

Jude looked back toward Anna, only to find that it was Marybeth sitting next to him on the bed now, face dirty, expression hard.

Craddock pulled down one of the shades, and the room darkened some more. Jude glanced out the other window and saw the greenery at the side of the interstate, palms, rubbish in the weeds, and then a green sign that said EXIT 9. His hands went *thum-thum-thum.* The air conditioner hummed, buzzed, hummed. Jude wondered for the first time how he could still be hearing Craddock's air conditioner. The old man's room was all the way down the hall. Something began to click, a sound as repetitive as a metronome: the turn signal.

Craddock moved to the other window, blocking Jude's view of the highway, and he ran down that shade as well, plunging Anna's room into darkness. Nightfall at last.

Jude looked back at Marybeth, her jaw set, one hand on the wheel. The blinker signal flashed repetitively on the dash, and he opened his mouth, to say something, he didn't know what, something like . . .

41

W hat are you doin'?" His voice an unfamiliar croak. Marybeth was aiming the Mustang at an exit ramp, had almost reached it. "This ain't it."

"I was shakin' you for about five minutes, and you wouldn't wake up. I thought you were in a coma or somethin'. There's a hospital here."

"Keep going. I'm awake now."

She swerved back onto the highway at the last moment, and a horn blared behind her.

"How you doin', Angus?" Jude asked, and peeked back at him.

Jude reached between the seats and touched a paw, and for an instant Angus's gaze sharpened a little. His jaws moved. His tongue found the back of Jude's left hand and lapped at his fingers.

"Good boy," Jude whispered. "Good boy."

At last he turned away, settled back into his seat. The sock puppet on his right hand wore a red face. He was in dire need of a shot of something to dull the pain, thought he might find it on the radio: Skynyrd or, failing that, the Black Crows. He touched the power button and flipped rapidly from a burst of static to the Doppler pulse of a coded military transmission to Hank Williams III, or maybe just Hank Williams, Jude couldn't tell because the signal was so faint, and then—

Then the tuner landed on a perfectly clear broadcast: Craddock.

"I never would've thought you had so much in the tank, boy." His voice was genial and close, coming out of the speakers set in the doors. "You don't have any quit in you. That usually counts for something with me. This ain't usually, of course. You understand that." He laughed. "Anyplace will do. You know, most people like to think they don't know the meaning of the word 'quit,' but it isn't true. Most people, you put them under, put them under deep, maybe help 'em along with some good dope, sink them into a full trance state, and then tell them they're burnin' alive? They'll scream for water till they got no voice left. They'll do anything to make it stop. Anything you like. That's just human nature. But some people— children and crazy folks, mostly—you can't reason with, even when they're in a trance. Anna was both, God love her. I tried to make her forget about all the things that made her feel so bad. She was a good girl. I hated the way she tore herself up over things—even over you. But I couldn't ever really make her go all the way blank, even though it would've saved her pain. Some people would just rather suffer. No wonder she liked you. You're the same way. I wanted to deal with you quick. But you had to go and drag this out. And now you got to wonder why. You got to ask yourself. You know, when that dog in the backseat stops breathing, so do you. And it ain't going to be easy, like it could've been. You spent three days livin' like a dog, and now you have to die like one, and so does that two-dollar bitch next to you—"

Marybeth thumbed the radio off. It came right back on again.

"—you think you could turn my own little girl against me and not have to answer for it—"

Jude lifted his foot and slammed the heel of his Doc Marten into the dash. It hit with a crunch of splintering plastic. Craddock's voice was instantly lost in a sudden, deafening blast of bass. Jude kicked the radio again, shattering the face. It went silent.

"Remember when I said the dead man didn't come for talk?" Jude told her. "I take it back. Lately I been thinking that's all he came for."

Marybeth didn't reply. Thirty minutes later Jude spoke again, to tell her to get off at the next exit.

They drove on a two-lane state highway, with southern, semitropical forest growing right up to the sides of the road, leaning over it. They passed a drive-in that had been closed since Jude was a child. The giant movie screen towered over the road, holes torn in it, offering a view of the sky. This evening's feature was a drifting pall of dirty smoke. They rolled by the New South Motel, long since shut up and being reclaimed by the jungle, windows boarded over. They glided past a filling station, the first place they'd seen that was open. Two deeply sunburned fat men sat out front and watched them go by. They did not smile or wave or acknowledge the passing car in any way, except that one leaned forward and spat in the dirt.

Jude directed her to take a left off the highway, and they followed a road up into the low hills. The afternoon light was strange, a dim, poisonous red, a stormy twilight color. It was the same color Jude saw when he shut his eyes, the color of his headache. It was not close to nightfall but looked it. The bellies of the clouds to the west were dark and threatening. The wind lashed the tops of the palms and shook the Spanish moss that straggled down from low-hanging oak branches.

"We're here," he said.

As Marybeth turned into the driveway, the long run-up to the house, the wind gusted with more force than usual and threw a burst of plump, hard raindrops across the windshield. They hit in a sudden, furious rattle, and Jude waited for more, but there was no more.

The house stood at the top of a low rise. Jude had not been here in more than three decades and had not realized until this moment how closely his home in New York resembled the home of his childhood. It was as if he had leaped ten years into the future and returned to New York to find his own farm neglected and disused, fallen to ruin. The great rambling place before him was the gray color of mouse, with a roof of black shingles, many of them crooked or missing, and as they drew closer, Jude actually saw the wind snag one, strip it loose, and propel the black square away into the sky.

The abandoned chicken coop was visible to one side of the house, and its screen door swung open, then banged shut with a crack like a gunshot. The glass was missing from a window on the first floor, and the wind rattled a sheet of semitransparent plastic stapled into the frame. This had always been their destination, Jude saw now. They had been headed toward this place from the moment they took to the road.

The dirt lane that led to the house ended in a loop. Marybeth followed it around, turning the Mustang to point back the way they'd come, before putting it into park. They were both staring down the drive when the floodlights of Craddock's truck appeared at the bottom of the hill.

"Oh, God," Marybeth said, and then she was out of the Mustang, going around the front to Jude's side.

The pale truck at the foot of the drive seemed to pause for a moment, then began rolling up the hill toward them.

Marybeth jerked his door open. Jude almost fell out. She pulled on his arm.

"Get on your feet. Get in the house."

"Angus . . ." he said, glancing into the back at his dog.

Angus's head rested on his front paws. He stared wearily back at Jude, his eyes red-rimmed and wet.

"He's dead."

"No," Jude said, sure she was mistaken. "How you doin', boy?"

Angus regarded him mournfully, didn't move. The wind got into the car, and an empty paper cup scooted around on the floor, rattling softly. The breeze stirred Angus's fur, brushing it in the wrong direction. Angus paid it no mind.

It didn't seem possible that Angus could just have died like that, with no fanfare. He'd been alive only a few minutes ago, Jude was convinced of it. Jude stood in the dirt next to the Mustang, sure if he just waited another moment, Angus would move, stretch his front paws, and lift his head. Then Marybeth was hauling on his arm again, and he didn't have the strength to resist her, had to stagger along after or risk being toppled.

He fell to his knees a few feet from the front steps. He didn't know why. He had an arm over Marybeth's shoulders, and she had one looped around his waist, and she moaned through her clenched lips, dragging him back onto his heels. Behind him he heard the dead man's pickup rolling to a stop in the turnaround. Gravel crunched under the tires.

Hey, boy, Craddock called from the open driver's-side window, and at the door Jude and Marybeth stopped to look back.

The truck idled beside the Mustang. Craddock sat behind the wheel, in his stiff, formal black suit with the silver buttons. His left arm hung out the window. His face was hard to make out through the blue curve of glass.

This your place, son? Craddock said. He laughed. *How could you ever stand to leave?* He laughed again.

The razor shaped like a crescent moon fell from the hand hanging out the window, and swung from its gleaming chain.

You're gonna cut her throat. And she's goin' to be glad when you do. Just to have it over with. You should've stayed away from my little girls, Jude.

Jude turned the doorknob, and Marybeth shouldered it inward, and they crashed through into the dark of the front hall. Marybeth kicked the door shut behind them. Jude threw a last glance out the window beside the door—and the truck was gone. The Mustang stood alone in the drive. Marybeth turned him and shoved him into motion again.

They started down the corridor, side by side, each holding the other up. Her hip caught a side table and overturned it, and it smashed to the floor. A phone that had been sitting on it toppled to the boards, and the receiver flew off the cradle.

At the end of the hall was a doorway, leading into the kitchen, where the lights were on. It was the only source of light they'd seen so far in the entire house. From the outside the windows had been dark, and once they were in, it was shadows in the front hall and a cavernous gloom waiting at the top of the stairs.

An old woman, in a pastel flower-print blouse, appeared in the kitchen doorway. Her hair was a white frizz, and her spectacles magnified her blue, amazed eyes to appear almost comically large. Jude knew Arlene Wade at a glance, although he could not have said how long it had been since he'd last seen her. Whenever it had been, she'd always been just as she was now—scrawny, perpetually startled-looking, old.

"What is this business?" she called out. Her right hand reached up to curl around the cross that hung at her throat. She stepped back as they reached the doorway to let them by. "My God, Justin. What in the name of Mary and Joseph happened to you?"

The kitchen was yellow. Yellow linoleum, yellow tile countertops, yellow-and-white-check curtains, daisy-patterned plates drying in the basket next to the sink, and as Jude took it all in, he heard that song in his head, the one that had been such a smash for Coldplay a few years before, the one about how everything was all yellow.

He was surprised, given the way the house looked from the outside, to find the kitchen so full of lively color, so well kept up. It had never been this cozy when he'd been a child. The kitchen was where his mother had spent most of her time, watching daytime TV in a stupor while she peeled potatoes or washed beans. Her mood of numb, emotional exhaustion had drained the color from the room and made it a place where it seemed important to speak in quiet voices, if at all, a private and unhappy space that you could no more run through than you could make a ruckus in a funeral parlor.

But his mother was thirty years dead, and the kitchen was Arlene Wade's now. She had lived in the house for more than a year and very likely passed most of her waking hours in this room, which she'd warmed with the everyday business of being herself, an old woman with friends to talk to on the phone, pies to bake for relatives, a dying man to care for. In fact, it was a little *too* cozy. Jude felt dizzy at the warmth of it, at the suddenly close air. Marybeth turned him toward the kitchen table. He felt a bony claw sink into his right arm, Arlene grabbing his biceps, and was surprised at the rigid strength in her fingers.

"You got a sock on your hand," she said.

"He got one of his fingers taken off," Marybeth said.

"What are you doing here, then?" Arlene asked. "Shoulda drove him to the hospital."

Jude fell into a chair. Curiously, even sitting still, he felt as if he were still moving, the walls of the room sliding slowly past him, the chair gliding forward like a car in a theme-park amusement: *Mr. Jude's Wild Ride*. Marybeth sank into a chair next to him, her knees bumping his. She was shivering. Her face was oiled in sweat, and her hair had gone crazy, was snarled and twisted. Strands stuck to her temples, to the sweat on the sides of her face, to the back of her neck.

"Where are your dogs?" Marybeth asked.

Arlene began to untie the sock wound around Jude's wrist, peering down her nose at it through the magnifying lenses of her glasses. If she found this question bizarre or startling, she showed no sign of it. She was intent on the work of her hands.

"My dog is over there," she said, nodding at one corner of the room. "And as you can see, he's quite protective of me. He's a fierce old boy. Don't want to cross him."

Jude and Marybeth looked to the corner. A fat old rottweiler sat on a dog pillow in a wicker basket. He was too big for it, and his pink, hairless ass hung over the side. He weakly lifted his head, regarded them through rheumy, bloodshot eyes, then lowered his head again and sighed softly.

"Is that what happened to this hand?" Arlene asked. "Were you bit by a dog, Justin?"

"What happened to my father's shepherds?" Jude asked.

"He hasn't been up to takin' care of a dog for a while now. I sent Clinton and Rather off to live with the Jeffery family." Then she had the sock off his hand and drew a sharp breath when she saw the bandage beneath.

It was soaked—saturated—with blood. "Are you in some kinda stupid race with your daddy to see who can die first?" She set his hand on the table without unwrapping the bandages to see more. Then she glanced at Jude's bandaged left hand. "You missin' any parts off that one?"

"No. That one I just gouged real good."

"I'll get you the ambulance," Arlene said. She had lived in the South her whole life and she pronounced the word *amble-lance*.

She picked up the phone on the kitchen wall. It made a noisy, repetitive blatting at her, and she jerked her ear away from the receiver, then hung up.

"You crashed my phone off the hook in the hall," she said, and disappeared into the front of the house to right it.

Marybeth stared at Jude's hand. He lifted it—discovered he had left a wet red handprint on the table—and put it weakly back down.

"We shouldn't have come here," she said.

"Nowhere else to go."

She turned her head, looked at Arlene's fat rottie. "Tell me he's gonna help us."

"Okay. He's going to help us."

"You mean it?"

"No."

Marybeth questioned him with a glance.

"Sorry," Jude said. "I might've misled you a bit 'bout the dogs. Not just any dogs will do. They have to be mine. You know how every witch has a black cat? Bon and Angus were like that for me. They can't be replaced."

"When did you figure that out?"

"Four days ago."

"Why didn't you tell me?"

"I was hoping to bleed to death before Angus went and croaked on us. Then you'd be okay. Then the ghost would have to leave you alone. His business with us would be done. If my head was clearer, I wouldn't have bandaged myself up so well."

"You think it'll make it okay if you let yourself die? You think it'll make it okay to give him what he wants? Goddam you. You think I came all this way to watch you kill yourself? *Goddam* you."

Arlene stepped back through the kitchen doorway, frowning, eyebrows knitted together in a look of annoyance or deep thought or both.

"There's somethin' wrong with that phone. I can't get a dial tone. All I do get, when I pick up, is some local AM station. Some farm program. Guy chatterin' about how to cut open animals. Maybe the wind yanked down a line."

"I have a cell phone—" Marybeth began.

"Me, too," Arlene said. "But we don't get no reception up in these parts. Let's get Justin laid down, and I'll see what I can do for his hand right now. Then I'll drive down the road to the McGees and call from there."

Without any forewarning she reached between them and snatched at Marybeth's wrist, lifting her own bandaged hand for a moment. The wraps were stiff and brown with the dried bloodstains on them.

"What the hell have you two been doin'?" she asked.

"It's my thumb," Marybeth said.

"Did you try to trade it to him for his finger?"

"It's just got an infection."

Arlene set the bandaged hand down and looked at the unbandaged left hand, terribly white, the skin wrinkled. "I never seen any infection like this. It's in both hands—is it anywhere else?"

"No."

She felt Marybeth's brow. "You're burnin' up. My God. The both of you. You can rest in my room, honey. I'll put Justin in with his father. I shoved an extra bed in there two weeks ago, so I could nap in there and keep a closer eye on him. Come on, big boy. More walkin' to do. Get yourself up."

"If you want me to move, you better get the wheelbarrow and roll me," Jude said.

"I got morphine in your daddy's room."

"Okay," Jude said, and he put his left hand on the table and struggled to get to his feet.

Marybeth jumped up and took his elbow.

"You stay where you are," Arlene said. She nodded in the direction of her rottweiler and the door beyond, which opened into what had once been a sewing room but was now a small bedroom. "Go on and rest in there. I can handle this one."

"It's all right," Jude said to Marybeth. "Arlene's got me."

"What are we gonna do about Craddock?" Marybeth asked.

She was standing almost against him, and Jude leaned forward and put his face in her hair and kissed the crown of her head.

"I don't know," Jude said. "I wish like hell you weren't in this with me. Why didn't you get away from me when you still had the chance? Why you got to be such a stubborn ass about things?"

"I been hangin' around you for nine months," she said, and stood on tiptoe and put her arms around his neck, her mouth searching for his. "I guess it just rubbed off on me."

And then for a while they stood rocking back and forth in each other's arms.

42

When Jude stepped away from Marybeth, Arlene turned him around and started him walking. He expected her to march him back down the front hall, so they could go upstairs to the master bedroom, where he assumed his father lay. Instead, though, they continued along the length of the kitchen to the back hall, the one that led to Jude's old bedroom.

Of course his father was there, on the first floor. Jude vaguely recalled that Arlene had told him, in one of their few phone conversations, that she was moving Martin downstairs and into Jude's old bedroom, because it was easier than going up and down the stairs to tend to him.

Jude cast one last look back at Marybeth. She was watching him go, from where she stood in the doorway of Arlene's bedroom, her eyes fever-bright and exhausted—and then Jude and Arlene were moving away, leaving her behind. He didn't like the idea of being so far from Marybeth in the dark and decayed maze of his father's house. It did not seem too unreasonable to think that they might never find their way back to each other.

The hall to his room was narrow and crooked, the walls visibly warped. They passed a screen door, the frame nailed shut, the screens rusty and bellied outward. It looked into a muddy hog pen, three medium-size pigs in it. The pigs peered at Jude and Arlene as they went by, their squashed-in faces benevolent and wise.

"There's still pigs?" Jude said. "Who's carin' for them?"

"Who do you think?"

"Why didn't you sell them?"

She shrugged, then said, "Your father took care of pigs all his life. He can hear them in where he's layin'. I guess I thought it would help him know where he was. Who he was." She looked up in Jude's face. "You think I'm foolish?"

"No," Jude said.

Arlene eased the door to Jude's old bedroom inward, and they stepped into a suffocating warmth that smelled so strongly of menthol it made Jude's eyes water.

"Hang on," Arlene said. "Lemme move my sewin'."

She left him leaning against the doorway and hastened to the little bed against the wall, to the left. Jude looked across the room to an identical cot. His father was in it.

Martin Cowzynski's eyes were narrow slits, showing only glazed slivers of eyeball. His mouth yawned open. His hands were gaunt claws, curled against his chest, the nails crooked, yellow, sharp. He had always been lean and wiry. But he had lost, Jude guessed, maybe a third of his weight, and there was barely a hundred pounds of him left. He looked like he was already dead, although breath yet whined in his throat. There were streaks of white foam on his chin. Arlene had been shaving him. The bowl of hand-whipped foam was on the night table, a wood-handled brush sitting in it.

Jude had not seen his father in thirty-four years, and the sight of him—starved, hideous, lost in his own private dream of death—brought on a fresh wave of dizziness. Somehow it was more horrible that Martin was breathing. It would've been easier to look upon him, as he was now, if he were dead. Jude had hated him for so long that he was unprepared for any other emotion. For pity. For horror. Horror was rooted in sympathy, after all, in understanding what it would be like to suffer the worst. Jude had not imagined he could feel either sympathy or understanding for the man in the bed across the room.

"Can he see me standing here?" Jude asked.

Arlene looked over her shoulder at Jude's father.

"Doubt it. He hasn't responded to the sight of anything in days. Course it's been months since he could talk, but until just a little while ago he did sometimes make faces or give a sign when he wanted something. He enjoyed when I shaved him, so I still do that ever' day. He liked the hot water on his face. Maybe some part of him still likes it. I don't know." She paused, considering the gaunt, rasping figure in the far bed. "It's sorry to see him die this way, but it's worse to keep a man going after a certain point. I believe that. There comes a time, the dead have a right to claim their own."

Jude nodded. "The dead claim their own. They do."

He looked at what Arlene held in her hands, the sewing kit she was moving off the other cot. It was his mother's old kit, a collection of thimbles, needles, and thread, jumbled in one of the big yellow heart-shaped candy boxes his father used to get for her. Arlene squeezed the lid on it, closing it up, and set it on the floor between the cots. Jude eyed it warily, but it didn't make any threatening moves.

Arlene returned and guided him by the elbow to the empty bed. There was a light on a mechanical arm, screwed to the side of the night table. She twisted the lamp around—it made a sproingy, creaking sound as the rusted coil stretched itself out—and clicked it on. He shut his eyes against the sudden brightness.

"Let's look at that hand."

She brought a low stool to the side of the bed and began to unwind the sopping gauze, using a pair of forceps. As she peeled the last layer away from his skin, a flush of icy tingling spread through his hand, and then the missing finger began, impossibly, to burn, as if it were crawling with biting fire ants.

She stuck a needle into the wound, injecting him here, and here, while he cursed. Then came a rush of intense and blessed cold, spreading through the hand and into his wrist, pumping along the veins, turning him into an iceman.

The room darkened, then brightened. The sweat on his body cooled rapidly. He was on his back. He didn't remember lying down. He distantly felt a tugging on his right hand. When he realized that this tugging was Arlene doing something to the stump of his finger—clamping it, or putting hooks through it, or stitching it—he said, "Gonna puke." He fought the urge to gag until she could place a rubber trough next to his cheek, then turned his head and vomited into it.

When Arlene was finished, she laid his right hand on his chest. Wrapped in layer upon layer of muffling bandage, it was three times the size it had been, a small pillow. He was groggy. His temples thudded. She turned the harsh, bright light into his eyes again and leaned over for a look at the slash in his cheek. She found a wide, flesh-colored bandage and carefully applied it to his face.

She said, "You been leakin' pretty good. Do you know what type of motor oil you run on? I'll make sure the amble-lance brings the right stuff."

"Check on Marybeth. Please."

"I was going to."

She clicked off the light before she went. It was a relief to be joined to darkness once more.

He closed his eyes, and when they sprang open again, he did not know whether one minute had passed or sixty. His father's house was a place of restful silence and stillness, no sound but for the sudden whoosh of the wind, lumber creaking, a burst of rain on the windows. He wondered if Arlene had gone for the amble-lance. He wondered if Marybeth was sleeping. He wondered if Craddock was in the house, sitting outside the door. Jude turned his head and found his father staring at him.

His father's mouth hung agape, the few teeth that were left stained brown from nicotine exposure, the gums diseased. Martin stared, pale gray eyes confused. Four feet of bare floor separated the two men.

"You aren't here," Martin Cowzynski said, his voice a wheeze.

"Thought you couldn't talk," Jude said.

His father blinked slowly. Gave no sign he'd heard. "You'll be gone when I wake up." His tone was almost wishful. He began to cough weakly. Spit flew, and his chest seemed to go hollow, sinking inward, as if with each painful hack he were coughing up his insides, beginning to deflate.

"You got that wrong, old man," Jude told him. "You're my bad dream, not the other way around."

Martin continued staring at him with that look of stupid wonder for a few moments longer, then turned his gaze to the ceiling once more. Jude watched him warily, the old man in his army cot, breath screaming from his throat, dried streaks of shaving cream on his face.

His father's eyes gradually sank shut. In a while Jude's eyes did the same.

43

He wasn't sure what woke him, but later on Jude looked up, coming out of sleep in an instant, and found Arlene at the foot of the bed. He didn't know how long she'd been standing there. She was wearing a bright red rain slicker with the hood pulled up. Droplets of rain glittered on the plastic. Her old, bony face was set in a blank, almost robotic expression that Jude did not at first recognize and which he needed several moments to interpret as fear. He wondered if she'd gone and come back or not yet left.

"We lost the power," she said.

"Did we?"

"I went outside, and when I came back in, we lost the power."

"Uh-huh."

"There's a truck in the driveway. Just settin' there. Sort of no particular color. I can't see who is settin' in it. I started to walk out to it, to see if it was someone who could maybe drive somewhere and call emergency for us—but then I got scared. I got scared of who was in it, and I came back."

"You want to stay away from him."

She went on as if Jude had said nothing. "When I got back inside, we didn't have power, and it's still just some crazy talk radio on the telephone. Bunch of religious stuff about ridin' the glory road. The TV was turned on in the front room. It was just runnin'. I know it couldn't be, because there isn't any power, but it was turned on anyway. There was a story on it. On the news. It was about you. It was about all of us. About how we was all dead. It showed a picture of the farmhouse and everythin'. They were coverin' my body with a sheet. They didn't identify me, but I saw my hand stickin' out and my bracelet. And policemen standin' ever'where. And that yellow tape blockin' the driveway. And Dennis Woltering said how you killed us all."

"It's a lie. None of that is really going to happen."

"Finally I couldn't stand it. I shut it off. The TV came right back on, but I shut it off again and jerked the plug out of the wall, and that fixed it." She paused, then added, "I have to go, Justin. I'll call for the ambelance from the neighbors. I have to go. . . . Only I'm scared to try and drive around that truck. Who drives the pale truck?"

"No one you want to meet. Take my Mustang. The keys are in it."

"No thank you. I seen what was in the back."

"Oh."

"I got my car."

"Just don't mess with that truck. Drive right over the lawn and through the fence if you have to. Do what you need to do to stay away from it. Did you look in on Marybeth?"

Arlene nodded.

"How is she?"

"Sleepin'. Poor child."

"You said it."

"Good-bye, Justin."

"Take care."

"I'm bringin' my dog with me."

"All right."

She took a sliding half step toward the door.

Then Arlene said, "Your uncle Pete and I took you to Disney when you were seven. Do you remember?"

"I'm afraid I don't."

"In your whole life, I never once saw you smile until you were up in them elephants, goin' 'round and 'round. That made me feel good. When I saw you smile, it made me feel like you had a chance to be happy. I was sorry about how you turned out. So miserable. Wearin' black clothes and sayin' all them terrible things in your songs. I was sick to death for you. Wherever did that boy go, the one who smiled on the elephant ride?"

"He starved to death. I'm his ghost."

She nodded and backed away. Arlene raised one hand in a gesture of farewell, then turned and was gone.

Afterward Jude listened intently to the house, to the faint straining sounds it made in the wind and the splatter of the rain falling against it. A screen door banged sharply somewhere. It might have been Arlene leaving. It might have been the door swinging on the chicken coop outside.

Beyond a feeling of gritty heat in the side of his face, where Jessica Price had cut him, he was not in great pain. His breathing was slow and regular. He stared at the door, waiting for Craddock to appear. He didn't look away from the door until he heard a soft tapping sound off to his right.

He peered over. The big yellow heart-shaped box sat on the floor. Something thumped inside. Then the box moved, as if jolted from beneath. It titched a few inches across the floor and jumped again. The lid was struck from within once more, and one corner was knocked up and loose.

Four gaunt fingers slipped out from inside the box. Another thump and the lid came free and then began to rise. Craddock pulled himself up from inside the box, as if it were a heart-shaped hole set in the floor. The lid rode on top of his head, a gay and foolish hat. He removed it, cast it aside, then hitched himself out of the box to the waist in a single, surprisingly athletic move for a man who was not only elderly but dead. He got a knee on the floor, climbed the rest of the way out, and stood up. The creases in the legs of his black trousers were perfect.

In the pen outside, the pigs began to shriek. Craddock reached a long arm back into the bottomless box, felt around, found his fedora, and set it on his head. The scribbles danced before his eyes. Craddock turned and smiled.

"What kept you?" Jude asked.

44

Here we are, you and me. All out of road, the dead man said. His lips were moving but making no sound, his voice existing only in Jude's head. The silver buttons on his black suit coat glinted in the darkness.

"Yeah," Jude said. "The fun had to stop sometime."

Still full of fight. Isn't that somethin'? Craddock placed one gaunt hand on Martin's ankle and ran it over the sheet and up his leg. Martin's eyes were closed, but his mouth hung open and breath still came and went in thin, pneumatic whistles. *A thousand miles later, and you're still singin' the same song.*

Craddock's hand glided over Martin's chest. It was something he seemed to be doing almost absentmindedly, did not once look at the old man fighting for his last breaths in the bed beside him.

I never did like your music. Anna used to play it so loud it'd make a normal person's ears bleed. You know there's a road between here and hell? I've driven it myself. Many times now. And I'll tell you what, out on that road there's only one station, and all they play is your music. I guess that's the devil's way of gettin' straight to punishin' the sinners. He laughed.

"Leave the girl."

*Oh, no. She's going to sit right between us while we ride the nightroad.
She's come so far with you already. We can't leave her behind now.*

"I'm telling you Marybeth doesn't have any part in this."

*But you don't tell me, son. I tell you. You're going to choke her to death,
and I'm going to watch. Say it. Tell me how it's going to be.*

Jude thought, *I won't,* but while he was thinking it, he said, "I'm going
to choke her. You're going to watch."

Now you're singin' my kind of music.

Jude thought of the song he'd made up the other day, at the motel in
Virginia, how his fingers had known where the right chords were and the
feeling of stillness and calm that had come over him as he played them.
A sensation of order and control, of the rest of the world being far away,
kept back by his own invisible wall of sound. What had Bammy said to
him? The dead win when you quit singing. And in his vision Jessica Price
had said Anna would sing when she was in a trance, to keep from being
made to do things she didn't want to do, to block out voices she didn't
want to hear.

Get up, the dead man said. *Stop lazin' around, now. You have business
in the other room. The girl is waitin'.*

Jude wasn't listening to him, though. He was focused intently on
the music in his head, hearing it as it would sound when it had been
recorded with a band, the soft clash of cymbal and snare, the deep, slow
pulse of the bass. The old man was talking at him, but Jude found that
when he fixed his mind on his new song, he could ignore him almost
completely.

He thought of the radio in the Mustang, the old radio, the one he'd
pulled out of the dash and replaced with XM and a DVD-Audio disc
player. The original radio had been an AM receiver with a glass face that
glowed an unearthly shade of green and lit up the cockpit of the car like
the inside of an aquarium. In his imagination Jude could hear his own
song playing from it, could hear his own voice crying out the lyrics over
the shivery, echo-chamber sound of the guitar. That was on one station.

The old man's voice was on another, buried beneath it, a faraway, southern, late-night, let's-hear-it-for-Jesus, talk-all-the-time station, the reception no good, so all that came through was a word or two at a time, the rest lost in waves of static.

Craddock had told him to sit up. It was a moment before Jude realized he hadn't done it.

Get on your feet, I said.

Jude started to move—then stopped himself. In his mind he had the driver's seat cranked back and his feet out the window and it was his song on the radio and the crickets hummed in the warm summer darkness. He was humming himself, and in the next moment he realized it. It was a soft, off-key humming, but recognizable, nonetheless, as the new song.

Do you hear me talkin' to you, son? the dead man asked. Jude could tell that was what he said, because he saw his lips moving, his mouth shaping the words very clearly. But in fact Jude could not really hear him at all.

"No," Jude said.

Craddock's upper lip drew back in a sneer. He still had one hand on Jude's father—it had moved up over Martin's chest and now rested on his neck. The wind roared against the house, and raindrops rapped at the windowpanes. Then the gust abated, and in the hush that followed, Martin Cowzynski whimpered.

Jude had briefly forgotten his father—Jude's thoughts pinned on the echoing loops of his own imagined song—but the sound drew his gaze. Martin's eyes were open, wide and staring and horrified. He was gazing up at Craddock. Craddock turned his head toward him, the sneer fading, his gaunt and craggy face composing itself into an expression of quiet thought.

At last Jude's father spoke, his voice a toneless wheeze. "It's a messenger. It's a messenger of death."

The dead man seemed to look back at Jude, the black marks boiling in front of his eyes. Craddock's lips moved, and for a moment his voice wavered and came clear, muted but audible beneath the sound of Jude's private, inner song.

Maybe you can tune me out, Craddock said. *But he can't.*

Craddock bent over Jude's father and put his hands on Martin's face, one on each cheek. Martin's breath began to hitch and catch, each inhalation short, quick, and panicked. His eyelids fluttered. The dead man leaned forward and placed his mouth over Martin's.

Jude's father pressed himself back into his pillow, shoved his heels down into the bed, and pushed, as if he could force himself deeper into the mattress and away from Craddock. He drew a last, desperate breath—and sucked the dead man into him. It happened in an instant and was like watching a magician pull a scarf through his fist to make it disappear. Craddock *crumpled,* a wad of Saran Wrap sucked up into the tube of a vacuum cleaner. His polished black loafers were the last thing to go down Martin's throat. Martin's neck seemed, for a moment, to distend and swell—bulging the way a snake will bulge after swallowing a gerbil—but then he gulped Craddock down, and his throat shrank back to its normal, scrawny, loose-fleshed shape.

Jude's father gagged, coughed, gagged again. His hips came up off the bed, his back arching. Jude could not help it, thought immediately of orgasm. Martin's eyes strained from their sockets. The tip of his tongue flickered between his teeth.

"Spit it up, Dad," Jude said.

His father didn't seem to hear. He sank back into the bed, then bucked again, almost as if someone were sitting on top of him and Martin was trying to throw him off. He made wet, strangled sounds down in his throat. A blue artery stood out in the center of his forehead. His lips stretched back from his teeth in a doglike grimace.

Then he eased gently down onto the mattress once more. His hands, which had been clutching fistfuls of the sheets, slowly opened. His eyes were a vivid, hideous crimson—the blood vessels had erupted, staining the whites red. They stared blankly at the ceiling. Blood stained his teeth.

Jude watched him for movement, straining for some sound of breath. He heard the house settling in the wind. He heard rain spitting against the wall.

With great effort Jude sat up, then turned himself to set his feet on the floor. He had no doubt his father was dead, he who had smashed Jude's hand in the cellar door and put a single-barreled shotgun to his mother's breast, who had ruled this farmhouse with his knuckles and belt strap and laughing rages, and whom Jude had often daydreamed of killing himself. It had cost him something, though, to watch Martin die. Jude's abdomen was sore, as if he had only just vomited again, as if something had been forced out of him, ejected from his body, something he didn't want to give up. Rage, maybe.

"Dad?" Jude said, knowing no one would answer.

Jude rose to his feet, swaying, light-headed. He took a shuffling, old man's step forward, put his bandaged left hand on the edge of the night table to support himself. It felt as if his legs might fold beneath him at any moment.

"Dad?" Jude said again.

His father jerked his head toward him and fixed his red, awful, fascinated eyes on Jude.

"Justin," he said, his voice a strained whisper. He smiled, a horrifying thing to see upon his gaunt, harrowed face. *"My boy. I'm all right. I'm fine. Come close. C'mon and put your arms around me."*

Jude did not step forward but took a staggering, unsteady step back. For a moment he had no air.

Then his breath returned, and he said, "You aren't my father."

Martin's lips widened to show his poisoned gums and crooked yellow teeth, what were left of them. A teardrop of blood spilled from his left eye, ran in a jagged red line down the crag of his cheekbone. Craddock's eye had seemed to drip red tears in almost just the same way, in Jude's vision of Anna's final night.

He sat up and reached past the bowl of shaving lather. Martin closed his hand on his old straight razor, the one with the hickory handle. Jude hadn't known it was there, hadn't seen it lying behind the white china bowl. Jude took another step away. The backs of his legs struck the edge of his cot, and he sat down on the mattress.

Then his father was up, the sheet slithering off him. He moved more quickly than Jude expected, like a lizard, frozen in place one moment, then lurching forward, almost too quick for the eye to follow. He was naked, except for a pair of stained white boxers. His breasts were little trembling sacks of flab, furred with curling, snow-white hairs. Martin stepped forward, planted his heel on the heart-shaped box, crushed it flat.

"Come here, son," his father said, in Craddock's voice. *"Daddy's going to show you how to shave."*

And he snapped his wrist, and the razor flipped out of the handle, a mirror in which Jude was briefly able to see his own astonished face.

Martin lunged at Jude, slashing at him with the straight razor, but Jude stuck out his foot, jammed it between the old man's ankles. At the same time, he pitched himself to the side with an energy he didn't know he had in him. Martin fell forward, and Jude felt the razor whicker through his shirt and the biceps beneath, with what seemed no resistance at all. Jude rolled over the rusted steel bar at the foot of his cot and crashed to the floor.

The room was almost silent except for their harsh gasps for breath and the shrieking of the wind under the eaves. His father scrambled to the end of the bed and leaped over the side—spry for a man who had suffered multiple strokes and not left his bed in three months. By then Jude was crawling backward, out the door.

He made it halfway down the hall, as far as the screen door that looked into the pigpen. The hogs crowded against it, jostling for the best view of the action. Their squeals of excitement drew his attention for a moment, and when he looked back, Martin was standing over him.

His father dropped onto him. He cocked his arm back to slash the razor across Jude's face. Jude forgot himself and drove his bandaged right hand up into his father's chin, hard enough to snap the old man's head back. Jude screamed. A white-hot charge of pain stabbed through his ruined hand and raced up into his forearm, a sensation like an electrical pulse traveling right through the bone, withering in its intensity.

He caught his father flush and drove him into the screen door. Martin hit it with a splintering crunch and the tinny sound of springs snapping free. The lower screen tore clean out, and Martin fell through it. The pigs scattered. There were no steps below the door, and Martin dropped two feet, out of sight, hitting the ground with a dry thud.

The world wavered, darkened, almost disappeared. *No*, Jude thought, *no no no*. He struggled back toward consciousness, like a man pulled deep underwater, churning toward the surface before he ran out of breath.

The world brightened again, a drop of light that widened and spread, blurred gray ghost shapes appearing before him, then coming gradually into focus. The hall was still. Pigs grunted outside. An ill sweat cooled on Jude's face.

He rested awhile, ears ringing. His hand ringing, too. When he was ready, he used his heels to push himself across the floor to the wall, then used the wall to work his way up into a sitting position. He rested again.

At last he shoved his way to his feet, sliding his back up the wall. He peered out the wreck of the screen door but still could not see his father. He had to be lying against the side of the house.

Jude swayed away from the wall, sagging toward the screen door. He grabbed the frame to keep from falling into the pigpen himself. His legs trembled furiously. He leaned forward to see if Martin was on the ground with a broken neck, and at that moment his father stood up and reached through the screen and grabbed for his leg.

Jude cried out, kicking at Martin's hand and recoiling instinctively. Then he was a man losing his balance on a sheet of black ice, pinwheeling his arms foolishly, sailing back down the hall and into the kitchen, where he fell yet again.

Martin pulled himself up through the torn screen. He crawled toward Jude, made his way to him on all fours, until he was right on top of him. Martin's hand rose, then fell, a glittering silver spark falling with it. Jude brought up his left arm, and the straight razor struck his forearm, scraping bone. Blood leaped into the air. More blood.

The palm of Jude's left hand was bandaged, but the fingers were free, sticking out of the gauze as if it were a glove with the fingers snipped off. His father lifted the razor in the air to strike again, but before he could bring it down, Jude stuck his fingers in Martin's glimmering red eyes. The old man cried out, twisting his head back, trying to get free of his son's hand. The razor blade waved in front of Jude's face without touching skin. Jude forced his father's head back, and back, baring his scrawny throat, wondering if he could push hard enough to break the cocksucker's spine.

He had Martin's head back as far as it would go when the kitchen knife slammed into the side of his father's neck.

Marybeth was ten feet away, standing at the kitchen counter, beside a magnetized strip on the wall with knives stuck to it. Her breath came in sobs. Jude's father turned his head to stare at her. Air bubbles foamed in the blood that leaked from around the hilt of the knife. Martin reached for it with one hand, closed his fingers feebly about it, then made a sound, a rattling inhalation, like a child shaking a stone in a paper bag, and sagged to his side.

Marybeth snapped another wide-bladed knife off the magnetic rack, then another. She took the first by the tip of the blade and chucked it into Martin's back as he slumped forward. It hit with a deep, hollow *thunk,* as if she'd driven the blade into a melon. Martin made no sound at this second blow, aside from a sharp huff of breath. Marybeth started to walk toward him, holding the last knife in front of her.

"Keep away," Jude said to her. "He won't lie down and die." But she didn't hear him.

In another moment she stood over Martin. Jude's father looked up, and Marybeth whacked the knife across his face. It went in close to one corner of his lips and came out a little past the other corner, widening his mouth into a garish red slash.

As she struck at him, he struck at her, lashing out with his right hand, the hand that held the razor. The blade drew a red line across her thigh, above the right knee, and the leg buckled.

Martin pitched himself up off the floor as Marybeth started to go down, roaring as he rose to his feet. He caught her in the stomach in an almost perfect flying tackle, smashed Marybeth into the kitchen counter. She slammed her last knife into Martin's shoulder, burying it to the hilt. She might've pounded it into a tree trunk for all the good it did.

She slipped to the floor, Jude's father on top of her, blood still foaming from the knife planted in his neck. He slashed his straight razor toward her again.

Marybeth grabbed her neck, clutching it weakly with her bad hand. Blood pumped through her fingers. There was a crude black grin dug into the white flesh of her throat.

She slid onto her side. Her head banged the floor. She was staring past Martin at Jude. The side of her face lay in blood, a thick, scarlet puddle of it.

Jude's father dropped to all fours. His free hand was still wrapped around the base of the knife in his own throat, fingers exploring it blindly, taking its measure, but doing nothing to pull it out. He was a pincushion, knife in the shoulder, knife in the back, but he was interested only in the one through his neck, didn't seem to have noticed the other pieces of steel sticking into him.

Martin crawled unsteadily away from Marybeth, away from Jude. His arms gave out first, and his head dropped to the floor, his chin striking with enough force to make his teeth audibly click together. He tried to push himself up and almost made it, but then his right arm gave out, and he rolled onto his side instead. Away from Jude, a small relief. Jude wouldn't have to look into his face while he died. Again.

Marybeth was trying to speak. Her tongue came out of her mouth, moved over her lips. Her eyes pleaded for Jude to come closer. Her pupils had shrunk to black dots.

He pulled himself across the floor, elbow over elbow, dragging himself to her. She was already whispering. It was hard to hear her over his father, who was making the cough-choking sounds again and kicking his heels loudly against the floor, in the throes of some kind of convulsion.

"He's not . . . done," Marybeth said. "He's comin' . . . again. He'll never . . . be done."

Jude glanced around for something he could stick against the slash across her throat. He was close enough now so his hands were in the puddle of blood surrounding her, splashing in it. He spotted a dishrag hanging from the handle of the oven, pulled it down.

Marybeth was staring into his face, but Jude had an impression of not being seen—the sense that she was staring right through him and into some unknowable distance.

"I hear . . . Anna. I hear her . . . calling. We have . . . to make . . . a door. We have to . . . let her in. Make us a door. Make a door . . . and I'll open it."

"Stop talking." He lifted her hand and pressed the rolled-up dish towel against her neck.

Marybeth caught at his wrist.

"Can't open it . . . once I'm on . . . the other . . . side. It has to be now. I'm gone already. Anna is gone. You can't . . . save . . . us," she said. So much blood. "Let. Us. Save. You."

Across the room Jude heard a fit of coughing, then his father gagging. He was choking something up. Jude knew what.

He stared at Marybeth with a disbelief more intense than grief. He found his hand cupping her face, which was cool to the touch. He had promised. He had promised himself, if not her, that he would take care of her, and here she was, with her throat cut, saying how she was going to take care of him. She was fighting for each breath, shivering helplessly.

"Do it, Jude," she said. "Just do it."

He lifted her hands and put them against the dish towel, to keep it pressed to her open throat. Then he turned and crawled through her blood, to the edge of the puddle. He heard himself humming again, his song, his new song, a melody like a southern hymn, a country dirge. How did you make a door for the dead? Would it be enough just to draw one? He was trying to think what to draw with, when he saw the red handprints he was leaving on the linoleum. He dipped a finger in her blood and began to draw a line along the floor.

When he judged he had made it long enough, he started a new line, at a right angle to the first. The blood on his fingertip thinned and ran dry. He shuffled slowly around, turning back to Marybeth and the wide, trembling pool of blood in which she lay.

He looked past her and saw Craddock, pulling himself out of his father's gaping mouth. Craddock's face was contorted with strain, his arms reaching down, one hand on Martin's forehead, the other on Martin's shoulder. At the point of his waist, his body was crushed into a thick rope—Jude thought again of a great mass of cellophane, wadded up and twisted into a cord—which filled Martin's mouth and seemed to extend all the way down into his engorged throat. Craddock had gone in like a soldier leaping into a foxhole but was hauling himself out like a man sunk to his waist in sucking mud.

You will die, the dead man said. *The bitch will die you will die we will all ride the nightroad together you want to sing la la la I'll teach you to sing I'll teach you.*

Jude dipped his hand in Marybeth's blood, wetting it entirely, turned away again. There was no thought in him. He was a machine that crawled stupidly forward as he began to draw once more. He finished the top of the door, shuffled around, and started a third line, working his way back to Marybeth. It was a crude, meandering line, thick in some places, barely a smear in others.

The bottom of the door was the puddle. As he reached it, he glanced into Marybeth's face. The front of her T-shirt was soaked through. Her face was a pallid blank, and for a moment he thought it was too late, she was dead, but then her eyes moved, just slightly, watching him approach, through a dull glaze.

Craddock began to scream in frustration. He had pulled all of himself out except for one leg, was already trying to stand up, but his foot was stuck somewhere in Martin's gullet, and it was unbalancing him. In Craddock's hand was the blade shaped like a crescent moon, the chain hanging from it in a bright, swinging loop.

Jude turned his back on him once more and looked down at his uneven blood doorway. He stared stupidly at the long, crooked red frame, an empty box containing only a few scarlet handprints. It wasn't right yet, and he tried to think what else it needed. Then it came to him that it wasn't a door if there was no way to open it, and he crawled forward and painted a circle for a doorknob.

Craddock's shadow fell over him. Ghosts could cast shadows? Jude wondered at it. He was tired. It was hard to think. He knelt on the door and felt something slam against the other side of it. It was as if the wind, which was still driving against the house in furious, steady gusts, were trying to come up through the linoleum.

A line of brightness appeared along the right-hand edge of the door, a vivid streak of radiant white. Something hit the other side again, a mountain lion trapped under the floor. It struck a third time, each impact producing a thunderous boom that shook the house, caused the plates to rattle in the plastic tray by the sink. Jude felt his elbows give a little, and decided there was no reason to stay on all fours anymore, and besides, it was too much effort. He fell to his side, let himself roll right off the door and onto his back.

Craddock stood over Marybeth in his black dead man's suit, one side of his collar askew, hat gone. He wasn't coming forward, though, had stopped in his tracks. He stared mistrustfully down at the hand-drawn door at his feet, as if it were a secret hatch and he had come close to stepping on it and falling through.

What is that? What did you do?

When Jude spoke, his voice seemed to come from a long distance off, as by some trick of ventriloquism. "The dead claim their own, Craddock. Sooner or later they claim their own."

The misshapen door bulged, then receded into the floor. Swelled again. It seemed almost to be breathing. The line of light raced across the top of it, a beam of brightness so intense it couldn't be looked at directly. It cornered and continued on down the other side of the door.

The wind keened, louder than ever, a high, piercing shriek. After a moment Jude realized it wasn't the wind outside the house but a gale wailing around the edges of the door drawn in blood. It wasn't blowing out but being sucked *in*, through those blinding white lines. Jude's ears popped, and he thought of an airplane descending too rapidly. Papers ruffled, then lifted off the kitchen table and began to swirl above it, chasing one another. Delicate little wavelets raced across the wide pool of blood around Marybeth's blank, staring face.

Marybeth's left arm was stretched out, across the lake of blood, into the doorway. When Jude wasn't looking, she had pulled herself over onto her side, reaching out with one arm. Her hand rested over the red circle he had drawn for a doorknob.

Somewhere a dog began to bark.

In the next instant, the door painted on the linoleum fell open. Marybeth should've dropped through it—half her body was stretched across it—but she didn't. Instead she floated, as if sprawled on a sheet of polished glass. An uneven parallelogram filled the center of the floor, an open trap, flooded with an astonishing light, a blinding brilliance that rose all around her.

In the intensity of that light pouring from below, the room became a photographic negative, all stark whites and flat, impossible shadows. Marybeth was a black, featureless figure, suspended upon the sheet of light. Craddock, standing over her, arms flung up to protect his face, looked like one of the victims of the atom bomb at Hiroshima, an abstract life-size sketch of a man, drawn in ash on a black wall. Papers still whirled and spun above the kitchen table, only they had gone black and looked like a flock of crows.

Marybeth rolled over onto her side and lifted her head, only it wasn't Marybeth anymore, it was Anna, and spokes of light filled her eyes, and her face was as stern as God's own judgment.

Why? she asked.

Craddock hissed. *Get away. Get back.* He swung the gold chain of his pendulum in circles, the crescent blade whining in the air, tracing a ring of silver fire.

Then Anna was on her feet, at the base of the glowing door. Jude had not seen her rise. One moment she was prone, and in the next she was standing. Time had skipped, maybe. Time didn't matter anymore. Jude held up a hand to shield his eyes from the worst of the glare, but the light was everywhere, and there was no blocking it out. He could see the bones in his hand, the skin over them the color and clarity of honey. His wounds, the slash in his face, the stump of his index finger, throbbed with a pain that was both profound and exhilarating, and he thought he might cry out, in fear, in joy, in shock, in all those things, in what was more than those things. In rapture.

Why? Anna said again as she approached Craddock. He whipped the chain at her, and the curved razor at the end drew a wide slash across her face, from the corner of her right eye, across her nose, and down to her mouth—but it only opened a fresh ray of brilliance, and where the light struck him, Craddock began to smoke. Anna reached for him. *Why?*

Craddock shrieked as she gathered him into her arms, shrieked and cut her again, across her breasts, and opened another seam in the eternal, and into his face poured the bountiful light, a light that burned away his features, that erased everything it touched. His wail was so loud Jude thought his eardrums would explode.

Why? Anna said, before she put her mouth on his, and from the door behind her leaped the black dogs, Jude's dogs, giant dogs of smoke, of shadow, with fangs of ink.

Craddock McDermott struggled, trying to push her away, but she was falling backward with him, falling toward the door, and the dogs raced around his feet, and as they ran, they were stretched and pulled out of shape, unraveling like balls of yarn, becoming long scarves of darkness that wound around him, climbing his legs, lashing him about the waist, and binding the dead man to the dead girl. As he was pulled down, into the brightness of the other side, Jude saw the back of Craddock's head come off, and a shaft of white light, so intense it was blue at the edges, slammed through and struck the ceiling, where it burnt the plaster, causing it to bubble and seethe.

They dropped through the open door and were gone.

45

The papers that had been swirling above the kitchen table settled
with a faint rustle, collecting into a pile, in almost the exact same spot
from which they'd risen. In the hush that followed, Jude became aware
of a gentle humming sound, a deep, melodic pulse, which was not heard
so much as felt in his bones. It rose and fell and rose again, a sort of inhuman music—inhuman, but not unpleasant. Jude had never heard any
instrument produce sounds like it. It was more like the accidental music
of tires droning on blacktop. That low, powerful music could be felt on
the skin as well. The air throbbed with it. It seemed almost to be a property of the light, flooding in through the crooked rectangle on the floor.
Jude blinked into the light and wondered where Marybeth had gone.
The dead claim their own, he thought, and shivered.

No. She hadn't been dead a moment ago when she opened the door. He
did not accept that she could just be gone, no trace of her left on the earth.
He crawled. He was the only thing moving in the room now. The stillness
of the place, after what had just happened, seemed more jarring and incredible than a hole between worlds. He hurt, his hands hurt, his face
hurt, and his chest tingled, a deadly icy-hot prickling, although he was
fairly certain, if he was meant to have a heart attack this afternoon, it

would've happened by now. Aside from the continuous humming that was all around him, there was no sound at all, except his sobs for breath, his hands scratching at the floor. Once he heard himself say Marybeth's name.

The closer he came to the light, the harder it was to stare into it. He shut his eyes—and found himself still able to see the room before him, as if through a pale curtain of silver silk, the light penetrating his closed lids. The nerves behind his eyeballs throbbed in steady time with that ceaseless pulsing sound.

He couldn't bear all the light, turned his head aside, kept crawling forward, and in that way Jude did not realize he had reached the edge of the open door until he put his hands down and there was nothing there to support him. Marybeth—or had it been Anna?—had hung suspended over the open door, as if on a sheet of glass, but Jude dropped like a condemned man through the hangman's trap, did not even have time to cry out before plummeting into the light.

46

*T**he sensation of falling—a weightless-sick** feeling in the pit of his
stomach and the roots of his hair—has hardly passed before he realizes that
the light is not so intense now. He lifts a hand to shade his eyes and blinks
into it, dusty yellow sunshine. He makes it midafternoon and can tell somehow, from the angle of the sun, that he's in the South. Jude is in the Mustang again, sitting in the passenger seat. Anna has the wheel, is humming
to herself as she drives. The engine is a low, controlled roar—the Mustang
has made itself well. It might've just rolled off the showroom floor in 1965.*

*They travel a mile or so, neither of them speaking, before he finally
identifies the road they're on as State Highway 22.*

"Where we goin'?" *he asks at last.*

*Anna arches her back, stretching her spine. She keeps both hands on
the wheel.* "I don't know. I thought we were just drivin'. Where do you
wanna go?"

"Doesn't matter. How about Chinchuba Landing?"

"What's down there?"

"Nothing. Just a place to set and listen to the radio and look at the
view. How's that sound?"

"Sounds like heaven. We must be in heaven."

When she says this, his left temple begins to ache. He wishes she hadn't said that. They aren't in heaven. He doesn't want to hear talk like that.

For a time they roll on cracked, faded, two-lane blacktop. Then he sees the turnoff coming up on the right and points it out, and Marybeth turns the Mustang onto it without a word. The road is dirt, and trees grow close on either side and bend over it, making a tunnel of rich green light. Shadows and fluttering sunlight shift across Marybeth's scrubbed, delicate features. She looks serene, at ease behind the wheel of the big muscle car, happy to have the afternoon ahead of her, and nothing particular to do in it except park someplace with Jude and listen to music. When did she become Marybeth?

It is as if he has spoken the question aloud, because she turns and gives him an embarrassed grin. "I tried to warn you, didn't I? Two girls for the price of one."

"You warned me."

"I know what road we're on," Marybeth says, without any trace of the southern accent that has muddled up her own voice in the last few days.

"I told you. One that goes to Chinchuba Landing."

She turns a knowing, amused, slightly pitying glance upon him. Then, as if he hadn't said anything, Marybeth continues: "Hell. After all the stuff I've heard about this road, I expected worse. This isn't bad. Kinda nice, actually. With a name like the nightroad you at least expect it to be night. Maybe it's only night here for some people."

He winces—another stab of pain in the head. He wants to think she's mixed up, wrong about where they are. She could be wrong. Not only isn't it night, it's hardly a road.

In another minute they're bumping along through two ruts in the dirt, narrow troughs with a wide bed of grass and wildflowers growing between them, swatting the fender and dragging against the undercarriage. They pass the wreck of a pale truck, parked under a willow, the hood open and weeds growing right up through it. Jude doesn't give it more than a sidelong look.

The palms and the brush open up just around the next bend, but

Marybeth slows, so the Mustang is barely rolling along, and for the moment anyway they're still back in the cool shade of the trees bending overhead. Gravel crunches pleasantly under the tires, a sound Jude has always loved, a sound everyone loves. Out beyond the grassy clearing is the muddy brown sea of Lake Pontchartrain, the water ruffled up in the wind and the edges of the waves glinting like polished, new-minted steel. Jude is a little taken aback by the sky, which is bleached a uniform and blinding white. It is a sky so awash in light it's impossible to look directly into it, to even know where the sun is. Jude turns his head away from the view, squinting and raising a hand to shield his eyes. The ache in his left temple intensifies, beating with his pulse.

"Damn," *he says.* "That sky."

"Isn't it somethin'?" *Anna says from inside Marybeth's body.* "You can see a long way. You can see into forever."

"I can't see shit."

"No," *Anna says, but it's still Marybeth behind the wheel, Marybeth's mouth moving.* "You need to protect your eyes from the sight. You can't really look out there. Not yet. We have trouble lookin' back into your world, for whatever it's worth. You maybe noticed the black lines over our eyes. Think of them as the sunglasses of the livin' dead." *A statement that starts her laughing, Marybeth's husky, rude laughter.*

She stops the car at the very edge of the clearing, puts it into park. The windows are down. The air that soughs in over him smells sweetly of the sun-baked brush and the unruly grass. Beneath that he can detect the subtle perfume of Lake Pontchartrain, a cool, marshy odor.

Marybeth leans toward him, puts her head on his shoulder, puts an arm across his waist, and when she speaks again, it is in her own voice. "I wish I was driving back with you, Jude."

He breaks out in a sudden chill. "What's that mean?"

She looks fondly up into his face. "Hey. We almost got it right. Didn't we almost get it right, Jude?"

"Stop it," *Jude says.* "You're not going anywhere. You're staying with me."

"I don't know," *Marybeth says.* "I'm tired. It's a long haul back, and I don't think I could make it. I swear this car is using some part of me for gas, and I'm about all out."

"Stop talking that way."

"Were we going to have some music?"

He opens the glove compartment, fumbles for a tape. It's a collection of demos, a private collection. His new songs. He wants Marybeth to hear them. He wants her to know he didn't give up on himself. The first track begins to play. It is "Drink to the Dead." The guitar chimes and rises in a country hymn, a sweet and lonely acoustic gospel, a song for grieving. Goddam, his head hurts, both temples now, a steady throbbing behind his eyes. Goddam that sky with its overpowering light.

Marybeth sits up, only it isn't Marybeth anymore, it's Anna. Her eyes are filled with light, are filled with sky. "All the world is made of music. We are all strings on a lyre. We resonate. We sing together. This was nice. With that wind on my face. When you sing, I'm singin' with you, honey. You know that, don't you?"

"Stop it," *he says. Anna settles behind the wheel again and puts the car into drive.* "What are you doing?"

Marybeth leans forward from the backseat and reaches for his hand. Anna and Marybeth are separate now—they are two distinct individuals maybe for the first time in days. "I have to go, Jude." *She bends over the seat to put her mouth on his. Her lips are cold and trembling.* "This is where you get out."

"We," *he says, and when she tries to withdraw her hand, he doesn't let go, squeezes harder, until he can feel the bones flexing under the skin. He kisses her again, says into her mouth,* "Where we get out. We. We."

Gravel under the tires again. The Mustang rolls forward, out under the open sky. The front seat is filled with a blast of light, an incandescence that erases all the world beyond the car, leaving nothing but the interior, and even that Jude can hardly see, peering out through slitted eyes. The pain that flares behind his eyeballs is staggering, wonderful. He still has Mary-

beth by the hand. She can't go if he doesn't let her, and the light—oh, God, there is so much light. There's something wrong with the car stereo, his song wavering in and out, drowning beneath a deep, low, pulsing harmonic, the same alien music he heard when he fell through the door between worlds. He wants to tell Marybeth something, he wants to tell her he is sorry he couldn't keep his promises, the ones he made her and the ones he made himself, he wants to say how he loves her, loves her so, but cannot find his voice and cannot think with the light in his eyes and that humming in his head. Her hand. He still has her hand. He squeezes her hand again, and again, trying to tell her what he needs to tell her by touch, and she squeezes back.

And out in the light, he sees Anna, sees her shimmering, glowing like a firefly, watches her turn from the wheel, and smile, and reach toward him, putting her hand over his and Marybeth's, and that's when she says, "Hey, you guys, I think this hairy son of a bitch is trying to sit up."

47

Jude blinked into the clear, painful white light of an ophthal-moscope pointed into his left eye. He was struggling to rise, but someone had a hand on his chest, holding him pinned to the floor. He gasped at the air, like a trout just hauled out of Lake Pontchartrain and thrown onto the shore. He had told Anna they might go fishing there, the two of them. Or had that been Marybeth? He didn't know anymore.

The ophthalmoscope was removed, and he stared blankly up at the mold-spotted ceiling of the kitchen. The mad sometimes drilled holes in their own heads, to let the demons out, to relieve the pressure of thoughts they could no longer bear. Jude understood the impulse. Each beat of his heart was a fresh and staggering blow, felt in the nerves behind his eyes and in his temples, punishing evidence of life.

A hog with a squashy pink face leaned over him, smiled obscenely down, and said, "Holy shit. You know who this is? It's Judas Coyne."

Someone else said, "Can we clear the fucking pigs out of the room?"

The pig was booted aside, with a shriek of indignation. A man with a neatly groomed, pale brown goatee and kind, watchful eyes, leaned into Jude's field of view.

"Mr. Coyne? Just lie still. You've lost a lot of blood. We're going to lift you onto a gurney."

"Anna," Jude said, his voice unsteady and wheezing.

A brief look of pain and something like an apology flickered in the young man's light blue eyes. "Was that her name?"

No. No, Jude had said the wrong thing. That wasn't her name, but Jude couldn't find the breath to correct himself. Then it registered that the man leaning over him had referred to her in the past tense.

Arlene Wade spoke for him. "He told me her name was Marybeth."

Arlene leaned in from the other side, peering down at him, her eyes comically huge behind her glasses. She was talking about Marybeth in the past tense, too. He tried to sit up again, but the goateed EMT firmly held him down.

"Don't try and get up, dear," Arlene said.

Something made a steely clatter nearby, and he looked down the length of his body and past his feet and saw a crowd of men rolling a gurney past him and into the hall. An IV bag, pregnant with blood, swung back and forth from a metal support rod attached to the cot. From his angle on the floor, Jude could not see anything of the person on the gurney, except for a hand hanging over the side. The infection that had made Marybeth's palm shriveled and white was gone, no trace of it left. Her small, slender hand swung limply, jostled by the motion of the cart, and Jude thought of the girl in his obscene snuff movie, the way she had seemed to go boneless when the life went out of her. One of the EMTs pushing the gurney glanced down and saw Jude staring. He reached for Marybeth's hand and tucked it back up against her side. The other men rolled the gurney on out of sight, all of them talking to one another in low, feverish voices.

"Marybeth?" Jude managed, his voice the faintest of whispers, carried on a pained exhalation of breath.

"She's got to go now," Arlene said. "There's another amble-lance comin' for you, Justin,"

"Go?" Jude asked. He really didn't understand.

"They can't do any more for her in this place, that's all. It's just time to take her on." Arlene patted his hand. "Her ride is here."

ALIVE

Jude was in and out for twenty-four hours.

He woke once and saw his lawyer, Nan Shreve, standing in the door of his private room, talking with Jackson Browne. Jude had met him, years before, at the Grammys. Jude had slipped out midceremony to visit the men's, and as he was taking a leak, he happened to look over to find Jackson Browne pissing in the urinal next to him. They had only nodded to each other, never even said hello, and so Jude couldn't imagine what he was doing now in Louisiana. Maybe he had a gig in New Orleans, had heard about Jude nearly being killed, and had come to express his sympathies. Maybe Jude would now be visited by a procession of rock-and-roll luminaries, swinging through to tell him to keep on keepin' on. Jackson Browne was dressed conservatively—blue blazer, tie—and he had a gold shield clipped to his belt, next to a holstered revolver. Jude allowed his eyelids to sink shut.

He had a dark, muffled sense of time passing. When he woke again, another rock star was sitting beside him: Dizzy, his eyes all black scribbles, his face still wasted with AIDS. He offered his hand, and Jude took it.

Had to come, man. You were there for me, Dizzy said.

"I'm glad to see you," Jude told him. "I been missing you."

"Excuse me?" said the nurse, standing on the other side of the bed. Jude glanced over at her, hadn't known she was there. When he looked back for Dizzy, Jude discovered his hand hanging empty.

"Who you talkin' to?" the nurse asked.

"Old friend. I haven't seen him since he died."

She sniffed. "We got to scale back your morphine, hon."

Later Angus wandered through the room and disappeared under the bed. Jude called to him, but Angus never came out, just stayed under the cot, thumping his tail on the floor, a steady beat that kept time with Jude's heart.

Jude wasn't sure which dead or famous person to expect next and was surprised when he opened his eyes to find he had his room to himself. He was on the fourth or fifth floor of a hospital outside of Slidell. Beyond the window was Lake Pontchartrain, blue and wintry in the late-afternoon light, the shoreline crowded with cranes, a rusty oil tanker struggling into the east. For the first time, he realized he could smell it, the faint briny tang of the water. Jude wept.

When he'd managed to get control of himself, he paged the nurse. A doctor came instead, a cadaverous black man with sad, bloodshot eyes and a shaved head. In a soft, gravelly voice, he began to fill Jude in on his condition.

"Has anyone called Bammy?" Jude interrupted.

"Who's that?"

"Marybeth's grandma," Jude said. "If no one's called her, I want to be the one to tell her. Bammy ought to know what happened."

"If you can provide us with her last name and a phone number or an address, I can have one of the nurses call her."

"It ought to be me."

"You've been through a lot. I think, in the emotional state you're in, a call from you might alarm her."

Jude stared at him. "Her granddaughter died. Person she loves most in the world. Do you think it will alarm her less getting the news from a stranger?"

"Exactly why we'd rather make the call," the doctor said. "That's the kind of thing we don't want her family to hear. In a first phone call with relatives, we prefer to focus on the positive."

It came to Jude that he was still sick. The conversation had an unreal tinge to it that he associated with a fever. He shook his head and began to laugh. Then he noticed he was crying again. He wiped at his face with trembling hands.

"Focus on what positive?" he asked.

"The news could be worse," the doctor said. "At least she's stable now. And her heart was only stopped for a few minutes. People have been dead for longer. There should be only minimal—"

But Jude didn't hear the rest.

Then he was in the halls, a six-foot-tall, 240-pound man, fifty-four years of age, the great bush of his black beard in ratty tangles and his hospital johnny flapping open in the back to show the scrawny, hairless cheeks of his ass. The doctor jogged beside him, and nurses gathered about, trying to redirect him back to his room, but he strode on, his IV drip still in his arm and the bag rattling along beside him on its wheeled frame. He was clearheaded, all the way awake, his hands not bothering him, his breathing fine. As he made his way along, he began calling her name. He was in surprisingly good voice.

"Mr. Coyne," said the doctor. "Mr. Coyne, she isn't well enough—you aren't well enough—"

Bon raced past Jude, down the hall, and hung a right at the next corner. He quickened his step. He reached the turn and looked down another corridor in time to see Bon slip through a pair of double doors, twenty feet away. They gasped shut behind her, closing on their pneumatic hinges. The glowing sign above the doors said ICU.

A short, dumpy security officer was in Jude's way, but Jude went around him, and then the rent-a-cop had to jog and huff to keep up. He shoved through the doors and into the ICU. Bon was just disappearing into a darkened room on the left.

Jude went in right after her. Bon was nowhere in sight, but Marybeth was in the only bed, with black stitches across her throat, an air tube poked into her nostrils, and machines bleeping contentedly in the dark around her. Her eyes opened to puffy slits as Jude entered saying her name. Her face was battered, her complexion greasy and pale, and she seemed emaciated, and at the sight of her his heart contracted with a sweet tightness. Then he was next to her, on the edge of the mattress, and gathering her into his arms, her skin paper, her bones hollow sticks. He put his face against her wounded neck, into her hair, inhaling deeply, needing the smell of her, proof she was there, real, proof of life. One of her hands rose weakly to his side, slid up his back. Her lips, when he kissed them, were cold, and they trembled.

"Thought you were gone," Jude said. "We were in the Mustang again with Anna, and I thought you were gone."

"Aw, shit," Marybeth whispered, in a voice hardly louder than breath. "I climbed out. Sick of being in cars all the time. Jude, you think when we go home we can just fly?"

50

He wasn't asleep, but thinking he ought to be, when the door clicked open. He rolled over, wondering which dead person or rock legend or spirit animal might be visiting now, but it was only Nan Shreve, in a tan business skirt and suit jacket and nude-colored nylons. She carried her high heels in one hand and scuffled quickly along on tiptoe. She eased the door softly shut behind her.

"Snuck in," she said, wrinkling her nose and throwing him a wink. "Not really supposed to be here yet."

Nan was a little, wiry woman, whose head barely came to Jude's chest. She was socially maladroit, didn't know how to smile. Her grin was a rigid, painful fake that projected none of the things a smile was supposed to project: confidence, optimism, warmth, pleasure. She was forty-six and married and had two children and had been his attorney for almost a decade. Jude, though, had been her friend for longer than that, going back to when she was just twenty. She hadn't known how to smile then either, and in those days she didn't even try. Back then she was strung out and mean, and he had not called her Nan.

"Hey, Tennessee," Jude said. "Why aren't you supposed to be here?"

She had started toward the bed but hesitated at this. He hadn't meant to call her Tennessee, it had just slipped out. He was tired. Her eyelashes fluttered, and for a moment her smile looked even more unhappy than usual. Then she found her step again, reached his cot, planted herself in a molded chair next to him.

"I made arrangements to meet Quinn in the lobby," she said, wiggling her feet back into her heels. "He's the detective in charge of nailing down what happened. Except he's late. I passed a *horrible* wreck on the highway, and I thought I saw his car pulled over to the side of the road, so he must've stopped to help out the state troopers."

"What am I charged with?"

"Why would you be charged with anything? Your father—Jude, your father attacked you. He attacked both of you. You're lucky you weren't killed. Quinn just wants a statement. Tell him what happened at your father's house. Tell him the truth." She met his gaze, and then she was speaking very carefully, a mother repeating simple but important instructions to a child. "Your father had a break with reality. It happens. They've even got a name for it: age rage. He attacked you and Marybeth Kimball, and she killed him saving the both of you. That's all Quinn wants to hear. Just like it happened." And in the last few moments, their conversation had ceased to be friendly and social in any way. Her plastered-on grin had disappeared, and he was back with Tennessee again—cold-eyed, sinewy, unbending Tennessee.

He nodded.

She said, "And Quinn might have some questions about the accident that took off your finger. And killed the dog. The dog in your car?"

"I don't understand," Jude said. "He doesn't want to talk to me about what happened in Florida?"

Her eyelashes fluttered rapidly, and for a moment she was staring at him with unmistakable confusion. Then the cold-eyed look reasserted itself and became even colder. "Did something happen in Florida? Something I need to know about, Jude?"

So there was no warrant on him in Florida. That didn't make sense.

He had attacked a woman and her child, been shot, been in a collision—but if he was a wanted man in Florida, Nan would already know about it. She would already be planning his plea.

Nan went on, "You came south to see your father before he passed away. You were in an accident just before you reached his farm. Out walking the dog by the side of the road, and the two of you got hit. An unimaginable chain of events, but that's what happened. Nothing else makes sense."

The door opened, and Jackson Browne peeked into the room. Only he had a red birthmark on his neck that Jude hadn't noticed before, a crimson splotch in the rough shape of a three-fingered hand, and when he spoke, it was in a clownish honk, his inflections soupy and Cajun.

"Mr. Coyne. Still with us?" His gaze darting from Jude to Nan Shreve beside him. "Your record company will be disappointed. I guess they were already planning the tribute album." He laughed then, until he coughed, and blinked watering eyes. "Mrs. Shreve. I missed you in the lobby." He said it jovially enough, but the way he looked at her, his eyes hooded and wondering, it sounded almost like an accusation. He added, "So did the nurse at the reception desk. She said she hadn't seen you."

"I waved on the way by," Nan said.

"Come on in," Jude said. "Nan said you'd like to talk to me."

"I ought to place you under arrest," said Detective Quinn.

Jude's pulse quickened, but his voice, when he spoke, was smooth and untroubled. "For what?"

"Your last three albums," Quinn said. "I got two daughters, and they play 'em and play 'em at top volume, until the walls shake and the dishes rattle and I feel I am close to perpetratin' dough-mestic abuse, you understan'? And this is on my lovely, laughin' daughters, who I wouldn't under normal conditions want hurt for any reason nohow." He sighed, used his tie to wipe his brow, made his way to the foot of the bed. He offered Jude his last stick of Juicy Fruit. When Jude declined, Quinn popped the stick into his mouth and began to chew. "You got to love 'em, somehow, no matter how crazy you feel sometimes."

"That's right," Jude said.

"Just a few questions," Quinn said, pulling a notebook out of an inner pocket of his jacket. "We want to start before you got to your father's house. You were in a hit-and-run, is that it? Some awful kind of day for you and your lady friend, huh? And then attacked by your dad. Course, the way you look, and the condition he was in, he probably thought you were . . . I don't know. A murderer come to loot his farm. An evil spirit. Still, I can't think why you wouldn't have gone to a hospital after the accident that took off your finger."

"Well," Jude said. "We weren't far from my daddy's place, and I knew my aunt was there. She's a registered nurse."

"That so? Tell me about the car that hit you."

"A truck," Jude said. "A pickup." He glanced at Nan, who nodded, just slightly, eyes watchful and certain. Jude drew a deep breath and began to lie.

51

Before Nan left his room, she hesitated in the doorway and looked back at Jude. That grin was on her face again, the stretched, forced one that made Jude sad.

"She really is beautiful, Jude," Nan said. "And she loves you. You can tell the way she talks about you. I spoke to her. Only for a moment, but . . . but you can tell. Georgia, is she?" Nan's eyes were shy, and pained, and affectionate, all at once. She asked the question like she wasn't sure if she really wanted to know.

"Marybeth," Jude said firmly. "Her name is Marybeth."

52

They were back in New York two weeks later for Danny's memorial service. Marybeth wore a black scarf around her neck that matched her black lace gloves. The afternoon was windy and cold, but the gathering was well attended nonetheless. It seemed everyone Danny had ever chatted up, gossiped with, or blabbed to on the phone was there, and that was a lot, and none of them left early, not even when the rain began to fall.

In the spring Jude recorded an album, stripped down, mostly acoustic. He sang about the dead. He sang about roads at night. Other men played the guitar parts. He could handle rhythm, but that was all, had needed to switch back to making chords with the left, as he had in his childhood, and he wasn't as good at it.

The new CD sold well. He did not tour. He had a triple bypass instead.

Marybeth taught dance at a tony gym in High Plains. Her classes were crowded.

54

Marybeth found a derelict Dodge Charger in a local auto grave-yard, brought it home for three hundred dollars. Jude spent the next summer sweating in the yard with his shirt off, restoring it. He came in late each night, all of him tanned, except for the shiny silver scar down the center of his chest. Marybeth was always waiting just inside the door, with a glass of homemade lemonade. Sometimes they would trade a kiss that tasted of cold juice and motor oil. They were his favorite kisses.

55

One **afternoon,** close to the end of August, Jude wandered inside, sweating and sunburned, and found a message on the machine from Nan. She said she had some information for him and he could call her back anytime. Anytime was now, and he rang her in her office. He sat on the edge of Danny's old desk while Nan's receptionist patched him through.

"I'm afraid I don't have a lot to tell you about this George Ruger person," Nan said without any preamble. "You wanted to know if he's been mentioned in any criminal proceedings in the last year, and the answer to that appears to be no. Maybe if I had more information from you, as to exactly what your interest in him is . . . ."

"No. Don't worry about it," Jude said.

So Ruger hadn't brought any kind of complaint to the authorities; no surprise. If he was going to bring a suit, or try to have Jude arrested, Jude would've known about it by now anyway. He hadn't really expected Nan to come up with anything. Ruger couldn't talk about what Jude had done to him without risking that it would come out about Marybeth, how he'd slept with her when she was still in junior high. He was, Jude remembered, an important figure in local politics. It was hard to run a really effective fund-raiser after you'd been accused of statutory rape.

"I had a little more luck concerning Jessica Price."

"You did," Jude said. Just hearing her name made his stomach knot up.

When Nan spoke again, it was in a falsely casual tone, a little too cool to be persuasive. "This Price is under investigation for child endangerment and sexual abuse. Her own daughter, if you can imagine. Apparently the police came to her home after someone called in an accident report. Price drove her car into someone else's vehicle, right in front of her house, forty miles an hour. When the police got there, they found her unconscious behind the wheel. And her daughter was in the house with a gun and a dead dog on the floor."

Nan paused to allow Jude a chance to comment, but Jude didn't have anything to say.

Nan went on, "Whoever Price drove her car into took off. Never found."

"Didn't Price tell them? What's her story?"

"No story. See, after the police calmed the little girl down, they took the gun away. When they went to put it back where it belonged, they found an envelope with photos in it, hidden in the velvet lining of the pistol's case. Polaroids of the girl. Criminal stuff. Horrible. Apparently they can establish that the mother took them. Jessica Price could be looking at up to ten years. And I understand her girl is only just thirteen. Isn't that the most terrible thing?"

"It is," Jude said. "Just about."

"Would you believe all of this happened—Jessica Price's car accident, dead dog, photos—on the same day your daddy died in Louisiana?"

Again Jude did not reply—silence felt safer.

Nan went on, "Following her lawyer's advice, Jessica Price has been exercising her legal right to remain silent ever since her arrest. Which makes sense for her. And is also a lucky break for whoever else was there. You know—with the dog."

Jude held the receiver to his ear. Nan was silent for so long he began to wonder if they'd been cut off.

At last, just to find out if she was still on the line, he said, "That all?"

"One other thing," Nan said. Her tone was perfectly bland. "A carpenter doing work down the street said he saw a suspicious pair in a black car lurking around earlier in the day. He said the driver was the spitting image of the lead singer of Metallica."

Jude had to laugh.

56

On the second weekend of November, the Dodge Charger pulled out of a churchyard on a red clay dirt road in Georgia, cans rattling from the back. Bammy stuck her fingers in her mouth and blew rude whistles.

57

Oﾠne fall they went to Fiji. The fall after, they visited Greece. Next October they went to Hawaii, spent ten hours a day on a beach of crushed black sand. Naples, the year following, was even better. They went for a week and stayed for a month.

In the autumn of their fifth anniversary, they didn't go anywhere. Jude had bought puppies and didn't want to leave them. One day, when it was chilly and wet, Jude walked with the new dogs down the driveway to collect the mail. As he was tugging the envelopes out of the box, just beyond the front gate, a pale pickup blasted by on the highway, throwing cold spray at his back, and when he turned to watch it go, he saw Anna staring at him from across the road. He felt a sharp twinge in the chest, which quickly abated, leaving him panting.

She pushed a yellow strand of hair back from her eyes, and he saw then that she was shorter, more athletically built than Anna, just a girl, eighteen at best. She lifted one hand in a tentative wave. He gestured for her to cross the road.

"Hi, Mr. Coyne," she said.

"Reese, isn't it?" he said.

She nodded. She didn't have a hat, and her hair was wet. Her denim jacket was soaked through. The puppies leaped at her, and she twisted away from them, laughing.

"Jimmy," Jude said. "Robert. Get down. Sorry. They're an uncouth bunch, and I haven't taught them their manners yet. Will you come in?" She was shivering just slightly. "You're getting drenched. You'll catch your death."

"Is that catching?" Reese asked.

"Yeah," Jude said. "There's a wicked case going around. Sooner or later everyone gets it."

He led her back to the house and into the darkened kitchen. He was just asking her how she'd made her way out to his place when Marybeth called down from the staircase and asked who was there.

"Reese Price," Jude said back. "From Testament. In Florida. Jessica Price's girl?"

For a moment there was no sound from the top of the stairs. Then Marybeth padded down the steps, stopped close to the bottom. Jude found the lights by the door, flipped them on.

In the sudden snap of brightness that followed, Marybeth and Reese regarded each other without speaking. Marybeth's face was composed, hard to read. Her eyes searched. Reese looked from Marybeth's face, to her neck, to the silvery white crescent of scar tissue around her throat. Reese pulled her arms out of the sleeves of her coat and hugged herself beneath it. Water dripped off her and puddled around her feet.

"Jesus Christ, Jude," Marybeth said. "Go and get her a towel."

Jude fetched a towel from the downstairs bathroom. When he returned to the kitchen with it, the kettle was on the stove and Reese was sitting at the center island, telling Marybeth about the Russian exchange students who had given her a ride from New York City and who kept talking about their visit to the Entire Steak Buildink.

Marybeth made her hot cocoa and a grilled cheese and tomato sandwich while Jude sat with Reese at the counter. Marybeth was relaxed and sisterly and laughed easily at Reese's stories, as if it were the most natural thing in the world to play host to a girl who had shot off a piece of her husband's hand.

The women did most of the talking. Reese was on her way to Buffalo, where she was going to meet up with friends and see 50 Cent and Eminem. Afterward they were traveling on to Niagara. One of the friends had put money down on an old houseboat. They were going to live in it, half a dozen of them. The boat needed work. They were planning to fix it up and sell it. Reese was in charge of painting it. She had a really cool idea for a mural she wanted to paint on the side. She had already done sketches. She took a sketchbook from her backpack and showed them some of her work. Her illustrations were unpracticed but eye-catching, pictures of nude ladies and eyeless old men and guitars, arranged in complicated interlocking patterns. If they couldn't sell the boat, they were going to start a business in it, either pizza or tattoos. Reese knew a lot about tattoos and had practiced on herself. She lifted her shirt to show them a tattoo of a pale, slender snake making a circle around her bellybutton, eating its own tail.

Jude interrupted to ask her how she was getting to Buffalo. She said she ran out of bus money back at Penn Station and figured she'd hitch the rest of the way.

"Do you know it's three hundred miles?" he asked.

Reese stared at him, wide-eyed, then shook her head. "You look at a map and this state doesn't seem so gosh-darn big. Are you sure it's three hundred miles?"

Marybeth took her empty plate and set it in the sink. "Is there anyone you want to call? Anyone in your family? You can use our phone."

"No, ma'am."

Marybeth smiled a little at this, and Jude wondered if anyone had ever called her "ma'am" before.

"What about your mother?" Marybeth asked.

"She's in jail. I hope she doesn't ever get out," Reese said, and she looked into her cocoa. She began to play with a long yellow strand of her hair, curling it around and around her finger, a thing Jude had seen Anna do a thousand times. She said, "I don't even like to think about her. I'd rather pretend she was dead or something. I wouldn't wish her on anyone. She's a curse, is what she is. If I thought someday I was going to be a mother like her, I'd have myself sterilized right now."

When she finished her cocoa, Jude put on a rain slicker and told Reese to come on, he would take her to the bus station.

For a while they rode without speaking, the radio off, no sound but the rain tapping on the glass and the Charger's wipers beating back and forth. He looked over at her once and saw she had the seat cranked back and her eyes closed. She had taken off her denim jacket and spread it over herself like a blanket. He believed she was sleeping.

But in a while she opened one eye and squinted at him. "You really cared about Aunt Anna, didn't you?"

He nodded. The wipers went *whip-thud, whip-thud*.

Reese said, "There's things my momma did she shouldn't have done. Some things I'd give my left arm to forget. Sometimes I think my Aunt Anna found out about some of what my momma was doing—my momma and old Craddock, her stepfather—and that's why she killed herself. Because she couldn't live anymore with what she knew, but she couldn't talk about it either. I know she was already real unhappy. I think maybe some bad stuff happened to her, too, when she was little. Some of the same stuff happened to me." She was looking at him directly now.

So. Reese at least did not know everything her mother had done, which Jude could only take to mean that there really was some mercy to be found in the world.

"I am sorry about what I did to your hand," she said. "I mean that. I have dreams sometimes, about my Aunt Anna. We go for rides together. She has a cool old car like this one, only black. She isn't sad anymore, not in my dreams. We go for rides in the country. She listens to your music on the radio. She told me you weren't at our house to hurt me. She said you came to end it. To bring my mother to account for what she let happen to me. I just wanted to say I'm sorry and I hope you're happy."

He nodded but did not reply, did not, in truth, trust his own voice.

They went into the station together. Jude left her on a scarred wooden bench, went to the counter and bought a ticket to Buffalo. He had the station agent put it inside an envelope. He slipped two hundred dollars in with it, folded into a sheet of paper with his phone number on it and a note that she should call if she ran into trouble on the road. When he returned to her, he stuck the envelope into the pouch on the side of her backpack instead of handing it to her, so she wouldn't look into it right away and try to give the money back.

She went with him out onto the street, where the rain was falling more heavily now and the last of the day's light had fled, leaving things blue and twilighty and cold. He turned to say good-bye, and she stood on tiptoe and kissed the chilled, wet side of his face. He had, until then, been thinking of her as a young woman, but her kiss was the thoughtless kiss of a child. The idea of her traveling hundreds of miles north, with no one to look out for her, seemed suddenly all the more daunting.

"Take care," they both said, at exactly the same time, in perfect unison, and then they laughed. Jude squeezed her hand and nodded but had nothing else to say except good-bye.

It was dark when he came back into the house. Marybeth pulled two bottles of Sam Adams out of the fridge, then started rummaging in the drawers for a bottle opener.

"I wish I could've done something for her," Jude said.

"She's a little young," Marybeth said. "Even for you. Keep it in your pants, why don't you?"

"Jesus. That's not what I meant."

Marybeth laughed, found a dishrag, and chucked it in his face.

"Dry off. You look even more like a pathetic derelict when you're all wet."

He rubbed the rag through his hair. Marybeth popped him a beer and set it in front of him. Then she saw he was still pouting and laughed again.

"Come on, now, Jude. If you didn't have me to rake you over the coals now and then, there wouldn't be any fire left in your life at all," she said. She stood on the other side of the kitchen counter, watching him with a certain wry, tender regard. "Anyway, you gave her a bus ticket to Buffalo, and . . . what? How much money?"

"Two hundred dollars."

"Come on, now. You did something for her. You did plenty. What else were you supposed to do?"

Jude sat at the center island, holding the beer Marybeth had set in front of him but not drinking it. He was tired, still damp and chilly from the outside. A big truck, or a Greyhound maybe, roared down the highway, fled into the cold tunnel of the night, was gone. He could hear the puppies out in their pen, yipping at it, excited by its noise.

"I hope she makes it," Jude said.

"To Buffalo? I don't see why she wouldn't," Marybeth said.

"Yeah," Jude said, although he wasn't sure that was what he'd really meant at all.

HEART-SHAPED ACKNOWLEDGMENTS

Raise your lighters for one last schmaltzy power ballad and allow me to sing the praises of those folks who gave so much to help bring *Heart-Shaped Box* into existence. My thanks to my agent, Michael Choate, who steers my professional ship with care, discretion, and uncommon good sense. I owe much to Jennifer Brehl, for all the hard work she put into editing my novel, for guiding me through the final draft, and especially for taking a chance on *Heart-Shaped Box* in the first place. Maureen Sugden did an extraordinary job of copyediting my novel. Thanks are also due to Lisa Gallagher, Juliette Shapland, Kate Nintzel, Ana Maria Allessi, Lynn Grady, Rich Aquan, Lorie Young, Kim Lewis, Seale Ballenger, Kevin Callahan, Sara Bogush, and everyone else at William Morrow who went to bat for the book. Gratitude is owed, as well, to Jo Fletcher, at Gollancz, in England, who sweated over this book as much as anyone.

My deepest appreciation to Andy and Kerri, for their enthusiasm and friendship, and to Shane, who is not only my compadre but who also keeps my web site, joehillfiction.com, flying with spit and imagination. And I can't say how grateful I am to my parents and siblings for their time, thoughts, support, and love.

Most of all, my love and thanks to Leonora and the boys. Leonora spent I don't know how many hours reading and rereading this manu-script, in all its various forms, and talking with me about Jude, Marybeth, and the ghosts. To put it another way: She read a million pages, and she rocked them all. Thanks, Leanora. I am so glad and so lucky to have you as my best friend.

That's all, and thanks for coming to my show, everyone. Good night, Shreveport!

Turn the page for a tantalizing taste
of Joe Hill's next twisted and terrifying tale,

1

Ignatius Martin Perrish spent the night drunk and doing terrible things. He woke the next morning with a headache, put his hands to his temples and felt something unfamiliar, a pair of knobby pointed protuberances. He was so ill—wet-eyed and weak—he didn't think anything of it at first, was too hungover for thinking or worry.

But when he was swaying over the toilet, he glanced at himself in the mirror over the sink and saw he had grown horns while he slept. He lurched in surprise and for the second time in twelve hours, he pissed on his feet.

2

He shoved himself back into his khaki shorts—he was still wearing yesterday's clothes—and leaned over the sink for a better look.

They weren't much as horns went, each of them about as long as his ring finger, thick at the base, but soon narrowing to a point as they hooked upward. The horns were covered in his own too-pale skin, except at the very tips, which were an ugly inflamed red, as if the needle-points at the ends of them were about to poke through the flesh. He touched one, and found the point sensitive, a little sore. He ran his fingers along the sides of each and felt the density of bone beneath the stretched-tight smooth-ness of skin.

His first thought was that somehow he had brought this affliction upon himself. Late the night before he had gone into the woods beyond the old foundry, to the place where Merrin Williams had been killed. People had left remembrances at a diseased black cherry tree, the bark peeling away to show the flesh beneath. Merrin had been found like that, clothes peeled away to show the flesh beneath. There were photographs of her placed delicately in the branches, a vase of pussy willows, Hallmark cards warped and stained from exposure to the elements. Someone, Merrin's mother probably, had left a decorative cross with yellow nylon roses sta-pled to it, and a plastic Virgin who smiled with the beatific idiocy of the functionally retarded.

He couldn't stand that simpering smile. He couldn't stand the cross ei-ther, planted in the place where Merrin bled to death from her smashed-in head. A cross with yellow roses. What a fucking thing. It was like an electric chair with floral-print cushions, a bad joke. It bothered him that someone wanted to bring Christ out here. Christ was a year too late to do any good. He hadn't been anywhere around when Merrin needed Him.

Ig had ripped the decorative cross down and stamped it into the dirt. He had to take a leak and he did it on the Virgin, drunkenly urinating on his own feet in the process. Perhaps that was blasphemy enough to bring on this transformation. But no—he sensed there had been more. What else, he couldn't recall. He had had a lot to drink.

He turned his head this way and that, studying himself in the mirror, lifting his fingers to touch the horns, once and again. How deep did the bone go? Did the horns have roots, pushing back into his brain? At this thought, the bathroom darkened, as if the light bulb overhead had briefly gone dim. The welling darkness, though, was behind his eyes, in his head, not in the light fixtures. He held the sink and waited for the feeling of weakness to pass.

He saw it then. He was going to die. Of course he was going to die. Something was pushing into his brain, all right: a tumor. The horns weren't really there. They were metaphorical, imaginary. He had a tumor eating his brain and it was causing him to see things. And if he was to the point of seeing things, then it was probably too late to save him.

The idea that he might be going to die brought with it a surge of relief, a physical sensation, like coming up for air after being underwater too long. Ig had come close to drowning once, and had suffered from asthma as a child, and to him, contentment was as simple as being able to breathe.

"I'm sick," he breathed. "I'm dying."

It improved his mood to say it aloud.

He studied himself in the mirror, expecting the horns to vanish now that he knew they were hallucinatory, but it didn't work that way. The horns remained. He fretfully tugged at his hair, trying to see if he could hide them, at least until he got to the doctor's, then quit when he realized how silly it was to try and conceal something no one would be able to see but him.

He wandered into the bedroom on shaky legs. The bedclothes were shoved back on either side and the bottom sheet still bore the rumpled impression of Glenna Shepherd's curves. He had no memory of falling into bed beside her, didn't even remember getting home; another missing part of the evening. It had been in his head until this very moment that he had slept alone and that Glenna had spent the night somewhere else. With someone else.

They had gone out together, the night before, but after he had been drinking a while, Ig had just naturally started to think about Merrin, the anniversary of her death coming up in a few days. The more he drank, the more he missed her . . . and the more conscious he was of how little Glenna was like her. With her tattoos, and her paste-on nails, her book-shelf full of Dean Koontz novels, her cigarettes and her rap sheet, Glenna was the unMerrin. It irritated Ig to see her sitting there on the other side of the table, seemed a kind of betrayal to be with her, although whether he was betraying Merrin or himself he didn't know. Finally he had to get away—Glenna kept reaching over to stroke his knuckles with one finger, a gesture she meant to be tender but which for some reason pissed him off. He went to the men's room and hid there for twenty minutes. When he returned he found the booth empty. He sat there drinking for an hour before he understood she was not coming back, and that he was not sorry. But at some point in the evening they had both wound up here in the same bed, the bed they had shared for the last three months.

He heard the distant babble of the TV in the next room. Glenna was still in the apartment then, hadn't left for the salon yet. He would ask her to drive him to the doctor. The brief feeling of relief at the thought of dying had passed, and he was already dreading the days and weeks to come: his father struggling not to cry, his mother putting on false cheer, IV drips, treatments, radiation, helpless vomiting, hospital food.

Ig crept into the next room, where Glenna sat on the living room couch, in a Guns N' Roses tank top, and faded pajamas bottoms. She was hunched forward, elbows on the coffee table, tucking the last of a donut into her mouth with her fingers. In front of her was the box, containing three-day old supermarket donuts, and a two-liter bottle of Diet Coke. She was watching daytime talk.

She heard him, and glanced his way, eyelids low, gaze disapproving, then returned her stare to the tube. My Best Friend Is A Sociopath! was the subject of today's program. Flabby rednecks were getting ready to throw chairs at each other.

She hadn't noticed the horns.

"I think I'm sick," he said.

"Don't bitch at me," she said. "I'm hungover too."

"No. I mean . . . look at me. Do I look all right?" Asking because he had to be sure.

She slowly turned her head toward him again and peered at him from under her eyelashes. She had on last night's mascara, a little smudged. Glenna had a smooth, pleasantly round face, and a smooth, pleasantly curvy body. She could've almost been a model, if the job was modeling plus sizes. She outweighed Ig by fifty pounds. It wasn't that she was grotesquely fat, but that he was absurdly skinny. She liked to fuck him from on top, and when she put her elbows on his chest, she could push all the air out of him, a thoughtless act of erotic asphyxiation. Ig, who so often struggled for breath, knew every famous person who had ever died of erotic asphyxiation. It was a surprisingly common end for musicians. Kevin Gilbert. Hideto Matsumoto, probably. Michael Hutchence, of course, not someone he wanted to be thinking about in this particular moment. The devil inside. Every single one of us.

"Are you still drunk?" she asked.

When he didn't reply, she shook her head and looked back at the television.

That was it then. If she had seen them she would've come screaming to her feet. But she couldn't see them because they weren't there. They only existed in Ig's mind. Probably if he looked at himself now in a mirror, he wouldn't see them either. Only then Ig spotted a reflection of himself in the window, and the horns were still there. In the window he was a glassy, transparent figure, a demonic ghost.

"I think I need to go to the doctor," he said.

"You know what I need?" she asked.

"What?"

"Another donut," she said, leaning forward to look into the open box. "You think another donut would be okay?"

He replied in a flat voice he hardly recognized. "What's stopping you?"

"I already had one and I'm not even hungry anymore. I just want to eat it." She turned her head and peered up at him, her eyes glittering in a way that suddenly seemed both scared and pleading. "I'd like to eat the whole box."

"The whole box," he repeated.

"I don't even want to use my hands. I just want to stick my face in and start eating. I know that's gross." She moved her finger from donut to donut, counting. "Six. Do you think it would be okay if I ate six more donuts?"

It was hard to think past his alarm and the feeling of pressure and weight at his temples. What she had just said made no sense, was another part of the whole unnatural bad-dream morning.

"If you're screwing with me I wish you wouldn't. I told you I don't feel good."

"I want another donut," she said.

"Go ahead. I don't care."

"Well. Okay. If you think it's all right," she said and she took a donut, pulled it into three pieces, and began to eat, shoving in one chunk after another without swallowing.

Soon the whole donut was in her mouth, filling her cheeks. She gagged, softly, then inhaled deeply through her nostrils, and began to swallow.

Iggy watched, repelled. He had never seen her do anything like it, hadn't seen anything like it since junior high, kids grossing other kids out in the cafeteria. When she was done, she took a few panting, uneven breaths, then looked over her shoulder, eyeing him anxiously.

"I didn't even like it. My stomach hurts," she said. "Do you think I should have another one?"

"Why would you eat another one if your stomach hurts?"

'Cause I want to get really fat. Not fat like I am now. Fat enough so you won't want to have anything to do with me." Her tongue came out and the tip touched her upper lip, a thoughtful, considering gesture. "I did something disgusting last night. I want to tell you about it."

The thought occurred again that none of it was really happening. If he was having some sort of fever-dream, though, it was a persistent one, convincing in its fine details. A fly crawled across the TV screen. A car shushed past out on the road. One moment naturally followed the next, in a way that seemed to add up to reality. Ig was a natural at addition. Math had been his best subject in school, after ethics, which he didn't count as a real subject.

"I don't think I want to know what you did last night," he said.

"That's why I want to tell you. To make you sick. To give you a reason to go away. I feel so bad about what you've been through, and what people say about you, but I can't stand waking up next to you anymore. I just want you to go and if I told you what I did, this disgusting thing, then you'd leave and I'd be free again."

"What do people say about me?" he asked. It was a silly question. He already knew.

She shrugged. "Things about what you did to Merrin. How you're like a sick sex pervert and stuff."

Ig stared at her, transfixed. It fascinated him, the way each thing she said was worse than the last, and how at ease she seemed to be with saying them. Without shame or awkwardness.

"So what did you want to tell me?"

"I ran into Lee Tourneau last night after you disappeared on me. You remember Lee and I used to have a thing going, back in high school?"

"I remember," Ig said. Lee and Ig had been friends in another life, but all that was behind Ig now, had died with Merrin. It was difficult to maintain close friendships when you were under suspicion of being a sex-murderer.

"Last night, at the Station House, he was sitting in a booth in back and after you disappeared he bought me a drink. I haven't talked to Lee in forever. I forgot how easy he is to talk to. You know Lee, he doesn't look down on anyone. He was real nice to me. When you didn't come back after a while, he said we ought to look for you in the parking lot, and if you were gone, he'd drive me home. But then when we were outside, we got kissing kind of hot, like old times, like when we were together—and I got carried away and went down on him, right there with a couple guys watching and everything. I haven't done anything that crazy since I was nineteen and on speed."

Ig needed help. He needed to get out of the apartment. The air was too close, and his lungs felt tight and pinched.

She was leaning over the box of donuts again, her expression placid, as if she had just told him a fact of no particular consequence: that they were out of milk, or had lost the hot water again.

"You think it would be all right to eat one more?" she asked. "My stomach feels better."

"Do what you want."

She turned her head and stared at him, her pale eyes glittering with an unnatural excitement. "You mean it?"

"I don't give a fuck," he said. "Pig out."

She smiled, cheeks dimpling, then bent over the table, taking the box in one hand. She held it in place, shoved her face into it, and began to eat. She made noises while she chewed, smacking her lips and breathing strangely. She gagged again, her shoulders hitching, but kept eating, using her free hand to push more donut into her mouth, even though her cheeks were already swollen and full. A fly buzzed around her head, agitated.

Ig edged past the couch, toward the door. She sat up a little, gasping for breath, and rolled her eyes toward him. Her gaze was panicky and her cheeks and wet mouth were gritted with sugar.

"Mm," she moaned. "Mmm." Whether she moaned in pleasure or misery, he didn't know.

The fly landed at the corner of her mouth. He saw it there for a moment—then Glenna's tongue darted out and she trapped it with her hand at the same time. When she lowered her hand, the fly was gone. Her jaw worked up and down, grinding everything in her mouth into paste.

Ig opened the door and slid himself out. As he closed the door behind him, she was lowering her face to the box again . . . a diver who had filled her lungs with air and was plunging once more into the depths.

SPELLBINDING TALES
from JOE HILL

HORNS
A Novel
ISBN 978-0-06-114796-8
(paperback)

"[...] compulsively [rea]dable supernatural [thr]iller . . . Hill spins [a s]tory that's both [mo]rbidly amusing and [em]otionally resonant."
—*Publishers Weekly*

20th CENTURY GHOSTS
ISBN 978-0-06-114798-2
(paperback)

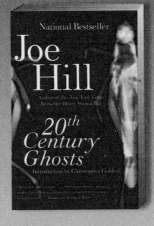

"The collection of short stories ranges from creepy to sweet, with an impressive arsenal of tactics to attack your psyche."
—*Boston Globe*

HEART-SHAPED BOX
A Novel
ISBN 978-0-06-194489-5
(paperback)

"The shocks in Hill's riveting debut novel can be lurid and blood-drenched, or as quietly chilling as a casual phone call from an old, dead friend."
—*Entertainment Weekly*

www.JoeHillFiction.com

Praise for *The Me I Used to Be*

Sisters
and
Secrets

Also by Jennifer Ryan

STANDALONE NOVELS
The Me I Used to Be

WILD ROSE RANCH SERIES
Tough Talking Cowboy • *Restless Rancher*
Dirty Little Secret

MONTANA HEAT SERIES
Tempted by Love • *True to You*
Escape to You • *Protected by Love*

MONTANA MEN SERIES
His Cowboy Heart • *Her Renegade Rancher*
Stone Cold Cowboy • *Her Lucky Cowboy*
When It's Right • *At Wolf Ranch*

THE MCBRIDES SERIES
Dylan's Redemption • *Falling for Owen*
The Return of Brody McBride

THE HUNTED SERIES
Everything She Wanted • *Chasing Morgan*
The Right Bride • *Lucky Like Us*
Saved by the Rancher

SHORT STORIES
"Close to Perfect"
(appears in *Snowbound at Christmas*)
"Can't Wait"
(appears in *All I Want for Christmas Is a Cowboy*)
"Waiting for You"
(appears in *Confessions of a Secret Admirer*)

Sisters

and

Secrets

A Novel

JENNIFER
RYAN

WILLIAM MORROW

An Imprint of HarperCollins*Publishers*

P.S.™ is a trademark of HarperCollins Publishers.

SISTERS AND SECRETS. Copyright © 2020 by Jennifer Ryan. All rights reserved. Printed in the United States of America. No part of this book may be used or reproduced in any manner whatsoever without written permission except in the case of brief quotations embodied in critical articles and reviews. For information, address HarperCollins Publishers, 195 Broadway, New York, NY 10007.

HarperCollins books may be purchased for educational, business, or sales promotional use. For information, please email the Special Markets Department at SPsales@harpercollins.com.

FIRST EDITION

Designed by Diahann Sturge

Chapter opener image © Irina Mos / Shutterstock, Inc.

Library of Congress Cataloging-in-Publication Data has been applied for.

ISBN 978-0-06-294446-7

20 21 22 23 24 LSC 10 9 8 7 6 5 4 3 2 1

For all of you out there who need to rebuild or renovate your life, this one is for you. Let go of the past and anything that doesn't bring you joy. Fill your life with laughter and love. You deserve to be happy.

Chapter One

Flames burned bright orange and red on both sides of the two-lane road as they consumed and destroyed everything in their path. Homes, businesses, multimillion-dollar vineyards. Nothing was spared as the fire climbed over the Napa Valley hills, unrelenting in its destruction. Sierra prayed it spared everyone on the road leading out, especially her sons.

She drove, heart pounding, fear amped to infinity, with her clammy palms locked on the steering wheel. Bumper to bumper, traffic moved at a snail's pace. Like her, the other residents had been notified too late to gradually evacuate. The sheer number of people trying to escape all at once down a single lane prevented them from racing away from the flames. The other lane was left open to emergency vehicles that occasionally sped into the belly of the beast. Everyone had to feel exactly like her: desperate to flee before this dark and dangerous road became their grave.

She loved watching the flames dance in her woodburning stove, but driving through a wildfire made her feel like she was inside an inferno. Trapped. A wave of terror shot through her, cold fear dancing down her spine. She wanted out. Now.

Sierra glanced at her two small sons in the back seat, danger inches away outside. Helpless to eradicate it, she sucked in a breath to calm the fear and focus on getting them out of here as safely as possible. Every instinct told her to stomp on the gas, jump in the other lane, speed past everyone, and get them to safety no matter what. But like everyone else, she tried to stay orderly and calm.

Noxious fumes, unbelievable heat, and fire surrounded them. Nothing and no one was a match for Mother Nature's firestorm. Ash, smoke, and sparks blew all around them while the satellite radio cut in and out, the signal blocked by the thick smoke obliterating their view of the night sky. Fear knotted her gut and rising panic sped up her heartbeat. Every second trapped within the blaze raging on both sides of them made it harder to keep it together for her two little boys.

She thought about their lives, how they'd already suffered a great loss when their father died, and all they had ahead of them. She didn't want it to end this way. She wanted to see them grown, happy, healthy, living the life they chose and thriving.

"Mom." Danny's voice shook. "The window is hot."

"Don't touch it." She'd flipped the vent system to recirculate, but the smoky stench permeated the car along with the immense heat. The acrid scent turned her stomach and left a sour taste in her mouth.

Oliver held his favorite blanket over his mouth and nose. His eyes held a world of worry, too great for one five-year-old to face and understand beyond the fact that the scene outside was scary as hell and he wanted to be far away.

So do I.

Frustration got the better of the guy in the pickup truck behind her and he laid on the horn. Where did he expect her to go?

The line of cars had only moved ten feet in the last two minutes. At this rate, they wouldn't get out of the fire zone before dawn.

At least, it felt that way.

A rush of adrenaline shot through her again, signaling the flight-or-fight response she'd felt when she'd seen the smoke and fire headed toward their home. She could neither fight it nor flee from it when it literally surrounded her. And so she tried her best to stay alert, remain calm, and pray this all worked out.

Three more fire engines sped past in the opposite lane. Reinforcements for the dozens she'd passed on the tedious and exceedingly dangerous trip out of here.

We'll make it out. We have to.

She'd worked too hard the last eleven months to keep her head above water after her husband's tragic car accident to have it all end like this . . . in a car, on a dark road, consumed by fire.

It felt too eerily close to how they lost David.

Sierra gripped the steering wheel even tighter to stop her hands from shaking and focused on the car in front of her, following it around another curve, not getting her hopes up when their speed increased even marginally, but telling herself *steady as she goes* was good enough, so long as they got out of this alive.

The thought of anything happening to her babies . . . She couldn't go there. It stopped her heart. But that fear drove her to keep her head and do everything possible to get them out of this situation even as thoughts of their home, her job, and the future swamped her mind. She'd barely made it by these last many months. If she lost everything . . . What then?

How would she support herself and the boys?

More flashing red and white lights glowed against the thick

smoke ahead. She inched her way toward the emergency vehicles, the cars slowing ahead of her as they approached what must be an intersection. Fire trucks and police cars blocked the cross street, drawing everyone's attention and slowing them down as everyone stared to the side to see if the fire had destroyed everything down that road. Ahead, cars shot forward as if they were racehorses released from the starting gates as they passed the commotion and the open road broke free of the fire border.

Relief hit like a crashing wave.

We made it.

Now what?

She didn't really have a plan for where to go. She ran out of her house with the clothes on her back, her purse, an armful of personal files, and her two sons in tow with the stench of smoke heavy in the air and flames devouring the houses only six streets away. By now, for all she knew, her house and all those on her block were gone.

Bile rose to the back of her throat, the thought so terribly upsetting, their future left uncertain.

Right now, though, she'd take the thirty-five-mile-an-hour speeds, the open land and road ahead of her as she outran the fire and smoke and spotted the sign for Yountville and the acclaimed restaurant the French Laundry.

"Is the fire gone?" Oliver asked.

She wished. "We're getting farther and farther away from it."

"Where are we going?" Danny leaned toward his brother so he could see through the windshield.

Now that the flames weren't licking at the sides of the car

and bearing down on them, Sierra took a moment to think about her next move. She needed a place to put the boys down to bed tonight. In the morning, there'd be news of the firefighters' efforts to stop the massive blaze and whether or not her home had been spared. She hoped, but her heart sank with the realization it didn't seem likely and they'd lost everything.

Chapter Two

A wasteland of ash and blackened trees spread before Sierra. It looked like an apocalyptic scene from a movie. But this was her neighborhood, the site where her home used to stand, its welcoming garden inviting you to the front door and the safe place she used to love.

Nothing stirred but the wind. The quiet unsettled her.

An officer escorted her into the fire zone and dropped her off, just as he had with some of her neighbors.

Driving through the eerily empty neighborhood, having to try extrahard to decipher where she was and where she used to live, left her stomach clenched in a knot. The park where the kids used to play was nothing more than a few burnt trees, their empty blackened branches reaching for the bright blue sky from barren ground. Many of the trees had burned to ash. The play set was nothing but some metal bars sticking out of the sunken cement rectangle with pools of melted plastic from the slides, seesaw, and swings.

Tears stung her eyes as memories of her boys playing and laughing with their friends assailed her.

It was nothing compared to standing in her driveway and seeing nothing but her blackened washer and dryer shells, twisted metal from her stove vent hood, and half her chimney standing, the top part in a heap of brick where the hearth used to be. She remembered hanging stockings from the thick wood mantel every Christmas and dashed a tear from her cheek with her finger.

The loss felt like a sledgehammer to what was left of her broken heart.

The boys' photo albums from birth to now, gone. She had the digital photos stored in the cloud, but she'd painstakingly put the albums together with other mementos. The hospital bands they wore when they were born. The ticket stubs from their first movie. The armbands from their first visit to the zoo. The pictures they colored on their first day of preschool. The colored and stained kids' menu from breakfast with Mickey at Disneyland. The prayer card from their father's funeral.

It killed her when they asked if all their father's things were gone. She'd promised them she'd find everything she could.

She thought of the cuff links he wore at their wedding. She'd hoped that one day the boys would wear them when they married the person of their dreams. She'd kept his golf clubs, despite how many times she'd resented him taking off for eighteen holes of solitude and fun when she barely got an hour to herself each day. But she'd hoped her boys would give the sport a try and find some commonality with their father. She pictured them standing on the course and taking a moment to think about him every time they played.

David died so young. It wouldn't be long before the boys lost the sharpness of their memories of him. She feared Oliver would forget him altogether.

She'd kept as much as she could of David in the house to

remind them, despite how those reminders triggered her resentments and anger.

Sierra reminded herself that she didn't need the things in the house to remember all they'd shared under that roof. The good times. The bad. She still carried them with her.

David's sudden death left her the keeper of his memory for the boys. She tried to keep him alive for them, but the fire took everything of his, all the mementos the boys needed to help them remember their father.

His stuff may be gone, but he'd left her with suspicions and doubts about the many months leading up to his death. Those didn't burn up in the fire. But anything that might have revealed the truth was gone.

Sierra didn't know if she could live without knowing, but what choice did she have now?

The fire had wiped the slate clean of every possession and tie to the past. She had to rebuild from the ground up.

No home. No job. A dwindling savings account.

It had taken hours to complete her claim with the insurance company, but a payout was weeks if not months away.

Rebuilding could take years with all the government red tape. But the cost of rebuilding . . . The insurance probably wouldn't cover it.

Added to her worries, she no longer had an income. The property management company she worked for had burned down, too, along with many of the properties they oversaw.

She faced a long journey ahead of her to figure out what to do with the home she no longer felt a connection to.

It felt like one more thing David had left for her to deal with on her own.

What am I doing here?

There's nothing left.

But she had promised the boys she'd take back anything she could salvage. She hoped to find at least one thing for each of them. The stuffed fish David won Oliver at the fair knocking down milk jugs with a baseball wasn't even worth consideration. Neither was Danny's science fair certificate he was so proud of winning. The memory would have to be enough for both of them. But maybe something survived.

She walked toward the property site and slid the respirator mask she'd been given over her head to cover her nose and mouth. She didn't want to breathe in all the soot, ash, and toxic chemicals from everything that had burned and melted.

With the layout of the house ahead of her obscured by debris and simply unrecognizable without the walls defining the space, she started at the cement porch steps that led to where her door used to be. She stepped up to what used to be the entry and surveyed the destruction with a lump in her throat, tears in her eyes, and a very heavy heart.

Nothing in the living room, kitchen, dining room, or bathrooms was worth sorting through all the wreckage to find. She visualized the house and made her way to where the boys' rooms were located, her rubber boots crunching over the remains of what used to be their home.

She tried not to think too hard about all they'd lost. Dishes, furniture, TVs, computers, clothes—all of it could be replaced, she reminded herself. That didn't help ease the ache in her chest or the wanting to have it all back. The baby clothes she'd saved. The crib she'd stored in the garage just in case one day they had another baby.

Not possible for them now.

But she'd liked knowing it was there if she needed it.

Just like her grandmother's quilt wrapped in tissue and stored in a box in the hall linen closet.

With the destruction spread out before her, it seemed ridiculous to even think something survived the flames and heat.

Sierra found what she thought was Danny's room and where his desk and bookshelf used to stand. She pulled on thick work gloves and dug into the debris, hoping to find something recognizable. Ten minutes in, her fingers brushed something hard. She picked up the disk and stared at it, not believing her eyes. The outside of the pocket watch had blackened, but when she opened it, the inside wasn't that bad off. The glass had cracked and the clock mechanism didn't work, but Danny would love to have it, anyway. She and David bought it for him at some downtown antique shop on their vacation up to Jamestown where they took the kids gold panning in an old abandoned ghost town turned into a tourist attraction. The kids had even made candles.

The memory along with finding the pocket watch eased her heart a bit. She had something to give to Danny besides the metal frame of what might be a Ford Mustang Hot Wheel with no tires and the paint melted completely away.

She spent ten more minutes rummaging through what was

left of Danny's room before working on Oliver's space. She didn't find much until she made it to where his toy box had sat below his window. There, she found a treasure that brought tears to her eyes. His marble collection had survived inside a tin that had once held Hershey's chocolate they'd bought at the chocolate factory they'd toured in the Central Valley.

Oliver would be so happy.

She lifted a half-burnt board and found two dirty but perfectly intact plastic dinosaurs. How they didn't melt escaped her, but she'd take the little guys back to Oliver. The mound of burnt plastic ten inches away had to be the bin that held all the others. She didn't even bother trying to pull it apart to see if anything in the middle survived. She just moved on, brushing things this way and that hoping something else caught her eye.

Even though her thighs and ankles hurt from crouching, she moved on to her bedroom, strategic in where she looked. She started where she thought the closet used to be, hoping that even if her wooden jewelry box hadn't survived, some of her jewelry had, especially the pieces she'd put into a metal lockbox.

Metal hangers told Sierra she was in the right place. But she didn't find anything resembling the few pieces of jewelry she owned until she started backing up toward where the bed used to be. Her foot kicked something and the metallic thump of it hitting something else made her heart pound and hope rise. She shoved debris aside to get to the blackened rectangle with the lock still intact. She hugged the box to her chest and heard several things inside rattle. She didn't have the key to open it, but with some tools, she hoped to bust it open and find her and

David's wedding rings, along with her pair of diamond studs, and a couple other rings and a diamond heart pendant David gave her their first Christmas as a married couple.

"Find something?" the officer who dropped her off asked from the road as he stood outside his patrol car.

She stood, pulled her mask off, and found a smile. "Yes. I did."

"It's getting late. We'll close the neighborhood off to visitors for the night soon. It's time to head back. You can return tomorrow if you'd like."

They'd closed off the neighborhood to keep looters from trying to sort through homes looking for anything that survived the fire.

Some people suck.

It wasn't bad enough the people who used to live here lost everything; someone wanted to profit off them.

Which made her think of all the paperwork and hoops she'd had to jump through to file her insurance claim and put in for federal assistance.

It sucked that the process was so hard and convoluted.

She put the metal box into the bucket she'd brought with her that now contained her treasures, planted her hands on her knees, and pushed herself up. Her legs ached, but her heart felt lighter. She'd found what she'd come here for, and Danny and Oliver would be so happy to have a small piece of their past to hold on to when everything had been taken away, including the school they used to attend.

They couldn't stay here much longer.

She needed to get the boys somewhere they could settle in and go back to school.

She also needed to call her mom and have the talk she'd put off because immediate concerns took precedence to actually making decisions that extended beyond their need for a roof over their heads and dealing with the aftermath of the fire.

She'd done what she needed to do with the property.

There truly was nothing left for her to do here.

Overwhelmed by what came next and the abundance of decisions that had to be made to start a whole new life, Sierra trudged through the wreckage, walked down the porch steps one last time, her heart heavy that this was probably the last time she'd ever come here, and headed for the police car. She opened the back door, set her bucket on the seat, then turned back and looked at what used to be.

Emotion flooded her, sending tears down her cheeks. She pulled off a glove and brushed them away with clean fingers.

"You can rebuild," the officer assured her.

Yes, I will. Just not here.

Her boys were counting on her.

But she had to face reality and listen to her heart. She didn't want to be here anymore.

She wanted to go home to Carmel.

* * *

"Hi, sweetheart."

"Hey, Mom." Sierra stood outside the motel room door on the balcony overlooking the pool with her cell phone to her ear, so happy to hear her mother's reassuring voice.

"It's been a couple of days. I worried."

The days since the fire had left Sierra drained. "I'm sorry.

I went to the house yesterday. There's nothing left but ash and burnt trees. Everywhere I looked . . . there was just nothing."

"I can't imagine." Emotion tightened her mom's soft voice. "We spoke about this the other day, but I'll say it again. I'm happy to help in any way you need."

"I appreciate that."

"Just tell me how much you need and I'll get it to you."

She didn't want to rely on her mother for financial support. That was more her little sister Heather's MO. "Right now I need something besides money."

"Anything."

"I want to come home, Mom."

"I've got your old room and the spare bedroom all ready for you."

Relief swept through her. Her mom offered the second she found out the house was lost. Overwhelmed in the moment, and since, Sierra hadn't been able to really think or plan.

"When will you be here?"

"Tomorrow?" She hated to impose, but she also wanted to get the boys settled.

"I can't wait." Her mother's excitement eased Sierra's mind.

"Thank you for this. I'm out of options." At least it felt that way.

"I'm always here for you, Sierra. This is still your home no matter how old you get."

Tears clogged her throat, but she pushed the words out. "I love you."

"I love you, too, sweetheart. Everything is going to be okay."

She really needed to hear that right now.

Sierra outlined her plans for the trip home, thanked her mom one more time, and said good-bye with a lighter heart and a belly full of anticipation.

This felt right. With everything of her old life literally left in ashes, she needed a fresh start.

So did the boys. They'd been through so much this past year, losing their father and now their home.

She walked back into their latest rented room and stared at her boys sitting on the queen bed in the fourth motel they'd moved to in the last three weeks. Their treasures she'd found at the house yesterday sat on the nightstand beside them. They'd been so surprised and excited to get them, but also sad that the few items had been all that was left of their belongings. She felt the same way.

One of the guys at the fire victims center took a hammer and screwdriver to the lockbox and popped it open for her. David's cuff links had survived. So had their wedding rings. The jewelry hadn't come out unscathed. The metal had turned black and tarnished, but the diamonds were eerily bright and sparkly. Maybe one day she'd have them reset into new men's rings for the boys. They could wear a piece of what bound her and David together.

Backs against the propped pillows, Danny and Oliver were deep into a cupcake baking show on the Food Network. Eventually, they'd ask to go to the local grocery store to pick up some treats.

They deserved something sweet for being such troopers. They missed their friends, their own things, and even school.

Sierra pressed her hand over the stack of papers sitting on

the small table by the window. They were all she'd managed to grab on her mad dash out of the house to beat the fire. All these months after David's death, she still couldn't account for the personal loan he'd taken out without her knowledge.

Fifty thousand dollars.

This past year, she'd struggled on her income combined with David's Social Security to pay the bills and keep a roof over their heads. And now she didn't even have the house or a job.

She had this motel room for the next two days, another lined up for one night, but she needed something more permanent. The boys needed stability. They needed routine.

And so did she.

All this uncertainty left her a live wire of anxiety, sadness for all they'd lost, and uncertainty about how she'd get them all back on track and thriving again.

As a mom, she thought she could do it all. She tried.

Most days, until the fire, she did a pretty good job.

You can't have everything. Something's gotta give. But right now, overwhelmed by their circumstances and uncertainty about the future, she needed help.

Her family knew of their troubles. They wanted to help. She appreciated it, but until now she'd gone from hour to hour, day to day, trying her best to deal with the aftermath of the fire and keep the boys entertained.

But she needed to start thinking of the bigger picture. Especially because she was running out of money and racking up credit card debt. Yes, there was help out there for the fire victims. She'd taken advantage of the free clothes, everyday necessities, like toiletries, and even a few toys for the boys to take their minds off all they'd lost.

Truly, when she thought about all the *things* they needed to replace, it overwhelmed her.

And yet, she had moments where she embraced the fact that this was a chance to start over, start fresh.

But there was so much of the past still left unsettled.

While the community had come together to provide free meals and assistance to navigate the process and red tape involved in a disaster, it was still so overwhelming. All she wanted to do was hand the whole job over to someone else. She wanted to turn back time and go back to her life before the fire destroyed everything.

That thought only reminded her that life hadn't been happy and carefree for a long time. Certainly not since her husband's death and, if she was honest with herself, it started before that. There'd been a distance building between them for some time. The more she thought about it, the more she realized that she'd never get the answers she desperately wanted from David.

Right now, that didn't matter.

Her boys deserved better than dingy motel rooms and another takeout meal.

Sierra glanced around the messy room. Plastic shopping bags with their meager belongings on the floor and dresser, discarded takeout containers scattered across the small table by the window, the boys' bath towels on the tile floor by the vanity with the dripping faucet, both beds a mess of tangled sheets littered with toy cars and stuffed animals, and her boys sitting among the chaos eating a bag of chips instead of a healthy snack.

The untidy room reflected the current state of her life.

She needed to clean up the mess, clear her mind, and come up with a plan for their new life.

"What do you guys think about going to visit Grandma and Aunt Amy and Aunt Heather?" Asking for help had never come easy, but Sierra really needed some right now. She'd reached that point where there was so much to tackle she didn't know where to start.

The boys rolled up to their feet and jumped up and down on the bed. "Yes!"

Danny bounced and landed on his butt. "When can we go?"

"Now!" Oliver begged.

Yep, they needed family. Stability. Something familiar.

Truth be told, so did she, but that meant going home. It felt like the right decision, but sometimes going home was easier said than done.

She hoped she wasn't trading one drama for another.

Chapter Three

Heather pulled onto the shoulder and parked the car next to the mailboxes. She checked the car seat behind her and found her daughter, Hallee, still slumbering, her face soft and sweet. Every time she looked at her little girl, she saw a glimpse of the man she'd loved and lost.

Cars drove by on the main road. She climbed out and inhaled the slightly salty scent in the air, though they were a ways from the beach. She loved it here in Carmel Valley. So much so, she'd never left.

Not like Sierra.

She couldn't imagine all her sister had been through these last weeks.

Her mother had called an hour ago, said she'd heard from Sierra, and asked Heather to stop by after work to talk about Sierra and the boys.

She missed her sister. But as much as she wanted to help, she dreaded Sierra's return. Everyone would start asking questions about Heather's daughter again.

Family. They wanted all the details about your successes and mistakes.

Hopefully, Sierra's troubles would keep them all occupied and off her back.

Life had always been about her older sisters. This time would be no different.

Amy seemed to have a new crisis every week. If you could call motherhood a crisis. Amy seemed to think everything had to be perfect in her perfect life.

Heather rolled her eyes at that. Sometimes the messy things gave you the most satisfaction and joy. She glanced at her sweet sleeping angel. Yep. The mess, the pain, the bad choices . . . totally worth it.

Even if she had to live with the consequences and secrets.

A Mercedes pulled in front of her car as she retrieved the mail from her mother's box. It had been a long time since she'd seen the sexy man who climbed out and stopped short when he saw her.

Mason Moore. Superhot next-door neighbor. Now a successful divorce attorney. They met him the day they moved here after their mom married husband number four. As teens, at one time or another, she, Amy, and even Sierra had a crush on him.

He had an odd profession for a guy who didn't seem to enjoy other people's drama. But Mom said rumor had it he'd helped an old flame out during a nasty divorce, managing to get her full custody of her kids from an ex-husband who liked to hurt the people he supposedly loved.

Mason would want to be the guy who protected people like her and the child.

He was just a good guy.

Maybe if she'd gone for someone like him instead of the bad

boys she preferred . . . Well, that's what happened when your heart wanted what it wanted.

Her heart sped up just looking at him.

"Heather. Hey. What are you doing here?"

Thinking about getting out of this rut and dating again. God, you're gorgeous.

It had been a long time since she'd enjoyed a night out with a guy. She missed the flirting, listening to a man's deep voice, having all his attention focused on her.

No offense to her sweet girl, but Mama needed some affection, too, sometimes.

She held up the stack of envelopes and catalogs. "Grabbing the mail for Mom on my way to see her."

"How is she?" He unlocked his box and pulled out his mail, his focus more on the bills than her. Unfortunately.

"Fine. Getting the house ready for company."

One eyebrow raised above his dark sunglasses. "Company?"

"Sierra and the boys."

The eyebrow went up again. "Sierra's coming home?" A hint of anticipation and hope filled the question that sounded way more like a statement he needed to hear to believe it.

She couldn't see his eyes, but she felt his interest in the answer, not her. "They'll be here tomorrow."

"How are they? I mean, they must be devastated after the fire."

"It's been difficult. They've been moving from one hotel or motel to the next while Sierra sorts out the mess with the insurance and government assistance. There's not much left up there for them. Sierra's job is gone along with everything else they owned, so . . ." She shrugged. "I guess this is her only choice right now."

Mason tilted his head. "She's smart. Resourceful. I'm sure she'll be back on her feet in no time. But it will be good to have her home."

Heather wasn't so sure about that. She loved her sister, but when they got together, they fell back into childhood roles. Heather wanted Sierra to see her for who she was now, not the impulsive spoiled brat Sierra used to call her. Of course, her sisters and mom never let her forget her mistakes and missteps. "I'm looking forward to seeing the boys." That at least was wholly true.

"Please tell Sierra, if there's anything she needs, I'm happy to help."

Yeah, everyone had scrambled to help Sierra after David died. They'd do the same now after the fire. She'd be everyone's priority.

Mason glanced at the back of her car. Hallee gave him a bright smile and waved. Mason waved back, smiling for the first time. It made him even more handsome, and Hallee ate it up, covering her face with her stuffed elephant, then moving it away and smiling at him again.

Mason turned his attention back to her. "She's really sweet."

"Growing like a weed."

"She'll probably love having the boys around."

Heather wished she could see his eyes. Something in his voice hinted at an underlying message she couldn't decipher. "Uh, yeah. We haven't seen Sierra and the boys in a while."

He leaned his weight on one leg in a casual stance, but she felt his focus. "How are you getting on all by yourself? It can't be easy being a single mom."

"I'm doing okay." It sucked. She wished she had a loving husband. Hallee deserved a father who loved her and showed her what a good man looked like.

Hallee's father had loved her. He had wanted her.

It just wasn't meant to be.

"Good to hear it." That same edge she'd heard before came again. "Well, it's been a long day and I have to get home and check on the horses. Say hi to your mom for me. Maybe I'll stop by to see Sierra and the boys once they've settled in."

"I'm sure she'd love to see you."

The innocuous statement made him pause for a second. "She's been through a lot. I hope she finds some happiness here."

Why did she hear a deeper meaning in the things he said?

Heather held up the mail. "I better get going, too." She stopped him just before he opened his car door. "It's nice to see you, Mason. It's been too long. We've known each other forever, yet we hardly take the time to say hi anymore."

"It's been a long time since you girls were jumping fences and begging me to ride the horses."

"Maybe I'll make a point to stop by and do just that."

She got another of those stares from behind his glasses that she couldn't see or read. "Tell Sierra if the boys need a distraction, I'm happy to saddle up a couple horses for them." With that, Mason slid into his car, started the engine, and pulled back onto the road, taking the long driveway just past her mother's.

"He's a strange one. But sexy as all get out." Maybe she

would take a chance and stop by for a *ride*. The images that evoked made her warm all over.

Definitely time to get back in the dating saddle.

But first she needed to meet her mom and Amy about Sierra. Because just like Mason's comments, everything right now for everyone was about *her*.

Chapter Four

Sierra pulled into the driveway.

Dede's stomach fluttered with anticipation. She hoped she, Amy, and Heather had gathered everything Sierra and the boys needed to settle in here.

With four marriages under her belt, Dede feared the only thing she'd taught her daughters about love and marriage was that neither lasts. With Amy on the verge of a divorce she wouldn't see coming with her blinders on, Heather a single mom with zero interest in finding a partner, and Sierra a widow with two young sons, it didn't look like any one of them would find the kind of love that lasts.

Despite not finding it for herself, she wanted her daughters to find their soul mates—if such a thing even existed.

But, oh, those daughters of hers!

Amy held on so tight to her husband and the image she showed the world—perfect marriage, perfect kids, perfect life—that she didn't enjoy any of it. The moments were lost, despite how much she loved to share the perfect pictures. She didn't seem to savor the memories or reflect on how lucky she was to have a man who really loved her and the kids. Amy was so busy creating a moment, she didn't share it with her husband and kids. Her family was perfect without all the fuss and polish

Amy heaped on them. And Rex was getting tired of feeling like he didn't matter as much as the Instagram-perfect meal Amy set in front of him each night.

Dede rolled her eyes at a memory of their last family meal together, a moment when Rex had tried to lean in and kiss his wife. Amy had nudged him out of her way so she could get the star-shaped cucumbers out of the fridge. They needed to go on top of the salad or it just wasn't finished. Rejected for cucumbers. Dede sighed. No wonder Rex was frustrated and feeling underappreciated.

But Amy would say no one appreciated all the fuss and bother she put into everything.

Dede had tried to tell her to relax and stop taking on so much. Of course, her oldest wouldn't listen. She had to be right about everything.

And maybe she got that from Dede, too.

Heather, on the other hand, just wanted to be with her little girl and soak up Hallee's bright smiles and joyful giggles. She loved being a mother. And yet, for all the happiness Dede saw in Heather when she and Hallee were together, Dede sometimes caught moments when that joy was replaced by a look of deep sadness and regret Dede wished she understood.

But Heather had always liked her secrets. As a kid she'd spy on Amy and Sierra. She knew which one of them ate the last of the cookies without permission. As a teen she knew who snuck in late. Heather relished knowing her sisters' secrets and letting you know she knew.

She loved sneaking around and listening in when she shouldn't. Those little things she knew were fun.

But withholding the name of Hallee's father—and not letting everyone know—seemed to wear on Heather. Still, she refused to divulge the information. And things didn't quite add up. She said the man knew about Hallee but wanted to remain in the background. In the beginning, he provided for Heather and Hallee, but lately it seemed evident by the number of times Heather asked to "borrow" money he wasn't even peripherally involved in their lives anymore. And that sadness she saw in Heather seemed to grow.

Dede didn't mind helping her daughters out when they needed it. But Heather relied on it a little too much. Her fault for spoiling the baby of the family.

And poor Sierra. How much could one young woman take? David had died tragically and unexpectedly nearly a year ago and now she'd lost everything in that devastating wildfire.

Dede barely heard from Sierra these last many months since David's death. She hadn't wanted to pry or seem to hover. Sierra thought herself capable and invincible. Dede agreed. But even someone as strong as Sierra could only take so much.

Though she suspected Sierra would come home to evaluate her options, the vulnerability she'd heard in her daughter's soft voice when she called asking to come home had made Dede's heart ache. It actually made her pause and think about all the times Sierra swore she was okay, she could take care of . . . whatever, but maybe she'd just been putting on a good front. Sierra always stood on her own two feet, ready for anything. But though she got through it, Dede wondered if she'd let Sierra down by not noticing that deep down Sierra needed her help and support.

Not this time.

This time I'm going to make sure Sierra feels safe and protected and that this new beginning is what she truly wants.

Because Dede suspected Sierra had settled in the past for what she thought was enough instead of reaching for what she really wanted.

Amy came up behind her and glanced out the front windows. Her two children, P.J. and Emma, ignored the plate of sliced apples slathered in almond butter in front of them. Instead, they devoured a second cupcake each.

"Mom, seriously, you couldn't have gotten something better for them to eat?"

"You don't have to be the sweets police all the time. A cupcake once in a while doesn't hurt. And I'm their grandmother. It's my job to spoil them."

She'd made the cupcakes for Danny and Oliver, hoping something sweet would make them feel welcome. They hadn't visited since they stayed a couple of days after David's funeral. The time before that had been during her own husband's funeral. She never thought to have that in common with her daughter, but life happens. Tragedy strikes. She wanted to give her grandsons something good to associate with visits with her, something besides death.

And all kids love cupcakes.

"I'm trying to teach the kids to make healthy choices."

Dede shrugged, wishing Amy would loosen her rigid control over her kids. "You can feed them quinoa and kale all you want. When they're here, let them be kids instead of organic-health-nuts-in-the-making and enjoy the simple pleasure of a sugar rush."

Amy turned to P.J. and Emma, who'd been avidly watching to see if Grandma won this argument. "Put the cupcakes down and eat the apples."

Loud and upset groans punctuated the kids dropping the treats and pushing the plate of apples away.

Dede rolled her eyes. "Moderation, Amy. Teach them that, so they can find balance and not feel like you're taking things away from them."

"You never let us gorge on cupcakes before dinner."

"Unless it was a party or holiday. You know, there's a time and place for everything, including letting kids be kids."

Amy needed to ease up in every part of her life. She was wound so tight, she was bound to snap and unravel. Dede pushed because she didn't want to see that happen. Amy needed to have some fun and relax. No one could be that anxious and obsessive about things and not suffer some consequences.

Amy clearly swallowed a retort when the front door opened. Her eyes went wide at the sight of Sierra and the boys standing there. "Poor thing. She looks worn out."

Of course Sierra heard the not-so-subtle stage whisper.

Instead of responding to Amy's comment, she simply said, "Hello, Amy," and stroked a hand over Danny's head, nudging him inside with his bundled blanket, backpack, and several overflowing plastic bags. Like a mini vagabond, he held his precious few belongings.

Oliver followed his brother in, his arms not quite as full, but still the five-year-old held what little belonged to him, including a cute stuffed brown puppy.

Dede rushed to greet them and make them feel welcome. "Oh my, you boys have grown so much."

"I have to pee," Oliver announced.

"The bathroom is this way." Amy held her hand out toward the hall.

Sierra smiled down at her littlest. "Go ahead. Aunt Amy will take you. Say hi to Grandma first."

Oliver gave her a shy smile. "Hi, Grandma."

Dede brushed her hand over his dark head. "Hey, sweetie. I'm so happy you're here."

Oliver glanced at the cartoon on the TV. "Motel TVs are hard." With that, he ran after Amy to get to the bathroom.

Danny looked up at Dede. "The remotes are weird." He leaned into her for the hug she wrapped him in.

"Well, soon your mom will have a new place for you to live maybe with a TV easier for you to use. Until then, I'm so happy to have you here with me." She released Danny, noting how much he reminded her of his father. "Your room is up the stairs. Second door on the right. You'll find a surprise on the bed for you and Oliver."

Danny gave her a smile, glanced briefly at his mom for an approving nod for him to go ahead, and he dashed up the stairs with a speed Dede could no longer achieve in her advanced age. But it did her heart good to hear him squeal with delight when he found his gift.

His shouted "No way!" made Sierra raise an eyebrow.

"I got him and Oliver new tablets. The nice boy at the electronics store said they're exactly what kids are using these days."

"Mom, you didn't have to do that."

"I wanted to give them something familiar. They lost everything, and you said it was the one thing they were missing the most."

"They read these online graphic novels and the newest one came out last week and they've been dying to see it."

"There you go, they're reading."

"Oh, they play their fair share of games and watch videos, too." Sierra hitched up the laundry basket she carried under one arm before it slipped off her hip and she dropped it.

"Your room is ready upstairs. Set your stuff down. Take a breath. When you're settled, come down for lunch . . . or a cupcake."

Sierra smiled. "Thanks, Mom." Weariness shadowed her eyes. "It's been a long few weeks."

"And now you're here, where help is just a request away."

Momentary relief shone in Sierra's eyes.

"I set up an appointment with the elementary school for tomorrow morning at ten. They have a terrific after-school program you can look into when you find a job and are back to work. Until then, I'm happy to watch them after school while you go on interviews."

Sierra nodded. "I'll see what I can find and what makes the most sense."

Dede put her hand on Sierra's shoulder. "There's no rush, Sierra. Take your time. Figure out what's best for *you*."

Sierra raked her fingers through her long dark waves. "I've just been trying to get through each day and do whatever needs to be done right now." That was Sierra. Make a list, check the box, keep moving forward. "I haven't had time to really process."

"Then take the time."

Sierra set the basket on the floor and hugged her. "Thanks, Mom." She held on like she hadn't done since she was young.

Dede teared up and held on to her little girl who had grown up and had the problems to show for it. This couldn't be fixed with a bandage and a kiss on the owie. No, this required thoughtful planning and a lot of hard work to create a new life for her and the boys.

Dede had done it after each of her divorces. It wasn't easy to face things alone. To know that your children were counting on you for their happiness and the stability they needed.

Sierra carried the load well, but it would take time for her to find solid footing again when so much was up in the air right now. Once she found a job, settled with the insurance company, sold or rebuilt her place up north, and found a new place here to make a home, she'd find happiness again.

Sierra slipped free and went to the sofa, leaning over to hook her arms around P.J. and Emma. One at a time, she nuzzled her nose into both their necks. "Not even a *hi, Auntie.*"

"Hi, Auntie," they said in unison, both giggling.

"You better save me a cupcake."

"Mom won't let us have any more." P.J. fell back into the sofa with a dramatic sigh.

Emma looked up at Sierra and snagged a handful of her long hair. "It's so pretty." She brushed a lock against her cheek.

Sierra smiled down at her and tugged Emma's caramel-colored straight hair. "You got the better color. Mine's just plain brown. Yours is shot through with sunshine."

Emma beamed.

Amy led Oliver back into the room and went right to Sierra and hugged her. "Look how skinny you are." Amy squeezed Sierra's middle. "Two kids and I still haven't lost the baby weight." She stepped back and rubbed her hand over the barely there belly pooch.

Sierra had a matching one, even if her sister was kind enough not to point it out.

Dede saw it as a badge of honor. A sign your body had done something amazing. And it had. Her daughters had created life and given her beautiful grandchildren.

Amy rolled her eyes. "The last ten pounds are the worst."

Fit. Toned. Amy worked out and ran after her kids nonstop. But Amy always found fault in something about herself. Dede worried that sometimes Amy put too much pressure on herself for no reason, battling her insecurities by trying to be perfect all the time.

Sierra looked her sister up and down with a frown. "You're right. You're fat. More cupcakes for me."

Amy pursed her lips. "I'm sure you're ready for something better than sweets and takeout by now."

"You have no idea. I never thought I'd say this, but I miss cooking."

Amy shrugged. "It's all I can do to get a decent meal on the table some nights. The kids' schedules are so packed. Dancing. Baseball. Swimming. Music lessons."

"Stop signing them up for everything under the sun," Dede remarked. She didn't understand why Amy thought the kids needed to be occupied every second of the day. It left no time for them to be creative and use their imaginations without it being a planned activity.

"They enjoy it. And it makes them well-rounded kids."

"So does riding their bikes with their friends on the street and playing in the backyard." Dede wrapped her arm around Oliver. "Head up the stairs and find your brother. There's a present up there for you."

Oliver carried his bundle of things and ran up the stairs.

Amy sighed. "I wish I had his energy." She turned to Sierra. "How are they doing after the fire and everything?"

"They miss the house and are sad we moved away from their friends. They're heartbroken that all of David's things are gone. It's like they lost him all over again." Sierra took a second to compose herself. "They seem to have an easier time getting through the day and accepting whatever we have to do in the moment. To be honest, they were getting bored and restless. Living in a motel room lost its shine about four days in. They just wanted to go home, but they knew there was no home to go back to and that made it even harder. The uncertainty about what we were going to do got to them. And me." Sierra shifted from one foot to the other. "I had to make up my mind and get them settled either up there or here. Long term, this seemed like the best choice with you all here." She let out a huge sigh. "No more moving around every couple days."

"I'm happy you're back." Amy brushed her hand down Sierra's

arm. "It'll be nice for the kids to spend time together. And Mom won't be rattling around this house all alone."

Dede took exception to that. She had a very full life. "I'm not alone. I have my clubs and friends. There's something to be said about being solely responsible for only yourself." She'd finally learned after four marriages how to be alone and be okay with it.

Oliver's little feet pounded on the hardwood upstairs seconds before he shouted down to them. "Mom! Look!" He held up his new tablet.

Sierra smiled for the first time since they'd arrived. "Awesome!"

Oliver ran back to his brother and Sierra turned that smile on Dede. "Thanks, Mom."

"You're welcome, sweetheart."

"Mom took care of keeping the kids occupied. I took care of the basics." Amy pointed to the bags of clothes sitting one after the next going up the first four steps. "I got three outfits for each of you, plus a couple basics. Socks. Underwear. I know you'll do a big school spree soon, but I thought you'd like something to tide you over."

"Amy, you didn't have to do that." Sierra's eyes glassed over at her sister's generosity.

Amy took it in stride. "Of course I did. I just hope I got all the sizes right. I can't have you wearing a Tweety Bird sweatshirt to school drop-off." Amy wrinkled her nose, hip cocked; she wore her designer yoga pants and workout top that made her look chic and casual.

Sierra looked like she'd just stepped off an eight-hour bus ride with no air conditioning and a dozen screaming kids from Disneyland.

Someone knocked three times, then opened the front door. Heather walked in with Hallee. The eighteen-month-old toddled next to her mother in a pair of purple tennis shoes that lit up around the bottom with every step.

Emma scrambled over the back of the sofa.

"Hey, we don't do that," Amy scolded.

That didn't stop Emma one bit. She ran for Hallee, took both her hands, and helped her walk into the living room area. Hallee smiled up at her older cousin and babbled some nonsense.

Heather sidestepped the laundry basket Sierra had left in the entry and stopped short of hugging Sierra. "Hey, sis. How are you?"

Dede wondered why Heather didn't embrace her sister, but she didn't say anything.

Sierra glanced at Hallee. "Look at her, Heather. She's walking."

"You were right. It goes by way too fast. Before I know it, she'll be dating bad boys with rock T-shirts and leather boots."

"So she'll take after you," Amy teased. "I'm guessing that's the description of the father-who-shall-not-be-named."

Of course Amy was teasing, but the menacing tone and mocking grin only made Heather glare at her older sister.

Heather dismissed Amy and turned to Sierra. "Where are the boys?"

"Upstairs glued to the new tablets Mom got them."

"How are they doing?"

"It's been hard, but they're resilient. Once they're in school making new friends, I think they'll be happy here."

"This isn't just a visit to figure out what to do next? You're staying for good?" Heather's surprise and disbelief mixed with a hint of disapproval didn't set off anything obvious in Sierra, but Dede wondered why Heather might not want her sister moving home.

What was with her odd behavior?

A bad day? Feeling that Sierra would get all the attention instead of her for a while?

Dede hated to admit that as a romantic at heart she'd sometimes gotten caught up in finding love and spending time with the men in her life, leaving the girls to jockey for her attention. She'd sometimes been selfish and distracted.

Sierra became self-sufficient early on. She reasoned things out and solved her own problems. She knew what needed to be done and got to it.

Amy turned into a perfectionist, hoping Dede would notice how excellent she was at everything. She craved acknowledgment and accolades for making things pretty, or getting the best grades, or having the perfect family.

Admittedly, because Heather was the youngest, Dede always found time for her. Sierra and Amy picked up the slack when Dede wasn't around. Basically, Heather thought anything and everything she wanted would be handed to her.

"The fire put a lot of things in perspective. It's been hard since David's death, trying to do everything on my own. The expenses . . . the bills piling up . . . I feel like I've been treading water for so long. The boys need to get back in school. And I'm tired. I have no time to myself." Sierra's eyes filled with defeat. "I need some help. Or at least to know you guys are around if I need you. Over the last year, I've lost friends simply because I didn't have time for anything but work and the kids."

Dede put her hand on Sierra's arm. "You're here now. You don't have to do it all alone anymore. You've always been so independent."

"Is that a nice way of saying stubborn?"

Dede squeezed Sierra's arm. "Yes." Dede shared a smile with Sierra and a moment of remembrance for all the memories they shared where they clashed or disagreed. Not in anger, but in that natural way young girls want to prove themselves to their mothers. "It's that inner strength and determination that will see you through this, too." She gave her daughter a reassuring smile.

Heather pressed her lips together. "What about your house? Your life in Napa?"

Sierra scoffed. "There's nothing left. Rebuilding could take years. The insurance might not even cover it. And my boys can't be displaced and their lives left up in the air that long. I don't have the luxury of waiting to see what happens up in Napa. I need to have a plan to get things back to as normal as possible for Danny and Oliver. That means finding a job, a new place to live, and getting them back in school and on a routine."

"I guess it makes sense, I just didn't think you wanted to move back *here*, that you liked your life up there away from us." Heather shrugged one shoulder, a hint of pain in her eyes.

Dede brushed her hand down Heather's back. Maybe she had missed her sister and wished she'd moved back sooner.

"I've wanted to move back for a long time. David didn't want to leave his job and connections he had up there. It was a good job with great benefits, so I couldn't really complain. I understood why he didn't want to give that up."

Heather's eyes went wide. "Really? I didn't know all that."

Sierra tilted her head. "It doesn't matter now."

Heather frowned. "I guess it doesn't. Not anymore." Sadness clouded Heather's usually bright eyes.

David's death had had a huge impact on all of them. Dede missed him. And more than that, she, along with Amy and Heather, wished David, Sierra, and the boys had lived out the promise of a happy life together everyone wants when they get married and start a family.

"Anyway, we're here now, and we're going to stay." Sierra went to pick up the basket she'd left in the entry. "I'll take this upstairs, then come back for the clothes Amy bought us." She settled the basket against her hip. "I've got more things in the car."

Amy headed for the door. "On it. We'll get you settled in no time."

Dede hoped everyone would settle into this change in their lives.

The girls had always been close but competitive with one another. Amy and Heather had both seen Sierra's life up in Napa from the outside looking in, only seeing what they wanted to see and thinking she had an ideal life. They admired her for it and were jealous because of it.

Heather had the child, but not the loving husband.

Amy had the loving husband—at least for now—and children, but still thought the grass was greener in Sierra's world.

From a distance, things may seem greener, but look closer and you'll find the weeds.

Dede hoped the girls would set aside comparisons and past hurts and insecurities and come together now to help Sierra and the boys start this new chapter in their lives.

Chapter Five

Sierra stood with her sisters on the porch, hands braced on the railing. She stared out across the yard to the wide pasture beyond that belonged to the Moore family and her thoughts turned to Mason. She remembered the last time she'd seen him. Husband number four's funeral. Poor Charles. Dead of a heart attack far too young. Mason came to pay his respects to her mother at the house. He'd done the whole cordial neighbor thing, saying hello, asking about the family, making sure everyone was well.

He and David had once been close friends. And that day, as they reminisced about the past, David jovial and teasing, most people watching them might've thought that closeness remained. Not her. While Mason joined in, he didn't have the same enthusiasm or level of engagement David displayed. Mason held back and didn't rise to David's teasing about the new lady in Mason's life.

Carrie. Christie. Something like that. Sierra didn't really pay attention because she didn't want to know.

She hadn't been able to keep her gaze from straying to Mason when he was in the same room. She watched him as he actively avoided her. Not that it was hard when she was rushing around trying to keep her then three- and five-year-old in line.

David opted to socialize anywhere the kids weren't demanding his attention, which had left her frustrated and looking like a frazzled maniac.

When she finally got a second of nearly a private moment to speak to Mason, he'd kept it short, asked about her, the kids, then gracefully departed with an "I'm happy you're happy," and walked away like they hadn't been friends for years. The whole time they talked she'd been assailed by memories. Them riding horseback out to the creek, racing across the fields on the way home. Summers out at the pond sitting on the dock talking, teasing, and having fun. Watching the Fourth of July fireworks in the pasture his dad set off every year. Holiday parties. Summer barbecues. School events. Though he was two years older than she, they still managed to see each other a lot.

When her sisters were running late for school, she'd rush out to the road, hoping to hitch a ride with him. He never said no. Not to the ride to school or when she showed up in his barn asking to go horseback riding. Mason always saddled a horse for her and let her ride. Most of the time, he went with her. Sometimes when he could tell she just wanted to blow off steam from a bad day, a fight with her sisters, or an argument with her mom, he'd let her go alone, but he'd always watch her from the stables to be sure she never got hurt.

And in the end, she'd treated him badly one night at a bar by holding back what she really wanted to say in an awkward exchange that ended with mixed signals and hurt feelings.

"Daydreaming about our hunky neighbor?" Amy bumped her shoulder, bringing her back to the here and now. A mischievous grin tilted her lips, and an *I-know-I'm-right* look lit her eyes.

"I never heard whether or not he got married." Of course he didn't invite her after . . .

"They broke up before they ever set a wedding date." Of course Amy knew. She was hooked in to the Mommy Grapevine in this town.

No doubt every single mother wanted a sexy, successful husband, and the last time Sierra saw Mason he certainly fit the bill to a T.

Heather fell in beside Sierra, leaning the opposite way on the railing and looking at her sideways. "I saw him at the mailbox yesterday when I visited Mom. He looks good."

Amy leaned back and met Heather's gaze. "Did you score a date with your dream guy?"

Heather tried to contain a soft smile as her cheeks pinked. "We had a nice conversation."

"I bet." Amy took on a far-off look. "We all had a mad crush on him at one point or another."

Sierra eyed Amy, surprised by her admission. Maybe it was inevitable back then. Amy and Mason were the same age and in the same high school class. But Sierra spent the most time at his place because she loved to ride.

Heather stared down at her feet. "As usual, he was nice. Hallee loved him."

"I think every female who sees him falls a little in love with him." Amy patted her heart, her eyes wistful with a touch of mirth.

Heather didn't let it go. "He's a good guy. I could use one of them."

"He's definitely a better choice than the deadbeat dad you picked." Amy sometimes didn't know when to keep her thoughts to herself.

Heather glared. "He wasn't a deadbeat dad. You don't know what happened, so shut up."

Amy held her hands up in surrender. "Okay. Touchy subject. Got it. But one of these days you're going to have to spill the beans about your baby daddy."

Heather bounced off the railing and headed for the front door. "Leave it alone." She walked in and slammed it behind her.

Sierra would have gone after her, but she wanted a little while longer out on the porch in the peace and quiet of a beautiful starlit night while the kids watched a Disney movie. "You shouldn't badger her about Hallee's father."

"Don't you want to know who it is?"

"I'm curious, but I also know it's none of my business."

Amy bumped shoulders with her again. "Come on. You know you can't stand not knowing. I think she keeps it a secret because she had a one-night stand and doesn't even know the guy's name."

"Why not just say that then?" It would suck not to know. People would judge. But in this day and age of swipe right Sierra bet there were a few thousand kids out there with moms who didn't know their hookup's real name.

"Too embarrassed. Who wants to admit that?" Amy stared up at the night sky. "Maybe the guy is married or a serial killer."

Sierra laughed. "A serial killer who left Heather pregnant and alive? There's a few holes in that scenario."

"Maybe she slept with one of her friend's boyfriends and now she can't say anything because she doesn't want to lose her friend."

Sierra shrugged. "Whoever it is, he isn't in the picture. Maybe she doesn't say anything about him because she and Hallee are better off on their own. Maybe the guy turned out to be a real shit. Maybe he hit her. Maybe he's a total loser with no job and no prospects and Heather did the grown-up thing for her kid and shut *him* out so she didn't have to take care of two children."

Amy frowned. "You're better at this than me. That sounds exactly like the kind of guy Heather used to like, only out for a good time, sponging off others, and never taking anything seriously."

Sierra could imagine it. "She discovers she's pregnant and grows up fast. You have to be an adult sometime, and expecting a baby will put your life into a whole new perspective."

Amy braced her hands on the rail, much like Sierra stood. "Poor Heather."

"What about me? I'm a single mom to two boys. I'm outnumbered."

"Yeah, but you've always had your shit together. Heather's a dreamer, always looking for someone to take care of her and looking in all the wrong places."

"*We* always took care of her."

"What are big sisters for? I'm still helping her out. I watch

Hallee when she's sick and can't go to day care. I've come through with the school treats for holidays, taken her late-night calls when Hallee is sick and she doesn't know what to do, and generally been her go-to help the last few years you've been away."

"I've taken my fair share of what-do-I-do phone calls. Though she hasn't done much of that since David passed." A lot of people stopped calling, asking her for things or her time. They didn't want to bother her. They didn't know what to say to the widow. "Well, I'm back and happy to help with the load." She wanted to be part of her sisters' lives in a real way now.

"I'm surprised you came back."

Sierra glanced at her sister. "Why?"

"You seemed happy up there, just you and David and the kids living your picturesque life."

"Napa Valley is beautiful, but expensive."

"So is Carmel."

True. But Napa lost its shine. Carmel still held a wealth of happy memories and you couldn't beat the beautiful valley and gorgeous beach. "There's too many memories and nothing left up there. You know?"

Amy pressed her lips tight. "Yeah. I know. I'm real sorry, Sierra. It sucks that you lost your husband and your home all in one year. One's bad enough, but both." Amy shook her head in dismay.

Sierra changed the subject. "How's your hunky husband? How come he didn't stop by? And don't give me that shit about him working late."

"I asked him to give me tonight with you and Heather. It's

been too long since it was just us with Mom. Plus, he'd be the odd man out, so he was happy to steer clear of the estrogen party."

"The boys would love to see him."

Amy nodded, her lips pressed tight. "They miss their dad."

"Every day. I try to be there for them and give them what they need, but I know there's a huge hole in their hearts and lives without him here with them."

"Have you thought about dating again?"

It had been almost a year. And Sierra really hated being alone. "Who has time to think of such things with two kids and a job? It's all I can do to keep up with them, work, the house, the bills." And dating after all these years seemed scary. She was out of practice. She couldn't remember the last time she'd even flirted.

Amy grew quiet for a long moment. "Don't lose yourself taking care of everyone else. You deserve to be happy, too." With that, Amy walked back into the house to check on the kids, leaving Sierra alone on the porch.

As she looked out across the land and saw a glimpse of light across the way that could only be a light from Mason's place, Sierra felt as alone as she'd ever felt after David's death and wondered how long she'd feel this way before she did something about it.

Chapter Six

Sierra peeked through the ajar door into the boys' dark room and smiled at them sleeping. Her mom had redecorated, swapping out the neutral "guest-room" quilts for blue-and-red-striped comforters. She'd added stained wood toy boxes at the foot of each twin bed. The comforters and toy boxes were for the boys to keep when they moved into their next home. They'd get to take something familiar with them, instead of another round of entirely new things.

New was fun and exciting to a point. Then, you just wanted to be around the things that made you feel comfortable, that made you feel like you belonged there because they were your things. You saw them, surrounded yourself with them and the memories they held.

With the boys settled for the night and happy to be here with their family, Sierra headed downstairs for the talk she knew her mother wanted to have about what came next.

She found her mom in the living room on the sofa, feet tucked up beside her under a blanket, and a mug of tea in hand. Sierra rounded the sofa, picked up her mug off the table, sniffed the fragrant apple cinnamon tea that reminded her of Big Red gum, and sat in the corner of the sofa, facing her mom.

"It can't be easy to go through what you've been through this past year. Losing your husband . . . Well, I never thought you'd go through something like that so young. I know the fire took everything you owned, but you still have what's important. Those boys. Your family."

"Really, that's all that matters, Mom. Getting the boys to safety . . . It was scary." Even now, thinking about it made her heart race. "For a little while there, sitting in the car, surrounded by the heat, caustic smoke, and flames so close . . . I really thought . . ." She swallowed back the fear and took a sip of tea to calm her nerves.

Dede leaned forward and put her hand on her thigh. "You made it out. Now what? You as much as told Heather you're planning to make a life here. Is that what you really want?"

Sierra sighed. "I don't have many options."

"That's not an answer."

Sierra had made up her mind the second she called home and knew that's where she belonged. "Yes. I want to live here. I think the boys would be happy here. Going back to Napa . . . Well, there are too many memories."

"Good memories that make you sad, or memories you want to escape?"

Leave it to Mom to dig deep.

"If we still had the house, I'd want the boys to be there, so they'd have an easier time remembering their father. But without the house, there's only the ghost of him and our life there. It's going to be a long time before everything's rebuilt. I've been told it could take more than two years. That's too long to make them wait. I don't want them to settle in here then uproot them again. It's too much. We're staying put."

"Okay, that's settled. You'll enroll them in school here, find a job, and once the insurance settlement comes through, you can buy your own place and start fresh."

"I'm afraid the insurance settlement won't be enough for me to buy a house here. At least not right away."

"What do you mean?"

"There's the outstanding mortgage and—"

Her mother eyed her over her mug. "And?"

"Before David died, he took out a large loan."

One eyebrow shot up. Her mother carefully asked, "Were you having financial difficulties?"

"No. Everything was fine until he took out the loan."

Questions lit her eyes. "What did you use the money for?"

"*I* didn't use it for anything. I only found out about it after he died." Her gut tightened just thinking about that huge sum and the daunting task ahead of her to pay it off.

Dede sat up straighter. "You have no idea what David used the money for, do you?"

"No."

"An investment of some sort?"

"Not that I could find."

As always, her mother went the direct route. "An affair?"

Sierra shrugged and tried to stave off the ache in her chest and the anger that wanted to surge. "That would have been my guess, too, but I can't find any evidence of one." She couldn't prove it one way or another. Which left her in a constant state of wonder and suspicion and second-guessing everything she knew and thought about her husband.

Sure, they'd had their problems.

But she didn't think they'd had secrets.

She'd been wrong.

"Did you find anything in his office when you cleaned it out? In any of his papers?"

"After he died, I glanced through the boxes that arrived from his office."

"You didn't clean it out yourself?"

She shook her head. At the time, she simply couldn't deal with the mundane task. Not when she had two heartbroken kids at home missing their father and wondering if she'd die, too. Oh, the questions they'd asked. Hard questions like *Where did Daddy go?* Easier ones like *Can I put my toy truck in his casket?*

Sierra didn't need to ask why Oliver wanted his father to have his favorite truck. He'd wanted his father to remember him wherever he went.

It broke her heart.

And as sad and overwhelmed and lonely as she'd been those first few weeks, she'd also felt extremely guilty. Her mind spun a million things she wished she'd said to David. They carried on a hundred imagined conversations in her head that she wished they'd had in person. Ever present was the nagging feeling that the distance and silence she felt from David those last few months leading up to his death were fraught with his indecision. And she didn't even know the questions he pondered. She'd catch him about to say something to her, then he'd stop himself and turn away or say something mundane about dinner or Danny's homework. Once he'd even commented on the weather when it had been warm and sunny for days so there wasn't much to say about it.

Why didn't I just ask him what he wanted to say?

She'd asked herself that question a thousand times.

She'd been scared of the answer, afraid that her suspicions were true. Either he was having an affair, or he simply didn't want her anymore.

There'd still been love there, especially for their children, but they hadn't truly connected in a long time. They went through their days and lived together, but the intimacy in their relationship suffered. They didn't put their relationship ahead of everything else.

And frankly, at the end of a long day, she hadn't been all that receptive to his needs. Switching from mom to wife when she walked through their bedroom door hadn't been as easy as flipping a switch.

She saw the marriage suffering, but she hadn't made a real effort to fix it. She blamed the distance he put between them, the sneaky way he'd shut down his computer screen when she walked into his office and covered by saying he was done with his work email, and the way he explained away overnight trips he had recently started taking when his company had never asked him to travel in the past.

She made excuses for him. He didn't have a lot of time to himself. Neither did she. She got it. Maybe he shut down his computer because he didn't want work to interfere with their home life. Maybe his company really did need him to visit a customer here and there to make them happy or seal a deal. Maybe he snuck away to recharge so he could be better for them. Lord knows, she'd thought about a weekend retreat, maybe a few days with her sisters in Carmel and a long day being pampered at the spa where Heather worked.

He didn't mean to snap at her, he'd had a long day.

He didn't want to miss Danny's soccer game, but work needed him to be out of town.

Dinner out wasn't an option because he had a call with a client and would be home late.

"The last thing I wanted to do after the funeral was pack up his office and go through his things. I took what they sent me and put it in the garage. He was gone and I missed him and I was angry he left me and the boys. I know that's terrible to say because it was an accident, but that's how I felt. I had two little boys who missed their father and grieved for him and I blamed him for taking that last-minute trip instead of being home with us."

Her mom leaned over and squeezed her hand. "Grief is a lot of different emotions all balled up and tangled into a mess. Don't fret over the fact your marriage wasn't perfect. Whose is? People make mistakes, they tell lies, they drift apart, but all that can be forgiven when there's love. Maybe you two hadn't gotten to that point in the particular valley you found yourselves in at the time of his death, but that doesn't mean that whatever was going on couldn't have been fixed. You just didn't have the time to do it. That's not your fault, Sierra. And yes, it's a shame you had doubts and suspicions about your husband. I wish he was here to answer your questions and account for that money. But he's not. But that doesn't mean you can't get some answers another way."

Sierra cocked her head. "What do you mean?"

"Ask Mason to help you."

The answer surprised her. "What can Mason do?"

"He's a divorce attorney. He has investigators who uncover everything the opposing spouse is hiding, including hidden bank accounts and such. Perhaps he can figure out why David took out the loan and what he did with the money. If it's sitting in a secret bank account, that money belongs to you. It would go a long way to getting you back on your feet."

Sierra hadn't thought of that. But the idea gave her hope that maybe she could recover the money, or at least part of it, and that she could use it to help take care of the boys.

Although asking Mason for help sounded easy, it was anything but.

A long time ago . . . A lifetime ago, they'd had a moment. There'd been a spark. But she was with David. She'd chosen him.

And maybe a time or two she'd asked herself if she'd made the right decision.

"Sierra." Her mom snapped out her name like it wasn't the first time she'd said it.

"Huh. What?"

"I said you could go over and see him tomorrow. Take the boys. You know how much they love to see the horses in the pastures. An up-close look might take their mind off everything else going on."

"I can't ask him to look into their father's past with the boys right there."

"Be discreet, of course, but ask Mason all the same."

"Maybe I'll call his office and make an appointment."

Dede rolled her eyes. "You've known him since you were thirteen. You don't need an appointment."

Sierra sighed. "Mom, it's been a long time since we were friends and neighbors. I'm asking him to do something that isn't exactly his job. I think approaching him with the request as a business arrangement—"

"Pishaw. This isn't business. It's a friend asking a friend for help."

"It's a business transaction. I don't expect him to have his investigator do the work for free."

"I'm not saying you shouldn't pay him, but you don't have to make the request so formal."

"Mom. Let me handle it my way." If she even asked him. Seeing him again . . . Well, he might not want to see her at all.

Her mother conceded with a wave of her hand.

Sierra went on, "Besides, depending on the cost, I may not be able to afford his services." Mason was one of the best divorce attorneys around. Wives loved it when he stuck it to their husbands. Husbands loved that he kept their wives from taking them to the cleaners.

She knew Mason. He'd always been fair-minded, honest, and a great negotiator. He'd settled more than one dispute between her and her sisters back in the day.

She wanted to believe he'd been a little more on her side than her sisters', but that might be her teenage heart locked in a crush on the boy next door talking.

"You know I'm more than happy to help you through this difficult time." Dede hadn't exactly taken her exes to the cleaners, but she'd come out of every divorce with a hefty payout.

She could afford to help Sierra. But she had taught her girls to be independent and never rely on others when you were perfectly capable of taking care of yourself.

Well, Sierra had taken that to heart, unlike Heather, who sponged off Dede all the time.

"I appreciate you letting us stay here until I find a job and a place of our own, but I need to take care of the rest."

"Sierra, honey, I love you. It's never been easy for you to accept financial support, but I want to help. I have the means."

"I know. I appreciate it." But it made her feel guilty and a little bit like she couldn't take care of herself and the boys on her own when she'd worked so hard to do that alone this past year.

The possibility of discovering what David did with that money gave her hope that she might get out from under at least part of the debt. "If I can't afford to pay Mason for the investigation myself, I'll let you know, so long as it's not too much." If she found the money, she'd have no trouble paying her mom back.

"Peace of mind is worth the cost."

Careful what you wish for. "What if I discover something I don't want to know?"

"Sometimes knowing the worst is still better than being in the dark. Maybe it will allow you to put your relationship with David to rest. You deserve that, honey. Then you can move on with a clear heart and mind."

She hoped so, because the questions swirling in her mind sometimes grew quiet, but they never went silent.

Right now, though, Sierra settled into the sofa and finished her tea and thanked her lucky star to have a mom who loved her and welcomed her home with open arms.

She soaked up the warmth of home, her mother's steady and familiar presence, and knew that though things may be difficult the next days, weeks, and months, she and her sons had a roof over their heads, the love and support of her family, and everything, eventually, would be all right.

Chapter Seven

Sierra leaned back against the hood of her SUV and watched Danny and Oliver playing on the playground at their new school. She'd gotten them enrolled and taken them to meet their new teachers. They were hesitant at first about a new place and new people. She saw it in their little faces when they realized that leaving their old life behind meant losing friends and the familiarity of all they'd known.

Since the fire most of the families they'd known had also scattered to find new homes while they dealt with the aftermath of losing everything. They all had to start over.

She explained that to the boys just before setting them loose on the playground. They seemed to get it, but it didn't make it easier. And she wished they didn't have to learn so many hard lessons or suffer so much tragedy in their young lives.

"Look at me, Mom!" Oliver plopped down on the slide and whooshed down, his feet hitting the thick pad at the bottom before he jumped up, gave her a huge smile, and ran to climb back up to the platform and do it again.

For the first time in a long time, her heart felt lighter seeing the boys simply play and have fun.

Amy pulled in next to her car in her white minivan. The side door slid open the second the car stopped and P.J. and Emma leaped out and ran to the playground.

"I want to slide, too." Emma climbed up the wide steps behind Oliver.

P.J. grabbed a swing, scooted into the seat, and pumped his legs to get going. Danny took the swing next to him. It only took a second for them to see who could fly higher. Their smiles and delight as they tried to outdo each other made Sierra grin.

"We used to be them." Amy copied Sierra's pose against the front of the SUV with her arms crossed as she stared out at their four kids playing together.

They were them. Competition and trying to one-up your siblings never changed. At least in Sierra's experience. As the oldest, Amy always wanted to be the best at everything. She wanted to have everything first.

"How are you, sis?" It had been a long time since Sierra had a good long catch-up with her sister. Dinner the other night had been fun, but they spent most of the evening trying to corral the kids and get them to eat.

"Good. Great." That was Amy's way of saying "Fine" when she didn't really mean it.

"I got the boys enrolled in school. Oliver and Emma are in the same class, but Danny is with Ms. Franks's class."

"She's good, but Ms. Simms is better. She knows how to command the classroom. She pushes the kids. Their test scores are higher than the other teachers' classes."

That might be true, but Ms. Franks seemed kind and understanding of what Danny had been through. She'd promised to focus on making sure Danny felt accepted and found new friends so he settled in and felt welcome. She understood that was important for kids starting over at a new school. If he didn't feel connected to school, he wouldn't put the work in to getting good grades.

Sierra let it go because convincing her sister that good grades weren't the most important thing was pointless. She wouldn't change Amy's mind.

"Does P.J. like his teacher?"

Amy scoffed. "No. He hates her. He thinks she's mean. He hates all the homework."

At this age and especially during this difficult time the last thing Sierra wanted was for the boys to hate school. With so many years left to go, she didn't want them turned off and checked out because of a bad experience. Sierra believed school should be fun and engaging, not just a chore.

"Danny and Oliver liked their teachers. Once they make some friends, they'll settle in." And having their cousins around at school would be a help, too.

"Of course they will. They're kids. They're resilient. What about you? What are you going to do now that you've decided to stay?"

"I'll start with a job and go from there. I checked a few apps this morning, but none of the postings seemed quite right."

"We don't always get what we want. You'll have to settle for what you can get."

Very supportive.

Sierra turned slightly and hid the eye roll. "How's Rex?"

"Busy as ever at work. When he's not working, he's golfing. He says he needs his downtime."

"We all do."

Amy huffed out a breath. "I'd like to know when it's my turn."

"Don't you have some time when the kids are in school?"

As a stay-at-home mom, Amy should be able to carve out a little time for herself.

"You'd think, but no. I spend Monday, Wednesday, and Friday volunteering at Emma's classroom for two hours. Tuesday and Thursday in P.J.'s. When I'm not in the class, I'm working on organizing the school events, attending PTA meetings, cleaning house, picking up and dropping off Rex's dry cleaning, doing the shopping, paying the bills, and running all over after school for dance class, swimming, music lessons, baseball, and art classes. Not to mention helping with homework and school projects. You'll see, this school is no joke. It demands all your time."

Sierra understood that homework and projects did take a lot of a parent's time. "Why do teachers assign things the kids can't do mostly on their own? Isn't the point of it for the kids to do the work, not the parents?"

"Right?"

"Maybe you should cut back on the extracurricular activities." Sierra wanted her kids to have the opportunity to do whatever they wanted, but they needed downtime, too. Overextending their schedules strained her schedule. Sierra liked balance.

It sounded like Amy had scheduled away all her children's free time.

"They're important to building their character and making them well-rounded individuals. It will help later in life."

"Yeah, but it's driving you crazy."

"You sound just like Rex. He thinks some of the stuff is too expensive and that the kids don't even like it."

Sierra asked the obvious question. "Do they?"

Amy scoffed. "They don't know what's best for them."

That wasn't an answer.

She went on, "You should see Emma in her little bat costume for her dance recital. She's so cute."

Sierra got it. The pictures would look great on Amy's social media. Everyone would comment and Amy would feel like a good mother.

Sierra tried again. "What do you do for fun?"

"I live for my wine o'clock."

Sierra laughed under her breath. "Your what?"

"That half hour every night after the kids go to bed and I clean the kitchen and have a glass of wine and soak up the quiet." The absolute need for that half hour shone in Amy's eyes, but the sadness that shadowed it struck Sierra as a red flag that something deeper was going on with Amy.

"Where's Rex while you're enjoying your glass of wine?"

"Upstairs reading books to the kids."

Aw. "That's sweet."

A wistfulness replaced the sadness. "Yeah. He always makes time for the kids. Bedtime has always been his time with them because he's at work all day."

"That's really nice. I'm sure they love spending that time with him."

Amy nodded, her eyes going soft. "They do."

If Sierra read things right, Amy wanted that kind of time with Rex. Something wasn't quite right in Amyland.

"Is everything okay between you and Rex?"

Amy snapped her head toward Sierra. "Of course it is. You know how it goes. You have kids and it's all about them. Rex is busy. I'm busy. But we're great. We've got everything we ever wanted."

Be careful what you wish for.

The thought popped into Sierra's head because on the surface everything did seem fine with Amy. But Amy tended to focus on the surface and not look deeper. Everything needed to appear perfect to her sister, even when the undercurrent was sucking her down.

"If you want me to watch the kids one night so you and Rex can have a date night, I'd be happy to do it."

Amy sighed. "I'd have to check with Rex to see what his schedule is like, but thanks."

"Anytime." She really meant it. She didn't want to see what happened to her and David happen to Amy and Rex.

Amy said, "And I can watch the kids if you have an interview or something you need to do."

"I appreciate that." Though Sierra felt reluctant to add to Amy's packed schedule. "Mom said she'd help, too."

"You'll find Mom doesn't spend a lot of time sitting around the house. She's got her gardening club, tennis, lunch dates, hiking club, pinochle, not to mention the country club socials she attends."

"Is she working on husband number five?" Sierra gave Amy a mischievous grin and tapped her elbow to Amy's.

Amy rolled her eyes. "God, I hope not."

"Why? She deserves to be happy. No one likes to be alone."

"She's got her friends." Amy sighed. "And her admirers." A grin tugged at Amy's lips, but she stopped it before it turned into a real smile. "Losing number four hurt her."

Sierra's heart clenched. "She really loved him."

"She loved them all." Amy paused for a pregnant moment, then asked, "Have you spoken to Dad lately?"

They all loved their dad, but he tended to let time slip away between calls and relied on them to contact him rather than the other way around. Though he was always up for a long chat. He just wasn't one to pick up the phone unless prompted by his new wife.

"Just before I left the Napa area. He seems happy in Arizona with Loran."

"I thought after the divorce he'd be a bachelor forever."

"Loran changed that. They've been married . . . what? Five years?"

"Six." Amy wrapped her arms around her middle. "She's younger than him." Amy let that hang for a minute. "Do you think guys are like that? As they get older, they think about replacing the old model with . . . well, a model."

Sierra chuckled. "Maybe some guys, but not Dad. Loran is only five years younger than him. It's not like he hooked up with some twentysomething."

"I know, but . . . Never mind."

Sierra caught on quick. "Amy, you're beautiful and smart and a great mom. Rex would be crazy to let you go."

Amy stood up straighter. "Of course he would. But he'd never leave me. We're good. Great."

Yes, everything is fine in Amyland.

Sierra checked her watch. "I'm so glad you made time to meet us here today so the kids could play, but I've got to get them home and fed. They start school tomorrow and I want to get them back on a schedule."

"I hear you." Amy whistled at the kids and waved her hand, calling them back from the playground.

The boys jumped off the swings, playfully pushing at each other, saying one or the other had leapt the farthest. Oliver and Emma climbed down from the ride-on rocking bear and dog that sat atop huge metal springs.

Emma ran up to her mom. "Can we get ice cream?"

Amy shook her head and brushed her hand over Emma's hair. "It's time to go to music class before dinner."

"Ugh. Mom. No. I hate violin."

"You just need to practice more and you'll be good at it."

"I hate it!" Emma scrunched her little face into a deep frown and stormed off to the car, climbing in the side door behind P.J.

Amy rolled her eyes. "They're so fun." She hugged Sierra. "Call if you need me to watch the kids after school or whatever."

"Call me about that date night," Sierra countered. She really hoped Amy took her up on it. It seemed like she and Rex needed a night, or two, to reconnect.

Sierra understood all too well how things could turn monotonous and routine in a marriage. Maybe if she'd scheduled a few more date nights instead of avoiding the talk she and David needed to have but always put off . . .

She couldn't change the past. She needed to let it go.

"Mom?" Danny called from beside the car. "Are we going? I'm hungry."

"Yes. Climb in. Make sure Oliver is buckled in his seat, please."

Sierra got behind the wheel, started the car, backed out of her spot, gave a honk good-bye to her sister, who was turned in her seat talking fast to the kids in back in what looked like an argument, probably about Emma not wanting to go to music class. Sierra headed out of the lot and turned toward their temporary home, thinking about what kind of life she wanted here with the boys.

Certainly not one filled with so much to do you didn't have time to really enjoy life. She wanted balance for the boys. And herself.

She thought about her mother and those socials at the country club. She loved that her mom was putting herself out there.

Sierra wondered if she'd ever be ready to try again.

* * *

Sierra stopped at the mailbox, pulling in behind a sleek Mercedes. She stared at the back of the tall blond in a navy suit who got out of the car. She thought he looked familiar, but from behind wasn't sure it was . . .

Mason turned and smiled at her.

She caught her breath at the sight of him and smiled before she even thought about it. "I'll just be a second, boys." She rolled the windows down and got out.

"Hey there, stranger." Mason stood in front of her before she knew it and put his hand on her shoulder. "I was so sorry to hear about your troubles. If there's anything you need, I'm happy to help."

She should ask him about helping her track down the money

her husband didn't tell her about, but all she could do was look up at him and wonder how men got so much better-looking as they aged.

"Sierra? You okay?"

She mentally shook herself out of her head and nodded. "Yes. Fine. I'm sorry. I didn't expect to see you here."

"I took over Mom and Dad's place about eight or nine months ago when they wanted to downsize. Dad didn't want to spend all his time tending the land and animals anymore. I didn't want to let go of the ranch."

"You must have some really great memories of that place."

He stared down at her for a long moment. "I do. Sorry to hear you lost your home. You guys doing okay?" He cocked his head toward her boys. "They're huge."

She laughed. "They refuse to stop growing up."

"Kids," he scoffed. "They never do what they're told." Same old Mason. Always good-natured, ready with a warm smile and a joke to make her laugh.

"They're great boys. And we're doing okay. In fact, I just got them enrolled in school."

Mason shook his head. "Ugh. Moms. Always doing what's best for their kids."

She found herself chuckling again. "Well, I did let them have a cupcake after breakfast this morning."

"Mom of the year." His smile made her heart trip over a couple beats.

"It was a bribe to get them to meet their teachers today. They've been out of school for a few weeks now and aren't anxious to get back to it."

"New place. New school. You don't know anyone. Yeah, I get their reluctance."

"Me, too, but they need to take this first step into their new life."

Mason tilted his head. "You're staying, then?"

She nodded, pleased for no reason at all that he seemed happy about it. "I want to be closer to my family. Mom is getting older, I need the help, and though my sisters and I stay in touch, it's not the same as being here all the time."

"I know what you mean. My parents and I used to see each other all the time, but with work and their social life, we don't get together as much." He got a far-off look. "Of course, I avoid them sometimes because of all the 'Why aren't you married yet?' questions."

She couldn't help the quick glance from head to foot and back before she asked, "Why aren't you married?"

He chuckled. "Lots of reasons, but"—his gaze turned to a hard stare—"I guess I've been waiting for the right woman."

Uneasy under his direct gaze, she went around that statement. "I thought maybe it was because of your job."

"That's what a lot of people think. I see couples in the worst possible situation. They've lost the love and can't communicate anymore. But that doesn't mean I don't think relationships can work. My parents are great together. I want that."

"I love your parents. I was jealous of you."

"Me. Why?"

"You were close with your mom and dad. I sometimes felt like a Ping-Pong ball between mine. They both tried to make everything seem normal and perfect, but when you aren't with one parent all the time, it feels like they don't really know you."

"I try to make my clients see that equal time with their kids is important. Some of them though . . . They don't want to give up custody out of spite, not because it's what's best for their kids."

"Divorce sucks."

"Yep." He held up his stack of mail. "But it pays the bills."

Probably quite well based on what she'd heard about him being in high demand.

"So, Sierra, what are you going to do now that you're back?"

"I need to find a job. I can't afford not to get back to work right away."

"I imagine settling your affairs for the house in Napa is going to take a while."

"I'm probably going to be the loser in the whole thing, too."

He nodded, a half frown tilting his lips. "California. It costs more to rebuild than insurance covers a lot of the time."

"Tell me about it."

"Are you still interested in property management, or do you plan to do something else?"

She tried not to show her surprise that he remembered what she did for a living. "Beggars can't be choosers, but I'd love to get a job doing what I know. I really enjoyed working with clients and renters."

"I might know someone who's looking for help. I could make a call."

The offer touched her deeply. "Oh, well, that's so nice, but I don't want to put you out."

"It's no trouble. I know a lot of people in this town. It's a simple phone call to see if something's available."

Hope surged. A job would solve a lot of problems and eliminate most of her anxiety. "Really? You'd do that for me."

He stared at her for a long moment. "Yeah, Sierra, I'd do that for you."

"Thank you, Mason."

"You're welcome, Sierra." He glanced at the boys again. "When are you going to take me up on my offer?"

She tilted her head and narrowed her eyes in question. "What are you talking about?"

"Bringing the boys over to ride." He watched her for understanding, then added, "Heather didn't tell you."

She shook her head and frowned. "No. I'm sorry, she didn't say anything to me about you." Probably because Heather wasn't the most reliable person when it came to delivering messages.

"I'm not surprised," he said under his breath. "Um, I saw her the other day and told her to tell you that anytime you want to bring the boys to see the horses and go for a ride I'd be happy to have you at the ranch."

"Can we, Mom?" Danny called from the back of the car.

"Horsies!" Oliver yelled.

"Nice, putting me on the spot like that," she teased Mason.

He winked. "I want you to come over. It's been a long time since we went for a ride."

It *had* been too long time since she and Mason spent time together and she let the giddy feeling building inside her loose. Nothing serious had ever happened between them, but she'd always felt like if they just gave it a chance something could happen.

"Please, Mom." Danny gave her those big puppy dog eyes that made it impossible to say no.

"Are you busy Saturday?" she asked.

"Not anymore." Mason smiled at Danny and Oliver when they both yelled, "Yes!"

"I don't want you to cancel plans or anything."

"It's just a football game. I can record it. Come up to the house at eleven."

Danny leaned over the window. "Are the Patriots playing?"

"They sure are. You like football."

Danny fell back in his seat. "I used to watch with my dad."

Mason walked over, planted his hands on the open window frame, and leaned down. "I knew your dad."

"You did?"

"Once upon a time we were friends. Every now and then we caught a game together. How about we go for a ride in the morning, you stay for lunch, and we watch the game together."

"Really?"

Mason tilted his head and looked at her. "If it's okay with your mom."

Sierra hadn't realized how much Danny missed watching the games with his father. "I think that's a great idea."

"Will you make chili cheese dip?" Danny leaned forward, his face so earnest and hopeful.

"Yes, honey. Anything you want." Anything to make him feel the connection he had to his dad.

"I want pigs and blankets," Oliver requested.

"Me, too," Mason added, his face just as hopeful as her boys'.

"I expect you guys will keep your room clean and do as you're told until Saturday, including any homework you get this week."

"We will, Mom," Danny assured her.

"Promise," Oliver added to his brother's vow.

"Promise," Mason echoed, making her laugh. "I'll get all my work done so we can spend the day together."

She shook her head, trying to hide her smile. "You're crazy, you know that. You have no idea what kind of mess those two monsters can make of a bowl of chips and chili cheese dip."

He shrugged that off. "I've got a sponge and mop and a leather couch that wipes clean. No problem."

She hoped he meant it. "Okay. We'll see you Saturday."

"I can't wait." He held his fist out to Danny. "See you this weekend."

Danny pounded it. "Yes!"

Oliver leaned way over his seat to fist-bump Mason's hand, too. "Horsies!"

"You can pet all of them and ride one."

Oliver sat back with a huge grin.

Sierra waited for Mason to turn back to her. "You made their day."

"I hope I made yours, too."

"You made me smile. Thanks."

"You're welcome, Sierra." He pulled out his phone and tapped a couple times, then handed it to her. "Put your info in there for me."

She typed in her name and cell number, then handed the cell back to him.

He touched a few more things on his phone and hers dinged with a text in her back pocket.

"Now you've got my number. See you Saturday." He touched her shoulder before heading back to his car. With a wave he drove off.

She watched him go until his car disappeared.

Grabbing the mail from her mother's box, Sierra climbed back into her car thinking about the way she still felt the imprint of his big hand on her shoulder and the warmth spreading through her.

Her heart felt lighter after seeing Mason and how he made her kids smile and excited about something again.

It had been so long since she'd seen Danny that animated that she hadn't even realized how subdued he'd been since his father's death. He hadn't mentioned football at all. But she remembered how they'd watch the games together cheering on their team and letting out long and overblown groans when there was a bad call or their team lost. They ate junk food, had burping contests, and wrestled and laughed together.

The sound of it had filled the house, and she missed it, too.

The fist bumps were supercute, and the looks in her boys' eyes as Mason paid attention to them . . . They needed that kind of male bonding in their lives.

She was Mom. She did her job, loved them with her whole heart, and they needed her. But it wasn't the same as having your dad around, or a man who took a real interest in them.

Mason had invited them over to be a good neighbor and distract the boys after all they'd been through. She appreciated the gesture.

She found herself looking forward to the weekend along with her boys. Maybe they all needed a man like Mason in their life. Someone open, honest, and kind.

* * *

It wasn't until she got the boys settled watching a movie while she made dinner that she remembered to check her text and save Mason's number in her contacts. She stared at the text, enthralled by Mason's words, and jumped when her mother tapped her on the shoulder and said, "The pasta is boiling over." She tore her gaze from her phone to deal with dinner.

But she didn't need to see it to remember exactly what it said and how it made her feel.

Mason: I've missed you. Welcome home. I can't wait to see you this weekend. Sooner, I hope.

Was it strange to feel like she'd been waiting to come back home and realize that maybe he was the reason why? It didn't make sense, but then again with their history, maybe it did in some strange way.

Chapter Eight

Mason couldn't stop thinking about Sierra. Hope and anticipation had been building inside him since Heather told him Sierra was coming home. Those feelings got stronger when Sierra confirmed she planned to stay for good.

If he could contribute in any way to encouraging her to make a life here again, he was all in.

He'd missed her. He thought he knew how much, but it didn't even scratch the surface of how he felt when he saw her yesterday.

Such a simple meeting, but he hoped it led to something more.

He'd let her get away years ago because he'd been too focused on building his career and thinking that she'd always be there for him, that she wasn't going anywhere.

Stupid. Of course someone else saw her beauty and everything wonderful about her and wanted her for himself.

It still pissed him off that David snuck right in there and stole her before Mason made his move.

He wouldn't make that mistake again.

Unless . . . No. Revealing that kind of secret would do no good for Sierra. She'd been through enough. And he didn't know for sure that what he *thought* he knew was even true. Making an accusation like that would only stir up trouble.

And if he was wrong, he could do some serious damage.

Better to keep his mouth shut and his unfounded suspicions to himself.

He walked into the top realtor in town and smiled at the beautiful woman walking out of her plush office to greet him.

"Mason. I'm so happy you called. I can't wait for you to spend all the money I paid you during my divorce on a gorgeous new house."

He chuckled and shook Marissa's hand. "Sorry to disappoint, but I'm here to talk about a job."

Her perfectly sculpted eyebrows shot up. "Handing in your lawyer card to sell real estate?"

"Not a chance."

She held her hand out toward her office past the cubicles where everyone eyed them and answered the ringing phones. "Come. Let's talk."

He followed her into her office, closed the door behind him, and waited for her to take her seat behind her desk before he took the chair in front of it.

She leaned forward and folded her arms on top of the mahogany desk. "You got me a huge settlement and kept my husband from taking my kids. So what can I do for you?"

"Are you still looking for a property manager?"

"I've done several interviews and have someone in mind. I plan to make the offer this afternoon. Why?"

Thank God. He was just in time. "I would like you to consider one more candidate."

"Of course. What's *her* name?"

He smiled, trying not to let on that this was indeed very personal. "Sierra Silva." He didn't use Wallace. He wasn't sure she'd gone back to her maiden name, but he didn't like tying David's last name to her. Not when he thought—

"Does she at least have experience?" Marissa cut into his thoughts.

"Yes. She worked at a property management company in Napa. Her home and place of business burned to the ground in the wildfire."

Marissa lost the knowing smile and turned solemn. "I'm so sorry to hear that. It must have been devastating."

"Her husband passed away almost a year ago. After the fire took everything, she moved back here where she's got family to rebuild her life. She's got two sons to support. They'll be attending the same school as your kids."

Marissa shook her head. "So much tragedy."

"She needs a break, something to go her way. I'm hoping you'll give her a chance."

"Yes. Of course. Ask her to please give me a call. We'll chat, but if you're recommending her, I'm sure we can work something out."

Relief washed through him. "You don't know how much I appreciate this."

Marissa gave him another smile, filled with more understanding than teasing. "You want to make sure she stays."

"I want her and the boys to be happy again."

"You're a good man, Mason. But I know this means something to you."

He tried to play it cool. "Why do you say that?"

"Because you could have simply called me about this. Instead, you came down here to plead your case if need be."

He sat back and spilled the truth. "She's the one that got away."

A romantic at heart, Marissa simply said, "Then we will give her a reason to stay so *you* can make her happy."

His plan, exactly. Mason stood. "Thank you, Marissa, for doing this favor for me. I owe you."

She waved that away. "We aren't even even, Mason. You helped me keep my business and everything I worked for during the marriage. I may have started with my husband's money, but I made this." She held her hands up to encompass the realtor office. "He never liked me working. But I needed this to fill the hole our awful marriage left inside me."

"Even without his money, I know you would have been a huge success all on your own. He knows it, too."

"If your lady friend has even half the skills I'm looking for, she's got the job, and I'll make it worth her while."

"She's smart, kind, spunky, and driven. She won't disappoint. In fact, I think she'll surprise you." He was really going out on a limb here. He'd taken the safe route in the past, though, and ended up without Sierra. This time he'd put it all out there.

"This side of *you* surprises me."

"I'm not just a cutthroat lawyer, you know. I have a soft side." He used it to be sure the kids involved in the divorces were taken care of properly and got equal time with their parents, so long as those parents deserved it, too.

"Don't let my ex or anyone else's you represent know that."

"Never." He held up his phone. "Expect a call from Sierra shortly. I can't wait to tell her."

Marissa gave him another of those knowing smiles and waved good-bye as he hit the speed dial for Sierra and walked out of the office and onto the sidewalk as the phone rang for the third time and he suspected he'd have to leave Sierra a message instead of talking to her.

"You better have some refrigerator magnets."

He didn't expect that answer. "Um. I have a couple, I think. Why?"

"Oliver wants to thank you for inviting him to go horseback riding by giving you a dozen pictures of horses he drew for you."

The smile hit him with the outburst of laughter that bubbled up from his gut. "Awesome. I don't have enough horse pictures."

Sierra's soft chuckle made his gut tighten. "Well, good, because he'll probably draw you some more when he gets home from school."

"The more the better." He added stopping at the store to pick up some magnets to his mental to-do list. He didn't want to disappoint Oliver by not displaying them.

"Aren't you supposed to be working or something?"

He felt Sierra's nervous energy through the phone. "I've been working on something for *you*. Get a pen and paper and take down this name and number."

"What for?"

"Write this down." He rattled off Marissa's full name and her office number. "She's expecting your call. She's got a job for you."

"What? She's the biggest realtor in the county, like major successful. Multimillion-dollar listings and famous clients."

"And she needs a property manager. Call her now. She's ready to make an offer to someone else if you don't want the job."

It took Sierra a full ten seconds to say something. "You're not kidding."

He couldn't help the smile on his face. He loved shocking her. "Why would I joke about this?"

"I don't know. But she's . . . huge."

"You need a job, she's got one. Call her."

Another long five seconds passed. "Is she doing this just because you know her? Is she your girlfriend or something and this is a pity job?"

"No. No. And hell no. It is not a pity job. You're exactly what she's looking for. Yes, she's a client. I helped her with her divorce. I knew she needed someone and I'm hooking her up with the best candidate."

"Mason, that's sweet, but you don't know that I'm the right fit."

Yeah, I do.

"I know you're smart, meticulous, good with people, and able to multitask and handle a crisis with a steady hand and level head. You will rock this job, Sierra. I know you will."

Dead silence.

"Sierra?"

"Thank you for the vote of confidence." Her voice was soft and filled with gratitude.

"It's the truth, Sierra."

"It may be difficult to get ahold of references right now."

"The only reference you needed was me. Trust me, Sierra. You deserve this opportunity." Nothing but silence, but he had her full attention. "Did I mention it comes with a huge salary?"

"I'll call her right now." No delay this time.

"Good." He breathed out a huge sigh of relief. "It's going to be okay. The boys are back in school and you've got a job."

"If she likes me."

"She's going to love you." His phone alarm went off. "Listen, I'm late for a meeting."

"Go. I'll make the call and let you know how it goes."

"Promise." He knew she'd get it, he just wanted to hear her tell him all about it.

"Yes. And thank you, Mason. It means a lot that you'd do this for me and put your reputation on the line for it."

"You're a safe bet, Sierra. You're going to do great." He hung up and spent the rest of the day going from one meeting to the next waiting to hear from her. When he didn't by the end of the day, he almost called Marissa to demand she tell him what happened but restrained himself.

* * *

Tired and annoyed Sierra hadn't called him to tell him how it went, Mason drove home, parked in front of his dark and lonely house, dragged his tired self out of the car and up the porch steps. When the automatic light came on and spotlighted the bottle of wine with the bow and card in front of the door, he stopped in his tracks, stared at it, and smiled for the first time since he'd spoken to Sierra on the phone today.

He picked up the bottle, tucked it under his arm, and pulled the card off it. He opened the white envelope, swore he could smell her on the paper, and pulled out the note.

> *I got the job! Thank you so much!*
> *I owe you one.*
> *Sierra*

Smiling, he unlocked the front door, went in through the foyer and back to the kitchen, turning on lights along the way. He set the bottle of wine on the counter, dropped his briefcase on a barstool, and pulled out his phone and typed with his thumb as he tugged the knot on his tie loose.

Mason: Any chance you can come over and share this bottle of wine with me? We'll toast to your new job!

He set the phone on the island counter and shrugged off his suit jacket.

When his phone dinged with a text, butterflies took flight in his stomach. He felt like a teenager waiting on a girl to call.

Sierra: I wish! Bedtime stories with the kids. And I have to be up early for my new job!

Disappointment sent those butterflies dropping dead.

Sierra: Rain check?

And they were resurrected.

Mason: Anytime.

Sierra: Thank you again.

Mason: My pleasure. Good luck tomorrow. I know you'll kill it.

Sierra: You have no idea what this means to me.

Mason: You deserve everything good in this world.

Sierra: I appreciate that. And I mean it. I owe you one.

Mason: I will collect! ☺

Sierra: Gotta go. Boys are waiting. Story time.

Mason: Say hi from me.

Sierra: I will. ☺

Mason sighed, set the phone back on the counter, and went to the fridge. He opened the door and stared at the leftover takeout, decided to pull a frozen pizza out instead, and flipped on the oven to heat while he went and changed into sweats and a tee. He'd save the wine for when Sierra came over and crack open a beer to go with the pizza and his lonely night in front of the TV.

He settled on the couch half an hour later with his pizza, beer, and thoughts of Sierra sitting around a table with her kids and mom having a family meal. He'd like to be included in that homey scene.

He couldn't wait to see her and the boys on Saturday.

Chapter Nine

At the end of a very long second day at work, Sierra fell into the couch, and put her feet up on the coffee table. She leaned her head back and closed her eyes. At last she could take a break, hang out with the kids, maybe watch a TV show after dinner.

"Long day?" Amusement filled her mother's voice.

She opened her eyes and stared up at her mom. "It's only been two days and I'm exhausted." She never expected Mason's phone call to lead to an hour-long phone interview with Marissa feeling out her strengths, weaknesses, and whether or not she was up for the demanding job. She hadn't sugarcoated the workload or sheer number of clients she represented, but Sierra hadn't been prepared for the unrelenting pace. Of course, she had a learning curve. Once she mastered her duties things would be easier. Until then, though, trying to do everything perfectly without making any major mistakes or making Mason look bad for recommending her was exhausting.

"You'll settle in and learn the routine," Dede said.

"I know, it's just I don't want to screw this up. It's a great job. A dream job. And the pay . . . Wow!" She never expected to find anything that paid so well. Not to start. And now she wouldn't have to rely on her mom to bail her out. She had some financial breathing room.

Sierra didn't mind working her way up, but starting at this level, it came with an expectation that you were the best. She hoped she was up to it.

She already loved Marissa. She didn't want to disappoint her, either.

"How were the boys this afternoon?" Her mother had agreed to pick them up after school for now. They both wanted to give the boys stability and familiarity.

"They were great. I love having them to myself for a couple hours. I get to spoil them."

"If it's too much . . ."

"Nonsense. They're my grandkids. This is why I got old." Her mother chuckled.

So did Sierra. "Thanks, Mom. It makes me feel better to know they're with you."

"Don't forget Heather is expecting you tonight for dinner. You better get a move on."

She forgot her mom had a *thing* at the country club and Heather wanted the kids to come over to play with Hallee so they could get to know each other better.

"I can't wait to see her place."

"It's really cute. You'll love it."

"Don't forget the boys and I are going over to Mason's place tomorrow."

Her mother's eyes twinkled. "I heard he went down and spoke to Marissa personally about that job for you."

Sierra hadn't known that until Marissa mentioned it, saying

how out of character it was for Mason to see her in person instead of making a phone call. "I appreciate that he went out of his way to help me. I really needed the job and the income." When Marissa told her the base salary, plus the size of the bonus she could earn for bringing in new clients, Sierra thought it was a joke. But no. The money would allow her to pay off her debt and hopefully buy a small house for her and the boys. Not just yet, but sooner than she thought possible. Of course, her mom would help with the down payment if she needed it, but she hoped to settle the Napa property and avoid having to ask her mom for help.

Dede patted her leg. "I'm just saying he obviously likes you."

"We've been friends for years."

"Timing is everything."

She played dumb. "What are you talking about?"

"You're single. He's single. One and one makes two." Her mom was having too much fun with this. The sparkle in her eyes made Sierra smile.

A romantic at heart, her mother couldn't help herself.

"You're always looking for love."

Mirth turned to a serious look in her mother's eyes. "You deserve to be loved, Sierra. Don't forget that while you're raising your children and working to make a good life for them. You want them to have everything. Don't leave yourself out."

"I've got a lot on my plate right now." She thought about Mason inviting them over for horseback riding and a football game. She deserved to have some fun, something good in her life when for so long it felt like she'd been treading water, just trying to stay afloat in her life instead of really living it.

"This is your chance to reinvent your life. Take it, Sierra. Figure out what you want, what really makes *you* happy. Leave the past behind."

"I'm trying." She really was, but David's odd behavior and that damn loan still haunted her. Maybe once she figured out what he needed that money for, she'd let it go, no matter if it was good or bad. At least, she'd know the truth and be able to move on.

Chapter Ten

S ierra is having dinner at Heather's place tonight." Amy waited for her husband to look up from his phone.

He didn't. "Are you going over there to join them?"

"*I* wasn't invited. Mom told me about it."

"Didn't you see Sierra earlier in the week for a playdate with the kids?" He didn't glance at her even once.

She didn't see what that had to do with anything. "Why are they getting together without me? Why not make it a big family thing?"

Rex sighed and finally made eye contact for the first time since he walked in the door an hour ago. "Heather's place is small. I'm not sure we could all pack into her place."

"We could have had a barbecue in the backyard."

"Maybe that's not what she had in mind. She hasn't seen her sister in nearly a year. Maybe she wants some time with Sierra, just the two of them."

Amy gritted her teeth and wondered if they were over there talking behind her back, sharing secrets like they did when they were kids.

Rex sighed. "If it bothers you so much, call Heather and invite yourself over to join them."

"Yeah, right."

He eyed her, grinning. "You know you want to. You hate being left out."

"What does that mean?"

The smile disappeared. "You can't stand it. If there's something going on at school, in town, with your family, you need to be in the middle of it."

Her shoulders and neck tensed. "That's not true."

Rex tapped his finger on the color-coded calendar hanging on the pantry cupboard next to him. "Really? There's not a single day on the calendar that you don't have something scheduled. You take on too much. You should scale back, have some time for yourself. Maybe then you wouldn't fall into bed every night exhausted."

Her defenses went up and she attacked without thinking. "It's not like you ever want to do anything with me."

He stuffed his phone in his pocket and pinned her in his gaze, glanced at the calendar, then back at her. "You've made it clear you don't have time for me. When I ask you to do something, it's always P.J. has baseball, or Emma has ballet, some class project, or . . . I don't know, a bake sale that requires you to make a thousand cookies."

"You're the one who plays golf every Saturday and most Sundays."

He held her gaze but waved his hand toward the calendar. "Because my family isn't home. The only time I see the kids is when I'm driving them somewhere you planned, and we don't even do that together. I see more of you on Instagram than I see you in real life."

That stung. She wanted to deny it outright but couldn't. "I want you to be there with us."

"I'm working all week to pay for all the things that take you guys away from me." He sighed and stared up at the ceiling for a moment before looking at her again. "I get they need something to do. But they don't need to do everything, all the time. By the time we finish with Spanish lessons, swimming, and whatever other sport you've got them in for the season, the weekend is gone. It'd be nice to go to the beach or hiking together. Hell, I'd love a whole weekend at home just hanging out playing board games and watching movies and stuffing ourselves on microwave popcorn."

That sounded like bliss. "We could do that."

"When? In the hour between one playdate and a birthday party for some kid in their class they aren't even friends with?"

"All the kids get invited to the parties so no one gets left out."

"That doesn't mean they have to go to every single one. They need to know that family time matters."

Frustrated and at her wit's end, she snapped. "What does that have to do with us going on a date?"

"Time. And the fact you don't have any for me."

"Are you guys fighting?" P.J. asked from the kitchen entry.

"No," Amy said.

"Yes." Rex dared her to contradict him again with a sharp look. "Put your shoes on, kiddo. Let's give Mom the night off from cooking and go pick up burgers."

"Yes!"

Rex waited for P.J. to run to his room to get his shoes before saying, "Something needs to change around here, Amy. You're always telling me to tell you how I feel. Well, I feel left out. I feel like you schedule all this stuff because you don't want to be with me."

"That's not true." She hated that he felt that way.

He glanced at the damn calendar again. "Really? Sure looks that way to me."

P.J. and Emma appeared in the entry, side by side, looking nervous about them arguing in the kitchen.

Emma smiled up at her dad. "I want to go, too."

Rex scooped her up and hugged her close. "Absolutely, princess. I bet you want french fries."

"And a chocolate shake?" Hesitation and hope filled her soft voice.

Amy didn't even bother to try to deny her daughter the sweet treat or Rex a moment to spoil the kids with junk food.

"Shakes all around," Rex announced, as he touched P.J.'s back to get him moving toward the front door. "Say good-bye to Mommy."

P.J. and Emma said in unison, "Bye, Mommy."

The front door closed behind them and Amy felt her stomach drop. She and Rex had had this same argument over and over again the past couple years, but now they rehashed it every few weeks.

She wanted to give her kids everything. She wanted them to experience all kinds of things.

She wanted more time with Rex.

More family time would be so nice.

She looked at her color-coded life hanging on the pantry door and thought about all she'd given up to be a mother. Oh, she loved it. But the satisfaction and joy waned as she lost herself in it. Everything she did was for the kids. She barely had time for herself. She couldn't remember the last time she did something fun just because she wanted to do it.

Sierra got that great job.

When did her own life turn into one endless art project, bake-off with the other moms, and cheerleading for her kids?

Amy wiped her palms down her chic yoga pants. She couldn't remember the last time she put on a sexy dress and heels. Hell, she barely remembered the last time she didn't go to bed in an old T-shirt and flannel shorts, let alone the last time she and Rex spent an hour or more making love.

The last time they had sex, she'd given in to his advances, not really feeling it because she was tired. She'd made sure he got what he wanted and fell beside him, unsatisfied and blaming him for it, when really it was her fault.

She'd just wanted the chore over.

Making love to her husband shouldn't be a task on her list.

The kids' schedule shouldn't be an endless loop of chauffeuring them around and keeping them busy because she didn't know what to do with herself if she wasn't doing something for them.

Rex was right. Something needed to change.

She needed a change.

Chapter Eleven

Heather sat Hallee on her play mat in front of her tower of toys then answered the door. She smiled at the resolute knocks from her sister, and the two other little pitter-patters from the boys' small fists.

She turned the knob and swung the door wide, loving the smiles on all three of their faces as they held their hands up mid-knock. "Hello, munchkins. Was that you pounding on my door?" She gave them a mock angry face, but it only sent them into a round of giggles. Heather found her sister's eyes were full of mirth, too. "Hey, sis."

"Hey. This place is so cute. Away from the road, and you've even got a little white picket fence with the flowers blooming along it."

"Thanks. I got lucky when I found it." She held her hand out toward the living room, hoping her sister didn't see it shaking. She didn't know why she was nervous. Okay, she did, but she shouldn't be. "Come in. Hallee is playing with her toys."

The boys raced past and fell on their knees beside Hallee, quickly picking up toys and engaging her. Heather took a second to watch them and enjoy the moment, seeing her little girl with the boys.

She closed the door behind Sierra, who stood in the tiny

foyer checking out the living room and through to the small kitchen and dining area.

"It's so you. Boho chic with a touch of elegance."

Heather didn't have much, but she made the most of her little space. She loved the wood-framed daybed with the colorful pillows she'd added in green, blue, and a pop of dark pink. They picked up the vibrant colors in the rug. Gauzy white drapes covered the window. Intricate woven baskets hung on the wall in a cluster as art. A simple wood oval coffee table served as a place for Hallee to play with some of her toys and Heather to prop her feet.

She'd added the elegance in the pretty antique chandelier-style lighting. Crystals gleamed and sparkled in the light. A collection of mercury glass candle holders lined the fireplace mantel.

Sierra touched her arm. "I love this place. It seems so perfect for you and Hallee."

"It's just what we needed. Her room turned out so great. I found this beautiful chandelier with golf-ball-sized crystals and she's got a sleigh bed crib that she's growing out of way too fast. I'm going to have to get her a big girl bed soon. I painted the walls a pale lavender and hung these cute butterflies from the ceiling."

Sierra took her gaze from the room at large and focused on her. "The kids seem happy. Show me."

Heather led Sierra on a tour of her house that didn't take more than a few minutes. They ended up in the kitchen where Heather had left two wine glasses on the counter next to a bottle of Moscato.

Sierra stared out the back window. "What a cute little patio. I love how you hung the lights and wrapped them around the tree. It gives the garden you planted out there a magical feel."

"I want Hallee to have a place that feels warm and inviting and fun at the same time, where she can touch things and run around without worrying that she'll break something. And if she does"—Heather shrugged one shoulder—"so what. She's missing something in her life, but my hope is that she'll always feel at home here and know she's loved."

Sierra's eyes went soft. "Isn't there any chance that her father will be a part of her life?"

"No." Heather's heart broke for her daughter. She deserved to have a wonderful father in her life. But it wasn't meant to be.

Heather had been selfish, threw caution out the door, took what she wanted, and her daughter paid the price.

At one time, Heather thought it would work out in some way, but no.

So she'd take the secret of who fathered her child to the grave. She still didn't know what she'd say to Hallee when she grew up and asked about her dad. Right now, it was easy to distract her when she pointed at her preschool friends' dads and said, "Dada."

"Maybe he'll change his mind."

She appreciated Sierra's optimism, but some things were absolute. "I thought there was a chance for us once. But . . ." She shrugged, not wanting to think about the mess she'd made and how it ended.

Sierra rubbed her hand up and down Heather's arm. "I'm sorry. It can't be easy to raise her on your own. But from what

I see, you've made a great home for her. She's got you and all of us to love her."

Choked up, Heather swallowed the emotions clogging her throat. "That means a lot." More than her sister knew.

"What smells so amazing?" Sierra inhaled the garlic and tomato sauce smells filling the kitchen, then sighed in pure appreciation.

Heather chuckled. "I call them meatloaf balls." She lifted the lid on the frying pan on the stove and revealed the meatballs simmering in sauce. "I hope the kids like them."

"They look fantastic."

"I'll serve them over rice, if the kids want, with broccoli on the side."

"We'll let them decide. And look at you with the healthy meals, veggies and all. I remember a time when you ate pizza just about every night."

"I worked at a pizza place. Who wouldn't eat pizza all the time when it's free?" Heather picked up the open bottle of wine and poured for Sierra, then herself. She set the bottle down and held her glass up to Sierra. "I'm really happy you're home."

Sierra clinked glasses with her, took a sip, then narrowed her eyes. "I didn't think you were thrilled about me moving back."

"I was just surprised you'd want to stay when you and David had made your life up in Napa. Is it true? You really did want to come back sooner, but David wanted to stay up there?"

Sierra lifted one shoulder and let it drop. "I missed you guys. I wanted all our kids to grow up together. He considered moving back, but then he said he couldn't do it. He loved his job and thought we had a good life up there and he didn't want to change that."

Heather took a bigger sip of wine. "Well, you're here now, and you've got a great new job."

"It's an amazing opportunity. And the money is great. More than I was making at my old job." Sierra glanced around the house. "I can't afford to buy anything just yet, but I'd love a cute little place like this for me and the boys."

"With two of them, you'll need another room. I'm sure once you get your settlement, you'll be able to get something."

"I don't know about that. I was barely getting by. The fire wiped out what little I had in savings paying for motel rooms and basic necessities. I'll get the settlement for the contents of the house, which will help, but the mortgage doesn't go away. And I've got a huge personal loan to pay off."

"Really?" That concerned Heather.

Sierra waved it away. "I'll figure it out. The fire is still so fresh in my mind. The loss. If I hadn't found this job so soon, I don't know what I would have done. Mom has been so great, letting us move in until I can figure out what to do next. It's just so overwhelming."

"I always thought you and David were doing really well." Heather had no idea they'd taken out a big loan. "I wish I could help, but I sunk all my money and then some into this place. My job covers costs and day care and a little extra, but Hallee and I . . . well, we've got what we need."

"I totally get it. Like I said, the insurance will help, but rebuilding isn't an option for me. I need to move on."

"It must be hard to know that the house you and David shared is gone. All those memories."

"I still have the memories. But there's nothing left that I want to go back to. David's been gone almost a year and it's time to settle into my life without him."

The optimistic tone surprised Heather. "Are you thinking about dating again?"

"It's been a long time since I went on a date. It's kind of scary. But also . . . I don't know . . . maybe it's time. I don't want to dedicate everything to raising the boys and miss out having someone in my life to share it with. I'm sure, just like me, you get lonely sometimes."

"It's been especially hard this past year, watching Hallee grow so fast and do so many new things." Heather nodded. "I want to share it with her father, but I can't, so yeah, having a partner, someone special, in my life would be great." She thought about her encounter with Mason at the mailbox. A sexy lawyer would do fine. Someone stable. Someone available and open to a relationship that could potentially turn into a lifetime of memories.

She loved being a mother. She'd love to have another baby.

Mason had never had a family. Maybe he'd like to be a father.

"You're thinking about someone," Sierra teased.

Since Sierra knew Mason, Heather didn't want to give away her secret thoughts. "I've just recently been reacquainted with someone and . . . I don't know. Maybe there could be something there."

Sierra held her glass up. "Go for it, sis. Life is too short."

Heather clinked it again. "Yes. It is. In the blink of an eye, you can lose everything. Why wait to have what you want."

"Here, here." Sierra took a sip, then glanced in the living room where Hallee let out a big belly laugh as Oliver held up a puppet and made fart noises. "Boys." Sierra shook her head, but a smile tugged at her lips.

Heather soaked up the scene with the boys entertaining Hallee. "This is nice."

Sierra met her gaze. "Yeah. It is. I'm glad you invited us."

"I hope we get to do this a lot more often. I'd like Hallee to really get to know Danny and Oliver."

"Me, too. We better feed them."

Heather, caught up in the moment and her emotions having Sierra and the boys in her home, impulsively hugged Sierra.

"What's this for?" Sierra held her close.

"I'm so glad I didn't lose you."

Sierra squeezed her harder. "You'll never lose me."

Heather hoped Sierra kept that promise.

Chapter Twelve

Sierra parked the SUV in Mason's driveway and tried to wrangle the butterflies into submission with a hand to her belly and a deep breath. This wasn't a date. It was just two friends getting together to watch a football game. Mason meant it as a kind gesture to make her sons happy.

"Can we see the horses first?" Danny asked.

Both boys watched the ones grazing in the nearest pasture. They were beautiful.

She missed riding and the freedom of it.

"We'll see." She opened the car door just as Mason walked out the front door with the ease of a confident man.

Nervous, anxious, and yes, excited, Sierra felt anything but confident. More like self-conscious.

She wasn't the same young lady he knew from their youth. She'd grown up, filled out, and had two kids that made her body dip and bulge in new ways that defied all exercises meant to flatten and tone certain areas.

How did he look the same after all these years?

She stepped out of the car and waved.

"Sierra, you look fantastic. I'm so glad you came."

The ridiculous amount of giddiness that single compliment shot through her made her feel like a teenager with her first crush.

Did she still have a crush on Mason?

Had she ever stopped crushing on him?

"Thank you again for inviting us." She closed the driver's-side door so Danny didn't hear her. "Danny is really looking forward to this. It means a lot that you'd spend time with him."

Mason brushed that off with a wave of his hand. "I'm happy to have a buddy to watch the game with me. Otherwise, it's just me, all alone in this big house."

She wondered if he spent his nights alone, but didn't dare ask or let her mind go down that road. Not her business.

He'd been kind to help her get the job, but she didn't want to assume he held any interest in her other than being a friend and neighbor.

Mason took a step closer. "And I'm hoping you and I can spend some time catching up, getting to know each other better now that you're back."

"There's not much you don't already know."

"I know the outline. I'd like the details."

"Horsies!" Oliver jumped out the back door and ran for the fence.

Danny ran after him.

Mason let out an earsplitting whistle.

The boys stopped in their tracks and turned back to him. "Not so fast. There are ranch rules you need to learn and follow."

The boys' faces dropped into disappointment at the prospect of new rules to follow, but they stood still and waited to hear Mason out.

"First rule. No going into the pastures or climbing on the

fences without your mom or me with you. Horses are big, they may not see you, and they can step on you and hurt you really badly. Second rule, no feeding the horses anything unless I give it to you. They like carrots and apples, but other things can make them sick. Third rule, you always stay within eyesight of me and your mom. There's lot of things here where you can get into trouble or get hurt. Any questions?"

Both boys shook their heads.

"Okay, then let's have fun. The game starts in half an hour. Who wants to pet a horse?"

Both boys raised their hands and jumped up and down yelling, "Me! Me! Me!"

Mason took Sierra's hand, walked a couple steps pulling her along with him, before he let her loose and caught each of her boys around the belly and picked them up under each of his arms. They shouted in surprise and laughed as Mason bounced them up and down as he walked toward the stables.

Sierra stopped in her tracks and watched them. Her delighted boys. And Mason. Strong. Intriguing. Engaging. Fun. And kind.

He'd known David. They'd been friends once upon a time. Mason knew the boys missed their dad. Here he was, trying to give them a good day and a memory to keep after all the ones they'd hopefully forget.

"Hey, you coming with us?" Mason stood facing her, one wiggling boy under each arm like they didn't weigh him down one bit.

She walked to catch up. "Sorry. I got lost in thought."

Mason set the boys on their feet and took their hands. "I've got a real pretty mare you'll want to meet. And I'm sure Tom is around here somewhere."

She'd forgotten about Tom the cat. "He's got to be pretty old by now. He was old when I last saw him."

"This is Tom the third."

"Excuse me?"

"We named every adopted cat Tom."

"Why?"

Mason grinned like one of her little boys. "You know, Tom and Jerry."

She smiled back at him. "Old school."

"What's Tom and Jerry?" Oliver looked up at Mason, confused. Not surprising. The boys watched cartoons, but they were mostly newer ones.

Mason stared down at Oliver, hands on his hips. "Your education is seriously lacking. If you get bored with the football game, I'll queue up the cartoon on my tablet for you."

Oliver beamed Mason a smile. "O-tay."

They all headed into the stables. Horses greeted their entrance into the darker interior with sweet whinnies that made the boys gasp with surprise.

"They talk, Mama." Oliver's eyes were filled with wonder.

"They're happy to see you, buddy." Mason picked up Oliver and held him close to the beautiful buckskin's head. "Give him a pet down the nose."

Oliver ran his hand down the horse's tan nose, then reached up higher and felt his black mane. "He's soft."

The horse moved his big head closer to Oliver, who giggled. "He likes me, Mama."

Danny stepped close and reached up to pet the horse. He was a bit too short to get a good feel.

"Come down this way," Mason directed and led them three stalls down. He set Oliver on his feet, then swung the stall gate open wide. A beautiful bay mare stepped forward, dark brown coat gleaming. She nudged her nose into Mason's hand, looking for a treat. "Sorry, sweetheart, I don't have anything for you right now, but I'll bring you something later."

"Apples?" Danny asked, remembering what Mason told them earlier.

"She loves green apples."

"What's her name?" Oliver touched her high shoulder.

"Star."

"Because of the white patch on her head." Danny pointed up at it, unable to reach her head.

"That's right. She's a sweet girl. Who wants to go for a ride?"

Both boys raised their hands and bounced up and down on their toes.

"Step back with your mom while I get her out." Mason unhooked the rope across the stable door, took a lead rope from the wall next to the stall, hooked it on Star's bridle, and walked her out of the stall.

He turned to the boys. "Okay. Rules for riding. No yelling or screaming. You'll spook her. She's very sensitive. No kicking. You'll sit on top of her and I'll lead her around the pasture. If you want to stop or get down, you let me know and I'll lift you off her, but no jumping down. You could hurt yourself or fall under her and get stepped on." Mason pointed down at Star's hooves. "See those? They can break your bones if she steps on you. She's a calm girl. As long as you're nice to her, she'll be nice to you. Understand the rules?"

Both boys nodded.

"Great. Who wants up first?"

Oliver ran forward, arms up.

Mason scooped him up and set him on Star's back. "Okay, buddy, you hold on to her mane like this." Mason placed Oliver's hands around two fistfuls of black hair. "Don't pull or hold too tight."

Oliver nodded.

Mason turned to Danny. "Ready?"

Danny held up his arms.

Mason lifted him up to the horse to sit behind his brother. "You hold on to Oliver's waist and make sure he doesn't slide off."

Danny nodded, looking unsure as the horse shifted under him.

Mason put his hand on Danny's thigh to steady him. "She's going to move a lot while she walks. Move with her."

Danny nodded.

Sierra moved in next to the boys as Mason took the lead rope at Star's head. Mason caught her eye and nodded, acknowledging that she'd walk alongside just in case the boys got scared or nervous or slipped off.

"Here we go." He clicked his tongue and gently tugged the rope to get Star moving.

Both boys' faces lit up with bright smiles when the horse started moving under them and they walked out of the stables, down the driveway, and into the pasture.

"Oh my God. She's so tall." Danny looked over and down at the ground.

Sierra fixed her hand at his waist. "Sit straight up, or you'll fall." Without a saddle and stirrups to keep the boys in place, they needed to focus on staying upright.

Oliver whispered, "This is so cool."

And just like that, the weight of all their troubles lifted off Sierra's shoulders. She smiled up at her boys, who were amazed and filled with wonder, riding their first horse and falling in love with it.

Oliver leaned over and hugged Star's neck. "Can we keep her, Mama?"

"Star is Mason's horse, honey."

"You can come visit her anytime you want," Mason offered. "She'd like it if you did." Mason turned and gave Sierra a *So would I* look.

One part of her hoped she read that right. Another part wondered if it was too soon to start dating again. Maybe she should focus on the boys and getting them a new home. But those were excuses for not putting herself out there.

Truth be told, Mason was hard to resist, especially when he was so kind and sweet to her precious boys.

But that wasn't all that drew her to him. There had been something there when they were younger. So much so that at one point before she married David, she'd had a moment where she wondered if a relationship with Mason was the better choice.

She chalked it up to nerves about getting married. Nothing but cold feet. Everyone experienced it. Second-guessing her compatibility with David just so she could be with another man, one she found intriguing and exciting and sexy as hell. They'd been friends so long, she knew so much about him.

But she'd convinced herself they would only ever be friends because she didn't want to risk losing that bond.

In the end, she'd felt like she and David married thinking the other person fit the image of what they wanted, but down the road they each turned out to be unable to fulfill the other's needs. David didn't think she was spontaneously fun or outgoing enough. She saw David's wild streak—at first so entertaining— as off-putting. He didn't think things through.

They turned into devoted parents but distant partners.

She didn't know when or why they both accepted that was their life, that the spark and fire between them had slowly burned out to ash. By the time David unexpectedly died, she'd been wondering for months if he wanted out of the marriage.

They didn't fight. They didn't disagree. They didn't care enough to do that. They simply lived their lives under the same roof for their children.

Looking back, it made her sad to think he died unhappy and unfulfilled in their marriage.

Still, she wondered if he'd had his foot out the door for a while.

Mason broke into her dark thoughts. "You okay?"

She nodded and smiled for the boys' benefit. "Fine." She checked her watch. "We should head back. The game starts in ten minutes and I've got to get the cooler of food out of the car and some of the things into the oven."

Mason studied her for a moment, then turned Star back to the house.

"Oh, come on, Mom, just a few more minutes," Danny pleaded. "I want to ride by myself."

"Not this time," Mason interjected. "But we'll definitely do this again. Come on, you don't want to miss kickoff."

Mason slowed his pace, letting the boys get every last second they could of the ride before he plucked them both off Star's back and set them on their feet again.

Oliver gave Star's leg a hug and glanced up at Mason. "I like her."

Mason brushed his hand over Oliver's head. "I'm glad you had fun. You can come see her before you go home later tonight."

"If I lived here, I'd sleep with her," Danny announced.

Mason chuckled. "She sleeps standing up."

"Nuh-uh." Danny stared up at the big horse.

"She sure does."

"I'm going to try that tonight." Oliver closed his eyes and wobbled before he opened his eyes again.

"Not so easy, is it?" Mason waved the boys back so he could put Star in her stall. He gave her a pat all the way down her back. "You made those boys' day." He pulled a roll of spearmint candies from his pocket, unwrapped one, and fed it to Star.

He walked out of the stall, secured the door, and held the roll of candies out to the boys. "Want one?"

"Horse treats." Oliver shook his head.

Danny peeled one off. "They're candy. Duh."

Oliver wanted everything Danny had and peeled one off for himself. He hesitantly stuck it in his mouth, then smiled when the sweet, minty taste hit his tongue.

Mason held the roll out to Sierra. "Want one?"

"I'm good. Thanks."

He stuffed the roll back in his jeans pocket, then touched his hand to her back as they walked up to the house. Every nerve in her body flared to life at that simple touch. He didn't crowd her but he didn't remove his hand, either.

She glanced up at him and caught him staring at her.

"I'm glad you decided to come today."

"Me, too. It's been a long time since I saw the boys smile and enjoy themselves this much."

"I liked seeing *you* smile."

"I haven't had a lot to smile about lately."

"Then I'm glad I'm part of why you did."

She stopped and stared up at him as the boys continued toward the house. "What is this, Mason?"

"It's a start to something that seems a long time coming." The words and sentiment rolled off his tongue so easily, like this was as inevitable as he claimed. He took her hand and gently tugged to get her to continue following the boys up to the house.

The warmth of his skin pressed to hers spread up her arm and through her whole body. She didn't pull away like she thought she should, but settled into the moment and the feel of his hand clasped with hers.

It had been so long since Sierra felt connected to someone, since a man touched her. Holding hands with Mason seemed like such a simple thing, but her heart melted at the thought that he wanted to start something with her.

At the end of her marriage, she'd felt undesirable and lacking in some way.

Mason made her feel wanted.

It made her stand a little straighter and feel lighter and giddy all at the same time.

She'd been unsure about coming home, thinking she didn't have anything besides family to come back to that would really make a difference in her life.

But Mason proved her wrong.

She'd wanted to find a way to get by. Mason gave her hope for something more.

Chapter Thirteen

Mason didn't know what to call the feelings running through him. An hour into the football game and he simply felt . . . great. Happy.

Sierra, looking beautiful in her dark pink top, long dark hair falling past her shoulders, stood in his kitchen, pulling a baking tray from the oven. She set it on top of the stove, then looked through the cupboards until she found the plates. She didn't hesitate to make herself at home in the kitchen he barely used.

The boys sprawled on the sofa. Danny watched the game, cheering with him when their team scored. Oliver watched *Tom and Jerry* on his tablet, giggling every so often and completely engrossed in the classic cartoon.

This is what this house needed. A family.

This is what his life needed.

He'd wanted this for a long time.

Once, he'd thought he'd get a chance to have it with Sierra.

If this was the start of his second chance, he'd make it count. This time, he wouldn't let her walk away without a fight.

Only one thing could screw it all up: the secret he'd kept since her stepfather's funeral.

His clients were falsely accused of wrongdoings all the time.

Divorces could cause hurt feelings, and the parties sometimes lashed out, making things worse.

He knew better than to present something without evidence to back it up.

If he said something and it turned out to be wrong, he risked her being angry at him for telling tales. She'd question his motives.

"Mason. You okay?"

He met Sierra's inquisitive gaze and smiled just because having her here made him so damn happy. "Yeah. Fine. Just got lost in thought." He tipped his chin toward the plate of pigs in a blanket. "Those look really good."

Danny took one and tried to see the TV around her hips. "Mom, move."

"Please," she prompted him.

Danny fell back into the cushions. "Please." He leaned over to check out the play on TV and groaned over the incomplete pass.

Sierra set the plate on the coffee table. "I'll get the rest of the goodies."

Mason rose and stood next to her. Close enough to smell her sweet floral scent. He'd missed that about her. She always smelled so good. "Let me help." He followed her into the kitchen, pulled the bottles of root beer and vanilla cream soda from the fridge and out of their cardboard holders, and placed them in the metal bucket he'd left on the counter.

"I love cream soda."

"I remember." He tried to play it off like it didn't mean anything, but Sierra stared at him, getting that he'd stored away a lot of memories and tidbits about her. He didn't know what it was about her, but she made him pay attention.

Maybe if he'd paid attention to his fiancée the way he did when Sierra was around, he'd have made it down the aisle and filled this house with his own family.

"I'm sorry, Mason."

At first he didn't know what she meant, then he caught the remorseful look in her eyes. "We don't need to do this, Sierra."

"I do. I've held on to it all this time. I've wanted to say something to you for so long, I just didn't know what to say."

"You don't need to apologize for being in love with David and wanting to be with him." It sucked. But Mason couldn't change the way she felt. Back then, he'd hoped maybe there was something deeper than friendship between them. Maybe there was, but she'd still picked David. Admittedly, he'd known she would. She and David had been seeing each other for a good long time. So Mason had swallowed his feelings and everything he'd wanted to say to her until it was too late and what little he had said hadn't been enough for her to really believe he wanted her to take a chance on him.

She shook her head. "I apologize for . . . whatever that weird scene was between us. I wanted to say something, then I didn't, and you didn't know what to say to me acting so weird, and then every time we saw each other afterward it was . . . strange. I made it weird."

"Look, I'm not going to deny that I hoped maybe you thought David wasn't the man for you."

"Wait. What?"

Mason thought she knew, but it looked like he'd been wrong. Great. What did that mean for them now? He didn't know, but he continued anyway because he'd been caught. "You and I were always friends, but I hoped we could be something more. David was my friend, but I still hoped you and I . . . Well, I shouldn't have made things more awkward when you were with him."

Her head tilted to the side and her gorgeous dark hair draped down her arm. "More awkward?"

Shit. He hadn't meant to bring this up. "David knew I had a thing for you."

"He did? You did?"

Her disbelief made him chuckle without any real humor. He laid it on the line. "It's more accurate to say *I do*."

Her brown eyes filled with surprise.

"Come on, Sierra, I might have been trying to hide it when you were with David, but I think I've made it clear now that I'm interested in seeing if there's something between us."

"I'm . . . not good at this. It's been a long time since I dated anyone. You and I have history. We're friends."

"And I hope that never changes, but I want more." He took a step closer, drawn by her wide eyes, so filled with disbelief, wonder, and hope, he couldn't stop himself from falling into them.

If they were going to rehash the past, he was going all in. "David knew you and I were friends when he started dating you. Let's just say David and I had a friendly rivalry, always trying to best the other. He got the girl I wanted."

She wrapped her arms around her middle. "Are you saying

he was playing some one-up game with you?" Anger and resentment flashed in her eyes.

He wanted to dispel that immediately. "I think he saw what I saw in you and in no time he fell in love with you. You're kind and generous and caring. He was drawn to you just like I was. I was caught up in building my career and I let my personal life slip. I let you get away. I didn't go after what I really wanted and David did."

She raked her fingers through the side of her hair. "I'm having a hard time resolving the past and right now. I wished I'd known how you really felt."

He gave her the God's honest truth. "I want you. That's how I feel right now. That's what I should have said to you back then. Not that it would have made a difference. You didn't feel the same."

Her gaze dropped to the floor and she slid the tip of her shoe along the hardwood. "Actually, I did feel something for you back then."

Blown away, he didn't know what to say. "Seriously?"

She finally met his gaze again. "I just wasn't sure what I thought I saw in you wasn't just wishful thinking."

Mason didn't think, he simply went with his gut, cupped her face, and kissed her, letting all his pent-up feelings and need loose. Her hands gripped his sides and her lips opened to him. He slid his tongue along hers and tasted the same need he had for her.

"Touchdown!" Danny yelled.

Mason certainly felt like a winner having Sierra in his arms.

Sierra broke the kiss and held him away.

He caught the desire in her eyes a second before he turned and caught Danny doing his own version of an end zone victory dance, pretending to spike the ball. Oliver barely glanced up from the tablet.

He turned back to Sierra. "I should have done that that night in the bar."

She chuckled under her breath, a pretty pink blush brightening her cheeks. "And started a fight with David."

"I wanted to start something with you."

She pulled him in a step and laid her forehead against his chest. "I don't know what to do with that now after everything that's happened. I married David. We had a good marriage for the most part."

He wanted to dive into that *for the most part*, but left it alone because he didn't want to talk about her and David. He wanted to talk about them and the here and now.

He cupped her face again and made her look at him. "The past is the past. Let's focus on right now. Do you want to be with me? Do you want to see where this thing between us goes?"

A shyness he'd never seen in her filled her eyes as her gaze fell away, then came back to meet his. "Yes." The whispered word rang loud and clear in his brain.

He brushed his thumbs across her pink cheeks and smiled down at her, his heart light, excitement thrumming through him. "Now we're getting somewhere." He leaned down and kissed her softly. "I'm so glad you came back."

She snuggled into his chest and he held her close. "Me, too."

The oven buzzer went off and she pulled away, but he took

her hand to keep the connection between them. "Pick a day that you can get a babysitter for the kids. Let's go out to dinner."

A smile bloomed on her soft lips. "A date?"

He squeezed her hand. "It's long overdue."

The smile went megawatt. "I'd like that."

He wanted to make her that happy all the time. "I want to spend a lot more time with you." He squeezed her hand to let her know he meant it and mentally kicked his ass for not being this open and honest with her back in the day.

She reached over and turned the incessant buzzer off, then opened the oven door, letting loose a blast of heat and the aroma of barbecue pulled pork.

He couldn't help himself. "That smells so good."

"I can't take credit. I picked it up at the Barbecue Pit. I'm just reheating it."

"I love that place."

"I know." She gave him another shy glance. "You're not the only one who paid attention."

"Mom, I'm thirsty." Danny spoke around the chunk of hot dog in his mouth.

Sierra turned to Mason again. "You get that I'm a package deal, right?"

"Rug rats and all. Got it. They're great boys. I like having them here. I like *you* here."

She cocked a hip and leaned heavily on one side. "How come we never got together in high school?"

"Because I was a dumbshit back then."

"You swore." Oliver appeared at his side out of nowhere.

Mason frowned. "Sorry, buddy, just telling your mom the truth."

"Are there any grapes?"

"In the cooler." Sierra took Oliver's hand and led him over to it, pulling out the covered bowl filled with green and red grapes. "Do you want a slider to go with that?"

"Yes, please. No slaw."

"I know." Sierra pulled the cover off the grapes and handed the whole thing to Oliver. "Go sit at the coffee table. I'll bring you your sandwich."

Oliver went back to the living room, sat on the floor, set the grapes on the table, and ate while watching some car insurance commercial.

"Are you sure you don't mind them eating in there?"

"It's no big deal. If they spill something, I can have the carpet cleaned." He went to the freezer, pulled out the ice container, and dumped the ice into the metal bucket filled with sodas.

"You sure you want to give them soda? They'll be hopped up on sugar for a couple of hours."

"Relax, Sierra. I don't care if they make a mess, jump on the furniture, and just be rowdy boys. I used to be one, you know."

She sighed. "I just want this to go well."

"It is. It will." He stopped in front of her with the bucket under his arm. "Are you talking about today, or us?"

He loved that she always met his gaze when she had something serious to say. "I don't want to mess this up. You've been so nice, getting me the job, and asking us over here."

"Stop. I didn't do those things so you'd say yes to a date, or to manipulate you into saying yes."

She put her hand on his chest like touching him was so easy now.

He loved it.

"That's not what I meant at all. I'm grateful for the help you've offered, but that isn't why I'm here." She raked her fingers through her hair again. "I appreciate what you've done and I'm so glad we've reconnected."

"Me, too." He saved her from trying to explain herself further when he got that this meant something to her. He mattered. "Let's eat before the boys start chewing on the furniture."

She smiled and went to make up the sliders where she had everything set out next to the stovetop.

He took the drinks into the living room and set the bucket on the coffee table.

"No way. Root beer in bottles. Cool." Danny pulled one out and stared at the cap.

Mason took it, twisted off the top, and handed it back.

Oliver held up a bottle to him. "Me."

Mason uncapped his and handed it back. Both boys took deep sips, burped, then fell into a fit of giggles. Mason took a big swig of his own bottle and burped long and loud just to make them laugh.

Sierra stared at him from the kitchen island, smiling, and shaking her head, but enjoying it all the same.

* * *

The rest of the evening went smoothly. The boys ate too much and ended up on either side of Mason and Sierra on the sofa where their legs touched the whole time but he resisted the urge to hold her hand or hook his arm around her shoulders and pull her into his side because he didn't want the boys to see how close they were getting before Sierra was ready to talk to them about her moving on. The boys loved their father, missed him, and may not be ready for a new guy in their mom's life.

He got that and kept a respectful distance for their sakes.

The game ended with their team winning. Danny jumped up and fist-pumped the air. Oliver was half asleep watching the tablet next to Sierra.

They worked together to clear the food and put everything away. Mason loved that she rummaged through his kitchen looking for plastic containers and appreciated that she stored the leftovers in his fridge for him to eat later in the week. He hoped to spend more time with her and the boys and not eat all his dinners alone anymore.

"Ready to go, boys?" Sierra stood by the entryway with the cooler she'd brought at her feet, holding the kids' jackets.

"Can't we ride Star again?" Danny dragged his feet on his way to get his jacket and gave Mason a pleading glance.

"Next time you come over. It's too late to do it tonight."

"You boys need to get home and take your baths and get ready for bed."

"But Mom . . ." Oliver walked with his shoulders slack. "Please. I'm not tired." The yawn he let loose said otherwise.

"Come on. Say thank you to Mason."

"Thank you." Danny frowned, not making the words sound so appreciative, but Mason got that he wanted to stay and have more fun. He chalked that up to a win for today.

"Thank you, May. Son." Oliver barely kept his eyes open.

"Maybe you guys can come over tomorrow for another ride."

Both boys shot their mom a pleading look.

She eyed him, then addressed the boys. "We've got some errands to run tomorrow, but maybe we can stop by in the afternoon before dinner."

The boys bounced on their toes, excited. "See you tomorrow, Mason." Danny ran out the door to the car, eager to get to tomorrow, it seemed.

Oliver trailed after his brother with a wave good-bye.

"What errands?" he asked, curious about what she had planned.

"My mom is going to see a play. I promised to do the grocery shopping. I also need to get some new work clothes, since everything I owned went up in flames. I'll have to take the boys with me, which means it will take twice as long and require tablet time bribes to get them to cooperate and not have a total meltdown in the dress department." She shrugged and rolled her eyes, looking exasperated already.

"I can watch the boys."

She held up her hand. "Oh, that's nice of you to say . . ."

"I mean it. I don't mind. Drop them off on your way into town."

Her head tilted to the side as she eyed him. "Don't you have your own plans for the day?"

"I'll be doing ranch chores. The boys can help. I'll let them ride again. We'll have fun."

"Mason, I don't want to take advantage . . ."

"You're not. I'm offering."

She hesitated a second, one side of her mouth drawn back

in a half frown-smile thing that made him think she really wanted to say yes, but felt she shouldn't.

"Sierra, seriously, bring them over. You'll get your stuff done faster and without the hassle of dragging them along with you. They'll be bored and acting out. At least here, they'll be doing something outdoors and having fun. It's for them, really," he teased, knowing it would really be a huge help to her if he took the boys for a few hours.

"You have no idea what you're asking for."

"A chance to get to know them better, and let them get to know me, too. We know each other, so dating is just a next step for us, but the boys may see me as intruding in your life, or taking their father's place. I don't want to do that. I want them to see me as a friend and someone who likes their mom and wants to make her happy."

Sierra's shoulders went slack. "I don't know what to do with you being sweet like this."

Which made him think David hadn't been all that sweet during their marriage if a simple babysitting gesture made her go all gooey on him.

Sierra went on, "You don't know how much your offer means to me. Things have been really hard lately, but thanks to you, they're looking up." She needed something to be easy and hassle free.

He could do that.

Mason put his hand on her shoulder and kissed her forehead. "I know you've got a lot on your plate with settling your affairs back in Napa and starting a new job here and getting settled again. If I can help, I will."

"You really mean that."

She didn't pose it as a question, but he assured her anyway. "Yes. I do. So drop the boys off tomorrow, go do what you need to do and take your time about it, and I'll see you when you pick up the boys and I'll get to do this again." He tugged her the two steps out of the doorway and into the kitchen so the boys couldn't see them, leaned in, and kissed her, long and deep. He broke the kiss far sooner than he'd like and smiled down at her. "I'm really glad you came over today."

"Me, too."

He picked up the cooler, took her hand in his free one, and walked her out to the car. He put the cooler in back and waved to the boys before placing his hands on the driver's-side open window and staring in at Sierra.

A soft smile made her even more beautiful. "See you tomorrow."

"I'm here whenever you need me," he assured her, then stepped back and waved them all good-bye.

He watched them drive away, knowing they weren't going far, just next door, but wishing they'd stay because the empty house behind him didn't feel the same without them in it anymore.

Chapter Fourteen

Sierra sat at the kitchen island counter listening to the boys upstairs brushing their teeth before she took them to school. She sorted through the envelopes in front of her.

Her mom sipped her coffee, then stared at her over the rim. "I know that frown isn't about Mason. Not after you've come home every day from his place with a smile on your face."

Sierra couldn't contradict her mother's assessment. She and the boys went over every night to help Mason feed the horses and spend time with him. The boys loved it. They were learning a lot about taking care of the animals.

She herself liked getting to know who Mason was now. They were both the same but different, and she enjoyed discovering new things about him.

They'd kept things light this past week because they'd both been busy at work and having the boys around all the time meant they had to be careful about what they said and did.

"Mason is great. The boys love him." Her feelings were growing deeper the longer she spent with him.

Dede said, "What's not to like? He's got a cat and horses for the boys to pet and ride. They like his company because having a big strong man around to let them be rowdy and wrestle is a lot of fun. And hey, you get to just look at him and kiss him."

Her mother's eyes twinkled with delight. She hadn't actually seen Sierra and Mason kissing, but it was a good guess that she was still smiling when she came home because of it.

"We do more than kiss, you know. It's nice to spend time with him. I miss coming home and having someone to talk to about my day."

"Have you asked him to help you with your David problem?"

How could David be such a problem after his death?

Sierra brushed her hands over the bill in front of her. She didn't like where her mind went every time she thought about it. She hated the monthly reminder that her husband kept a big secret from her.

Dede pressed her. "Why are you stalling? If Mason can figure out where the money is, you can get rid of that loan and leave it in the past where you should leave David." Bitterness filled those words. "If you can't deal with it, let me pay it off and be done with it."

Sierra appreciated her mother's anger and resentment that David left her carrying the debt. She had to admit she didn't have a lot of kind thoughts when it came to David and the loan, but she wasn't one to bury her head in the sand, either. Still, the thought of taking that kind of money from her mom didn't sit right, even if her mom could easily afford it.

"Between David's death, struggling to get by after he was gone, helping the boys through their grief while I worked through mine, and losing everything, I'm not sure I can take one more blow. Our marriage wasn't perfect. I know that. No one's is. But I don't want to find out it was broken and I didn't even know it."

"Don't blame yourself for something you didn't do."

Sierra's stomach knotted. "That's just it, I don't want to know what he did with that money."

"So you're just going to worry over it, pay it back, and just take it?"

Part of her wanted to, but no, she wasn't one to just let it go. "Who am I supposed to make pay for and answer for it? David isn't here." That really ticked her off.

"It's your decision, but I think this has more to do with the fact you're afraid to ask Mason for help because you don't want him or anyone else to know that David wasn't the great guy and husband everyone thought he was. You don't want anyone, Mason especially, to know that David pulled one over on you."

No, she didn't. "Is it so hard to understand why? I feel stupid and duped and like I didn't even know him if he could do something like this behind my back. He lied to me for months before his death by not telling me he took out the loan. What else was he lying about?"

Her mom thumped the coffee mug on the counter. "That's a very good question. If it were me, I'd want to know so that if something else comes at me out of the blue from his past I'd be prepared. If you know, you can protect the boys. And yourself, Sierra. Who knows what he was into that cost that kind of money."

She'd like to think it was a bad investment, or gambling, though that really seemed unlikely. David had never been a gambler. Maybe he was helping out a friend and didn't want her to know for whatever reason. Sierra hoped it was something easily explained.

The boys stomped down the stairs and headed for their backpacks by the door. She scooped up the mail, set her mug in the sink, and met her mother's inquisitive gaze. "I need more time to think about it."

She needed superpowers. She'd love to resurrect David and shake some answers out of him.

Instead, she headed for the door to take the boys to school and get herself to work. The boys ran out the door and she turned back to her mom. "I appreciate the push and that you've kept this between us."

"I only want to help, honey. If there's a way for you to recover some of that money, it will make your life easier." Her mother paused, then sucked in a steady breath. "I also think that if you're really hoping to move on with Mason, you should put the past to rest with a clear head and heart." Dede held up her hands and let them drop. "That's my two cents."

In other words, Sierra should be honest with Mason about her and David's relationship. She should trust him to help her with this problem without judgment.

David had shaken her ability to trust. He'd made her cautious. Where her desire was to jump into a relationship with Mason now, she'd cautiously erected a wall between them, using the boys to keep him at a distance and make things uncomplicated.

"Damn. I'm still letting him influence my decisions and get in the way of what I want."

Her mother's eyes narrowed. "What do you mean? Why wouldn't David let you have what you want?"

She drew back one side of her mouth in a half frown, thinking back to how David subtly manipulated her into doing what he wanted most of the time. "I wanted to move back here. I talked to him about it, but he refused. He didn't want to change jobs or be so close to all of you. He wanted us to have *our* life." As in separate from her family. "I went along because I thought what he wanted was me and the boys."

"And now you're not so sure that's what it was."

"I think something was keeping him in Napa Valley and it wasn't me and the boys." She shrugged. "Maybe I'm wrong." And in that moment, it became clear. "I guess I'll find out."

Chapter Fifteen

Mason stared at the change on his calendar and wanted to smile, but found he was more confused than happy about his next appointment. He walked to his office door and found his assistant at her desk, typing.

"Louise, when did Sierra call for an appointment?"

"This morning. You had a cancellation. She said she's a friend of yours, so I made the appointment."

"Did she say why she wanted to meet with me?"

The object of his inquiry walked in the door.

"Hey," Sierra said, her eyes darting between him and Louise, who couldn't stop looking from him to Sierra like she could see the sparks flying between them.

"I hear you need a lawyer."

Sierra bit her lip, glanced at Louise, then back at him. "Um. Not really, but kinda."

That made him nervous. If she wasn't in need of a lawyer . . . Well, he hoped she wasn't here to break up with him.

Then again, who made an appointment to do that?

"Mason?"

"Yeah?"

"If you don't want to help me . . ."

"Of course I want to help you." A strange sense of ease went through him. She wanted help. She didn't want to break up. And she wasn't here because she'd found out what he suspected but never told her. "Come into my office and tell me what you need."

Louise's gaze bounced from him to Sierra and back. She gave him a knowing look. "I'll hold all your calls."

He waited for Sierra to pass before closing the door on Louise's inquisitive gaze. She'd grill him later. She knew him well enough to know that Sierra, a friend, wasn't here about a divorce.

Normally he'd greet Sierra with a kiss on the cheek or a brush of his hand on her arm in front of the boys. He'd like to kiss her now, the way he did when the boys were distracted and he stole one from her. But she didn't take a seat or look like she came here to make out in his office for an hour. Pity.

Sierra simply stood in front of his desk and stared at him, looking unsure and nervous as hell.

"Do you want to do this standing up or sitting down?" Okay, that sounded dirty even to him.

Sierra raised an eyebrow and dropped into one of the chairs.

He went with her prompt and took a seat behind his desk, keeping this professional. She'd made the appointment. He'd give her his full attention.

Sierra stared at him for a good long moment, then pulled a stack of envelopes from her purse along with a slip of folded paper. She set it on the desk, opened it, and slid the check toward him. "Your assistant said a five-hundred-dollar retainer would do."

He knew she was still short on ready cash, so the five hundred had to be a stretch for her to come up with for . . . whatever it was she wanted him to do for her. Maybe she borrowed it from her mom or Amy.

"I don't want your money, Sierra. I'm happy to help you with whatever you need."

"If I pay you, that means you're my attorney and you can't say anything to anyone about what I'm about to tell you."

That confused him. Didn't she trust him? "Anything you say to me is between you and me. You don't need to pay for my silence. You just have to ask."

"You're mad."

A little bit. "I thought I made it clear what I wanted with you, and it's not to be your lawyer."

She deflated in the chair, her shoulders sagging and all the air going out of her lungs in a loud sigh. "So you won't help me."

"Of course I'll help you. I just don't get why you didn't just ask me about this the half-dozen times you've seen me over the last week instead of making an appointment."

Sierra stood and paced back and forth. "I didn't want you to think I was taking advantage of our friendship."

"I hope we are moving into a deeper kind of friendship where you trust me and know that I'd do anything for you."

She stopped in her tracks and stared at him, looking for something, then deciding she saw whatever it was she needed to see to sit back down and tell him what she needed. "This is awkward. You and I . . . We're seeing each other now. I don't want to screw that up."

"Hundreds of people have sat where you are ready to end relationships because they couldn't trust the other person enough to have a civil conversation about what they needed and wanted from the other person. So, Sierra, what do you need from me?"

She sucked in a breath. "I need your help to find out if David was having an affair or in some kind of trouble that cost him, *us*, fifty thousand dollars."

He thought she needed help navigating the insurance and red tape on her property up in Napa. He never thought this had anything to do with David.

No wonder she'd been apprehensive to bring it up to him.

Mason fell back in his seat and tried to get his thoughts together and figure out a way to navigate this. He started with the simple question. "Why do you think he was having an affair?"

Sierra pulled some papers out of one of the envelopes and slid them across the desk. "He took out a fifty-thousand-dollar loan nearly two years ago. For what, I have no idea. I didn't know anything about it until after his death and the bank contacted me about delinquent payments I knew nothing about. He had the bills sent to his office, not the house. Once the bank contacted me, I went through the boxes his assistant had packed up and delivered to the house after his death."

"Okay. He took out a loan you didn't know about. Did he use it to pay off debts the two of you accrued during the marriage?"

"Of course I checked that first." Annoyance replaced her earlier trepidation.

"I'm just trying to cover all the bases." He didn't want to dig into their marriage, but she'd come to him for help. This was a can of worms he hoped to avoid. "Did you receive any statements for an account you didn't know about?"

"No. That's what I need you to help me find out. If this

money, or even part of it, is sitting in some other account that I can access, I need to find it. Then I can pay off the loan—or at least some of it with what's left." She raked her fingers through her hair, distress and despair in her eyes. "I have been struggling the last year to pay this and the other bills on my own." Tears glistened in her eyes.

David had left her a mess and a mountain of bills.

"Didn't he have life insurance?"

She rolled her eyes. "By the time I paid off the funeral costs and credit card debt we had, hoping to make the monthly expenses more reasonable on just my salary, I only had a small amount left to put into school accounts for the boys. My plan was to use part of the survivors' benefits money from David's Social Security to pay bills and transfer what's left into their college funds. Then I got hit with this." She tapped her finger on the loan notice. "The job you got me is a huge help. I make more, so I can afford to pay this, but it's an expense and I have nothing to show for it."

Mason suspected he knew where the money went, but he didn't want to be right. "Did you find any evidence of an affair?"

"His phone is locked. His fingerprint is required to get into it. Because the phone he used was provided by his company, I don't have the bills for it, so I can't see who he called or texted."

Smart, hiding his conversations and texts from his wife.

Bastard.

"I'm guessing you didn't find any notes or unexplained receipts among his things."

"No. I have no hard evidence that he was having an affair. It makes me sick to think that he hid something like this so well that I didn't even notice. But I think about the two years leading up to his death and I think about how everything had become so stale and routine. As a family, everything seemed fine, but between David and me . . . We lost something along the way."

"You suspect he pulled away because he had someone else." Mason's stomach knotted. The bastard didn't see what he had right in front of him, a beautiful, kind, loving woman.

"I think we drifted so far apart that I didn't see or suspect he was seeing someone else. Like I said, everything seemed fine between us. I knew we needed to spend more time together as a couple, but work and kids took over our lives. We didn't have big, blow-up fights. He mentioned just as much as I did that we needed to get away, just the two of us, but we never did. I don't know how to explain it, except that we were living our lives and it seemed both of us were thinking that as the boys got older we'd have more time for each other.

"I did feel like there were days and weeks where he was pre-occupied with something he didn't want to talk about. He went on more business trips the months leading up to his death. The night of the accident, he was driving down south to meet with clients the next day."

Are you sure?

Mason had his doubts.

She answered his unspoken question. "At least, I think that's where he was going. I was so lost in my grief and taking care of the boys right afterward, making sure they were okay, I never asked his boss about it. I just went through the motions each day, trying to get whatever needed to be done, done."

Mason held his hand out to her across the desk. She laid her hand in his and he squeezed to let her know he was there. "You know none of this is your fault, right?"

"I wasn't paying attention. Maybe I just didn't want to know."

"A lot of my clients feel that exact same way. Women and men. They aren't exactly happy in their marriages but there isn't enough strife to end it. There's still hope that they'll find their way back to how they felt when they got together and married. They let things slide. They make excuses, like staying together for the kids. They don't open up about how they're feeling or what they want to change. Sometimes things just fizzle out and they end up here. Other times, someone finds what they need with someone else and they still end up here."

"Is that why you never married?"

"I came close. Once." But his ex felt like he'd been holding out on her. Maybe he had been, because he'd been carrying a torch for the woman in front of him for a long time. And the engagement with his ex ended right after he saw Sierra at her stepfather's funeral.

Sierra showing up here and telling him about this situation made him feel guilty for keeping his secret, even though he didn't know if what he saw was what he thought he saw.

"Mason?"

Jarred out of his thoughts, he met Sierra's inquisitive eyes. "Yeah? What?"

"Do you think David was having an affair?"

"I'm not sure. But I have an investigator who can look into it. He can try to track the money." But if the money led where Mason suspected, he didn't know what he'd tell Sierra. The last thing he wanted to do was break her heart. Or lose her because he'd kept quiet about what he suspected.

Love blinds us all to people's faults. When love fades, sometimes those flaws are all too clear.

He wished for Sierra's sake that she could let David rest in peace with a clear heart.

Instead, she'd been left with suspicions and come to him to clear them up. Mason didn't know if he could do that for her without wrecking the new, fragile feelings developing between them.

He should tell her what he suspected, but he didn't want to accuse a dead man of something he couldn't prove. David wasn't here to speak for himself. And Sierra would only have Mason to take out her feelings of betrayal on, whether he was right or wrong.

"Thank you, Mason. This means so much to me. I've been sitting with this all alone for a long time. I wanted answers, I just wasn't sure how to get them. If your investigator can find anything out for me, I'll be so grateful."

Mason suspected grateful was the last thing she'd be.

"I'd appreciate it if you kept this between us. My mom knows, but I don't want my sisters to find out. David was your friend. I'm sure you're not thrilled to be investigating him. But I need to know the truth."

How did he get himself into this pickle?

Because he couldn't say no to the woman sitting across from him. Because he wanted her to be happy. Because he'd let her get away once and wouldn't let that happen again.

Investigating David and the money meant it might be that much harder to convince Sierra how much he cared.

"David and I knew each other a long time ago. I know he wasn't perfect. He could be competitive." And go after the girl Mason liked just to see who got her. He had a feeling David learned that winning didn't mean you got what you wanted and he went looking for someone else without thinking about the devastation he'd leave in his wake. "Maybe all this is, is some kind of deal he made that went south and he had to pay back the money or something."

Sierra dismissed that with a shake of her head. "I hoped so, too. But I've come to terms with the fact that I would have found some evidence of that in his papers. I looked for some business proposal or investment. I didn't find anything." She stared at their joined hands. "I think my intuition was telling me he had someone else and I just didn't listen to it."

"You'd be surprised how many wives say that same thing. You should listen to that gut instinct. I've found based on the number of women who come in here, it's usually right."

"Well, my gut's telling me you're not happy about doing this for me."

He tried to smile but didn't quite pull it off to ease her mind. "I'm afraid that uncovering the truth will only hurt you and that's the last thing I want to do."

"Don't worry. I won't shoot the messenger."

He was afraid she wouldn't be able to keep that promise.

Chapter Sixteen

Sierra stood just as the office door opened. Mason walked in looking fine in a navy suit, white shirt, and blue-and-purple tie. The color made his hair appear even more golden, his eyes a brighter blue. He looked good and had to know it. Every woman still left in the office noticed as they tracked his progress across the entry and through the cubicles to her desk.

Mason stopped in front of her, his eyes diving down her new lilac-colored dress to her sparkly black strappy heels, then coming up to meet her gaze. "That dress is killer. You're gorgeous."

"I was just thinking the same thing about you." That got her a huge smile from him. She was glad for it because things had been casual and guarded between them since she appeared in his office three days ago asking for his help with her David problem.

Mason stepped closer, the woodsy smell of him drawing her in. "I'm so glad we're finally doing our dinner date. I love the boys, but I've wanted you all to myself for a while now."

"I feel the same way. Amy has the kids. They're having a sleepover with their cousins."

Mason leaned in close. "Are we having a sleepover tonight, too?"

She'd thought about it all day, which meant thoughts of him

distracted her from doing anything really productive. "If you play your cards right." She was teasing, but she'd planned for this, hoping it would happen sooner rather than later.

"Well, then I'll do my best to impress you with some good food, better wine, and charming conversation."

"All of that sounds amazing, but really all I want to do is spend some time alone with you." It had been so long since she'd dressed up and took the time to make herself feel pretty. Sierra couldn't remember the last time a man paid her a compliment. It had been far too long since she'd been held. Even longer since she'd had sex.

Even more than that, she wanted to feel a man against her, inside her, and all around her. She wanted to feel needed and desired again.

The look Mason gave her went a long way to bolstering her courage and resolve that tonight they wouldn't stop at a few hot kisses while the boys weren't looking.

Tonight was about being a woman again, not just Danny and Oliver's mom. She'd needed that for a long time.

Mason's fingers brushed her face. "I lost you. What's wrong?"

She focused on Mason, the man who'd made it clear he wanted a real relationship with her. A man who'd gone out of his way to make her and her kids feel at home with him and at his place.

"Nothing is wrong. I'm with you." With that, she went up on tiptoe and kissed him right there in her office. The surprise she felt in him disappeared immediately and he took over the kiss, sliding his tongue along hers as his arms enfolded her and held her close.

He'd always initiated the intimacy between them. He seemed to like her taking the lead. She'd have to remember that later.

"Hi, Mason. I see my new employee is more than just a friend you wanted to help."

Mason broke the kiss with a huge smile on his face and turned to Sierra's boss without letting her go. "Hi, Marissa. How are you?"

"Not as good as you, judging by that big grin you're wearing."

Mason chuckled and loosened his embrace of Sierra, but he didn't release her, keeping his arm banded around her waist. "Sierra and I go way back. We've recently reconnected."

Marissa eyed him with a knowing look. "I see that. And I hate to admit it, but you were right about her. She's fantastic. She's brought in three new clients since she started. All of our clients adore her."

Mason squeezed her to his side. "So do I."

Sierra glanced up at him and caught her breath at the wide smile and absolute adoration in his eyes.

"Looks like you two are headed out for a nice evening together. I just wanted to say hi. Have a great night." Marissa turned to Sierra. "I knew you had great taste when you picked out the furniture and decorations to stage the last rental property. Now I know you've also got excellent taste in men, and you must be something special, because I've asked him out at least half a dozen times and gotten turned down flat every time."

Mason chuckled. "I don't date my clients."

"From what I've seen and heard, you hardly date." Marissa gave her another bold smile. "I'm glad you changed that. He deserves someone who knows what a great guy he is."

"I've known that for a long time." She'd nearly canceled her engagement because she thought Mason was a better choice for her than David.

Mason didn't know that though.

He'd asked for a second chance of sorts because he'd let her go. She didn't know that at the time, either, but he'd said as much to her since she'd moved back.

Maybe this was a chance for both of them to get it right.

"See you tomorrow, Marissa." She took Mason's hand. "Let's go."

Mason gave Marissa a good-bye smile and walked with Sierra out of the office and onto the sidewalk. "The restaurant is up two blocks. Mind walking?"

"Not at all."

They started down the street and she couldn't help but smile up at him.

He caught her staring. "What?"

"This is nice. It's been a long time since I felt this light."

He squeezed her hand. "I'm glad. Something feels different about you tonight."

"I guess I want to set aside all the worries and just enjoy being with you."

"You've had a lot on your mind and to deal with since coming home."

She didn't want to ruin the night with talk of David, but had to ask, "Has your investigator found anything out yet?"

Mason frowned and kept walking without looking at her. "No. Not yet. Something came up on a divorce case and he needed to work on that for me first."

"Of course."

Mason held the restaurant door open for her. "If there's something to find, he'll find it." She walked in and settled into his side when he stood beside her with his arm around her waist in front of the reservation desk. "I just hope whatever we discover doesn't upset you."

"I can't be more upset than finding out he took out a loan and messed with my credit, made it difficult to support the kids, and never said a word about it to me."

"I know the why is important, but sometimes it's worse than the deed itself."

"I'm already expecting the worst."

"Mr. Moore," the hostess greeted them. "We're so happy to have you back. The table you requested is ready. This way." The hostess led them into the dining room and to the right where a private booth was set up with half a dozen tiny candles, a pretty pink-and-white floral centerpiece, a bottle of white wine in an ice bucket, and a dozen red roses bundled with greenery on the table.

Mason picked them up and handed them to her. "For you."

She leaned in and inhaled their heady scent. "Thank you. They're beautiful."

"Like you."

The hostess smiled. "I hope everything is to your liking, Mr. Moore."

"With her here, it's perfect."

Sierra's heart fluttered and melted all at the same time. "Mason, this is . . . wonderful."

"I want you to remember our first date."

The hostess left them alone.

Sierra slid into the booth, followed by Mason.

She set the flowers on the table, brushing her fingers over the delicate petals, and turned to Mason. "My favorite memory of you is when we rode out to that pretty spot along the creek, tied up the horses, and swam in that little pool of water, then laid out in the sun, just talking and being quiet."

"That was a good day. I wanted to kiss you so bad."

"I wanted you to kiss me, but you didn't."

"I was older than you. I didn't want to take advantage."

"You're still older than me," she pointed out, teasing.

"Yeah, but I grew out of stupid and I know what I want now. Back then, I didn't want to mess up our friendship."

"And now?"

"Now I want to grow our friendship, strengthen it, make it better."

Good answer. She wanted the same thing. "I guess when you're young you think it's one or the other. Friends or lovers. But a real relationship is built on that friendship. Everything you add to it only makes it better. Without the friendship, how can you have real trust and intimacy?"

Mason pulled the wine from the bucket and poured two glasses. She took hers and clinked it to the one he held up. "To building on our friendship."

Feeling nostalgic, she reminisced about the past. "I don't know how we got from the cute guy next door who let me come over whenever I wanted to ride horses and just hang out to you being the man who goes out of his way to take my kids' minds off the move, a new school, and missing their father, getting me a dream job, and taking me out to dinner with flowers and candlelight."

Mason settled back into the cushion. "I liked being your friend. You were easy to talk to and be with despite the draw we both felt but let simmer in the background. You liked to have fun and ride and just enjoy yourself."

"And yet, we never got together."

Mason's smile dimmed. "I blame Amy. She tagged along more often than not."

Sierra put her elbow on the table and planted her chin in her hand. "She had a mad crush on you."

"And I didn't want to hurt her feelings. Because you knew she had a crush on me, you never seemed open to allowing yourself to want more between us."

True. "She's my sister. She was in your class at school, and I was two grades behind, so she seemed like the girl you'd want."

"And yet, I liked you. She was . . . don't take this the wrong way, but too high maintenance and fussy and needy."

Sierra frowned and laughed under her breath at the same time. "All true. Poor Amy. That's not very flattering."

"Some guys don't mind. It doesn't appeal to me. She showed off and constantly wanted my attention. At first, it was flattering. But then it got old. You always seemed so secure in your skin."

"Oh, believe me, I went through that awkward stage where I thought everything was wrong with me."

"Amy fussed and complained about all that stuff. If she didn't like herself, how was anyone else supposed to like her?"

He held up a hand. "Don't get me wrong, she grew out of it, but at the time, seeing you two together, you were so much easier to be around. I could be myself with you. Amy seemed to have a vision of what I'd be with her that didn't fit who I am. Does that make sense?"

Sierra actually got that very well. It was what she realized about her marriage. She'd built up a vision of what she and David would look like together as a married couple. In reality, they were the same people they'd always been.

"You can't make someone like you, or even love you." She'd learned that a long time ago. "You can try to live up to their image of you, but in the end, you are who you are." In the end, David didn't want her.

"You see me for who I am because we have history. You knew me before I was successful." Mason glanced up, then back at her. "I apologize for this." He cocked his chin toward the man walking up to their table.

"Mason, man, good to see you." The gentleman came right up, hand extended to shake Mason's.

"Allen. It's been a while. I'd like to introduce Sierra Silva. Sierra, Allen. A former client."

Sierra took the gentleman's hand. He glanced down at her other hand, looking for a wedding ring she hadn't worn in more than six months. "I see Mason's untangled you from the dummy who let you go."

Mason took her wrist, drew her hand away from Allen's, and linked his fingers with hers. "She's not a client. She's my date."

Allen frowned. "Lucky you. Disappointing for me."

Mason chuckled. "Last I saw you, you and a beautiful brunette of your own were on your way to Fiji for a couple of weeks to celebrate your divorce."

"And celebrate we did." The gentleman turned solemn. "Listen, I won't take up your time, but my ex is back with more gripes about how I'm not keeping her in the lifestyle I afforded her while we were married and she wants more child support. If Sabrina wants horseback riding lessons, fine, but I want to be the one to take her."

"Got it," Mason agreed.

"Sorry to interrupt your date with this."

"No worries. Make an appointment with Louise, we'll get this settled."

"Appreciate it." Allen gave Sierra a soft smile. "Nice to meet you."

Mason nodded and waited for the gentleman to take his leave. "Sorry. I was hoping we'd have the evening to ourselves and some privacy."

"It's fine. You obviously helped him out of a rough situation."

Mason chuckled. "Allen loves his daughter. He loves his ex. They just can't seem to have a civil conversation anymore. Not that I blame her; she did catch him kissing her best friend, made a scene, it ended up going viral on someone's Twitter. A 'friend' posted a video of the epic yelling match between the two women, Allen standing there dumbstruck not knowing what to do until he ultimately had to physically separate them before the cops showed up."

"Oh man, that sucks."

"I have dealt with so many people who lost their minds in

the moment and regretted it almost as soon as it was over. Allen begged his ex to forgive him. She couldn't. Not after he'd embarrassed her in public like that." Mason sighed. "It's too bad, too, because if they'd tried, they might have come out of it stronger."

"And Sabrina wouldn't be caught in the middle."

Mason nodded, looking solemn, then took a sip of his wine.

Sierra went on, "Your job is so complicated and emotionally straining."

"My clients aren't happy to be ending their relationships; the anger is just a mask for the pain. Mostly they're hurt and bitter. They think they want revenge, but what they really want is to be able to move past the pain and anxiety over starting a new life without their partner. Change is scary. Most of them are better off after the divorce, emotionally, but it takes time and perspective to get there."

She squeezed his hand. "It took me a while to get there after David's death. I felt rocked by it. I didn't know how to go on without him. I was his wife. I didn't know how to be a widow and what was expected of me. I just knew I was still a mom and I needed to be there for the boys. But I still needed to figure out how I felt and what I wanted now that my life had changed."

"And then the fire happened and your life is upended again."

She appreciated that he got it. "So much is still in flux, but I feel anchored here now."

Mason brushed his thumb against her skin, sending ripples of warmth through her hand and up her arm, spreading out to every part of her body. "I hope I'm part of the reason you feel at home here again."

"It seems like everything in my life has been hard lately. Then you came back into my life and I don't know . . . it just seems so easy to be with you."

"Because we're friends?"

"That part's always been easy. Hiding the attraction in front of the kids is a bit harder."

Mason leaned in close, his breath whispering against her cheek. "You don't have to hide anything tonight." His lips brushed her skin in a light kiss that left her wanting even as every nerve in her body lit up with lust.

Mason sat back and smiled at their waitress. "We need another minute to decide what we want."

Sierra didn't need even a second to know she wanted Mason.

The sexy smile he gave her said he knew it, too.

She took a fortifying sip of her wine, picked up the menu, and tried to concentrate on the words and not every breath Mason took, or the way his arm brushed hers when he opened his menu.

"They do a great steak. The potatoes au gratin are amazing. But you might like the roasted chicken with white wine sauce. It comes with a side of mac and cheese. I know you can't resist that." He knew her all too well.

"I kind of want it all."

Mason turned and locked his gaze on her. "You can have anything you want." He let that hang for a moment and her heart beat faster and her breath hitched when his gaze dipped to her mouth. "I'll get one. You get the other. We'll share." His blazing blue eyes met hers again. "What do you say?"

"Yes. Okay." She had a feeling she was answering a question he hadn't asked, but needed to be answered all the same.

"You make it hard to concentrate."

His deep voice and the thoughts he invoked did the same to her. "You make me think about all the things I've been missing."

His eyes darkened with desire and the sexual tension grew thick and heady between them. She pressed her thighs together to ease the ache of it, but she didn't take her eyes off his gorgeous face.

"You're coming home with me tonight, right?"

"Yep." The word popped off her lips.

He chuckled, humor and frustration all packed into the light sound. "Why didn't I think to just make you dinner at my place?"

To ease the tension and make him smile, she teased, "Well, you can't be brilliant *all* the time."

This time the laugh was straight from his gut and filled with self-deprecation. "Don't tell my clients."

"Cross my heart."

His gaze dipped to the V in her dress. "Your heart is what always drew me to you. Your ability to always be kind amazed me."

She tried. "I imagine your clients don't come to you with a lot of kindness for their exes. I'm sure dealing with their anger and demands all day can get to you."

"I have to say, coming home and seeing you and the boys every night for a few hours erases everything bad from my day."

That touched her deeply and brought a sheen of tears to her eyes. "I appreciate that, Mason. I find myself looking forward to seeing you at the end of the day, too. The second I walk in the door, the boys are asking to go to your place."

"I hope that doesn't change." A suspicious edge tinged that nice sentiment.

She didn't have time to wonder about it, or second-guess why she thought she heard something in his words that maybe wasn't there. The waitress approached the table and Mason placed their order, then refilled her wine glass.

* * *

They enjoyed the rest of the evening, talking about their day, people they knew from the past that Mason was still acquainted with, plans to take the boys on a long ride and picnic over the weekend, and eating and sharing the amazing food.

Sierra loved reconnecting with Mason, sharing a simple but lovely meal, and focusing on each other. He asked questions, trying to fill in the pieces he didn't know about her life in Napa. He didn't shy away from the fact she'd been married to David. He didn't mind that David naturally came up in conversation. In fact, he asked about him, which made it easier to remember they'd once been friends and Mason missed him, too.

In all the time since David's death, she finally found a kind of peace about his absence. Talking to Mason about him settled her in a way that she'd tried to find this past year, but it had seemed so elusive. Now she got it. No one talked to her about David. They all tiptoed around the fact that he was dead. They stopped asking if she was okay or offering condolences because they didn't want to make her sad. But talking about the good times and fond memories of David with Mason made her miss him and, at the same time, lessened her grief.

Mason had no trouble filling her in on his family, either. She asked a ton of questions because she wanted to know more about him. She wanted to know everything about his life now.

"So my dad joined a yoga class after he hurt his hip. My mom thought it was a good idea. She dropped him off, went to run an errand, then came back, walked in to pick him up, and found him bent over with a twentysomething hottie leaning over him from behind helping him with the pose and stretching his hips. She says my dad had a grin on his face and was enjoying himself far too much. She dragged him out of there and wouldn't let him go back."

Sierra busted up laughing. "She knows the lady was just doing her job, right?"

"Mom told him if he went back to her, she'd hire me to represent her in the divorce."

Sierra laughed even harder. "Oh no. I take it he didn't go back."

"Oh, he went back, but to a class that has a male instructor. The guy is very handsome according to my mother. Based on my father's frowns about that, I don't think he likes my mother sticking around to watch the class and stare at the instructor."

Sierra's cheeks hurt from smiling so much. "Oh dear. So I guess you might be working for your father if she goes after the sexy instructor."

Mason shook his head. "I'm staying out of it."

"How is your dad's hip now?"

"Better. He goes to a massage therapist once a week, too. It's helping. He's moving better. He hates being inactive. Worse, he hates that he can't ride the way he used to."

"Do they come to the ranch often?"

"Less and less, but we keep in touch. They're always hounding me to settle down and start a family." Mason rolled his eyes. "Settle down? Like I'm out partying all the time or something."

"It's not easy to find someone. I guess you're more aware of what you want and don't want because of your job."

"Believe me, I've learned that real kindness means more than a pretty face and a fat bank account."

"I've learned that trust and the truth are really important, too."

Mason signed the check the waitress discreetly left on the table during their talk, then turned to her. "The truth is, Sierra, I can't wait to get you home."

She put her elbow on the table, planted her chin in her hand, and gave him a sexy smile. "Well, what are you waiting for?"

Mason slid out of the booth and held his hand out to her. She took it knowing she was taking the next step in their relationship and a giant step out of her past and into a future she got more excited about each and every time she was with Mason.

Chapter Seventeen

Amy thought she had a plan to keep four kids happy until bedtime but that plan went south the second smoke filled the kitchen and the smoke detector blared through the house.

Distracted with getting the kids to clean up for dinner, the organic pizza she put in the oven had burned to a crisp.

The blaring sound made Danny's and Oliver's eyes go wide with terror.

Oliver freaked and ran out the front door screaming, "The house is on fire!"

Danny followed him at a dead run.

Amy tossed the burnt pizza on top of the stove and ran after them. She found Oliver in the yard sitting in the middle of the lawn with his knees bent, arms tightened around them, crying. Danny stood next to him patting his shoulder, cooing, "It's okay."

She knelt next to Oliver and brushed her hand over his hair. "Sweetheart, I'm so sorry. There's no fire, only a very burnt pizza."

Oliver looked up at her, bottom lip trembling. "Is anyone dead?"

Her heart broke. "No, honey. Everyone is fine." She glanced up at P.J. and Emma standing at her side. "See, your cousins are fine and there's nothing but smoke in the house." She wiped at Oliver's tears with her thumbs. "Come on. Let's see if I have another pizza in the freezer and get that smoke detector to stop that incessant buzzing."

The last tear spilled down Oliver's soft cheek. "It's scary."

Her heart was still pounding. "I know, but it's all over now."

She picked up Oliver, hugged him close to reassure him, and stood. She walked back into the house, scrunching her nose at the burnt smell and smoke still lingering in the air.

"P.J., Emma, and Danny, grab a magazine off the table and wave it in the air and try to get the smoke to blow out the door." She set Oliver on a stool at the counter and picked up the burnt-to-a-crisp disk from off the stove. "I'll be right back, sweetheart. Let me get rid of this." She walked out the back door and went to the trash bins on the side of the house. She dumped the ruined pie into the trash and slammed the lid.

Where the hell is Rex? He should have been home an hour ago.

Of course he picks tonight to leave me alone with four kids.

She walked back into the house and sighed. All four kids were running around, flapping magazines pretending to be helicopters and windmills. Oliver seemed back to his old self. Thank God. The house smelled slightly better, but the smell of smoke would linger for a while.

She kicked the oven door shut, found another pizza in the freezer, tossed it on the counter, and snagged the phone from the charger. She hit the speed dial and waited three rings before Rex finally picked up.

"Where are you?"

A long silent pause on the other end made her stop and think she should have at least said hello first.

"I can't talk right now. I'll call you back in an hour." The clipped tone set her off.

"I'm here with four kids and no backup. I need your help."

"Hold on."

Her patience nearly snapped when she heard his muffled "Please excuse me for a moment. I need to take this," and a woman said, "Sure. No problem."

She got even angrier when it took him another minute to come back on the line.

"What is going on?" he demanded in a hushed whisper.

"Who was that woman?"

"A client."

"You didn't say anything about a business dinner tonight."

"I called you three times today and left you two messages, but apparently you were too busy to listen to them."

She couldn't refute that. After she picked up all four kids at school, took them to the park to play, out for frozen yogurt, got them back to the house to wash up and do homework, then started dinner, she hadn't even looked at her phone . . . until now.

"Can you get out of the dinner and come home and help me?"

"No." He didn't say anything more.

"But I have Sierra's boys here. They're sleeping over. It's crazy. I burned dinner, the smoke alarm went off, and Oliver freaked out."

"I'm sure you've got it covered. I need to get back to my client."

"That's all you have to say."

"We've been over this too many times to count at this point. According to your master plan, the kids were supposed to be at the park carnival thing tonight. I figured you weren't expecting me, since you didn't tell me about it, or even ask if I wanted to go with you."

"Of course we wanted you to go, but there was no way I was taking four kids on my own."

"And you prove my point for me. You thought you'd be doing that alone and changed your plans without telling me a thing."

The anger and frustration in his voice only made her angrier. "So I'm expected to plan your schedule, too."

"I thought we were a family. One that does things together. But lately, you're so busy keeping busy you forget I exist. It took you over an hour to realize I wasn't home at the usual time. Instead of listening to my messages, you interrupt my business meeting and insinuate I'm out with a woman behind your back."

True. Still . . . "It's not like you're hot for me when you get home."

"Most of the time you don't notice I'm even there unless you need me to do something with the kids. It's all I can do to get you to stop whatever you're doing to kiss me hello. It used to be that I couldn't leave or come home without kissing you. Now, it feels like it's just one more chore for you to do. Most of the time, it doesn't make even one of your lists."

True. Damnit. This wasn't all her fault. "That's not fair."

"I'm the first one who'll say no, it's not. I used to have a wife. Now I've got the mother of my kids. You're so wrapped up in that, you don't have time for anything else, including me, and while I get it, I'm tired of it."

That scared her all the way to her soul. "What are you saying?"

"Something needs to change. We've talked about it to death,

but you refuse to cut back and spend more time at home. Your priorities don't include me. My needs and wants rank dead last to the kids and their activities and you wanting to make it seem like we've got the perfect life. The photos are great, Amy, but have you ever noticed I'm not in most of them? Where are the ones of us doing things as a family?"

She didn't know what to say.

"We planned tonight as our first date night in God knows how long. Do you remember that?" He didn't give her a chance to respond. "But instead of putting that on your precious calendar, you scheduled yet another thing for the kids to do."

"The park carnival only happens once a year. I thought the kids would love it, but then Sierra asked if I could watch her boys, too."

"That just sounds like excuses to me about how unimportant our date was to you. *I* was looking forward to it. I had a reservation and a plan to seduce my wife. But she wasn't interested. She made other plans. So I made other plans, and I need to get back to them. At least my boss will appreciate my extra effort."

Desperation seized her heart. "Rex, please. Come home, we'll talk about this."

"I've said everything I have to say. You know how I feel. I know you're not going to change. Maybe it's time I did something about it."

"What are you talking about?"

"You're always complaining you have no time to yourself. You obviously don't want to spend it with me, so maybe we fix that and I take my fair share of time with the kids."

She turned her back on the kids who were tearing pages

out of the magazines and making them into paper airplanes and tossing them all over the living room. "Are you saying you want a divorce?" She kept her voice low, so the kids didn't hear her say that last word she'd never thought would come out of her mouth when talking about her and Rex. They loved each other. They swore they'd be together forever. They promised that nothing would ever come between them.

"I'm telling you that if something doesn't change *now*, it's not looking good for us."

She stood stunned, listening to the dead line.

He'd hung up on her.

What the . . .

How did this all become her fault?

She glanced at the color-coded calendar.

Green for sports.

Blue for art class.

Orange for music class.

Red for birthday parties. The bold color to help her remember to pick up a gift.

Purple items for the things she volunteered to do: working in the kids' classrooms, school and community events.

She had a rainbow collage of events listed that should have made her life feel full and satisfying. So why did she feel like a bedraggled athlete coming in last at the end of a triathlon every day? She made it through, but she didn't feel like a winner. She didn't feel like she'd enjoyed it.

"Aunt Amy, I'm hungry." Danny stared up at her, his finger in his mouth.

"Don't put your fingers in your mouth. They're dirty."

Danny pulled his finger free and showed her the long paper cut that welled with blood and dripped down to his palm. "It hurts."

Yeah, every accusation Rex lashed her with tonight felt like a stinging paper cut, throbbing in her mind. But when he insinuated they were headed for a divorce and it was all her fault, she felt the dagger to the heart.

Amy fought back tears, her anger and frustration, along with the fear and uncertainty about the future.

She wanted to fix this, but also felt paralyzed, because it all overwhelmed her.

She'd been dealing with those feelings for months. Because she liked everything perfect and organized, trying to untangle her life only made it seem that much harder to do, so she didn't do anything but get through the next marathon day.

Right now, she needed to feed four kids and get them settled for the night.

As always, the kids came first and she came last.

She got that's what happened when you had kids. Most days, she didn't mind. But right now, she'd like a few hours to herself to think about everything going on in her life instead of what fruit or vegetable she'd serve with the pizza and how many bedtime stories it would take to get the kids to go to sleep.

"Can I call my mom?" Danny asked.

Sierra was probably having the night of her life out with Mason at a fancy restaurant that probably didn't even serve chicken nuggets and had linen napkins and fancy cocktails.

Amy desperately needed an adult beverage right now.

"Let's fix that cut. You can call her after dinner." She held her hand out to her nephew and walked with him to the bath-room, leaving the other three loud children tossing paper air-planes trying to outdo one another with the distance they got on their throws.

She didn't feel like she was getting anywhere but older in her life.

Chapter Eighteen

Mason kicked the front door closed, tugged Sierra's hand to get her to turn to him, then took her mouth in a searing kiss that made his heart slam into his ribs, then beat double time. She tasted like wine and honey. Sweet on his tongue. A fire in his arms. She gave back everything he poured into showing her how much he wanted her.

He'd waited so long to have her all to himself and in his arms like this.

He didn't want to waste a second of it. And yet, he had all night to take his time.

She hooked her leg around his thigh, her arms locked around his neck. He grabbed her ass and pulled her in close. About to pick her up and carry her to his bedroom, she jolted and pushed away when her phone rang.

She sucked in a much needed breath and smiled up at him. "Sorry. It's probably the kids calling to say good night."

Reluctantly and with a lot of effort, he let her loose.

She swiped the screen to accept the video call and held up the phone so the boys could see her. "Hey, you guys. Are you having fun?"

"Aunt Amy set the house on fire," Oliver announced.

"What?" Sierra gasped. "Are you all okay?"

"Everyone is fine," Amy yelled. "I burned a pizza, not the house."

Sierra's shoulders sagged with relief. "Sounds like you had some excitement. What else did you do today?"

"All kinds of stuff. I won the airplane-flying contest and ate the most pizza." Danny beamed his mother a smile. "P.J. beat me on the race car game. Emma wanted us to play tea party, but there wasn't anything in the cups, so we went out back and played on the swings. P.J. can go really high."

"You've been busy. I hope you helped Aunt Amy clean up."

"We did. First one to finish their area got to pick the books for bedtime. I won."

"Awesome." Sierra's adoration for her boys and their accomplishments showed in her bright eyes. "Did you brush your teeth and wash up for bed?"

"All done." Danny leaned in close to the screen. "Where are you?"

With nothing but a blank wall behind her, she had no trouble lying. "At home. I'll be there first thing in the morning. We'll have breakfast with Aunt Amy, then come home."

"Can we go riding with Mason? He said he'd teach me to go backwards."

"Why do you want your horse to go backwards?"

"Cuz."

Sierra glanced at Mason. He nodded that he'd take the boys horseback riding. "I'm sure Mason will take you and Oliver riding again. Now I want you to be good boys, be quiet while

Aunt Amy reads books, and go right to sleep so you'll be rested and ready to ride with Mason tomorrow."

"Okay." Danny yawned. "You'll be here in the morning. Right?"

"Yes, honey. I'll be there."

"Night, Mommy." Oliver blew a kiss.

Sierra pretended it smacked her on the cheek and smiled. "Night, baby. I love you both. Make sure you thank Aunt Amy for a great day."

The boys waved good-bye and Amy took the phone and turned away from the screen, making sure the boys left. "I hope you had a good night because four kids all going in different directions is chaos."

Sierra chuckled. "*You* said you wanted to keep them for the night."

"Because I don't know how to say no. Except to Rex. Who's pissed at me, by the way."

"Because you offered to babysit the kids?"

"No. Yes. We were supposed to have date night and I forgot."

"Oh, Amy, I'm sorry."

"Yeah, well, it is what it is. So while my relationship is falling apart and yours is heating up, I expect details over breakfast about your fab night because I'm living vicariously through you until Rex decides if he's going to keep me or not."

Sierra stared at her sister stunned, then found her words. "Um, I'm sure Rex just got caught up and said some things he didn't mean."

"Oh, he meant them." Amy waved it all away. "Sorry. I'm

bumming you out on your hot date. You're still with him, aren't you?"

Sierra turned the phone so Amy could see him standing next to Sierra.

Amy covered her face with her hand and shook her head. "Oh god. I'm an idiot. Go back to . . . whatever you two were doing. I've got the kids. Don't worry about anything. See you in the morning." And just like that Amy hung up, and Sierra and Mason stared at each other.

Sierra's eyes filled with worry. "I had no idea she and Rex were having trouble."

"Me, either. She always seems so . . . on it." He shrugged. "I'm sure they'll work it out."

"I hope so."

Mason wanted to erase everything from her mind and bring her back to him. To their special night together. A night years in the making. He wanted her only thinking of them.

"The kids are fine. Amy and Rex will work out their own problems. Tonight, let's focus on us, because I finally have you all to myself. And I don't want to waste a second of it."

Chapter Nineteen

Sierra stared into Mason's eyes, awed by the depth of sincerity and desire filling them.

Had any other man ever looked at her like that?

In that moment, she let any reservations that they were moving too fast fall away. This was Mason. Her friend. The guy she'd nearly called off her engagement for on a flicker of hope they might have something worth holding on to forever.

And now here was the chance to find out.

He held her face in his hands and stared deep into her eyes. "I've been waiting for you and to feel this way again for a long time." His lips touched hers in a soft kiss that packed a punch of longing and need so raw it echoed through her.

She wrapped her arms around his neck, went up on tiptoe, pulled him close, and took the kiss deeper, letting the walls around her heart drop and allowing him and the rush of feelings in.

Excitement.

Need.

And yes, love.

New and blossoming.

Fragile but hardy, with the possibility to thrive if they nurtured it.

So Sierra let go of everything and focused on them and the way he made her feel. Safe. Wanted. Needed. Important and vital.

A thrill of excitement swept through her as his hands slipped beneath the hem of her dress and brushed up her thighs.

Thoughts about cellulite, unshed baby weight, and pudge flew out of her head the second his hands clamped on her ass and he groaned with pure male appreciation. He effortlessly lifted her snug against him, her legs wrapping around his waist bringing her aching center into exquisite contact with his hard length. She tightened her legs and rubbed against him.

Mason broke the kiss and squeezed her ass. "You're killing me."

"Wait 'til I get your clothes off."

Without a word, he gave her a searing kiss and walked out of the entry, hopefully to his room. Though she didn't much care where they landed so long as he didn't stop kissing and touching her.

It had been way too long since she felt like a desirable woman. It had been too long since her body felt this alive.

And she reveled in it.

Mason clamped his hands at her waist and nudged her off him. Her feet hit the floor and the backs of her legs brushed against the bed. He dipped his hands under her dress again and pulled it up and over her head. The slinky material sailed across the room and landed in a puddle, looking like a pale purple flower on the dark hardwood.

His gaze swept down, taking in her pink lace bra and the matching cheeky panties that she had to admit were well worth the splurge because they made her ass look great. The blaze of heat in his eyes said he thought so, too.

She slipped her hand inside his suit jacket and pushed it down his arms. He shrugged it off while she attacked his dress shirt buttons. He pulled the tie over his head. She took in his broad chest and wide shoulders while he undid the cuffs, took the shirt off, and tossed it.

She swept her hand from his shoulder to his pecs and over his heart. It thumped wildly against her palm. The heat from his skin seeped into hers.

Eyes locked, he sank his fingers into her hair and held her head. "I've wanted this for so long."

"Me, too." Deep inside, she realized she *had* been waiting for this. For him.

They had a connection. She felt it vibrate through him and into her where her hand pressed to his chest. She felt it in the way he looked at her. She couldn't deny that whenever they were in the same room, something drew her to him.

She'd fought it for so long.

They were friends.

That meant something to her.

But this . . . It meant so much more than she ever anticipated or expected.

So she dove in, knowing everything would be different. Better.

They'd be connected in a new way. And she hoped it turned into even more and lasted.

Her heart was ready to move on and find happiness again.

The last of their clothes disappeared in a blur of hands needing to touch flesh, their lips seeking a tempting taste, and their bodies desperate to be laid out and pressed together. When Mason rose on his hands and stared down at her, his hard shaft sinking into her beckoning core, she felt the depth of their joining all the way to her soul.

He leaned down, kissed her reverently. Time stopped and she took in the moment and branded this amazing feeling on her heart.

Then he moved and she lost herself in the rhythm, the feel of him deep inside her body and soul, remembering what it felt like to be loved and freed and lost in ecstasy and to come back to herself with a man holding her close, safe and protected and loved.

She wallowed in the heady buzz and snuggled into his side, letting the quiet surround her and the newfound joy fill her up.

She pressed a kiss to his chest. "It doesn't get better than this."

"I accept that challenge."

She laughed, loving the sound of his deep, completely satisfied and sated voice, and the assurance he put into those words.

Just as she was about to fall asleep, comfortable and happy in his arms, she found herself beneath him once again, thoroughly convinced that with him, everything just got better and better.

In the morning, he proved it again.

* * *

Sierra was still smiling, every nerve still tingling with the memory of their first night together, when she knocked on her sister's door to pick up her kids feeling like a completely new woman.

In the very back of her mind she wondered, with everything that had happened these last two years, if this abundance of joy would last or whether the other shoe would drop soon.

Chapter Twenty

Sierra stared at Amy and didn't know what to say about her frazzled state. It had been years since she'd seen her sister in complete disarray. Hair a mess, no makeup, her eyes swollen and underscored by dark, puffy circles, she appeared to have smeared pancake batter or butter or both on her black pajama shirt. Her sister didn't usually rub her dirty hands on her clothes. No, she'd have her handy Wet Wipes standing by for such things.

"What happened to you?" Anxiety tightened her gut. She worried Amy was in the midst of some sort of crisis.

Amy's bloodshot eyes narrowed. "I gave up my life to have kids."

Those kids were making a ruckus in another room down the hall.

Amy's gaze bore into her before moving to Mason standing behind her. "Looks like you two had a good night."

Sierra couldn't help smiling up at Mason, thinking of the wonderful night they'd spent in each other's arms and what it meant going forward.

Looking back at her sister, she felt a bit guilty. But not much. It was too hard not to feel this good.

Mason put his hands on her shoulders and squeezed.

"Yeah, you two look cozy now, but that won't last." Amy swung the door open wider, revealing Rex sitting on the couch, a blanket draped haphazardly across his lap as he rubbed the heel of his hand into his eye socket. He was still wearing what looked like yesterday's clothes: slacks and a wrinkled dress shirt. "The party's over."

"Amy, I'm not sure what's going on here, but I can take all the kids out to breakfast and give you and Rex some time alone."

Amy's eyes glassed over and filled with frustration and desperation. "I already made the pancakes." She combed her fingers into her hair, loosening the messy topknot even more. "It's fine. Everything is fine." The desperate tone didn't back up her words.

Rex turned and stared at her. "Everything is a mess." The announcement made Amy pale.

Yes, the house looked wrecked. The kids had done a number on the living room. Toys littered the floor. The coffee table was covered in scraps of paper. A paper airplane stuck out of the leaves of a potted plant by the window. The kitchen looked like a tornado hit it. Frozen pizza boxes lay discarded on the counter. The makings for pancakes and eggs cluttered together at one end. Two pans were on the stove. And the house still smelled like burnt pizza from last night.

To Sierra, it wasn't so bad. Messy to the eye, but easily cleaned up. But this was Amy's house. She liked things in their place. Everything scrubbed clean and immaculate.

Amy herself looked like she was a second away from losing her shit.

Guilt settled in Sierra's heart. She wished she'd known her

sister wasn't exaggerating about the kids running wild. Over-whelmed, Amy had lost control of the situation.

Mason stepped into the house, taking charge. "I'll go get the kids to settle down and make sure they're dressed."

Amy stood immobile by the front door like she couldn't make a decision about what to do next.

The only way to get her sister back on track was to put things back to the way she liked them. Sierra tried to be normal and keep things light. "Morning, Rex. Can I get you a cup of coffee?"

Rex turned and stared over his shoulder but he didn't look at her; instead, he locked eyes with Amy. "Sure. That would be great."

Sierra went into the kitchen, got a mug from the cupboard, poured him a cup, added a dollop of milk like she remembered he liked it, took it to him in the living room, then went back to the kitchen.

Yep. Definitely taking the kids out.

With that settled, she put the kitchen to rights, tucking the food back in the fridge, then loading the dishwasher. She found some plastic wrap in a drawer, covered the bowl of pan-cake batter, and set it in the fridge for later.

"You can have breakfast for dinner. The kids will love that."

Amy hadn't moved from the entry. She stood there like a zombie staring at Rex's back like she could will him to fix this.

Clearly, they needed to talk.

Sierra could only imagine what was going on in her sister's mind knowing she and Mason walked in on this mess.

Sierra had never cleaned so fast in her life, but at her sister's look of pure appreciation when she finally did take her eyes off Rex and glanced at the kitchen, Sierra felt she'd helped. At least a little bit.

Mason appeared in the hallway entry, four kids lined up behind him. "Everyone is dressed, teeth brushed, hands washed. All the toys have been put away, sleeping bags rolled up, beds made. Let's go eat." He led the kids to the front door. Amy kissed her kids on the forehead as they passed and accepted the thank-yous from Danny and Oliver as they followed Mason and their cousins out to the car.

Rex set his coffee mug on the cluttered table, rose, and walked out the front door in his black dress socks without a word or glance for Amy.

Sierra went to her sister and wrapped her arm around her shoulders. Rex put the kids' booster seats in her SUV, kissed each of his kids, and got them settled in the back. He closed the door and stood with Mason, chatting. Their voices didn't carry, but they both looked serious.

"Do you think he's asking Mason to represent him in the divorce?"

Stunned by her sister's words, Sierra gasped and turned to face Amy. "Did he ask you for a divorce?"

"Not yet. But it's coming." Amy's forehead wrinkled with worry.

"Are you sure? Can't you guys work whatever this is out?"

Amy folded her arms across her chest. "I'm not sure it can be fixed. I've put everything I am into this family." Amy's sad gaze met hers. "I don't have anything left. I do everything I can to make them all happy."

But Amy wasn't happy. Not anymore.

She acted like she'd tapped all her resources and had nothing left.

"Oh, Amy. I feel that same way, too, sometimes. I don't want to wipe one more nose, solve one more problem, make one more school lunch, let alone give my husband the attention and affection he wants and needs. But it will pass."

Amy looked unconvinced.

Work, children, life could really take it all out of you.

But those frustrations were temporary.

Because then you'd have those moments where life filled you up. Your child did something that touched your heart. Your husband washed the dinner dishes, and damn, that was sexy as hell. A song on the radio reminded you of something from your past. Your first date. A dance at your wedding. A long drive you took, just the two of you. The kids made you something special at school and were so proud and excited to present it to you.

Their exuberant laugh made you laugh with them and wish that they laughed like that every day for the rest of their lives.

Your husband kissed you like it was the first time he realized he loved you all over again.

Amy got lost in the storm of life. She just needed to ride it out and find the calm.

Every relationship had ups and downs. They'd work this out and find their way back up to the peak again.

"You and Rex need to take a breath and talk this out."

"We talk *at* each other constantly. Nothing changes."

Sierra took Amy by the shoulders. "Then tell him how you really feel. Tell him you're unhappy. Tell him what you really want him to know. He can't read your mind." Sierra remembered all too well how she wished David would see everything roiling inside her when she needed him to, but he didn't. She wished she'd spoken up. This time, with Mason, she'd do better. She'd make their relationship a priority. "Rex knows you, but you can't expect him to know exactly what's going on in your head. You need to tell him."

Amy's hands came up, dropped, and slapped her thighs. "I don't know what I want." Amy sighed and hugged herself. "I'm tired." She glared at Rex. "I'd like to see him do everything I do for this family. Then he'd know how hard I work, how little time I have for myself."

"Great. Take a day off. Rex is home today. Let him take care of the kids. Go to the spa. I'm sure Heather can fit you in. Get a massage. Have a mani-pedi. Indulge in doing nothing but letting others pamper you."

Amy didn't answer.

"I'll take the kids to breakfast and have them back in about an hour and half."

Amy nodded, turned, and walked down the hall toward her bedroom.

Sierra walked out onto the porch and met Rex on his way back to the house.

"How bad is it?"

She didn't really know. "You two need to talk."

"I've talked until I'm blue in the face. She doesn't hear me. She wants everything her way. I get she likes things a certain way, but I'm asking for some compromise and she won't budge." He raked his fingers through his disheveled hair. "I want more time with my family. I don't think that's too much to ask."

"I'm not sure your sleeping on the couch says you want more time with *her*."

"Yeah, well, when I got home last night, she had Emma sprawled in bed with her. I could have put Emma back in her bed, but what was the point. Amy's so exhausted, the last thing she wants to do is work things out with me. In her mind, everything will be fine once the kids are older. I can tell you, things haven't been fine in years. I'm tired of it."

"I said this to her, now I'm saying it to you. Tell her how you feel and what you want. Don't expect each other to know."

"Your sister has her whole life scheduled. I'll see if I can get an appointment." With that snarky comment, he walked into the house and slammed the door.

Sierra didn't take offense. His anger wasn't directed at her. She understood that his frustration got the better of him.

"Hey, sweetheart, you okay?"

She stared up at Mason, so completely taken by his sincerity and that gorgeous face. "I'm great." She touched her hand to his chest and smiled up at him. "I'm feeling a little smug for being this happy and guilty about it because my sister and Rex are having trouble connecting."

"They'll work it out."

"So he didn't ask you for legal advice?"

Mason's head snapped back. "No. He apologized for the uncomfortable scene and thanked us for taking the kids for a little while. He said Amy needed a break, she's just too stubborn to take one."

Sierra shrugged. "That's my sister."

"That's all the Silva sisters," Mason teased. "Stubborn."

She socked him in the gut, her fist striking nothing but lean, strong muscles. "Not nice."

"But true," he teased again.

"Are you sure you're up to taking four kids to breakfast?"

"I know the perfect place. They've got the best pancakes." He slipped his hand around her waist and drew her toward the car. "Plus, I get to spend my morning with you."

"Sweet talker."

He nuzzled his nose into her hair and kissed her head. "I'll be talking you back into my bed later."

"I think I'm going to owe you a nice reward after you've shown such patience and understanding this morning."

He squeezed her to his side. "I can't wait to collect."

Sierra smiled up at him as he held the car door open for her and she slipped into her seat.

Yeah, the beginning was the best part.

And just like that, she spun dreams of a future with him. A future that looked very different from the one she'd imagined with David. Mason treated her like she was exactly what he'd been waiting for. David made her feel like he'd settled for the simple life they'd created together.

She refused to let another man settle for her again. She wouldn't stand for lies. Spoken or unspoken. She wouldn't hide the way she felt or put her needs on the back burner to make someone else happy.

Sierra made sure the kids were all engaged with one another in the back as they passed some kind of cartoon cards back and forth before she quietly asked Mason, "Have you discovered anything about that thing I asked you to look into?"

Mason kept his eyes on the road. "My investigator is working on it, but I don't have anything concrete yet."

An uneasy feeling settled in her gut.

Did she really want to know?

Should she let well enough alone and just be happy with the new life she was creating for herself and the boys?

Maybe. But she didn't think the nagging feeling in her gut would ever go away if she didn't uncover the truth.

Chapter Twenty-One

Amy walked out of the bathroom wrapped in a towel, her hair brushed back off her face, and her skin pink from the exfoliating scrub she'd used in the shower.

Rex sat on the edge of the bed, wrinkling the comforter after she spent five minutes making it perfectly smooth. "We need to talk."

"Later. Right now, I'm going out. You need to take care of the kids today when they get back. I need a day." She sucked in a breath. "I'm taking a day."

Rex nodded. "Great. Fine. Take a day. But we still need to talk about what is going on between us."

Like she didn't know she was putting off their conversation. She hoped to find some calm and perspective at the end of a much-needed massage. This wasn't going away. They needed to work things out. But she needed a minute to get her head on straight.

One horrible thought made it difficult to do that, so she blurted out her worst fear. "Are you having an affair?"

All the air went out of him. His gaze stayed on the floor for a good ten seconds before he looked up at her again. "Is that what you think of me? You think that's the kind of man I am?"

She held her hands up and let them fall to her sides. The

knot in her gut tightened. "I don't know what to think any-more. You spend more time at work than you do here."

"Amy, we've been through this. Why should I be here in this house alone when you're constantly out doing something with the kids?"

"Maybe if you were here, we'd stay here, too."

Rex shook his head. "Do you hear yourself? You put this on me. I'm not the one out there trying to impress everyone with how much I do with the kids, how great they are, or how organized I am and able to manage so much on my plate like it's easy."

"It's *not* easy!" She vibrated with frustration.

"I know. But your quest for perfection . . . It's changed you. You used to be fun." He stood and unbuttoned his wrinkled shirt. "When's the last time you had fun doing anything?"

She watched his fingers work the tiny buttons through the holes. Lust for her husband warred with her rising anger. She hadn't felt this way in a long time, but arguing with him, watching him fight for what he wanted and for them turned her on. It gave her hope, even in the midst of feeling like he was putting this all on her. "You get to be the fun parent. I'm the one who disciplines and has to do all the real work."

The shirt hung wide open, exposing his gorgeous chiseled chest. "Is that so? I guess my bringing home the paycheck and keeping a roof over our heads and food on the table isn't real work at all. It's just me being selfish and spending time away from you."

She sighed. "That's not what I mean."

They'd agreed when they decided to have children that she'd

quit her job and be a full-time mom. They'd wanted their children to come home to a parent after school and not be stuck at some day care for hours. Financially, it made sense, because day care would have eaten up most of her salary anyway.

Amy didn't mind giving up the job. She just never expected taking care of the kids and the house would take up every waking moment and not leave her any room for herself.

She expected Rex to feel pressure as the sole breadwinner, but she never expected him to feel burdened by it, or that he'd think she didn't appreciate how hard he worked for them.

Rex threw up his hands and let them drop back to his sides. "You resent me for going to work. Then you resent me for not spending enough time with the kids and not paying attention to you. Well, I resent that you use my job as an excuse to make me feel guilty for not being here. I resent that you make your life and the kids so busy you don't have time for me. I resent that you think you and the kids have to be doing something for everyone to see instead of just hanging out together as a family. I resent that when I asked you to spend more time with me, to go out on a date, you volunteered to babysit your sister's kids instead."

Exasperated, she spit out the obvious. "She needed my help."

"She wanted an evening alone with the guy she's seeing. Great. Good for her. But if you had told her we had plans, she would have hired a babysitter or picked a different day. Better yet, *you* could have called the sitter to watch all the kids and made time for me."

"Four kids for one sitter," she scoffed.

"Why not? You have it in your head that you're the only one

who can handle four kids. You're the only one who can volunteer in the classroom or organize the bake sale or 5k charity run. You're the only one who can do everything at school and home and for our kids. I'm really not sure what you need me for anymore." Rex stormed past her and slammed the bathroom door. A few seconds later, he turned on the shower.

They were home alone for the first time in months with at least an hour before the kids returned and instead of falling naked into bed, they were fighting.

Amy couldn't remember the last time they made love.

She kind of remembered it had been a pity fuck because she'd been tired but felt like she owed him because it had been so long.

And that was a terrible thought and way to show her husband she loved him.

Now, Rex couldn't be bothered to even notice her standing in front of him naked underneath only a towel. It was like he didn't even see her that way anymore.

He thought she didn't need him.

Well, she needed him to see what she was going through.

It wasn't that no one else could do all the things she did; it was that she didn't know what she'd do if she wasn't doing those things.

She thought she'd be so happy being a mother.

And she was, except she didn't want to be just a mother because . . . what would she be when her kids didn't need her anymore? They were already getting so big and independent.

She micromanaged their lives, frustrating them because they wanted to do things their way and make their own decisions.

Over the last year, she'd seen them trying to rebel against her rigid control. She didn't want her kids to resent her the way her husband did.

With her mind swirling with thoughts and feelings too overwhelming to deal with all at once, Amy dressed quickly, swept her hair into an easy ponytail, and did something she never thought she'd do—she left. She didn't let the guilt get to her that she hadn't said good-bye, leaving Rex to deal with the kids when they returned from breakfast. She didn't let herself second-guess her decision or turn around to do the responsible thing instead of the selfish thing.

It wasn't selfish to take care of herself.

She needed a day. A little time to think without the kids asking her for a million little things or feeling Rex's silence and the distance he kept building between them with his resentments.

She didn't smooth the comforter before leaving their room. She didn't even peek into the kids' bathroom to see what kind of mess four kids left after brushing their teeth. She walked right past Emma's and P.J.'s rooms without even a glimpse to see if their beds were made, toys tidied. Nope. She didn't bother to clean up the living room. She sent her sister a halfhearted silent thank-you for cleaning the kitchen, though the hasty job had left a few crumbs on the counter and the floor needed to be swept. She ignored everything, grabbed her purse and car keys, and left the house, her mind set on what she wanted to do today. And none of it involved cleaning up the mess in her life.

* * *

Heather had everything set up—last minute with little notice—thanks to a phone call from Sierra, when Amy walked in the spa steaming as much as the sauna. She tossed her purse on the counter, folded her arms on top of it, and blurted out, "My husband is an asshole."

"So glad I don't have one of those." The lie came easily, but it sent a wave of regret through Heather's system.

Amy tilted her head the way Sierra did sometimes, making Heather wonder if she had the same mannerism. "Are you really?"

It took her aback for a second. She'd longed to make a life with Hallee's father, but she'd known from the start she probably would never get what she really wanted, even if she deluded herself into thinking somehow, some way it would work out like magic. But magic wasn't real. "Um, I thought we were talking about you."

"Right. Today is about *me*. I want the works." She waved her hands in the air to encompass everything she was asking for but had no clue what that included.

Heather rolled her eyes. "I pulled off a full day of pampering for you. And you can use my employee discount, too."

"Really?" Tears glistened in Amy's eyes. "That's so nice."

"Oh god. You've really lost it if you're crying over a discount."

Amy sucked in a steadying breath. "You know me. I love a coupon."

Heather rolled her eyes. "Me, too." These days it was all she could do to get by on her salary and keep her growing little girl in shoes and clothes. Recently she'd been looking into preschools. She nearly choked on the monthly cost. She'd had a wonderful sitter these last few years at half the cost, but soon

Hallee would need to be in a class, working on her primary skills before she hit kindergarten.

Heather reminded herself the exorbitant childcare costs wouldn't last forever but would diminish over time, especially when Hallee spent most of the day in public school and only a couple hours in day care until Heather picked her up after work. But that was a few years off.

She wished she had a husband and could work part-time or even be a stay-at-home mom. She'd love to give Hallee a brother or sister. She'd considered doing it on her own. Why not? She'd been doing just fine with Hallee. Of course, Hallee's father had provided financial support until recently. Now everything was different . . .

She stopped that train of thought and focused on her emotionally drowning sister.

"Come with me. I'll get you set up for your massage. That will relax you and maybe you'll start thinking more clearly about the amazing life you have with Rex and the kids."

Amy's shoulders sagged. "It is amazing. Most of the time. But lately . . ."

Heather hooked her arm around Amy's skinny waist and drew her away from the counter and toward the massage room. "Give yourself a break. There's no contest for raising your kids with the most skills and talents. So what if they can't play an instrument or score a million soccer goals? No one cares if they don't make the swim team."

"I don't want them sitting around the house staring at a screen all day."

"They're barely home at all."

"You sound just like Rex."

She didn't want her sister to think she'd taken sides. "Do you like doing all that stuff with the kids? Do they like it?"

Amy stopped in the massage room, turned, stared at her, and shrugged.

Her sister without words didn't compute. Amy had an answer for everything.

Heather took Amy's purse and set it on the chair. "Strip. Climb on the table. Put the sheet over you. Lie there. Think of nothing. Do nothing. Allow yourself to be quiet and still. Take it in, Amy, and see if you can let things go."

"I won't let Rex take the kids from me."

"From what Sierra said, he wants to spend more time with all of you."

"He was talking to Mason."

"I'm sure that was nothing but two friends catching up."

Amy's bottom lip wobbled. "I'm not so sure."

"Mason knows both of you. If anything, he'd try to talk Rex into making up with you. Everyone knows you two are meant to be together."

"I used to think so, too."

"You're best friends. You love each other. He makes you laugh and you spoil him. You two just work like it's supposed to."

"It used to be so good and easy."

Heather hugged Amy. "You're tired, sis. Take a breath. Relax. Things will get better. You'll see."

Amy sighed. "I hope so."

Heather couldn't help herself. Ever since she'd seen Mason, she couldn't stop thinking about him. "How did Mason look?"

"Good. It's Mason. He always looks great. He doesn't have two wild kids and an upset spouse to deal with."

"Do you think he wants a wife and kids?" Hope filled her heart and made it beat faster. She'd really love a real, grown-up relationship. Mason had always seemed the strong, steady, reliable type. She needed some of that in her life.

Amy found a halfhearted smile. "He sure looked like it earlier."

Heather had heard he'd been spending time with Sierra's boys lately, teaching them to ride and watching them when Sierra worked late. He and Sierra had always had an easy kind of friendship.

Mason might have always been the guy next door, but now Heather saw him in a whole new light. She wanted more than a friend in the successful lawyer. She wanted love. Uncomplicated and real and out there for everyone to see.

Maybe then her family would see that she'd grown up and found a real partner, a legitimately good man.

Wouldn't it be amazing to live on his sprawling ranch, have more kids with him, and have the security being married to a man like him would give her?

She'd thought a lot about Mason since their chat at the mailbox. Maybe she needed to spend more time at her mom's place and "accidentally" run into him again.

Maybe she'd ask him out on a date.

Heather tried to persuade Amy out of her glib outlook. "Rex doesn't want a divorce. You guys will work this out. He's your forever."

And maybe Mason could be mine.

With that thought in mind, she left her sister to her massage, went back to work, and started thinking up ways to put herself in Mason's path. If she wanted a different kind of life, one with a sexy, rich husband, then she'd have to go after it.

It would be so different from her last relationship.

Of course, she got Hallee out of that wild time, where rational thought and consequences meant nothing compared to what she wanted and how she felt in the arms of the man of her dreams.

God, how she missed him. And hated him. And wished for him, even knowing how bad they were for each other.

She couldn't help loving him.

She'd always love him.

But she needed to move on. And this time she'd play it smart and get what she wanted for Hallee and herself.

A second chance at love.

And no one would keep her from having it.

Not this time.

Chapter Twenty-Two

Mason slid the papers his investigator gave him yesterday into his briefcase and wondered how he was supposed to break the news that they contained to Sierra. He wished she hadn't asked him to look into that damn loan, but he couldn't bring himself to refer her to someone else. Everything had been so great between them. He didn't want anything to mess it up. He didn't want to be the messenger who turned her suspicions into reality and ripped open a wound that might never heal.

David was gone, but the ripple of his mistakes continued to lap at Sierra's life, causing more grief and trouble than she deserved.

David's betrayal would tear a hole in Sierra's heart, make her rethink everything she thought about the man she married. She'd second-guess every detail of their marriage.

Was it real?

How long had David been lying to her?

What did she do now with the information?

What happened when her family found out?

He wished he could keep the revelations to himself and save her the heartache and mess this would create in her life.

Selfish?

Yeah.

It took him this long to finally get the woman of his dreams. They had a real shot at a life together. He wanted it. Bad.

He wanted to marry her. He wanted to be a father to her boys. He wanted to create a life and family with her by his side.

They could be so good together.

They would be, because he wasn't going to let David tear them apart from the grave.

"Hey. The boys are waiting to go down to the stables to ride." Sierra walked into his home office, her gaze going directly to the folders in his briefcase.

He closed the lid and turned all his attention to her and held his hand out. She took it without hesitation, smiled sweetly, then went up on tiptoe when she got close and kissed him. He poured everything he was feeling into the kiss. He wanted her to know how much he loved having her here. He wanted her to know how deeply he cared about her.

He loved her.

He loved her boys.

He suspected she loved him, too.

The night they made love for the first time, he'd felt it in the way she gave herself over to him, the way she held him, the way she made him feel.

He wrapped her in his arms and held her close, needing to feel her warmth and the way she snuggled into him whenever they were alone like this.

She looked up at him, her gorgeous brown eyes inquisitive. "Did you have a lot of work to catch up on this morning?"

"Not more than usual."

"Are you working on a particularly upsetting case?" She

studied him, probably seeing the worry about what he knew about David but hadn't told her written all over his face.

"All my cases are difficult, which is why I'm so happy to have you and the boys here to make my day better."

"I'm happy here with you, too. More than I thought possible." Her candor surprised him.

"You mean that."

She rubbed her hands up his chest. "Can't you tell? We spend practically all our free time here."

He loved that they'd made themselves at home. Last night, they'd showed up with shopping bags. The kids did their homework at the table while he and Sierra made dinner. He wished they could do that every day.

"I wish I could spend more nights with you, but . . ."

She needed to be home with the boys. They stole a couple of hours alone this week when Dede took over bedtime with the boys while he and Sierra had a "date." They'd been in each other's arms burning up the sheets. Until she had to go home to her kids.

He took a chance and asked a bold question, knowing he might be pushing things too far too fast. "You feel at home here, right?"

She narrowed her gaze and stared at him. "Yes. Of course. Why? Are the boys making too many messes?"

He shook his head. This wasn't going the direction he wanted. "They're fine. They're kids. Messes come with the territory and they're really good about cleaning up the best they can." He held her hips and tried to get her to understand. "Do you ever think about staying here?"

Her smile dimmed. "I wasn't planning on going anywhere."

Mason shook his head. "No. I mean, do you see yourself living here. In this house. With me."

Sierra's hands clamped onto his arms. "We haven't been together that long."

"We've known each other since we were teens."

"I know. But . . ."

"But what? We're great together. The boys love it here. You love it here."

Her head tilted back and she stared up at the ceiling. "I'm still dealing with the house up in Napa and figuring out what we'll do next."

"Fair enough." He put one hand at the back of her neck and tilted her head back to look at him. "But have you considered making us more permanent and making this your home?"

The wobbly smile and nervous laugh gave him hope. "Mason, I would never presume to think that's what you want."

"That's exactly what I want." He squeezed her hips. "Have you thought about us long term?"

It took her a second to work up the courage to say, "Yes." The shy smile bloomed into a pretty blush on her cheeks. "We've always been friends. At one time, I thought maybe we could be more. But that was a long time ago. Now that we are together, it's . . ."

"What?"

"So much better than I imagined. We have this easy way about us. It's like everything is as it should be. I find myself leaving here and wishing I was still with you. I can't wait to see you every day. I think about you constantly." She brushed her hands up his arms. "When I watch you with the boys . . ." Her eyes turned dreamy and so sincere. "You're wonderful with them. They really love you. The longing and missing their father I always saw in their eyes has dissipated. Don't get me wrong, they still miss him and wish he was here, but now they have you to do things with them and show them how to be good men when they grow up. You filled a void in their lives. And in mine, too."

"I love you. I love them."

She sucked in a surprised gasp and leaned back in his arms, her eyes wide. "Is this happening right now?"

This time, he let loose a nervous laugh. "Yes. I want you to know how I feel about you. I want you to know I'm all in with you, the boys, and *our* life together."

"Mom! Are you coming, or what?" Danny called from the kitchen.

Mason deflated, knowing the rest of this conversation would have to wait. He let loose his hold on Sierra and gave her some space.

She fisted her hand in his tee and held him still, then called out to the boys. "We'll be right there." She locked eyes with him and said the words he needed to hear. "I love you, too. I think I have since the beginning."

He didn't know if she meant since they got together or from back in the day when their friendship had been just as easy and essential in his life as it was now.

"As much as I want to leap into this with you, I have to think about the boys. Their whole lives have been uprooted. They're adjusting to a new place, a new school, and making new friends. I'm not sure they're ready for more."

He opened his mouth to make his case, but she touched her fingers to his lips to stop him.

"I love that you want us to be part of your life *right now*. My heart says yes to all of it."

"But you want to talk to the boys, see where they're at with you and me and moving in here."

"Yes. They didn't get a say in their father leaving, or their house burning down, or us moving back here. Everything has just happened to them. If you and I are going to build a life together, I want them to have their say."

"I'm pretty sure they'll be happy here."

She smiled. "So am I. You're here."

"So are the horses and Tom." The boys loved the animals. Maybe he'd finally get a dog. The boys would love that.

"I think they like you more."

He caressed her face and kissed her softly. "I like *you* more than anything."

Her eyes softened as she took that in.

He kissed her again, knowing she understood how he felt and what he wanted. He could even appreciate that she wanted to do right by her boys and put them first. Too many of his clients never gave a thought to what their kids wanted.

"Mom! Seriously. You're taking forrrr-everrr."

Mason chuckled. "I think they're getting restless."

"When aren't they?" She stepped back. "I forgot to tell you. I got the insurance settlement for the contents of the house in the mail this morning. I planned to use it to get me and the kids a new place, but I guess I'll have to rethink that idea." She gave him a knowing smile, brightening his day even more.

"Put it away for the boys' college."

She nodded and tipped her head. "If your investigator would hurry up and tell me what happened to the fifty grand, I could make better decisions. I've still got the loan, plus the mortgage on the house to pay. Do I rebuild, then sell, or simply sell the property and get out from under it?" She held her hands up, then let them drop, unsure what she should do.

She tapped him in the gut. "I hope you have news for me soon."

He let her walk out of the office without him saying anything about the file in his briefcase and what he knew.

He should tell her. Now.

But he didn't want to ruin the day or have her think back to the first time he told her he loved her and then crushed her with bad news.

He'd waited this long to speak up. It could wait a little while longer. He didn't relish confirming what deep down she suspected about the father of her children. Guessing was one thing: knowing was another matter entirely.

Damn David for being a son of a bitch, for lying to his wife and going behind her back the way he did. He was just as bad as some of Mason's worst clients.

Mason vowed he'd never treat Sierra like that.

It suddenly struck him that if he didn't tell her the truth now, he was lying to her. And he'd never lie to her. He'd love her and the boys and give them the life David promised them but destroyed.

David had been a coward. Mason refused to be the same.

I need to tell her the truth. Now.

"Sierra," he called, walking out of the office before he stopped short and found Amy with her two kids in his living room.

"Look who stopped by." Sierra smiled at him but her eyes held a question.

"I'm so sorry to just show up. I just need to know . . . I have to figure this out," she rambled, then pushed her two kids toward Sierra. "Go with your aunt. I need to talk to Mason alone for a minute." The frantic energy coming off Amy made him wonder what happened to make her rush here to talk to *him*.

This time, he sent a questioning look to Sierra. She shrugged and gathered her niece and nephew into her sides. "Let's go see what kind of snack Mason has in the kitchen."

Mason called after her. "I need to tell you something."

Amy cut him off from going after Sierra. "Please. This can't wait."

"Later." Sierra gave him an apologetic smile and disappeared into the kitchen.

Mason huffed out a sigh and focused on Amy. "What can I do for you?"

"Did my husband speak to you about divorcing me?"

Taken aback, he shook his head. "No." He didn't want the kids to overhear, so he held his hand out toward his office. "Let's step in here and talk about this."

Amy walked in ahead of him, paced back and forth in front of his desk, then turned to him. "He's planning to leave me. I know he is."

"Did he say so?"

"No. But since the weekend you took the kids to breakfast, we've barely spoken. He spends even more time at the office.

He walks in the house, looks around, then just . . . I don't know, goes quiet."

"It sounds like you need to talk to Rex about this."

"I need you to tell me what happens if he wants a divorce. Will I get the kids? The courts side with the mother, right?" She paced away, then spun back around. "He can't take my kids."

Mason had never seen Amy this out of sorts and agitated. "Why don't you take a seat and tell me what is really going on between you and Rex?"

She fell into the chair and folded her arms across her chest, defensive and angry. "I do everything for him. I cook. I clean. I do all the shopping. The man hasn't bought a single article of clothing for himself in years. I take care of the kids. Is that enough for him? No."

"Is that what he said?"

In his practice, he'd learned that often people perceived the other person thought something they'd never said. They put words in the other person's mouth without ever really talking to them or asking how they really felt. Communication was the one thing people forgot to do when things fell apart. So many of his clients would still be together if they'd simply stopped assuming they knew what the other thought and started talking about it. And listened.

People didn't really know how to listen anymore. They made everything about them. They wanted to be heard.

"He wants me to change the way I do things. He wants me to change my whole life. Like I'm the only one who has to change to make this work."

"What exactly does he want you to change?"

She sat up and shouted, "Everything!" She fell back into a pout and folded her arms.

Mason took a breath and tried again, making this about Amy, not Rex. "What do you want to do?"

She opened her mouth, then shut it. It took her a second to finally respond. "I don't know." She dropped her gaze to the floor, then looked back at him. "That's just it. I'm stuck. I created the life I wanted, but . . ."

"Now it's not working," he guessed.

"Yes. And no." She unfolded her arms and sat up. "I know something has to change, but it's just so much. What if it's not enough?" She went quiet, silently winding herself up again with the thoughts running through her head and making her eyes narrow. "I'm taking the kids. He can see them every other weekend. That's it."

Mason sighed. "Is that what you really want?"

"I want him to realize that my life isn't that easy. I don't sit around all day watching TV and eating ice cream. It takes skill to organize two kids, school, their activities, playdates, homework, managing the house, and getting dinner on the table. I'd like to see him do the grocery shopping. He'd never know what to buy organic and what kind of toilet paper we use. He doesn't have to think about the dozens of things I have on my plate, the decisions I have to make for our home and family. No. He just comes home, enjoys a home-cooked meal, plays with the kids and puts them to bed. You'd think that's the end of my day. You'd be wrong. I've still got to make lunches for the next day, make sure their homework is in their backpacks and not left on the table, put their instruments or sports gear together and by the door so we don't forget it, then clean up the dinner dishes and make sure the house is put to rights before I finally get to go to bed. I'm lucky if I get to watch a whole episode of . . . anything."

"Have you asked Rex to help with any of that stuff?"

"He doesn't know how to do it or doesn't do it right and I have to fix it. I might as well do it myself."

Mason raised an eyebrow. "He doesn't know how to wash the dishes?"

She rolled her eyes. "He loads the dishwasher completely wrong."

"So long as the dishes are in there, does it really matter? You'd get that time back?"

"You sound just like him. Why do I have to change the way *I* do things? Why can't he learn to do things the way I want them done?"

"Have you shown him how you want it done without it sounding like a lecture or that you're criticizing him?"

"Great. Now I'm a bitch for wanting things done right."

Mason held up his hand and shook his head. "No. That's not what I'm saying at all." He tried another way to make her understand. "I find that with most of my clients the one thing they neglect to do is express what they want when things are good. Instead, they let resentments and anger build up and then demand the other person do what they want. They fall into patterns and never take the time to break them by having a civil conversation."

"You want me to go to Rex and explain to him how to fill the dishwasher."

He held his hands out wide. "Why not? If you told him that if he took over that chore in the evening it would free you up to spend time with him, don't you think he'd be open to doing it for you? He knows you. He understands you like things done a certain way. I think if you told him it's important that he does it your way so you aren't anxious or worried about how it's done, you could relax and enjoy your time with him without feeling like you had to do everything yourself."

Her mouth scrunched with uncertainty tinged with anger, but he had her attention.

"I bet Rex could even pack the kids' lunches or do some of the other things, like get their gear together for the next day, if you showed him how you want it done."

She didn't say anything, but he could see the wheels turning.

"If what he wants is more time with you, then put some of the things from your plate on his. Consider trimming some of the things on your to-do list that maybe aren't so important to you or the kids. This is your life, Amy. If you aren't happy and fulfilled doing the things you're doing, let them go. Life is too short to be saying yes to everything only to be miserable doing them." He took the seat next to hers and put his hand on her knee. "You are an amazing mom. Your kids are fantastic. I see how much you love them. I know a little bit about how much work kids can be from having Danny and Oliver here. After just a few hours, I'm exhausted sometimes. But I love being with them, just like I know you love being with P.J. and Emma. You want them to have everything possible. Which is why I know you don't want to divorce Rex and take his kids away from him. You know your kids love and need their father. You love and need Rex. He wants things to change. So change by making him change with you. Talk to him. Teach him how to help you. Show him how to make you happy and less anxious."

"You mean less of a bitch."

"I doubt very much that's how he feels. I bet he wants to make things better for you but he doesn't know how. He's trying to tell you that, but doesn't know how to do that, either. You're wanting something from him but not telling him what that is and how you want it done.

"You guys are great together when you work together. Things have gotten complicated and busy and it maybe feels like things have taken over your life together and you're not really living it."

Tears gathered in her eyes. "Yeah. It feels like that. I try to make time for myself, for him, and it all gets away from me."

"You want to be everything to everyone. I've known a lot of women like you, who find it hard to say no. They take on everything. They are smart, capable, strong women just like you. And I have seen them find a new kind of happiness in taking back their lives."

"You mean after they divorce their husbands."

"Most of the time, yes. But what if you could find that happiness without losing the love of your life?"

They both caught sight of Sierra in the doorway. "He's right, you know. You both want to be together. That's worth fighting for, Amy."

Amy wiped the tears from her cheeks. "I didn't know you were eavesdropping."

"I came to see if it's okay if I take Emma and P.J. down to

the stables, but I'm glad I heard Mason's sound advice. I could have used some of that with David."

"You two were having problems?" Amy didn't hide her surprise.

"Every couple goes through periods where things seem off. Most of the time, you right them by reconnecting. Talking. Other times, you let things go and then it seems like this *thing* between you. I get it, Amy. Relationships are hard. Some can't be salvaged. Mom will tell you that. She's been divorced three times. But you and Rex . . . You two can renovate your relationship."

Amy laughed at that turn of phrase. "Renovate, huh?"

"It's been a lot of years. It's time to revise the chore list, redo the one-on-one time you used to make a priority, and gut the schedule that leaves you no free time for yourself. You are important, Amy. Rex wants to make you a priority, he's just tired of trying to catch you coming or going all the time."

Amy wiped away a few more tears, then turned to Mason. "I'll take everything you've said under advisement. I'll talk to Rex. If this doesn't work"—she looked from him to Sierra—"will I get the family discount if I need a lawyer?"

Mason didn't know what to say.

Sierra laughed. "Subtle, Amy."

"Well, you've been kind of quiet about how much time you and Mason have been spending together. I know about the one date, but you've been stingy with the details about how it went."

Sierra radiated happiness. "Mason and I are very happy together. We're talking about plans for the future."

Amy sat up straight. "Seriously? How come I didn't know things were moving so fast?"

"Because I have to consider the boys and what they want."

Amy deflated a bit. "Yeah. I get that."

"So I'd appreciate it if you kept things quiet until Mason and I decide it's time to let the boys in on how serious our relationship is and that we want to make things more permanent."

Amy's eyes went wide. "Wow. Just wow. Like I knew you had a thing for each other, but this is so . . . great. I'm happy for you. Both of you."

Mason stood and went to Sierra, wrapping his arm around her. "Thank you. We're working toward something really special. I want the boys to be happy to be here with us."

"Are we staying here?" Oliver asked from the doorway.

Mason turned to him, then glanced at Sierra, who took over. "We're going for a ride."

"You said that forever ago." With slumped shoulders, Oliver walked to Mason and put his arms up to him.

Mason scooped the little guy up against his chest. "What's up, bud?"

"Can we go now? Ple-ease?"

Mason chuckled and tickled Oliver's softly rounded belly. "Yes. Let's go." He turned to Amy. "Want to stay a while and let Emma and P.J. ride?"

"Sure."

Sierra put her arm around Amy's shoulders and led her out of the office. "It's going to be okay. You've got this. If anyone can reorganize their life, it's you."

Chapter Twenty-Three

Sierra looked around Amy's immaculate house and smiled. Things looked back to normal in the house even if she and Rex hadn't set their relationship back on the path to bliss. Tonight, she'd give them a chance to talk in peace without their two little ones listening.

"Emma. P.J. Aunt Sierra is here to take you over to Aunt Heather's for dinner."

Sierra loved that she got to spend more time with her sisters and the kids. She'd missed this.

"What time will Rex be home?"

"Half an hour if he isn't still avoiding me."

Sierra brushed her hand up Amy's arm and squeezed her shoulder. "You two will work this out."

Amy huffed out her frustration. "I told the kids' teachers I can only come in two days a week now. I was home today for the first time and didn't know what the hell to do with myself."

"Did you go for a walk? Read a book?"

Amy rolled her eyes. "I reorganized the hall closet."

"You'll get better at doing nothing. Maybe you'll find a hobby or something that you like."

"Easy for you to say. Everything comes easy to you. I always feel like I should be doing something."

"You need to learn to give yourself a break. Instead of or-ganizing closets, meet Rex for lunch. Spend some time recon-necting with him."

"Like you've reconnected with Mason." A knowing twinkle brightened Amy's eyes.

"It seems it was a long time coming. Like it was inevitable. I can't explain it." Sierra checked to be sure Danny and Oliver were still upstairs with their cousins and out of earshot. "He told me he loves me."

Amy did the eye roll thing again. "Of course he loves you. He loved you when you were dating David."

That stopped Sierra's heart and set off an alarm. Mason told her he had had feelings for her for a long time, but what did Amy know about it? "What are you talking about? We were friends, but there wasn't anything romantic going on."

Amy held her hands up and let them drop. "I guess it doesn't matter if you know now, but Mason told me one night before you got engaged to David when we were all out that he wanted to tell you how he felt about you."

Sierra put the pieces together. "And you told him not to say anything."

Amy shrugged. "You were with David."

Anger flashed inside her. She couldn't believe Amy could be so callous about this. "Was this before or after I confided in you that I wasn't sure a life with David was what I wanted?"

"Before. After. What does it matter now?" The question sounded like a plea for Sierra to drop it.

Maybe it didn't matter now. Not after all this time. But still, she needed to know. "When did you tell him I didn't have feelings for him?"

"It wasn't exactly like that. I just never told you he had feelings for you and made it clear that you and David were solid."

Her stomach dropped. "But you knew differently. I told you David and me, we were fine, but I felt like the relationship wasn't as strong as it should be."

"You mean you felt like David loved you but wasn't *in* love with you."

She didn't remember saying it like that, but the description fit. Even now, looking back, it seemed exactly right.

Amy shrugged. "Some people don't get the love of their life."

"You did. Rex is crazy about you."

"Mason is crazy about you."

Sierra thought so, but appreciated that her sister saw it, too. "I've never been happier."

"Everyone has second thoughts when faced with the rest of their lives with one person. Sounds like with Mason, you don't have any." Amy tried to make her focus on now and not what happened then.

Sierra wouldn't let her get away with it. "Exactly. Yet you kept quiet about the fact that I had second thoughts about David because of my feelings for Mason and that Mason had feelings for me. Why?"

"You picked David. It worked out fine. You had two kids and a good marriage. Now you've got Mason. It even looks like he's been waiting for you all this time. Lucky you." It didn't sound like Amy was really happy for her.

"What was it really, Amy? Why keep the secret?" She really wanted to understand why Amy would keep her and Mason apart for no reason.

"Everything was always so easy for you. You had two great guys who wanted to be with you. David wanted to marry you. After years of just being friends, out of the blue, Mason decides he has feelings for you. While I believed him, I thought that maybe it was possible he didn't want to lose you to his buddy, but he also didn't want to give you what David offered: marriage, family, a good life. So I kept it to myself because I didn't want to see you give up all those things I thought you wanted. You were ready for them. At the time, Mason was married to his job."

Sierra had to admit, that was true. Mostly. She still wondered, if given a chance, like they had now, would Mason have married her back then? Would they have been happy all this time?

"He could have told you about his feelings no matter what I'd said back then. It's clear *now*, the two of you are meant for each other. Is that because you're both ready for each other now because you know what you don't want?"

Maybe.

"I'm sorry if you think I purposely set out to hurt you. I didn't."

Sierra wasn't so sure about that. Amy could be selfish. "It's hard for me to hear that maybe if I'd listened to my heart I'd have been happy with Mason all this time." Maybe David would have been happier with someone else, too.

And then she heard what she'd just said and sighed. "I don't mean that."

She'd chosen David instead of going to Mason and telling him how she felt. She was responsible for her choices and her life.

Amy touched her hand, trying to make amends for not telling her Mason had feelings for her. "You and David made a good life together. You had the boys. David's death was a tragedy, but now you and Mason have a second chance at forever."

Exactly.

This time, she'd go for what she wanted and not settle for anything less than a truly happy life.

Amy traced her fingers along the gray lines in the marble countertop. She glanced at the front door for like the tenth time, her gaze turning worried as she waited for Rex to return.

This talk with Rex was long overdue. With Amy's ingrained need for everything to be perfect, she had to be worried about this going well and making sure she said and did the right thing to make this better. Despite still being a little pissed Amy kept things about Mason from her, Sierra covered her sister's hand on the counter, stopping her nervous motions before she wore a hole in the stone. "You and Rex want to work this out, which means you will. He wants you to be happy, Amy. We all do."

"Don't you think I want to be happy?"

"I think you need to figure out what makes you happy now. Things change. What we thought we wanted before kids, after kids, at the beginning, somewhere in the middle, at the end, it's not the same as when we started. Allow yourself to let go of what's not working and find something that makes you feel fulfilled again."

"That seems easier said than done."

Sierra squeezed her sister's hand. "Talk to Rex. Figure out what that looks like together."

Amy nodded, then met Sierra's gaze. "I really am sorry. I

should have told you what Mason confided in me. The truth is, I was jealous for no reason. You know I had a thing for him back in the day, but he never looked at me the way he looked at you."

"You mean the way Rex looks at you," Sierra pointed out.

Amy found a genuine smile.

Sierra knew Amy's other secret. "You would have preferred Rex and Mason both wanting you."

Amy always had to be the center of attention. She gave Sierra a mischievous grin. "I wouldn't have hated it."

Sierra let it go. She didn't want to fight with Amy or resent her for a past she couldn't change.

"How about you get Rex back and I'll keep Mason and we both just be happy for each other?"

Amy nodded, relief in her eyes. "Deal." Though her eyes clouded with worry as she looked toward the front door again.

"Kids! Let's go." Sierra picked up the tote bag by the front door that Amy had packed with sweatshirts and snacks for her kids. Just in case.

No doubt Heather had everything the kids would need for dinner and a movie tonight.

The four kids rushed down the stairs and headed for the front door just as Rex walked in. "Hey. What's all this?"

P.J. as the oldest led the way. "We're going to Aunt Heather's. Bye." He hugged his dad and ran out the door.

Emma followed up with a hug for her dad. "Bye."

Rex let Emma loose, gave Danny and Oliver a pat on the head as they passed, then focused on Amy. "You're taking the kids over to your sister's?"

Amy held her hands clasped together in front of her. "Sierra's taking them for a couple of hours so we can talk."

Rex stared at his wife for one long moment, then turned to Sierra. "No Mason tonight?"

"He's got dinner with a client."

"He told me he's head over heels for you."

"I feel the same way."

"Good for you guys. I hope it works out."

"Thank you, Rex. With everything that's happened over the last year, it's nice to have something good in my life. He makes me happy."

"You deserve it."

"Are we going or what?" Danny yelled from the porch.

"And that's my cue to get going."

Amy hugged her and held on for an extra moment before Sierra headed to the door.

Rex gave her a quick hug. "Thanks for taking the kids."

"No problem." She turned to Amy. "I'll have them back at nine."

Rex walked into the kitchen to get something out of the fridge. With his back turned to them, Sierra mouthed, *You've got this*, to Amy, gave her a big thumbs-up, and headed out the door to take four little rascals to dinner.

She hoped Mason's investigator helped her resolve her issue with her deceased husband and she could let the past go and move on.

Chapter Twenty-Four

It took ten minutes to get all the kids to agree on a movie, but Heather and Sierra got them settled in Heather's big bed.

Hallee's eyes drooped as sleep crept in, but she fought to stay awake. Heather would come back in ten minutes and move her to her crib. For now, she let her daughter hang with the big kids. She looked adorable tucked up against Oliver's side as he lay on his back, one knee bent, his other leg crossed over it, swinging.

Danny and P.J. lay down the center, their heads at the foot of the bed. Emma lay across from Hallee and Oliver, with her own little bowl of plain popcorn because she didn't like it salty or drenched in butter.

Sierra tapped Heather's shoulder. "Adult beverages in the kitchen."

Heather stared at all the kids. "Look at them. We need to do this more often."

"So long as you don't mind washing melted butter off your bedspread and sleeping in popcorn crumbs, sure. Let's do this again." Sierra chuckled, but the nostalgia and joy in her eyes said she loved the sweet scene just as much as Heather did.

"We used to crawl in Mom's bed together and watch movies."

"It's been a minute since we did that." Sierra cocked her head and narrowed her eyes. "Is that a Metallica T-shirt sticking out under your pillow?"

"Yeah. David turned me on to them. Remember?"

Sierra's eyes went soft. "He loved them. I surprised him for his thirtieth birthday with tickets. We drove to San Francisco to see them play with the symphony. I don't think I've ever seen him smile so wide or enjoy something so much." Sierra stared at the shirt for a long moment, nostalgia and sorrow in her eyes before she turned and headed down the hall, her head downcast.

Heather sympathized with her sister. David left a hole in all their hearts. Deeper in some of them.

She took in her little girl one last time, so happy to be included and trying so hard to keep her eyes open, then followed her sister to the kitchen.

Sierra handed her half a glass of wine, because kids.

Heather clinked her glass against Sierra's. "To late-night movies with the ones you love."

Sierra sipped, then turned solemn. "The boys slept in my bed for a month after David died. I'd turn on a happy cartoon to chase away their sadness. Some nights, we'd all talk like Scooby-Doo and laugh. Other nights, we sat quietly and just let the tears fall and held each other. I can't tell you how it heals my heart to see them in there with their cousins happy and laughing. They'll remember nights like these just like I remember you, me, and Amy sleeping in our blanket forts trying to scare each other with wild ghost stories."

"You used to scare the pants off Amy with Franny Fright."

Sierra busted up laughing. "One of my best stories."

"I hope you haven't told the boys that one."

Sierra shook her head. "The ones I told you and Amy were far too scary for them. Instead, I made up cute little rhymes about Franny as a mischievous witch. Maybe when they're older I'll tell them the really scary ones. I'll be sure Amy is around when I do." The devilish smile died quickly.

Heather read the heavy sorrow her sister carried. "How are you doing? Today is so hard."

Sierra took a seat at the table and stared into her wine. "I can't believe David has been gone a whole year. It seems my every other thought this past week has been about this day. I knew it was coming, and still, I find myself unprepared to deal with my thoughts and feelings. I miss him. I'm angry he's gone. I wish he was here to see how much the boys have grown. I think about what he's missing all the time. It goes by so fast."

"I know what you mean. Sometimes I look at Hallee and I feel like I can see her growing right before my eyes. She does so many new things, all faster than I can really take them in, and I think if I don't pay attention, I'll miss it myself." Her father missed it all. Heather wished she could change that, but it was impossible. It wasn't all Hallee's father's fault. Heather took the blame for her bad decisions and regretted all the way to her soul that Hallee paid the price.

But she hoped to find a good man to love them. Someone who would love being Hallee's dad. She thought about Mason. She hadn't really stopped thinking about him. But being a single, working mom left little time to pursue a guy who didn't even know she was interested in him.

"I can't believe it's been a year. I can't believe we lost the house, everything of his, and we started a whole new life here."

"Maybe, in some ways, it's better that way. A fresh start for you and the kids. From what you said over dinner, you love your new job and the kids are settling in at school. You said they seem really happy here."

"They are. Part of that comes from being around family. They love it when Mom wakes them up with tickles in the morning. Riding the horses has really given them a sense of accomplishment and confidence."

That was interesting. "So they spend a lot of time with Mason."

"Several nights a week if Mason doesn't have any late-night meetings. He loves having the boys over. His horses like the exercise. Danny is in love with this mare named Goose."

The name made Heather smile. "After the bird or *Top Gun*?"

Sierra chuckled. "I'll have to ask Mason."

"I bet Hallee would love to see the horses."

"You should bring her over tomorrow afternoon. Mason takes the boys riding after lunch on the weekends."

"Do you think he'd mind if I just showed up?"

Sierra waved that away. "Not at all. We'll all be there."

"So it's like old times. You and Mason picked up where you left off." She'd always thought it weird that her sister was better friends with Mason than most of the girls she went to school with.

"In a lot of ways, it seems that way. He's been so great with the boys. They've really come out of their shells around him. I can see how much they miss their dad and Mason is so good about being that guy in their lives who teaches them things and shows them how to be a good man. They need that. They love him."

"I wonder if he thinks about getting married and having kids."

Sierra picked up her wine glass and said over the rim, "He's hinted at it," before taking a sip.

"I wonder why he and his fiancée broke things off."

Sierra shrugged. "People break up for lots of reasons. Mason's been career oriented for a long time. He wanted the relationship to work, but in the end his feelings weren't deep enough. Relationships only work when both people put everything into it. I'm sure you know how that goes." Sierra set her glass back on the table. "Any hope for you and Hallee's dad getting back together?"

Heather gave her the truth. "At one time, I dreamed it could all work out. He'd marry me. We'd raise Hallee together and be happy that we had each other. But . . ."

Sierra's hand covered hers on the table and Heather swallowed the lump in her throat. "But what? What happened? Why doesn't he visit you and Hallee? Why isn't he in her life?"

Everyone always wanted to know *who* he was, not why he wasn't here. The why tore her apart. "Not everyone gets to keep the love of their life." She was never meant to have Hallee or her father. But she'd loved him with her whole heart and didn't regret the time they shared, only the consequences.

Sierra sat back in her seat. "I'm sorry you lost him, Heather."

They sat quietly, both of them thinking about what they'd lost, the pain and sadness a match, though they'd experienced it all in different ways.

Heather had to live with the choices she'd made, taking what she wanted when she knew it would be impossible to keep and cause so much pain despite the unbelievable joy and love she'd felt and the wonderful gift she'd gotten out of it.

She'd been selfish.

She'd loved and lost and had no one to blame but herself for how it ended. She didn't know heartbreak could hurt this much and cut so deeply.

Tears glistened in her eyes but she didn't let them fall. She didn't expect Sierra to comfort her. Not today. Not on the day she'd lost her husband, the boys' father, the man she thought she'd spend the rest of her life with and had to learn to live without.

Heather understood that kind of pain and wouldn't make this about her.

She didn't deserve that selfish indulgence.

Chapter Twenty-Five

Amy couldn't remember the last time she'd felt this nervous about talking to her husband. If she didn't get this right, it could mean the end of them, their marriage, the family their children knew.

The urgency of the situation tied her stomach in knots.

She and Rex needed to fix this. Now.

Amy needed to be brave and figure out what she really wanted.

Rex sat at the counter with a glass of water, the gold band on his left hand softly tapping against the glass. He did that all the time. The habit sometimes drove her crazy.

Every tap seemed to mark another second of silence.

So she started. "I don't like the way we've been treating each other lately."

He shifted on the stool and stared at her over his shoulder but didn't say a word.

She moved into the kitchen and stood across from him. "I try so hard to make everything perfect for this family."

"You're amazing." His sincerity touched her. "And a little crazy." She'd always loved that sexy half grin.

The smile he wanted from her came easily when he teased her like this. And if they could still find humor in their situation and life, they still had a chance. She hoped.

"You're always telling people how your wife is so great at keeping things together. How much I spoil you and the children and you love it, so I try even harder to live up to that. But then you're angry that I'm trying so hard to make you proud of me and our family."

"Amy, I am proud that I have a kind, caring, loving wife and mother of my children. I'd still be proud if you did even half the things you do for us."

And that was the crux of their problem. "You're angry that we don't spend enough time together."

"I'm unhappy that you seem to go out of your way to schedule me out of the picture. As I said before, it's like the only thing I'm good for is bringing home the paycheck."

Anger flashed, but she tamped it down and gave herself a moment to absorb how he felt. "That's not true. And I'm sorry I made you feel that way. It's not my intention to leave you out or make you feel like we don't want you with us." She sucked in a breath, ignoring the look on his face that told her clearly he didn't believe her. "I've thought about all you've said and how you feel."

"Look, Amy, I've tried to be understanding about your need to be involved in the kids' school and their lives. They're your whole world. I get that. They're mine, too. But I used to be important to you, too." Rex leaned back, his shoulders sagging. "How the hell did we get here?"

"Rex, I hate the way we are now. I want us to find our way back to the way things used to be." She waited for his gaze to meet hers. "I'm tired." She relaxed her tense shoulders and her arms sagged. "Like all the time. I always feel like I'm rushing around doing things but I never feel like I'm doing them right."

Rex's mouth drew tight. "Amy, you're great at everything. I don't know how you do so much and make it look so effortless."

"It's not. Trust me. It's stressful and time-consuming, and half the time the kids are complaining because they don't want to do a lot of it." She took another breath. "I haven't been listening. To you. To the kids. To my own feelings. So I'm going to sit the kids down with the schedule and ask them what they really want to do and what they can drop."

Rex's eyes went wide. "Seriously?"

"Yes. I don't want them to feel like I'm making them do things. I want them to love what they do. Instead of just signing them up for activities, I'm going to ask them if they even want to do it."

"I think they'd like that. P.J. isn't really into the music thing."

"He hates playing the trumpet."

"Emma seems to like art class."

Amy shrugged one shoulder. "She likes to please. I worry she does it for me, not because she really likes it. But I'm not going to assume that. I'm going to ask her if *she* wants to keep going. The last thing I want to do is turn her into me, someone who can't say no."

Rex eyed her. "Are you going to go nuts with less to do?"

Of course he knew she didn't like to be idle. "When we got married, I really wanted to be a mom. That's all I thought about."

"You're a great mom."

"But I'm also your wife."

His mouth drew back on one side into a half frown filled with sadness. "We live in the same house, but I still miss you."

She knew exactly what he meant. "It's not that we've lost the love."

Rex nodded his agreement. "We've lost the time we spend together. We don't connect like we used to."

"I want more time with you. So with the extra money we'll save on not doing the stuff the kids hate, I will pay the babysitter on date nights. For real this time."

"I'm going up on your schedule?" He eyed the bane of his existence hanging on the cabinet with a teasing light in his eyes and voice, but he was serious.

"I'm getting my priorities in the right order. Bake sales and school plays don't come before you anymore. In fact, I'm putting you back where you belong. At the top of my list."

"Listen, sweetheart, I know the kids need you."

"You need me, too. And I need you. I'm tired of feeling like I'm doing all this on my own." She held up her hand to stop him from unnecessarily defending himself. "I did this to myself and blamed you for not wanting to do everything I set up without asking you about it in the first place. You want to see the kids more, too. You want to make family time a priority."

"Yes. And I want to spend time alone with my wife."

She put her hand over his. "I want that, too. We both deserve more downtime."

"I wouldn't mind sleeping in on a Saturday. Especially if you're in bed with me." The devastatingly handsome smile she hadn't seen in too long appeared and melted her heart.

She smiled back. "That sounds really good." She hoped she could rein in that feeling inside her that she should be doing something. Being lazy and unoccupied with something to do made her antsy.

But doing her husband sounded like a good way to pass the time, too.

"About our sex life . . ."

Rex rolled his eyes. "What sex life?" Again that teasing tone didn't mask the seriousness in his voice.

"I made it another item on my list."

Rex tilted his head and another sorrowful frown took hold of his handsome face. "Pity sex is not sexy. I don't want to be something you check off."

"I know. And I'm sorry. I'd like to work on that, because I don't think we can get back to where we used to be without finding our way back to each other in every way."

"You know, if you tell me what you need, I'll try to give it to you."

She smiled at the innuendo, but Rex remained completely focused, which told her this was important to him. Her happiness mattered. Their marriage mattered.

"Okay. I'd like your help to free up my time and make the evenings more relaxing for me. I'd appreciate it if you'd do the dinner dishes and make the kids' lunches for the next day each night while I get them ready for bed."

Skepticism filled his eyes. "I've tried to help you with chores around the house. The only thing I seem to do right is take out the trash."

"I know. Which is why I'm going to show you how I want the dishwasher loaded." She waited out his eye roll. "Not because you do it wrong, but because I like it a certain way or I get anxious and feel like I have to do it myself."

Rex caught on quick with a nod. "Okay. I get it." A smile crept across his face. "Why don't you make me a diagram?"

Not a bad idea. And though he was teasing her, he knew her well enough to know that was exactly how she'd be able to let go of the chore and let him do it. "I will."

"I'll still read them stories while you relax. I love that time with them."

"I love that time, too. Let's switch off, or do it together."

"Sounds good."

"Once I've got the new schedule finished with the kids, I'd like to go over it as a family. I'd like it if we could do the things that stay on it together, your work schedule permitting."

"I'd like that."

"Okay. I'd like your Thursday nights for our dates."

"You can have any night you want."

"I'd appreciate it if you made the plans."

"My pleasure. It will be my job to wine and dine you." He held his hand out to her.

She reached out, took it, and moved around the counter, closer to him. "Thank you for understanding. That's exactly what I needed to hear you say."

"You put us all first, sweetheart. Deep down, I think you want someone to do that for you. That's my job. And I haven't done it well these last months."

"I pushed you away."

"I let you because I felt like you didn't need me."

She touched her hand to his cheek. "I always need you."

"I see that now. You pushed me away and filled up the empty space with things to do to fill your time and the hole inside you."

"I didn't mean for it to happen."

"I know. I'm glad we had this talk. I see what's been happening. I hope you do, too, and we can move forward and come back together. I'm really looking forward to having you all to myself on Thursday night."

She leaned in and kissed him softly. "We're alone right now."

He shifted on the stool, wrapped his arm around her waist, and drew her in between his strong legs and up against his wide chest. "What should we do?"

For a split second she thought about teasing and telling him she'd teach him how to load the dishwasher. Instead, she showed him what she really wanted: more of him.

She kissed him with all the intention she had for where she wanted the kiss to lead.

Rex took direction well, even if it was unspoken. He slipped his hands down her hips and grabbed her ass. His lips left hers to travel down her neck and back to her ear. "I've missed you so damn bad."

"Me, too," she said on a breathless sigh.

She missed feeling this way. Wanted. Needed. Like she mattered.

She bet Rex felt the same way and poured everything into loving him.

If they only had a couple hours until the kids came home to show each other they wanted this to work and their love was still very much alive and as deep as it used to be, she'd make the most of it.

She broke the searing kiss, stepped back, took Rex's hand, and pulled him up and out of his seat and toward the stairs. "Come with me."

"I'd follow you anywhere."

"Still?" She smiled up at him, knowing full well he meant it.

"Always."

The mischief came back into his eyes. He tugged her hand, so she walked toward him. He dipped his shoulder and hoisted her over it. She lay like a sack of potatoes down his back. She smacked his ass and laughed because he hadn't carried her like this since they were dating.

"Put me down before you throw your back out."

He smacked his hand over her ass and left it there, the heel of his hand pressed intimately to her sorely neglected lady parts. "Not a chance. I've got until nine o'clock to show you how much I've missed you. I'm pretty sure it's going to take every minute from here to then to prove it to you."

He didn't have to prove anything to her, but the second he tossed her down on their bed and swallowed her giggles with a deep, searing kiss, he made good on his promise.

* * *

In fact, Rex made good on his promise so well and thoroughly, Amy answered the knock on the front door on shaky legs, wearing nothing but her bathrobe.

Sierra stared at her, taking in Amy's tousled hair, rosy cheeks heated by the embarrassment she felt getting caught doing the naughty with her husband, the robe, and her bare feet. Sierra's knowing smile amplified her embarrassment as well as the vixen inside her who was completely satisfied and smug about it.

Sierra's gaze swept over Amy, then met her eyes. "Hello. I remember you."

Amy felt a lot more like her old self than a haggard mom. "I'm feeling pretty damn good."

Emma stared up at her. "You swore."

"Mommy gets a pass tonight." Rex walked down the stairs in an old worn pair of jeans and a white T-shirt, his hair mussed, too. "Did you have fun with Aunt Sierra and Aunt Heather?"

P.J. yawned. "We had pizza with basil on it. It wasn't bad."

Not a ringing endorsement, but he'd tried something new and didn't hate it. Amy put that in the win column.

Emma hugged her. "I missed you, Mommy."

Amy held her daughter, cherishing the warm feeling in her heart. "I missed you, too, baby. Head upstairs with your brother. Daddy and I will be up to kiss you good night."

Emma trudged up the stairs behind P.J.

"Thank-yous for Aunt Sierra, please."

They didn't stop their ascent, but obediently called out, "Thank you!"

Rex stepped up to Sierra and hugged her. "Thank you for taking the kids and giving Amy and me some time together." He let her loose.

Sierra smiled up at him. "Looks like you two put the time to good use."

Amy shoved her sister toward the door. "Thank you. We appreciate it. Now take your kids home so Rex and I can say good night to our kids and finish what we started."

Rex glanced at her, a gleam and hope in his eyes. "We're not done?"

"*I'm* not done with you."

"Lucky me." He headed for the stairs. "I'll say good night to the kids then. Bye, Sierra."

"Bye, Rex."

Amy stood in the open door as her sister stepped out onto the porch.

"I'm happy for you, sis."

Amy thought about their earlier conversation. "I'm sorry I interfered in your relationship, Sierra. I should have listened to you and told you what I knew about Mason and his feelings for you. I withheld that from you because of my own selfish reasons. It wasn't right. I was wrong. And I'm sorry."

Sierra took a few second to absorb that before she closed the distance between them. "It was wrong. You did it for spite because you didn't want me to have him even though you had Rex and had no intention of doing anything about that old crush. But . . ."

"But?"

"Mason should have come to me if he had feelings and wanted me to reconsider my decision to marry David. Instead of telling you, he should have told me. I was conflicted but I never went to him and said my piece, either. That's on me." Sierra gave her sister a hug good-bye, then stepped back. "Let's leave this in the past where it belongs. Things are different now.

We've all changed. I know how Mason feels. He knows how I feel. We're both in a place where we make sense."

"You two seem really great together."

"I feel that way, too, which is why I'm going to start talking to the boys about how I feel about Mason and where I'd like to see us in the coming months."

"Really?"

"Yeah. After everything we've been through, I keep asking myself what I'm waiting for. Why I am waiting at all when time is too precious to waste." She headed down the porch steps. "Stop wasting time, Amy. Rex is waiting for you upstairs."

Amy took her little sister's advice, closed and locked the door, and headed up to the man who made her life so much better in every way because he got her kind of crazy and loved her anyway.

Chapter Twenty-Six

Sierra stood on the porch, holding the boys' hands. Her mother stood beside them as Mason pulled into the yard, the truck cab filled with green balloons. So many that she couldn't even see him through the passenger window.

"What are all the balloons for?" Oliver looked excited for a party that wasn't going to be exactly joyous, even if they were celebrating. A different kind than they were used to, but a way that was necessary and simply part of life.

"We're going to send messages to your father in heaven with them."

Danny's head whipped toward her. "What?" Tears gathered in his eyes.

She released Oliver's hand and touched Danny's wobbly chin. "Your dad passed away a year ago. I thought we should celebrate his life and how much we loved him by sending him our love up into the sky."

A tear trickled down Danny's cheek. "I thought you forgot."

So Danny had been paying attention to the day. She should have known, though he'd been strong and gotten through yesterday without a word. She hated to think of him suffering his sadness in silence. It broke her heart and brought tears to her eyes.

At seven and five, she didn't think they'd remember the exact date. Her mistake. One she'd never make again.

"No, honey. I will never forget your dad."

"But you're with Mason now, right?"

Oh yes, kids paid attention to everything.

She and Mason tried to keep their affection in check around the boys, but she knew they'd caught them innocently touching hands, had noticed the way Mason hugged her good-bye when he really wanted to kiss her, and how he paid so much attention to her.

"I like Mason a lot." She tried to be low-key about it. "We have feelings for each other. We've been friends for a long time, even before I met your dad."

"Is he your boyfriend?" Oliver asked, biting his bottom lip, his eyes filled with uncertainty.

"I suppose you could call him that. Is that okay?"

Oliver nodded. "He's nice."

"So is he going to be our dad or something?" Danny asked, a touch of anger in his voice.

She hadn't anticipated having this conversation today. She hoped to use the next couple of weeks to ease the kids into accepting Mason into their lives permanently. They liked him. They saw him as a friend, but not as Mommy's special friend. Not as the man she loved and wanted to make a life with.

She and Mason hadn't had a chance to get on the same page about this, either.

"Mason wants to be part of our family. He really likes being with you boys. You like doing things with him, too, right?"

Danny reluctantly nodded. "The horses are fun."

Oliver raised his hands as Mason approached the steps with the bundle of balloons in one hand. He caught Oliver in his free arm when he launched himself off the steps and into Mason's chest. "Mom says you're going to be our new dad."

Sierra's cheeks burned with embarrassment. "I said Mason wants to be a part of our family."

Her mom tried to help her out of this awkward situation. "Maybe we should table this for now."

She met Mason's eyes. "Sorry. I know we haven't had time to talk about this."

Mason focused on Danny, who wore a frown, but his eyes were filled with hope. "Well, I know how I feel. You see, your mom and I really like each other. In fact, I love her. I love you." Mason made a point to look at both Danny and Oliver so they could see he meant it. "I don't want to take your dad's place. David will always be your dad. I know he's watching over you both each and every day. I hope he thinks I'm doing a good job teaching you to ride and helping you with your schoolwork and just being here to help your mom take care of you. I know he's with us when we catch a game on TV and hang out with each other. I hope he's happy that I'm with you guys and that I'm here for you no matter what you need me to do and be in your life because he can't be here with you like I know he wants to be. He was my friend. I miss him, too. I wish he was here for you and your mom. I don't want to take his place. I want to make my own place in your lives."

Danny scrunched his lips, then spoke softly. "Sean at school has two dads. They're married to each other, but still . . . He's got two. I don't see why we can't have two."

Oliver hugged Mason's neck. "I like you."

Mason chuckled and squeezed Oliver to his chest. "I like you, too, bud." Mason handed the balloons to her, then took Danny in his arms and looked him in the eyes. "I'm not the replacement. I'm extra."

Danny hugged Mason and his brother at the same time, then shyly backed away.

Her mom dabbed at her eyes with the sleeve of her blouse. "Wow. Um, that was very well said, Mason."

"Thank you, Dede." For the first time, Mason kissed Sierra right in front of the boys. "Hi."

She smiled up at him and Oliver, who stared down at her with a big smile on his face. "Hi."

Her mom waved them over to the porch table where she'd set out slips of paper and colored pencils. "Let's write our messages for your dad."

Danny frowned. "Are we always going to do this for Dad's death?"

It seemed ominous, but Sierra hadn't wanted the first year to pass without them doing something. "Only this year. From now on, we'll celebrate his birthday."

"That sounds better." Danny picked up the green pencil. "His favorite color."

Mason put his hand on Danny's shoulder. "That's why your mom asked me to pick up green balloons. Your dad wore green ties with his suits all the time."

Danny smiled up at Mason. "We gave him a new green tie every birthday. He liked them." Danny frowned again. "They all burned in the fire."

"He drank green beer once and his tongue was all green." Oliver scrunched up his face. "It was yucky."

"The beer or his green tongue?" Mason teased.

"I can't drink beer." Oliver stated that with all seriousness.

Mason tickled his belly. "Silly me. What was I thinking?" He set Oliver back on his feet and handed him the light green pencil. "What do you want to write to your dad?"

"I miss him."

"That's perfect, bud. Let's get on that. If you can't think of what else to say, you can draw him a picture." Mason held his arm out so Sierra could slip in beside him. He held her to his side as they watched the boys write their messages.

Oliver stuck his tongue out a little while he carefully printed his block letters and tried to spell the words correctly.

Danny kept his hand over what he wrote, wanting his message to be private.

She glanced up at Mason and mouthed, *Thank you*. He'd made today easier for the boys. He'd given them permission to never forget their dad even if they were lucky enough to get an *extra* one like Mason.

Mason took a slip of paper and wrote a message, then read it aloud. "David, your boys are amazing. Thank you for bringing them into my life."

Danny and Oliver stared at him for a long moment before they both smiled.

Oliver held up his note. "I drew him a picture of Horse." Oliver couldn't remember all the horses' names, so he just called them all Horse.

"Love it." Mason turned to Danny. "Did you finish yours?"

Danny held up six or seven rolled pieces of paper. "Do you think he'll know what they say?"

"I think he hears everything in your heart."

Danny turned to Sierra. "What did you write?"

She held up the first note. "I love you and miss you every day." She showed him the second one. "Thank you for leaving me the boys so I'll never be lonely without you because I see you in them every day." She wanted Danny and Oliver to know that they reminded her of David. That she'd never forget him because she had them. She wanted them to know she thought about David every day.

She showed him the last one. "I got a great job. We have a new home. We're happy."

Danny hugged her. "He'll be happy to know that."

"That's all he wants for us. I know this past year has been hard. We miss him. We wish he was here. But he'd rather see us smiling than sad for him."

"I'm glad we moved to Grandma's," Oliver announced.

Dede rolled up the slip of paper she'd finished writing. "I just told your father how happy I am to have you all here with me." She tied the note to one of the balloon strings. "How about we send these to your dad?"

Mason helped tie each of Danny's and Oliver's notes to the balloons. Sierra tied her own.

They gave all the balloons to the boys in the front yard.

"One at a time, or all at once. Doesn't matter," she coaxed the kids.

Oliver meticulously pulled one at a time free from his bunch and let it loose, marveling as each rose up into the sky.

Danny divided the bundles between his hands and let them go together, his hands raised, eyes to the sky as they floated away.

Sierra stood with Mason, his arm around her back. Tears gathered in her eyes. Grief over David's sudden passing, missing what they had, wondering if they'd have fixed things or gone their separate ways, grateful for the time they had, and still suspicious about what he'd kept from her—her thoughts and emotions were all over the place.

Mason kissed her on top of the head. "You okay?"

"It just hits me sometimes. He's gone. He's not coming back. He's going to miss so many things in the boys' lives. And I still have questions about why he needed that loan and if he was hiding something even bigger from me."

"About that . . ."

She turned to him, but Oliver ran over and slammed his little body into her leg and hip.

His arm gripped her leg and he looked up at her. "Mommy, look at them. They're all going straight up to Daddy."

She stared up at the sky with Oliver and brushed her hand over his head, so happy she'd done this with the boys. "I have something else for you and Danny."

"Really? Can I have it?"

"Danny. Come up to the porch." She waved him in from the yard.

Her mom stood on the porch with the two wrapped packages for the boys.

Sierra leaned down and kissed Oliver's nose. "Grandma has a special present I made for you and Danny."

Oliver took off up the steps to take his package from her mom.

Mason touched her arm. "Sierra, about the information you wanted . . ."

"Did your investigator get back to you?"

"Yes. I didn't want to do this today, but I don't want to keep it from you any longer."

She studied his serious face. "What do you mean 'longer'?"

"I've actually had it for a little while. I just didn't know how to break the news to you."

She didn't like the sound of that. "It can't be worse than what I'm imagining. Just tell me."

He glanced at the boys and her mom waiting on the porch. "Not here. We'll go over it after the boys' ride this afternoon. Maybe Dede can watch them while we talk."

Her stomach tied into a knot. "It's that bad?"

"If I've learned anything in my law practice, it's that secrets are always bad. I wish I didn't have to tell you what I know, but . . . you deserve the truth. I just hope you're prepared to hear it."

"Mom! Can we open these?" Danny called out.

Sierra touched Mason's arm. "We'll talk about this later." She headed for the porch, then remembered what she was supposed to tell him about their ride. "Heather and Hallee are joining us at the ranch later."

Mason stopped in his tracks behind her. "Why?"

She caught herself and turned back to him. "She wants to introduce Hallee to a horse."

"I wish you'd told me about this sooner."

His reluctant tone made her raise an eyebrow. "Have you run out of horses?"

He shook his head. "No. It's just . . . we really need to discuss the information I received from my investigator. But you didn't know, so we'll deal with it later." The postponement frustrated him. He seemed to want to get it over with, but she wasn't so sure she wanted to know given his dire tone.

He touched her back to get her moving up the stairs to where the boys waited at the table, their presents in front of them, hands ready to tear into the packages. "Let's do this and save the rest for later."

Sierra let it go, tried to shake off her worry, and focused on the boys. "Okay, you two, I don't want you to think you're going to get presents every year but after the fire and we lost everything of your dad's I made some calls to our friends in Napa and downloaded what I had and made you these." She nodded for them to go ahead and open the gifts.

They tore open the wrapping paper and tossed it away. Danny and Oliver both stared at their photo books, a picture of each of them with their dad on the cover.

"Our friends sent all the pictures they had of you guys with your dad. Aunt Amy and Heather and Grandma gave me some from family gatherings. I used all the ones I had stored on my phone and put them all together in these books."

Danny flipped through pages, tears rolling down his cheeks.

Oliver simply stared at the cover, his face solemn.

Her mom wrapped her arm around Sierra's middle. "They're gorgeous, Sierra. When you told me what you were doing, I never expected it to turn out like this. It's like a photography book."

"You custom-make them online." She addressed the boys then. "I wanted you to remember all the good times we had with Dad. Now any time you miss him, you can look at these pictures and see his face and remember how much he loved you."

Choked up, she swallowed back her own tears.

The books had taken quite a bit of time to design, but they turned out so well. She customized each one to focus on either Danny or Oliver, though of course many of the pictures showed both of them. But there were lots that were just one of them with their dad and her.

She vowed to make new ones for them every few years, so they had their memories to look at instead of all the pictures simply sitting in the cloud doing nothing for anyone in cyberspace.

Sierra hoped this helped heal their hearts. She couldn't give them back everything lost in the fire, but this had been a way to bring the memories back to life for them.

They were so young. She didn't want those memories to fade away without them having something to help bring them back to life in their minds and hearts.

Danny finally looked up at her, so much sorrow in his eyes. "Thanks, Mom." He clutched the book to his chest. "Thanks."

She hugged him close. "You're welcome, sweetheart." Tears tracked down her cheeks.

Oliver pressed his face into her side. She put one arm around him, too, and held both her boys close.

This had been a hard day. Necessary, but difficult. They

needed this chance to remember and keep the healing going and the memories of David alive.

Her phone rang in her back pocket. She let the boys go and pulled out her cell and read the caller ID. "It's work."

Mason moved into her place next to the boys. "Your mom told me about the books. I'd love to see them." Mason and her mom kept the boys occupied while she took the call.

"Hi, Mike. How's the Gilmore place coming along?"

"One of the subs hit the gas line. We're shut down. Emergency services is on the way. We've cleared the area, but we're going to need the owner down here."

"I'll call him and meet him there as soon as I can." She raked her fingers through her hair and silently swore.

Mason touched her arm. "What is it?"

"A work emergency. I need to meet the owner at a property."

"Dede is meeting her friends for lunch. I'll take the boys. Join us at the ranch when you're done."

"Are you sure?"

He squeezed her hand. "It's part of being a family, right? We look out for each other."

The sweet sentiment touched her heart. "You make everything easy."

"It's not supposed to be hard. I don't mind taking the boys. Soon, we'll be together all the time. I hope."

She wondered why he added the last. "You know that's what I want, right?"

"Yes." His excitement shone through. "And I hope nothing changes." That drained the enthusiasm right out of him.

"What would change that?"

"I'm nervous about telling you what I know."

Anxiety tightened her gut. "Nothing David did would make me change the way I feel about you." Her phone buzzed with a text from Mike. She quickly read it. "I need to deal with this. I'll be back as soon as I can, then we'll talk about David." She went up on tiptoe and kissed him quick, gave the boys hugs good-bye, wondering about Mason and the way he spoke about what he'd discovered about David, and questioning if she'd come home to an even bigger problem than the one facing her now.

Chapter Twenty-Seven

Mason heard a car pull up just outside the stables. He hoped Sierra had finished her work emergency early. He didn't like the way they left things.

He'd wanted to be wrong about David, who loved his family. He wanted to believe David would never do anything to hurt them.

But David had hurt them. He'd done something he couldn't take back.

And he wasn't here to answer for it.

Which made it even worse, because Sierra deserved an explanation and an apology at the very least.

A car door slammed.

Mason plucked Danny off the stall door and set him on the ground. "I think your mom is here."

Oliver gave Jezebel's big head a hug. "Bye, Horse."

Mason pulled Oliver off the gate, then swung him around in a circle and set him on his feet. Oliver giggled and smiled so big Mason smiled with him.

He really loved having the boys here. "Let's see if your mom wants something to eat before we ride. She probably missed lunch."

Danny tagged Oliver in the back. "You're it!" He ran for the open stable doors just as a second car door closed.

Oliver caught up to Danny. Only because he stopped to hug Hallee.

Mason joined them and greeted Heather. "Hey. I forgot you were coming."

Heather touched her hand to her chest, partially covering the cleavage revealed by the one too many buttons undone on her black-and-white plaid flannel. In tight black jeans and boots, she looked ready to ride. "You certainly know how to make a girl feel welcome."

She teased, but he just wanted her out of here before Sierra came home, so they could pick up their conversation where they left off.

But thinking the word *home* made him pause. He wanted Sierra to feel like this was home. He wanted her and the boys to live here. The boys accepted him in their mother's life. But he didn't want to get ahead of himself. He'd waited this long for her. He could wait for her to make the decision about where to live when she felt they were ready for it.

He just wanted to give her everything and make her happy.

He wanted to start each day with her.

And maybe one day, they'd have another child together and give Danny and Oliver a brother or sister. He didn't care which. He just wanted to see his eyes and Sierra's smile on his little one.

He wanted that future so bad.

But it all hung on the secret he knew and had to break to Sierra.

Heather stuffed her hands in her back pockets, widening the gap in her shirt as her chest thrust forward. "Hallee loves animals. I thought she'd love to see a horse up close and she can play with Danny and Oliver. It's so nice to have Sierra home. I love seeing all the kids playing together."

Mason bit back what he really wanted to say.

Oliver tugged on the hem of his shirt. "I have to pee." He buried his face in Mason's side.

Mason brushed his hand over Oliver's dark head. "Okay, bub. Why don't you and Danny go up to the house and take Hallee with you. There are Popsicles in the freezer. You can each have one." To Danny he added, "Hold Hallee's hand. Help her up the steps. Do not let her out of your sight."

"Got it." Danny took Hallee's hand and walked with her while Oliver ran for the house to use the bathroom.

Mason watched them go, startled when Heather put her hand on his bicep and squeezed.

"It's so nice of you to let us come over and go for a ride. I've been thinking about you ever since we saw each other at the mailbox. I've been meaning to come by, but it's hard to find a spare minute being a single mom and all."

He stepped away, putting a comfortable distance between them. "It must be really hard to do it on your own with Hallee's father out of the picture."

"It is. I hardly have any time to myself." She bit her bottom lip and edged closer. "That's why I wanted to see you. I thought maybe you and I could go out and have some fun."

Stunned, he didn't know what to say or do.

She had to know he and Sierra were seeing each other. Right?

Then again, they'd kept things quiet so the boys could get used to them seeing each other.

Heather closed the distance and put both hands on his chest and went up on tiptoe, her body brushing his, her face inches from his. "It's been a long time and I really want to get to know you better."

His brain finally caught up to what she meant. He took her by the shoulders and gently nudged her away while he let her go and took two steps back.

"This isn't going to happen. Sierra and I, we've been seeing each other."

Heather took a step back, her eyes filled with skepticism. "Really? I mean, you were like brother and sister when we were younger."

"It was never like that and you know it."

"She said she's been coming over to see you, but I thought that was just so the boys could learn to horseback ride."

"It's a lot more than that. Sierra and I have a good thing."

Doubt filled her eyes. "Sierra is just so serious all the time. Doesn't that get boring?" She took a step closer again. "We could be so much more."

Angry she didn't back off when he told her he and Sierra were together, he blurted out, "Is that what you told David?"

The sexy smile died on her lips. She simply stared at him.

He let her know what he'd suspected all this time. "Danny and Hallee have the same eyes." Hers went wide. "Their father's eyes."

They both jumped at the gasp that sounded behind them.

Before Mason even turned toward the stable, he knew who'd be standing there. He never heard a car because she'd walked across the pasture instead. He instantly knew he'd made a huge mistake in not talking to Sierra about his suspicions before confronting Heather himself. And the look of betrayal he saw in Sierra's eyes now said she blamed him for keeping this from her.

Sierra dismissed him without a word and focused on Heather. "Hallee is David's daughter."

Heather's eyes filled with tears. "I'm so sorry."

Sierra looked so brittle the dust on the wind might shatter her to pieces, but it was Heather's words that set her off.

"You're sorry? Like you were sorry when you stole Miss Maisey when you were four and wanted my baby doll for yourself so you took her? Sorry like when you borrowed my makeup and clothes and never gave them back? That kind of sorry?"

Distress lined Heather's forehead. "I never meant for it to happen the way it did."

"But you did mean to sleep with *my* husband. Were you hoping he'd leave me for you?"

"At first, it was just something that happened."

"At first? So it wasn't a onetime thing? You were carrying on an affair behind my back."

Heather caught herself with a gasp. "It wasn't like that."

Oh, yes it was. And Mason felt every ounce of pain he saw etched on Sierra's face along with her anger.

"You weren't sneaking around behind my back fucking my husband every chance you got? Without protection? For God's sake, Heather, you got pregnant with his child."

"That was an accident."

"Right. You tripped and fell on his dick in the dark and didn't realize he wasn't wearing a condom."

Heather's mouth drew into a tight line. "You're angry. Maybe we should talk about this once you've calmed down."

"This is as calm as I will ever be when it comes to you fucking my husband. And this is the last time we will *ever* speak. Period."

Heather's eyes pleaded. "You don't mean that. Hallee is Danny and Oliver's sister. They deserve to know that and grow up knowing each other."

"Is that right? So you want to tell those two little boys that their father lied to their mother and cheated on her by sleeping with her own sister. Their *aunt.* How do you think that will make them feel about their father? You think they'll think he was a good man?"

"We can explain it in a way that doesn't make them upset with David."

Sierra laughed without any mirth in a nearly hysterical sound. "You stupid bitch. You didn't think about anything but yourself. You just took what you wanted, consequences be damned. You didn't think about how this would hurt me, let alone the children. Tearing up a family didn't even give you pause."

"I didn't want anyone to get hurt. David and I had this amazing connection. He said I made him feel alive."

"Stop talking," Mason warned Heather, knowing every excuse out of her mouth was a dagger through the back and straight into Sierra's heart.

Sierra stood rigid. "No. Go ahead. Tell me how much David wanted you."

"He loved me," Heather whispered.

"Did he tell you that while he was fucking you, then coming home to me?"

Heather looked unsure. "I knew he did. I felt it." Sierra laughed again and it set Heather off. "You don't know what we had."

"No. I don't. Because I was taking care of my kids while you were trying to steal their father and break up their home." Sierra paused, then shook her head and laughed under her breath. "When I arrived, you were surprised I wanted to move back home. You thought David was the one who wanted to move back here and I didn't want to leave Napa. You thought that because that's what *he* told you." She hit Heather with another hard truth. "What did you think he'd do, move us all down here and you two would carry on your affair right under my nose? He didn't want to get caught. He didn't want to lose his family. He didn't want to be with you, Heather. If he did, he'd have left me. All he did was give you excuses."

Hurt, Heather retaliated. "Yeah, well, while you thought he was on a business trip, he was actually with me."

"I got that. Stupid me for believing my husband, thinking that he cared about me and would never hurt me. I knew there was something wrong between us and I didn't do anything about it. I ignored it, because I had faith we'd make it right. And we had a good life despite the growing distance between us."

Heather just stared at Sierra.

"What? Did you think we were fighting like cats and dogs?"

Sierra sighed. "You don't know anything about us, Heather. You weren't there when we sat down to dinner and talked about the boys and our day. You weren't there when he played with the boys and put them to bed and spent the weekends hanging out with all of us. You broke a family that could have been saved given some time for David and me to find our way back to each other, because we probably would have. At the core of our relationship we were always friends."

"You put all the blame on me, but he betrayed you, too."

"He did. But you're my sister. I thought that meant something. I would have done anything for you." Sierra's eyes filled with disgust before she closed them for a second. "Just looking at you makes me sick."

"I hoped you'd never find out."

"I bet. How long did you plan to carry on the affair? Until David and I celebrated our ten-year anniversary? Twenty years? Fifty?" Sierra frowned. "No. You were hoping to celebrate all those anniversaries with him. You hoped he'd leave me and the boys and pick you."

"Yes! I wanted him to pick me, but I also knew it would never work out even after we had Hallee."

"Was he there for the delivery? Did he help you pick out her name? Did he paint the nursery especially for her?"

Heather's gaze fell to the dirt.

"No. He didn't. Because he was at home with his family. And now he's not here at all." Sierra gasped and put her hand over her mouth. Her eyes were so wide and filled with an accusation she didn't look like she wanted to speak.

Mason prayed it wasn't what he was now thinking.

Sierra dropped her hands and sucked in a breath and took a menacing step toward Heather. "He died on Highway 1 when it was socked in with fog. He was coming to see you."

The accusation hung in the air, thick and menacing and fraught with Sierra's rage.

Heather wrapped her arms around her middle. Tears cascaded down her cheeks in rivulets. "Hallee got sick. Her temperature was so high. I had to take her to emergency. She had pneumonia. I was so scared I'd lose her, I called and begged him to come. She needed him."

Sierra and Heather stared at each other for a long moment, then Sierra broke the tense silence. "Should we tell the boys you're the reason their father is dead, too?"

"It's not my fault."

"No? Then whose fault is it? David should have been home in bed with me instead of crushed to death on the highway."

Mason turned at the sound of the house side door closing.

Sierra stared at her boys, each of them holding one of Hallee's hands, helping her down the porch steps. That's when the tears fell.

Heather and David deserved her anger.

The kids sparked her grief and sadness.

Sierra brushed away the tears and stared at her sister. "You took my husband. You destroyed my memories of him." She gave Mason a sharp look, then turned back to Heather. "And now I know why David needed that loan. For you. You took money that should have gone to my children. That cute little house you love so much, *I'm* the one paying for it. You just took and took and took and didn't care one bit. Well, let me tell you, I care. I will never forgive you for this."

"Sierra, please," Heather choked out.

"No. You don't get to ask me for anything ever again. Stay away from me and my children. I never want to see you again." Sierra cut off her words before the kids got too close to hear. She closed the distance to the boys and held her hands out to them. "Come with me."

The boys let Hallee loose and took their mother's hands. She turned and headed for the pasture. "We're going home." She directed that right at Mason.

Mason's heart broke and his throat constricted. His chest felt so tight he couldn't breathe. He'd blown this by confronting Heather without telling Sierra what he knew first.

"Sierra, this isn't fair," Heather called out to her as she held Hallee close to her chest and cried.

Sierra didn't even turn around when she shouted, "You should have thought about that when you took what didn't belong to you and killed it."

Heather burst into tears and heaving sobs.

Torn between going after Sierra and trying to make her listen to him and Heather crying all over a bewildered Hallee, Mason chose to save the little girl from her mother and plucked her right out of Heather's arms.

"Take a minute to get yourself together. I'll take Hallee to see the horses." If he couldn't fix things with Sierra right now, at least he could make a little girl happy.

But damn his heart felt like it had been hit with a sledgehammer. He couldn't bear to see Sierra so upset. He'd explain his part. She'd understand.

He'd show her that no matter what, through good times and bad, he'd be right beside her, on her side, ready to love her through it.

Chapter Twenty-Eight

Sierra tried her best to hide her rage. The boys felt the vibe coming off her and remained watchful as they walked home. They didn't understand why she'd made them suddenly leave, without letting them go for their ride, without even saying good-bye to Mason or Aunt Heather.

But *she'd* said her good-byes. And that was enough for now.

Mason understood exactly what she'd meant when she said they were going home. She meant forever.

Sierra's mind raced.

He must have known, or suspected, something about Heather, David, and Hallee.

That's why he'd put off telling her whatever his investigator discovered.

He'd kept a huge secret from her.

After her husband's lies and betrayal, she wouldn't stand for another man in her life to keep things from her.

If she couldn't trust Mason, they had nothing.

As for Heather, her betrayal cut so deep she didn't think the wound would ever heal. Right now, every beat of her heart pumped out anger and hurt, filling her up to the point she felt like an explosion waiting to happen.

Tears stung her eyes when she thought of David and the last

year of their marriage. And she couldn't help but wonder why, if he wanted to be with Heather, did he stay up in Napa with her?

And if he hadn't wanted to be with Heather, why didn't he come clean about the affair and beg her forgiveness?

Lying, cheating bastard.

Her conclusion: he hadn't wanted to face what he'd done, wanted a family with her and the boys and to keep Heather and Hallee on the side. Unable to face the consequences of his actions, he'd simply bided his time, hoping to not have to ever explain himself.

But a secret like that always comes out.

Sierra was surprised Heather kept her mouth shut this long, never revealing to anyone who Hallee's father really was.

And while she wanted to blame her sister for everything—Heather was impulsive, reckless, and always felt like she was entitled to whatever her sisters had—David was equally to blame.

He'd carried on with Heather behind Sierra's back for God knows how long. He'd fathered a child with her sister. He never said a damn thing to her about it. He never voiced even a hint that he wanted out of their marriage.

Of course she knew he'd been hiding something. But he still maintained their relationship. He was the perfect father. They still talked about their days, spent time together, kissed each other hello and good-bye, and yes, they'd had sex. Not as much as they used to, but they'd have a great night and then she'd wake up hopeful everything would go back to the way they were before, but then David would be distant again.

His guilt built a wall between them.

She hadn't known what it was at the time. She'd blamed

herself, thinking that it must be something she did—or didn't do—that built the barrier between them.

But it had been David's actions that had ruined them as a couple.

He had doomed them, and he'd known it.

Instead of doing the right thing and confessing and letting her go, he'd hid his dirty deed.

All those months she'd wanted to confront him. Yes, she'd kept silent, hoping things would get better and she wouldn't have to upset the boys by fracturing their family.

But David had torn their family apart the second he slept with Heather.

The boys didn't know the full truth, but they'd felt something off in the house. Just like they felt her dark mood now.

And just like David had done, she was going to have to hide the truth from them, for now anyway.

When she finally got to the house, she found her mom sitting on the porch reading the mail when they walked up the steps. She took one look at Sierra and the smile she'd had for them died on her lips. "What's wrong?"

Sierra walked the boys to the front door, opened it, and stared down at them. "Please go upstairs, wash your hands, then you can have an hour of screen time. I need to speak to Grandma privately."

Danny stared up at her, eyes wide and filled with worry. "Is everything okay? Will we go see Mason later?"

She touched Danny's soft cheek. "I'm sorry, honey, but no. Something happened between us and I need to figure out what happens next."

"I thought you liked him." The concern in Danny's eyes turned to dismay. "Tell him to apologize."

"I wish it were that simple, sweetheart."

"Don't you want it to be okay?"

She put her hand on his shoulder and leaned over to look him in the eye. "I need some time to figure things out." Her anger made it hard to think reasonably and rationally.

Danny's eyes narrowed with frustration that she didn't give him an answer that made sense. If she could make sense of her feelings right now, it would be a lot easier.

She'd asked Mason to find the truth about the money and what David had been doing with it. But now she thought he'd already known. Or suspected it. Either way, he must have known to look in Heather's direction.

Danny took Oliver's hand and tugged him into the house.

She closed the door and turned on her mother. "Did you know?"

Her mother's head drew back at her angry tone. "I don't know what's got you so upset, but I do not appreciate being spoken to that way."

Sierra took a few steps toward her mom and pinned her in a hard glare. "Did you know that Heather was having an affair with my husband and Hallee is David's child?"

All the color drained from her mom's face and her eyes went wide. "What? No." She shook her head back and forth saying, "No. No, no, no. She wouldn't do that."

"She *did* do that. Again and again and again. She thought David was going to leave me for her."

"Do you believe that?"

"That he was telling her the truth? No. I think he got caught up with her *and* wanted to somehow keep me and the boys. He strung her along, probably hoping he'd come up with some way to fix this."

Dede stood and embraced her. "Sierra, I'm so sorry."

Sierra didn't want to hurt her mother's feelings, but she didn't want to be touched or held right now. And because she didn't want to take things out on her mom, she gently pushed her away and took two steps back, her body tense, her chest aching with the expanding ball of emotions she tried to contain, but wanted to get rid of all at the same time.

"I think Mason knew about it."

"What?"

"I don't know how, or when he figured it out, but I think he suspected they had an affair and that Hallee belonged to David. He never said a word to me. Nothing." She pressed her hand to her forehead. "I think that's why he was reluctant to track down the money."

Dede gasped. "The house. I thought Heather saved up for it."

Sierra sneered. "Their private little getaway. David would sneak away from us, pretending he had a business trip, and slip right into her bed."

Even more anguish filled her mother's eyes. "Oh, Sierra. I'm sorry. I wish I knew what to say."

"There's nothing to say. David's not even here to defend himself. Not that he could after what he's done. No, he left me to clean up the mess." She paced away, then back. "But you know what, I'm not cleaning up anything. As far as I'm concerned,

Heather is just as dead to me as David is. They can both go to hell for all I care."

Her mom touched her arm. "You don't mean that."

She snatched her arm back. "Don't I? This isn't the same as her stealing the keys to my car and taking it out on a joyride. She slept with my husband and had his child and hid it all this time, soaking up all the sympathy we showered on her because Hallee's father wasn't in the picture and poor Heather had to do it all alone." It made her seethe inside to think of all the times she'd tried to soothe and sympathize with Heather. "She played on all of our heartstrings. We went out of our way to help and support her this past year and half. I've been such a fool." She raked her fingers through her hair. "And to top it off, she's the one who begged David to come see her the night he died."

"What? No. What are you saying?"

"Hallee got sick. Heather panicked. She called and begged David to come. So he made a mad dash to get to her and crashed his car on the highway in the fog."

Her mother pressed her fingers to her mouth and her eyes filled with sympathy and understanding. "He wanted to get to his sick child. Surely you must understand that."

She fisted her hands. "I'm not some coldhearted bitch. But he might have thought about the children he had at home."

Sierra went on. "Of course he wanted to get to Hallee and make sure she was okay. But it should have never happened because Hallee was never supposed to happen in the first place."

"It's not Hallee's fault."

She knew that but it didn't ease her anger. "Of course not.

It's her parents' fault. And now Hallee, Danny, Oliver, and I are paying for their selfish, heartless deeds."

"Isn't there any way this can be fixed?"

She glared at her mom. "Why? How?" She held her arms out and let them drop. "Why would I want anything to do with Heather? So she can stab me in the back again? She was hitting on Mason when I showed up. Hell, she's probably sleeping with him right now." The thought turned her stomach and broke her heart even though she'd heard Mason loud and clear turn Heather down flat.

"I can't imagine Mason would do something like that to you." Dede let her head fall back and stared up at the porch ceiling before looking at Sierra again. "Your sister was always audacious."

"She's a home-wrecking whore."

Anger etched lines on her mom's forehead. "Sierra, that's enough. I know you're angry and hurt—"

"I'm furious. And I deserve to be."

"Of course you do, but you need to take a breath and give yourself time to sort this out."

"Why? So I can go back to paying for a loan that put a roof over *her* head. Should I give her the okay to go after Mason? Why not? She gets everything she wants and doesn't care who she steamrolls over to get it."

"You're right. She's selfish. She expects others to make her life easy. And she gets what she wants. Maybe that's my fault for spoiling the baby in the family."

"We all did. Amy and I took care of Heather. We watched over her. We gave in to her just as much as you did to keep her happy. I helped create the monster, I shouldn't be surprised she stabbed me in the back."

"If you feel that way, then teach her to take responsibility for what she's done."

"How? What can she possibly do to make this right in any kind of way that counts? Can she bring David back so Danny and Oliver have a father again? Can she not sleep with my husband? Can she in any way, shape, or form erase what she did? Can she make me stop second-guessing every interaction I had with David from the time she sank her claws into him? Can she make me feel less like a failure or that I drove him into her arms?"

"This is not your fault. All marriages have issues. That doesn't mean someone cheats."

"No. It opens the door for someone to want something and someone else."

"Sierra, honey, I've divorced three men, including your father, and each time I felt like I'd done something wrong. I took on all the blame. It had to be me. The marriages fell apart because there was something wrong with *me*."

Sierra shook her head.

"I finally realized there's nothing wrong with me. Those relationships ended because we didn't fight to keep them together. David gave up on your marriage. Instead of fixing it, he let the issues between you fester. He made a mistake. Of course you sensed something was wrong, so you were hesitant to keep your whole heart in the relationship. You didn't want to get hurt."

"It was already too late. I just didn't know it." She sucked in a steadying breath. "I didn't want to know it."

"Trust me, I understand. No one wants to know the person they love lied or cheated or simply doesn't want to be with them anymore. Whatever the problems, we want that love to survive. We don't want to feel the pain."

"It's all I feel now. All my memories are tarnished. Can I believe anything he said to me in the end? Was he just placating me, hoping I wouldn't find out? Were we happy, or did we just settle into our life and accept it?"

"I saw the two of you together. You were happy. He adored you and the boys."

"Are you sure? Because if he could sleep with my sister, not some stranger, but someone that close to me, I wonder if he loved me at all?"

The silence stretched while Sierra wallowed in her hurt and pain. Her mom tried to come up with something to say to make this better when nothing would change this.

"This is an impossible situation."

"This is a bad episode of shock TV. I'm trapped in my own real-life version of some sordid talk show where they reveal your sister slept with your husband and your niece is really your kids' half sibling."

"I don't even know how to help you through this."

She appreciated her mom's honesty.

"I know you want some magic way to make this all right, that somehow Heather and I can work this out. For the children's sake," Sierra tossed out, because that's what couples tried to do when they wanted to keep things together for the kids.

"Have you thought about what you'll say to the children?"

"How are they supposed to understand this, when I can barely wrap my head around it?"

"They are siblings. I suppose, at some point, they should be told."

"I agree. At some point. But how do I tell my sons that their father was a cheater? How does that news impact them? Will they think it's okay to do that to a woman because, hey, their father did it to their mother? Or will they think it's the worst thing you can do to your partner and that their father is a bad person? No matter what David did, I don't want them to think less of their father."

"The truth is that David was human. He made mistakes. The boys can learn from them. You can make them understand that what David did was hurtful and wrong, but that doesn't mean he didn't love his children, that he wasn't a good father to them."

"He didn't think of what his actions would do to those boys. He didn't think about anything but what he wanted and his own selfish desires. This wasn't a onetime lapse in judgment. He carried on the affair for however long, maybe even up until his death."

"I'm sure Heather can fill in the details."

"I don't *need* the details. I don't want to hear her excuses or apologies. Nothing she says will make this better. Nothing will change my mind about what I think about her now and how I feel."

Dede deflated with a heavy sigh and sank into the chair. "What about Mason?"

"What about him? Am I supposed to trust him when he kept this from me?"

"You don't know for sure Mason knew before he investigated the loan. You love him. Not the same way you loved David. It's deeper. Don't let this come between you. Give him a chance to explain."

She would. But right now, she was mad at herself and the world, and she didn't think anyone could say anything to change that.

"All I know is that I don't want to see her ever again. I don't want to be confronted with what she and David did every time I see her. I don't want to feel this way over and over again."

"Please, Sierra, take some time to let all this sink in and settle before you make any drastic decisions."

"I don't have a choice. I have to think of the boys. I can't just do what I want to do like Heather does without thought to how it affects others. No. I have to be responsible and thoughtful and considerate and decent while she does whatever the hell she wants, consequences be damned."

Her mother allowed the bitter snarkiness without comment. "All I'm saying is take some time. Think about who's at fault and who's not. What's best for your kids?"

Yeah, that last part was the hardest. The boys deserved to know Hallee was their sister. Lies had a way of coming out eventually, and they would have to learn the truth.

She was expected to be the bigger person. But it was damn hard when she was the one wronged in so many ways.

"Would you please watch the boys? I need to get out of here for a while."

"Where are you going?"

"I don't know. Away from here."

"You can't outrun this, sweetheart."

"I know. But I can at least be alone with it for a while and not have to worry about what everyone else wants me to do and how they want me to feel and what they expect me to do to make this all right for everyone. I want to just be mad."

Because being hurt and sad just might break her.

And she didn't want the boys to see her curled into a ball, crying her heart out over a man who broke her heart and a sister who crushed it to pieces.

Chapter Twenty-Nine

Sierra found herself at the ocean, sitting in the sand, staring at the waves crashing on the beach, seagulls screeching overhead, her thoughts a swirl of emotions as wild as the wind blowing her hair back. Tears streamed down her cheeks unchecked. They dripped on her shirt and still she stared out at the wide expanse of water, out to the horizon, and fought the urge to just walk right into the waves and let them carry her away.

She didn't really want to die. What she really wanted was to not hurt anymore. She wanted to erase what she knew from her mind and heart.

She wanted to believe people were good and kind and did the right thing.

David. Heather. They betrayed her. They lied.

How could her sister sleep with her husband?

How could David break every promise and vow and hurt her that way?

If he was that unhappy, if he wanted someone and something else, he should have said so. Ending their relationship would have hurt, but it wouldn't have been this devastating.

Not only had he cheated, he'd done so with her sister.

The thought cut so deep, she couldn't bear it. She hugged

her knees to her chest, but nothing eased the pain. Her head pounded with every horrible thought that kept rolling in like the waves, the onslaught of second-guessing all their conversations and everything he did all those months he was seeing Heather behind her back.

Now it all made a horrible kind of sense.

Looking back, she had had her suspicions, but she'd never come right out and accused him of an affair. Part of her didn't want to know. The other part didn't want to mess up the life their boys blissfully enjoyed, not knowing one iota of the troubles facing their parents.

She hadn't wanted to burst their happy bubble. She had wanted to protect them. And her heart.

Ignorance is bliss.

Until you're forced to face the truth.

David did cheat. He lied. He betrayed her and broke their vows.

He left her with a hell of a mess.

She hated David for what he'd done. But David wasn't here. She couldn't yell at him or force him to hear all the terrible things she wanted to say. He'd taken that from her.

But Heather was here. She hated Heather.

She'd have a thousand excuses for her behavior. She'd romanticize their relationship, say it was meant to be, that David's and her love couldn't be denied.

She'd already sworn she never meant to hurt Sierra. But what did she expect would happen when Sierra found out?

And the kids. Oh god, how would she ever explain to Danny and Oliver that their father slept with Heather and had a child with her? They may not understand the ramifications of that now, but they'd understand when they got older.

She hated David for leaving it to her to explain to their children.

Because she couldn't get away with not telling them. Hallee was proof of what happened, and eventually she'd have to be told the circumstances of her birth and that she had two brothers.

What would she think when she discovered Sierra hated Heather because of it?

She sensed her mom wanted to find a way to reconciliation, but Sierra couldn't see past her rage and hurt to a time when she wouldn't feel this way when she looked at Heather.

Just thinking about her brought on a new wave of anger that she had no way of expending. It just built inside her like a volcano, the pressure pushing against everything inside her, wanting to explode.

The salty mist clung to her hair and chilled her skin. She could use a sweater and something hot to drink.

She could use a friend, someone who'd let her scream about all the injustices dealt her these last two years.

She didn't deserve this. She tried to be a good mom, wife, lover, and friend.

None of that mattered to David.

He'd taken what he wanted, their marriage and her be damned.

Her phone beeped with yet another text or voice mail she wanted to ignore. Her mom wondering where she was and if she was okay. Maybe Amy. Heather probably went to her, hoping to get Amy on her side. Sierra doubted Amy would be sympathetic.

But Amy would be happy to open a bottle of wine and trash-talk Heather and David all night with her. Deep down, Sierra knew that wouldn't really help.

Another beeping notification followed quickly by another. Maybe Mason. He was the hardest to ignore.

She didn't take out her phone. She didn't worry about what they needed or wanted. The last thing she wanted to do right now was make this okay for everyone else while her heart lay in pieces at the bottom of her battered soul.

She laid her head on her knees and let the grief swallow her as the tears came in a torrent she couldn't stop or hold back anymore. She let the pain and grief pour out, but the ache of it never seemed to cease, it just kept throbbing. Even when the tears dried and the hiccups disappeared and the sun fell into the ocean, the grief, the pain, they were still there, claws sunk deep in her heart and mind, unrelenting, just like the waves battering the shore and the wind blowing against her, chilling her to the bone.

Sierra stood on stiff legs, hands numb with cold, and gave one last solemn look at the beautiful ocean and headed back to her car.

The boys were probably wondering what happened to her and why she wasn't home to get them ready for bed. She knew her mom would take care of them, but they expected their own mother to care for them.

She couldn't dwell on her problems forever, but she'd needed these last several hours alone to think and grieve and be angry and upset without having to explain herself to anyone.

Now, she'd be the adult and mom and gather herself up and forge ahead because what the hell else was she supposed to do.

Life sucked. People disappointed and hurt others all the time. And tomorrow was another day to deal with it all and figure out what she did from here.

The boys deserved the best of her. One day they'd appreciate all she'd sacrificed and given for their happiness.

Being the adult and the mom sucked, because it meant she had to do all the hard stuff so her kids were happy.

After everything she'd been through with David and Heather, she wished there was one person wholly and unequivocally on her side.

Someone who knew all that happened and said, *You deserved better. They suck. Fuck them*, and stood beside her through all that still needed to be done to get her life back on track.

Chapter Thirty

Mason sat on the porch steps waiting for the woman he loved to come home, knowing he had one shot at explaining himself. If he blew it, his whole life's happiness would disappear.

He'd spent far too many years wishing for her.

He'd fix this and make her happy the rest of her life because he didn't want to live without her.

He'd show her every day how much he loved her. She'd never have cause to question how he felt about her and that he was completely, irrevocably devoted to her.

Now if he could only figure out how to make her believe him.

All his texts thus far had gone unanswered. He didn't take it as a bad sign. She hadn't answered any of Dede's calls or texts, either.

The front door opened behind him. He turned and stared up at Dede. "Have you heard from her?"

She gave him a sad frown. "No. Not yet. I thought she'd be home for dinner or at least in time to put the boys to bed."

He completely deflated and hung his head. "She'll be here soon." The assurance didn't ease his mind or heart. It probably did nothing for Dede, either.

"I told you, you didn't have to wait out here."

"I didn't want to intrude."

"Well, they heard your truck pull in earlier and they refuse to go to bed without a bedtime story from you."

He glanced at Dede over his shoulder. "I'm not sure Sierra would appreciate that given how she walked away today without giving me a chance to explain."

"The boys don't know that. They're anxious and worried that their mom isn't here. They didn't buy that she had to go to work, especially after they saw how upset she was earlier. I think you might have a better chance of convincing them she's okay than I did."

He sucked in a breath and let it out, but it did nothing to loosen the band of regret and worry wrapped around his chest, making it hard to breathe.

He couldn't deny the boys or let this opportunity to see them go.

He stood and faced Dede, letting loose one of the apologies he thought he owed. "I'm sorry about how this went down. I wanted to talk to her today about what I knew about David, but after the balloon ceremony this morning and her getting called away to work, I let it go, hoping we'd have time alone after the boys' ride to talk."

"Sierra told me a little of what happened with Heather. I'm beside myself. I don't know what to do. Heather won't take my calls, either. I'll give her time to get herself together."

"Then what?" The bitter question put Dede on the spot, but Mason didn't care. Heather didn't deserve any coddling from her mom. She'd wronged Sierra in the most hurtful way possible. And he'd gotten caught up in her web of lies and deceit.

He had no sympathy for Heather.

If David were alive, he'd kick his ass for treating his wife so callously and leaving her to deal with the fallout of his bad behavior.

There was no good way out of this for Sierra.

She had to live with knowing her husband and sister betrayed her. Worse, she had to explain to the kids and try to do it in a way that didn't make her the bad guy by disparaging their father and aunt. Impossible.

But Sierra had a big heart and she'd try, all the while her heart would be breaking. But she'd suck it up and do right by her children because she loved them enough to take the hit herself.

"Both my girls are hurting."

"Heather doesn't deserve sympathy for what she's done to Sierra."

"David was a part of this, too."

"And Heather is your daughter and you're loyal to her. I get that it's easier to blame David. He's not here to answer for what he did. But you should have seen Heather today, she outright came on to me. She didn't even ask if I was seeing someone. She just thinks she can have whatever she wants."

"Did Sierra hear that?"

"I'm pretty sure she heard the whole exchange. Heather didn't seem to know Sierra and I are *seeing* each other. We've kept our relationship quiet. But she does know Sierra and I have always been close and we were spending time together with the boys at the ranch. Amy knows because she watched the boys while we went on a date, but Sierra never had a reason to say anything about it to Heather other than in a casual way because the boys were always around."

Mason rubbed his hand over his tense neck. He thought about their conversation. "I don't think Heather really likes me. We barely know each other, but I'm a good catch." He didn't say that out of conceit, but because it was true for Heather. "To Heather, I look like great husband and father material. I've shown that I want a family of my own, so she decided to insert herself into my life as the perfect potential wife."

Dede put her hand to her chest. "How did we go from talking about you being a father to those boys this morning to this?"

He held his hands up and let them fall. "It's been a hell of a day." And he hated that he'd hurt Sierra. "I better get upstairs to the boys before they get restless and more worried about their mom."

He left Dede on the porch lost in her thoughts about the day and her daughters and how they were going to fix this. Mason wasn't so sure it could be fixed, but for Hallee's sake, he hoped Sierra was willing to try.

Mason stood in the doorway and stared into Danny and Oliver's room. The night-light between the two twin beds highlighted their faces and solemn eyes. He hated seeing them upset and worried about their mom.

"Hey, why aren't you guys asleep yet?"

"Where's Mommy?" Oliver's bottom lip quivered.

"She'll be home soon."

"Something is wrong." Danny sat up and studied Mason, looking for any sign that he knew why their mom wasn't here.

So Mason gave it to them straight. "Your mom is very upset right now. She and Heather had an argument. Your mom is deeply hurt and sad. She needed some time to herself to sort out her thoughts."

"She's mad at you, too, isn't she?" Nothing much got past Danny.

Mason wondered if he'd picked up on the tension between his mom and dad when David was still alive.

"I kept something from your mom. I should have told her right away, but I didn't want to hurt her, either. I ended up hurting her anyway because I waited too long to say something."

"What?" Oliver asked.

Danny leaned forward, wanting to know, too.

"That's between me and your mom. I was wrong. I will apologize as soon as I see her." That was the best he could do to show the boys that even adults screwed up sometimes and had to take responsibility and apologize when they did.

Mason moved into the room and stood by Danny's bed. He leaned over and pointed at the books on the blanket. "Want me to read these?"

Danny hesitated a moment, still taking Mason's measure and deciding that he wasn't going to dismiss him yet. He nodded and scooted over so Mason could sit beside him, propped against the headboard.

Oliver jumped out of his bed and climbed up onto Mason's lap, lying down his chest, his head on Mason's shoulder.

Mason opened the first book and started reading about pirates and treasure. He got the words out, but his focus was on Oliver and Danny so trusting and sweet, pressed against him.

He loved these boys.

He already thought of them as his own. He wanted a thousand more nights like this with them. And Sierra.

He read one book and then another. The boys settled in and relaxed, their eyes drooping by the time he started book three. They were asleep before the last page, but he read it through anyway, wanting the boys to know he was there watching over them. He settled into the quiet, one arm wrapped around Oliver on his chest, the other around Danny at his side.

Nothing had ever felt this right and poignant and like a wish come true.

If only—

That thought cut off when Sierra appeared in the doorway, fulfilling his thought.

She was finally here.

She stared at him, trying so hard to hide her feelings, but he saw the longing that she wanted this to be their lives and the disappointment that he'd kept something important from her.

Determined to fix it, he gently slipped his arm from Danny's back, letting him settle into the pillow. He adjusted Oliver into his arms and rose from the mattress, laying Oliver in his own bed and settling him under the covers. Filled with love for the boys, he leaned over and kissed Oliver's brow, then turned and did the same to Danny.

With one last glance to be sure the boys were settled and sleeping peacefully, he headed to the door and caught up to

Sierra at the stairs. He couldn't help reaching out and brushing his hand down her hair.

She flinched and glanced over her shoulder, giving him a warning glare.

Undeterred, he looked her in the eye and hoped she saw the remorse overflowing from him. "We need to talk."

Chapter Thirty-One

S ierra walked down the stairs, barely spared her mother a glance, and went right out the front door onto the porch.

"It's not fair that you come over here and cuddle with my kids and think that will soften me up." Okay, it had, because, damn, the scene she walked in on was sweet and filled with sincerity because she'd seen the way he held the boys and kissed them good night and it was . . . perfect.

"I came here to talk to *you*. Spending time with Danny and Oliver was a bonus I didn't expect, but they knew I was here waiting for you and wanted me to read them bedtime stories. And you know what, I loved it. I love them. And I love you." He paused.

She stared out at the yard with him at her back, fighting the urge to turn and face him, but knowing she had to because they couldn't leave things like this.

She tried to mentally prepare herself to look at him and not feel anything, but the second she turned and saw the agonizing pain in his eyes she caved and her heart swelled with the love she couldn't deny and didn't want to let go of without giving him a chance. "You lied to me. I asked you to look into the loan, but you already knew what David did with the money."

"No, that's not true. I suspected, but I had no facts to back it up. It would be wrong to make an accusation like that to you, not knowing if it was really true or not. What if I'd told you I thought David and Heather had an affair and Hallee belonged to him and it wasn't true? Do you think I wanted to put you through that without being absolutely certain?"

Sierra sighed. Everything he said made sense. She'd been so obsessed with thinking about David and Heather, what they did behind her back, she hadn't really thought it through.

Mason had been trying to do the right thing, the right way.

"I'm guilty of withholding my suspicions, and yes, not telling you the second the investigator had all the proof to back them up. I didn't know how to tell you. I didn't want what they did to hurt you the way it has. I wanted to figure out a good way to tell you, but there wasn't one. The few times I tried to tell you, we were interrupted. I couldn't just blurt it out with other people around. And I hate the way you found out."

"You mean while watching my sister hit on you."

"You also saw me turn her down flat."

He did. No hesitation. Not even a hint that the prospect of seeing Heather intrigued him.

After everything she'd already lost, Sierra couldn't bear to lose him, too, despite the fact this wasn't completely resolved. "I'm still mad."

"You have every right to be about all of this. But you know in your heart I did plan to tell you everything. I tried to tell you this morning but the timing wasn't right. I told you we'd talk after the boys' ride."

She held up her hand to stop him defending himself further.

She remembered all that, it had just gotten buried under everything else for a while.

"Of course Heather picks today to stab me in the back after I spent all that time trying to give the boys a chance to remember their father in a meaningful way."

He pleaded with her again. "I should have told you what I knew sooner, but . . . God, Sierra, the last thing I wanted was to see you like this and know I had any part of it."

"You didn't want to investigate David."

"No, I didn't, because I didn't want what I suspected to be true. But I went ahead with it because you deserved to know the truth."

Mason might be the only person who'd give her the unvarnished truth. "Why did you suspect them?" She stood waiting, afraid to hear the details but feeling like knowing was better than letting her mind torture her with a million scenarios.

"Remember Charles's funeral?"

"You barely spoke to me. You were here with your fiancée."

One side of his mouth drew back in a half frown. "Feeling like a total ass because the woman I really wanted to be with married my friend. I stayed away from you because I didn't want my fiancée to see how much I wanted you. I guess I didn't hide it well enough because we ended things shortly after that day. I couldn't go through with a marriage to a woman I loved but wasn't wholly *in* love with."

"Mason, you can't tell me that you broke it off with her and stayed single all this time because you were waiting for me."

"Why not? It's true." He shrugged. "I didn't do it consciously.

I told myself, one day I'd love someone the way I loved you. I dated. I had short-lived relationships. But that day never came. Until you moved back home. The second I saw you, I knew I wasn't going to let you get away again without my doing everything possible to show you how much I love you." He raked his fingers through his hair. "I blew it today."

She couldn't let him blame himself for something David and Heather did. "No. You didn't."

His gaze came up and met hers. The desperate hope in his eyes softened her heart and erased all the anger she'd directed at him.

"You loved me enough to turn Heather's offer down flat."

"I only want you."

"You confronted her for me about David and Hallee. You made her tell the truth for once."

"I should have spoken to you first, as I planned to, but in that moment I was so angry for you. I couldn't stand there and let her try to do with me what she did with David behind your back."

"How did you come to suspect them?"

"Everyone gathered here after the graveside ceremony. People were packed into the house. You were chasing after the boys, keeping them in line."

"And David was nowhere to be found." After the long car ride the day before, the boys not sleeping in the strange house, having to stand still and be quiet through the long ceremony, and stuffing themselves with goodies when they got back, well, they were acting out. David lost his patience and made himself scarce. Truthfully, their days were filled with those types of outbursts from two energetic boys.

She'd spent most of that day feeling frazzled and resentful that David had checked out on her.

"I saw him with Heather out back sharing a drink and talking. I didn't think much of it. You guys didn't get back often, so I thought they were just catching up."

David and Heather had always had a close relationship. Sierra never thought anything of the way they joked with each other. She appreciated that her husband and sister got along so well, especially since Heather, as the youngest, wasn't often included in her and Amy's outings growing up. The age gap meant she couldn't hang out at the bar with them.

"But you saw the closeness between them."

"I saw a woman flirting with your husband. I expected David to brush it off, take a step back, and go inside to be with you."

"But that's not what happened."

"Heather may have been flirting, but David's the one who took her hand and tugged, coaxing her to leave with him. They started walking across the yard together. Away from the house and the others milling around on the back porch and garden area. Heads together, talking, laughing, they disappeared around the back of the house out toward the pond."

"And the shed out there." Dede had allowed her girls to turn it into a fort of sorts when they were teens. They had a mini fridge, a large rug where they used to sleep in their sleeping bags and tell ghost stories all night, and an old worn leather sofa. It was their hideaway just inside the woods, shaded by trees, and just rustic enough for them to feel like they were in their own world.

And Heather turned it into a lovers' hideaway with *her* husband.

"I couldn't follow them without making it obvious."

"So you're not sure what really happened."

"I suspected, so I waited for them to return. When I saw them, I knew by the looks on their faces, the way they touched hands, trying to make sure no one saw. The way she brushed her hand down her thigh to smooth her skirt and over her hair. David scanned the whole yard, looking to be sure you weren't out there, seeing him return with Heather. I saw the guilt. But I couldn't be sure what he was guilty of. A stolen kiss? More?"

"But you suspected you knew exactly what was going on."

"Yes. And it turned my stomach to watch him go back inside to you and act like nothing happened. He said something to you and you smiled at him. Heather glared at the two of you from across the room."

"After all that, you still didn't think to tell me something?"

"David accused me once when we were all out together of being jealous."

She understood. "He knew you liked me."

"I don't know how I managed to hide it from you all the time, but David saw it. Maybe it's a guy thing. We tend to have radar for other men looking at our girlfriend or wife."

"Do you remember telling Amy that you wanted to tell me how you felt?"

"Of course. I wanted you to know so bad, but she said you

were happy with David. You loved him. Telling you would do me no good and probably end our friendship. I didn't want that. I wanted you to be happy."

"I get that, but you should know she also didn't tell you what I told her about you."

He took a step closer, his eyes narrowed with confusion and anger. "What do you mean?"

"I told her that I was having second thoughts about marrying David because of my growing feelings for you."

Mason fell back a step. Eyes wide, he sputtered, "What?"

"My sisters seem hell-bent on meddling in my relationships." Sierra shook her head and pressed on. "Amy encouraged me to stay with David because she thought you were still married to your job and David offered me what I really wanted. Plus, she'd always had a crush on you and she didn't want me to have you."

"Seriously?" Mason rubbed his hand over the back of his neck. "I can't believe she held out on both of us." The frustration in his words matched her own.

"Trust me, I wasn't happy when I found out, either. But here I am, stuck with the aftermath of what my sisters did. Amy's petty interference seems insignificant compared to what Heather did, but both of them changed my life." She pinned him with her gaze. "And you should have told me, not Amy, that you had feelings for me."

He held her gaze. "You have no idea how much I wish I had done just that." He really meant it.

"On one hand I wish I'd made a different choice. On the other . . ."

He nodded, his eyes going soft with understanding. "You have Danny and Oliver."

"Exactly. Now what? What's done is done. I can't change the past or what David and Heather did."

"Everything would have been different if we'd just confessed our feelings."

"Maybe. But we were different people back then. At the time, were we right for each other? Would we have gotten married, had kids, and lived a happy life together?"

"Yes." No hesitation. Just absolute assurance. Mason knew how he felt and what he wanted. "We can still have all of that if you can just forgive me."

"I do forgive you. It's easy to do because you really didn't do anything wrong. You wanted to protect me. That's more than my own sisters ever did for me."

Mason closed the distance and cupped her face in his warm hands. "I love you, Sierra. Let me prove it to you. Let me show you."

"I see it in everything you do, Mason. I let my anger get the better of me earlier despite the fact you'd made it clear you had news for me about David."

"Does this mean we're still together, that you're not going to leave me?"

She placed her hands on his wrists and leaned into his palm. "I don't want to lose you. You and the boys are the only good things I have in my life. I love you." She did. And she trusted Mason. "But I don't know what comes next with all this."

"I want to help you through it. I'm here for whatever you need." He pressed a kiss to her forehead.

"I appreciate that." Unable to look him in the eye and say the next part, she stared at his chest. "I'm just not sure that I can stay here and see Heather and Hallee and not tear open this wound every time I do."

He nudged her face up so she'd look at him. "Don't let her take away your happiness again. If you leave, and we can't be together, I don't know . . . somehow it feels like she wins."

That was the last thing Sierra wanted.

"But if you truly can't live here, then I'll go wherever you want to go."

Stunned by his words, she met his gaze with her wide-eyed one. "Mason. You can't leave your home and your law practice for me."

"Why not? I love you. What good is a job and a home if you aren't with me and I'm alone and unhappy?"

They'd wasted a lot of time trying to build a life without each other, always feeling like something was off or not quite right. They were missing each other and the deep, true love they shared. She didn't want to let go of the way she felt right here, right now, standing with the man who not only would say he'd give up everything to be with her, but meant it.

"Ever since you came back, I spend my days desperate to see you. I think about you all day, to the point I'm distracted on calls and in meetings and people think I've lost my mind. I have. And my heart. Over you. I think about the life we could have together. I think about the boys growing up at the ranch with the horses. I think about us being a family and you and I having more kids."

"Kids?"

"One. At least. Two if you're up for it. However many you

want. You can quit your job and be with the kids. Or keep your job. Cut your hours. Take a different job. I don't care. Settle all this other stuff the best you can and be happy with me."

She knew it wouldn't be easy to live with what happened, but she'd find a way, so she could be happy with him. "Okay."

"Really?" Genuine surprise filled his voice. "I thought I'd have to do a hell of a lot more convincing."

"Why? No one has ever loved me the way you do. I want the boys to grow up with a man like you to look up to. I want a husband who thinks my happiness is the most important thing in the world. I want to show you that the love you give me is appreciated by loving you the same way. I want to be ridiculously happy. And maybe part of being happy is letting go of the past and the people who have hurt me."

"I'm not sure you'll really be happy without your sister in your life."

"I don't know if I'm capable of forgiving her. I know I'll never trust her again."

Mason frowned. "Are *we* good?"

"Yes. When I got home tonight, my emotions were raw and all over the place. I was angry and hurt and just a mess. But I pulled into the drive and saw your truck, and though I didn't want to feel anything, a spark of joy burst because you came to see me even after I ignored you. You didn't give up."

"Never."

"Then I saw you with the boys and it was so obvious that you love them. You owned up to what happened and told me the truth about what you knew even though you didn't want to paint a picture of how my husband and sister betrayed me right here at my home, right under my nose, even though I knew they'd been together."

Mason rubbed his hands up and down her arms. "It makes it harder and more real to know the details."

"Yes, it does. It's all part of the same betrayal. I can't escape what happened or how it's changed my perspective of the past and how I feel about David, our marriage, and my sister. Nothing is the same. I'll need time to come to terms with all of it. But I don't need time to evaluate how I feel about you. That is so clear in my mind and heart. David's death, the fire, they've taught me that time is precious. I don't want to waste any more of it or give anyone else a chance to interfere in our lives again. I love you. I want to build a life with you. I won't let anything or anyone come between us again."

"Then let's make it happen."

"Okay." She didn't hesitate to go after what she wanted.

Mason stared down at her with a smile that lightened her heart when she thought nothing would today. "Okay. Where do you want to start?"

"I could really use a hug."

"Come here, sweetheart." Mason pulled her in to his chest and held her close.

She slipped her hands around his sides to his back and hugged him close.

"Best thing that's happened all day." Mason kissed her on the head.

She loved that he tried to make her focus on the good. Right now, she had the best in her arms. And she wouldn't let him go, not for anything.

"It's late. You've had a hell of a day. You must be tired. I don't want to let you go, but . . ."

"Don't." She leaned back and stared up at him. "I don't want to lie in bed alone all night with my head spinning."

"Come home with me. I'll hold on to you." That's exactly what she wanted him to say and do. "I'll make sure you're up and home before the boys wake up. Tomorrow, we'll figure out the rest."

"As long as it begins and ends with you and me, I think we'll be okay."

Mason kissed her softly. "My whole world begins and ends with you."

That beautiful statement wiped away any and all lingering doubts trying to creep in and spoil this reconciliation. Sierra let all the bad get washed away by the wave of love she felt for him.

She'd have to deal with what she knew about David and Heather, but she didn't have to do it alone. Mason would stand beside her. He'd hold her when she needed it. He'd love her through the bad and fill her up with nothing but good.

If he could do that for her today of all days, she bet he'd have no problem making her happy and feel like she was wanted and needed like she did right now every day for the rest of their lives.

She didn't want much, but she refused to live another day without love and trust.

Mason made her feel safe.

He had her back.

He'd lift her up when she was down just like he'd done for her today with his open honesty and heartwarming love.

Chapter Thirty-Two

Heather stood next to the stove in the late-morning light lost in thought until the high-pitched whistle of the teakettle broke into her reverie. That's when she realized the *other* sound she heard was someone pounding on the front door.

She turned off the stove and headed for the loud knocks, ready to send whoever it was on their way.

Her mother stood on the stoop, dark circles under her bloodshot eyes. She'd pulled her silver-streaked brown hair back into a sleek bun, which had the effect of making her look even more tired. "If you slam that door on me, you will regret it."

Heather checked the urge to close the door on the inevitable scolding and refrained from rolling her eyes. "What are you doing here? Shouldn't you be home judging me?"

Dede brushed right past her and stood in the living room. "After what you've done, you deserve a good talking to from your mother." She glanced into Hallee's room. "Where is she?"

"Day care. I needed some time alone."

"I bet. Your sister is really angry. I taught you better than this."

This time, Heather did roll her eyes. "Please. Four husbands. Don't tell me you never strayed." Their lives growing up had been a revolving door of men coming and going. Dede tried to be discreet with the dating, but they knew what was going on.

"When I was done, I left. I never cheated. I never went after someone who wasn't available. David wasn't free to love you. He had a wife and a family. He was bound to them. No matter how it happened, you knew that and you participated in ruining that marriage."

That hurt, but deep down Heather knew it was true.

"He degraded you. He made you his dirty secret, knowing you two would never really end up together, not with so much standing in your way."

Harsh!

"And you went along with it."

Because I loved him. I thought the time we had together would be enough.

Heather had dreamed about the beautiful life they'd share raising Hallee, knowing it was only a figment of her imagination. Nothing but wishful thinking.

She'd worked so hard to suppress her feelings about Sierra's family, so she could wallow in their love.

Naïve. Stupid. Callous. Scared. Selfish.

She called herself all those things and more. She knew it couldn't last forever, but she never expected things to end with David's death.

"You were the *other* woman. Not *his* woman."

Her heart ached knowing that was true, too.

"You don't know what we had." No one understood how David made her feel, what they shared when they were together.

"Sex isn't love, Heather. It's a thrill. It's temporary."

She knew that all too well. Because the second David walked out the door and went back to Sierra, she felt his absence. All the wonderful feelings inside her dissipated and she wondered if he'd be back. Did he care? Did he really love her? Was the regret in his eyes because he had to go or because he hated himself for cheating on his wife?

"David was married to Sierra. That's a bond not easily broken."

Heather had felt it. Though David was with her, in the back of his mind he was thinking about Sierra. He worried about what would happen if they got caught. He feared losing his boys.

"He had no trouble breaking his vows." That wasn't exactly true. After that first time, she had to push. Every time she asked him to come visit, she had to coax and tempt him. But still he came to her every time.

She'd felt a sense of power in that.

He'd been drawn to her. But he'd also been pulled back by Sierra and the boys.

"So it's true. You went after him like you did with Mason."

She resented how that made her sound. "It wasn't like that with either of them. I didn't know about Mason and Sierra. And David and I had a connection." It had been fragile and tenuous. She'd been careful to never give David an ultimatum because she feared he'd choose his life with Sierra and the boys. Where would that leave her and Hallee?

Exactly where they were now. Alone.

Her mom shook her head in dismay. "Maybe there was something good between you. I hope David didn't betray his wife and children for nothing. But you can't honestly believe the relationship could hold up to a divorce and the two of you being together after you both destroyed your relationship with Sierra. Did you think she'd happily allow the boys' visitation with their father here with you, the woman who stole her husband and tore her family apart? What do you think the boys would think of you? Of their father? How would they deal with seeing their mother upset and sad and hurt?"

"I never dreamed things would go so far. Hallee was a surprise and a blessing I never expected. The relationship became so much bigger than David and me. But none of that matters now. He's dead. We'll never be together again."

"It matters a hell of a lot to Sierra. It will matter to those boys and Hallee when they learn the truth. Maybe you can delude yourself into thinking it all ended with David's death, but it didn't."

"I don't think that. I'm just saying that I don't get to be with him anymore. He's gone. Sierra got all the sympathy when he died, but I lost him, too. *I* loved him. *I* grieve for him. Hallee will never know her father. She won't have a single memory of him. The boys will. Sierra does. But I'm not allowed to have my feelings or express my grief or even share my memories with anyone."

"Whose fault is that?" The snap in her mother's tone conveyed her anger all too well.

"It's my fault. And David's." She wasn't the only one who did the wrong thing. "We did this." She combed her fingers through her hair and pushed the wild waves back. It made her momentarily think of the way David would do the same thing a second before he kissed her with a passion and desperation she'd never felt with anyone.

She didn't know why he went behind Sierra's back. She didn't care. She had just wanted him. If she could give him what Sierra couldn't, it somehow made her feel like she was the better woman for him.

But he'd never chosen her over Sierra. Not in a permanent way.

When she asked him when they'd finally be together, he changed the subject, distracted her with sex, or simply said he needed more time to figure out a way to tell Sierra that didn't mean he'd lose his boys.

But that was never going to happen.

Revealing their relationship meant the destruction of others.

And now that's exactly what happened.

Sierra hated her. Her mother was disappointed and angry with her. When Amy found out, she'd take Sierra's side. Mason had looked at her with such contempt she still felt the impact of it even now.

Heather folded her arms around her middle, wishing her mother understood. "I never meant to hurt Sierra. I didn't want to break up her marriage. I only saw that David was unhappy." She reconsidered. "He was restless. I felt the same way. None of my dates ever gave me the spark I felt when I was with David. He was kind and funny and paid attention to me. We kept it friendly at first, but I wanted more. And then all of a sudden, teasing turned to serious flirting and the line blurred until I couldn't see it and I found myself in David's arms. I thought I'd get everything I wanted."

"You thought you'd get what your sisters had. A loving husband. Children. A home."

As shameful and deluded as it was, Heather had allowed herself to think that sometimes. "I wanted all those things."

"Well, you got them. Of course, the husband belonged to

someone else. The child didn't have a full-time father. And the home didn't include you all happily living together."

"Right. I got what I deserved. Believe me, I know. The guilt eats at me every day. But Hallee doesn't deserve to pay for my mistakes."

"She suffered from day one. It was always going to end this way. You had to know that. Or were you okay giving up your family for a man who'd cheat on his wife?"

She hated that her mom put it that way, but reality slapped her in the face.

Dede didn't wait for an answer Heather didn't really have. "Do you think David would have felt that way? That he didn't care what Sierra, his boys, the rest of the family thought about what you two had done?"

"Obviously he cared. He didn't leave her. He tried so hard to hide what we'd done."

Dede's head tilted to the side. "Did you two stop seeing each other before he died?"

Damn. She hadn't meant to let that slip.

"When I told him I was pregnant . . ."

Dede nodded, filling in the blanks. "Reality hit. He couldn't hide what you'd done anymore. He knew it would eventually come out. He stopped sleeping with you."

Raw pain pinched her heart. "Yes. He said he couldn't do it anymore. He promised to support us, but all the love and affection disappeared. When he looked at me, it was like he regretted every second of our time together." And it broke her heart even now to remember it.

"Guilt is a heavy burden. He wronged Sierra, his boys, even

you. And you willingly participated with him. You could put Sierra out of your mind, but he couldn't. Not when he had to go home and face her and his children and their life." Dede frowned. "Didn't you see the toll your affair was taking on him?"

"Yes. Of course I did. I told him everything would be okay. That he didn't have to stay with Sierra if he wasn't happy."

"But he didn't leave her. What ate away at David was that he wanted things to work out with her, right?"

She pressed her lips tight, not wanting to confirm it. Not wanting to feel the hurt that he wanted Sierra more than he wanted her.

"There was no way to fix things. Once she found out about us, she'd leave him."

"And you'd be there to pick up the pieces. I'm surprised you didn't tell her yourself." Her mom leveled the accusation with such conviction.

Heather glanced out the window at the blooming flowers, not feeling as cheerful as them by a long shot.

"You thought about it," her mother answered for her. "Wow. How selfish can you be?"

Very.

But it didn't mean she didn't feel for Sierra, that she didn't feel guilty and rotten about herself for what she'd done. It didn't mean she didn't regret her choices at the same time she cherished her memories of David and that she got Hallee.

"Why does she get everything and I'm left with nothing?"

"Nothing? You have this house. You have Hallee. What have you left Sierra with? A cheating husband. Questions about how he really felt about her and their marriage. She can't even grieve the man she loved because of his betrayals. She has to put on a good front for the boys. She has to preserve his memory for them because she doesn't want her children to know what a bastard their father was to their mother. She has to find a way to tell them they have a sister. That means a talk about how their father had sex with her sister and produced a child. Can you imagine?"

Yes. Because she'd have to have that same discussion with her daughter someday.

"She has to face the whispers and stares from others when they find out the children are all siblings and that her husband cheated on her with her sister."

"I'm the one who will get the worst of that."

Dede glared at her, waiting for Heather to get it.

She did. But she didn't have to like it.

"I'll keep my distance."

"Right. Like you won't run into each other. This is a small town. Be realistic, Heather. For once, think things through."

"What do you want me to do? I don't have a lot of options. I'm a single mom on a fixed income with no support."

"You have a fifty-thousand-dollar payout that your sister has been paying for because you slept with her husband. David took out a loan to get that money. Did you know that? And how do you think that makes her feel to be paying her husband's mistress who happens to be her sister? Did you even think about that when you accepted that money?"

"I didn't know about the loan. I thought he was well off enough to give it to me to support his daughter. What was I supposed to do? The bills from the hospital were piling up. I needed a place for me and Hallee that wasn't some dump in an apartment complex I could barely afford along with day care while I worked."

"Right. So now do you expect your sister to foot the bill for her husband's affair?"

"I expected Hallee's father to do his part!"

"Were you also hoping Mason would make your life considerably better? You barely know him, yet you went to his home with a clear purpose and it had nothing to do with horseback riding with Hallee."

Getting called out by her mom sucked.

"Mason is a great catch. He's never been married. He's been spending all that time with the boys, so he obviously likes kids. I thought maybe he wanted some of his own. He's got a great job, makes lots of money, and Hallee would love growing up on a ranch."

"Except you didn't even ask him if he was seeing someone before you threw yourself at him."

She took her shot. "I had no idea he and Sierra had a thing."

"Really? Then you're the only one who can't see that man is obviously head over heels in love with her."

Frustrated and angry to be the bad guy in everything, Heather rolled her eyes. "Everyone loves Sierra. I got the memo a long time ago."

Her mother fisted a hand and took a step forward, rage rolling off her. "You knew Sierra and the boys were spending a lot of time at Mason's ranch. Didn't it occur to you that something might be going on?"

"She never said a word about it to me when we spoke."

"She kept it quiet because of the boys. She wanted to be sure their relationship was solid before they told the kids."

"Yeah, well, he turned me down flat and outed me to Sierra. Now she's pissed and probably out for revenge."

"What can she possibly do to you that's worse than what you've done to her? What's the point? Nothing will change what you've done. No apology will be enough to erase the hurt."

Heather knew that, but deep down she'd hoped that somehow, some way . . . "So it's a lost cause to even try to make her understand."

"Understand what? You can't expect her to sympathize with you. You certainly didn't care about her feelings or what would happen to her and the boys if David left them."

"I did care. But there was no going back. So what am I supposed to do now?"

"Apologize. Take responsibility for what you did. Ask for forgiveness. Tell her what you hope can happen going forward with the kids and between you and her. Show her that you have a heart despite how you've acted."

Heather didn't know if that would be enough to get Sierra to even look at her again. "Are you going to be mad at me forever, too?" She hated the way her mother looked at and spoke to her. She didn't want to lose her mother's love and support. Her disappointment tore at her heart. If her mom turned her back on Heather, she'd be devastated.

"Mostly I'm disappointed that you'd do this to your sister and her children. You were always spoiled, but that's my fault, though your sisters spoiled you, too. You got away with a lot.

But I never thought you did anything hurtful, until now. I hoped you'd see the mistakes I made with men and do better. I hoped you'd see your sisters' happy marriages and want that for yourself."

"I can't help who I loved."

"No. But you didn't have to act on it."

She hadn't been able to stop herself. "I know it was wrong. I'm sorry I hurt Sierra and fractured the family. I'm sure Amy will be just as angry and upset about this as you. I feel terrible that I snuck around with David. I even feel bad for loving him, even though I couldn't help myself." Tears fell down her cheeks. "And I will forever carry the weight of regret and guilt for begging him to help me and Hallee when she got sick and he drove down in the fog to be with us. I never meant for him to die trying to get to us."

Her mother stepped forward and gave Heather a hug she didn't deserve but badly needed. "I know you didn't. It was a tragic accident. Of course you wanted David there to help take care of Hallee in her time of need."

"Sierra blames me for his death." Heather blamed herself, too. But at the time, she'd done what she thought was right. Hallee had needed her father.

"She's angry and hurt and dealing with a lot. Give her time to sort things out for herself. Maybe you two will never come to an understanding, but she will find perspective when she's had time to think. And you need to tell her you are sorry." Dede pulled back and held her by the shoulders. "Heather, take some time and a really good look at what you did and the consequences. You can't go to Sierra and ask for forgiveness until you truly understand the cost of what you did. That includes the fact that David wouldn't have been on that road if not for your affair."

"You said it was a tragic accident."

"It was. But it was also an accident that should have never happened. If you want to make things right, put yourself in Sierra's place. Put yourself in Hallee's, Danny's, and Oliver's places. See this affair from their perspective. Understand how they will see the affair and all that happened. Imagine how they will feel. Only then will you really understand the impact your choices had and will continue to have on yourself and everyone else."

"I don't want to keep punishing myself for loving him. It hurts too much."

"How can you forgive yourself for what happened unless you take responsibility for all of it?" Dede released her and headed for the door. Before she left, she turned back. "You can't hide here forever. You will need to face them. You'll need to look at yourself. I hope you find a way to do that with sincerity and an open heart, knowing that you may not get the forgiveness you want, but that it's the only way you will have a shot at having some kind of relationship with your sister. Sierra loves you. She has been there for you your whole life. You deserve your feelings and hurt and grief, but so does she. And you're the one who caused them. It's up to you to try to make amends."

"I just want to move on."

"That's your choice, too. But think of what it will cost you before you put this in the past and live your life without dealing with this first." Dede never stopped being Mom.

She walked out leaving Heather with *I'm disappointed in you*, and an implied demand that she make better choices.

She should have gone to work today instead of trying to hide and just take a day to figure things out. Of course her mom showed up to hold her accountable. She wanted all her daughters to get along. She wanted them all to be happy.

Heather was pretty sure happiness was a myth.

A picture of Hallee caught her eye and she dismissed that thought altogether. All of a sudden she understood her mother a lot better. Of course she wanted this to all be sorted out and for her girls to get along and be happy. She wanted to go back to holiday get-togethers and birthday parties with everyone smiling and happy for each other.

Heather wouldn't take back what she'd done, but she could accept the blame.

For Hallee, and because she really did love her sister, she'd do everything possible to make up with Sierra, so they could have some semblance of a relationship where they could be cordial and all the kids stayed connected. They shared David's loss. Maybe being with her siblings would someday help Hallee connect to him through her brothers.

Heather walked back into her kitchen and stared at the kettle. A cup of tea wasn't going to make her feel better. She needed to do what her mother said and dig deep, put herself in others' shoes, and understand that, yes, her feelings mattered, but not more than theirs because she was the one who did the harm.

She knew that. Of course, she did, but she'd been hiding

behind lies, omissions, and delusions to keep her secret instead of facing the truth and putting her heart out there to make things right.

Not anymore.

Time to take responsibility and do the right thing, even if it was hard and meant more heartbreak for her.

Chapter Thirty-Three

Sierra leaned back into Mason, loving the feel of his arms around her. Yesterday had been one of the worst days of her life. But she woke up next to Mason with a sense that if she focused on their future, everything would be all right. More than that, she believed they could have a happy life together.

"What do you think?" Mason asked.

Sierra stared at the room that used to be Mason's when he was a teen and lived here with his parents. Since then he'd redone it and turned it into a guest room with basic wood furniture and a queen bed covered in an old quilt. "If we paint and update the pictures and bedding, I think one or both of the boys will love it."

"The off-white walls are kind of dull. Abstract art probably isn't the boys' thing. The bedspread was something left over from when my parents lived here. We'll go shopping. New bedding. They can pick the wall color and decorations. What did you think of the other room?"

Sierra glanced through the Jack and Jill bathroom at the room beyond. "Same. Paint and updates to the bedding and decorations." She glanced up and over her shoulder at Mason. "It's time the boys get to have their own space and make it theirs."

"When do you want to talk to them about us?"

"What do you think about getting the rooms ready first? We could surprise them. We could ask some questions about what they'd like their new rooms to look like in a general kind of way, letting them know I'm thinking of moving us to our own place. That will give them a chance to talk about what they want and how they feel about moving again."

"We'll do it slow," Mason agreed. "Take all the time you need."

She stepped out of his embrace and turned to face him. "I don't need more time to decide what I want, Mason. This past year, I grieved for a man who— You know what? I'm not going there. I'm not going to keep putting energy into my anger and what didn't work. This is my life. If I keep dwelling on what happened and what I've lost instead of what has come into my life and what makes me feel good, then all I'll do is end up sabotaging myself all over again."

"You didn't sabotage your relationship with David."

"Didn't I? I definitely made things worse by not voicing my concerns about us. I let things go. I *hoped* they'd get better. But I didn't do anything to fix it." She thought about all her small attempts to get David to talk, or how she'd tried affection and outright seduction. She'd gotten a response, but it never lasted. "I should have seen what seems so obvious now."

"Do you want to know why I never got married?"

"Why?"

"Because I saw all those couples come through my office miserable and hating the person they once loved like nothing could ever change that. I got engaged thinking the same thing. But then I realized why all those relationships ended, like mine, was because those people didn't feed that love. They let it starve."

That hit her right in the heart. "Yes. That's what happened. We let everything else get in the way of us."

"No matter how hard you'd tried to fix things, once David cheated and lied and spent all that time covering it up, you were doomed. One person can't fix a relationship. One person can't hold it together, but one person can destroy it all."

Mason closed the distance and touched her face. "I'm not worried about us, Sierra. You know why? Because I don't expect you to be someone different when we get married. I know life won't always be easy, but I'll have you beside me to get through the rough times. I want to be there for you, because I want to see you smile every day of your life. I love you. And the way that makes me feel . . . It's something I never want to lose. So I will do everything and anything I can to show you how much I love you every day because I don't want to lose *you*."

She stared up at him. "*When* we get married?"

"Yes. When." He kissed her softly. "But you'll have to wait a little bit for that. I have plans."

She smiled, her heart light because he understood that she needed his open honesty. "Plans for me?"

His eyes filled with desire at her seductive tone. He'd been sweet last night, holding her while she let her mind sort through the anger, sadness, betrayal, and confusion over how this all happened. When the sadness set in and she let the tears fall, he'd buried his face in her hair and whispered soothing words and affirmations that everything would be okay.

And she believed him, because she believed he was the kind of guy who stuck it out. He wouldn't quit on them.

She hadn't stopped loving him all these years. It had lain

dormant in her heart, but now that she was free to love him, she wouldn't stop. Not ever. The way he made her feel . . . Well, she wanted to feel this way all the time. It's what she'd been looking for, what she'd missed, what she craved.

And right now, she wanted to show Mason how much she appreciated him for being the man she needed.

"I have plans to keep you here. Plans to make you happy." He slid his hands down her neck, over her shoulders, and along her spine until his big hands covered her ass and pulled her closer. "Plans . . ." He covered her mouth in a searing kiss that sparked every nerve in her body and lit a fire between her legs, especially when he squeezed her ass and lifted her right off her feet. Wrapped in all his strength and love, she held him close and kissed him like her life depended on it.

She wanted to lose herself in loving him. She wanted to feel something good and sexy and hot and let everything else get wiped away.

She was so tired of feeling stupid and taken advantage of and left in the dark.

Mason made her feel desirable and necessary. Especially when he talked about their future and seduced her right out of her sorrows and into his arms like this.

He turned with her in his arms, feet dangling at his shins, and stopped short of walking out of the spare bedroom door when a car pulled up out front.

His eyes opened and his lips left hers and she missed the intimacy and building need. "Someone's here."

"I don't want to see anyone but you. Preferably naked. And horizontal."

He smiled. "I like the way you think, but it could be Amy with the boys."

"I'm not supposed to pick them up for another hour." But something could have come up and Amy needed to bring them back early.

Mason kissed her one last time, slowly, putting all the promise of more to come in the sexy kiss.

He set her back on her feet and smiled down at her. "You're bouncing back really well."

"Don't get me wrong, I'm still angry and upset. It overwhelms me sometimes. But being with you helps a lot. You take my mind off it. You make me see the possibilities of what we can have together. Something that's honest and built on mutual love and respect."

"I respect the hell out of the way you've handled this."

A car door slammed out front, drawing Sierra's attention to the bedroom window that looked out over the front of the house. She spotted Heather's car and all the anger she'd tucked away this morning came flooding back in a hot wave of rage.

"If you knew what I was thinking right now, you'd think a hell of a lot less of me."

Mason swore under his breath. "What the hell is she doing here?"

"Making things worse." Sierra didn't want to hate her sister, but that's exactly how she felt right now. "I'm not doing this with her."

Mason tilted his head, his face and eyes filled with sympathy. "She's your sister. You can't leave things like this forever. You two should talk."

"All I want to do right now is scream at her." Her whole body vibrated with pent-up anger. "No. She doesn't get to pick the time and place and just expect me to do what she wants. Not after what she's done."

"Absolutely not. I just want you to consider that eventually you two should talk and try to come to some sort of resolution."

"I get that mediating for your clients is a big part of your job, but I'm not ready to come to the table and hear anything she has to say."

"Fair enough. I'll tell her now isn't the time and send her away."

She followed Mason down the hall. "We spent the morning talking about our future, my moving in here with the boys, and she had to show up and ruin it."

Mason ignored the knock on the door and turned to her. "Nothing has changed about all we talked about this morning. That's all going to happen. We will have our life together and no one is going to come between us or ruin it for us."

She deflated. "I'm sorry."

"You don't have to apologize for feeling the way you do. I get it. If it were me, I'd be looking for a fight. You've at least maintained your composure."

"You didn't see my total meltdown on the beach yesterday."

He brushed his hand over her hair and held her head. "I hope you know I wanted to be with you."

She leaned into his hand. "I know. I just needed to be alone for a while."

"You never have to be alone again if you don't want to be."

Heather knocked again, this time softer, more hesitant.

Sierra glared at the door. "I'd appreciate it if you took care of that. I'm going to head over to Amy's and pick up the boys. I'm sure she's got a million questions, and I could use some time with her."

"Your sisters have always been important to you. You guys have always been really close. I'm sorry this is tearing you apart."

"Heather did it all on her own. She crossed a line and I'm not sure I will ever be able to forgive her for it."

"Maybe not now, but for the kids' sake, I know you'll try." Mason had a lot of faith in her.

She grabbed her purse and pulled out her keys. She turned back to him and gave him a half frown. "You're right, but right now, I don't have it in me to even look at her." She went up on tiptoe and kissed him softly. "Thank you for understanding and being so supportive."

"Always." He kissed her again, brushing his thumb across her cheek in a soft sweep as he stared into her eyes. "Bring the boys back here. Let's just spend some time together before we're back to work and life tomorrow."

"Sounds amazing. But you're cooking dinner."

He smiled. "Deal."

They shared another quick kiss, then she turned, opened the front door, barely spared Heather a look before she said, "No," and walked right past her and to her car.

Heather called after her, "I just want to talk."

Sierra climbed into her SUV, turned it on, and pulled out of the driveway without another thought for her bitch of a sister.

Instead she thought about what she and Mason talked about this morning. She focused on their future, not her messy past.

It may be too fast or too soon to move in with Mason, but she didn't care. She wanted to start the life Mason painted for her this morning with his plans to make her and the boys part of his life permanently.

In her mind, despite what happened with David, she believed that life with Mason would be a happily-ever-after kind of love.

She deserved that.

And she wouldn't let anything get in her way.

Chapter Thirty-Four

Heather stared at the back end of Sierra's car driving away. "She hates me."

"Yep." Mason didn't sugarcoat it at all. "Right now anyway. Can you blame her?"

"No." She sighed and faced Mason. "That's why I came. To apologize. To see if we can work this out."

"Nice try, showing up unexpectedly and forcing her to deal with you." The sarcasm came across loud and clear. "Don't you think she deserves some time to process all this?" Mason shook his head. "Yesterday she spent the morning memorializing David with Danny and Oliver, then she finds out he was having an affair with her sister and her niece is actually her boys' half sister. You expect her to accept all that in less than a day?"

"Can we talk about this inside?"

"I'm not inviting you in without Sierra here. I won't give her any reason to question me, especially when it comes to you."

"I'm not going to do anything. I just thought that maybe you and I—"

"Stop right there. There is no you and I. Sierra and I are together. We are going to be a family. Right now, that doesn't include you."

Heather's heart sank. "She's never going to talk to me, let alone forgive me, is she?"

"Do you blame her if she doesn't after what you did?"

"I'm sorry. I really never meant to hurt her."

"I'm sure she didn't even cross your mind." The harsh statement was unfortunately mostly true. "If she did, you didn't care enough to stop what you were doing."

I couldn't stop loving David.

Heather sighed. "I wasn't the only one who hurt her. David did, too, but I'm the only one everyone is mad at."

"That's not true. She's devastated by what David did to her and their children. He ruined their relationship and marriage. He had everything, but he turned his back on Sierra and what they'd built together."

"He wasn't happy. He wanted to be with me."

"Neither of those things excuses what he did or erases the hurt he's caused. For either of you. Sierra is devastated."

"How do you think I feel? He's gone. I loved him, too. I miss him, too. But I'm not allowed to show that because we weren't supposed to be together."

Mason eyed her. "Do you really mean you weren't supposed to be discovered?"

Yes. And no.

"He wanted to be with me." She kept telling herself that, but couldn't convince herself anymore that it was wholly true.

"He was never really yours. He got caught up in something exciting and thrilling in the moment but it ultimately left him feeling bad about himself and worried that he'd lose everything over something that didn't really mean anything to him." She wanted to deny that. "I've seen it a lot. A husband cheats think-ing it's just sex. It doesn't mean anything. He's got no real feel-ings for the woman. He still loves his wife. As long as she doesn't find out about it, it's no big deal. But women have intuition. They know their husband better than anyone. Maybe they don't want to see it, but they know. Sierra knew. And David sensed she knew. I bet he even let on to you that she was suspicious of him."

She spoke David's worst fear. "He thought she'd take the boys from him."

Mason dismissed that with a shake of his head. "The courts would allow him visitation and Sierra would never keep those boys from their father because she knows they needed him in their life. I bet what David feared was losing a brilliant, loving, kind, generous woman like Sierra."

"He had me."

"And you gave him a reason to always be in your life."

It took her a second to understand his meaning. "Hallee wasn't planned."

"Maybe not, but she sure did ensure you kept David coming back to you. He was coming back to you the night he died."

True. But . . . "That's not fair."

"No, it's not. Neither is what you did to Sierra."

"I want to make it right." She did, because she'd lost David and she didn't want to lose her sister, too.

"'Right'? What does that even mean? You can't change what you did or that you have a child by *her* husband."

She fell in love with the wrong, right man. She had a baby with him when he couldn't—or wouldn't, she sadly confessed to herself—be with her.

She never expected to be a single mom.

She never thought she'd lose David.

"I love Sierra, even if I've done a poor job of showing it. I want her to be happy. And if that is with you, then I wish you both the best." Heather sucked in a breath. "I'm embarrassed and sorry about my behavior yesterday. I'm sorry I put you in the middle of me and Sierra. I have a lot of making up to do. It won't be easy, but I want my sister back. I want our kids to grow up together."

"She's still sorting out her feelings. I don't know *if* or *when* she'll be able to consider talking to you or getting the kids together."

Heather appreciated that he'd given up that much, but hated the way he phrased it because it implied Sierra had no intention of keeping Heather in her life. It made her sad and the guilt piled on.

"For what it's worth, I think you'll be great for her and the boys." She shrugged. "That's all I was looking for, for me and Hallee."

"Look for it with someone who isn't already with someone else."

"Good advice." She meant it despite the mirth and sarcasm.

"I hope you take it." Mason sighed. "Look, I don't know if this can be fixed between you and Sierra. Right now, she doesn't want to hear anything you have to say. To her, it all sounds like excuses and empty apologies. She doesn't want to hurt the kids. She won't take it out on Hallee. And she doesn't want her boys to think less of David, or even you. She's not ready to have that talk with them. Until she is, I'm not sure she'll be ready to hear anything you have to say about it."

"Understandable. I always knew I'd have to explain to Hallee about who her father was and how we fell in love. We both look bad, but I want her to know that despite what David and I did, she was born out of real love. Sierra probably doesn't want to hear that, but it's true. I hope she can find it in her heart to understand I couldn't turn my back on that love and as much as I regret hurting her, I am incredibly grateful to have Hallee."

She didn't know how else to explain it, except that for all the bad she caused, she got something so great out of it.

"Thank you for listening to me and being so good to Sierra and her kids. I appreciate it. If she stays, maybe one day soon we'll be able to . . . well, maybe not settle this, but put it behind us. I really would like Hallee to know her brothers."

"In time, I think Sierra will want that, too. But getting there may take some time."

"I understand." She gave him a halfhearted smile. She hadn't accomplished what she'd come here to do, but maybe this was better. Mason would tell Sierra the details of their conversation. Maybe coming from him, she'd hear what Heather wanted her to know. Maybe she'd think about it. Sierra wasn't mean or vindictive. She'd come around eventually.

I hope.

"Please tell Sierra I'm not giving up, but I will give her some space."

"I'll tell her."

Heather nodded her good-bye and walked down the porch steps to her car. She'd pick up Hallee from the sitter and spend the rest of the day with her. She needed Hallee's sweet smile and unconditional love to see her through this dark time.

She'd been alone a long time, but she'd never felt this lonely. Her whole family would rally around Sierra. Her mom had already let her have it. Amy probably wouldn't waste any time saying her piece.

Heather had made herself the outcast in the family. She deserved their scorn.

She hoped to earn their forgiveness.

She loved her family and needed their support. Especially now.

Which meant she needed to show them she took responsibility for her actions.

Chapter Thirty-Five

S ierra stood in Amy's kitchen wondering if her sister had been swapped with an alien.

Rex stood at the sink filling the dishwasher. Amy didn't make a single comment, issue a demand he do it differently, or take over the task because no one could do anything like her. Rex appeared completely at ease. In fact, the atmosphere in the house felt different. The kids calmly sat at the island. Danny and Oliver worked on a chore chart. Amy stood between P.J.'s and Emma's chairs looking at a brand-new activities calendar they were filling in.

"P.J., you're green." Amy handed him a green marker. "Emma, you're dark pink."

Emma took her pen. "I only have two things each week."

Amy pointed to the calendar. "Fill in your activities. We'll use purple for the things you and your brother do together."

"Dad is blue, right?" P.J. rolled the marker across the counter to his dad, who stood drying his hands with a towel.

Rex stopped the pen from rolling off the counter with a flat hand and caught Amy's eye. "All set?" He glanced toward the open dishwasher.

Amy checked it out and nodded. "Thank you. Would you mind running it?"

"Sure." Rex turned and took a detergent cube from a tub under the sink, dropped it in the dispenser, slid the lid closed, pushed the dishwasher door up, hit the start button, and turned back to help with the calendar.

The kids finished their part. P.J. had soccer Tuesday and Thursday with a game on Saturday. Emma had dance class on Monday and Wednesday. They both had art class together on Thursday before P.J.'s soccer practice and swim class on Saturday morning before P.J.'s soccer game.

"No more music classes?" The calendar looked far less cluttered with events than the original one still up on the wall.

Amy put a hand on both of her kids' shoulders. "They chose the activities they like the most. We're cutting back so we have more time at home." Amy took the teal-colored pen and wrote Family Time on every Sunday of the calendar, then looked up at Rex. They shared a smile and Rex gave Amy a nod of approval.

Sierra's heart soared that Amy and Rex not only had talked out their problems but were working to make each other happy by making changes in their relationship.

Amy used the same color to write Date Night on every Thursday. This time when she and Rex shared a knowing look, her sister's cheeks pinked.

Aw. Sweet.

They needed more time together.

She and Mason should talk about their schedules and how they were going to work out date night and taking care of the boys. It would be nice to have help getting them to their activities or simply having Mason there with her to cheer them on at soccer or whatever they chose to do in the future.

Danny had already asked about baseball. She needed to get on that and sign him up. Mason used to play in high school. He could coach Danny at home.

And that thought solidified her decision to speak to the boys about moving in with Mason soon. He'd be such a great father and role model for Danny and Oliver.

Rex stepped around the counter and touched Amy's shoulder, that closeness they used to share back on full display. "Hey, babe, why don't you let me finish this with the kids. When we're done, I promised them a kickball game in the front yard. You and Sierra can sit out back and catch up."

Code for *Go ahead and talk about Heather and the affair.*

Amy gave Rex a quick kiss, ruffled her kids' hair, and went to the fridge. She pulled out an open bottle of white wine and selected two glasses from the cupboard. "Come on, sis, let's talk."

Sierra went to the boys and gave them each a kiss on the head.

Oliver held up his chore chart. "Aunt Amy says I should get fifty cents for each chore, but I should ask for seventy-five and negotiate. I don't know what that means, but I want an allow ants."

Sierra sent her sister a disgruntled frown and glare.

Amy stuck her tongue out at her. "Hold out for the seventy-five cents, kiddo. Mommy can afford it with her awesome job. I bet if you ask Mason for chores at the ranch, he'd pay you a dollar."

Sierra scoffed. "Amy! Really?"

Amy winked at Danny and Oliver and headed out the back door.

Sierra stared at both the boys. "We'll discuss *allowances* later. Be good. Have fun with Uncle Rex."

Rex finished tearing down the old calendar and replaced it with the new one, a satisfied smile on his face when he studied it. "That's more like it."

She bet he appreciated that he had a spot on the calendar now and so did Date Night and Family Time.

"Who's up for kickball?"

All the kids scrambled off their stools and headed for the front door.

Rex caught her arm. "Hey, I'm sorry you're going through this. I had no idea about David and Heather. It sucks. I hope you're okay."

She put her hand over his. "Thank you. I will be."

Rex gave her a half smile and headed out after the kids.

Sierra walked out to the back to find her sister, knowing what she'd just said to Rex would be true one day.

She would be okay. She just needed time to let the feelings come, to reevaluate her life and what happened, and put it into perspective.

One day it wouldn't hurt this much.

There'd come a time when the anger didn't rush in and consume her.

One day it would be a memory that didn't sting so sharply.

Her happiness would overshadow the pain and betrayal.

"So I spoke to Mom this morning after she went to see Heather. We hate Heather, right?" Amy held up a glass of wine from her Adirondack chair in the garden.

Sierra took the glass, fell into the other chair, stared at the beautiful flowers, focusing on the pretty pink roses, and sighed. "I don't want to hate David or Heather, but they make it damn hard not to."

Amy clinked her glass to Sierra's. "Bastard. Bitch. What the fuck were they thinking?"

Sierra appreciated her sister's outrage. "I don't know." She took a sip of the sweet and smooth peach wine, loving the flavor and crispness. She needed more sweet in her life.

"It hurts." Her chest grew heavy with thoughts of what her sister and husband had done, scenarios of how they carried out their trysts, and how she'd been oblivious to it all. "I think it would be easier if it was some stranger, a random woman I didn't know. But Heather . . ."

"It keeps circling my mind. How could she? Why? How did it even happen?"

"That's the thing. I have some of the details, but it doesn't really matter how, when, why. They did it without thinking about what would happen when they were discovered."

Amy turned her gaze from the flowers, focused on her, and put her hand on Sierra's arm. "They had a child together."

"Hallee." Just saying her name hurt Sierra's heart something fierce. That poor girl. Caught in the middle of all this. The living reminder of how her parents hurt and betrayed Sierra. An innocent child. "I don't know what to do about her. She's Danny and Oliver's half sister. How do I explain that to them?"

"They're too young to understand what really happened. Maybe it's better to tell them now in a simple way. She's their sister. They have the same father. Leave it at that. When they're older and they understand more, they'll ask questions and you can tell them more of the real story."

Sierra thought that might be the best way to handle it.

"But if you tell them, they'll want to see Hallee, which means . . ." Amy let the rest go unsaid.

She'd have to see Heather. She'd look at Hallee and bring back all the hurt.

She didn't want to keep reliving this nightmare. But she also didn't want to punish the kids or keep them apart.

"David and Heather have put me in an impossible position. If I don't let the boys see their sister, I'm the bad guy. If I do, I have to deal with Heather and the affair coming up over and over again for me."

"Well, if you're okay with the boys seeing Hallee, they can have playdates here, then you won't have to deal with Heather. Anyway, David left our sister holding the bag on this one." Amy sipped her wine and looked at her over the rim of the glass. "Do you think if he'd lived, he'd have left you for Heather?"

She'd asked herself that a hundred times. "I don't know. My gut says he wanted to stay with me and the boys. That's why he tried so hard to hide the affair." Sierra shrugged. "Or he just put off telling me, trying to avoid a fight. That's what we did . . . avoid things."

"Been there. Done that."

She studied Amy. "But you and Rex are back on the same page."

"And better than ever. The past week or so has been great. We've found our way back to each other. I feel like I can go to him with stuff now. He feels like I listen to him now." Amy smiled. "I'm trying anyway. We both are."

"The closeness is back."

"Great sex will do that." Amy's bright smile disappeared. "I'm sorry. That was insensitive given what you're going through."

"Hey, I like great sex. I just prefer my husband is having it with me." Sierra couldn't believe she was able to joke about this, but it felt good to find some humor in all the drag-me-down feelings running through her.

"She really fucked up."

Sierra took another sip of wine. "Yes, she did. And the thought of running into her, other people finding out and gossiping . . ." She didn't know if she could take it.

"Fuck them. You know what people are going to be talking about? The fact that you landed the hottest, most eligible bachelor in the state."

Sierra chuckled. "Mason has been a light in all this dark mess."

Amy met her gaze. "And you've been a light in mine. I've missed you. I need you to tell me when I'm turning into a batshit crazy control freak. And"—Amy held up her glass—"who else will have afternoon wine with me?"

"I'm sure Rex would love to sit out here with you sipping wine."

Amy's smile softened into a dreamy grin. "I met him for lunch this week. It was so nice to sit together and have a nice meal and talk about anything but the kids."

"Mason and I really haven't been together that long—"

Amy waved that away. "You've known each other forever."

"Which is why it's so easy to be with him. We know each

other. We connect. When I'm with him, I'm really happy. Before I knew about"—she circled her hand in the air to encompass the affair and Heather and David without having to say it again—"I felt guilty that I liked being with Mason so much."

"You felt like you were somehow betraying David." Amy closed her eyes and shook her head, then opened them. "Don't. Even without the affair, David would have wanted you to be happy after he died. He wouldn't have wanted you to stop living your life. He'd want someone for you and the boys. I know that."

So did Sierra, but now all her thoughts were muddled up with the affair and she second-guessed her memories and what she thought David would say and want for her and the boys.

"Since I found out about the affair, I don't feel guilty about seeing Mason anymore. After all, David had already left me before he died. Well, I guess I feel a *little* guilty about being with someone else when the past is so present at the same time."

Amy leaned forward and put her hand on Sierra's knee. "Give yourself a break. David died a year ago. You grieved. It's okay to move on. Just because you know about the affair now doesn't mean you have to start the process of grieving him and your relationship all over again. The clock doesn't start over. Yes, process what happened, but don't sacrifice the happiness you could have with Mason. If you want to be with him, *be* with him. Love him. Let him love you, Sierra. You deserve it. Don't let them take that from you."

"Mason wants us to move in with him."

"Do it. The best revenge against the ones who hurt you is to live your life, happy and carefree, doing what you love, being with the one you love, and having a great life with your family."

"Heather is part of my family."

Amy sat quietly contemplating the scenery, lost in thought. "I don't know what to do about Heather. I'm angry she hurt you. I want to understand why, but I don't think anything she says will satisfy that question because who can accept that she was simply selfish and heartless? What she did was despicable. But would I judge her so harshly if she had an affair with a married man we didn't know? What if the wife was some other woman? How would I feel then? I'd be upset by her actions, but would I feel this disappointed and disheartened?" Amy locked gazes with her. "It's because she did this to you that I find it hard to see a path to redemption for her. I'm not sure that I can forgive her, and I'm not the one she hurt."

"I feel guilty that this has fractured the family and that it affects your relationship with her and her relationship with Mom."

"She's the one who should feel guilty."

"I can't help it. I thought moving back here would mean we'd all share our lives. Our kids would grow up together. We'd have birthday parties and holidays together. It would be so fun and the kids would take those memories into the future and have that with their kids. The years and distance made our relationships less intimate, but I hoped we'd grow closer again and things would be like they used to be."

"Where we bickered but loved each other." Amy smiled, nostalgia in her eyes along with the humor in that all-too-true statement.

"Yes. We three are so different from each other, but we always managed to get through the rough patches."

"Because we're family."

"Now what?" Sierra asked Amy, because she really didn't know how to get through this, this time. An "I'm sorry" wouldn't fix it. She couldn't look at Heather without thinking about what happened. She couldn't trust her.

"I wish I knew, sis, because this sucks." Amy downed the last of her wine in one gulp. "All I know is you can't let what happened stop you and Mason from moving forward with your relationship. Marry him. Make a beautiful blond-haired, green-eyed baby with him. Live on that ranch and spend every day grateful for your second chance and the happiness you deserve."

Amy painted a beautiful picture of what could be.

No. What *would* be. Because Sierra wanted that life.

And nothing was going to stand in her way of having it. Not even herself.

"I think I'll talk to the kids tonight about moving in with Mason."

"Great idea. While you're at it, pack them up and just show up on his doorstep."

Sierra laughed. "Mason wants to fix up two of the rooms in the house and surprise them."

"See, that's a good man, thinking about making it fun for the boys. He wants them to see that he wants them there. You can't give up a guy like that."

"I have no intention of letting him get away again." But she did want to find a way to put all this other stuff in the past where it belonged, so she could move on with Mason with a clear and open heart.

Amy checked her watch, then settled back in the seat, closed her eyes, and turned her face to the sun. "I've been making myself learn to do nothing but relax."

"Self-care is important."

"I'm not very good at it yet, but I'm trying. Rex and I are taking the kids out to dinner tonight. I don't have anything to do until then that absolutely has to be done."

"I bet Rex and the kids will play for at least another twenty minutes." Sierra settled back in her chair much the same way as Amy and let the sun warm her face.

"It's going to be okay," Amy whispered.

The talk with her sister helped Sierra to settle many of the thoughts running around her mind, but sitting in the silence out in the garden with that whispered promise eased her heart even more. It came with all her sister's love and understanding that there was no easy answer, except to move forward and accept that eventually everything would work out the way it was supposed to because Sierra had people who loved her in her life.

Chapter Thirty-Six

Sierra stood outside the car, the boys ready to go home and in their car seats, and stared up at Mason. "Thank you for dinner."

"My pleasure. I'm glad your talk with Amy earlier helped."

Sierra put her hand on his chest. "It affirmed for me that moving forward is the best way to put the past behind me. I don't want to get lost in what happened, the why, the how, the what-ifs. It's just so overwhelming and disheartening. It takes all the energy out of me. I loved coming back here and watching you and the boys man the barbecue."

"They need to know how to make the perfect burger."

"I think they've got it now, thanks to your expert tutelage." She couldn't help the smile. The boys had hung on Mason's every word and off his arms and back as they tried to wrestle him to the ground while the burgers cooked.

Mason brushed his fingers across her lips. "I love it when you smile."

"You always knew how to make me smile. Now, you do it for the boys."

"They're little monkeys." He stretched his back, pretending he was sore. "I'm getting old."

She tapped him in the gut, her hand hitting rock-hard

muscle. The ranch kept him in great shape. "Whatever you say, grandpa."

He locked his hands at her back and pulled her close. "I'm not too old to sweep a pretty girl off her feet." He did just that, grabbing her waist and picking her right up.

She giggled and clasped her arms around his neck. "Put me down."

He hugged her tighter. "You don't mean that."

In fact, she held on and leaned in close, her mouth an inch from his, their eyes locked. "I want you to hold on to me this time."

The mirth in Mason's eyes turned to sincerity. "I won't ever let you go." He kissed her softly, then broke the kiss and stared at her again. "I won't ever give you a reason to leave. I promise, Sierra, you're all I want or will ever need."

Tears sprang to her eyes. She hadn't known how much she needed to hear that until Mason gave her the words. "How can my heart be broken and battered and so full of love all at the same time?"

"Because you care. About me, the boys, your family, and even David and Heather. If you didn't care, it wouldn't hurt so much. And because you use your whole heart in everything you do, including the way you love me. I feel it, sweetheart. I'm humbled by it. I want more of it. I can't wait for you to move in and for us to be a family."

She pressed her forehead to his. "Soon. I promise. I don't want to wait, either."

He kissed her one last time, keeping things relatively tame because they had eyes on them. He set her on her feet, opened the door for her, waited for her to climb in before he looked into the back seat. "I'll see you guys tomorrow."

"Night, Mason." Danny waved.

"Bye." Oliver yawned.

"I better get them to bed. It's back to school tomorrow. Don't work too hard."

Mason remembered the case files he'd brought home and hadn't touched this weekend. "I won't." If she wasn't staying with him, then he'd spend the next couple hours in his office, alone with his files instead of her. "Call me if you need me."

She smiled. "I will. Promise."

When she was home, alone, in the quiet, that's when it was the hardest to shut off the thoughts. He knew something about that, because though he'd get his work done, the rest of the night he'd be thinking about her, them, and what he wanted their life to look like for their future.

He closed her door, waited for her to turn the car toward the main road, and waved good-bye before heading in for the night.

Drawn to the brilliant stars overhead, he looked up and stared in wonder at the sheer number of them. He picked one that seemed to wink at him.

I wish for a long and happy life with Sierra by my side. I want to watch those boys grow up into good men and find someone to love who loves them the way I love Sierra and she loves me. I want all of us to be happy.

More than anything, he wanted Sierra to find peace here on the ranch with him.

* * *

Sierra walked in the front door behind the boys and spotted her mom cleaning up the toys the boys left out. "Mom, I'll do that."

"I'm almost done." Her mother tossed toy cars into the bin and pulled apart the racetrack.

Sierra helped the boys out of their zip-up hoodies and hung them on the coatrack. "Go upstairs and brush your teeth. Change into your pj's and I'll be up in a few minutes to read books."

Her mom finished pulling apart the last piece of the track and tossed the two plastic pieces into the bin. "Lord, it's been a long time since I had to pick up after kids." She put the toy bin next to the other two the boys had brought down from upstairs.

"You won't have to do it much longer."

Her mother gave her a knowing smile. "Is that man of yours getting impatient?"

A smile tugged at her lips. "Honestly, we both are."

Her mom put her hand on the coffee table and used it to help support her while she rose from sitting on her feet. She rubbed at her sore knees before she stood straight. "It's been just as long since I spent that much time on the floor. I hope Mason knows what he's in for."

Sierra listened to the water running upstairs while the boys brushed their teeth. "We talked this morning about turning two of the rooms in his house into the boys' rooms."

"They'll love that. Lord knows he's got the space and then some in that big house." Dede studied her for a moment. "I take it things with Amy went well."

"Believe it or not, she had some great advice. She made me feel better. She thinks moving forward is the best thing for me."

Her mom nodded. "I agree." Her eyebrows drew together. "I spoke to Heather."

"She stopped by Mason's but I left without really talking to her."

"I hope she apologized to him about her behavior."

"She did."

"I understand your frustration with her, Sierra. What she did . . . It makes no sense, and yet, I understand what she wanted."

"You may want a chocolate bar, but stealing it still comes with consequences."

"She's feeling those consequences. And I understand you need time and distance. But I'd like you to consider something that I hadn't really thought about until I spoke to her. I was so angry about what she did, I didn't think about the similarities you share."

Sierra wasn't sure she wanted to hear this.

Her heart pounded as the answers came to mind and her mother spoke out loud.

"You both lost the man you love. You both have children who will grow up without their father. You both have to explain to them how they are connected. You both have to keep David's memory alive for your kids." Dede held up her hand, cutting off words Sierra couldn't get out her constricted throat anyway. "I know it's the same but different. I just wanted you to think about that. Heather scolded me for not understanding that she has her feelings, too. I guess what I'm saying is that you both have a side. She was wrong to do what she did, but she did love him. Not that that's an excuse, but . . . I don't know. It's so hard to articulate and reason out."

Sierra bit back the anger and focused on her mother and how hard she tried to make Sierra understand that somewhere in all this mess, with a little sympathy and understanding, Sierra could see her sister as a woman who'd loved and lost and who grieved like she had once. Heather faced a future similar to hers and a time when she'd have to explain David to Hallee and how their relationship started and ended. It was a tragic love story that might have ended differently if it had been born of truth and honesty instead of mired in lies and deception.

"No matter how you explain it, what she did was wrong. I know you want us all to be the way we used to be. I just don't think that's possible. But . . ." She took a deep breath and tried to wrap her head around the next words she gave her mother even if she didn't wholly believe in them yet. "One day, I hope, Heather and I can understand each other and love more and hurt less."

Her mom's eyes overflowed with tears. "Yes. I'd like that very much." Dede closed the distance and hugged her close. "Thank you, Sierra, for keeping your heart open to possibility."

Sierra hugged her mom back. "I'm still angry. I still want to kill her. But I feel it a little less today than I did yesterday."

Heather had been coddled and pampered far too long. Not anymore.

Sierra was taking care of herself first this time.

Her mom released her, but touched her hand to Sierra's cheek. "I love you, sweetheart. I hope you know that I want the very best for you."

"I know you do. I know you want that equally for Heather."

"Well, maybe she gets ten percent less than you now."

Sierra appreciated the teasing tone, but knew her mother didn't mean it. And it was okay, because she'd have a hard time not wanting both her sons to be as happy as they could be, either.

"Does that mean you'll miss me when I move to Mason's?"

"I will, but still, it'll be nice to have the house to myself again. I hope my grandsons find their way here often."

"I bet they will." After all, they only had one wide pasture to cross to get here. She smiled for her mom. "And so will I."

"That's a promise, then."

Sierra nodded. "Good night, Mom."

"Good night, sweetheart."

Sierra made it up the stairs just as the boys turned off their bedroom light, leaving the room in shadows, the heads of their beds bathed in a soft glow from the night-light.

Danny held two books on his chest. Oliver sat on Danny's bed, waiting for her to take her place next to Danny so Oliver could sink between them.

"Mom?" Danny studied her, his eyes serious.

"Yeah?"

"Is everything okay? Everyone seems upset about something."

Of course the boys had picked up on the strange vibes. She tried to hide her anger, but they knew something was off.

"You're right. I discovered some upsetting news when we were at Mason's house."

"Did Aunt Heather make you mad?" Oliver played with the ends of her long hair.

"Yes. She did. She took something that belonged to me."

Danny turned on his pillow to face her. "I hate it when Oliver takes my stuff."

Oliver crossed his little arms over his chest. "I do not."

"Yes, you do! All the time."

"Enough. Anyway, it made me angry and I needed to be by myself for a little while to think about it. But then I talked to Mason and I felt better." She wanted to turn this conversation to the future. "He made me think about everything that's happened and all we've lost, and you know what? It made me think of all the new things we can have now."

"Like new Legos." Oliver looked up at her, hopeful he'd get a new set soon.

"Maybe. But I was thinking about us moving into a new place and you two having your own rooms." She didn't give them time to ask questions about where and when. "What color would you like your room to be?"

"Blue." Danny's favorite color.

"Green and orange." Oliver could never pick just one.

"Those are great colors for your rooms."

"We're moving in with Mason, aren't we?" Danny eyed her, a soft smile on his face.

"What do you think about that?"

"It would be awesome!" Danny's smile grew and brightened his eyes. "He said if I keep working at it, I'll be able to ride one of the horses by myself soon."

"I want to, too, but he said only in the ring and only if he holds the rope. I told him Horse won't run away with me, but he didn't believe me." Oliver scrunched his face, not happy with that at all.

Sierra tried to hold back a laugh. "He's concerned about your safety, honey. That's all."

"I can ride by myself." Oliver frowned far too grumpily for such a sweet little boy.

"Well, if we live with Mason and you get much better at riding I'm sure it won't be long before you can ride Horse all by yourself."

Oliver nodded his approval of that like it would happen when he said so. She let him believe that for now.

Danny fidgeted, trying to dig deeper into the mattress. "Are you going to marry him?"

"He hasn't asked me, but I hope so. I love him a lot." She wanted the boys to know that.

"He watches you all the time. At first I didn't like it, but . . . I like the way he looks at you now."

Mason had won Danny's approval.

It touched her to know her son had been looking out for her.

Sierra brushed her fingers over Danny's hair, understanding completely. "Loving Mason doesn't change that I loved your dad. My heart is big enough to love both of them, just like I love both of you."

It wasn't easy to say that out loud, but in her heart she knew that the love she had for David, the love that created their two perfect sons, was still buried deep inside, waiting for the day when she could look back on it and remember the good times they shared, not just the bad stuff she discovered after his death.

"It'll be fun to live with Mason. He's good at bedtime books. He does voices." Oliver handed her the first book, his eyes already drooping.

"I guess if we move in with him you'll want him to read all the time."

Oliver shook his head. "You can share."

She chuckled. "That's a great idea."

Danny turned his head away.

"What is it?" She waited him out, because Danny had always been the one who took his time.

"Does this mean we won't celebrate Dad's birthday and stuff?"

She brushed her fingers over his hair again. "We will celebrate it every year. David is still your father."

"Mason is extra," Oliver said, then snuggled into her side.

"Okay." Danny nodded his chin toward the book in her hand, ready for the story and to move forward with their life with Mason.

So simple. Easy. Decision made.

She wished being an adult was as easy as being a kid.

Chapter Thirty-Seven

"A re you ready?" Mason wasn't sure *he* was ready for this.

Danny stared down at him from atop the horse. "I've got this."

Mason kept his grip on the horse's bridle and glanced over his shoulder at Sierra, who watched from the other side of the small arena, her phone at the ready to snap a picture. "All right, start at a walk, then you can trot once around the circle." Mason's heart raced, but he let loose and stepped back so Danny could kick his mount into a walk.

Danny glanced at Mason, making sure he'd really let him go on his own. "I'm doing it." He sat straight in the saddle, the reins loose in his hands, and moved with the horse.

Mason let out his breath, relief swamping his system. So far, so good.

"Go, Danny!" Sierra cheered, taking a picture.

Oliver stood beside her waiting his turn. Big brother got to go first. Oliver wasn't happy about it, but Mason hoped one day he'd have a little sister or brother who wanted to do everything Oliver got to do first.

Mason had plans to make Sierra his wife. But first, he needed to make sure the boys were okay with it. If their questions about when they were going to move in said anything, they were ready to be a family, but he had to be sure.

The last two weeks had been quiet. Normal.

When he was home alone in the evening, he worked on their rooms. Sierra bought the boys new bedding and desks. He took care of the painting. Next on his list, he wanted to tackle the bathroom.

For that, he had a contractor coming this week. He also wanted to do something for Sierra to make the house feel like hers, too. She mentioned how much she loved the kitchen in her old house, how cheerful and soothing she found it, with its pale green walls, white counters, and dark cabinets. He had the dark cabinets, but the granite counters were earth tones, gold, brown, tans, that wouldn't go with a bright pale green. So he'd ordered new countertops, and also a bigger sink, because she complained how small his was when the boys generated dirty dishes at an astronomical rate. He'd also asked the contractor to build a raised garden bed off the kitchen door so Sierra could plant a vegetable garden like she used to have in Napa.

They were little things, but he hoped it helped her understand that this was her house, too. He hoped it allowed her to feel free to change things to make the house hers.

They were taking their time while working toward making a life together happen.

Mason liked the thoughtfulness behind how they were doing this, but he really wanted Sierra, Danny, and Oliver moved in and settled with him as soon as possible. He'd waited a long time for a wife and family. He wanted it now. His excitement and enthusiasm grew each day.

And today, after the promised horseback riding with the boys, he planned to take them to get one of the things he needed to make Sierra his.

Danny kicked the horse into a trot, kept his balance, back straight, reins loose, wearing a big smile that lit up his face. He was a natural. Soon, he'd be riding like he was born to the saddle. They'd all be going on family rides.

It made Mason think of all the times when they were teenagers when he'd found Sierra haunting the stables, spending time with the horses, ready to go out with him at even a hint that he wanted to ride.

Something about having her near just always felt right, and now having them all here made him happier than he'd ever been.

Sierra walked up beside him as he kept a close eye on Danny. "You look pleased."

"He's doing great."

"You taught him well."

"I always knew I wanted this." He indicated Danny up on the horse, Oliver hanging on to the fencing, cheering on his brother, and her right beside him. "I just didn't know how much."

She smiled up at him. "I didn't know what I was going to do when I moved back, except the abstract, find a place for me and the kids. I never imagined it would be this place. With you. I didn't dream that big. You've helped me to allow myself to want more."

He put his arm around her waist and drew her to his side. "From now on, it's you and me. Let's always dream big."

She snuggled into his side. "This is great already."

Oliver ran up to them. "My turn."

Mason picked him up and settled him on his hip. "You ready?"

Oliver nodded.

Mason was ready, too, for a life filled with moments like this.

"Danny, rein him in and come to a full stop."

Danny gently pulled the reins, bringing his horse to a halt. He patted the horse's neck, then leaned over and hugged him. He sat up straight, keeping hold of the reins. "That was awesome!"

Mason approached and set Oliver on his feet next to the horse, then said to Danny, "Dismount like I taught you."

Danny swung his leg over the back of the horse and dropped to the ground. He pulled the reins over the horse's head and stood next to him, holding the horse still.

"Very good."

Danny beamed him a smile, pleased with the praise. "You can do this," he encouraged his brother.

Mason took the reins from Danny. "Help your brother mount." He'd taught Danny how to help Oliver into the saddle. Mason could pick him up and settle him atop the horse, but he wanted the boys to learn to work together.

Danny cupped his hands. Oliver grabbed the saddle, one hand on the front, the other on the back, put his foot in Danny's hands, and pushed himself up, laying his belly over the saddle, then swinging his leg over the horse and righting himself in a seated position. He clutched the pommel and held on. "Got it."

"That's great teamwork."

Danny adjusted the stirrups so Oliver's feet rested in them.

Mason pulled the reins over the horse's head and handed them to Oliver, who adjusted them in his hand like he'd been taught.

"Ready?"

Oliver smiled and nodded, his focus straight ahead.

Mason made a big show of letting go and holding his hands up. "You're on your own."

Sierra snapped a photo.

"Walk him around the circle," Mason coaxed, holding his breath but confident Oliver would ride as well as his big brother.

Oliver lightly tapped his heels into the horse's side.

Mason chose Kit for his mild temperament. Still, putting one of the boys on him and letting them loose put a knot in his stomach. If something happened, he'd never forgive himself.

But Oliver rode like a champ. He kept the pace slow, happy to just be in the saddle and on his own.

"I'm doing it." Oliver pulled the reins gently to the left to make the horse turn along the circle curve. Not that he really needed to—the horse had to follow the fence—but Oliver was doing great. Mason couldn't be more proud.

They gave Oliver a good ten minutes to ride circles around them. His smile never wavered.

"Does this mean we can ride out in the pastures with you on our own now?"

Mason planted his hand on Danny's riding helmet and stared down at him. "One step at a time. Oliver isn't quite ready. You both need a little more practice. But soon."

Just as he said that, Oliver got tired of slow circles and kicked the horse into a nice trot. At first his eyes went wide with surprise, but then he laughed and enjoyed the faster pace.

Sierra took a video, then looked up at him. "What were you saying?"

"They're fearless."

"You gave them the tools and training to know they can do it."

He gave her a worried look. "We're in trouble with them. You know that, right?"

"I think we can handle it."

He hoped so. Because if anything happened to one of the boys, he'd be devastated.

This is what it feels like to be a parent.

It hit him all at once. He'd accepted that the boys came with Sierra. He welcomed them in his life. He thought of them as his. But for the first time it really hit him what that meant. A lifetime of worry and hoping that they had safe and happy lives.

Sierra looked up at him and read his mind. "Scary, right? You want everything good for them, but there's so much that could go wrong, so much that you can't control. Including that they're their own people and have a mind and will of their own."

"Can we lock them up until they're at least thirty?"

She laughed. "They're good kids. Discipline and boundaries. The rest is just hoping they use their heads and hearts."

Oliver brought the horse around in front of them and reined in like he'd been riding forever. He turned to his mom with another big smile. "Did you see?"

"I saw it all, baby. You were fantastic."

Mason felt like he'd lost at least a year off his life worrying about the boys, but he had to admit, they rode well and followed all his directions and rules.

He was so impressed with Oliver, he plucked him right out of the saddle and swung him around. "Excellent job." He grinned down at Danny. "You, too." He set Oliver down next to his brother. "I think this calls for a guys-only lunch in town."

He'd already spoken to Sierra about taking the boys for a couple hours. Time enough for her to decorate the boys' rooms with all the things she'd bought for them.

"Yes!" the boys said in unison, then turned to their mom. "Please."

"Okay, but you need to go up to the house and wash your hands before you go."

The boys took off for the house.

With an arm around Sierra, Mason took the horse's reins and walked with her and Kit back toward the stables. "We're so close to really making this happen."

"The boys are going to love their new rooms."

"I mean everything. You and me. A life together."

She smiled up at him. "I can't wait."

* * *

Mason had no intention of making her wait long. Mostly because he was impatient to make her his wife.

Danny and Oliver demolished a cheeseburger, fries, and shakes. Chocolate for Danny. Vanilla with caramel sauce for Oliver.

Mason finished his burger, but he'd barely tasted it with his stomach tied in knots and filled with butterflies. "So, guys. I thought we'd stop at a store before we head home and buy your mom something."

Danny sucked on the straw, but with barely any shake left, all he did was make loud gurgling noises. "What?"

Oliver stared at him, waiting patiently for the answer.

Mason dove in. "I love your mom. You know that, right?"

Two dark heads bobbed across from him.

"We've talked about us living together and being a family."

"Mom said soon, but so far nothing's happened," Danny pointed out.

"Right. Your mom and I are working on it. But I want to make sure your mom knows moving in means a lot more than just us sharing a house."

Both boys' heads tipped to the side, their eyes filled with questions.

"I want her to be my wife."

"She said you guys might get married." Oliver stared at him, letting him know they'd covered this and to get on to something new.

"I'm going to ask your mom to marry me, but before I do, I wanted to make sure that you're both okay with that."

"I'm pretty sure that's what she wants." Danny abandoned the empty shake and pushed the glass away. "She smiles a lot more now. So that's good."

Oliver nodded his agreement at that assessment of their mom and Mason's relationship.

He'd obviously stressed about this talk a lot more than needed. The boys were happy their mom was happy. They liked being with him. Sierra and he had laid the foundation for the boys to know this was coming and they accepted it because they were all happy being together.

"Do you guys want to help me pick out a ring?"

Both boys sat up straighter.

Danny's eyes filled with excitement. "Really?"

"What kind?" Oliver asked.

"A sparkly one."

They slid out of their side of the booth, ready to get the job done. He thought about asking Amy to help him with the perfect ring for Sierra, but he wanted the boys to be a part of everything they did, including getting engaged.

Mason tossed some bills on the table to cover their lunch and the tip and ushered the boys out of the diner and across the street to the jewelry store. He'd gotten several recommendations from the ladies who worked in his office as well as a couple clients. The place was pricey but they were known for their custom designs. He wanted Sierra to have something special.

The boys walked along the cases, checking out all the pieces.

"May I help you?" the woman behind the counter asked, smiling at him and keeping an eye on the boys.

"I'd like to see your engagement rings."

Her smile widened. "Of course. They're at the end." She waved her hand toward the back of the store and walked along with him that way. She stopped in front of a case filled with diamond rings in all kinds of shapes and sizes. Some simple. Others ornate and ostentatious.

The boys flanked him and stared into the case.

Oliver looked up at him. "Very sparkly." He pointed at a ring that had about thirty diamonds. It was huge. "That one."

Mason inspected it for a moment, then scrunched his lips into a half frown. "I see why you like it. It's got a lot of sparkle, but I think your mom might like something simpler." He glanced at the saleswoman. "She'd probably like something classic, but . . . pretty." He didn't know how to explain it.

Danny pointed to a set of three rings. "That one."

Oliver stared, too. "Yes. That's it." He leaned down and pressed his face to the glass, then looked up at Mason. "Get that one."

The woman opened the case and pulled out the three rings stacked on a cylindrical holder. Mason loved the classic round diamond solitaire, but the two bracketing bands really made it special. The gold had been molded to look like a twining vine set with four blue diamond-shaped sapphires on each band.

"It's a three-carat certified diamond. Marquis-cut sapphires in the bands. The set together is classic, delicate, and very pretty with that standout diamond." She turned the dangling price tag. "The GIA certification details as well as the price."

He expected the hefty price tag and didn't even blink or hesitate when he realized he could buy a car for the amount of the rings. If he'd been here alone, he'd have picked this set for Sierra. That the boys picked it, too, for her made it even better.

He thought he might have to steer the boys to something that would suit Sierra, but they knew what their mom would like just as well as he did.

Oliver seized Mason's hand and pulled it down so he could inspect the rings up close. Danny hovered over them, too.

"Are they good enough for your mom?"

"She'll really like it," Danny confirmed.

"Very sparkly." Oliver touched his finger to the diamond, then moved Mason's hand so the diamond caught the light and sparkled even more.

Mason glanced up at the clerk. "We'll take them."

"A beautiful choice. She'll love it." The woman looked at both boys. "You guys have great taste. That's my favorite set."

The boys stood taller, pride lighting their eyes.

"Thanks for your help, guys. I couldn't have done this without you. I really wanted to be sure I got your mom the very best."

"I can't wait to give it to her." Oliver clasped his hands at his chest.

Mason handed the rings along with his credit card over to the saleswoman. "Um, listen, buddy, we need to keep this a secret for a little while. I want to ask your mom to marry me in a special way."

"When?" Danny asked.

"I was thinking next weekend." The house would be done and ready for them to move in. He wanted his ring on Sierra's finger when that happened so she'd know he meant for them to be together forever.

"Do you guys think you can keep a secret that long? No hints. No telling her what we bought, or that I'm going to ask her to marry me."

Danny and Oliver both looked a little reticent about having to wait but they nodded.

"I'll need your help with the proposal, too."

That perked them up.

"You think you can help me surprise her?"

Both boys nodded, their heads bouncing up and down with their renewed excitement.

Mason signed the sales slip.

The clerk opened the beautiful wood box, revealing the three rings inside, cushioned in white velvet. "Congratulations."

He smiled, knowing that Sierra's yes was a given, but still nervous about making the proposal perfect for her.

The woman placed the box inside a small white bag with the jewelry store's logo on it. "I hope you have a long and happy life together."

Mason held the bag by the strings, took both boys in hand, and walked out of the store with them beside him, excited to give Sierra the rings they'd picked for her and so ready to start the rest of his life with her.

Chapter Thirty-Eight

Sierra met her mom at the bottom of the stairs. Something in her eyes made Sierra suspicious.

"Is everything okay? Where are the boys?" They were supposed to go horseback riding with Mason before they surprised the boys with their redecorated rooms.

"Today's the day." Her mom looked both happy and sad about them moving into Mason's house.

"We've been talking about it for weeks. Mason says all the work is finished at his place, though he hasn't let me come over and see any of it this past week."

"It'll be a surprise for all of you." Dede touched her arm. "You've been so resilient. I'm amazed at how well you've managed to deal with everything. I know it hasn't been easy, but I see how hard you try to stay focused on what you want and the future."

"It's the only thing I can do. Being with Mason makes it easier to let it go and move on."

"He makes you happy."

Sierra didn't understand the trace of a question in that statement, but it was easy to reassure her mom. "Yes. So happy. I see him with the boys and I fall deeper in love with him. He's made us a priority in his life." Mason still worked hard, but now instead of spending late hours at his office because he didn't have anything pulling him home, he was happy to find a work-life balance for himself.

Her heart melted every time she saw him and his eyes lit up. Then he'd give her a wide smile and kiss her like he hadn't seen her in forever.

She loved talking about their day over dinner and how they traded off reading stories to the boys at night. They'd done that here at her mom's place this past week, but she imagined them doing it at Mason's from now on.

The ranch would be their home.

And she couldn't wait.

"Mason loves us. I'm excited about our future. So are the boys. They light up around him. They even mimic him." She smiled to herself. Every night Mason stood to clear his plate from the table and the boys did the same thing and followed him into the kitchen. Mason rinsed his plate and put it in the dishwasher. The boys followed his lead and did the same.

They looked up to him.

They wanted to be like him.

She loved that.

With Mason, everything seemed easy and possible.

"I just want you to be happy." Her mom searched her face for any sign she had second thoughts about moving in with him.

"Mom, I was happy when David and I moved in together and started our family. With Mason . . . I wish I could express how joyfully blissful I am. I think about him and I smile. I see him and all I want to do is hug him and kiss him and just be with him. When we talk, I know he's listening and wants to know about my day and what I want and need in my life. From the start, he's talked about *us*. It's not about him or me, but what *we'll* do going forward. How we'll raise the boys. The life we'll share."

"That's how it should be."

"After all this business with him investigating David and learning about Heather, I know I can count on him to have my back and stand beside me. I know that if we disagree or he does something I don't like, he's willing to talk it out, apologize, and make things right." Sierra appreciated his openness so much. "I know that if we hit a rough patch, he'll speak up about what he needs and that we'll talk it through together. He's seen so many relationships fall apart. He knows how devastating David's betrayal was for me. Our relationship is different. It's better. When Mason is happy, I'm happy."

"Then you're truly fated."

For some reason, that sparked a memory from the past. Something she'd forgotten, but suddenly wanted to share with Mason. It shifted something in her heart and eased the sting of what David had done to her.

"Where are the boys? We need to get going."

Dede checked her watch. "Mason picked them up twenty minutes ago and took them over to the ranch to get the horses ready for your ride."

Mason taught the boys all about chores and caring for the horses.

"Strange. I told him last night we'd head over together."

Dede shrugged and looked away. "He must be anxious to have you all there together today."

Sierra had spent the morning packing up their rooms while her mom kept the boys occupied downstairs with breakfast and cartoons.

"Well, I'm headed over there. We'll be back later to pick up the bags and boxes." They'd use Mason's truck, because they'd accumulated a lot of new stuff since arriving.

Excited, Sierra's belly fluttered with anticipation. She couldn't wait to merge their lives together. She wanted to be his partner in every way, and that included finally being together every night. She wanted to wake up with the man of her dreams every morning.

She couldn't think of a better way to start and end her day than being with Mason.

"Go. Have fun."

Sierra took a step toward the door, then turned back and wrapped her mom in a huge hug. "Thank you for everything, Mom. For being my sounding board, welcoming us home when we had nowhere else to go, and understanding that I need time when it comes to Heather."

"If I could erase that from your heart, I would."

"I know. Thank you for all the support. I appreciate it even when I'm stubborn and try to do everything on my own."

"I'm always here when you need me."

"I always need you, Mom, even when I make it seem like I can fix everything on my own.

"Stubborn is right." Her mom hugged her tighter anyway.

"I love you, Mom."

"Oh . . ." Choked up, her mom gulped. "I love you, too,

sweetheart." Her voice shook with the emotion-filled words and Sierra's heart grew two sizes too large for her chest.

She sucked in a deep breath, released her mom, gave her a smile, and headed for the door. "See you soon."

"Enjoy today. Take it all in."

Sierra raised a brow at how she said that, but thought it good advice and headed out to meet her guys.

She smiled at the thought and moved a little faster to get to the ones she loved.

Chapter Thirty-Nine

Mason's gut had tied itself into a knot so tight he could barely breathe. He kept a close eye on Danny riding alone beside him. Sierra rode on his other side with Oliver seated in front of her. The two of them looked sweet riding together.

He offered to have Oliver ride with him, but the little guy wanted his mom today.

The boys had helped him set up this surprise. They kept glancing at him, their smiles and excitement evident.

Mason hoped Sierra attributed it to the fact they were headed to the creek where the boys loved to fish and splash in the wading pools.

He'd been waiting for this day a long time. He'd never been more nervous in his life. He wanted to give Sierra something amazing and wonderful.

The creek came into view. Danny reined in his horse and dismounted just like Mason taught him. The horse cropped grass and remained docile with Danny holding the reins.

Mason dismounted and plucked Oliver from his mother's lap. "This is going to be so good."

Mason appreciated the little guy's enthusiasm and optimism. "What is all this?"

Mason gripped Sierra's hips and lifted her right off her horse, drew her body to his, and let her slide down him until she stood close in his embrace. "A celebratory picnic."

Her gaze left the blanket spread out under one of the huge oak trees with the food basket and cooler to meet his. "What are we celebrating?"

"Us." He took her hand and drew her toward the creek.

Danny had already tied off the horses' reins to the bushes like Mason had shown him earlier in the morning when they rode out to set everything up while Sierra packed up their stuff. Tonight, they'd all sleep under the same roof for the first time.

Mason couldn't wait.

But first, he needed Sierra to answer one question.

"Do you remember this spot?"

"We came here all the time when we were in high school. We'd skip stones and just hang out listening to the water. I poured out all my secrets to you."

"We share some history." Mason drew her to a stop in the shade next to the rolling creek, the cascading water gurgling over rocks next to them, and took her hands in his. "I'm looking forward to us making more together."

Danny and Oliver appeared on either side of him and stared up at their mom. She glanced down at them.

"What's going on?"

Danny pulled out his hand from behind his back and showed Sierra the small white box.

Mason explained. "This represents our past."

Danny flipped the lid open on the box and revealed the charm bracelet Mason had had made for her. "A horse for all the rides we took together. A diamond for all the nights we spent staring up at the stars and talking. Whether it was in the back of my truck, out in the pasture, or right here, those are some of my best memories."

Sierra's eyes misted with tears. "Oh, Mason."

"And a daisy."

She laughed. "For all the times you picked a wildflower and plucked the petals off in exactly the right order to land on *he loves me not* for whatever boy I had a crush on."

"Even back then, I wanted to keep you all to myself. I was just too stupid and focused on other things to see that what I really wanted was right in front of me."

A single tear slipped down her cheek.

Oliver drew his surprise out from behind his back.

Mason held Sierra's questioning gaze. "The bracelet is for the past. This one is for the present."

Oliver pulled the lid off the white box and revealed the set of keys on a heart-shaped key chain.

"Keys to *our* house."

She smiled and pressed her lips together as her eyes glassed over again. "I can't wait to make it our home."

"Tonight will be the first night of the rest of our lives where we go to sleep and wake up together."

Both boys heads turned up to him.

He glanced at both of them. "Did I forget to tell you you're moving in today?"

The boys looked to their mom for confirmation. She nodded. "That's right. We are."

"Yes!" the boys said in unison, their big smiles conveying their excitement.

Mason squeezed Sierra's hands to draw her full attention back to him. "Before you do and I show you the surprises I have for you at the house, there's one more thing I want to give you." He slipped his hand in his front pocket but didn't draw it back out just yet. "This one is for our future." He pulled out the wood ring case, used his thumb to open the lid, and held it out in his palm as he sank to one knee.

Sierra gasped, put her fingertips to her lips, and stared from the ring to him to the ring and back again. "Mason."

"I love you. So much that it fills me up and I feel like I can't possibly feel this much for one person. Then you smile at me and that feeling gets bigger and my whole world gets brighter. I want to build a life with you. I want a lifetime of memories filled with you and our children."

Her head was already bobbing up and down, but he kept going because she deserved to hear it all and have him ask the question.

"I want you to be my one and only. I want you to be my wife. Will you marry me?"

She kept nodding, tears falling down her soft cheeks, her lips trembling when she said, "Yes!" She leaned down and kissed him. "Yes." She kissed him again. "Yes. Yes. Yes." She kissed him for one long moment.

He stood, pulling her into his arms and kissing her more deeply.

The boys cheered and gave them bear hugs, their little arms around his and Sierra's legs.

Mason managed to step back, take her hand, and put the diamond engagement ring on her finger.

"Where's the rest?" Oliver checked the box in his hand.

"The other part is for the wedding day." Mason took Sierra's hand and kissed her knuckle right above the ring. "Do you like it?"

"I love it." She stared at the diamond.

"The boys helped me pick it out."

Her gaze shot to his. "Really?"

"I got their permission to ask you, then we went shopping."

She chuckled under her breath. "That's really sweet."

"We're going to be a family," Oliver announced.

Danny took his mom's hand and checked out the ring again. "It looks really good. Wait 'til you see the rest. It's awesome."

Relief hit Mason in a wave. Sierra said yes. The kids were excited about them getting married, and Sierra looked happy that he'd pulled off the proposal and included the kids.

"When are we getting married?" Oliver asked.

"Not *we*," Danny scolded Oliver. "*They* are getting married."

Mason ruffled Danny's hair. "It's definitely we. My commitment to your mom is a commitment I make to you, too. We will be family." He hugged the boys to his sides. "I, for one, can't wait."

Sierra kissed him again. "Me, either."

Oliver wriggled away and handed Sierra the box with the keys in it. He ran off to the picnic. "It's time for cake!"

Danny handed over the bracelet and ran to catch up to Oliver.

Sierra raised an eyebrow. "I thought you brought lunch."

"I was told that a celebration required cake." He tilted his head to the boys pulling the cake out of the cooler.

Sierra laughed. "Absolutely."

Mason took the bracelet out of the box and fastened it around Sierra's wrist. He brushed his fingers over her skin and stared deeply into her eyes. "Were you surprised?"

"In the best way." She linked her fingers with his. "I knew we'd get here, I just didn't expect it to be today."

"Why not today? You're moving in. I wanted you to know I want it to be forever."

She turned into him. "I never doubted you wanted me."

He looked into her eyes. "Always."

He kissed her softly, then she backed away, pulling him along with her. "I can't wait to show you how much I love you tonight. In our bed." She shook the keys in the box.

Mason suddenly had second thoughts about bringing the boys with them for the proposal. He'd love to lay her out on that blanket and make love to her under the tree.

But the boys smiled at them and he decided this was good, too.

This would be a memory all of them cherished.

* * *

Sierra held her hand out to her mom to show off the gorgeous engagement ring. Mason had really outdone himself. She couldn't wait to see the wedding bands the boys kept talking about while they ate cake and drank sparkling cider by the creek.

It truly had been a wonderful proposal, filled with poignant moments. Mason had put a lot of thought into it and her gifts.

Her mom touched the charms on the bracelet. "This is lovely, Sierra."

"Mason wanted to remind me of the past we share. It was really beautiful."

Her mom looked from her to Mason, standing right behind her, his hands on her shoulders. "I wish you both a lifetime of happiness together."

"Thank you, Dede."

Sierra touched her fingers to Mason's hands on her shoulders. "Mom. If you don't mind watching the boys for just half an hour before we take them to Mason's—"

"*Our* house," Mason corrected.

An uncontrollable smile spread across her face. "Yes. Our house. I wanted to show Mason something out by the pond."

"Sure, honey. Take your time."

"Thank you." She took Mason's hand and tugged him toward the back door.

"Why are we going to the pond?" A sparkle in his eyes hinted at what he hoped they'd be doing by the pond.

"It's not what you think."

His face fell in disappointment, but he rallied. "Are you sure?" He stepped behind her, took her hips in his hands, and kissed the side of her neck, nuzzling his nose in her hair.

She leaned back into him. "Come on. You'll see." She grabbed his hand again and pulled him along.

They made it to the garden gate before Mason slowed his pace. "Sierra, why are we going out there?" He meant the place where David and Heather snuck away to so long ago.

Funny how it felt like a lifetime ago now.

It was hard to be mad when she felt so excited and happy and hopeful.

"It's not what you think. There really is something I want to show you. I didn't remember it until this morning when I was talking to my mom. And then you proposed and now it seems even more important to show it to you."

Mason reluctantly went along, holding her hand all the way to the pond. She stopped near it and stared out at the two ducks floating in the water.

"How many summer days did we spend out here?"

"A lot. Amy strutted around in her bikini."

"How many times did she pretend to have a leg cramp so you'd help her out of the water?"

Mason chuckled and shook his head. "She tried, I'll give her that. But I always preferred hanging out with you."

"Funny how we never took it further back then."

"Maybe we always knew there was time and we'd be together eventually."

Sierra's heart sped up. "I think you're right. And I can prove it." She grabbed his hand and led him to the shed they used as a little cabin. She didn't hesitate to push the door open and step inside. Memories assailed her as she stared at the board games stacked on a bookshelf, the old afghan and mismatched pillows on the worn leather sofa, the blue-and-cream braided rug on the floor they had sat on during countless card games, bowls of snacks spread around them.

But it was the dozens of pictures they'd tacked up on the walls over the years that caught and held her attention.

Sierra spotted the one she remembered this morning and walked over to it, Mason right behind her. She plucked the old Polaroid from the wall, the tack still stuck in the top. She turned to him and showed him the picture of the two of them sitting on the small dock that stretched into the pond that they used to jump off all the time.

They were sitting so close together their shoulders and arms touched. She was looking up at him and he was looking down at her, both of them smiling.

She traced her finger over the picture. "I don't even remember someone taking this shot of us."

They'd often been lost in conversation together, avoiding everyone else, happy to just keep things between the two of them.

"It could have been taken any number of days."

He bumped his arm to her shoulder. "We spent a lot of time together. I'd bring my friends out here. You and your sisters would have yours. It was always a party. Nothing wild. Just fun."

"I really loved our friendship. I had my sisters, but somehow you were always easier to talk to and be around."

"Probably because I was an only child, I liked hanging out with you guys. It was better than being alone at the ranch. And you liked doing everything I liked to do."

"But there's something else that's special about this picture that I remembered this morning. Even back then, I think I knew we'd always be together." She turned the picture over and showed him what she'd written on the back. Inside a big red heart she had written Sierra + Mason.

"I don't know why I wrote it like this. We were just friends, but I knew I loved you. Not the way I do now. It's so much bigger now, but still . . ."

He linked his fingers with hers. "We laid the foundation.

Now we're both ready to build on the love that started all those years ago."

"You get it. I know it's sappy." But she didn't care.

"No, it's not." He tapped the picture. "Sometimes we wish for something and feel like it will never come true. Maybe that's how you felt when we didn't take things to the next level back then. But here we are back together and getting married."

Her smile came fast and filled with joy. "We're getting married!"

He tapped the photo. "Because Sierra plus Mason equals a whole lot of love." He kissed her then, drawing it out, letting her feel how much he loved her.

He broke the kiss and stared down at her. "I'm glad you showed me this. After Amy told me you weren't interested before you married David, I thought I was the only one who harbored feelings from back then. I know now that wasn't true, but this just really seals it for me."

"I always knew what I wanted, but I guess we both had to experience what didn't work so we could really appreciate what we have now."

"That's a great way to put it."

She hadn't exactly wasted that time. She had the boys to show for it, and she'd never regret her relationship with David for that reason alone.

And maybe it was a little petty, but she found it fitting to know that David and Heather came here to this little hideaway and carried out their betrayal and all the while this picture hung on the wall with her wish clearly stated on the back.

Standing next to Mason, his ring on her finger, a future of happiness on the horizon, Sierra found it easy to let go of the past. Life had led her to this home when she was a teen and she'd found her first friend in this new place with the boy next door. When circumstances turned her life upside down and took everything but the boys from her, she'd landed here again and found that friendship with the boy who'd turned into a very good man was even more necessary. And the love she'd harbored for him all these years was free to grow and fill her up like nothing else she'd ever had in her life.

Sierra tacked the picture back up on the wall.

"You don't want to take that with you?"

"It'll be here waiting for me if I need it." Just like Mason had been here waiting for her all these years. "Let's go home." She took his hand and walked out of the shed, leaving her hurt behind, knowing she had everything she needed to be happy.

She had her boys.

She had Mason.

Chapter Forty

Sierra woke up with Mason's big body plastered to the back of her, his arm draped over her hip, and his face buried in her long hair. A sense of all-encompassing contentment filled her up. She'd have liked to spend the rest of her life just like that, nestled in Mason's arms, feeling that much love and joy at just being with him.

It had been that way for the past two weeks.

The boys had settled in without any apprehension. They loved their rooms and pretty much took over the rest of the house like they'd always lived here. Mason didn't mind at all, but he'd made it clear his office was off-limits.

They'd found a routine that worked for all of them.

Mason left early for work each morning, using the extra hour in his office before any of the other staff arrived to catch up on paperwork or go over his cases for the day. Sierra dropped the kids at school, then went to work. When their schedules permitted, she met Mason for lunch since they worked so close to each other. Mason picked the kids up right after school on Fridays, saving them from going to after-school care. He took the boys horseback riding before Sierra got home.

Mason cooked Friday to Sunday. Sierra did the cooking during the week.

She loved that they found a rhythm and everything synced so easily.

Seeing Mason embrace the new structured chaos in his life and enjoy it so much made her feel safe and secure. Mason took on her and the boys with enthusiasm.

Sierra now sipped her coffee in the kitchen Mason had redone just for her.

Not only had he welcomed them into his home, he'd made it feel like theirs, too.

"What are you thinking about?" Mason walked in and went to the sink to wash his hands.

The boys chatted down the hall in their bathroom doing the same after helping Mason feed and water the horses.

"I'm standing in our beautiful kitchen thinking about how much I love living here with you."

Mason shot her a surprised and exuberant look. His smile made her heart melt. "Everything about this place has changed. Especially the feel of it."

She knew exactly what he meant. This was a big place for a bachelor to live in alone. Now, the house had a family. It was cozy.

It felt like home. A place where they laughed and loved and shared their lives.

Mason dried his hands, hung the towel from the oven door handle, then closed the distance between them. "You look amazing in that dress." His gaze skimmed down to her toes and back up again, momentarily stopping at the deep V in the pretty wrap dress she'd chosen for the engagement party her mom was throwing them in half an hour. The simple white dress had tiny pink flowers sprinkled over it. It felt feminine and flirty.

With Mason's hot gaze sweeping over her, she felt sexy and desirable.

She placed her hands on his chest. "I thought you might like it."

Mason traced his fingers along her shoulder and settled his warm hand on her neck. "Are you ready for today?"

She heard what he didn't ask in that question. "I asked my mom to invite Heather and Hallee to the party."

His eyebrow shot up. "You did?"

"I listened to your argument, thought about it, and decided you were right. I can't ignore her forever. What she did doesn't erase the fact we are family and at some point I need to accept that the boys have a sister they should get to know better."

"And you and Heather need to have a real talk about what happened. It's not good to keep your feelings all bottled up."

"I know. I heard you, Counselor. I'm not sure today is the day to do that, but as you said, I don't want to look back and miss having everyone together to celebrate with us." She wanted to see if she could be in the same vicinity as her sister and not want to kill her. "If nothing else, this will make my mom happy. It's the least I can do, since she's throwing us the engagement party."

"Wait until she finds out we're getting married in less than three months."

Sierra felt the nervous butterflies in her stomach. "We have so much to do in such a short time." The ocean view boutique hotel she fell in love with had a cancellation and because the owner and Mason were friends, they got first dibs on booking the date. They planned to keep the guest list to family and close friends, but on Mason's side that meant a lot of people because of his status in the community. She didn't mind. Not when it meant she'd be Mason's wife.

"We have a lot to celebrate."

They sure did. Besides their upcoming wedding, Sierra had sold the property in Napa for a better than decent price to a developer thanks to Mason's brilliant negotiations on her behalf. Most of the insurance money she'd received went to paying off the loan and setting up college funds for the kids, but she invested the property money and set aside a chunk in savings for a rainy day.

Going forward, she and Mason would combine their funds. Mason's income far exceeded hers. He'd told her she could quit her job or scale back her hours. Whatever she wanted to do. He had no problem supporting them. At first, she'd balked at the thought of not working. After what David had done to her financially, she wanted to know she had the money if something happened. But then she reminded herself that Mason wasn't David. He didn't hide things from her. He didn't lie. She trusted him.

So she talked to her boss and scaled back her hours to thirty a week so long as she was available by phone for emergencies. After the wedding, her new hours would take effect.

And who knew, maybe she'd quit altogether when a new baby came along. Talk of marriage had sparked talk of expanding their family. They planned to start right after the wedding, and Sierra couldn't wait. She wanted another child. Mason loved the boys, but he dreamed of a child of his own. She wanted to give him one. Maybe two.

"You've got that sweet smile again."

"This year we'll celebrate our wedding. Maybe next year we'll celebrate the birth of our child."

Mason's hand brushed down her arm and swept over her hip. "I can't wait."

"A few months ago, I had nothing left of my old life. The boys and I came here with next to nothing. We have a whole new life and it's wonderful and so full I couldn't ask for more."

"I didn't know how much I was missing in my life until you came back into it. I can't help but feel like this is how it was always meant to be." He kissed her softly.

"Kissing again," Oliver announced to Danny who followed him into the kitchen.

"Aren't we supposed to leave now?" Danny finished buttoning his white dress shirt.

Oliver had also changed into his party outfit.

The boys looked great in their black pants and white dress shirts.

"I guess I better get dressed." Mason kissed her on the forehead and gave each boy a shoulder squeeze on his way out.

She smiled at Danny and Oliver. "How lucky are we?"

They both stared back at her, wondering what she meant, but deep down they understood. In the years to come, with the life she and Mason would give them, they'd understand.

Home is where you are always loved and welcome.

Chapter Forty-One

D ede wanted the party to be everything Sierra and Mason deserved for this happy occasion. So far, the guests seemed happy, the food and drinks were plentiful, and everyone gathered in small groups to chat on this beautiful sunny day.

She checked her watch. Almost time for the cake and a toast to the happy couple. The caterer was already setting out the plates and forks.

The poster by the cake table caught her eye again. She loved how Sierra had blown up the old Polaroid of her and Mason sitting on the dock when they were teens. Amy had snapped a new picture of the pair in the exact same pose. The poster showed the two pics side by side. They'd grown up, but their smiles—and the way they looked at each other—were the same.

"Thank you so much for the party, Mom. It's beautiful."

Dede encircled Sierra's waist with one arm and used her other hand to point to the poster and the old photo. "Those two belonged together."

"It took us a while to get here, but we're really happy."

Dede turned and faced Sierra. "Thank you for including Heather and Hallee. I know it's hard, but I think it's important for both of you to keep a connection no matter how tenuous."

Sierra put her hand on Dede's shoulder. "I mostly did it for you, Mom, but I also wanted to see if I could do it without making today about the past. And I can. Today is about me and Mason and our love story." She held her glass up toward the poster, the past and future represented. "I want to keep looking forward, not back."

"I hoped you'd feel that way."

Sierra glanced over at Mason talking to his friend and neighbor, Luke Thompson, with Oliver hanging on Mason's back, his chin propped on Mason's shoulder. "Look at him. At them. How could I not be happy today?"

"I just want you to know I know it's there under all the good and I appreciate that you're strong enough to bury it and appreciate what you do have, not what you lost."

"Maybe it's callous . . ." Sierra frowned. "Or maybe it's just my way of coping, but what Mason and I have is so much bigger and better than what I had with David. Don't get me wrong, it wasn't all bad."

Dede touched Sierra's hand. "I've been married and divorced three times, sweetheart, I know what you mean. The love you have for Mason is different from what you felt for David. It's okay to feel that way. It's okay to celebrate it without feeling like you're disparaging David's memory and what you had with him before it went bad."

"I don't feel bad. I've gotten to a place where I can hold on to the good and not let the bad steal the joy from that. We loved each other. We had two children together. That's worth holding on to fondly without letting the bad taint it."

"Good for you, Sierra." Dede hugged Sierra again and whispered her wish, "Maybe in time, you'll be able to do that with your sister."

* * *

The caterer waved her mom over and Sierra took a minute to appreciate her mom for being the rock she needed and the thread that tied Heather, Amy, and Sierra together.

"I know you invited her, but are you ready for me to ask her to leave?" Amy pointed her wine glass at Heather, who walked back into the garden area from the path that led to the pond and shed.

It made Sierra think of how Heather and David snuck off there. Anger flared, but the sad look in Heather's red-rimmed eyes drew sympathy from what she thought was her hardened heart.

Sierra thought about her trip back to the shed with Mason and how the memories came back and filled her with all the emotions she'd felt then and now for him.

Heather missed David. She'd loved him. They'd had a child together.

If David hadn't been Sierra's husband and she saw her sister in this state over a man she'd loved and lost, how would she feel?

She'd sympathize. She'd want to comfort and console her sister.

No one had done that for Heather because David had been Sierra's husband.

What they did was wrong, no doubt. It caused a lot of damage.

Heather deserved to feel terrible for what she'd done.

But for the first time Sierra put herself in her sister's place. Heather mourned David. She missed him. She wished for him.

Sierra felt all those things when he died and she was just a widow, not the wife of a philanderer. That's who David turned her into after she grieved and found out about what he did.

That's not who David was to Heather.

"I need to talk to her."

Amy scoffed. "You're not seriously going to forgive her for what she did."

Sierra met Amy's disbelieving gaze. "She's been carrying the weight of what happened for both her and David."

"Because she deserves it."

"She knows that. But I can't keep feeding this anger. I'm working harder at hating her than I am on forgiving her. Maybe if I did it the other way around, this pit in my stomach every time I think about her would go away, because I don't want to hate my sister." It hurt her heart to shut her sister out like this, to think such terrible things about her, to wish bad things for her. She couldn't do it anymore.

Amy sighed. "I know what you mean. It's hard. She left me a message last week asking if I'd call her with the name and number of a good babysitter. I don't know if she didn't want to ask me to watch Hallee for her, or she wants someone as backup, or what. I want to see my niece. I want her to know that I'll always help with Hallee and that if she's really in a bind, I'm here."

"That's just it. You and Mom got sucked into our drama. I'm sure Heather feels like it's us against her because of what she did. I don't want it to be that way. I don't want Mom to feel like she's stuck in the middle of us for the rest of her life, like she can't support both of us without feeling guilty or disloyal to either of us. As a mom, I feel for her, because I don't know that I could do that with Danny and Oliver."

"Me, either. P.J. and Emma have their squabbles. I help them work it out. Mom can't fix this with forced apologies and making you two talk it out. This is a deep kind of hurt. Talking about it will only hurt more."

"Maybe the only way past this is through the hurt." Sierra grasped Amy's arm. "Thanks for being on my side, but I want you to know it's okay to have her back, too."

"You're a kinder person than I am. I don't think I would have worked my way through this the way you have and gotten to a point where I could even contemplate talking to her, let alone trying to work it out."

"I feel like if I don't try, I'll regret it. If David was still here, I'd want to find a way to at least be civil with each other for the kids' sake. The least I can do is give my sister the same courtesy for the same reason."

"When you put it like that, yeah, it makes sense." Amy bounced her gaze from Sierra to Heather and back. "We do a lot for our kids." Amy hugged her, then gave her an encouraging smile.

Sierra walked toward Heather, stopping briefly to clasp hands with Mason who'd stood by watching her and Amy quietly talking alone. He had to know the gist of the conversation and where she was headed. He gave her a reassuring smile and let her move on toward her sister.

Heather sat alone, her head down, holding a drink she

hadn't touched. Her head snapped up when Sierra approached the table and took the seat across from her.

"Uh. Hello."

"Hi." They had to break the ice somehow. Inane greetings seemed a good way to start, but Sierra wanted to make this as quick and painless as possible. "You hurt me."

"I know." Heather looked her in the eye, hers filled with remorse and pain. "I'm sorry."

Sierra took that in and let it settle in her heart. "I believe you."

"You do? Why? After what I did . . ." She shook her head. "I can't take it back."

"I sincerely doubt you'd want to." Otherwise it wouldn't have continued after the first encounter. And then there was Hallee.

One side of Heather's mouth drew back in a half frown and tears glistened in her eyes. "I don't know what to say to you."

Because they weren't meant to share the details. Those memories belonged to Heather. Sierra didn't need to pile on to the hurt by hearing all the sordid specifics.

"I was just talking to Amy."

Heather glanced over at their sister spying on them from across the yard. "She hates me, too."

"No, she doesn't. And I don't want to hate you, either. But you made it damn hard not to. You're my sister. I used to clean and bandage your skinned knees and push you on the swing and talk to you about boys and kissing. I'm pretty sure I'm the one who gave you the sex talk."

Heather's cheeks pinked. "Mom's idea of a sex talk was telling me not to do anything you and Amy were doing."

They shared hesitant smiles and it felt like it cracked the shield Sierra put between them to keep Heather away. "I suppose we should have taught you to be careful who you fall in love with."

"I'm sorry, Sierra. I never meant—"

Sierra held her hand up to stop her. Heather's mouth snapped closed. She deflated, her shoulders sagging.

"I don't want to hear any more apologies. What I told Amy was that if you were David, I'd make an effort to be civil. That's probably the best I can do right now. The kids deserve at least that much from us. I don't want to necessarily tell them they're siblings right now. But I don't want to keep them apart, either."

Heather's gaze went to Emma and Hallee out on the lawn, rolling a soccer ball back and forth between them. Danny and P.J. sat nearby eating a bunch of grapes from the fruit plate they served earlier.

Sierra sighed. "I don't want them to miss birthday parties and holidays together because you and I can't be in the same room with each other."

"I don't want that, either. I've been trying to figure out a way to make things up to you in some way. I didn't want to do this today, but I went to my boss and applied for a promotion that I deserve but probably would have gone to someone else because I tend to think everything will be handed to me, and that's not how things really work."

Sierra had pointed that out to her.

"I told my boss that I deserved that position. I'd earned it. I did half the work already without being paid." Heather stared down at the table, then met Sierra's gaze again. "I want to provide for my daughter and give her the best life I can. I want her to know that I worked hard to better myself. And I'm working on it."

"What does this have to do with us?"

"I want you to know I'm working on being a better me. And that starts with standing on my own two feet, taking responsibility for what I've done, and finding a way to pay you back for the money David gave me. So I got the promotion I deserved and the raise that goes with it, so I could get a loan to pay you back half the money David gave me." She shrugged. "I didn't do it for the whole amount because I believe David should support his daughter."

Sierra reluctantly agreed with that.

"I'll get the check to you this week. I didn't know he took out the loan. I didn't really think about him taking money away from you and the kids." Heather sighed, her eyes filled with regret. "Let's face it, I tried really hard not to think about you."

Sierra appreciated the honesty, even though it stung.

Heather kept going. "I will never be able to apologize enough or make this right, but if you're willing to set this aside, at least for the kids, then I'll follow your lead on how you want to handle getting them together and how and when we tell them the truth."

"Hallee is too young to understand. The boys might get the concept, but they're still too young to grasp the gravity of what having a sister means. Maybe when Hallee is old enough to understand the concept of siblings we'll tell them. Until then, let's stop rehashing what happened and live in the moment. We can be civil. Who knows, maybe one day we can even be friends again."

Heather pressed her lips together, eyes watery, and nodded. "Thank you. It's more than I deserve."

"No more talk like that, either. All the energy I poured into being angry, all the energy you put into thrashing yourself over this, it's not good for either of us."

"Why are you doing this now? Or at all?"

"I'm about to get married to a man I really, really love. I have a chance to have the life I always wanted with a man who only wants to love me back and make me happy. The last thing I want to do is carry this with me and let it drag my heart down. I don't want to carry this weight with me into something that is so . . . perfect."

Heather gave her a sad smile. "I'm happy for you."

Sierra stood and stared down at her sister and gave her the truth. "I hope one day I'll be happy for you, too." She turned to go and spotted the kids playing Duck, Duck, Goose on the lawn. She smiled when Oliver goosed Hallee and the little one jumped up and tried her best to chase Oliver, who was faster and steadier on his legs than the toddler. Hallee lost, but the sweet grin on her face said she didn't care. She started around the circle of kids, touching each of their heads, saying *Duck* each time.

Sierra hadn't put a lot of thought into the wedding details, but one thing she absolutely wanted was all the kids to participate. Danny and Oliver would share the duty as best man to Mason. She'd ask Amy to be her matron of honor. But Emma and Hallee would be adorable flower girls. P.J., though older than the rest of them, would still make a great ring bearer.

She turned back and found Heather staring at the kids, too, a single tear rolling down her cheek.

"I'd love it if Hallee was a flower girl in my wedding."

Heather's surprised gaze shot to hers and she gasped.

"I'll get her a pretty dress. *All* the kids will be included."

Including Hallee in her life seemed an easier way to move forward. With Heather, she'd need to take baby steps to rebuild the trust that had been shattered. It would take time. Maybe they'd never get back to what they had, but Sierra would try to find peace with what happened and with her sister.

She left Heather and went back to Mason and their celebration, content she'd not only salved the discord with her sister but made wedding plans that amped her anticipation for their big day.

She couldn't wait to get married and look back on it knowing she'd done her best to leave the past behind and start fresh with the man she knew would be her perfect partner.

Chapter Forty-Two

Sierra stood at the back of the ballroom in her gorgeous white wedding gown feeling like a princess. The wedding coordinator handed her the bouquet. The heady scent of white roses filled the air. The simple bouquet complemented the lavender hydrangea, pink peony, and white spider mum bouquets decorating the tables at the back of the ballroom and the aisle leading to the temporary stage in the middle of the dance floor.

Mason stood there with Danny and Oliver waiting for her grand entrance. They all looked dashing in their black tuxes. P.J. stood just inside the door holding a white satin pillow with the rings tied to it. He tugged at the collar of his dress shirt.

Amy stood next to him wearing a gorgeous fuchsia A-line chiffon off-the-shoulder dress, looking spectacular. She brushed P.J.'s hand away from the offending collar. "Stop fidgeting."

Emma and Hallee stood behind them in their matching pale pink dresses with the tulle overlaid skirts and, tied around their waists, fuchsia satin ribbons that matched Amy's dress. So sweet and cute.

The florist handed them each a basket filled with pink rose petals.

Hallee spotted her and ran over, the basket bouncing against her side. She set the basket down and grabbed fistfuls of her beaded wedding gown. "Pretty."

Sierra stared down into Hallee's beautiful hazel eyes. For the first time, she allowed herself to really see the resemblance to Danny's eyes and she saw David in the little girl. There was of course a hint of her sister in Hallee's pert nose and bowed mouth.

Hallee threw her arms around Sierra's legs. "Auntie. Pretty."

Sierra's eyes teared. She patted Hallee on the back, then dipped down and traced her finger along the curve of Hallee's sweet face, admiring her dark curls that always seemed to be in disarray. Just like Heather's. "You look like a princess in your dress, too."

Hallee spun around and almost toppled over with the momentum, but Sierra caught her waist and kept her upright.

"It's time to start," the wedding coordinator announced.

P.J. started out first.

Sierra touched her fingertip to Hallee's nose, making her smile. "It's your turn, sweetheart. Go with Emma."

The girls followed P.J. down the aisle tossing flower petals into the air and watching them fall in disarray on the white draped aisle.

Amy took the edges of Sierra's dress, pulled and shook it out, then let it drop. "Gorgeous, sis."

Sierra smiled, but a pang in her heart made it stop before it hit maximum wattage. For a heartbeat she wished things were better between her and Heather. She'd excluded her from all the wedding preparations. She hadn't even included Heather in picking out Hallee's dress.

She'd needed the space and to keep the preparations and wedding happy and all about her and Mason.

"Don't tell me you're having second thoughts." Amy studied her, then glanced over her shoulder as the girls stepped up on the stage, making it Amy's turn to go.

"Not at all. Mason is my future." She waved Amy to go. "Hurry up. I want to kiss my husband."

And later, she'd thank her sister for letting Hallee be a part of the wedding and attending despite how frosty things were between them. Maybe it wouldn't be the same as it used to be, but they could definitely be better than this.

Amy glided down the path, turning her head slightly to give Rex a sexy smile on the way. Sierra had no doubt they'd make it to their rocking chairs on the porch watching their grandkids play in the yard.

The wedding march started. She didn't hesitate to take her place in the double door entrance and paused to take in the smile on Mason's face when he saw her. She took him in, standing with their sons, and that smile. The connection they shared drew her right to him.

She felt the stares from their avid audience of friends and family, but she only had eyes for the man who stepped forward and held his hand out to her. She took it and stepped up onto the stage.

"God, you're beautiful." Mason gave her a soft kiss.

Sighs erupted in the audience along with a few woots from the guys.

Mason smiled down at her, then gave his neighbor and

buddy Luke, who'd become certified online to perform their ceremony, a sheepish grin.

Luke teased him. "Give me five minutes and you can kiss her all you want."

Everyone burst out with laughter.

Sierra handed her bouquet to Amy and took Mason's hands and lost herself in his steady, loving gaze and the simple ceremony. His declaration of love and devotion along with the promises he made filled her up. She didn't hesitate to give him back all he'd given her and before she knew it they'd exchanged rings and said, "I do," and Luke pronounced them husband and wife.

Mason kissed her again, taking his time, the cheers washed out by the sheer joy emanating from both of them.

"I give you Mr. and Mrs. Moore."

Hearing that felt so right.

Everything about being with Mason felt like it was meant to be.

Amy handed her back the flowers.

Sierra and Mason faced their friends and family as husband and wife and she couldn't smile big enough to convey the happiness bursting out of her.

They'd planned their exit for the photographer to get an amazing shot.

Emma and Hallee led the way with Danny, Oliver, and P.J. next, Amy at the side behind them, and she and Mason following them all back down the aisle, smiling for the pictures she knew would be amazing and capture the moment.

They left their guests to find their way to their tables for lunch while she, Mason, and the wedding party took more pictures in the hotel's amazing gardens.

Twenty minutes later, they rejoined their guests to rousing applause and she and Mason took to the dance floor for their first dance. The kids joined in, making everyone smile again.

Mason danced with her mom and she danced with his dad, then she danced with her boys together before dancing with her dad while Mason danced with his mom.

They finally took a break to eat and chat with guests.

She spotted Heather sitting quietly by herself, the other guests from her table on the dance floor. Heather looked so alone. It should make her happy to see her sister get a little of what she deserved, but it didn't. It made her sad. She didn't want to feel this way today of all days. She wanted everyone, including Heather, to be happy and celebrating.

She didn't have a solution that would bring her and Heather closer but she'd think on it later. Right now, she wanted to live in the moment and wallow in her happiness.

Sierra let it all go for now and enjoyed the rest of the reception by her husband's side. She pulled Mason back out onto the dance floor for a slow song and found peace as they swayed to the music.

When it came time for them to leave for their honeymoon, their guests lined the exit and stairs to the waiting limo.

Sierra stopped and kissed her boys good-bye. "Be good. We'll call you tomorrow and send pictures." She looked forward to spending the next week in Hawaii at a luxury resort, soaking up the sun, and working on a brother or sister for the boys.

She intended to spend every second with Mason, not just getting through the days, but living them to the fullest for the rest of her life.

She hugged her mom. "Thank you for always being there for me."

"Be happy."

"Done. I couldn't get any happier than I am right now."

Amy stepped away from Rex's side and pulled her in for a hug. "I'm so glad you moved back home."

"Me, too. See you when I get back."

Mason let loose the boys, who practically strangled him with their hugs. He waved good-bye to her mom and sister and his family, then they finally made it down the steps under a rain of flower petals to the limo. She glanced over her shoulder to toss the bouquet, but spotted Heather standing with Hallee in front of her.

She squeezed Mason's hand. "Give me a sec."

He glanced at Heather and nodded.

Sierra walked up the two steps, smiled down at Hallee, then handed the bouquet to her sister. She leaned in close and whispered something for her sister's ears only. "I hope this brings you good luck and you find a man who is all yours and who loves you the way Mason loves me." She meant it. They both needed to move on.

Tears slipped down Heather's cheeks.

"Mom has the kids while we're gone, but I bet they'd love a sleepover at Aunt Heather's." Maybe they weren't ready to hang out like they used to, but the kids loved being with each other, and that shouldn't have to change.

Heather wiped away a tear, found a smile, and nodded. "I'd love that."

Sierra rejoined her husband, light of heart and filled with hope for the future, knowing no matter what, she didn't have to face anything alone again.

She had her family, the boys, and Mason.

Author's Note

Sierra loves reading her boys bedtime stories, but her favorite ones are the ones she tells about Franny Fright. When she was young, they were frightening tales she told to scare her sisters. But now, they're fun . . . and just a bit scary.

Here is just one of those tales . . .

FRANNY FRIGHT

Franny Fright took such delight
In making things go bump in the night
A clink and clang from her boa chain
A boo and ooh like a scary ghoul

Franny Fright plays her tricks
On the little ones she picks
Tickling toes
And chilling their bones

You'll hide under the covers when Franny Fright hovers
Squeaking floors

And slamming doors
Your delightful screams Franny Fright adores

So when the sky is dark
And the moon is bright
Watch out for Franny Fright

Acknowledgments

I am so grateful to the Avon Books/William Morrow team for all the support and enthusiasm for all the stories I bring to life. And I do mean team, because the books aren't finished and in readers' hands without the editorial, marketing, publicity, sales, and all the other support staff that have a hand in every book.

A very special thank-you to my amazingly talented and patient editor, Lucia Macro, for always diving deep into every story and making sure, in the end, it's the best it can be.

To my hardworking agent, Suzie Townsend, who takes care of business and has my back. I'm so lucky to have you as a friend and partner on this amazing journey.

And of course, thank you, readers, for picking up my books, giving me your precious time and attention, and spending time with my characters. I know I put you through a lot, but in the end, I promise you'll always find a happy ending.

About the author

About the book

Insights,
Interviews
& More...

Meet Jennifer Ryan

Steve Hopkins

New York Times and *USA Today* bestselling author Jennifer Ryan writes suspenseful contemporary romances about everyday people who do extraordinary things. Her deeply emotional love stories are filled with high stakes and higher drama, family, friendship, and the happily-ever-after we all hope to find.

Jennifer lives in the San Francisco Bay Area with her husband and three children. When she finally leaves those fictional worlds, you'll find her in the garden, playing in the dirt and daydreaming about people who live only in her head, until she puts them on paper.

For information about her upcoming releases, sign up for her newsletter at www.jennifer-ryan.com/newsletter.

Reading Group Guide

1. The novel is about the secrets people keep from one another. Discuss whether some secrets should remain just that—secret—and the kind of damage that secrets (revealed or not) might do to relationships.

2. What do you think might have happened to Sierra and David's marriage if David had lived?

3. As a reader, are you able to forgive Heather? Why or why not? Do you believe Sierra should forgive her?

4. Amy seeks perfection, especially "public perfection." Discuss the ways society today encourages this often false façade. Do you think it's harmless fun or damaging?

5. Why do you think the author chose to begin the novel the way she did? How do you think it sets the stage for and later reflects the rest of the book?

6. The Silva sisters' father is mentioned only in passing, but do you think their relationship with him—or lack thereof—might influence their current relationships with the men in their lives? How do you think their mother's idealism combined with bad romantic choices have also affected the sisters? ▶

7. The author made a choice in making Mason a divorce attorney. In what ways does Mason's profession inform his views on love and marriage?

8. Mason unconsciously waits for Sierra for most of his life. Is this sort of love possible in reality?

9. Heather makes a choice when she has an affair with David. Do you think she truly loved him or was she acting out of jealousy? In what ways does her rivalry with Sierra affect her actions?

10. Do you feel Amy's actions in warning Mason off Sierra when he confessed his feelings for Sierra to her were vindictive? Or did Amy act out of concern, actually thinking that Sierra had made her choice? 〰

Discover great authors, exclusive offers, and more at hc.com.